THE WORLD
FORGOT

THE WORLD FORGOT

BOOK THREE OF THE EVER-EXPANDING UNIVERSE

MARTIN LEICHT
AND ISLA NEAL

SAGA PRESS

LONDON SYDNEY **NEW YORK** TORONTO NEW DELHI

SAGA PRESS

AN IMPRINT OF SIMON & SCHUSTER, INC.

1230 AVENUE OF THE AMERICAS, NEW YORK, NEW YORK 10020

Text copyright © 2015 by Lisa Graff and Martin Leicht

Cover illustration copyright © 2016 by Tim O'Brien

All rights reserved, including the right of reproduction to reproduce this book or portions thereof in any form whatsoever. For information address Saga Press Subsidiary Rights Department, 1230 Avenue of the Americas, New York, NY 10020.

SAGA PRESS and colophon are trademarks of Simon & Schuster, Inc.

For information about special discounts for bulk purchases, please contact Simon & Schuster Special Sales at 1-866-506-1949 or business@simonandschuster.com.

The Simon & Schuster Speakers Bureau can bring authors to your live event. For more information or to book an event, contact the Simon & Schuster Speakers Bureau at 1-866-248-3049 or visit our website at www.simonspeakers.com.

Also available in a SIMON & SCHUSTER BFYR hardcover edition

The text for this book is set in Electra LT.

Manufactured in the United States of America

First Saga Press paperback edition March 2016

2 4 6 8 10 9 7 5 3 1

The Library of Congress has cataloged the hardcover edition as follows:

Leicht, Martin.

The world forgot / Martin Leicht and Isla Neal. — First edition.

pages cm. — (The ever-expanding universe ; 3)

Summary: Teen mom Elvie Nara searches the universe after her daughter has been kidnapped.

ISBN 978-1-4424-2966-6 (hc)

[1. Science fiction. 2. Teenage mothers—Fiction. 3. Human-alien encounters—Fiction. 4. Kidnapping—Fiction.] I. Neal, Isla. II. Title.

PZ7.L53283Wo 2015

[Fic]—dc23

2014024001

ISBN 978-1-4814-4288-6 (mass market pbk)

ISBN 978-1-4424-2968-0 (eBook)

For Lena and Bob

How happy is the blameless vestal's lot!
The world forgetting, by the world forgot.

—Alexander Pope, "Eloisa to Abelard"

PROLOGUE

Some days I sleep. Some days I pace. Some days, the days when they decide we have no need for light, I sit in absolute darkness.

Today I have no idea where I am. I haven't known much of anything for as long as I can remember. Since they brought me here. They moved me or didn't, and I simply can't remember. I can't seem to remember much of anything. Can't even remember which things I forgot and which things I never knew to begin with.

Today I do not know where I am.

It's loud. I know that much. Blaring horns, like an alarm or a whatdayacallit. Signage? Siphon?

It's loud. There are flashing lights. On and off and on again.

Siren. I remember the word. Siren, that's what's making so much noise.

A siren means something is wrong.

The others don't seem to care that something is wrong. Most of them are sleeping. Some of them, the ones who just came back from their tests, are sleeping the most soundly. You're always the most tired after a test.

After a while, I don't know how long, I drift off to sleep too. More time passes.

I wake up.

I pace.

I sit in the darkness.

The door hisses and clicks, and suddenly everyone's at attention. Everyone always wakes up when they open the door.

The white light that streams in when the door is opened is blinding. Two black silhouettes in the doorway.

"Number Twelve!" the first guard barks out. I don't know his name. Or maybe I just don't remember.

I rub a sore spot on my shoulder. I don't know why it's sore. I don't think I've taken a test recently. Around me I hear whispers, more shifting of weight.

"Number Twelve!" the guard shouts again.

There is a sharp poke in my back. *"That's you,"* one of them hisses at me.

"Oh!" The wheels click together in my brain. "Oh." I squint into the whiteness of the light beyond the door. "That's me," I tell the guard. My voice is hoarse, cracking. I guess that's what happens when you're stuck in one dark room after another—you stop talking so much, and then your voice goes hoarse.

Or maybe my voice was always like that. I can't remember.

The guard jerks his chin downward, a sharp nod.

"Come with us," he says.

I step out into the light.

As my eyes adjust to the brightness, I take in the guard who leads me by the arm—with swift, sure strides—and, four steps behind him, the other, shorter guard. I recognize him. I think I recognize him. He is young. Short blond hair, sharp blue eyes. And I think I remember that he is friendlier than the others.

"Hi," I greet him quietly.

"No talking," the first guard snaps at me. He yanks me forward with such force that I stumble, almost fall. The second guard steadies me.

I turn to thank him, to offer him a smile at least, and I see that he is turned away from me. He will not accept my gratitude.

Still, I think, *I will remember this small kindness.* I will try to remember.

I am led to a room. White, sterile, silent. There's nothing here that's memorable, and yet when we walk into it, I'm flooded with memories. I can feel the sore spot on my shoulder. I can hear crying. But it's not me. A baby? A baby's cries? I . . . had a baby once—didn't I? Thoughts whirl through my brain, and I can't remember which are real and which are imagined. The white walls blur into one another in my memories. The friendlier guard leads me to a high table, and he helps me hop up to sit on it. The taller, gruffer guard stays in the hallway to confer with someone else. I take my opportunity to talk. Use my voice.

"Why did the siren go off, before?" I ask. I'm pleased that I was able to remember the word before I got to ask.

The guard's eyes dart to the door. No one is listening.

"There was a breach," he tells me. I don't know what that means. It's a word I've forgotten, or never learned. But I don't want him to know I can't remember. I want him to think I'm the kind of person who knows what words mean. "But it's okay. We're safe now."

We talk no more after that, and he doesn't look at me. But I sit up a little straighter. Brush the tangles out of my hair when I think he isn't looking.

The person who enters the room next is not the first guard but an older man. A doctor, maybe? He wears a white coat, carries a lap-pad. I may have met him before. He glances down at the lap-pad. "Number Twelve," he says, reading.

"Yes, sir," I respond. *I know that I am Number Twelve,* I think proudly. I remembered.

"How have you been feeling?" the doctor asks me.

I try to remember. "Fine," I say.

"Aches or pains of the joints?"

"No," I tell him. I think that's right. "Oh! My shoulder is sore." I rub the spot again. Tugging at the neck of my tunic, I can make out a mark there—one short line that intersects another at a right angle, like a capital *L*. I rub at it again, but the mark will not go away.

The doctor ignores my observation. "Any stomach cramping, abdominal pain, chest flutters?"

"No."

"Disturbing dreams? Thoughts?"

"Thoughts? No. Would that be bad?"

"Could be. Psychological stresses could introduce unknown variables into the testing."

Tests. It's my turn for a test. What are the tests for again? I always get so sleepy after and forget. I glance back at the friendly guard. He gives me a small smile when the doctor is focused on his lap-pad. I smile back.

I remember how to do *that*, at least.

"I don't have any dreams," I tell the doctor.

The doctor nods, pleased with my answer. "Just one final question," he tells me, "and then we can begin the testing." I sit up a little straighter, waiting. "Do you remember anything from before your time here began?"

"Remember?"

"Yes. For instance, your name? Do you remember your name?"

I open my mouth to answer—such a simple question—and find that I can't.

"I . . . ," I start. A jumble of words circle frantically in my brain, but I can't quite grab at any of them. I look at the friendly guard. He's frowning. I want to tell them, *Yes, I know my name. I can remember things. I'm good at knowing things and remembering words. I remembered the word for the loud noise before. Didn't I? Surgeon?* "I can't remember. I'm sorry." I hang my head, ashamed.

The doctor smiles a kind smile at me and sets down his lap-pad. "Don't be sorry. Let's get you into the lab so we can begin testing."

I nod. I'm tired. That must be why I can't remember. I

turn to the friendly guard, who puts a guiding hand on the small of my back. "This way," he directs.

I have disappointed him. And after the testing I'll be even more tired. And I'll remember even less.

I allow the guard to lead me to the door, while I still search my mind. There must be *something* there. I probe the furthest corners, grab at the tumbling thoughts.

Until, finally, I reach one.

"Britta," I say quickly, spinning around to face the doctor. "That's my name. Britta McVicker." They both look stunned, but I know this is correct. *I know something.* I am elated. I smile at the friendly guard.

But he is not smiling back. He takes in a deep breath. I *feel* it, as though he has taken in the air I needed to breathe.

And I don't know why, but the skin on the back of my knees begins to tingle.

I face the doctor again. He is frowning.

"That's right, isn't it?" I ask him, even though I am sure of the answer. "My name is Britta McVicker?" How have I disappointed them with my remembering?

"Sir?" the guard says to him, as though to confirm something.

The doctor is poking around inside a drawer, looking for something. "Unfortunate," he tells the guard. "We do not have time for these setbacks." He does look up now, but not at me.

The doctor is holding something long and thin in his hand. What do they call it? A needle. I think that's the word. The doctor clasps the needle tightly in his gloved hand.

I don't remember when he put on the gloves.

"Sit back down, please," the doctor tells me. His voice is cold. "Hold her down." That he says to the guard.

Suddenly I feel sick. A cold feeling—dread—runs through me. It's as if in finding my name I have turned on a switch, and now light is creeping slowly through a dark room. A room like where they were holding me. With the others. All the others.

The others. Oh God. I remember. I know.

"Just relax," the friendly guard says. He's trying to smile as he holds my shoulders down, but his eyes are sad. "This won't hurt at all. You'll feel sleepy, and when you wake up, everything will be fine."

I look at his face, then the doctor's. I watch the needle go into my arm. And I know that he's lying.

Chapter One

IN WHICH WE ATTEMPT TO HIT THE GROUND RUNNING

•

Come on, already. Is it too much to ask for a little time to myself for once?

I spot Cole on the other side of the deck, where he slouches over the rail, staring out at the water. For a split second I consider turning around and heading back belowdecks, but Cole spots me before I make up my mind. He gives me a quick nod, then turns back to the water and takes a slug from a silver can. He makes no movement toward me, leaving me in the unenviable position of having to either be an antisocial jerk and ignore him or choose to hold an actual conversation.

You'd think that chatting with Cole would be easy enough, despite our current dire situation. I mean, we did conceive a child together. That kind of thing doesn't happen when you're communicating solely by semaphore. But after the realization I had back in Antarctica that I'm changing in really unexpected ways while Cole, for better or worse, is pretty much always going to be, well, Cole, I've been having a hard time acting normal around him. The fact that Cole's testing to see if I'll approach him is proof enough that even he has picked up on this.

I take up a spot about an arm's length away from him along the ship's railing and follow his gaze out to the horizon. The wind is superbrisk, but thanks to my Enosi hybrid genes, I adapted to the chill long before we even disembarked.

"Where's Ducky?" Cole says to me, still not looking in my direction.

"He's down in the bathroom. Barfing again."

"I'm surprised you're not down there holding his hair," Cole says. "You've barely left his side since we set sail from Cape Crozier."

"Cole, I've been with Ducky because Ducky's been with Marnie, and Marnie's been the one taking care of my dad. Remember? Harry Nara, middle-aged, out-of-shape engineer-slash-world's-oldest-and-most-chuteless-skydiver?"

Cole takes another long drag from his nondescript tin can, then hurls it overboard. I want to chastise him for being an ocean litterbug, but I somehow manage to stop myself. I guess I'm growing as a person. Cole bends down and pulls two more cans from a crate at his feet on his other side.

"You'd think he'd have his sea legs after two weeks at sea," he says, offering me one of the cans.

I don't take it. "He's spending twenty hours a day in a medical gel bath recovering from frostbite, hypothermia, and more than a few broken bones, Cole," I reply, more than a little rankled. "I hardly think sea legs are his biggest—"

"I meant Ducky."

"Oh. Well, I think he was hoping that Oates's contact would come pick us up in a fancy spaceship or something, instead of an old oil tanker. But I guess beggars can't be choosers when it comes to which smugglers aid in your escape from prison." I do take the can from him then, but I don't open it. It's shiny and silvery smooth, like a can of peaches with the label pulled off. I play with the pop-top, lifting it slightly up and then letting it snap back onto the lid. "Besides, I'm sure Ducky'd barf in a spaceship, too. I've yet to discover any form of transportation gentle enough for his world-class motion sickness."

"At least Oates had friends out there who could pick us up," Cole says. "Even if they are kinda shady. After those pricks on the elevator platform left us stranded."

"Well, the elevator was kinda sorta completely destroyed," I remind him. "Those guys didn't have any way to send a transport to pick us up before they left."

"They could have left us *something*," Cole argues. "Instead of scrambling back home with that weak-ass excuse about a 'communications blackout.' If it weren't for Oates's pals, we'd still be stuck in the snow."

I look at Cole's profile, a beautiful silhouette against the white sunlight. There are things we need to be talking about. Another conversation entirely.

I'm not sure I'm ready to have it.

"They're still fighting down there," I say, darting my eyes down to the deck below, where all the Almiri and Enosi trapped with us in Antarctica have been battling it out for the past several days. They stop only for meal breaks. "Oates is doing his best to referee, but no one's seeing eye to eye on the whole let's-go-back-to-Almiri-headquarters-and-hug-this-out plan we've got going."

"Well, probably because it's a shit plan," Cole says.

"It's the only option we have."

Cole turns and looks at me. "Elvs, the hybrids are never going to be okay with going to HQ. We Almiri have been huge dicks to them for centuries. And I don't see that changing anytime soon just because we all took a boat ride together."

"The Jin'Kai invasion is coming," I say, and I hate to admit it, but even I can hear the hint of desperation in my voice. "Marsden said as much. A fleet of those Devastators is on its way to Earth. Our only hope is to make sure everyone who calls Earth home—Almiri, Enosi, human—learns to play nice and form a unified resistance."

"That's all well and good to say," Cole says, "except that's not why you want to go back to HQ. You think Byron knows how to find Olivia."

"Yeah," I snap back. "And so what if that's my reason? You act like wanting to find my daughter is some sort of crime."

She stole her. My own mother kidnapped my daughter, right out of my hands, and handed her over to Dr. Marsden.

"*Our* daughter," Cole says, and when I give him a funny look, he bores his stony eyes into me. "You said 'my.' You keep forgetting that Olivia's my daughter too."

I do. I do keep forgetting that. Probably because Cole hasn't been acting much like a parent lately. Probably because he's been acting more like a whiny, entitled baby, sulking on the deck when he should be helping Oates to get everyone to play nice like I've been doing for two weeks straight. Suddenly I feel butterflies climbing into my throat. I haven't felt butterflies, not truly, since I was home in Ardmore, before any of this alien invasion craziness was a thing. A million years ago, in my bedroom in Ardmore, when Cole touched my hair, and I looked into his eyes, and he kissed me for the very first time.

Those were very different butterflies.

"I think we should break up," I say softly. The words hover in the air between us like they're in a cartoon speech bubble. Cole barely reacts at all, but I notice the corner of his mouth twitch. For several seconds the only sound is the crashing of the waves against the hull of the ship. I wait, as patiently as I can, for the explosion of feelings that's probably welling up inside him right now.

"Whatever," Cole says finally.

Not exactly what I was expecting.

"*Whatever?*" I snap back.

"What do you want me to say, Elvs?"

"Something more than 'whatever.' We have a *child* together, for Christ's sake."

"*You're* the one who just said you want to break up!"

I'm at a loss. I want so badly for Cole to understand. I want to tell him that he'll always be my first true love, that he'll always be the father of my child, and that there will always be a special place in my heart just for him. That I'll always want him in my life, but that I'm growing into a different person from who I was when we met, and that I need to figure out who this new person is going to be. I want to tell him I'm sorry.

"Fine. Whatever, then," I shoot back at him.

My mouth feels like I've been chewing on cotton balls. I crack open the silver can and take a huge sip, only to immediately spit it back out in a glorious spray over the bow of the ship.

"Jesus, Cole! What in the hell is this?" I run my finger along the lip of the can, picking up the thick white liquid. "Have you been drinking *condensed milk*?"

"It was all they had in the galley!" he shouts. "And, hey, I don't have to explain myself to you, because *we just broke up!*"

With that, he storms away, brushing past Captain Oates, who is walking toward us. Cole doesn't break his stride and starts running as he gets farther away from me. Oates looks back at him before turning to me with a concerned look on his face.

"Miss Elvie?" he asks. "You're crying."

"It's nothing," I say, holding up the can of syrupy milk. "Just went down the wrong pipe."

"Ah." Oates settles in right beside me and looks out at the water. I can tell he doesn't believe me, but he's way too British to let on. "It's quite lovely, isn't it?"

"Yeah," I say, sniffing.

"It's been too long since I've been on the water. I hadn't realized how much I truly missed it."

"Well, seems like you could have called your buddies here to escape from prison anytime you wanted to."

"I broke the law of my people, even if I felt that law to be unjust. If I wanted my actions to mean something, I could not run away from their consequences."

"I didn't realize extra hanky-panky was such a weighty

subject for you," I say. Seriously, I've always thought the Almiri "code" was a bit bogus—deciding who a dude gets to sleep with, and then locking him up indefinitely if said dude can't keep it in his pants—but my buddy Oates has taken things to a new level of bogusitude.

Oates looks me dead in the eye. Now I've done it. I should just keep my mouth shut for the rest of the trip so that I don't piss anyone else off.

"These sailors who aid us in our journey home . . . ," Oates begins.

"The smugglers? What about them?"

"They are not smugglers. Well, they are, but not in the manner that you suppose. They are freedom runners. They transport the, shall we say, recently liberated, to safer harbor."

"You mean like escaped convicts?" I ask.

Oates shrugs. "Perhaps, sometimes. But not always. They have been making their covert runs for centuries now."

"They're Almiri?" I'm stunned. I mean, I guess they were handsome enough dudes, but with this entire alien race war being such a sausagefest, I've been getting kind of immune to hot guys.

Oates nods. "They have helped to transport freed slaves. Illegal prisoners of war. And even men and women like yourself."

"Enosi," I say, slowly beginning to understand. "You mean they've helped hybrids escape from Almiri camps. But how did they . . ." And then it dawns on me, full force. "You!" I turn to face Oates straight on. "Cape Crozier wasn't originally for Almiri Code-breakers with extra ants in their pants, was it?

The Almiri held Enosi captive there, back when the continent was unexplored. And you . . . your trip to the South Pole in the twentieth century . . . you were *freeing* them."

Oates is way too classy a dude to even acknowledge his own heroics. He simply rubs the palms of his hands along the cool rail. Me, being not so cool or classy, I slap him on the arm.

"Why didn't you ever say anything? You helped rescue, what, a hundred Enosi prisoners? A thousand? You need to tell them that! They need to see that not all Almiri are raging prejudiced asshats."

"The time may very well be at hand," Oates agrees. "I am equally concerned with convincing the Almiri Council that they have been, as you put it so poetically, 'asshats.'"

"So you, what? Stayed in the prison as a statement to Byron and the others?"

"I did. And it has already had some positive effects."

"Such as?"

"Well, your grandfather sent you to me, did he not?"

Byron, aka James Dean, aka my grandfather. Who would have imagined that sending your granddaughter to an Antarctic prison could be considered a *relaxed* position in the whole Almiri-Enosi conundrum?

"So he sent me to you to keep me and Olivia safe," I say.

"That was the idea. God laughs at all our plans, child."

I feel the tightness in my chest that comes whenever I allow myself to think about my daughter. "Byron will help us get Olivia back, won't he? I mean, I know the world is coming to an end and everything, but . . ."

"We will find your daughter. I gave you my word. But you

must be patient. There are many developments that we must account for now, not the least of which is the imminent Jin'Kai invasion."

I clench my teeth and say nothing. I mean, I know he's right, that there are bigger things going on right now. That I need to be patient.

But that doesn't mean I can do it.

I grip the railing and smell the salty air as a frigid breeze blows across the deck of the rickety old boat. There's a bitter taste in my mouth, which can only be blamed in part on the milk residue on my tongue.

"How did you know?" I ask.

"Miss?"

"You stayed trapped for so long, because you thought it was the right thing to do. How did you know when it was time to free yourself?"

"We are all captains of our own destiny," he says, putting an arm gently around my shoulders. "When the time comes, you just know."

And for some reason that starts me bawling, crying like some sort of girl. I press my face into Oates's coat, letting it absorb my tears. He pats my back.

"There, there, Miss Elvie," he reassures me. "Everything's all right now. You're almost there."

And as I look out at the water, I can almost allow myself to believe it.

Hold on, I think to my daughter, wherever she may be. *Just hold on a little longer. Mama's coming for you.*

Hold on.

Chapter Two

IN WHICH THINGS ARE SEEN THAT CANNOT BE UNSEEN

"Wait," Ducky says as we walk down the narrow hall toward the med bay. "You *broke up* with Cole? Like, 'broke up' broke up?"

"Let's not make a thing about it, please," I say. "Let's file it under 'Old News.'"

"Old news? It happened, like, three seconds ago. And need I remind you that you've been swoony over that guy since you first laid eyes on him?"

"Seriously, Duck. Focus. We're almost home. Well, to the Poconos, at least. One short helicopter trip away from the Poconos."

Ducky clears his throat. "Helicopter. Goodie."

"Duck, you can barf out the window, okay? Nut up. We've got to be ready to leave as soon as we dock. And I've got one more Dad-shaped piece of luggage left to pack up."

We reach the med bay, and I knock gently on the door. There's no response, so I knock again and finally receive a very weak "Come in" from inside. Ducky and I enter quickly, closing the door behind us in order to give Dad some privacy from the hustle and bustle out in the hallway.

"Dad, everything's nearly ready to— *Oh my God!*" I spin around away from Dad and try to grab the door but instead smash head-on into Ducky.

Ducky slaps a hand over his eyes, but it's too late for him. For either of us. "Mr. Nara! I'm so sorry. Marnie told us you were almost ready to, um, go."

"Elvie, Donald, for heaven's sake, what's the matter?" Dad asks, his voice thin.

"Scarred. For. Life," I tell my father, emphasizing each bit of punctuation so that I really make my point clear. I push myself against the door, leaning my forehead against the cool metal surface. There's a hideous sloshing behind me, but I don't dare turn around again for fear of being subjected to the horrific sight another time.

"Dearheart, please don't be so dramatic," Dad scolds.

"Dramatic?" I shout, rather dramatically. "Did it ever occur to you that if someone has the decency to knock before entering that you should try to sink *below* the goo line if you're floating naked in a tub?"

"It's a medical recuperation bath, Elvie, and this 'goo' is healing my wounds. It's not like I'm in here enjoying a leisurely soak."

"That doesn't mean you should reenact *Welcome to My Dingle* for your daughter," I say. "Goo line. Get under it. I'm begging you."

Ducky still has a hand over his eyes, which is making it

difficult for him to find the doorknob and escape. "I just . . . I just . . ." He gives up and slithers to the floor, back against the wall, eyes still shut tight. "Don't mind me," he says. "I'll be over here. Not looking at anything."

"Dad, for God's sake, you've broken Ducky," I say.

"Please tell me you're not here to make me drink more of that vile tea," is Dad's only reply. His voice is wavering between legitimately enfeebled and playing the martyr. "Donald, tell your girlfriend her tea stinks."

Ducky manages the incredible feat of becoming even more flustered. With his eyes still squeezed shut, his face turns a crimson red, and he begins sputtering like a backed-up faucet. "She's not my girlfriend," he gets out at last.

"Dad, Marnie told me she was getting you out of the tub." I shield my eyes with my hand, in case Dad hasn't found the good sense to shift deeper into the goo yet, and turn to speak to him more directly. "It's almost time to leave."

Dad sloshes a bit in the tub, making a sickening *slorp!* sound. I try to keep down the little bit of food I managed to eat today. "I'd never make the trip, Elvie," he says, laying it on even thicker than the liquid he's currently marinating in. "Not in my condition."

"*Dad.*" I roll my eyes, which is a mistake, because the ceiling is reflective. "Marnie says you're more than capable of making the helicopter journey. And in any case, you don't have a choice. I'm not about to leave you here."

Dad's response is quiet. "I'm not well, dearheart."

I sigh the dramatic sigh a million girls have used on a million fathers before me. But the truth is that even though I'll probably have my father's disturbingly pudgy image burned into my brain until death or a severe head injury releases me, I'm really glad to still *have* a father who is able to flash me. And I totally get why he's hesitant to go back out into the elements. I mean, he was frostbitten *before* we had to bail out of that exploding space elevator car, and the blisteringly cold air and the whole semi-crashing into the snowy fields of Antarctica didn't do him any favors.

"We'll make sure you're all bundled up," I say. "The warmest suit we can fi— Dad, *seriously*, can't you, like, cover yourself with a washcloth or something?"

"I mean, we've never used the words 'girlfriend' or 'boyfriend' before," Ducky says, clearly off in another world that does not involve a buoyant parent in his birthday suit. "We were prisoners together, so we were bound to be close. But now that we're not in Antarctica anymore, I figure . . ." He trails off.

"Ducky," I tell him lovingly. "You adorable, idiotic dillhole. You and Marnie are totally boyfriend-girlfriend. You're practically joined at the hip. I'm surprised you don't break out in a rash when she eats fresh fruit. Now can we please focus on my father?"

"I don't know," Ducky says, eyes still squeezed shut. "I can't help thinking that this whole time I've just been her special camp friend."

Suddenly there's a new voice at the door. "Wha's this all about, then?" I turn to see Marnie, arms akimbo, wearing a very disapproving look on her face. "Dinnae I tell ye to get clear of that stuff twenty minutes ago?" she asks my father.

"I'm not *well*," he reiterates.

"Oh, ye poor wee bairn," Marnie says, the sarcasm slicing through her thick Scottish burr. I notice that she really lays into her accent when she's annoyed.

She pulls a thick bathrobe from a cabinet along the far wall. "Now come on outta there, and let's get the goop off ye," she says. "Hello there, Donald."

Ducky replies with little more than, "*Yeep!*"

Dad is still pleading his case. "I shouldn't be moved in my condition," he says. He's really working it now, all coughs and groans. Fortunately, and perhaps in an attempt to prolong his stay in the tub, he has submerged himself so that everything from the chin down is safely below the surface. I open my mouth to scold him, but Marnie holds up her hand, stopping me.

"Very well," she says, handing me the robe. She heads back over to the closet and starts rummaging through the now pretty bare supplies. Dad peeks over the edge of the tub to catch a glance at what she's up to. "I think I know why ye've been feeling so uncomfortable, Harry," Marnie calls over her shoulder. "Ye've been rolling around in that regenerative enzyme bath fer days now, and yer healing quite nicely, but there are . . . side effects."

"Side effects?" Dad asks squeamishly. His chin is resting on the edge of the tub, his eyes boring holes in Marnie's back as she digs out what she was looking for.

When she steps back from the closet, she is holding a large green synthetic cloth pad, a box of latex gloves, and what looks to be a small baby's bottle. "Yer stopped up, ye poor love," she says. "Constipated. Ye haven't moved yer bowels since we got ye in here, have ye, Harry?"

The goo makes another *slorp* sound as Dad moves to the far edge of the tub. "My . . . bowels?" comes his thin, worried voice.

"'Tis nothing to be ashamed of, Harry. We all get plugged up now and again. We'll just be givin' ye a wee enema to get things moving, and then ye'll feel much more able to move about."

"*Enema?*" Dad says, his eyes wide as, well, really wide eyes.

Marnie snaps a latex glove over her slender hand. "Of course, if that doesn't work right away, we can always try digital extract—"

The *slorp* turns into a *fwa-plop* as Dad practically levitates out of the tub and lands with a thud on the micro-tile.

"No need, no need!" Dad cries, suddenly sounding a *lot* less feeble. "You know, I'm actually feeling pretty mobile after all." As if to prove his point, Dad starts swinging his arms and legs around like he's getting a good stretch in after a run. Which, in case it weren't obvious, is *not* helping any with the whole buck-naked-Dad situation I'm having. I can only imagine the long-term trauma inflicted on my cerebellum by watching my father twist and flex while green ooze sloughs off his rotund nude body.

"What's happening?" Ducky cries, hand slapped over his eyes again. "What's going on?"

"Come on, Duck. Let's give Dad and your 'special camp friend' a little alone time," I say, and I yank him to his feet so we can hightail it out of the room as quickly as possible. Marnie gives me a quizzical look as we head to the door, and I realize I might have tipped Ducky's hand a little bit, which makes me feel bad. But not bad enough to stick around to explain myself.

"Dad, I'll be out here!" I call to my father. "Don't come out till you are *completely dressed*!"

With any luck, maybe someday I'll get kicked really hard in the head.

As modes of transportation go, helicopters most definitely rank in the top-ten loudest. That plus the invention of repulsor tech has really made them pretty obsolete. Before succumbing to a much needed nap, Dad subjected us to a mini-lecture on the copter we currently found ourselves riding in. A retrofitted Dragonfly 20 with magnetic stabilization, it was apparently one of the last helicopters ever mass-produced, back in the '50s. Originally a military craft, the only ones left in circulation tend to be used by emergency relief organizations with limited funds to transport personnel and/or supplies to destitute regions such as Africa, Eastern Europe, and Detroit. The thing is roomy enough that it easily houses half of our Antarctic contingent—Dad, Cole, Ducky, Marnie, yours truly, and the rest of the Enosi—while Oates flies on a second copter with the Almiri.

Of course, the novelty of flying on such a relic is somewhat muted by the Fantastic Barfing Twins huddled together over a bucket near the back of the copter.

"*Blaaaaaaargh!*" goes Ducky, face stuck in the bucket, hands tightly gripping the sides. Cole shoves him in the shoulder.

"Quit hoggin' it, Donalll . . . ," he slurs. Clearly, at some point between our little chat on the tanker and now, Cole managed to get into something quite a bit stronger than condensed milk. He tugs the plastic bucket toward him with the sloppy urgency that only the truly inebriated possess. The contents of the bucket slosh around as Cole envelops it in a nauseated bear hug.

"Oh God, Cole," Ducky gasps. "Please, give it back. I'm gonna . . . Oh, *blaaaaaaargh*!" He manages to grab the bucket just in time, but even as he's still yakking, Cole steals it back and shoves Ducky more forcibly, causing him to lose his balance and tip over.

"Hey, you leave him alone!" I have to scream to be heard over the whirring of the helicopter's blades.

"You don't get to tell me what to do anymore!" Cole screams back. "Because you *arnamygirfren*!"

"What?"

"You," Cole says more deliberately, staring daggers at me. "Arna. Mygirfren."

"They're quite the pair, aren't they?" Marnie muses. I'm sitting on the ground next to my snoozing father. (How he can sleep with all the racket/barfing is a true mystery.) Marnie sits on the other side of Dad, her back to the dueling vomiteers, and gives me a smile. She checks Dad's forehead with the back of her hand.

"Good," she says. "No fever. He's going to be fit to bring down a bear sooner 'n not."

"He was lucky to have such a good nurse," I tell her.

"Eh, give credit where it's due. The man has a will on 'im."

"Still," I say. "Thank you."

Marnie shakes me off. "So, I hear ye've called it quits with the cologne model, is that it?"

"Word gets around fast."

"Ducky's spoken of naught else since ye told him. He really loves ye, that one."

"Ducky?" I feel my cheeks getting red.

"No, the other lad who's followed ye around yer whole life," she says with a wink.

"Ducky's the best," I say. And I mean it.

"Can I ask ye somethin'?" Marnie looks back at the boys over her shoulder. "That thing ye said earlier. About 'special camp friends'?"

"Oh, that," I say, exhaling a breath I didn't realize I was holding. "I was just, um, having a go at Ducky."

"About what? About me?" Marnie arches her eyebrow, and I am reminded that she could probably judo toss me out of the helicopter in one fluid motion if she doesn't like my answer.

"Yes, but, I mean, not *about* you. I mean . . . How to put this? I think Ducky's afraid that, now that we're free and heading home, you're going to find him less compelling than say, some rugged Enosi freedom fighter from your past."

"Is that the truth, now?" she asks, smirking. She turns back to the boys. "And what if I'm afeart there's someone else he'll fancy now, seein' as how they're available?"

"Um, I don't know what you—"

"Donald Hunter Pence!" Marnie screams suddenly, rising up. Ducky snaps his head at the sound.

Marnie strides across the platform to where Ducky and Cole sit. Instinctively I leap up and follow her.

"Am I to understand that now that yer options are improvin', ye plan on castin' me aside, ye two-timin' rake?" Marnie fumes. Her blue eyes are wide with indignation, which—don't ask me how—seems to make her hair look redder.

"What?" Ducky asks, shock overwhelming his nausea. "Rake? Who? What? Don't speak so Scottish. I can't—"

"I'm onto ye, lad, and yer womanizing ways." She slaps him on the arm for emphasis. "Did ye enjoy yerself, anyway? Playing me heart like a bloody fiddle?"

"Who said? What? Who? What?" Ducky looks like he's being attacked by invisible mosquitoes all around his head.

"I'm yer special camp friend, izzat it?" Marnie continues. She's laying into the poor guy with everything she's got. Her eyes are wide, her finger's a-jabbing, and her brogue is turned to high. "Oh, ye've got all the time in the world for plain old Marnie when yer locked away in the blizzards. But with our Elvie being a single lass again, now that yer bloody soul mate is yers for the pluckin—"

"I knew it!" Cole interrupts, through a queasy burp.

"Elvie, what did you *say* to her?" Ducky asks me, shielding his face from a barrage of slaps.

"I may have said something about 'special camp friend,'" I admit with a cringe. "But that's it. I didn't mean to imply—"

"You've been after my girl the whole time!" Cole slurs at Ducky, lunging toward him awkwardly. Ducky dodges easily, and Cole crumples to the ground.

"Marnie, I swear," Ducky says, scrambling to his feet, "that's not what I meant."

"So you dinnae fancy Elvie, then?" Marnie asks.

"I was telling Elvie that I was afraid *you* didn't feel the same as me."

"And how izzit that ye feel, Donald?" Marnie says, looking him square in the eye.

"I . . ." Ducky looks around, possibly considering a head-first dive out of the helicopter to avoid answering. "I . . ." The rest of his words are mumbled into his chest so that I can't hear.

"Wha's that?" Marnie asks.

"I fancy you," he says, slightly more clearly.

Marnie's stern gaze immediately breaks, and she bursts out laughing.

"Do ye really think I'd be messin' with ye, prison or no, if I dinnae fancy ye back, ye nidderrodded dunce?"

"Um, I . . . ," Ducky says. "No?"

"Of course not." She grabs at his chest and clutches his shirt, pulling his face close to hers.

"Careful," Ducky says. "I smell like puke."

"And no doubt ye taste like it too." With that, Marnie plants a hard wet kiss on Ducky. "How's that fer a 'special camp friend'?" she says, before going in for a second smooch.

Cole turns to me, equal parts confused and queasy. "So, you didn't break up with me because of Ducky?" he asks.

I roll my eyes. "No," I tell him honestly.

"So, you really just don't like me at all?"

"Cole, I—"

A hand grabs at my sleeve. "Dearheart?"

I turn and look at my father. He's as white as a sheet. And not some ordinary run-of-the-mill sheet either. I mean like a really, really noticeably white example of sheetiness.

"What's the matter, Dad?" I ask, worried. "You feel sick?"

"You can have. the bucket if you need it, Mr. Nara," Cole offers.

"No. Elvie. We've arrived."

"We're in the Poconos already?" Time sure flies when you're fighting with a vomiting comedy duo. "Do we need to send them a signal or something, to let them know we're coming in? I don't know if they have defensive laser mounts embedded in their lodge-stronghold thing or not, but better safe than—"

"Elvie, it's gone," Dad says.

I feel a sudden pit in my stomach. They can't have left. I need Byron. He's the only one who might be able to help me track down my baby. "How can you be sure?" I am reaching panic levels again. *Hold on,* I repeat to myself. To somewhere-Olivia. *Hold on. Mama's coming.* "Have you tried to radio them? It's the middle of the night; maybe they're all asleep."

"Elvie," Dad says again, the concern practically exploding all over his face. "It's gone."

"The lodge?"

"The Poconos."

All I'm aware of is how warm my face feels. Like a million red-hot needles were all carefully inserted into my skin at the same time. I rush to the long window along the side of the helicopter and look down at the ski resort town below. There are no lights for as far as I can see, save for the dim orange glow of a dozen fires.

The Poconos are burning.

Chapter Three

WHEREIN OUR MERRY GANG ONCE AGAIN FINDS ITSELF IN A PICKLE

"Try it now, dearheart," Dad says, his butt sticking out from under the console. Seeing the site of all our hopes for humanity's salvation ablaze has given the man an unexpected burst of energy, and now he's on his hands and knees, attempting to reconnect power to the lone computer system that seems to have survived the devastation.

One computer terminal. That's what we've found in the still-smoking rubble of the Almiri ski lodge headquarters. One—count it, *one*—computer on the second floor that was only nominally scathed by whatever took place here. Everything else in the area has been completely decimated. An entire town annihilated. Once we tuned in to local news broadcasts, we got reports of an apparent catastrophic overload in the town's power grid that had caused a cascade of electrical fires and explosions. The area has been evacuated for the time being while folks try to figure out the safest way to proceed.

But the second we landed at the skeletal remains of the lodge and saw the concentration of damage surrounding it, I knew what had happened here. Perhaps the power grid overload in town was used as a distraction, but the damage to the lodge is different, specific, and familiar. The energy burns on the building façade. The pinpoint destruction of crucial support structures. This wasn't a power surge. This was the Jin'Kai.

But which Jin'Kai? It couldn't be the invasion. It wouldn't make sense for them to target this one spot and then disappear. No, when they do hit, they're going to hit hard and fast, and they won't go anywhere once they're finished. This hit and run has Dr. Marsden written all over it. His splinter group must have found a way to locate the Almiri and target them. But why? Were they looking for something, or just trying to eliminate an adversary when the adversary wasn't expecting it? With the Almiri gone, what hope do I have to track my baby now? It's taking everything I have to not melt into a puddle of tears.

Hold on, Olivia, I think again. But the voice in my head is growing weaker by the minute. *Hold on.*

There's a slight hum as the power turns on and the monitor in front of me flickers to life. Barely, but there's a flicker.

"It worked!" I shout. From underneath the console comes Dad's trademark "Hmmph" of triumph.

The victory, however, is short-lived. I let out a frustrated sigh as I take in the black cursor, blinking against a totally white screen. I punch the screen with the bottom of my fist. The already cracked display rains little shards onto the console.

"What is it, dearheart?" Dad asks, shimmying awkwardly

out from underneath the console. He rises up on his knees to take a look.

"The operating system's been wiped," I tell him. Through the empty blown-out window frame I gaze at where the two helicopters rest in the snow. *Hold on, Olivia.* "Completely erased."

"There must be something here to salvage," Dad says. "We'll run some recovery software, or . . ." But he trails off without even finishing the thought. We both know that Apple probably doesn't make any software compatible with an Almiri mainframe server.

When Cole enters the room with Ducky and Marnie, I decide, just for the moment, to pretend like I am okay. I steady my breathing. Straighten my back.

"Any luck?" I ask them. The gang's been searching the rubble and the surrounding grounds for survivors. But as soon as I see their faces, I know the answer. Ducky, for one, looks like he has just vomited. And not from motion sickness.

Marnie puts a protective arm around Ducky's waist. Cole's face is ashen.

"We found them," Cole says, and it's obvious he's been experiencing the world's worst sobering-up. I'm hoping somehow that he won't say what he does next, but of course he has to. "They're all dead."

The ice in my chest plummets into my stomach. "All of them?" I ask.

Cole merely looks at the ground.

"They were still in their rooms," Marnie says. "It looks like they were locked in. They couldnae get out when . . ." She trails off and motions with her eyes at the burning debris surrounding us.

"Oh God." I sink to the floor.

Cole is the one who sinks down to comfort me. "We'll find her, Elvie," he tells me.

I bury my head in my arms. "Will we?" I ask.

"We have to."

Hold on, Olivia.

"Byron might still be alive," Dad says, rubbing my shoulder. "He seems like a more than capable fellow. Perhaps he was able to—"

"Shhh," Ducky says suddenly.

"What d'ye hear?" Marnie asks.

Ducky shakes his head—he's not sure. When he points to the blown-out window, I quickly rise and make my way over.

I hear it now too.

Voices. Outside. I peek my head out to look.

Down below, our friends Rupert and Clark, along with a handful of other Almiri and Enosi, are near the first-floor rear entrance, most likely searching the perimeter of the grounds.

"They're talking to someone," I whisper to the others, holding a hand up for them to stay back away from the window. "I can't tell who."

"But who could be—" Cole starts at full volume, before Marnie leans down to slap a hand over his mouth. I strain to listen to the conversation thirty meters away.

"We belong to the cooperative that runs the lodge, officers," I hear Rupert say. "We were only trying to survey the damage."

"In the middle of the night?" comes the gruff reply.

Cops. Damn. They must have seen the helicopters landing. Or perhaps the local authorities left a small detachment to patrol the mountain. Either way, dealing with a squad of clueless policeman could get real complicated real fast. How exactly are we supposed to explain who we are or what we're doing here?

"Sir, I'm going to need you to keep your hands where I can see them," one of the officers barks.

Rupert's hands are up near his chest. Even I can seem them. "What we have here is a simple misunderstanding," Rupert says. He sounds like he's trying to be playful, so I can only imagine that the police officer is handsome. Still, Rupert, not the time. "We didn't realize the area was off-limits. Don't you think we can discuss this like two—"

"Hands *up*," the officer growls again. Honestly, I'm surprised by the guy's tone. I've yet to meet anyone, male or female, who can resist Rupert's charms when he decides to crank the sexy up to eleven.

"Dearheart," Dad whispers. He comes over to tug on my arm. "Get away from the window."

But my eyes are fixed on the scene below.

As Rupert takes a step back, the main cop he's been dealing with comes into view.

Strong jaw.

Five o'clock shadow.

"*No!*" I shriek at the top of my lungs. But it's too late, because before Rupert or any of the others can even register who's screaming about what, the Jin'Kai in police garb pulls out his ray gun and fires. Rupert takes the blast straight through the chest and collapses backward in the snow, dead. It's instant pandemonium as the other Jin'Kai raise their weapons and open fire on the remaining Almiri and Enosi. Clark, stunned by the sudden execution of his best friend, is a half second late in reacting to a shot in his direction. He catches the blast in the shoulder and spins full around before falling face-first into the snow. I scream again, which distracts Clark's assailant just long enough for Clark to jump back up and swipe the guy's legs out from under him. I don't see the rest, because my screaming has drawn the rest of the Jin'Kai's attention, and all at once shots are perforating what's left of the wall around me.

Marnie pulls me down away from the window. "We've got to get out of here!" she yelps.

"But the others . . . ," I start.

"There's no time. We haven't any weapons. We must leave. Now!"

And for once I think maybe I'll listen to someone's advice.

Marnie, Cole, Ducky, Dad, and I book it out of the room. We're halfway down the hallway before we realize we don't have the faintest clue where we're going. More shots ring out from below, followed by confused shouts as the Jin'Kai make their way into the building and take aim at our remaining comrades.

"There's no way to get to the helicopters," I pant as we run. Way to state the obvious, Elvie. "They probably have all the entrances blocked." Maybe when I'm done with all the running, I can go back to school to get my PhD in dur.

"Is there any other exit?" Marnie asks. "A service entrance, or a garbage chute, perhaps?"

Oh dear Lord, not another garbage chute.

Cole suddenly gets a look on his face like a lightbulb just went off. Which, honestly, is not a look I've ever seen on him before.

"This way. Follow me!" he barks. He directs us down the left hallway, around a sharp turn, and toward a flight of stairs. For the first time since we hightailed it off the *Echidna*, he actually looks like the commando that barged his way onto a ship full of baddies to rescue me. I didn't realize quite how much I missed that Cole until just now.

We're racing down the hallway, when suddenly the floor breaks away beneath Dad. He lets out a startled squawk, and his right leg disappears. Just vanishes into the floor, all the way up to the knee. Ducky and I swarm on him as quickly as we can and try to hoist him up, but he's too heavy.

"The knee!" he grunts. "Why is it always my knee?"

"Cole, help!" I call ahead of me. The sounds of our impending doom are growing louder behind us. Stomping. Chasing. Jin'Kai barking orders to one another. But no more screaming. No more shots. For all I know, everyone else is dead already.

Cole slides to a halt and doubles back to us.

"Step back, Elvie!" Dad says, before letting Cole grab him underneath the arms. "The whole floor is completely unstable." Cole lifts Dad easily, and together they start back down the hall. Cole stops, though, when he realizes I'm not following them. Instead I'm kicking at the hole Dad fell through, filling it with clouds of debris and splintered wood.

"Elvie, what are you doing?" Cole shouts.

"Only be a minute!" I holler back, still kicking. It's not

until I hear our pursuers around the far corner that I turn tail and run toward the others. Ducky is waving his arms in a windmill motion, urging me on.

That's when the "cops" turn the corner and open fire.

Ducky flinches as the shots fizzle around him. "Just go!" I shout. He obliges, turning and making his way up the stairs where the others are already racing out of sight. A few more shots whip by me as I follow. At least my efforts to not be blasted to death are aided by the wreckage the Jin'Kai have already produced. The hallway is so trashed that I have to zigzag around the mess, which probably makes me a slightly more difficult target to hit.

I'd also like to think that my time in Antarctica helped me shed most of the baby weight.

"Hurry, Elvie. They're getting closer!" Ducky calls from the top of the stairs.

That's exactly what I'm counting on.

The weakened floor gives way under the hot cops' stomping feet, and I whirl around just in time to catch the results of my considerable kicking skills. The first two dopes fall completely through and crash to the floor below. The third manages to grab the edge of the newly gaping hole, but all that serves to do is rip the edge of the floor away even further, which sends him and number four—who had managed to stop just short of the fall—tumbling after their buddies, who have landed in a heap of douche bag below us.

I catch up to the others, pretty pleased with myself.

"Congrats," Marnie says drolly. "Ye've bought us ten seconds. After costing us twenty."

I frown. There'll be time later to be annoyed with Marnie for being right. Hopefully. For now I run.

Cole, with my father in tow, leads us down the new wide hallway toward an atrium, where the high glass ceiling has completely shattered to the ground. The cold night air rushes in around me as we run to the far door, slushing our way through beads of safety glass. I'm trying to figure out why Cole is leading us *up*. I'm really hoping he isn't planning on all of us leaping off a balcony, having forgotten that not everybody can survive a twenty-meter jump.

But when we come out through the door onto the balcony, suddenly I wish that jumping had been Cole's plan all along.

"You've got to be flipping kidding me," I say.

"You got any better suggestions?" Cole asks as he races to the battery console against the far railing, where he rips off the front panel with one hand. "Mr. Nara, could you?" He is still holding my father.

"I suppose I could," Dad says, sliding out of Cole's arms and doing a pretty weak job of holding himself up as he bends down to inspect the panel's wiring. After a single moment of consideration, he shifts his gaze across the expanse beyond the balcony. "Although I'm not quite sure I *should*."

The balcony on which we currently find ourselves is a massive covered wooden structure where the Almiri probably had secret tea parties or something. Despite the blast damage to the surrounding lodge, this place has stayed relatively intact. (Good thing, or we'd be toast right now.) Each beam has been carefully engraved, and if I were super into woodcraft—or, you know, if I weren't in the process of fleeing for my life—I'd probably spend more than a millisecond taking in the intricate details of the wildlife scenes carefully carved into the wood: squirrels climbing trees, wildflowers and bunnies, cute baby deer, that sort of thing.

Right now, of course, I'm more focused on the goons behind us.

And, oh yeah, the *giant gaping chasm* below.

Because this is not just any artsy-fartsy balcony Cole has lead us to. Oh no. It is, in fact, the base of a chairlift that stretches horizontally across the peaks of two neighboring mountains.

"Are you kidding me with this crap?" I say to no one in particular. "Why is this a thing? Tell me, why do the Almiri have a ski lift with no safety net just dangling over the edge of Splatter Mountain? Were they kamikaze snowboarding in their spare time?"

"That's, uh, a really big drop," Ducky says as he looks out over the ledge to the slope below.

Marnie looks too, then glances behind us. I have a feeling she's thinking the same thing I am: Are we safer attempting to cross a two-hundred-meter drop when there's a band of angry aliens behind us with ray guns, or might we be wiser to, you know, *not* do that?

"We could try to slide down the slope," Marnie interjects.

Dad's still fiddling with the lift's operating panel. "That's about as straight a drop down as you could ask for," he says.

"Why would you ever ask for that?" I mutter. The drop reminds me of the Death Torpedo waterslide on the board-walk down the shore. Except instead of merely chafing your thighs and shooting you into a pool with a nose full of water, this one would knock you across an assortment of jagged rocks and leave you a giant jelly smear at the foot of the mountain.

"All set!" Dad cries, slapping a triumphant hand on the control panel.

"So," I say, glancing down the side of the mountain once more, then back to where the Jin'Kai—and our certain doom—quickly approaches. I grab tight hold of the nearest chairlift. "Me first, then?"

I slide into the chair, and Ducky sits down beside me. At first I'm surprised he's chosen to plummet to his death next to me and not his girlfriend. But then, of course, I notice that Duck's skin is ashen gray, and despite the cold, he's sweating bullets. He probably could've sat down next to Dr. Marsden and not have noticed. I try to get ahold of myself, in order to help Ducky get ahold of *him*self.

"Ducky," I say in as soothing a tone as I can muster, while Cole helps my father settle in next to Marnie in the chair behind us. "You can do this, Duck. It's just a chair. You sit in chairs all the time. All you have to do is sit and not look down." Ducky nods vacantly and pulls down the front safety rod (like a single strip of metal half a meter from our stomachs is *really* going to save us in the event of an emergency) and grabs hold of the bar beside him like it's a limited-edition Jetman figurine. "There you go," I say. "You can do it."

Ducky lets out a whimper.

"Ye'll be fine, love!" Marnie shouts from behind us. "Be a brave lad, yeah?"

And is it just me, or does Ducky sit up just the tiniest bit straighter after that?

As soon as Dad and Marnie are safely tucked into their seat, Cole dashes to the control panel and smacks the go button. The lift comes to life and starts us with a jolt across the gap. I turn around just in time to see Cole ripping the control panel away from the console and punching it through with his fist, sending sparks flying and assuring that the Jin'Kai can't simply hit reverse on us. A moment of real commando can-do from Cole.

"Nice thinking, Cole!" I shout at him.

"Feel bad for dumping me yet?" he shouts back.

"Let's discuss it at a different time, shall we?"

Ducky moans.

My feet dangle beneath me as the lift moves rapidly forward, swaying slightly back and forth. Our destination is obscured, and the cable disappears ahead of us into the dark. Ducky's breathing is raspy, and when I turn to him, I see that he has not followed my instructions at all and is in fact staring directly down at the gaping maw of death.

"Elvie, I'm not gonna make it," he says, voice trembling.

"You'll be fine, Duck," I tell him. "Just look ahead."

"No." Ducky shakes his head weakly. "No, I think . . . yeah, I think I'll pass out now."

And before I know it, Ducky has begun *sliding out of his seat*. His butt's almost off the bench before I manage to clutch at his jacket.

"Ducky!" I scream. One hand still tight on his jacket, I release my grip on the bar beside me and slap Ducky's face with everything I've got, to try to rouse him. But his eyes just roll around blankly.

"I'll be fine, Elvie," he mumbles. At this point I'm not even entirely sure he's conscious. "Just let me pass out for a little whi . . ." His voice trails off and he slides even farther. I grab him with both hands—one wrapped awkwardly around his back and the other clutching the material under his armpit—but he's far too heavy for me, and apparently he has far too great a death wish. His butt slips right off the seat, and his weight jolts my arms at the sockets and yanks us both full-force into the safety rod.

Which turns out to be a good thing, since the laser blast fired from behind us zips by directly where my head used to be, and singes the hood of my jacket. Several more shots zip by, all off target, which makes me think we must be far enough into the misty darkness that the baddies can't see us clearly. But the shots aren't far enough away to make me *not* want to totally crap my pants.

"Help!" I scream as Ducky's dead weight slips in my weakening grasp. His chin is on the safety rod at the moment, and I *might* be worried that the thing were cutting into his jugular, if it weren't currently the only thing holding him up. As for me, my gut's smashed so hard into the bar that I am *this close* to puking, but I'm keeping it together because Ducky has saved my ass more times than I can count. I'm a little peeved that this is the moment he decided to let me return the favor, but I suppose we can discuss that later.

At least the Jin'Kai seem to have ceased firing. Who cares why.

Suddenly I hear a clanging, and the chair begins to sway as the cable jostles violently. It takes me a long second to realize that the movement is *not* due to Ducky plummeting to his death below me but rather something moving on the cable above. With my grip still as tight as I can get around my bestie, I crane my neck as far as I am able, and to my surprise I see a figure *climbing toward me on the cable*.

"Ducky!" I scream. "Ducky, *wake up*! They're coming! They're—"

I look up again. It is not a Jin'Kai making his way hand over hand across the length of moving cable.

It's Marnie.

Holy shit, that girl's a badass.

"Make room!" she orders one second before swooping down to land beside me, where Ducky was once sitting. Thankfully, I managed to dart my head to the side just a few centimeters, avoiding a boot to the nose. As she squats in the moving chair, Marnie reaches down and manages to find a better purchase on Ducky's jacket. Together we haul him up, both of us grunting in equal parts exertion and frustration. Ducky is mumbling incoherently, making every attempt to slide out of our grips to his death, but after some tricky maneuvering and arm repositioning, Marnie raises the safety rod and we pull him safely back into the seat. I've got him by the feet, his upper body stretched across Marnie's lap. He looks for all the world like a napping baby.

"Remind me to murder him later," I tell Marnie.

"Not if I get 'im first," she replies.

I don't know if the cable has been jostling this whole time and in my concern for Ducky I simply didn't notice, but suddenly I am once again aware of lots of tugging and bouncing.

"Is that the Jin'Kai?" I holler at Marnie over the wind. If *she* can climb across on that cable, Lord knows those hunks of alien evil can do it too. I wrap my free arm tightly around the bar beside me and do my best to see what's causing the movement, but the fog here is thick.

"Probably Cole with yer da'," Marnie tells me. Sure enough, as soon as she says it, I can make out Cole, moving hand over hand across the cable just like Marnie did. Except that Cole's got my father hanging around his neck like a kid who's way too old for a piggyback ride. Dad—to put it mildly—looks freaked. I let out a breath of relief. "The Jin'Kai are comin' up behind them," Marnie goes on. "They'll be on us in minutes."

Looks like I sighed a little too soon.

"What do we—" I start. But Marnie's too quick for me.

"I've got a plan," she says, then without any warning pushes Ducky's full weight into my lap and stands up once more in the chair. We rock and clang and sway, and if Ducky were awake, I'm positive he would full-on motion-sickness-barf right in my face.

I cling to him more tightly.

"What are you doing?" I shout up at Marnie.

But she's got no time for me. She's gazing back at Cole and Dad. "Archer!" she shouts. "Gan, catch the chib!" And she pulls a slender knife out from the small of her back. How she kept it hidden from the Almiri this whole time is a mystery for another time—like, say, a time when she's totally not thinking of doing what I'm pretty sure she's thinking of doing.

She tosses the knife to Cole, who—despite the fact that he

is *clinging from a moving cable with a full-grown man on his back*—catches it one-handed.

"Cut the line!" Marnie shouts at him.

"Are you crazy?" I scream, eyes bulging.

She glances down at me. "Ye oughtta lower that safety bar," she says. Then she glances back at Cole again, apparently with just enough time to save us all from his deathly stupidity. "*Behind* ye, ye daft bampot!" she screeches. "Cut the line *behind* ye!"

Even from here I can hear Cole's sotto voce "D'oh!"

I slap down the safety bar and hold on for dear life.

Whatever type of blade Marnie's been packing must be the Ginsu's burlier cousin, because within seconds I hear the thick metal cord above us *twang*. I feel just the slightest of jerks—the cable beginning to snap.

As quick as lightning, Marnie squeezes herself back into her seat.

A second *twang*! And we jerk again.

"Donald, love," Marnie says to the boy in the fetal position between us. Ducky's eyes flutter open and roll lazily in her direction. "Remember that story ye were gabbing on about in such detail a ways back, to pass the time?" She reaches over to pet his head gently. "The one with the archeologist, carried a whip?"

He's waking up. "Um, yeah?" You can practically see him trying to make his way through the brain fog with a lantern.

Twang!

"Ye recall that bit in the middle?" Marnie goes on. "With the bridge and the mingin crocodiles?"

Ducky's eyes grow slowly but steadily larger, to the point where I think they might expand and take over his entire face. He rouses enough to reach back and grab hold of the arm of the lift chair, easing my burden considerably.

"Oh, sweet Mama Jama," Ducky exhales.

"That's it, dove," Marnie coos, leaning back in her seat to watch Cole slicing. She turns back to us. "Hold on ti—"

That's when the last cord breaks away, and the cable swings down, and we are immediately flung forward. Behind us I can hear the screams of the Jin'Kai as their end of the cable swings back toward the lodge. It's a very short-lived relief, since, you know, we're hurtling toward the side of a mountain at an increasingly alarming speed. I slide in my seat, but the inertia of our swing plus Ducky's mass keeps us both from falling out.

I'm going to have to apologize to that safety rod for mocking it earlier.

As we swing lower and lower, the snowy slope ahead of us comes into focus.

"Wait fer it!" Marnie calls over the whipping wind. How she can even manage to form words in this chaos is beyond me. "Hold . . ." We're a few dozen meters from the slope when she releases my buddy the safety rod and kicks off the back of the chair.

"Now!" she screams.

I drop below the chair and feel the seat whip over my head.

For a second it feels like I'm flying, but really what I'm doing is falling sideways, Ducky still clutched to my chest. The snow comes up at us, and I hit it with a *whompf!* losing hold of Ducky in the process. I hear the impact of the others in the snow as well, but I can't see them, because I'm busy rolling backward down the slope, head over heels, without any way to get my bearings. I roll around and around and around, until the large tall dark object I'm fast approaching reveals itself to be a giant tree, and I twist to crash back-first into it, which sends another shower of snow down on top of me.

As I start to lose consciousness, I wonder why I can't ever find myself running for my life somewhere like the Bahamas.

Chapter Four

IN WHICH HOPE, HAVING BEEN DASHED, MAKES A SURPRISING REAPPEARANCE

When I come to—seconds later? minutes?—I find myself still beneath the tree, looking up at the lightly falling snow. I decide that I must not have been out too long. Otherwise someone would have found me.

Assuming that they aren't all jelly stains on the mountainside.

"Dad? Ducky? Cole?" I call out weakly. "Marnie?" I get no response. I manage to sit up, my arms aching from the strain. I can feel what I imagine are some world-class bruises forming already. I look around in the dark, but all I see are the shadows of more trees. I rise slowly, unsure of what's making me so wobbly: my legs or my head. I wonder if I'm concussed. If that's the worst that comes out of falling off a kilometer-high ski lift and crashing into a mountain, then I suppose I'll count myself lucky.

There's a *shushing* sound out in the dark, coming toward

me. The dancing shadows are too much for my wonked-out vision to process, and I can't see who, or what, is moving in. As the *shushing* grows closer, I am able to determine that the rapid, synchronized footsteps are coming from farther down the slope. And they most definitely don't belong to my hobbled father or my extremely uncoordinated best friend.

I make a beeline away from the sound in a straight line, neither up nor down the hill. As soon as I start running, I hear the shushers change course in their pursuit. The snow isn't terribly deep, but the slope is steep enough that I am continuously losing my footing as I go. Ahead of me is a thick bramble of trees, and I move toward it, hoping to find cover among the pines.

"There she is!" one of them calls from behind me. In my panic my foot slips out from under me and I tumble, sliding on my ass through the dense tree coverage. I twist and turn in a series of comical contortions to avoid the trunks as best I can, and honestly I think I'm doing a pretty spectacular job of not smashing to death against an evergreen. I would probably give myself an A+ in Not Smashing, and that's not even grading on the curve. But I guess I've been too concerned about the trees and not enough about *huge honking boulders*, because suddenly one of those appears in front of me as though out of nowhere, and it's absolutely too late to move out of its way.

Well, we had a pretty good run there, Life.

I brace myself for the inevitable broken bones, praying I will somehow make it through the wreckage. . . .

And collide with the boulder with a dull *thud*.

A dull thud?

Sure enough, this particular boulder ends up being *soft*.

And warm.

And . . . furry?

"All right, human scum," says one of the three Jin'Kai I now find looming over me, ray guns pointed at my noggin. "Stand up, girl. Hands where we can see them."

The boulder behind me rumbles, and I smile at the suddenly confused looks on my attackers' faces. "Okay," I say. I rise from the ground, hands up over my head, and step to the side. "But before we go any further . . ." I nod toward the rumbling lump behind me. "Have you met my friend Drusilla?"

With that, the "boulder" rears up on its hind legs, revealing itself to be none other than Lord Byron's ursine companion, roughly 150 kilograms of bear-hurt. Drusilla is on top of the first Jin'Kai before he knows what's mauling him—pinning him to the ground and swiping at him with her massive paws.

The other two Jin'Kai open fire on the bear, and the smell of burned flesh and fur immediately fills my nostrils. I whip my head around to discover several large wounds they've opened in Drusilla's side. "No!" I cry out, throwing myself at one of the bastards. He merely tosses me aside, turning his gun on me.

But before he can fire, a flash of fur knocks his arm to the side, sending the shot astray. It takes me a second to realize that *this* lifesaver isn't Dru—she's still busy crushing her original prey, seemingly oblivious to the scorched wounds on her side. No, instead there are two dogs attached to my former assailant, and even in the commotion I recognize them as Thunder and Boatswain, Byron's pet pooches. They've got their jaws locked on the guy's forearm and crotch, respectively.

And the third Jin'Kai? Well, he has maybe a nanosecond to process the *When Animals Attack!* special unfolding in front of him before something smashes him in the back of the head and he drops to the ground, out cold.

Now, I spent a lot of boring days in Mrs. Kwan's English Lit class, daydreaming up elaborate scenarios in which Charles Dickens ran a cat orphanage, and D. H. Lawrence teamed up with Samuel Pepys in a traveling aerial burlesque act. (I was not, for the record, Mrs. Kwan's favorite student.) But I never, not even in my wildest imagination, pictured the poet Lord Byron and his menagerie of furry critters *performing kung fu in the snow*.

Where is my phone when I need to vidcap something?

Byron leaps into the air and sails over my head in what looks like a flying double roundhouse kick from Jetman, then punts the dog-entangled baddie square in the chest, sending the dude flying backward into the snow. The dogs fall back, perfectly content to let their master do the heavy lifting. They bark vociferously as Byron engages the Jin'Kai in mano a mano combat. It's a ballet of fists and knees and headbutts, complete with Byron's cocky carefree quips as they tussle.

"Have at thee, Mankin! Ha-ha-ha!" Byron spits.

Whatever it is Byron is talking about is totally lost on me—although I suspect it might make Mrs. Kwan chuckle.

The Jin'Kai retreats a step and reaches behind his back. But as he brings the weapon to bear (har, har), Drusilla's massive jaws clamp down on his arm, causing him to shriek. So the Jin'Kai might be superhuman alien killing machines, but it's nice to know that a good bear-chomping will still give them pause. The dude flops around like a rag doll as Drusilla whips him back and forth over her head, then finally flings him several meters through the air into a tree. When he lands, Byron is on him with several well-placed socks to the jaw.

"The great object of life," Byron tells the dude as he Hulk-smashes him, "is sensation." *Smash, smash, punchity-punchity, smash.* "To feel that we exist, even though in pain." He finishes off the dazed Jin'Kai with a spinning kick that forces the dude's head quite literally into the tree trunk, so that his suddenly limp body dangles from his anchored noggin.

"Feel that?" Byron asks.

There is no reply. All three Jin'Kai are out of commission, one with some pretty permanent reminders to never wrestle a bear.

"Hello, young Elvie!" Byron exclaims. "You look well."

"Uh, hey, Gramps," I reply. "By the by . . . what the hell is going on?"

Instead of answering me, Byron gives me a surprise shove down into the snow, which I appreciate in retrospect as a ray gun blast sizzles into the tree in front of me. I flip over onto my back to look down the hill, where I spy what appears to an entire platoon of Jin'Kai running straight for us, firing at will. Byron draws two firearms of his own from behind his back.

"This, sweet child? Why, this is the counteroffensive! Death and glory!"

As his dual-wielded blasters put an exclamation point on his battle cry, from over my head I hear several large electrical claps in response. At first when I look up, I'm not quite sure what it is I'm looking at. It just looks like moonlit sky, but somehow more . . . shimmery. I can make out the sparks from heavy weapon fire appearing from out of nowhere, raining down laser-y death on the Jin'Kai, who dive for whatever cover they can find. The shimmering effect above suddenly becomes more agitated, and the sky disappears and it's not the moon above me but a hovering ship.

A ship with a stealth cloak.

"Elvie!" Ducky cries from overhead. "I'm in a spaceship!"

"I can see that, Duck!" I scream back, super-relieved that he's still alive.

A cable lowers, dangling from a round porthole in the underbelly of the ship about half a meter in circumference.

"Elvie!" Byron shouts. "Connect me!"

Frantically I snatch the cable and search Byron for some kind of latch. I find it on his back, lock the catch into place, and then tug on the cable for good measure.

"Now grab hold, darling girl!"

I do as I'm told, wrapping myself around Byron in a big hug, with my arms placed securely under his so as not to obstruct the ass-whoopery he's still doling out. All at once the cable jolts, and we're flying up toward the porthole, which is sliding closed even as we hurtle its way. The Jin'Kai scatter in the face of suddenly uneven odds.

"Remember the Poconos!" Byron shouts as we pass into the ship. The porthole seals under our feet, and we land on the metallic surface with a *thunk*. Byron punches an intercom on the wall. "We're aboard. Now gather the animals and make haste!"

"We've got them, sir!" comes the response. I can feel the ship shift course.

"Well, aren't you a sight for sore eyes?" Byron says, looking down at me.

Slowly I release my death grip on Byron's chest. Looking around, I spy Ducky, Marnie, Dad, and Cole, each one with a bigger grin on their face than the last. "So I take it you're the cavalry?" I ask after finally taking a breath.

"This quaint little carriage?" Byron replies, unlatching himself from the cable. "No, dear." He accesses a vidscreen next to the intercom and brings up an image that I assume is a replica of the ship's main view screen. We are speeding away from the ground, already nearly a kilometer above the surface. The view is wavering with the now familiar shimmer of the Almiri stealth. Out of thin air an entire squadron of spaceships appears, a large command ship at the center of the formation.

"*There* is your cavalry."

"You've been building a fleet?" I ask, incredulous.

"'Fleet' implies a scale we have not attained," Byron says as he leads us through the hallways of the command ship toward the bridge. "We began construction a few years ago after the realization that the Jin'Kai might pose a serious threat. Our efforts had to be carried out in secret, of course. Mankind might have become a wee bit paranoid if advanced starcraft had suddenly appeared in the skies above them."

"You mean like in the way they did just now?" Ducky points out.

"Well, the situation has changed, hasn't it?" Byron explains. "The Jin'Kai have escalated things to another level altogether. They didn't just hit us, Elvie. Hundreds of humans, maybe more, died down there in the Poconos when they struck."

"It was Marsden," I say as we pass through a second hallway.

"We cannae ken such a thing fer sure, Elvie," Marnie chimes in.

"I *do* ken," I tell her. "Er, know. I know it. The computers at HQ were wiped. Not just destroyed. Wiped. And Marsden left one terminal operational for me to find. He's trying to tell me that I won't be able to find them."

"Yer sounding a wee paranoid, Elvie," Marnie says.

We come to a sealed door, and Byron flashes a card across the wall sensor.

"Access granted, Commander Byron." The door slides open onto a large command bridge. The room is a hive of activity, with Almiri officers buzzing about intently at work stations and running around to who-knows-where.

But the only person I see is Captain Oates.

"You didn't think a little gunfire could stop me now, did you?" he says as he absorbs the full brunt of my face-first bear hug.

"Of course not," I say, trying to suck the tears back into my eyes before anyone else sees them. "What about the others?"

"Clark is fine. A few others you probably don't know. We lost eight in all. Including Rupert."

Byron takes his place in the command chair at the center of the bridge and taps aimlessly at his arm console. "I'm sorry for your loss, old friend," he tells Oates earnestly. "I wish we had arrived sooner."

"That you arrived at all is the only reason any of us still draw breath, Commander," Oates says. He says it without a hint of malice—just a simple statement of truth.

"Elvie," Byron says to me. "You said Marsden was trying to send you a message? You personally? Why would he do that?"

"They have Olivia. My daughter. Your great-granddaughter. Marsden took her, with my mom."

"Your mother?" Byron says. He stops tapping and gapes at me. "Zee? She's alive?"

"Oh, right, yeah." I give Gramps the quickest version of "Previously: On Elvie's Shit Life" I can muster. "My mom faked her death after she gave birth to me and is actually one hundred percent alive. Hurray."

A glimmer of something flashes across Byron's face. Something like sadness? Regret, maybe? It's hard to tell with him, seeing as he's so melodramatic all the time regardless.

"This Marsden took her and your daughter?"

I almost don't have the heart to tell him.

"No," I say. "Zee's . . . with him. She sold out the Almiri at Cape Crozier, stole Olivia from me, and took off with Marsden to wherever it is evil douche bags go after daring aerial escapes."

Byron takes a moment to let the news of his estranged daughter's betrayal sink in. His eyes close and he tilts his head back, letting out a long sigh.

"Anyway," I say. I can feel a poem coming on, and I'd like to nip that in the bud if at all possible. I don't have time for self-pity from a guy who loves to hear himself talk. Not right at the moment, at any rate. "We came back to the ski lodge hoping you could help us track them down. Which is when we found the whole town barbecued."

"I warned them," Byron says, his head hanging. "But they weren't inclined to listen to me at that point."

"How'd ye ever make the slip out from such a hackit mess?" Marnie asks.

"I was not at the lodge for some time before the attack occurred."

At that, Cole chimes in for the first time. "Sir?" he asks. "Why not?"

"The Council has . . . seen fit to relieve me of my duties as commander."

Color me stunned. "You mean you're not the Head Almiri in Charge anymore?"

"My lenience with regards to the Enosi—and certain individuals within that larger group—caused me to fall out of favor," Byron tells us. "Rather quickly, by our standards. The Council allowed me to retain my rank, but my voice on policy matters has been somewhat muted for the time being." He looks at me, a wistful look in his eye. "My opponents had me stripped of power within a week of my shuttling you away to safety. Or what I thought was safety. My comrades aboard these vessels are the remaining few who still follow my orders."

Suddenly he pounds his armchair and jumps up with the theatrical flair you'd expect to find in a community production of Shakespeare in the Park.

"Curse my stunted vision! This is all my fault. Your mother. The base. All of it. I should have listened to you, Titus, from the start, and worked harder to reconcile the Almiri and their Enosi offspring. But no, I was the consummate politician, wasn't I? Compromising my morals into a vapor. Talking when I should have acted! The exact antithesis of the great Titus Oates! And now my own daughter, siding with the enemy, because of my failings. 'The thorns which I have reaped are of the tree I planted. They have torn me, and I bleed.'"

Please, please don't let this dovetail into twenty minutes of iambic pentameter or something. I think I'd rather fight the Jin'Kai again.

"We all find our conscience," Oates says. "You did what you thought was right. As you always have."

Dad steps in too. I guess it's not every day that you get to console your alien father-in-law. "We must live in the present, not the past," Dad tells him. He's using the voice he used to with me when I would sulk over a bad test grade. "It was quite fortuitous that you happened across us back on the mountain."

"Fortunate? Yes. But not a coincidence," Byron says.

I cock an eyebrow. "What do you mean?"

Byron reaches to the outer right side of his command chair and taps a sensor, which opens a small compartment. Several electronic devices rest inside. (I half-expected it to be a beer mini-fridge, but maybe that's on the other side.) Byron pulls out a long, flat device that looks almost like a bent Ping-Pong paddle, with an angled grip attached to an LED screen. It is beeping at a fairly rapid rate.

"What is that?"

Byron approaches me, and as he does, the beeping grows even faster. He hands me the device, and I look at the display. The majority of the screen is a faint blue, warbling around the edges with a slight purple distortion. But dead center is a bright flashing yellow dot, and in the bottom right-hand corner is a series of numbers. No, not just numbers.

Coordinates.

"Elvie?" Cole says, looking over my shoulder. "What is it?"

"This is me!" I gasp. "You've been . . . *tracking* me?"

Byron nods. "Since I sent you to Titus."

"How? Why?"

"I knew I needed to get you as far away from the Council as I could, at least until I could figure out a better course of action. I figured a remote, little-known location would be ideal, with Titus being the perfect guardian. I still wanted to be able to keep tabs on you, however, just in case. So I placed a tracer in you."

"You stuck something inside me without my knowledge or permission?" I ask. "You Almiri, man, you have some real issues."

"I didn't do anything so quaint," Byron says. "I wanted to be able to track you, but I also wanted to be the only one with such capabilities. A physical tag could be spotted too easily. A mutation, however . . ."

"This isn't going to end anywhere good, is it?" I say. I already feel sick to my stomach.

"To be blunt, my dear," Byron replies, "I altered your DNA."

"You did *what*?" I shriek. "What did you do?" I begin frantically searching my arms, like I'm going to, I don't know, spot a new mutated tracer mole or something. "Wasn't I hybrid enough for you before?"

"It wasn't anything serious. I promise. I simply gave you a little tweak to assign you a specific membrane potential—an electrical signature on a cellular level—that I would be able to detect even from great distances using the device you're holding."

"So leaving aside the great invasion to my rights as an individual and my serious *disgust* at the intrusion for just a second," I begin, and Byron nods, "you're saying that you picked up this signature of mine and knew I was headed to the Poconos . . ."

"And we doubled back, yes," Byron finishes for me. "We would have been here sooner, had we not first followed the other signal out into orbit."

"Other signal? What other signal?" My eyes go wide, and I can feel my ears do that weird thing where they move backward on my head without my having to touch them. "You put this genetic tracer mutation in Olivia too, didn't you?"

"Yes," Byron says. "The device tracks both frequencies on separate channels. When Olivia's signal began to move independently, I grew concerned. We lost the signal out in the Rust Belt. We would have continued the pursuit, but then I saw you headed for the Poconos, and into the Jin'Kai's waiting arms, so we doubled back."

My body turns to ice. "What do you mean, you lost the signal?" I say. "You couldn't track it anymore or . . ." I can't even bear to finish the sentence. I feel a hand on my shoulder. It's Cole. I shrug him off.

"The signal dissipated," Byron tells me. "We believed that to be due to interference in the belt, although of course we can't know for sure. That's why, when we saw your signal, we—"

"You *left* her," I finish for him. "You left her with *them*." Half of me wants to punch my grandfather in the kisser—for turning away when Olivia needed him most, for violating both of us for our own protection (because one must never forget that the high and mighty Almiri always know what's best for *everyone*). But honestly the other half of me wants to give him a big old kiss on the mouth—this horrible violation might be my only fighting chance at finding my daughter. I shake my head free of confusion. Focus on what's important. "What are we waiting for?" I ask him, pointing to the tracker in his hand. *Hold on, Olivia.* "Why aren't we heading back there this second? Let's go find her!"

"The fact remains that we have no point of trajectory to use as a locus for a search," Byron says, dousing my hope with a bladder full of buzzkill. "A full-scale sweep of the entire sector would be necessary."

"Well, then that's exactly what we're going to do!" I tell him. "Let's put all this flipping advanced alien tech to use for a change, for something other than your own selfish purposes!"

Byron looks at me with a stern expression. It's not quite angry, but we've entered into no-nonsense territory. It's like I can feel him winding up the hammer, ready to bring it down on all my remaining conviction.

"We simply don't have the manpower for that, Elvie, given our current situation. The Almiri—nay, the world, is under direct assault. The enemy has dealt the first blow, and we must regroup. My modest strike force alone cannot hope to repel the invaders. We must rally the forces of men and Almiri alike for the coming—"

"I want my daughter back, you son of a bitch!" I scream, flying at him. He doesn't flinch as I fall on him, slapping at his face and clawing at his shirt. Some of the crewmen on the bridge move to grab me, but Byron waves them off. It's Oates who puts his strong hands on my shoulders. He doesn't pull me, or wrap me up. He just holds me until I calm down. The tears are racing down my cheeks and dribbling off the edge of my nose. I'm sure I'm quite the sight, but I don't care. That's kinda the point.

"My dearest child," Byron says softly. "I promise you, when the time is right, I shall move heaven and earth to help you find your daughter. But we must focus on the bigger picture for now. We must force the Council's hand by making ourselves known to the leaders of Earth. And there are mysteries to be unlocked which may be our only hope of surviving the coming storm."

"Yeah, whatever," I say, wiping my nose. "You do that."

Byron turns to one of his crewmen. "Ensign, would you please take our guests to the quarters we've made up for them? You should all rest. We'll reach the rendezvous point with the rest of my men shortly. From there we will discuss how to proceed."

"Lord Byron, or, should I say, Commander," Dad says, stepping forward. "I would like to offer my services to you in any way possible. I know the Almiri are a race of superintelligent beings, and I don't want to toot my own horn, but I am probably the smartest person I know."

"It would be my honor to have you on our team, Mr. Nara," Byron says.

Dad wraps me up in a big hug and kisses my cheek.

"Get some rest, dearheart. I'll come see you shortly."

I don't answer, just return his hug. He pulls away and looks at me, sadness on his face.

"We must make our plans according to the problems before us," Dad tells me softly. I can see the pain in his eyes. "We'll find her," he says. "I promise."

"Sure," I say, and I even manage a nod. I turn back to Byron, the tracking device still in my hand. "Is it all right . . . if I hold on to this for now?" I ask. "I know she's not going to suddenly reappear while I'm napping, but . . ."

"Of course," Byron tells me. "There's no harm in holding out hope." He nods to his ensign, and the young crewman leads me, Ducky, Marnie, and Cole back out into the hall. The whole way down the corridor, Ducky's got his arm around me, and I rest my head on his shoulder.

Hold on, Olivia, I think. *Just hold on.*

"These quarters aren't so bad," Ducky says, bouncing his butt on the cot a little, taking in the 1970s-era sci-fi blandness that the Almiri let pass for décor. He nudges me in the arm. "I mean, considering we just spent a month underground at the South Pole."

"Yuh-huh," I say absently. In truth, I'm not paying attention. I'm counting in my head.

"I cannae imagine what yer goin' through," Marnie says. "But rest assured that when the time comes, I'll help ye find yer bairn. If she's been taken to the Rust Belt, the Enosi have contacts there. Folks that go unnoticed, and therefore notice everything."

"What's a Rusbell?" Cole asks from his bunk across the room.

"The Rust Belt," Marnie repeats. "Tha's where all the low-pin space stations are and all tha'. Cruisers, beat-up ships, lots of rubbish, mainly."

"Guys," Cole says to me and Ducky, "is it just me, or is Marnie talking gibberish?"

I attempt to act as translator. "The Rust Belt," I say. "You've been there, Cole. It's where the *Echidna* was stationed."

"Oh, the *Rust Belt*," Cole says. "I thought Marnie said 'Rusbell.' And I was like, 'Where's the Rusbell? I've never heard of that place.' And then the other part of me was like, 'Yeah, I don't know. Better ask.'"

"Thanks for that glance into your inner monologue, Cole," I say. I turn my attention to Ducky. "How long do you think it's been since they left us here? Five minutes?"

"Probably closer to ten," he replies. "Why?"

Without answering I spring up off the mattress and open the door.

"Elvie?" Cole says as I pass him into the corridor. "Where are you going?"

I look both ways down the hall. Empty. And why wouldn't it be? We're not prisoners anymore. We probably have free rein to go wherever we please on Grandpop's party boat in the sky.

Well, almost anywhere.

I'm already halfway down the hall toward the lift when the others realize I'm not merely stretching my legs. The three of them come bounding after me, and catch up just as I enter the elevator and hit the down button. They squeeze themselves in with me before the doors slide shut.

"Mind filling me in, Elvs?" Cole asks as we travel down to the bottom deck.

"Let the boys up there enjoy their explosions and heroics and other boring derring-dos," I say. "The Almiri can have their little race war. I'm getting my daughter back."

"Yer going to track down Marsden?" Marnie asks. "How?"

I wield the tracker. "With this." The elevator doors slide open, and we're down on the hangar level. I make a beeline for the sealed bay doors.

"Elvie, you heard the commander," Cole says. "That thing won't be able to penetrate whatever interference is mucking up the signal. You'd have to be, like, right next to Olivia for it to pick her up."

"Then I guess we have a needle in a haystack to find," I say. "Marnie, your contacts in the Rust Belt. Where can we reach them?"

"We've eyes 'n' ears on several installations," Marnie says. "I'd start on New Moon, the ozone refinery station."

"Very well, then. We'll start there. Maybe your guys have heard about some unsavory types lurking about, hiding with the rest of the floating garbage up there."

"And how do you propose we get there?" Ducky asks. "Swim?"

"If it wasn't already clear, I'm stealing a spaceship," I say. "One of those neat little numbers with the stealth shield."

Ducky slides in front of me, bringing me to a halt. "Elvie, you're not thinking." He turns and points at the bay doors. "Unless you've suddenly jumped several ranks in the military service of the aliens who *don't even like your kind*, you don't have the clearance to open those doors, let alone launch a ship."

"True," I say, twirling my grandfather's security clearance card around in my hand. "But Byron does."

"How did you get that?" Ducky asks.

"You son of a bitch!" I fake-cry as I pantomime slapping Ducky in the chest. I burst into a great big smile.

"Aren't ye the canny lass," Marnie says, a grin spreading across her face.

"When the need arises," I say. "Always have a plan."

"Even if you can get the ship started up," Cole counters, "they'll spot it and shut the outer doors down."

My smile only broadens as I turn to Cole. "Then I guess I have some pretty extraordinary hacking to get started on." *Hold on, Olivia. Mama's coming.* "Let's get to work."

Chapter Five

IN WHICH COMMUNICATIONS BEGIN TO BREAK DOWN

Not to brag or anything, but if they gave out medals for stealing invisible ships and piloting them away from your alien grandfather undetected, yours truly would grab the gold, easy.

"Okay," Ducky says after we've successfully broken away from the Almiri strike force and plunged into the blackness of space. His face is green, naturally, because we are moving, and he grips the armrests of his seat tightly. "So, like, *now* what?"

To that I have absolutely no response. But at least someone else does.

"We're thirteen-point-three-thousand clicks from the Rust Belt," Marnie tells us. The chick's been standing over my shoulder for the past fifteen minutes or so, watching me work the controls, and it's making me mildly claustrophobic. "New Moon is near the center of the densest cluster of ships. Tricky flying, but this ship's slight enough that we shouldnae have much trouble."

"What are spies doing sitting in the middle of an orbital

ghetto?" Cole asks, fiddling with the tracker. He wanted something to do so I let him hold it, but I'm getting worried he's going to break it.

"Cole!" I snap as he bangs the tracker with the heel of his hand. "Be careful with that."

"They're na' spies," Marnie tells him. "More as like they're untapped fonts of information."

"How much info can you get sitting on a defunct space station with the dregs of humanity?"

"Where d'ya reckon undesirables go when they want to do business?" Marnie says. "They go where they think no folks are watching. So, what better place to watch?"

"I'm confused as to why you would need contacts like that in the first place," Cole asks, still banging the tracker.

"We can't all be as selective about our friends as the Almiri," Marnie says.

"Ha-ha," Cole says. He flips another switch on the tracker, and it starts frantically beeping. "Holy shit, Elvs! I got it working!" He's waving the tracker around like a maniac. "Olivia's here! She's, like, two meters away or something!"

I roll my eyes. "Cole, any chance you switched it to frequency one again?"

He checks, then presses his lips together, all chagrinned-like. "Um . . . ," he says slowly. "It's possible, yeah."

"*I'm* frequency one," I tell Cole for, like, the four-billionth time. I grab the tracker from him to flip the switch back to stop the inane beeping. "Our daughter is frequency *two*."

"It's hard to remember," he says by way of defense as he takes the tracker back.

"Try to make up a mnemonic," Ducky calls from his chair. And he doesn't even need to turn around to sense that Cole is staring at him blankly. "A memory trick," he clarifies. "Like . . . 'Frequency two, which rhymes with 'coo,' which is what babies do.' So two for Olivia."

"Or how 'bout 'eejit,'" Marnie chimes in. "Cuz there's two *E*s in 'eejit,' and if yer so daft ye cannae remember that, then that's what ye are."

"I'll remember," Cole says.

"So," I say, turning my attention to Marnie. "To the Rust Belt, then? To find this contact of yours?" It's the best—sorry, *only*—plan any of us have had so far, and if anyone can give us information that leads to Olivia, I'm all for it. "All agreed?" I ask.

Marnie gives an emphatic "Aye!" Cole on the other hand . . .

"Guys!" he shouts. "I found her! I found our daughter! She's, like, two meters aw— Oh, wait. Frequency *two*, right?"

And that's when Ducky barfs on the floor.

Clearly, Marsden and his cronies don't stand a chance.

The station, designated New Moon A-1138 according to my navigational readouts, looms large in front of us as I bring the ship in closer. Did I say large? I meant *uge*, as in so huge that there isn't any room left for the *h*. I've been to New York City only twice, once on a middle school field trip to the Museum of Pretentious Art and once when Dad took me and Ducky to see *2 Fast 2 Furious* on Broadway for my eleventh birthday, so I don't have a great sense of the actual size of the island of Manhattan, but if I had to guess, I'd say it's roughly the same as the floating hunk of metal that I'm currently steering toward.

"Look at the size of that thing!" Cole whistles from behind me.

"Cut the chatter, Red Two," Ducky says, half-snorting.

"Red what?" Cole asks.

"It's just . . . It's from . . . Forget it. Hey, but, guys, I was thinking. We're working a reconnaissance mission, right? Gathering intel?" Ducky is still green, but it's an *excited* green. I can tell he's about to nerd out on all of us. "Don't you think we should all be incognito? Like, with secret identities and stuff? I've been working on mine." He sits up a little straighter. "Alfred Sniggle, new junior sanitation engineer. Thoughts?" He looks expectantly to the rest of us.

I am not the only person concerned with things besides Ducky's nerd fantasy, apparently.

"This thing's getting even wonkier," Cole says. He's still messing with the tracker. "Now *both* frequencies are buzzing in and out."

"It's the debris from all the derelict craft in this sector," Marnie tells him. "Radiation, magnetic fields, et cetera. Chops up yer signal, makes it cockeyed."

"You sure it's not just broken?" Cole asks, aiming the tracker at his head. No signal *there*, obviously.

"Cole, give me that thing," I say, attempting to snatch it from him with one hand while the other operates the ship's controls.

"Best leave it aboard, act'ly," Marnie tells me. "A precious object like tha' won't be safe where we're going. It'll get pocketed an' sold less than five minutes off the ship."

"I'll hide it somewhere *really* safe," I promise.

"Trust me," Marnie says. "Ye could hide it up yer own arse—those thieves'd have it off ye 'fore you even noticed they pulled down yer drawers. Much safer here."

"Hard to believe this isn't more of a vacation destination," I mutter. But I know Marnie's got a better sense of this place than I do. The tracker will stay on board.

Hold on, Livvie, I think as the station looms ever larger before us.

"I've never seen a station this big before," Cole says.

"Or so . . . gross," I add.

Even from this distance it's easy to tell that New Moon has seen better days. I didn't realize you could see rust from kilometers away, but if that's not what I'm looking at, then whatever it is is doing a pretty good rust impersonation. The blotchy brown patches on the hull of the station must be several hundred meters in diameter, at least, and from what I can see, they snake all over the surface. There are cracks, holes, and just plain shoddy construction running the entire length of New Moon from start to finish.

"It's amazing that thing doesn't break apart," I muse.

"Why in the heck do they call it New Moon?" Cole asks.

"That's no moon," Ducky begins. "It's a space—"

"Ducky, enough," I tell him.

"Alfred," he insists. "I'm Alfred Sniggle now. Don't forget. You'll blow my cover."

I roll my eyes. "Okay, then. Enough, *Alfred*. Now listen to this." And I begin reading the information from the heads-up display the console is feeding me. "According to the description here, New Moon is the largest orbital station ever constructed, and the second largest satellite of Earth after the actual moon. Built in 2043, it has been home to an ozone processing refinery, the only ever off-world supercollider, and for a brief period in the sixties served as the headquarters for the Psychedelic Tofreegan Collective before they were all committed. Now everything's gone except the refinery."

"Well, if you ask me," Cole says, "New Moon is the biggest hunk of crap I've ever seen."

"Can't argue with you there," I say.

"*That's* a first," Cole replies with a snort.

I sigh. I'm getting more than a little fed up with Cole's attitude. Sure, he agreed to steal a stealth ship with me and go flying off into the great unknown in an attempt to rescue our daughter, disobeying a direct order from his former Almiri supervisor, and potentially endangering the entire planet in the process, but he's been such a *drag* about it.

I flip the comm to an open channel as we begin our approach.

"New Moon control, this is, um, the U.S. . . . *Baby Chaser*," I say, shrugging at Ducky as he shakes his head at me. "Request permission to dock."

I leave the channel open, awaiting a response. All that comes back over the comm is static.

"New Moon control," I repeat, "this is—"

"Ye can save yer voice," Marnie tells me. "There 'nt a control to give clearance."

"Well, then how are we supposed to know where to dock?" I ask. "Not to mention avoid crashing into other incoming vessels?"

"I'll show ye where to land," Marnie assures me. "As fer the other thing, well, ye'll jes' have to show off some fine piloting skills, won't ye?"

Marnie does indeed seem to know her way around this place. She guides me past the prow, where I would have assumed the docking bay to be, and down along the seamy underbelly of the station.

"This is a really weird approach for a landing dock," I say. "How are you supposed to find it if you don't already know it's there?"

"Tha's the point," Marnie says.

"Well, at least there isn't any other traffic, so we don't have to worry about—"

On cue—because the universe absolutely adores using me as its straight man—three small ships come flying out of nowhere from underneath the station, screeching by so close that I can practically feel the paint scratching off our hull. For a moment I lose control and we swerve hard enough for Ducky to lose his footing at the console behind me. There is a violent *thud!* against the side of the hull as the last ship zips past.

"What the hell was that?" I shout, scrambling to regain control of the ship. "Did one of them hit us?"

"Negative," Marnie says, smiling a bit as she reads Ducky's display (Ducky being otherwise occupied, picking himself off the floor). "They jettisoned some rubbish out the back as they passed. It's nothin' to be afeart of. Jes' a friendly suggestion we watch ourselves."

"We should *watch ourselves*? Who where those jackasses?"

"O, Cowboys," Marnie tells us. "They take the ozone

bricks from the refinery and deploy them into the atmosphere, where they break down and revert to gas."

"They fly around in those little ships like that carrying ozone?" Ducky asks incredulously. "It's a miracle they don't blow up."

"They do, from time to time," Marnie says. "It's not the most stable career, to be sure."

I grunt in reply, but I have more important things to concern myself with than a bunch of alpha-apes. "Marnie, just show me where we're landing on this heap."

The docking hangar is long, wide, and decrepit. It seems like it might break away from the station and float off into space at any moment, which would be a real accomplishment for a structure that, technically, is just a hole in the side of the platform. It's from here that the cowboys have been disembarking, and the flow of small, possibly explosive transport crafts is steadier—but since I can see them coming now, it's far less nerve-racking. I approach at a low angle but don't waver on my course, letting these atmo-jockeys know that we belong. It wouldn't do to stick out like a sore thumb before we even land.

"Yer pretty good at the stick," Marnie says with a whistle. I try to suppress my smile as I angle us toward the nearest free landing pad. For some reason Marnie's approval feels incredibly rewarding, but I really don't want her to know that.

"It's not my first spaceship," is all I say. "Once I put her down, what's our first move?"

"Well, I dunnae about the rest of ye, but I could sure go fer a pint," Marnie says.

Typical Scot.

"Um, Marnie, honey"—and, oh my God, no one has ever said the word "honey" more awkwardly than Ducky just did— "none of the rest of us are twenty-one. So if they try to card us, we're screwed."

I can hear the smack as Marnie plants a big wet kiss on Ducky's forehead behind me.

"Ach, Donald. Yer a bonnie lad, aren't ye?" she says, and kisses him again. From the squelching noises Ducky's making, I can visualize the romantic Celtic headlock Marnie must have him in. Cole sits down next to me and gives me a look.

"You okay?" he asks me.

"I'm fine," I say, staring straight ahead out the viewport as we make our approach.

"You look . . . superfocused," he replies.

"Just making sure not to crash the ship and kill us all in a fiery blaze."

The kissing noises behind me stop.

So it turns out that landing a spaceship in a crowded hangar is a lot trickier than piloting it through the emptiness of space. It sure doesn't help that there's no landing guidance whatsoever to tell us where to go. The first pad that seems empty is apparently already spoken for by an incoming cowboy who decides to slip underneath us to sneak into the spot just as I'm about to engage the repulsors. Luckily I avoid crushing the maniac's tiny little ship as flat as a frat boy's used beer can. (Normally it wouldn't bother me to crush the guy, because I've always been of a mind that parking infractions should be punishable by death, but we're trying to keep a low profile here. Oh, and the whole thing where the guy might still have ozone bricks on board with him, which would've ended up with all of us in smithereens. Tiny details.)

Anyway, I'm finally able to navigate to a free space, although I do have to engage in a brief staring contest with a supply transport whose pilot seems just as weary of the etiquette up here as I am.

When the door slides open, it's all I can do to keep from gagging. In fact, it's more than I can do. I gag. I gag big-time. The stench on the docking platform is absolutely putrid, with the almost indescribable combination of oxidized metal, congealed grease, and something that smells like rotting possum but (one would hope) couldn't possibly be, all swirling together to form one of the most odiferous confections I've ever come across. I'd be hard pressed to ascertain when, if ever, this place had been sanitized.

"You look as green as I feel," Ducky whispers to me as we walk down the exit ramp.

"I don't think I've ever smelled anything like it," I say, choking back tears. "This must be where highway rest stops are born."

Marnie takes a deep breath and exhales gleefully as she traipses past us into the hangar. "Ye lot certainly are a bunch of delicate flowers, then, aren't ye?" she says. "Jes' remember, people live here. So dinnae be rude."

"Don't worry," I say. "We're not so dumb that we're going to go around shouting about how—"

"This place flipping reeks!" Cole shouts as he climbs down

the ramp behind us. More than a few heads turn to look at us.

I grit my teeth but choose to let Marnie give Cole the chiding glare this time. The truth is, even if Cole's lack of tact could probably get us stabbed with something seriously unhygienic, the dude's not wrong. I was prepared for this place to be run-down, but I have never, ever, seen anything like *this*. This place makes squalor seem like a resort spa.

We make our way hastily through the hangar, which is buzzing with activity. The place is packed to the gills with an array of raggedy ships, many of which look like they might be held together with staples and duct tape. People tinker on their vessels using equipment ranging in quality from automated repair drones to manual screwdrivers. One guy, I swear, is using a baseball bat to pound something into place. Our ship already stands out from the rest, since it's the only craft currently docked that looks like it could pass a legitimate safety inspection.

As soon as we exit the hangar, we find ourselves on a massive promenade, with cathedral-high ceilings and wide avenues snaking in every direction. The paths are congested with hundreds, if not thousands, of people who seem to be going nowhere in particular, but are rather just spinning about in random circuitous paths like atomic particles. Marnie has pushed well ahead of us, and were it not for her brilliant red hair, I would have immediately lost her in the gray-brown throng pressing against me on all sides. The metallic rotting smells of the hangar have made way for a far more organic but no less offensive stench. Warm bodies grind against me as I move forward, leading with my shoulder. I can feel the tangible grime from their clothes rubbing off on me as I go. From behind I feel something clutching at my shirt near my waist. Instinctively I twist around, expecting to see one of the pickpockets Marnie warned us about. But it's only Ducky.

"I'm trying not to lose you," he says over the din, reaching his hand out. I grab it and hold on for dear life as we keep moving.

"Where's Cole?" I ask without looking back.

"I'm here!" he calls, trailing well behind us. "Nobody worry about grabbing my hand! I'm just fine!"

"I'll hold your hand," Ducky says.

On either side of the path, barkers are hawking dilapidated wares. One olive-skinned old woman with a long crooked nose and only three teeth in her head jumps out and waves a dingy-looking length of woven cloth at me.

"Face-swath cheap's they come!" she spits, literally, in my face.

"E-excuse me?" I stammer, leaning away as far as I can.

"Wear's mask, use's scarf. Real wool synth. Five 'n' five ducks needs give!"

The woman shoves the gross cloth into my boob with one hand, while pulling forcibly on my arm with the other. Rattled, I shove her back, and she stumbles into the wall. Immediately three other vagrant-types are swarming me, shouting at me in their incomprehensible dialect and shaking their fists violently.

"Just back off!" I holler, feeling the heat rise in my cheeks. "I don't want your filthy rag." I feel Ducky and Cole flank me defensively. Just when I'm sure I've inadvertently ignited a brawl that will get us unceremoniously dumped out of the nearest air lock, Marnie strides through the crowd as if she were liquid metal seeping through the cracks of an old concrete wall.

"Cheap's they come?" she says, pointing at the cloth still clutched in the tooth-challenged woman's hand.

"Five 'n' five ducks," the woman replies from the ground.

Marnie sneers. "Two 'n' five's they lucky."

"Four's they go."

"Three 'n' five's we walk."

The woman lifts herself, using the already dingy cloth to push herself up off the even filthier floor. To my surprise she's laughing and smiling, putting all three pearly not-so-whites on display. She waves the dirty cloth in my direction again.

"I told you, I don't want—" I start, but instead of pushing me with the cloth, she drapes it over my shoulder and lets go, turning her cupped hand palm-up expectantly. Marnie drops three large coins and one smaller one into the woman's hand, which clutches the coins for dear life as they land. The other barkers are still shaking their fists, but now they're directing the gesture to the woman, who responds by shouting at them so rapidly that I have no shot at deciphering what she's saying.

"What in the hell was all that?" I ask Marnie as we start back through the crowd.

"'Grats, Elvie. Ye've jes' had yer first haggle," Marnie tells me.

"Haggle?" I say, staring down at the dirty cloth lying across my shoulder. "We bought this on purpose?"

"I know it can make ye a tad dizzy at first," Marnie says. "But yer instincts to push her off were good."

"Why do they talk like that?" Cole asks.

"Local patter. There's more than two hundred dialects that have been canoodling with one another up here fer decades. It takes the rules from each language and then ignores them all equally. Ye pick it up after a spell."

"And I thought you were hard to understand before," I mutter.

"C'mon, then," Marnie says, smiling. "Let's head down to one of the local watering holes. Good a place as any to start trolling fer information."

The promenade level where we first arrived is only one level of four, each stacked on top of the other and connected by magnetic elevators. Marnie ushers us into one of the elevators when it settles on our level, and we wait for the flood of people to pour off the platform around us before we're pushed forward by the throng behind us heading to the lower levels. I hold my grip on the railing and look down over the open-air car to the levels below.

"Ducky, do us all a favor," I tell him. "Don't look down." It's hard to estimate just how far down the station goes, but if I had to guess, I'd say you could drop the Empire State Building from the top and still have to wait quite a while to hear it hit the bottom. Even I can feel my knees wobble a little beneath me as I fathom the splatitude that would be the result of a fall from this height. At least I have this one creaky, hip-level metal railing to keep the two dozen or so other passengers from pushing me off the edge to my doom.

Safety was apparently not high on the station builders' list of priorities.

"Already on top of it," Ducky says, and when I look back, I see that he has covered his eyes with both hands like he's about to play the most death-defying game of peekaboo known to man. "And the *name*," he reminds me, "is Alfred Sniggle."

"Here, Alfred," Marnie says, slipping her arms around his waist from behind and snuggling against him. "Let me guide ye."

In this manner we make our way off the elevator, out to Level 1, and into what Marnie informs us is New Moon's classiest bar.

The whole place looks eerily like the cantina scene from *Star Wars*—after they yelled "cut" and the extras stripped out of their alien suits, revealing the pent-up funk of sweat and slime that results from spending twelve hours under hot lights while wearing a latex mask. Seriously, the room has a visible "stank smog" wafting around. If I vomited on the floor, it would be a marked improvement in hygiene.

"Go find yerselves a seat," Marnie urges. "And try to na' stick out too much."

"Us? Stick out?" I say, trying to coat my extreme nervousness in a hardy candy-coated shell of sarcasm. Marnie smirks and moves away toward the bar. Cole starts to follow her, when I grab his arm.

"Where are you going?" I ask.

"Don't worry about it, Elvs. You're not my girlfriend anymore, so you don't have to pretend to care what I do." And with that, he storms after Marnie toward the bar.

"Two days after our breakup, in the middle of a goddamn rescue mission in outer space, and he decides to go all Devin from *Martian Chronicles* on me," I seethe. Ducky leads me by the shoulder toward a booth in the back that has just opened up.

"Don't let it get under your skin," he says. "Let's sit down and wait to see what contacts Marnie still has up here."

We sit in the corner booth, which gives me a pretty good lay of the land. The clientele is markedly different from the mobs we found up on the promenade. It's mostly men, tough burly types that must all take turns sharing the same razor, because there's more than enough straggly facial hair to go around. They're loud and raucous, the kind of shouting where it's hard to differentiate camaraderie from the prelude to a knife fight. There's not much danger of any Jin'Kai types moving around incognito in here either. This is a decidedly unattractive group of dudes.

"I highly doubt we're going to find any useful information in a place like this," I say, raising my voice enough to be heard over the shouting coming from the next booth.

"You never know," Ducky says. "Marnie says tons of traffic comes through here. Being so far off the grid and all. Attracts all kinds."

"It's a shame it didn't attract any shower salespeople," I say. "I hope Marnie's right about this. I'd hate to have come all this way for nothing."

"Aw, wouldn't say nuffin, luff," says a broad, portly dude who seems to have just materialized in front of our table. "You've not had chances wif me weren't y'ere."

"Why don't you go peddle your sweet talk somewhere else, Romeo?" I reply, looking down at the table, trying to avoid staring at the creep's tooth-challenged mouth.

"Um, Elvie," Ducky whispers. He grabs my knee under

the table, and I look up to see that my scraggly suitor has three large friends with him. They're all wearing the same dirty gray coveralls, like a mechanic-themed boy band on an ill-advised comeback tour.

"Luff, seems we've launched with a bum rocket," the ringleader says. "Let's start again real nice, yeah?"

Without another word he slides gracelessly into the booth next to me, with two of his friends following after, shoving me into Ducky and nearly spilling Ducky onto the floor. Only one of them remains standing, hovering over Ducky.

"Look, f-fellas," Ducky stammers, "we don't want any trouble."

"Aw, son, none trouble here," the ringleader says. His breath reeks of heavy spices and vinegar, so strong that my eyes start watering. "Look at us to be the welcome wagon for you's new 'cruits."

The one standing over Ducky claps him on the shoulder and literally lifts him up out of the booth before resting him down on his feet.

"You's c'n be drinks," he says, sliding into Ducky's old spot. "New 'cruits be drinks, we's all friendly."

I look at Ducky with a slightly panicked expression that I'm hoping says, *Don't you dare leave me with these hairy mouth breathers.* In response Ducky furrows his brow and sticks his tongue between his upper teeth and lower lip, which clearly means, *Stay here while I go get Cole, or Marnie, or barring that, a whole bunch of drinks, and hopefully this lot will turn out to be more boorish than villainous. In the meantime, keep them busy, and try not to do anything to make them angry.*

What can I say? Ducky and I absolutely *kill* in charades.

"A round for the table, then," Ducky says, and disappears into the crowd, leaving me with my new friends pushing in close on either side.

"You's with the new bunch?" the ringleader asks, looking me up and down. He has the longest beard in the group, which may be how he got voted capo in the first place. "We's told they's Chinese." He squints at me. "You's Chinese?"

"Well, um, no," I say. Keep them busy. "But my grandfather was Japanese, though."

Long Beard looks to the fellow on his right—let's call him Scrungy Neck. "She's look Japanese?" he asks.

"Dunno she's look Japanese," Scrungy Neck responds. "Know she's look pretty."

Don't make them angry. "Why, um, thank you," I muster.

"Too pretty for gasworks."

Shit.

"Beg pardon?"

"Gasworks are for poor, dumb, desperate," says a third guy. Mr. Chip Tooth. "For those without another place. Look you's pretty white teeth. Listen to talk. You's no 'cruit."

"No, you're right," I say, trying to think on my feet. Or from my seated butt at least. "I didn't come here to work at the ozone refinery. I'm a, uh, pilot."

The fourth one, Stout N. Smelly, leans in with a deadly serious look on his face, so close that I'm afraid I won't be able to get the vinegar smell out of my hair for weeks. I wonder for a moment if he's going to clock me. But to my simultaneous relief and annoyance, he bursts into a fit of laughter.

"You's pilot! Ha-ha-ha!" Stout N. Smelly bellows, spittle wetting the whole side of my face. The others join in on the laughter. "Fellas, look it the lady pilot!" He calls to anyone within earshot, pointing at me. "Gov'ner must be dreggin' the mist if he's brung pretty things as pilot!"

The laughter is spreading, and it's getting under my skin. I keep telling myself to let it go and let these Neanderthals have their fun, but no one ever accused Elvie Nara of being without a temper.

"While I'm sure that would be funny if I had the slightest idea what it was you were trying to say," I say before I can stop myself, "I am a pilot. I flew to this piss bucket easy enough."

"Fancy pretty pilot with the mouf," Long Beard says, chortling. I give him my most condescending smile, the one I used to reserve exclusively for Britta McVicker.

"Smelly fat ass with the breath," I say. To my continued annoyance, my snark is simply making them laugh more loudly. And worse, I'm starting to gather an audience. Other bar patrons hover near the table, while my new would-be drinking buddies are crowding me on either side. I look around for my rescue, and as if on cue, Ducky parts the crowd and emerges in front of the table . . .

. . . carrying a tray of mugs.

"Hey there, guys," Ducky says sheepishly. "I, uh, didn't bring any credit with me, so, um, the bartender said he'd put it on your tab."

The table goes silent. Long Beard rises slowly from his seat directly across from where Ducky stands. His mouth has become tight and small, and his eyes seem to have grown to compensate. Ducky shakily puts the tray down on the table and lifts one mug in offering, with a look that says, *Please don't break my arms, cuz I'm really rather fond of them.* Long Beard reaches out—only, he doesn't take the mug. He grabs hold of Ducky's forearm and squeezes. His other hand shoots up and clasps Ducky around the back of the neck, and before I can move, he has pulled Ducky in toward him so that Ducky is leaning precariously across the table. Their faces are so close, I'm sure that the dude's breath is going to dissolve Ducky's corneas. Then, just when it appears the guy is going to make balloon animals out of Ducky's body, Long Beard lifts his head and plants a big wet kiss on Ducky's forehead.

"Luffly! Look, boys. Table serfice!" he bellows, and with that, all his cronies burst out laughing again, each grabbing a mug off the tray. Stout N. Smelly rises up, grabs Ducky roughly, and shoves him back into the booth next to me, slapping him on the back so hard that he nearly chokes.

"That went slightly better than I'd feared," Ducky says, checking his arms—to make certain they're still there, I suppose.

"I thought you were going to get help, not to actually get drinks," I hiss at him.

"I couldn't find Marnie anywhere," Ducky says. "She must have wandered off somewhere to find her contacts."

"Well, what about Cole?"

"He's, um, at the bar."

There's something in Ducky's voice that makes me think there's something going on with Cole that I definitely don't want to know about. So of course I tilt as far back in my seat as I can, so I can know about it.

"What the . . ." I start. Leave it to Cole to find the one woman in this entire bar and start hitting on her. Seriously, cliché much? He's leaning with one elbow on the bar, swishing a drink in his hand and making eyes at his new lady love.

Although, I notice that every three seconds or so he darts his eyes my way, to be sure that I'm noticing.

Ducky puts an arm on my shoulder. "Just leave it," he tells me. "He's not doing any harm. Let's talk to these guys and wait for Marnie."

"Yeah," hoots Long Beard. "Speaks t'us, luff." He turns his attention to Ducky. "You's pilot, same?" he asks.

"Oh," Ducky says, startled. "Oh." He looks at me. I know he's trying to get me to read something in his face again, but I'm only half-paying attention. I'm focusing every ounce of control I have on *not* turning my head again to look at Cole "Dingbat" Archer, who's over at the bar *ruining our only chance of finding our daughter, in order to flirt with some chippie*.

"Uuuuuh," Ducky says, drawing the syllable out as long as possible. "Uh. Actually, I'm a sanitation engineer, myself. Not a pilot, not me." He lets out a fake laugh. "Ho, ho! That's a good one. Right, Wanda?"

I'm assuming I'm meant to be Wanda.

"Sure," I say. "Right." I take a quick swig of my beer, and immediately regret it. "Oh God, that's bad!" I choke, allowing half the mouthful to dribble out onto my chin. "Duck, what did you *order*?"

"My name is Alfred Sniggle!" Ducky shouts, *much* too loudly. "I'm twenty-one years old! I've never been to prison, and my favorite cheese is bleu!"

Oh dear.

"He specky, this one?" Long Beard asks me. He looks pretty concerned. So do the other guys, actually, and the half dozen or so other patrons who have decided to stop doing whatever it was they were doing before and stare at us instead. Way to fly under the radar, Duck.

"He's fine," I say quickly. "Sometimes he has episodes. Alfred, did you take your medication this morning?" Ducky hunches back in his seat and nods painfully. And I think the stench of this place must be infecting my brain or something, because before I realize what I'm doing, I've lifted the mug to my mouth again and—"Shit, that's *terrible*!"

Fortunately for us, the group of dudes in front of us seems to find the whole thing rather hysterical. Perhaps they've decided that Ducky and I are this evening's entertainment. Long Beard lets out the most raucous laugh of all of them. "Needs getting used to," he tells me.

I set the mug down on the table with a clatter. "I don't think I could ever get used to that," I reply.

"Pinchin noses helps," Stout N. Smelly tells me.

"And shuttin eyes," adds Chip Tooth.

"And stoppin breathin," says Scrungy Neck.

"Here." Long Beard lifts my mug out toward me. "Give her 'nother go."

Well, at least I've managed to divert their attention from the master spy technique of Alfred Sniggle. "Hey, now," I say in my coyest voice. I take the mug from old Long Beard and smile at him. "If I didn't know any better, I'd say you were trying to get me drunk."

"Oh, the luff knows good," Long Beard says with another laugh. The others join in. Next to me, my buddy Sir Sniggle is starting to relax just the slightest. I have a feeling these guys have finally decided we're harmless weirdos, and are doing their best to initiate us into their group. I'm actually considering taking another sip of the vile concoction, when—I swear not on purpose—I glance back over at the bar and get my first good look at the woman Cole is talking to.

She's no woman at all. She's, like, my age. Skinny little tart with straight black hair, like mine but sleeker (as though she somehow managed to lay her hands on some styling cream in this hellhole, which must've been a feat). Thick arched eyebrows, like mine. Seems Cole went out of his way to find my prettier doppelganger just to flirt with her right in front of me. He gives her his nothing-up-my-sleeves-but-my-killer-biceps move, and then darts his eyes my way again.

Which I guess would explain why I'm not really in the right headspace when Long Beard reaches over toward my boob and declares, "Ain't this suffin, then!"

In a gut-reaction move of self-defense, I flick my mug at Long Beard, shooting the entire contents directly into the very large fellow's very dirty face.

Chairs screech across the bar floor. Mugs slam down on tables. All conversation stops.

It is only then that I realize that my bearded companion was reaching not for my breast but rather for the raggedy face-cloth still draped over my shoulder.

Oops.

"Way to blend, Wanda," Ducky whispers at me as he does his best to shrink into the wooden bench. There isn't a single person in this bar who *isn't* staring at us.

I am suddenly feeling like I played this very, very poorly.

Chapter Six

WHEREIN THE HITS JUST KEEP ON COMING

I've pulled a lot of chromer moves in my time. (Let's not even *discuss* the high-waisted shorts fiasco of '71.) But even I have trouble processing that I just dumped the universe's grossest beer on some dude the size of a yeti.

"Uh, sorry about that," I say lamely, making quick eyes at Long Beard across the table. I have no idea what the dude is thinking. Maybe he gets beers dumped on him every day and he thinks it's hilarious. Maybe he's contemplating how best to remove my head from my shoulders. What I do know is that I need to make this situation right as quickly as possible, or all our asses will be floating lifelessly out into space before Marnie can dig up any dirt, and then we'll *never* find Olivia.

"Everything okay here?"

And now here's Cole, who has ditched his hot date to come jump into the role of Elvie's manly protector. Like what we really need now is Cole using his righteous alien superstrength to punch some Neanderthal in the face, blowing our already shit cover for good.

"We're fine," I tell Cole. Long Beard is busy wiping his chin off on the hem of his shirt, and I still can't get a read on his face. His comrades are watching in stunned silence, presumably waiting for their leader to tell them precisely which grade of pulp we should be turned into.

"It's my fault," I tell Long Beard. "I saw you reaching out of the corner of my eye, and I just overreacted." I hand him my haggle rag so he can better mop his face. "I don't know what got into me. I'm an ass. Forgive me?"

Long Beard stares at the rag like I've just handed him a precious heirloom.

"No ass, luff," Long Beard says, mopping his face. He finishes and hands me back my rag like it's a lap-pad full of irreplaceable baby pics. "Things happen. We's move on."

Around us I can feel the energy of the bar shifting. People murmuring in begrudging acceptance. Even Ducky eases up a little on the bench. So kudos to me, I guess. Elvie, massager of awkward situations.

Perhaps unsurprisingly, however, Cole doesn't seem to get the memo re: chillaxing.

"You make friends wherever you go, don't you, Elvs?" Cole says.

"Wanda," I say, giving him a hard look. But Cole never was any good at charades.

"Wanda? What? What are you talking about? Why are you throwing drinks in people's faces?"

"It was an accident," I say. "You're not helping."

Cole's eye twitches. Oops. That must've been a chord I just struck.

"Not helping? What would you like me to do, then, Elvs? Should I start dousing people in cheap beer? Or maybe I should start a fistfight? Would that count as being helpful in your book?"

"Can you stop being you for just two seconds?" I ask.

"What's that supposed to mean?"

"If you weren't you, you'd know," I say. "Just . . . go away. Go flirt with your bar floozy some more."

"What do you care who I flirt with? I'm currently unattached, remember?"

"You are such an ass."

"I'm an ass? I'm. An ass. That's rich. Coming from the queen bee of asses."

"The queen bee of asses? Do you even formulate words in your head before you speak, or do random sounds just fall out of your mouth?"

Across the table Long Beard slowly rises to his feet. "Seems nuff from you's," he says, pointing at Cole. "Luff said sorry. You's do it now."

If I were Cole Archer, and a giant bearded redwood of a man were standing in front of me asking me to shut the hell up, I might think about obliging.

But Cole, as we know, doesn't have the sense God gave a mannequin.

"Apologize? She's the one who doused you with swill," Cole continues. "She's the ass, not me. In fact, I think I'm gonna write it on a cake. You'd like that, Elvie, wouldn't you?

You like cake. What if I have it written on a cake? 'Elvie's an ass,' in chocolate frosting." My eyes dart to Long Beard, whose face is dark and expressionless as he listens to Cole bluster.

"And I know what you're thinking too," Cole continues. "That I'm such a nimrod, I can't spell 'ass'? Well, how's this for nimrod?" He gets right in my face. "A." There is a bit of spittle on my left cheek. I bite my lip and pray for this whole ridiculous fiasco to end soon. Where the hell is Marnie? "S . . ."

Before he can get to the last letter, he up and gets cracked in the jaw with a beer mug.

"Whoops," says Long Beard. And I have to say, he's got Cole beat in the sarcasm department. "Guess 'haps I'm an ass too."

The crowd roars, dripping with joy. Ducky, for his part, looks like he's trying to melt into the bench and disappear completely. I'm pretty sure my eyes are frozen, watermelon-wide, in shock and terror.

And Cole?

"Ow," he says. With about the depth of feeling you might have if you accidentally drank orange juice right after brushing your teeth. Which is probably not the reaction the crowd was expecting from the dude who just broke a beer mug with his face.

"I mean . . ." Cole snaps a quick look at Long Beard, and then suddenly seems to remember that he's posing as a human and not a freakishly strong alien hunkazoid. "I mean . . . *ooooh*-OW!" he hollers, jumping completely to the other end of the pain spectrum. We're talking branding-iron-to-the-groin level. He collapses to the floor. *"Elvie, I think I'm dying! My jaw! He hit me so hard on my fragile human jaw!"*

I move to the ground next to Cole, although until I'm there, I don't know if I'm going to cradle his head or slap his face for making Ducky look like a world-class sleuth.

"What the bloody biscuits?" says Long Beard.

There is a chorus of agreement of that very sentiment.

"Do you think they bought it?" Cole whispers at me from the floor. He's clutching at his chin. "I'm acting hurt."

I tug him to his feet. Reach out for bench-Ducky, too. "I noticed," I say.

The skinny flirt at the bar, I see, has completely disappeared.

Not a terrible idea.

Or . . . not.

I don't take one step before Long Beard slaps a strong hand on my shoulder and forces me back into my seat. He doesn't look so interested in protecting my honor now. Neither, for that matter, do Chip Tooth or Scrungy Neck. Or really any of the other approximately four-point-eight-million people in the bar who are staring at us with more than a little curiosity. "Suffin fishy's startin ta rot," Long Beard says.

Understatement of the millennium, Mr. Beard.

"They's cahooting wif tha Guv'na!" someone calls out from the crowd.

And you know how you're not supposed to shout "Fire!" in a crowded theater because it makes everyone go raving nut bars? Apparently, here on New Moon, you shouldn't shout "Cahootin wif tha Guv'na!" in a cantina.

Major ruckus, that's what I'm getting at.

"We're not cahooting with anybody!" Ducky shouts over

the sudden chaos. Scrungy Neck has him by the collar and is probably trying to blind him with his vinegar breath.

Cole, who apparently would hold out approximately three seconds longer in a torture/interrogation situation than Ducky, shouts to the man at *his* throat. "I don't even know *how* to cahoot!"

For my part, I'm being pressed into the back of the booth by Long Beard's sausage of an index finger. "Luff, you bess tell us truths bout who yous is and what yous doing, or these lot might jess eat yous all, pretty or no."

"They're with me," comes a new voice from the crowd. A figure presses through, but when it reaches us, I have absolutely no idea who the person is. A man—no a boy, a teenager, probably not much older than me—with long dark hair and more than a bit of swagger in his step. "Hamish, ease up on them," this new mystery man tells Long Beard. "You don't wanna get involved, trust me."

Long Beard/Hamish darts eyes between his captives and the greasy-haired youth. "They's acting s'picious," he says. "Rousing in 'at."

"We're very roused!" calls one particularly loud local from the back.

Beside me Ducky is entering full-on panic mode, which is never a pretty sight. "I lied before," he tells Scrungy Neck. "About the cheese. My favorite's really ricotta. Please don't hurt me."

"Do what you will," Mystery Teen tells Long Beard. "But if you hurt them, Hux is gonna have your hide."

Well. You should hear the crowd go silent *then*.

Long Beard looks about as confused as I feel. "You's throw wit' Huxtable?" he asks me.

"Uh, yeah," I say slowly, following Mystery Teen's eyes as they dart sideways to Long Beard. He nods slightly: *Go with it.* And really, what have I got to lose besides my teeth? "Hux," I say. "We're, uh, working with Hux. For Hux. He's really gonna have your hide. Whew, boy."

Well, sign me up for CIA duty right now. I mean, I am *nailing* this shit.

Mystery Teen takes advantage of Hamish's confusion to reach out and tug me out of his grip. He does the same with Cole and Ducky, whose assailants aren't so thrilled about letting them go but grudgingly allow it. "Seems we should be going," he tells the crowd, and just like that, he pulls us from the fray.

It isn't until we reach the far less crowded corner of the bar that I notice Marnie, standing with her arms across her chest, shaking her head at us.

"Cannae take ye *anywhere*," she scolds. When Mystery Teen releases us into Marnie's custody, she offers him a peck on the cheek—and I *know* Ducky must be shaken up, because he doesn't even seem to notice. "Thanks, love," she tells him. Then she turns her attentions back to us. "Everyone, meet Dodge. Dodge, everyone."

Marnie's contact—and our new best friend—slides into the empty bench at the table Marnie has been guarding, and cocks his head to take us in, smirking. "Pleasure," he says. Then he turns back to Marnie. "I don't know what you're after, but the price just tripled," he tells her.

• • •

I'm staring at a plate of what I've been told is food, but you'd be hard pressed to convince me of that. If I'm being honest (and more than a little gross), I'd say this looks like something Ducky would bring back up after a particularly nasty trip in a space elevator.

"What is this?" I ask, poking the soggy lump of *something*. It's swimming in a thin blue-white liquid that I can only imagine unicorn tears must look like.

"It's a curry," Dodge says as he mops the substance up from his own plate with a hunk of rye. "Well, sorta. It's good if you sop up the juices with the bread."

I consider my own piece of bread, turning it over in my hand. A shower of crumbs falls onto my plate. I rip a piece off the edge and give it a munch.

"It's stale," I say, forcing it down.

"I know. Great, isn't it?" Dodge says. He slurps the soggy end of the bread in his mouth, sending the juices dribbling down his chin. "Usually you gotta pick out the maggots first, but we must've gotten lucky with the last shipment."

Marnie leans over to me. "Try it, Elvie," she says.

"I'm not all that hungry."

"Try it."

It's clearly not a suggestion. I look for sympathy from Cole or Ducky, but they're having their own curry issues at the moment. Cole is simply tilting the plate back and forth to watch the gelatinous substance slosh around. Meanwhile, Ducky looks like he's doing a pantomime of eating, complete with rubbing his stomach after each phantom bite.

"It's good," he says in a completely unconvincing voice.

Marnie's gaze has not left me, and now I realize that Dodge is watching me expectantly too. I take a deep breath, dip the hard bread into the slimy liquid, and take a tentative bite. Immediately my mouth is overwhelmed by the most pungent form of vinegar I have ever tasted. It spreads across my tongue like an electrical arc, making my eyes water. After the initial shock of the vinegar, I realize that my mouth is *on fire*. Like, fifty-two-alarm-chili level of spicy.

"Oh God!" I say, spitting the food out onto my plate and coughing. "What'd they do, drop a whole jar of devil peppers into this crap?"

"Elvie, fer Pete's sake," Marnie scolds.

"Oh, it's all right, luff," Dodge says, laughing. "I wouldn't expect a bunch of zoners to take to the seasoning right off the bat."

"What's a zoner?" Cole asks, using the question as a distraction as he clumsily pushes his own plate away.

"You lot," Dodge says. "Living planet-side, enjoying the little bit o' ozone we provide for you up here? Zoners."

"Why in the name of all that is holy would you eat this . . . *this*?" I ask.

"Bein' out here too long, your sense of taste and smell start to wane," Dodge explains. "After a few years you can't taste anything unless it's flavor-blasted."

"I think I'd rather eat that protein gel crap we had in Antarctica."

"Protein gel?" Dodge whistles. "Well, aren't we the fanciest of pants? You want protein here, best wait for the next bakery delivery and pray for maggots."

The conversation has turned Ducky a color not unlike the milky slop on our plates. He tries to mask a queasy burp as he slides his plate away, knocking my plate in the process and nearly spilling it over the edge onto my lap.

"Watch it!" I cry. "You think I want to smell like this stuff until the end of time?"

Dodge is laughing hard now. I guess watching others suffer amuses him? I dunno. He wipes tears away from his eyes and stands up from the table.

"Why don't I get you guys another round to wash the food down, eh?"

"That swill's not much better than this," I say. "Just thinner."

That gets Dodge laughing again, and he slaps my arm as he chortles. Marnie reaches into her pocket, but Dodge stops her.

"No, luff. This round's on me. For old times, yeah?"

He walks away toward the bar, still laughing and shaking his head.

"Well, he's a fun guy, isn't he?" I say. Ducky shrugs and uses the opportunity to dump his food onto Cole's plate.

"Hey!" Cole screams, shoving the plate toward Ducky.

I smirk at the boys' antics, but when I turn to Marnie, I drop the smile. To say that she's giving me the evil eye is to do a disservice to the evil eye, which is downright benign by comparison.

"What?" I ask. She doesn't answer me. I check the wall behind me to make sure I'm not sitting in front of a portrait of Pol Pot or something. But nope. It's just me. "What?" I ask again. "What did I do?"

When she replies, her voice is laced with barely suppressed rage.

"Yer actin' like a wee rotten princess," Marnie replies dryly.

Cole and Ducky freeze their food spat and stare at us, dumbfounded. Cole whistles through his teeth. Ducky tries once again to become one with the bench.

"Excuse me?" I say.

"Ye've been naught but a spoiled bairn since ye arrived here," Marnie says. "The lot of ye. I'm sick of it."

"I'm being *spoiled*?" I huff. "I'm being *spoiled*?" She nods, all sassy-like. "Would you mind explaining to me how traveling on a mission to find my kidnapped child makes me *spoiled*?" I feel like my face might burst into flames. "Or, no, wait. Maybe I got so spoiled after my mother *faked her own death* and ran off with your lot. Is that the part you were referring to? Or maybe it was the thing where I just, like, a month ago figured out I wasn't even a friggin' human. So, I apologize, *Marnie*, if with all that's going on I'm having a hard time feigning non-disgust regarding this failed science project masquerading as food. It's hard to be polite sometimes when your entire life is falling apart."

I may be a spastic lunatic of rage at this point, but Marnie is nothing but calm. "No one denies yer in a bad spot, Elvie," she says. "And I feel sorry fer ye, I do. But ye've done nothing but dismiss this place and these folk since we got here, and I might remind ye that these folks"—she jerks her head toward the crowd—"are most of them fine gents who've lived near their whole lives in this spot that ye wouldn't lower yerself to spit in. They work hard, they die quick, and fer what? So they can spend their free time and the little money they make shooting shite with their friends. And that 'swill,' as ye so disdainful put it? It's costin' Dodge what would go fer a day's wage round here, so ye jes' think about that 'fore ye turn yer nose up at it." I am starting to feel a little squirmy in my seat, but Marnie goes on. "And as fer learning about yer roots a month ago"— she leans forward on both elbows, never breaking her intense gaze— "I've been Enosi me whole life, which is how long I've been runnin' and hidin'. Cry me a river, ye ought. And even I wouldn't swap one day with one of these fellas."

I finally allow myself a breath. "Are you finished?" I say as she leans back in her seat. She gives me a look, daring a snarky comeback. Before I can speak, Dodge returns with a tray of beers. I can tell from the first sniff that this new batch is going to taste a whole lot like regurgitated sheep's feet.

"Here you go. These should be a little easier on your tongue than the last," Dodge says.

I take a mug from the tray. I can feel all eyes on me as I put it to my lips, tasting the bitter metal lip of the mug before the warm beverage fills my mouth. Yup. Sheep's feet.

"Thank you," I say quietly.

I look at Marnie, and she nods ever so slightly in my direction.

"Look, Dodge," Marnie says as Dodge settles back in at the table with his own mug. "We're in need of a favor."

"Anything for you, Legs," Dodge says with a wink. "I still owe you for the 'favor' you did me."

Ducky suddenly sits up as straight as an arrow in his seat. "Legs?" he asks no one in particular.

"Don't be crass," Marnie says. "Rake." Her freckles disappear into a sea of red blush, a development that is not lost on Ducky. "We're lookin' fer information."

"Who isn't, luff? Information on what?"

"There's a group of blokes, in deep with some bad bizzo. Nasty lot. Dangerous. Last place they were ken to be heading was up to the Belt."

"You just described everyone I know," Dodge says. "What're you after them for?"

"They took my daughter," I blurt out. Marnie gives me a quick sideways glance without moving her head. I think I detect the corner of her mouth tightening in a barely perceptible frown.

"Nappers, eh?" Dodge says, shaking his head with so much contrived sincerity that you'd think he was in a regional production of *Our Town*. "That's the worst. But again, not uncommon. Belt's a big place. You're going to have to give me more than that to go on."

"I dunnae that we are," Marnie says, narrowing her eyes. I give her a confused look, but she doesn't break her gaze away from our would-be informant. "Whaddya know, Dodge?"

I can feel my stomach twisting itself into a knot, and it's only partially the result of indigestion. Dodge grins at Marnie and gives her a wink, which does nothing to calm my nerves.

"Still read me like a book, dontcha?" he says. "Now that you mention it, I might know about some unusual goings-on, but aside from the beers, nuthin's free up here, luff."

"Dinnae take me fer a dobber," Marnie says. "We've got a line of credit, ye and I."

"But this here's delicate information, Red. The price is, oh, triple the old rate."

"Double," Marnie says, unwavering. Dodge takes a long draw from his mug. Without putting it down, he holds out his other hand expectantly. Marnie reaches into her pocket and pulls out a credits card. She slaps it down onto Dodge's palm. Before he can pull his hand back, she squeezes, pressing the card between their hands. She raises her eyebrows inquisitively, and he nods in answer. Only then does she release her grip. Dodge puts down his mug and pulls a card reader out of his jacket pocket. He swiftly swipes Marnie's card and plugs in an amount I can't see, before flashing the reader at Marnie for confirmation. She nods, and he pockets the reader, handing the card back to her.

"So, what do ye know, Dodge?" Marnie asks. "They hidin' in the outer shoals somewhere?"

"That'd be a grand place to lay low, to be sure," Dodge says. "But if you're looking for who I think you are, then you won't have to go nearly that far."

"How far, then?" I interject.

"Oh, maybe a dozen decks or so."

The information lands on the table like a bomb, as literally all of us fall back in our seats like we've been flavor-blasted.

"Dr. Marsden is *here*?" I gasp.

"Can't say I got names," Dodge says.

Marnie puts a calming hand on my forearm. "Let's slow down," she says, turning back to Dodge. "Awrite, what's yer tale?"

Dodge shrugs. "All I know is that a little while ago New

Moon got some new tenants downstairs. Secretive bunch. Set up shop in the unused facilities underneath the refinery."

"Jes' like that," Marnie says, a hint of disbelief in her voice. "That area's owned by the Federated Gas Minin' Conglomerate. And yer sayin' these bastarts waltzed in and took over the entire facility without any fuss?"

"Well, if all I'd done was seen 'em, I might've guessed they coasted by on their good looks," Dodge says. My heart is smashing into my rib cage. "But these guys are full bricks, yeah?"

"Full bricks?" Cole asks.

"They've got money," Marnie translates.

"That's the understatement of the year, luff," Dodge replies. "These guys have thrown so much money at the Governor, they can pretty much do whatever they please. They could be running around the ship taking anything they wanted, *if* that was what they felt like doing. But they've stayed out of sight, for the most part. Doing God knows what down there in those old medical facilities."

Medical facilities. Oh God. What are they doing to my poor baby?

"That's them!" I say a little too loudly. "It's got to be them. What are we waiting for?"

"Hold yer roll, Elvie," Marnie says. "Even if it is them, from what Dodge is sayin', they've got the protection of the local government."

"Calling it government, there's a laugh," Dodge says. "Just the Governor and his goons, really. Used to get by on squeezing whatever credit they could from the poor blokes living here. Now, with all the bricks comin' in from this new lot, they don't know what to do with all their wealth. Like giving a walrus a mandolin."

"They won't want anyone poking around their benefactors," Marnie says. "We best be dead careful, or we'll wind up stockaded."

"Or worse," Dodge agrees. "Having wealthy backers is making the Governor cocky. He was always a greedy, opportunistic prick, but times past he wouldn't rock the boat too much, for fear of interrupting his credit flow. Now, though, he fancies himself some kind of bloody kingpin. He's even pressing Huxtable a bit, hiring away some muscle."

"Who is this Huxtable guy?" Cole asks. But before he can get an answer, I stand up. This is a million times better than I even dared dream. Marsden's cronies, here, on this very space station? That places the odds that my baby is within crying distance at good to awesome. I reach into my pocket for the tracker, before remembering I left it on board the ship.

"What are we waiting for?" I ask the gang. All of my emotions are battling inside me—relief, fear, hope—and the adrenaline from it is making me shaky. I just hope I don't start bawling in the bar.

Marnie rises as well. "Best get back to the ship."

"Exactly," I say. "I'll grab the tracker. Then we'll be able to follow it to—"

"Elvie." Marnie offers me a sorrowful look. "We dinnae know fer certain that yer bairn is here. And even did we, we can't jes' go bargin' into a Jin'Kai stronghold, the four a us, no weapons. Tha's suicide."

I am confused. "But my *baby*," I say. I can feel my neck going rigid.

"I think I'm gonna leave you to it," Dodge says, taking in the rising tension around the table. "Marnie, always a pleasure, luff. Maybe next time you'll make a social call, yeah?"

He kisses her hand and disappears into the crowd so quickly that it's tempting to think he might never have been there in the first place.

"What does he mean by that?" Ducky asks.

"Forget about him," I say. "We need to find out how to get down to these secret facilities and rescue my daughter."

"What we need to do," Marnie tells me, "is head back to Oates and th' others, tell them what we learnt. Now we've found Marsden's base of operations, we need to inform someone who can do something about it."

"You want to abandon her here?" I ask in disbelief.

"I want to do what's in the greater good," she tells me. "And I want ye to wake up and do the same."

"But she's here!"

"Aye, and what do ye want to do about it? Blast yer way into a fortified base crawlin' with Jin'Kai? I thought we'd get a lead if we were lucky, something to point us in the right direction as we formulated a plan. We're not prepared for a rescue."

"I don't believe this bullshit," I say. I storm away from the table and head for the exit.

"Elvie, wait!" I hear Cole call from behind me. I stop and turn, to find him pushing his way toward me.

"What, Cole? You have something to add?"

"Only that, whatever you want to do, Elvs, I'm with you."

Finally, someone I can rely—

"Hey, handsome, you're not leaving so soon, are you?"

The chippie from the bar sidles up to us and puts an arm around Cole's.

"Excuse me," I say to her.

"You're excused," she replies, barely giving me a glance before turning back to Cole. "I didn't get your digits or anything," she tells him with a wink.

"Oh, um, hey," Cole says. He looks between me and his floozy hanger-on. "Um, this, um, isn't the best time right now."

I can barely muster an "Ugh!" as I storm away into the outer passageway. I'm halfway to the elevator banks when the gang catches up to me.

"Elvie, please, just think about this for a minute," Ducky says, panting.

I turn to my last and greatest ally. "Ducky," I say, "can you please explain to your girlfriend why we're not leaving here until we get what we came for? Thanks so much."

"Actually, Elvie, I, er . . ." Ducky trails off, rubbing his arm slowly.

"What?" I snap at him. "Afraid Marnie won't like you anymore if you tell her what you really think?"

"Elvie." Marnie's voice is soft. Sympathetic. "Yer the one he's afeart to tell."

I knit my eyebrows together. "What?" I say, looking back to Ducky.

Ducky is clearly hoping Marnie will do the talking, but when she only stands there, looking pointedly at him, he finally pipes up, his voice hoarse. "We have information now.

More than we could have hoped for. But Marnie's right, we aren't some kind of special forces strike force. We're just us."

"I was on a special forces strike force," Cole chimes in.

"And how'd that go?" Ducky counters. "Look, we can use this information. Give it to your grandfather. They'll know what to do."

"All they care about is the invasion," I say. "I need Olivia. If she's here, I'm going to find her."

"I'm sorry, Elvie," Ducky tells me. He sounds genuinely gutted. "I want to find Olivia too. I do. But this is the entire *world* we're talking about. These Devastator guys could literally *destroy the planet* if we don't act fast. When you weigh things that way . . . she's just one baby."

We are all silent, letting Ducky's words sink in.

"If we go back to Earth," Ducky says softly, placating, "we can tell people what we know. People who can do something. We'll get her back, Elvie. I promise."

She's just one baby.

"Don't you talk to me," I tell Ducky. My chest is frozen. "Not ever again."

She's just one baby.

Ducky reaches out an arm to try to make it up to me—leaving my baby in this place to die or worse—with a hug, I guess. But it's not happening. I give him a stiff arm, sending him stumbling back for Marnie to catch.

"C'mon, then," Marnie says. Her tone is conciliatory. "We'll go ahead and get the ship fired up. Give ye a few ticks to yerself."

"You do that."

Marnie heads off to the elevators, Ducky in tow. He turns and gives me a pitiful look, but I am in no way willing to feel sorry for that backstabbing creep right now. I hope his new squeeze is there for him the next time his infant is kidnapped by aliens, because if he expects me to lift a finger, he can just forget it. They get into the first open elevator and turn to face us.

"Archer?" Marnie asks. It's only then that I realize that Cole is standing right next to me.

"We'll catch up," Cole says. At this very moment I really wish that he'd put a strong, reassuring hand on my shoulder, like he used to. But he doesn't. He just stands dutifully beside me, like one of Byron's Newfoundlands. The elevator doors swish shut, leaving us alone with about four hundred other lost souls milling in and out of the bar.

"You okay?" Cole asks. The only way I know to answer him involves a lot of cursing or crying, so I say nothing. He turns to face me directly.

"Elvie, you say the word," he says. "You tell me what to do, and I'll do it. You just tell me the plan."

"What plan?" I say, the tears edging dangerously toward the corners of my eyes. "What are the two of us supposed to do against Marsden's whole gang? It's not like we can waltz in the front door."

"Actually," comes a voice from behind us, "it might be you could do exactly that."

I whip around to see Dodge leaning against a pillar several yards away from us, picking at something resembling slimy flat noodles from a flat square tin.

"Where did you—" I start to ask.

"I took off," he interrupts, walking up to us, "but I never left. Sometimes folks tell you a lot more when you're not there." He picks up one of the "noodles" from the tin and slides it down his throat like it's some sort of delicacy. He offers the tin to me, but I shake my head politely, because despite my tears, my nose still works. Dodge shrugs and closes the tin, then slips it into his jacket pocket.

"You must be a real ace mum," he says.

"Not yet," I say. "But I'll never get there without practice."

"Wish I'd had a mum like you. Mine sold me to the Conglomerate when I was ten, to pay off her debts. She's living somewhere planet-side now, rot take her."

"I'm sorry," I say. I'm not sure where this is going. "You said we could get in the front door? What do you mean by that?"

"Just what I said," Dodge answers. "These folks you're after, they're below the refinery, yeah? So the only way in is *through* the refinery. The security there is pretty tight—they don't want just anyone sneaking in and scampering off with any of their precious ozone bricks—but if you know the right scamp . . ."

"And you're that scamp," I finish. "We don't have any credits, Dodge."

Dodge waves me off like he's insulted. "Not everything's about money, luff." I give him a look. "Okay," he says, and smirks. "Most things are. Look, if I help you get your wee one back, all I ask is that you comp me a ride planet-side on your ship. If you're still feeling generous then, we can discuss further compensation later."

"Why would you help us like that?" Cole asks, suspicious.

"You know the going rate of a flight down?" Dodge asks. "I'm not talking a joy ride with any of these space jockeys, who are just as likely to blow up as get you anywhere. I mean an honest-to-goodness ride back to civilization? I couldn't afford it on ten years' scamming."

"You could have asked Marnie for a ride anytime you wanted," I say.

"Legs usually travels with that humorless bunch of sad sacks she calls her family. She's never had a proper ship. Like you."

"How did you—"

"Luff, this will go a lot faster if you just accept that I know a lot more than you think I should, without asking the why," Dodge says. "I've broken into the plant before. Ozone—even gas—fetches a fair price around here. I can get you in and out before your mates have even finished prepping the ship for takeoff. Whaddya say?"

Cole gives me a worried look, but when he sees my face, he must realize there's no use in arguing.

Hold on, Olivia, I think, the voice in my head growing louder by the second. *Just hold on.*

Chapter Seven

IN WHICH A PREVIOUSLY INCONSEQUENTIAL SOMEONE MAKES AN EXPLOSIVE REAPPEARANCE

"Here. Put these on," Dodge says, handing us two dirty pairs of coveralls. Not at all like the one I wore during my failed attempt to escape the *Echidna* in the trash compactor, or the ones the Almiri gave us when they first shuttled us onto the space elevator to the South Pole. No, these are decidedly . . . earthier. There's so much grease and assorted grime caked to the coarsely woven material that it feels crunchy in my hands as I unfurl it.

"Why?" I ask. Presently I am very unappreciative of my Enosi adaptive abilities. I would love to not be able to smell this jumper.

"Because you're a scrubber, remember?" Dodge replies. "We're being all sneaky-like."

"Oh," I say. "Right." I really wish people would leave the being-a-sarcastic-pain-in-the-ass thing to me.

"You too, pretty boy," Dodge tells Cole, who seems to be having similar difficulty in building the courage to slip the filthy cover over his own clothes. "You're going to stand out too much as it is, smooth little peach that you are."

"I am not a . . . peach," Cole says defiantly. But when he slips into the coveralls and zips the front up, he looks like a flat-pic superhero after a grueling but sexy battle in the mud, whereas I can only assume I look like a moldy prune someone dropped in a soggy trash can.

"Where's your disguise?" I ask Dodge.

"Disguise? Yours truly?" Dodge says, sounding sincerely and profoundly hurt. "My notoriety is a blessing here, my luffies, unlike yours, should you be caught trespassing. Don't you fret. With ol' Dodge as your guide, we'll have you where you're headed in no time."

Once we're in our crunchy coveralls, we exit the terminal booth. The crowds are thinner down here than they were up on the promenade or residential levels, which suddenly makes me feel very naked in spite of the rumpled disguise I'm wearing.

"So remember," Dodge says as we walk, "you're new scrubbers fresh off the latest transport, came here thanks to a generous donation on my part toward the purchase of two tickets for said transport, and we're going to set up your debit wage, with a thirty-five percent cut going to yours truly."

"Thirty-five percent?" I say, incredulous.

"It's not for real, luff. Don't get caught in a spot over it. It's got to look legit for us to get inside."

"Somehow even fictional indentured servitude gives me pause," I say.

"That's nothing," Dodge says. "Wait till you see the convenience and processing fees. A weekly wage of seven hundred dollars usually leaves a new scrubber with a debit card of under three hundred."

"How can they get away with that?" I ask, honestly indignant. "There are labor laws for that sort of thing."

"Laws is for zoners, luff."

"But why doesn't anyone do anything about it?"

"And here I thought rich girls didn't catch the activist bug until uni," Dodge tells me. "Look, it's a bloody awful system, luff. But it didn't come from nowhere. That's why I'm helping you. We uncover this big bad you think you're after, why, that can't help but shine a light on some of the other unmentionable things going on here. Just so long as you don't forget about all this back planet-side."

"I won't," I say. "I promise."

"Right, then," Dodge says. "A few more blocks to the facility gates."

The front of the refinery complex looks like the terminal of a decidedly fourth-rate airport. There are several rows of plastic chairs back-to-back, forming narrowing channels toward a barrier, a twelve-meter-high silver wall with six gates—three checkpoints on the right marked by a blue light above each doorway, while the three to the left are marked by a red light. Hanging from the ceiling are three spherical surround-view cameras taking in enough visual data to create a fully manipulable, examinable 3-D image of the grand foyer.

"That's some fancy security," I say, nodding upward.

Dodge smiles but doesn't look up. "New toys the Governor had installed not too long back," he informs us. "Among others. Not exactly standard issue for this kind of plant."

"The kind of toy that'd come in handy if you wanted to keep extra close tabs on who was coming in and out," I say.

"You think it's Marsden?" Cole asks, looking straight up.

"Maybe," I say, resisting the urge to tell Cole not to point his face directly at the camera.

The other thing I notice as we approach the entry is that there is suddenly a large cluster of people hovering near one of the gates. They aren't wearing work coveralls, and they don't look like they are here in any kind of professional capacity. They look like the throng flooding the promenade level.

"What's with the crowd?" I ask.

"Payday," Dodge says.

His meaning is made clear as we reach the gate. The crowd flocks toward us, clutching at our sleeves as they plead in the assorted dialects of the upper levels.

Beggars.

As we approach, a tone sounds through the room. For a split second I freeze, fearing that we've been found out (although, technically, we haven't done anything illegal yet). That's when I see the men and women start to exit the complex through the red-light marked doorways. The beggars immediately tear away from us and fly at the workers just ending their shift—presumably with a weekly debit payment in their pocket. Many of the beggars extend small digital card readers toward the scrubbers, hoping for a charitable swipe of a few credits, while some of the less fortunate futilely hold their bare hands out, palms up, on the off chance that someone might be carrying an actual piece of physical currency. Having just been told how measly their working wage is, I'm surprised to see that more than half of the two or three dozen scrubbers pause on their way home to transfer a few dollars here and there to those unable to get work. The only people who don't break their stride are a group of men wearing completely different uniforms—dark, trim jumpsuits. Pilot attire.

"Come on," Dodge says, eyeing the scene with a bitter expression. "Stick close once we're inside, and follow my lead."

Cole and I follow Dodge closely. He passes through the far right blue-lit doorway without incident, but the door lets out two soft dings as Cole and I walk through.

"Don't fret," Dodge tells us. "It's just 'cause you don't have a pass card." On the other side of the silver wall, there is another lobby, just as drab as the outer foyer. Along the right wall is a small glass office space, from which two men exit at the sound of the pings. Dodge opens his arms in a grandiose gesture as they approach, a smile twice as wide as his face.

"Bricks, Potter, how are ya, mates?" Dodge greets them.

"What's ya there, Dodge?" the one called Bricks says, gesturing at us.

"Fresh offerings from the below," Dodge says.

Bricks looks us over, unimpressed. "Zoners, eh?" He inhales what sounds like an inordinately large block of phlegm from his left nostril.

"Not anymore, they ain't," Dodge tells him. "Got the scrubber bug."

"They're really dreggin' the mists with these lot nowadays, eh?" Bricks says, smirking.

"That's the second time someone's said that about me," I whisper to Cole. "I'm starting to think it's not a compliment."

"The less they think of us the better, right?" Cole says with a shrug.

"All right," Potter says to Dodge. "So what's yer cut, then?"

Dodge turns to us and barks, "You's wait while we discuss business." And with that he disappears into the glass office with Bricks and Potter, an arm around each man's grime-encrusted shoulder.

"So, um," Cole says, looking around to see if there's anywhere to sit, which there isn't. "Once we're inside . . . then what, Elvs?"

I merely shrug. "I'm assuming Dodge will know where to go."

Cole raises an eyebrow. "To find this supersecret place where the supersecret Jin'Kai who might not actually be working with Dr. Marsden are doing supersecret things?" he asks.

"Um, yep," I say lamely. But I guess I get defensive when I see the look Cole offers me then. "No one said it would be easy," I say.

"No offense, Elvs," Cole says, "but I'm used to a little more planning from you on stuff like this."

"You know what, Cole, if you didn't like the plan, then why'd you even bother to come with me?"

I'm not actually angry at Cole, of course. The dude could not be more right. I do usually plan these things better. If my dad isn't already disappointed in me for stealing Byron's ship and going rogue, he'll most assuredly be chagrinned by this half-baked baby-rescue mission.

To my surprise Cole gets right in my face, and he looks fierce. "Why'd I come with you?" he snaps. "She's my daughter too, Elvie."

I think the fact that I can feel my face go white as I stumble back a few paces is enough to inform Cole that he's got me dead to rights.

"I'm . . . sorry," I say slowly. God, it seems like I've had to say that a lot lately. But Cole is right, and I guess I'd sort of let that detail slip out of my brain for a while. No matter what he and I are to each other, he is Olivia's father. Always will be.

Cole nods slightly. "S'okay," he mumbles, staring at Dodge and those guys in the glass booth.

As far as I can tell, Dodge is still BS-ing. I can't hear anything they're saying, but Bricks in particular looks confused, whereas Potter looks more concerned as he peppers Dodge with silent questions. I wish I were a better lip-reader.

After a few minutes Potter nods, seemingly in agreement. Bricks looks through the glass at us again and smiles, revealing several gaps in his crooked set of teeth.

"What's happening?" Cole asks, staring back at the glass booth trio. Dodge clasps Potter's hand in a firm shake. "Is that . . . good?"

I honestly don't know how to answer. Dodge walks to the door before spinning around and doing an elaborate curtsy for the two men. They each give him an equally exaggerated gesture with their hands, then turn to look at us with shit-eating grins.

"I don't like it," I say, feeling my body tense. "Something's not right."

Dodge is through the door with a smirk on his face. As he approaches, he gestures toward the long snaking corridor leading into the facility. "This way, lass and lad," he says without breaking stride. "Let ol' Dodge guide you through the gates of Dis."

"What was that all about?" I ask, running to catch up to him as he passes through the first archway. "What was with all that smiling?"

"Elvie, my dear," he says, "I'm sorry to inform you that Bricks and Potter'll each be getting a five percent kickback on your wages for letting you on the rolls."

"After your cut, we'll hardly have enough to live off," I say. Then I break into a grin. "Nicely played."

"You bribed them with fake money?" Cole asks.

"Don't feel too bad for 'em, Cole old boy," Dodge says. "I'm sure they'll get by on the backs of some other poor saps."

The winding corridor leads us farther into the heart of the factory. The first thing that hits me right away is the smell. It smells like a pool. The chlorine stench is so strong that my vision actually goes a little blurry. The second thing is the cold. While it doesn't bother me nearly as much as the smell, it's noticeably frigid.

"Why is it so chilly in here?" I ask as we pass underneath a large robotic crane arm shifting pallets of equipment from the ground level to the open upper deck.

"Keeping the temp down reduces the chance that the ozone will combust," Dodge says. "This is nuffin'. Wait till we get into the processing chambers. That'll chip the nips right off ya."

"Charming," I reply. I feel a hand on my back. It's Cole, guiding me forward slightly faster than I'd like. I turn to give him the old what-do-you-think-you're-doing? routine, but then I see that the crane we just passed under has jammed and is whirring loudly under the strain of a pallet that hasn't quite reached its destination. A team of workers on the top level rush to the edge and reach out precariously with grappling rods to pull the cargo up. "It's a wonder this whole place hasn't blown up already."

"Tech is old, run-down, but it works. Mostly. Problem is injuries. Even with his new cash flow, the Governor ain't dropped a credit toward upping safety standards for the floor crew. Only place he's put in a little dough is the compressor system what presses the bricks 'emselves. Guess he don't want 'em going boom right under his own arse."

We pass into a cavernous room, twice as big as the machinery floor we just left, and sure enough, the temp is probably half what it was before. My breath can see its own breath in here.

"Your brights are on, luff," Dodge says with a smirk. At first I don't know what he means. Cole, looking embarrassed, gestures at the half-zipped top of my overalls.

"Thanks for the heads up," I growl, zipping the overalls up to my neck. Dodge clucks his tongue in what I think is disappointment.

"Not trying to be vulgar. I am a great admirer of the female form." He punches Cole in the arm jovially, but Cole just stares back at him.

"So, what goes on in here?" I ask, trying to change the subject, lest Cole start to get chivalrous on my behalf at the worst possible moment.

"Here's where the ozone gas is pressed into brick form." Dodge points at the long chain of machines whirring along the left side of the room. "The gas feeds in through the venting system there, where's it's purified. Then the temp goes down to -112 degrees Celsius through them pipes, and the gas goes gooey." He gestures to the series of massive tubing that stretches for dozens of meters toward a tall, boxy machine. The contraption stands close to thirty meters high and runs almost the complete length of the room. "The goo goes in there, and the temp drops even further, gets fashioned into the bricks. Each brick's about half a cubic meter, weighing about one metric ton, and if one o' them popped, you'd feel it on the far side of the station, that's how much wallop they pack. They drop through that shaft you see at the end there, straight down, and get delivered to the factory hangar, where they're loaded into the flyers so they can be deployed into the atmo, and you zoners can keep going to the beach without having to use SPF 200 sunscreen."

"You sure know a lot about how the sausage is made around here," I say.

"You gotta know how things work, luff," Dodge says as we come to a stop at the end of the compression room. He pulls a security card from his jacket pocket. "Everything and everyone. Once you get that wired, you've got a shot."

He gives me a wink as he swipes his pass card across the door's security sensor, but the panel honks—the card's been rejected.

"That's odd," Dodge says, raising an eyebrow. He swipes the card across again, and gets the same honking response. "This should be working." He tries again, with the same response from the security sensor.

"Knock it off. You're going to draw attention to us," I hiss. I look around nervously. Despite the lack of visible security cameras in this area, I still have the uncomfortable feeling that we're being watched. I look across the floor, but there's no one else around. I glance up to the catwalk in the cooling/ventilation system above us—nothing. It's empty. Way too empty.

"Is there another way in?" Cole asks. He's getting anxious as well.

"No," Dodge says. "I'm afraid this is it."

The sensor pings in the affirmative, and it takes me a split second too long to realize that Dodge didn't swipe his card. I try to get Cole's attention, but before I can speak, the door slides open and five men come pouring out. Four of them are large and rough, wearing the same uniforms Bricks and Potter wore. They quickly surround us. The fifth man is of medium height and maximum width. Seriously, he's sporting the kind of girth that demands that you find employment in a lowered gravity environment.

"So's you've deliverated as promised, eh, Dodge?" the man says, a crooked yellow grin on his face. His clothes are remarkably posh compared to anyone else I've seen on the station— pressed white dress slacks, a bright blue dress shirt, and a purple sports jacket with a single button. I even recognize his boots (which seem quite ill-fitted for factory work) from last year's Macydale collection. Despite the quality of the outfit, the man wearing it doesn't match. His greasy dome of a head sports a messy thin comb-over, while several days' worth of stubble spreads unevenly down his cheeks to his collar, which is stained with sweat. All of his clothes stretch with uncertainty around the man's massive frame, threatening to bust loose at any moment. His pants are dingy at the knees.

"Evenin', Guv'na," Dodge says with a wink. "Your delivery, as promised."

"You sold us out?" Cole blurts.

Of course he did. Flip me. Why didn't I see this coming?

"Sorry, mates," Dodge says, clearly not sorry in the slightest. "You seem all right for zoners, but you're worth enough to get me off this rickety bucket once and for all."

"You could have come with us," I say.

Dodge merely shrugs. "Okay, so you're worth a ride plus a little more, monetarily speaking."

"More 'n a little, boy," the Governor tells him. "You'll not be wanting fer much." He unwedges a wrinkled handkerchief from his pants pocket and drags it across his brow—which, despite the chilly temp in here, is dripping with sweat. Then he nods to one of the large thugs, who hands Dodge an envelope. Dodge opens it and examines the contents: a passport book, something that looks like a bundle of different travel tickets, and a green debit card.

"No offense, 'mate,'" I say to Dodge, "but I hope you choke on your thirty pieces of silver."

"A terribly cutting insult, to be sure, luff."

"Cole," I whisper, "now might be a time for some thrilling heroics."

"I don't think so," he replies, gesturing toward the thugs. They're all touting high-powered pistols, ready to give the Swiss cheese treatment to anyone feeling particularly escape-y. I glance back at Dodge, who gives me one of his charming winks and begins to whistle as he walks away from us back the way we came. As he passes behind us, he raises his hand, index finger pointed upward, in one last dismissive farewell gesture. I have to credit Cole for his restraint. Armed goons or not, if I had Cole's quickness and strength, I'd probably leap over and snap Dodge's finger off before doing horrible, horrible things to him with it.

"So, you are our new snoops, intrudicating upon my affairs," the Governor wheezes when Dodge has disappeared for good. He rubs the back of his neck with his handkerchief, then brings it back around and jams it into his pocket, a good three times grosser than it was before. "Now, how a couple of zoners would get curiatized as to the comings and goings upon this most gesticulated spacial institution, that would perforate me most greatly."

There's a long pause as the Governor waits, looking at us expectantly. Finally Cole leans over to me.

"Elvie, we're in luck," he whispers. "I think he's having a stroke."

The Governor harrumphs and begins pacing back and forth in a clearly rehearsed and hilariously miscalculated attempt to look intimidating. If it weren't for the mortal peril we currently find ourselves in, the visual of this zeppelin waddling like a duck and spouting nonsense would be worthy of an autotune vid upload for sure.

"My benefactorous business associates will be most enjoyed upon finding such illicitating trouble-makers brought to their attention. I believe a bonus to our fiduciary concordance will present itself . . . presently."

So Dodge ratted us out only to the locals, which means the Jin'Kai don't know we're here yet. Maybe that gives us a chance, if I play this just right.

"I really don't think you want to do that," I tell the Governor, trying to muster as much cool as I can.

"Oh, do expound upon such statements," he replies with a smirk. "Under what guise of treacherating deceitedness do you boast so?"

"Well, I know you're a big cheese up here and all that," I say. Cool, Elvie. Icy cool. "But I don't think our boss will be too happy to know that you've interfered with us."

"And pray tell, who is your employifier?"

"We're on a special assignment," I say with a shrug. "For Huxtable."

There is a sound of air escaping as the thugs seem to gasp in unison. Even the Governor's smug smile drops, and a new swath of sweat speckles his forehead.

"You work for Hux—Huxtable?" he stammers. He's uncomfortable even saying the name. So, good. The boogeyman works on this lot as well. "Dodge never said anything about that."

"Well, Dodge had no need to know of our affiliation," I say.

The overfilled bowl of saturated fat peers at me through narrowed eyes. "What verifying evidentials do you have?"

"Hey, if you need proof, you can ask the man yourself," I say. And sure enough, that seems like it might be working. The Governor looks around hesitantly at his men, who are busy murmuring to one another.

"I dun want no trouble wit Huxtable," one of them mutters. The others mumble in agreement.

"Das nuf," the Governor says, his mannered speech faltering, if only for a moment. He grabs one of the thugs by the arm. "Go grab Dodge, the little rodent, before he's fled."

The thug holsters his gun and trots toward the front of the facility. One armed assailant down; three to go. Gotta get the odds in Cole's favor.

"You're in over your head with these new 'friends' of yours, 'Guv'na,'" I say, stretching my back in an exaggerated gesture of calm. "You don't understand the people you're dealing with."

"And what would you know about who I'm dealing with?" he says. The handkerchief is back out of his pocket as he furiously mops up his flop sweat again. "They don't cause any trouble. Not one fisticutory disturbance."

"Do you even know what they're doing on your own station?" I ask, laying on the disbelief. "Do you know what you've gotten yourself into?"

"I've no informatives on their practitions!" the Governor says, his eyes bulging in his fat head. "If they've come at odds with Huxtable's dealings—"

"Oh, but they have," I say. "In a big way. And you don't want to make him any angrier than he already is, do you?"

"Boss, mebbe we should cut 'em free," one of the thugs says.

The Governor stands frozen, like the OS in his brain needs a reboot. Maybe, just maybe, this guy is chump enough to buy this bluff long enough for us to—

"No!" he shouts suddenly, his face collapsing into a scowl even less attractive than his normal expression. "Huxtable thinks he calls all the shots here? Not anymore. I have money now. I have muscle behind me. I am the caller of shots. I am the decider!" He pokes the nearest thug in the arm. "Shoot these dregs."

Um, so, bluff backfired. I'm at a loss for a response.

"Shit," Cole says.

That works.

"Boss?" the thug responds, confused. "You's want to war with Huxtable?"

"Huxtable ain't scare me no more! I got uppers on 'im! I'm the real weight around here now," the Governor replies.

"No argument here," I mutter. Which actually gets a snicker out of the thugs.

But snickers don't save lives.

The thug next to the Governor raises his handgun and points it right at Cole. "Hope you's know what you're doin'," he tells his boss.

"Elvie . . . ," Cole says. His muscles are coiled tightly, ready to spring into action. He could probably take the guy out—he might be able to take them *all* out—but he knows as well as I do that there's very little chance that I can survive a firefight unarmed and surrounded. I want to scream for Cole to just go, run, smash everyone's face and break into the Jin'Kai base, find Olivia, save Olivia, go run away and raise her on an island somewhere that doesn't have mosquitoes and make sure she's happy . . .

The first shot is so unexpected that I don't even flinch. There's just a flash and we all stand still for a moment. Then my brain registers what has happened. It occurs to the thug with his gun trained on Cole too. Probably because he's the one who just got shot.

"Run!" one of the others shouts as his comrade collapses, dead, to the floor. More shots rain down from the catwalk above us. I look up to see who's up there playing Rescue Ranger. The shooter is in the shadows, but the green crackle of the energy blasts has a familiar glint to it.

The thugs scatter and take cover in the doorway as the Governor trips over his own fat legs trying to backtrack to safety. He rolls more than falls to the ground, whimpering, as his men grab hold of his purple jacket and pull him inside the cover of the entryway.

"It's Huxtable!" one of them shouts.

"What are you waiting for?" the Governor yells. "Shoot! Shoot! Perforate the transgressitators!" The thugs comply, firing blindly up at the attacker.

"Is it Marnie?" Cole asks as we duck down behind a bulkhead to avoid the cross fire.

"I don't remember her bringing an Almiri ray gun with her," I reply.

A shot strikes one of the coolant valves above us, causing steam to burst out in a violent rush. The shooter moves out of the steam's path, into the light.

"What are you conks waiting for?" the shooter calls. Female. Definitely female. "You don't actually *want* to be dead, do you?"

I look up, but it's not Marnie on the catwalk. It's not even Ducky, reduced to a squealing soprano brought on by the stressful situation.

It's the cheap floozy from the bar that Cole was hitting on.

"Dude," I say to Cole. "Just how much time did you two have to 'chat'?"

"Elvie!" Cole shouts, grabbing my arm to pull me out of the line of another shot. "Gift horse. Mouth."

"The ladder!" the chippie shouts down at us. I look to where she's pointing. A service ladder about a dozen meters behind us, leading to the catwalk. The little tart with the ray gun sends several blasts toward the doorway, forcing the thugs to hide behind their cover. "Now would be a good time!" she screams.

Cole pushes me from behind the bulkhead, and then I'm running like crazy. As soon as I reach the ladder, I grab hold of the first rung, and before I even start climbing, the girl slaps a control panel on the wall above, and the ladder begins to retract up into the ceiling. I scramble to maintain purchase on the rung as I fly upward, but I lose my grip and have to catch hold with the crook of my elbow.

"Cole!" I scream as I rise far above him. The floozy lays down a suppressive cover fire for her new boy toy, and Cole takes off from where he's been crouching, leaping the several meters to catch the bottom of the ladder. He lands against me with a thud and holds me safely in place as we zip the rest of the way up to the catwalk. When the ladder locks into place with a jolt, Cole lets go and drops to the ground, catching me as I release my dodgy grip.

"Cole," the girl says.

(She would just say his name like that.)

"What are you doing here, Chloe?" Cole asks.

(I never really noticed before how dumb a name "Chloe" is.)

"Someone had to save your skins," Chloe responds. "Follow me, pretty boy."

(Not the time, Elvie. So not the time.)

With that, Chloe takes off down the catwalk toward a

coolant system service shaft. "This way," she instructs, like the world's most obvious tour guide. I mean, where else does she think we're going to go? Back down toward the guys trying to shoot our heads off?

"Chloe," Cole calls as we run, heads ducked low, through the shaft. "How did you know I was here? And what are you doing with a gun?"

"You want answers?" Chloe says, leading the way. "Or do you want to get out of here in one piece? A ship?"

"Was that supposed to be a question?" I ask.

"A ship," she repeats over her shoulder, her voice indicating that she thinks *I'm* the chromer in this group. "Do you have one?"

"Our friends have a ship," Cole answers. "They were prepping to leave when we snuck off."

"Well, with any luck we'll catch them before they head off without you," Chloe says. We come up to a magnetically sealed service hatch that requires a pass key.

"And how do you propose we get there?" I ask, pointing to the door.

Chloe smirks (which someone should inform her is not flattering for her face shape) and pulls a pass card out of her pocket. She swipes the access card, and the door *hiss-pops* open.

"It's called being prepared," she says.

If she weren't saving our lives right now, I'd soooo punch her in her stupid teeth.

The service shaft leads to the same processing room we passed through earlier. The scrubbers below us mill about unawares as we scamper overhead. I'm starting to think that we might be able to sneak quietly by, but then my eyes land on Dodge on the factory floor. The guard who had been sent after him is now dragging him by the collar back to the Governor, Dodge kicking and squirming the whole way, pleading his case. That's when he happens to look up, and we lock eyeballs.

"Don't you do it," I whisper under my breath. "You slimy little—"

"Up there!" Dodge screams, pointing right at us. The guard looks up just as his companions run in and join him from the other room. "There they are! It's thems you want, not poor old Dodge!"

"Guys . . . ," I say.

Chloe turns, sees our pursuers, and fires off several shots down in their direction, scattering the scrubbers, who scream while looking for the nearest exit.

"Chloe, what the hell!" Cole shouts, grabbing her arm. "The ozone! You want to blow us to smithereens?"

If Cole's lecturing someone on safety, then you *know* they've pooched it. Even the Governor's men know better than to open fire in this room. Chloe looks around for a split second, then smirks again.

"Good thinking," she says, and before you can say "stupidest idea ever," she takes aim at one of the compressor units that's pushing out bricks, and fires directly on the exhaust grill. The compressor and the ozone feeders connected to it detonate in a chain reaction, setting off a series of massive explosions. Dodge and the Governor's men are instantly evaporated. The force of the blasts knocks me off my feet.

Cole catches me with one hand, his other tightly gripping the rail for support.

"Are you insane?" I shout at Chloe, my hands clasped over my ears. But Chloe doesn't respond—she simply keeps moving across the walkway through to the next service shaft. Cole and I exchange a glance, then follow after her.

The factory is on alert now, sirens blaring, emergency lights casting the entire place in a get-the-flip-out-of-here crimson glow. When the catwalk comes to an end, we run down the wobbly metal stairway to the ground level, where we are met by hundreds of factory workers rushing into the long hallway to the facility entrance.

"Time to blend," says the girl who just fired blasts into exposed ozone.

Chloe, Cole, and I pour out into the inner lobby, mixing with the throng. Several guys who look more like guards than scrubbers are near the entrance by the glass office, trying to stem the tide, searching over the crowd as it floods toward them.

Searching for us.

I stay crouched behind Chloe as the crowd pushes us toward the entrance. With all the commotion, I hope it'll be hard to spot us. Once we're outside, it will be only a matter of getting to the elevators, out of the view of those fancy 360-degree cameras, and praying that Ducky and Marnie haven't decided to leave our asses here for good.

Chloe is the first out the doorway into the outer foyer. As I run to catch up, I spot Potter, spinning on his heels as he scans the area. I'm running right at him—nothing else I can do with the push of so many people behind me. Sure enough, he spots me as I come bearing down on him. Recognition crosses his face, and he reaches for something inside his jacket.

"Here's your cut!" I holler at him, plowing into his groinal area knee-first.

Potter's air escapes him in a high-pitched *woof!* and he collapses onto the ground with me on top of him. I feel Cole lift me by my coveralls with one hand, landing a knockout punch to Potter's face with the other. He doesn't even break his stride as he heads for the exit, dragging me along with him.

Once we're outside, we shift gears, doing our best to stride calmly rather than run. Emergency services are streaming toward the factory—firefighters, medics, etc.—to see to any wounded. Chloe guides us to a bank of lifts that I hadn't noticed before, around a corner and out of the way. A few dozen other scrubbers walk in the same direction.

"What level is your ship on?" Chloe asks me quietly as we ride up. She's tucked her blaster out of sight into the folds of her tunic, and she stands casually with her hand on her hip like she couldn't care less where she was headed or when she'll get there.

"The hangar," I tell her.

"Which hangar?" she presses, the impatience in her voice somehow heightened by her hushed tone.

"I don't know. The big one. Right off that promenade with the crazy marketplace."

"Right. Let's head there straight off. Hopefully, we'll catch your friends before they bail on you."

"They're not bailing on us," I say, annoyed for I don't know what reason. "Well, not really. Technically, you could say we bailed on them."

"Whatever." As Chloe watches the floor indicator above us, I notice her foot tapping unconsciously in time with the thrumming of the lift. I look down at my own feet and realize that I'm doing it as well. I stop and look straight ahead.

"You gonna tell us who you are and why you're helping us?" I ask. "'Cause if this is just a big gesture to get into Cole's pants, I can tell you for a fact that there are easier methods."

Chloe gives me a look that could be read as disgust, bemusement, or possibly gas.

"Let's wait till we're safely on your ship," she says, super-condescending-like. "Then I'll explain everything."

"I think you should tell me now."

"Look, do you want to get your daughter back, or what?"

Boom. A perfectly timed emotional uppercut successfully landed. But if this chick thinks she is going to KO me with one big punch, she hasn't danced in the ring with anyone like Elvie Nara before. I grab her shirt and slam her into the elevator rail.

"How do you know about my daughter?" I shout, inches from her face.

"I know where she's being held," Chloe responds, as calm as a cucumber. The elevator comes to rest and the doors slide open. "I can take you to her. But we need to get to your ship. Now." She removes my hand from her shirt and brushes past me out onto the promenade.

Who *is* this chick?

The promenade is bustling, but no more than it was before. I hear murmurs about an accident inside the ozone factory. As we make our way to the hangar, a name is whispered more than once in quiet, reverential tones.

Huxtable.

"Seriously, who is this Huxtable guy?" I ask, for like the umpteenth time.

"He's not important now," Chloe says. "I'd concern myself with your own situation."

My situation. Olivia. This girl can get me to Olivia. She's right. Nothing else matters right now.

Inside the hangar a PA speaker blares a muffled message.

"Attention. Due to a minor incident on the factory level, all outgoing traffic is suspended to allow emergency vehicles clear airspace. Normal takeoff procedures will recommence shortly. Attention. Due to a minor incident on the factory level . . ."

Seeing our ship still in dock makes me want to reach out and kiss the hull. The outer door slides open, and Ducky rushes out.

"Elvie!" he exclaims, surprise and concern mixed into a panic cocktail all over his face. Only, he's talking not to me but to Chloe, who gives him a small, insincere smile. Ducky does a full-body double take. "Sorry. I thought you were . . . You look a whole lot like . . . Who *are* you?" Then, taking in the announcement over the PA, he turns finally to me. "What did you do?"

No time to answer this one. "This is Chloe," I tell him instead. "She's coming with us."

"We're na' goin' anywhere," Marnie says from behind Ducky. "Thanks to whatever stunt ye two've pulled, the hangar is on lockdown until further notice."

I push my way into the ship and bulldoze my way to the bridge, Cole and Chloe not far behind.

"If they close that door, I'm slamming through it. We're out of here now, or we're never getting free." I sit down in the pilot's seat and start to initiate the takeoff sequence.

"Elvie, enough," Marnie says, placing a hand on my forearm to stop me from reaching the control panels. "Ye cannae keep flyin' off half-cocked."

"Some new information has come to light, so we're changing course. But the plan hasn't changed. We're getting Olivia back."

"Elvie?" I hear Cole squeak behind me. A persistent beeping lurks at the outskirts of my consciousness, but I'm too riled up to pay it much mind. I pull my arm free from Marnie, who simply reestablishes her grip.

"Yer not thinkin' straight, daft girl."

"Get off me, Marnie, or I swear to God . . . ," I start, rising up to go toe-to-toe with her.

"Elvie," Cole says, a little more forcefully.

"Why don't we all calm down?" Ducky says, trying—and failing—to come between me and his girlfriend.

"*Elvie!*" Cole shouts.

"Cole, what?" I say, still not breaking eye contact with Marnie.

"The tracker . . ." That's when I notice the beeping again. "It's going nuts," Cole says.

"For the last time, Cole, you've got to set it to frequency two! You're picking up my signal again."

"No," he says, and his voice is shaky, like I've never heard it before. "I'm not."

I turn to look at him. He is as white as a sheet. And when he holds out the tracker to show me, I see it.

Sure enough, the tracker is picking up a second signal.

"But how?" I say, the threat of tears crackling in my voice. "I mean, where . . ." My voice trails off as I follow the direction of the signal. According to the tracker, our daughter should be right in front of—

"*You*," I breathe.

Chloe stands there, just outside in the center cargo area, smirking at us, and suddenly I start noticing things—her thin, straight black hair, her upturned chin, and even the shape of her eyebrows. It can't be. But it is.

"Olivia," I say.

And then I notice something perhaps even more obvious about her.

"I'm afraid you're all going to have to come with me now," Olivia/Chloe says, her blaster aimed directly at me. "Dr. Marsden will want to see you right away."

Chapter Eight

WHEREIN OUR PLUCKY HEROINE
COMPLETELY LOSES HER SHIT

Some days I sleep. Some days I pace. Some days, the days
when they decide we have no need for light, I sit in absolute
darkness.

Or perhaps it isn't even days. Perhaps I've been here for
only a matter of hours and it only feels like an eternity, because
I'm losing my mind.

Olivia, my mind wails as I slump against the dark, cold
wall for who-knows-how-long. *My baby. What did he DO to
her?*

My precious girl. Altered. Grown. Years ripped from
her, ripped from me. And it's not even that I wonder *how* it's
possible—I've seen Marsden's genetic experiments in action
before, when we found Britta's friend's baby in the ruins of
the *Echidna.* Bok Choy, an approximately two-week-old infant
who looked like he was six years old.

But I wonder *why.* What could possibly possess a monster

like Marsden to take such a perfect, tiny girl like my Olivia and . . .

My thoughts are lost in a storm of wails.

I pound the walls with my fists. I kick the door until I'm sure I've broken toes on both feet. I press my head against the cold metal and I scream until I'm hoarse.

A day passes. Maybe more. Maybe less.

I sleep.

I scream.

I weep in the dark.

Then, after a while, I just lie there.

I'm woken by the door lock clicking and the door sliding open, filling the room with a blinding white light. I guard my eyes with one hand, but still I blink fiercely.

A silhouette appears in the doorway between my eyes and the light—a momentary sanctuary of shadow.

"Elvie?" the voice says, not unkindly. The owner of the silhouette pronounces my name with familiarity, but it is a voice I do not recognize.

I slowly rouse myself from the floor. I am only vaguely aware of the tangles of my hair, the crusts of tears at the corners of my eyes, my nose, my mouth. I am weak, my thoughts and my skin tingly, fuzzy—whether from malnourishment or delirium, I neither know nor care.

I blink up at the man. I can do no more than that.

"I need you to come with me," the voice says. "Can you stand?"

I blink again. No answer. I do not know if I can stand.

It doesn't much matter to me.

Her first steps, I think. *I missed her first steps.* I'm not exactly sure what the noise that escapes from my mouth is. It could be crying, laughing, or just air pushing its way out of me in a nervous convulsion. Whatever it is, it gives my captor pause.

He stands still in the doorway for a long while, perhaps waiting for me to stop doing whatever it is that I'm doing.

"Here," he says finally. He bends down, offers his hand. "Let me help you up."

The man helps me up. Or he lifts me completely. I do not know. Not much penetrates the fog. Before I'm aware of it, we have left the dark room and are passing through a long white hallway. I squint as the man helps me along. I am still unaccustomed to the brightness. My feet work, they hold me upright. But only barely.

Where is she? I mean to ask the man. *Can I see her? I need to see her.* But I have forgotten how to speak, or perhaps I've become unable. I try again. *Where?* But the words do not leave my parched throat.

"Ssssh. It's okay, Elvie," the man tells me. "Just concentrate on walking. You're doing a great job."

Who is this man? I was not expecting kindness here. I don't deserve it—not when I've failed my daughter so miserably. My cheeks are wet. I'm crying again.

"Ssssh," the man repeats. He looks around the empty hallway, then softly rubs my back with one hand and, after a pause, begins humming into my ear.

It is a song I know.

I love you, a bushel and a peck.
A bushel and a peck and a hug—

A sob catches in my throat as I place the tune. I look up at the man's face for the first time.

"Hi, Elvie," Bok Choy says to me.

And I am wailing again, although I don't know why.

"Good morning, Elvie."

That's a voice I'd recognize anywhere. My stomach flops inside me as Bok Choy deposits me gently onto an examination table in the center of a white room—face-to-face with none other than the very man who stole my baby girl from me.

Marsden.

Instinctively all the strength in my body pools in my shoulder, and I slap him hard across the face.

He smiles at me.

I turn my head to whimper at Bok Choy, beg him to rescue me from this man, but he is out the door before I can remember how to form the words.

"I'm so glad you came to find me," Marsden tells me.

I think I fall asleep again. Maybe from exhaustion. Maybe I am drugged. I can't know for sure. I'm not sure I care.

"She lives!" Dr. Marsden says with a chuckle as I blink open my eyes again.

I am vaguely aware of a needle in my arm. Is the doctor taking blood from me? Giving me something?

My head droops on my neck, unable to hold itself up.

"We've got to stop meeting like this, Elvie," Marsden says. Which, when it penetrates my brain, makes me think perhaps this is not the first time I've been in this room, needle in my arm. Maybe there have been a dozen times. Maybe more.

How long have I been here? I mean to ask.

"Where?"

That is what I ask instead.

"Ah, so you do have a voice," Marsden says. "I was beginning to worry. You know, Elvie, I've been surprised by you. The others have adjusted to their surroundings quite well. And you, normally so feisty . . ." He clucks his tongue. "But I knew you'd come around." Again that fatherly smile, like he's *proud* of me. "To answer you're question, you are in my laboratory. Would you like to hear my mad-scientist laugh?" Another chuckle. "You can't know how happy I was to see you, Elvie. Apart from your general witty demeanor—these past several visits notwithstanding, obviously—I was in dire need of your DNA. After your mother—"

I have found my voice. "Where is she?" I croak out.

Marsden's face is a dark cloud. "That one? Run away. Gone. And good riddance."

That wasn't what I meant, I want to say. *Olivia. Where is my baby?*

But my words are caught in my throat again, and Marsden is back to his jovial self. "But let's talk about something more pleasant, shall we? It was so kind of you to bring me a plethora of DNA to add to my research. I can't tell you how unfortunate it was that my comrades failed to preserve any viable Almiri samples at the compound in the mountains."

"You slaughtered them," I say, slowly finding my voice. "The Almiri." *You're a monster.* But I don't have enough breath for the last sentence.

"Now with Mr. Archer here," he continues, ignoring me, "I have a small hope of isolating the gene I've been searching for." He pulls the needle from my arm. "So thank you again, Elvie, for that."

Cole. Cole is here. And perhaps the others, too.

"Where is she?" I ask.

This time the reply comes from the doorway.

"She's muttering," the voice says. "Want me to knock her out again?"

I turn, as best I can, and the small movement sends my brain spinning. When I steady myself and focus my vision, I take her in.

Chloe.

Olivia.

My baby.

I almost collapse to the floor. The other figure in the doorway—Bok Choy, I think—leaps to my aid and catches me just in time, righting me on the exam table. I try to reach out a hand to my daughter, but I don't think I manage.

I am going fuzzy again.

I close my eyes, try to focus my thoughts. "What did you do to her, you . . . you . . ." The words are nearly mush in my mouth.

Although I am fading, I can hear the smile in Marsden's voice.

"Remarkable, isn't it?" he says.

• • •

I am back in the hallway, walking, along with the help of Bok Choy and Olivia. *Chloe,* I think. *She's Chloe now. Not Olivia.* It's hard to think of them as the same person, even though I can tell they are. Same button nose, only less button-like. Same curved earlobes, only bigger.

Chloe.

As I pull out of the fog, I realize that my two guards have been talking.

"You should be kinder to her," Bok Choy is telling Chloe. I think he means me. "She's not so bad."

Beside me Chloe snorts. "When she's unconscious," she replies. But I turn just in time to see the look she gives him when he's not watching. She studies him carefully, a hint of a smile on her otherwise steely face.

"She's been through a lot," Bok Choy replies as he buzzes open the door to what I assume is my cell. "None if this is her fault. Being cruel to her doesn't further our goal."

And Chloe's eyes are soft, watching him. "I'll think about it," she says.

She has her father's eyes.

As Bok Choy deposits me in my cell, I get one last glance at Chloe. She makes some joke I don't catch to Bok Choy, raising a thick, arched eyebrow.

She has my eyebrows.

I rise to my feet, without even noticing the strain in my muscles. Grown or not, altered or mutated or I-don't-care-what, that is still my baby girl. And I'm her mother.

"Chloe," I say—but the door is already shut in front of me by the time I get the word out.

• • •

I do not sit.

I do not pace.

I do not sleep.

I do not weep.

That girl on the other side of the door is my daughter. And whatever the cost, I'm going to get her out of here.

Chapter Nine

WHEREIN OUR HEROINE'S WORST NIGHTMARE (NOT INCLUDING THE ONE WHERE SHE HAS TO PERFORM AN ELABORATE ICE-SKATING DANCE SHE HASN'T REHEARSED, TO THE TUNE OF "SEXY AND I KNOW IT") COMES TRUE

"All right, now. This will be the last sample we take today. Sound good?"

As Dr. Marsden guides the needle under my skin, his voice is as gentle and reassuring as someone who wasn't holding me captive and performing a series of invasive tests on my person.

"You've taken, like, six vials already," I mutter. "I hope you've got a sugar cookie hidden away somewhere."

"We'll make sure you're replenished."

By "replenished" Marsden means more needles—the kind where stuff goes *into* your arm as opposed to being drawn *out* of it.

"I bet people wouldn't mind your taking over the world so much if you guys had sugar cookies."

Marsden chuckles and shakes his head. "I do so prefer you this way," he says, a please-kick-me-in-the-teeth level of obnoxious smile on his face.

"What, you mean lucid?"

"I was going to say 'chipper,' but why split hairs?"

"Quick question," I say. "I mean, not that I'm not enjoying all this blood-taking and awesome bonding time with my baby's kidnapper, because, whew boy, it's been a hoot! But, uh, you mind sharing why you still haven't cracked the secret to hybrid fertility, even after all this time? I thought you were supposed to be a mad genius."

Marsden doesn't seem offended in the slightest. "Even mad geniuses must work through the science to reach their goals."

"So how come I get to have all the needle-pointy fun? Why do the others miss out?" This is my supersneaky way to try to figure out what Marsden has done with my friends.

"Don't worry. Mr. Archer has had his fair share of needle pokes."

So Cole's still alive, and even if they're poking and prodding him, that's a good thing. But . . .

"What about Ducky?"

"Ducky?" Marsden asks. Like I just ordered something that wasn't on the menu. I feel my stomach go icy.

"Donald?" I say. "Floppy hair? Skinny arms? Probably barfed a few times by now?"

"Ah, yes. Your human comrade. He's here. But what use would I have for his DNA?"

I settle down a bit. Ducky's alive. "So Duck gets a free pass from all these good times just for being normal? That hardly seems fair—not that I'm suggesting you start poking him, too."

"I'm looking for an evolutionary breakthrough for a superior species. I don't have time to muddle with apes. And to save you some more sleuthing, your redheaded hybrid friend is alive as well. Her samples are a helpful baseline to compare yours against. So no one's been executed. Does that satisfy you?"

"I suppose," I say. "Unless you're still considering my offer to have you surrender?" The snort from the doorway belongs to Chloe, who has been standing quietly at attention since she brought me here from my cell. I pretend to ignore her, even though what I'm saying is as much for her benefit as Marsden's, if not more so. "You know the Jin'Kai leadership will never understand what you're trying to do here. You could come with us."

"Come with you?" Marsden lets out a snort of his own. "To where? Another Almiri prison?"

"I'm guessing it'd be better than getting sliced up by Devastators, or Kynigos, or whatever the hell you want to call them. Who knows? In time maybe you and the Almiri could work together to find a way to help *both* of you."

"You seem to miss the point of what I'm trying to do here, Elvie," Marsden says. "The point is not to help everyone. It's to help me. My people. I don't care one wit about any of the rest of it, one way or the other. Hybrids, humans, Almiri, it makes no difference to me whether any of you live or die. I will be the savior of the Jin'Kai people. That's all that matters."

"If that were what you really believed," I say, wincing as he pulls the needle out of my arm and slaps a gel patch over the wound, "then you'd be looking for allies, instead of seeing enemies everywhere. You aren't a messiah. Hell, you're not even a patriot. You're a genocidal, racist piece of—"

I don't get to finish the epithet, because that's when Chloe clocks me across the jaw, sending me flying off the exam table onto the floor.

"Shut your filthy mouth, mutt," she hisses at me.

"That's quite enough," Marsden snaps, his voice slicing through the room like a knife. Chloe freezes up and stands at attention.

"Apologies, Doctor," she says. "I only meant—"

"Be quiet. Act out again and there will be punishment. Do I make myself crystal clear?"

"Yes, sir."

Chloe resumes her place by the door, her face sullen and red with shame, and Marsden lifts me up to my feet and guides me back to the table. He holds my head in his hand, examining my jaw.

"I'm fine," I tell him.

"I'll be the judge of that," he replies. He gestures toward Chloe. "You'll have to forgive it."

"'It'?" I say, pulling away from him. "That's my daughter, asshole."

"No, I'm not," Chloe shoots back.

"Look." I wrench my head around on my neck to face my daughter in the doorway. "They may have stolen you away, experimented on you, and filled your head with nonsense, but I *gave birth* to you, dammit. You literally shot out from my down below."

"And thank you so much for the imagery," she sneers.

"You really want to stay here? He just called you an 'it.'"

"I will play an important role in the future of the Jin'Kai

people," Chloe tells me, as if she's reading from a pamphlet.

"Oh, and what role is that? Is there a cheerleading team on this station? Because no daughter of mine is ending up a cheerleader."

When Chloe replies, there is more than a hint of pride in her voice. "I will host a new test subject, one with the engineered potential to save the Jin'Kai from extinction."

That's it. I snap. Snap hard. I'm on top of Marsden, clawing at his face. "You're going to make her a breeder, like you tried to do with me?" I screech. "She's not livestock, you rotten son of a bitch. *I'm* not livestock. We're *people*."

Marsden easily lifts me away from him, and it's Chloe who roughly slams me facedown on the table and binds my hands behind my back.

"Ah, but that's where you're wrong, Elvie," Marsden informs me coolly. "You were always livestock. Up until now you've just been free-range."

"If you think for a second that I'll allow you to violate my daughter like you did all those other poor girls—"

"No one's violating anyone," Chloe says, spinning me around. "I will be paired with a suitable partner, and I will nourish his offspring."

"Jesus Christ," I spit. "Chloe, don't listen to another word this man tells you, please, I'm begging you." Pain I can handle. Needles? Tests? Do whatever you want to me, Marsden. Just leave my poor daughter out of it. "You don't have to be *paired* with anybody. You should get to be a normal kid. Go ask Bok Choy out for a Coke or something, if he's the one you like, but don't wait for this shit monster to *pair* you."

° I can see from the way Chloe flinches that I've inadvertently hit a nerve. Meanwhile, Marsden's too busy looking smug. "I had forgotten your charming nickname for our little friend from the *Echidna*," he tells me. "But don't fear, Chloe. That creature would never be your match. He's far too rudimentary a subject to use for our purposes." He's jotting down notes on his lap-pad, about my samples, I'd wager. Hardly giving either of his "livestock" and our futures any mind. "I hadn't yet analyzed your hybrid DNA when I first started growing that one," he continues. "I hadn't even solved the decay problem at that point."

"Decay?" I say the word, but I can see in Chloe's confused face that the question is on her mind as well. "What do you mean? Bok Choy will . . ."

"Yes, in that first generation of subjects the gene accelerator unfortunately causes their cellular structures to break down fairly rapidly. The life span is far too short to create desirable offspring. Hardly a trait I want contaminating the results of future testing."

When Chloe sees me looking at her, she turns quickly away and wipes at her face as stealthily as she can.

"I'm sorry," I say softly.

"It's all right," Marsden replies. "I corrected the flaw in the second generation. There were some promising results with that round as well, as with the third and fourth. Soon enough I'll have a match suitable for you."

"Me?" I ask, jolted out of my empathetic mother-daughter mind-meld.

"Of course," Marsden says. "You. This one. The redhead.

I'll need all the reusable hosts that I can get. Time is running out, after all."

As Chloe leads me back to my cell, she walks with her head high, staring stonily ahead. But the wetness around her eyes doesn't lie.

Maybe I've found a crack in her armor.

"I really am very sorry," I tell her.

"Shut it," she snaps.

"Marsden's a monster," I tell her. "You can see that, can't you? He's *brainwashed* you, Chloe. You're a whole person, not some sort of breeding sow to be used up and discarded. You're not even Chloe. You know that, right? Your name's Olivia." She squeezes painfully on my arm, but still I keep talking. "We could find a way out of here," I say, my voice low. "There's a way, I'm sure of it. My mother escaped. We can too. Get home somehow."

"I said, *silence*," she tells me, wrenching my arm again.

"If he's so blasé about Bok Choy's life," I gasp through the pain, "what do you think he'll do with you once you're not useful to his research anymore? Or your baby?"

"It doesn't matter," she says. "So long as it's in the service of the Jin'Kai empire."

"You cannot be this stupid," I groan. "Not with half my genes."

She stops dead in her tracks and shoves me against the wall.

"Listen, mutt. The doctor said not to hurt you again, but there's *all kinds* of things that I could do to you that he'd never notice. Understand me?"

She's trying to sound tough, but her voice is trembling. I can feel the hurt coursing through her. *My poor baby*, I think. *I'm so sorry I couldn't stop them from doing this to you.*

"Look, you're confused, I understand, but I'm your mother. I can help you. Maybe if we could get out of here, we could even help—"

"What's going on here?"

We both turn to see Bok Choy standing in front of us, his arms crossed over his chest.

"Nothing," Chloe says, straightening up. "Just returning the prisoner to her cell."

"It doesn't look like nothing," he says. He approaches us and notices the swelling on the side of my face where Chloe hit me. He gives Chloe a harsh glance.

"Chloe . . ."

"Just . . . get out of my way!" she blurts out. Pulling me along, she brushes past Bok Choy.

I don't say anything the rest of the way. In her current state she wouldn't even hear me if I tried.

But I'm not done trying yet, *Olivia*.

"Think, Elvie," I mutter to myself as I pace the room. "*Think, think, think.*"

The door lock clicks open and distracts me from what I'm sure was about to be an absolutely brilliant escape plan. I back up against the far wall in a defensive position. What could they possibly want with me again so soon? They just extracted who-knows-how-much genetic-material-slash-unsavory-inside-fluids. I doubt there's anything useful left in me at this point.

The door slides open, and Bok Choy steps into the room. A duffel bag is slung over one shoulder.

"You going somewhere?" I ask him. "Do evil alien commandos get sleepovers?" I look past him into the hallway, but Bok Choy is alone this time. I rub the sore spot on my upper arm. "What do they want now? Don't tell me Marsden's discovered a way to save his species with my spit."

Bok Choy motions toward the door silently.

"What? Come on, speak. I know you can. You've learned quite a bit of English since I saved your life on the *Echidna*."

Again he motions me toward the door without saying a word.

"I'm sorry, sweetie," I say, folding my arms across my chest, "but stubborn crankiness is about all I have left at the moment, so I'm going to have to insist that you convey your evil alien demands to me out loud. I'm in no mood for pantomime."

Bok Choy leans his head back out into the hallway, looking side to side. I notice for the first time that he isn't holding his weapon—it's holstered at his hip with the clip fastened tightly.

"What's going on?" I ask. There's a feeling of anticipation rising in my gut, and I can't tell if it's hope or fear. Either way, it's a good thing they don't feed me much in here, or I'd be ready to yak all over the place. Bok Choy moves to me quickly, a nervousness in his step. He leans in, and for a split second I think he's going to kiss me, which would be all kinds of weird, since it wasn't that long ago that I saw his six-year-old didjeridoo.

"I'm here to rescue you," he whispers into my ear.

I jerk my head back and stare at him. His face is just as terrified as his voice, and his eyes are bulging wide. His chest moves up and down rapidly. It's the first time I've seen one of these superaliens even close to hyperventilating.

"You're here to res—" I start, before Bok Choy clamps a hand over my mouth.

"Shh!" he shout-whispers. "We don't have much time. There's about to be a guard shift in five minutes, and I think we might have a chance of getting you all out of here."

"Why are you doing this?" I ask. If I sound suspicious, it's because I totally am. (Although, to be honest, I cannot fathom what could be in it for Marsden to attempt to trick us like this. He might be a megalomaniacal madman, but mind-dickery just for the sake of it doesn't seem like his style.)

"I don't know a lot," Bok Choy says. "I mean, I'm learning things, but it's all very fast and confusing. I know I haven't . . . been here very long. I know there are things I can't understand yet . . . but there are things I just know. No, that's not the right word. Things I . . . *feel*."

Bok Choy takes the bag from his shoulder and hands it to me. I open it and find a spiffy zip-front sheath jacket. I slip the jacket on right away, immediately appreciating the warmth of the fabric. I hadn't realized how cold I'd been in here.

"It fits perfectly," I marvel, stretching out my arms. "How did you—"

"I've got an eye for sizes," Bok Choy replies with a shrug.

"But"—I switch over to a slightly more important topic of conversation—"aren't you going to get in a lot of trouble for this? Like, the kind of trouble that gets you dead?"

Bok Choy examines the floor as he speaks. "The doctor . . . ," he begins. "He tells us things. How he says things are. I've listened to him, and I've believed him, because, I don't know, I just have? Like there was no reason not to. I had no choice. But the things he's done here, the things he's doing. The things I've helped him with. None of it seems right. But you . . ." And that's when he looks up at me. "You sang to me. You're the only one who's ever done that. You sang to me when I was scared, and showed me kindness. Yours is the only kindness I have ever known."

Who says show tunes can't unite warring nations?

Without really thinking what I'm doing, I reach out and touch Bok Choy's cheek. It's a very motherly gesture, I realize.

Hard to believe you don't have much time left, I think, remembering what Marsden told me about Bok Choy's "viability." But I say nothing. I have a strong suspicion that the poor kid doesn't know.

"I think I figured out what my daughter sees in you," I tell him instead.

Bok Choy cocks his head to the side like a confused puppy. "Huh?"

"Nothing. We should go. Get the others."

Bok Choy nods. "Here." He hands me a pair of nifty Jin'Kai manacles. "This way."

We come out into the hall and make our way quickly down the corridor. I keep my hands crossed in front of me, the cuffs loosely placed around my wrists so that to a passing baddie it'll look like I'm a prisoner being transported. Bok Choy keeps a grip on my arm. When we turn a corner, we both freeze for a split second, hearing footsteps. But whoever the footsteps belong to is traveling away from us, so we continue on.

There are five cells lining the left wall, three of them with a solid red light above the doorway. Doors I've passed at least a dozen times now, wondering if any of my friends might be trapped inside. Sure enough, Bok Choy taps the wall console, and all three cell doors hiss and slide open, their red lights flashing blue. Marnie pops out of the first cell, and if she's surprised to see us, she does a good job of hiding it. I guess in her world there's rarely any time for explanations during life-and-death situations.

"What's going on? How did you get out?" Cole says as he sticks his head out of the far cell and sees us.

The center cell is quiet. No movement. I feel a growing lump of ice form in the pit of my stomach.

"Ducky?" I call. No answer.

I rush past Marnie and ignore Cole as he steps into the hallway, still confused by his sudden emancipation. I clamor down the two steps into the middle cell, expecting the worst. Or worse.

I find Ducky lying stretched out on his side on the hard metal bed slab jutting out of the far wall. He's resting his head in one hand, with the other draped over his hip. He's looking right at me, and the smirk on his face is tight and twitchy, like he's trying with all his might not to burst into a great big moony smile.

"Aren't you a little short for a storm trooper?" he asks, his voice one step away from a giggle.

I could pop him in the mouth, but he's just so happy at the moment that I don't have the heart.

"Ye wretched scamp!" Marnie chastises as she brushes past me into the cell. Ducky rises slowly from the bed, and I can tell he's in pain. They must have done a number on him at some point—doing what, I'd rather not know.

"You okay?" I ask.

Ducky waves me off like he gets tortured by space invaders all the time. "I'm just glad it was you this time," he replies. "The last ten times, the guards didn't think it was funny."

I move to Ducky's side opposite from Marnie, and we help lift him gingerly to his feet. All my friends are alive. I will count myself lucky.

"I don't reckon I'll ever understand yer particular brand of humor," Marnie says, looking at the two of us as we step out into the hallway.

"After the world doesn't end, I've got about a hundred flat pics for you to watch," Ducky tells her.

"Elvie, what's the plan?" Cole asks as he takes my place at Ducky's side, shouldering the brunt of the weight. Cole examines my handcuffs, and then Bok Choy.

"Who's this?" he asks.

"Cole, it's Bok Choy. Little naked boy from the *Echidna*?"

"Holy shit." Cole whistles. "You don't still bite, do you?"

"I, uh, no? Not recently," Bok Choy stammers.

"Can we trust him?" Cole asks me.

"We can trust him. We need to get out of here, see if we can find the ship. Hopefully it's where we left—"

"Halt right there!" a voice shouts at us from down the hallway. Three Jin'Kai guards are running toward us, weapons drawn. "What's the meaning of this?"

"Uh, prisoner transfer," Bok Choy says, reaching to his belt. "I have the order right here."

"Stay that hand, freak," the lead guard says, sticking his weapon right in Bok Choy's face. So I guess the prejudice against Marsden's pet projects extends even to his own loyal men. I can see why he's reluctant to have his superiors see his work before he has acquired the desired results. Bok Choy reluctantly moves his hand away from the blaster at his hip. The guard looks over his shoulder to the other guards. "Call it in. Let's see what Marsden—"

Before the dude can finish, Bok Choy has knocked the gun out of his hand and fallen on him. Cole springs into action immediately, ditching Ducky and leaping at one of the other guards. You can just tell that all this imprisonment has left Cole aching for a good fight, because I don't think he's ever whaled on anybody so enthusiastically. The third Jin'Kai turns his gun on Ducky, who immediately crumples to the floor—which seems to confuse the hell out of the guard. He looks up at Marnie for a split second in his confusion, giving Ducky the opening I *guess* he was looking for. In a move way more bold and coordinated than I ever would've expected of him, Ducky jumps across the floor and tries to leg-tackle his would-be attacker. The guard is thrown off balance for a brief second, and in that time Marnie does a nifty jump-kick move, popping his gun out of his grip and onto the floor. The guard counters with a backhand slap that sends Marnie crashing into the wall, dazed. Then he pulls one leg free from Ducky and kicks him hard in the stomach, eliciting a pitiful yelp.

Cue Elvie's turn to play the hero.

I lean down to reach for one of the fallen weapons—only to realize that the cuffs that I had loosely draped over my wrists have *actually locked into place*, the coiled metal bands giving me less than fifteen centimeters of leeway. My momentary hesitation gives the guard a chance to grab me by the arm and toss me hard at the wall. I land on Marnie—lucky for me but not for her. If she wasn't out cold before, she certainly is now. I decide to pull a classic Ducky and feign my own unconsciousness, which seems to work. Through the slits of my eyelids I see the guard swivel in place, trying to remove Ducky from his ankle.

That's when I spring up, jumping as high as I can and wrapping my manacled hands around the dude's throat. With all my might I pull back, pressing the bands deep into his neck. He jerks back, instinctively reaching for the cuffs in an attempt to pry them away. I press my knee hard into his back, using the leverage to really go for gold. The guard's gagging, unable to get any air, and his whole head goes red, the veins in his forehead throbbing.

It dawns on me in that moment that I am actively strangling another person, with the closest thing to my bare hands that I could get without leaving fingerprints on his throat. And I falter—just enough for the guard to get his fingers underneath the bands. Rather than thanking me for my momentary flash of humanity/mercy/what have you, once the Jin'Kai has a solid grip on the cuffs, he lifts them (and me) up, flipping me over his head and down hard onto my back.

Now I'm the one with the wind knocked out of me. Free from Ducky's grasp, the guard dashes to pick up his gun. But as his hand brushes across the weapon, he is tackled from behind by Bok Choy. Unfortunately for our plucky little gang, the guard is low to the ground, and Bok Choy comes in too fast. The guard easily uses Bok Choy's momentum to slide past him, scooping up the weapon and spinning around to line up a shot.

The crackle of energy sings through the air, and sends the guard flailing from the wound in his chest. I look up from my spot on the floor to see Bok Choy's savior—expecting it to be Cole, or Marnie, or perhaps Ducky (hey, anything is possible). Instead I see everyone in our little melee, including the remaining two Jin'Kai guards, frozen in place, staring at Chloe, her weapon still raised, standing only a few paces away.

The girl sure knows how to make an entrance.

"What are you doing?" one of the other guards asks. Not the most famous of last words, but they'll have to do, because with two more dead-on shots from Chloe, that's the end of our last two adversaries. Well, original adversaries.

"Chloe?" Bok Choy says, hunched in a crouched position amidst the pile of dead Jin'Kai. "Put the gun down, Chloe."

Chloe does not comply. Instead she shifts her aim and points the gun right at me.

"You," she says. Her voice is as still and cold as ice. "If I let you go, you'll take him with you? You'll be able to help him?"

Everyone looks between the two of us. Except for Marnie, of course, since she's out cold. I stand up very slowly. It's still hard to breathe, and I take little gasps in an attempt to build up a reserve of air.

"I . . . don't . . . even know . . . what they . . . did . . . to him," I say. When you've got an unstable person pointing a gun at you, the truth is usually your best strategy to remain unshot.

Chloe straightens her gun arm, making her gun more pointy-at-me'd than it already was. *"Will you help him?"* she asks again.

"What are you talking about?" Bok Choy says. He's edging carefully toward Chloe, probably in an attempt to put himself between the two of us.

"I'll try everything I can," I say. "I can't promise any more than that without being a liar."

"Everything in your power," Chloe presses.

"In my power, and in the considerably greater power of my friends."

Chloe lowers her gun and turns back down the hallway from which she came. "Come on, then. Let's get going."

Bok Choy gives me a curious look, then trots after Chloe. Cole has picked Marnie up off the ground, with Ducky uneasily supporting her head in an attempt to be helpful.

"What was that all about?" Cole asks me.

"Not now, Cole," I say.

"But who does she want you to help?"

"Not *now*, Cole."

We all make it to the end of the hallway, but then Chloe breaks left as Bok Choy heads to the right.

"Wait," Bok Choy tells her. "This way."

"Their ship is up on the factory subhangar," Chloe replies, looking over her shoulder but not breaking her stride. "Marsden gave it to the Governor as payment for my shooting his men."

"Well, at least it's closer than we thought," I say.

But Bok Choy still won't move. "Chloe, we have to get the others," he says.

"There's no time," she answers.

"Wait," I say, stopping dead in my tracks. "What others?"

"There's no time. We have to go now."

"What. Others?"

Chloe harrumphs and folds her arms across her chest in a pretty dead-on me impersonation. At least it would be if she realized she were doing it. She looks at Bok Choy expectantly.

"The other girls," Bok Choy tells me.

The words hit me like a ton of bricks. The other girls. Could it possibly be the girls from the Hanover School? Ramona. Natty. Maybe even . . .

"Where are they?" I ask Bok Choy. "How many of them are here?"

"You're wasting your time with that lot," Chloe says. "It's too risky. Not worth it."

I take a few steps toward her and jab my finger into her chest to emphasize every crucial point. "Now, you listen to me, you little brat. I don't have time to completely deprogram the Jin'Kai propaganda that Marsden's brainwashed you with, but know this—Every. Single. Person. Is. *Worth it*. You follow? A human life—a woman's life—whoever they may be, is every bit as important as those *you'd* risk everything for. *Comprende?*"

Chloe looks at her feet and mumbles something.

"I can't hear you," I snap.

"I said *all right*," she mumbles more loudly. "Jeez." She turns to Bok Choy. "If we're going to get them, let's get moving already."

"This way," Bok Choy says, and we all follow. I bring up the rear with my bratty-ass daughter.

"Someday you'll understand," I tell her.

"Whatever," she replies.

Teenagers.

Suddenly the floor rocks underneath us, and we find ourselves in complete darkness.

"Now what?" Ducky cries behind me.

As soon as the words are out of his mouth, backup lights illuminate the hallway in a dim, bluish hue. The hairs on the back of my neck stand up, tingling.

"A trick of yours?" I ask Bok Choy.

"No," he says.

"It's like before," Chloe says. "When the other hybrid escaped. She sabotaged the security systems by overloading the power grid. It lasted only ten minutes or so, but that was all she needed. Crafty for a mule."

"Don't call her that," I say, spinning around on Chloe. "That's your grandmother you're talking about. She's not a mule; she's an Enosi. And so am I. And so are you. If you want to call the woman anything, call her 'grandma.' Or 'lying, double-crossing bitch' works too. But never, *ever* 'mule.'"

"Sorry," Chloe tells me, rolling her eyes.

I look around in the dim light. "So who do you think's trying to escape now?" I ask the group. "Besides us, I mean."

"I don't know," Chloe replies. "But if it puts the whole base on high alert, then we're in trouble." She jerks her head toward Bok Choy. "Let's hurry up and grab the ditzes so we can get out of here already."

With Bok Choy in the lead, we make our way to the next detention area over, identical to the one we just left. There are five cell doors along the wall, but only one has a red "locked" light on. I follow Bok Choy directly to the door.

"I thought you said there were girls," I say. "As in plural."

"There are," Bok Choy tells me. "Marsden keeps them all in here."

Bok Choy punches the key code into the wall console, but nothing happens.

"It's stuck," he mutters. "The power, I guess." He grips the door and starts trying to pull it, even though there's no edge to grab. Cole lays Marnie gently down on the ground and lends Bok Choy a hand. Between the two of them, with their otherworldly alien strength, they manage to move the door exactly zero millimeters.

"*Boys*," I say with a sigh. "Chloe, you have anything that could jimmy this panel loose?"

"Step back," she says. And it's a good thing I do, because before the words are even out of her mouth, she has unslung her gun and fired off one precisely aimed shot to the immediate right of the console, sending sparks flying and blasting a clean hole through the metal plating. I pry the remaining fragments away to create a gap, giving me access to the wiring behind the panel.

"Okay. One second," I say, fiddling blindly.

"Careful," Chloe tells me. "You'll fry yourself." She hands me a pair of thin rubbery gloves from the pocket of her uniform.

"Thanks." I slip the gloves on and resume my work. Chloe slips in beside me, and together we piece through the wiring. I'm happy to learn that in addition to my smart mouth, Chloe has inherited at least a few of my other qualities.

"There," I say as the light above the door surges with a *vwoop!* This time, rather than switching from red to blue, the light blinks out completely.

"Um, Elvie, the door is still locked," Cole says.

"Wrong," I inform him. "The door is still *closed*."

Chloe and I exchange a glance and push against the door, much as Bok Choy and Cole did before—only, this time the dead door slides, with some resistance, into the wall.

"Voila," I say. "Open sesame, and such."

Inside, the room is completely dark. I peek inside.

"Hello?"

There is some low murmuring. Shadows flicker in the corners.

"It's all right," I say softly. "It's me. It's Elvie. We've come to rescue you guys. One more time, with feeling."

"Elvie?" comes a voice along the back left wall—but it's not said in recognition. It's as if the girl has never heard my name before.

Oh God, I think. *What have they done to these girls?* Because the voice, it's one I know all too well. And the name attached to it is *certainly* not one I'd ever forget.

"It's me, Britta," I say quietly. "We're going." Shockingly, I don't even feel annoyed at the thought that Britta McVicker—world's most obnoxious cheerleader and Cole's former girlfriend—is alive and well. Score one for personal growth!

"Going?" says another voice from the other side of the room.

Another eerily familiar voice.

"Um, yeah," I say. The hair on the back of my neck prickles once more, and I have not yet figured out why. "Come on, guys. Stop hiding back there. It's all right. We're getting you all out of here and going home."

"Home?" says another voice straight ahead of me. Or was that Britta again? "What is home?"

"Give me a light," I call to my friends behind me. The prickling has quickly morphed into nausea, creeping into my throat.

Behind me Bok Choy flashes a small LED lamp, chasing the shadows away with a harsh, cold light. And all at once I have an irrepressible need to puke my metaphysical guts out.

I am standing in a room, surrounded by more than a dozen girls.

And they're all Britta.

Chapter Ten

IN WHICH IT SEEMS EVERYONE HAS SOMETHING TO SAY ABOUT OUR HEROINE'S EX-BOYFRIEND'S BUTT

It's just a dream, I tell myself, eyes shut as tightly as I can force them. *A bad dream. A really, really, really bad dream.*

But when I open my eyes, they're all still here. It's not a dream, or a trick of the light, or some sort of stress-headache-induced hallucination. I am surrounded on all sides by Brittas. At least twelve exact duplicates of my least favorite person-who's-not-actively-trying-to-kill-me in the world. This is a new low, even for a lunatic like Marsden. I mean, homicide? That's bad. Attempted genocide? Not good at all. Imprisoning and torturing innocent young women? Really frowned upon.

But an *army of Brittas*?

The man must be stopped.

"What's the matter, Elvie?" Ducky calls from the hall behind me. "Are you okay in there?"

"Who's that?" a Britta asks, taking a tentative step forward and craning her head to try to see into the hallway.

"Are you taking us for more tests?" another Britta joins in.

"I just had my test," pouts a third Britta. "Please don't make me go back so soon."

Another Britta feels the need to chime in. "Your hair . . . did you make it look that way on purpose?"

"Can't we gag them or something?" Chloe asks me seriously. "Before we get permanently dumber from listening to them?"

Looks like my daughter and I might have more in common than I feared.

"We need to go, Brit—er, *ladies*," I say, trying to reassemble the toppled Jenga tower that is my brain. "We're getting you out of here."

"What's a britterlady?" one asks.

"Why are we leaving?" asks another.

"Who are you?"

"What's wrong with your face? You look like you smelled something bad. Did you smell something bad?"

From there things turn into a cacophony of Britta babble, each of the identical hell beasts bombarding me with questions and accusations that weave in and out of one another so unintelligibly that soon I hear nothing but one long hum of shrill, entitled, and apparently amnesiac voices.

"Look, just shut up!" I finally shout. "We've got to go, like, *now*." You'd think at this point I'd be more adept at explaining to a large group of imprisoned teenage girls why we need to get off a spaceship, but I find myself a tad flustered. And nothing I say stops them from whining at me.

That's when Cole decides to step into the room to see what all the fuss is about.

"Elvie?" he says. "What is going—*whoa*."

"Cole," I say. He's fallen into the same stupefied trance I just found myself in, but we really don't have the time to play out these reactions one at a time. There's still the matter of getting out of here un-murdered. I snap my fingers at him. "Cole!"

Suddenly I realize that the Britta Brigade has fallen silent. And it's not because of my authoritative tone.

"Cole?" one of the Britta's says, the question hanging in the air like a hopeful, half-remembered dream. Every girl is now staring intently at Cole, who manages to close his mouth just long enough for one comically perfect gulp.

"Um, hi," he says awkwardly.

"*Cole . . . ,*" another says with a sigh.

And then, in perfect, horrific unison, the Brigade bursts into terrifying, synchronized smiles.

"*Cole-eeeeeeee!*"

As the Brittas swarm around Cole, chattering like Brittas are wont to do, I am reminded of an old recording we once watched in history class of a band called the Beatles trying to escape a rabid crowd of young female fans, who were chasing and pawing at them with unbridled passion. This is exactly like that, only 300 percent more vomit-inducing.

The Brittas engulf Cole like a school of piranhas. I'm half afraid that when they finally swim off, there will be nothing left but Cole's head on top of a cleanly picked skeleton.

"Amazing," Bok Choy says. I didn't even notice him stepping into the room. "They know him."

"Well, he did date her back on Earth," I say. "I mean, one

of them, at least." Then I ask the obvious question. "How are there so many of them? Of *her*?"

Bok Choy winces as the Brigade squeals en masse, having just (re?)discovered how cute Cole's butt is. "The doctor needed . . . a controlled environment," he tells me. "To incubate his experiments. And he found himself with a limited number of hosts."

That's when I notice that one of the Brittas, sporting a thin tank top, has a dark letter *K* tattooed on her right shoulder.

Another sports a *D*.

And yet another, an *H*.

Clones.

"He couldn't have cloned literally *anyone* else?" I ask. "Was Lizzie Borden not available?"

"We have to go," Chloe reminds me, interrupting the shiver that is making its way down my spine. "Either you find some way to herd them, or we leave all their asses here. I won't bother telling you which option I prefer."

As much as I hate to argue for a world in which we actively attempt to rescue a dozen photocopies of my least favorite cheerleader, after my little "Everyone is worth it" speech earlier I don't seem to have much choice.

"Excuse me!" I shout over the din. "Excuse me! Brittas? Hel-*lo*? Hey, dummies!"

But they clearly can't hear/see/smell anything but Cole.

"Cole, flex your butt again!"

"Can I touch your butt, Cole?"

"No, I get to touch it. Cole, let me touch it."

"Cole?"

"Hey, Cole?"

"Cole?"

"Cole?"

Cole.

"Cole!" I call, adding to the din of voices shouting his name. But I guess I manage to break through. Cole whips his head around to face me, completely shell-shocked, and I give him an expectant look. "I think you're the shepherd we need for this particular herd of cats."

It shouldn't surprise me that Cole has no idea what I'm talking about.

"Huh?" he says.

I point down the hallway, in the direction where our ship (pleasepleasehopefully) lies. "Run!" I tell him.

"Ah," Cole replies, finally getting it. And bless his dumb, doofy heart, he makes a break for it, knowing full well that the gaggle of screaming Brittas will follow.

"We're right behind you!" I assure Cole—only to be elbowed in the stomach by a passing Britta.

"Hands off, lardo," she snaps at me. "That butt is *mine.*"

I am too confounded and exhausted to even attempt a comeback.

"Okay," I say to the others as the Britta Brigade pushes its way down the hall like a particularly unsavory hair ball down a drain. "Best get moving."

And that's when I notice that one of the Brittas is still in our midst.

Haggard, harried, dirtier than I've ever seen her, she stands stock-still, staring at the group receding around the corner.

And I am certain, without even checking her shoulder, that *this* is the Britta I've known and hated for so long.

She turns to me and rolls her eyes. "Tell me I'm not that annoying," she says, gesturing toward the others.

I laugh, despite myself. And something escapes my mouth that I never would've expected in the presence of Britta McVicker. "It's nice to see you," I tell her.

She regards me coolly. "Captivity's been *hell* on your complexion," she replies.

So far we haven't passed a single Jin'Kai guard, but I'm not counting on our luck holding out. There's a lot more hallway in this space station than I ever would've anticipated. If you'd told me two months ago precisely how much of my time I was going to spend running for my life through various hallways, I would've asked to see if your medical hallucinogen card had expired.

At least this time the Brittas are keeping things interesting.

"Has your hair *always* been so dreamy?" one asks Cole as we dash past several locked doors.

"Can I touch your biceps again?"

"No, me!"

"It's my turn. You got to touch his butt."

"It *is* a really nice butt."

Chloe is clearly on her last nerve. "I have a blaster," she reminds us.

"Go ahead," says Original Britta, hustling to keep up beside me. "You didn't have to share a room with those chromers."

"You do realize that's *you* you're talking about," Ducky puts in. Then he hesitates. "Isn't it?"

All but the Brittas are silent for a few minutes, perhaps pondering this very question, when Marnie, in Bok Choy's arms, at last begins to stir.

"Oh, thank God," Ducky says. "Cole!" he calls up ahead. "Cole, hold on one sec. Marnie's waking up. We have to make sure she's okay before we— Oh, Marnie, you're awake!"

Marnie blinks several times, as though testing her vision.

"How are you feeling?" Ducky asks her gently.

Marnie offers him a warm smile. "I'm fine, Donald, ye specky goose. I jes' had a bit a the—" Her gaze travels down the hall to the lot of identical blond cheerleaders, all staring directly at her. "I must've hit me head harder 'n I thought," she says. And with that, she's out again.

The floor trembles beneath us, and the emergency runner lights flicker. Sirens start blaring.

And here I thought our luck would give out.

"Crap!" Ducky says. "They're onto us."

"No," Chloe replies, pausing to listen to the muted honking. "Something's . . . off. Those aren't Jin'Kai alarms."

"What do you think it could be?" I ask.

Chloe tilts her head. "Those are station-wide alarms," she says. "Whatever's going on, it's going big."

Which is precisely when one of the Brittas up ahead shouts, "Someone's coming this way!"

"Get behind me!" instructs Bok Choy, passing the still-unconscious Marnie off to Ducky and crouching in a defensive stance with his weapon drawn. Chloe slides into position next to him, her weapon out as well.

A band of Jin'Kai guards comes rushing up the adjoining

corridor, large rifle-size ray guns slung down from shoulder straps in a let's-fuck-shit-up position. I count six of them. No way we survive this. No way.

Except they run right past us. Past all of us. All except the last one, who turns with a confused look on his face.

"What are you doing wasting your time with that lot?" he asks Bok Choy and Chloe, jerking his head toward the Brigade. "Get to your designated battle station. We're under attack!"

"Attack?" Chloe asks. "Almiri?"

"No, the fleet," he says as he runs after his compatriots. *"They're here."*

Well, if that don't put the donkey on the carousel, or some other expression that actually makes sense. (Forgive me, but I'm way too terrified to string words into phrases right now.)

The fleet.

The Jin'Kai invasion force that Marsden warned about.

They're here.

If an armada of Devastators doesn't make you stain your undies, I don't know what in this world will.

Suddenly there's an explosion from up ahead. Screams and gunfire. I race to the front and peer around the corner to get a look. The bodies of five guards lie motionless on the ground, while the sixth is dangling two meters above, held at the throat in a vise grip by a Devastator. This particular Devastator is bigger than the one I tussled with in Antarctica, if that's possible, and wearing full battle armor, a gray, bug-shell-like muscle suit, complete with jagged metal edges at the joints. You know, because apparently its massive claws and spiky exoskeletal protrusions alone aren't enough to eviscerate its prey. Three more

Devastators, similarly armed, stand behind the leader, seemingly unscathed by the firefight. The leader barks something at them, and the three giant uggos run off in another direction.

The remaining Devastator speaks menacingly to the Jin'Kai guard in his grip, in a language that sounds a lot like spoons in a garbage disposal. The Jin'Kai, meanwhile, still alive but wounded and defenseless, whimpers something in response. But I guess his particular mangled spoon response is not what the Devastator wanted to hear, because the creature unsheathes a long, serrated blade from its back and in one smooth motion skewers the helpless guard like a shish kebab. The guard dangles, twitching, on the hilt of the weapon, the blade jutting out of his back.

There's a shriek right in my ear. I turn to see Britta, white with fear, staring at the murder scene, still screaming.

"It's them! Them!" she screams. Like, guess who just arrived at the party.

My initial impulse is to clock her in the head, because *hello*, alerting the freaky monsters to our existence much? Of course, then I remember that Britta has been tortured for who knows how long, and prior to that she actually witnessed a Devastator decapitating her best friend (who was kind of a bitch, but *still*). So, with our own impending head-from-neck removals imminent, I decide, rather magnanimously, not to pile on.

When the monster looks up and roars, a chill of memory washes over me. I really need to start reevaluating my life decisions, I think, given the number of times lately I've found myself face-to-face with monsters who want to kill me.

Unable to quickly dislodge the dead Jin'Kai from his sword, the Devastator tosses his weapon away and charges at us, equipped only with four armored monster arms, endless rows of fang-like teeth, and about half a dozen enormous guns strapped across its heavily protected chest.

I pull Britta back around the bend of the hallway, and the other Brittas, perhaps instinctively, squeeze in to form a protective barrier around us. I'm afraid Ducky's going to go all noodle-boned on us again and collapse, but perhaps because he is holding Marnie, he remains upright, head held high.

Bok Choy exchanges a look with Chloe, who nods in agreement to something that he hasn't actually said out loud. The Devastator comes into view, spinning its head around on its massive neck to spot us. Bok Choy and Chloe open fire immediately, but the blasters leave only harmless-looking scorch marks on the creature's armor and exposed exoskeleton. The Devastator swings upward with its two upper arms, knocking the guns out of Bok Choy's and Chloe's hands, and then it kicks outward with its two heavier middle limbs, ramming Bok Choy and Chloe in their chests and sending them sprawling. The creeper looks up and spots me surrounded by the Brittas—which, I suddenly realize, makes me look a lot more like a valuable target than if an army of clones weren't creating a human shield around me.

"Gargle, gargle, kim chee!" it growls. Or something close to that. I left my universal translator in my Comic-Con swag bag.

Even if I don't speak monster, I'm picking up on the Devastator's body language just fine. It pulls yet another nasty pointy sword thing from its side (seriously, how many swords does a giant six-limbed death monster *need*?) and starts plodding toward me. That's when Cole decides to get heroically stupid and leaps with all his Almiri might right for the thing's arm—inadvertently pulling an impressive parallel bars maneuver and flipping right past his attacker into a heap of hurt on the floor.

I'm going to assume that wasn't the plan.

The Devastator clocks Cole with a nasty kick, and Cole is officially down for the count.

"Cooooooole!" the Brittas screech in unison. They all make to run toward their dashing leading man—I swear I hear one sob, "Is his butt okay?"—but then they seem to think better of it (because, one can only assume, of the scary-ass Devastator standing between said hunk and themselves). Together they whirl around and disperse down the length of the hall like cowardly little chicken shits, squealing in terror all the way.

Well, to be fair, some of them faint.

So my protective Britta-barrier has completely crumbled, and now the Devastator looms over me, ready for another shish-kebab-ing. But before I get the pointy end, Bok Choy leaps into the path of the blade.

It impales him, awkwardly, right in the side.

"No!" Chloe screams as Bok Choy cries out in pain. My heart constricts in my chest at the sound of Chloe's wail. She scoops up her blaster and fires at the Devastator.

I feel a tug on my arm and realize that Ducky is pulling me out of the way. As Ducky, Marnie (still unconscious, lucky dog), Original Britta, and I huddle behind a protective pile of rubble the Jin'Kai so thoughtfully left for us during their previous firefight, we can only watch helplessly as the scene in front of us seems to play out in slow motion.

Chloe runs straight at the Devastator, clutching her ineffectual pistol in her fist more like you would a rock than a firearm.

"Chloe!" I scream at my only child. My throat is hot, burning, as I watch her charge headfirst into danger. Britta has to physically restrain me to keep me from leaping after my daughter. (She gets an elbow to the gut for her efforts, but she doesn't let go.)

Chloe literally throws herself at the Devastator, and the creature opens its arms up wide, as if to catch her midleap. She crashes into his chest, and I can practically see the impact rippling through her. The monster's gargantuan arms wrap around my daughter and squeeze. I watch her grimace in pain as the grip around her tightens. The creature opens its massive maw, the strange, jointed teeth flexing in and out on the exposed mouth tendons, and I realize with unavoidable certainty that this beast means to bite my child's head off.

"Smile, you son of a bitch!" Chloe screams. After wiggling her arm free, she reels back and thrusts her fist deep into the Devastator's open mouth, still clutching her gun. The creature chokes and staggers back. Then Chloe flattens her arms against her body, goes limp, and manages to slide out of her assailant's grasp, rolling away as she hits the floor, shielding her face.

And then the Devastator's head explodes.

The headless body collapses to the floor. Without missing a beat, Chloe has flown to Bok Choy's side and cradles him in her lap. He winces in pain when she touches his side. Chloe, meanwhile, doesn't even seem to notice that I'm checking her all over like a prize pig at the fair. "If you ever do something that reckless again, I'll— You're *bleeding!*"

Long jagged gashes snake up Chloe's arm all the way to her elbow, bloody reminders that it can be hazardous to jam your entire arm down a space monster's throat. I fumble in my tunic, for what feels like an eternity, until I am finally able to pull out the ratty cloth Marnie purchased for me. I wrap it around Chloe's arm—the world's least hygienic bandage.

But Chloe will have none of it.

"Get off me. I'm fine." She yanks the rag off her arm and uses it instead to put pressure on Bok Choy's side. He's not looking good. He manages to sit up, but it obviously pains him. "We have to keep moving," he tells Chloe through gritted teeth. "There will be more of them any minute."

"He's right."

To my surprise this voice of reason belongs to none other than Original Britta. Even more surprising, she's busy looting the Devastator's body for weapons.

"What?" she says when she sees my look. "Some of this shit could come in handy."

Uh, who is this chick, and why didn't she take over Britta's body sixteen years ago?

"Hand me one of those knives," I tell Britta, reluctantly leaving my daughter's side. I look around and see that Cole has, thankfully, roused himself, although Marnie is still unconscious. "Cole," I say, "round up the Brittas." Cole aye-ayes and runs off immediately.

"Donald, was it?" Britta says to Ducky.

He gulps. I can't blame him—he went to school with Britta for twelve years, and this is the first she's deigned to speak to him.

"How much can you carry?" she asks him. Then, without waiting for an answer, she proceeds to drape him in supplies from both the dead Devastator and the Jin'Kai guards, making him look like a cosplay enthusiast with no sense of scale.

"I have a question," Ducky says as Cole returns with his flock of Brittas and scoops up Marnie. Britta shoves a blaster into Ducky's hands, and he tries his best not to hold it like you would a dead cockroach. "That Devastator's head just totally exploded."

"Yeah," I say. I'm scooping up my own share of weapons, whatever I can shove safely down the front of my jacket. "We were there, remember? And that wasn't a question."

"True," Ducky replies. "But, um, how, exactly, did that happen?"

"I overloaded the power cell on the blaster," Chloe says, still tending to Bok Choy.

"How'd you know how to do that?" Ducky asks. "Is that part of your training? Evil Alien Weaponry 101?"

"No," Chloe answers. "I just figured it might work."

Ducky smiles broadly at me. "I'd like to think of a clever way to say 'the apple doesn't fall far from the tree,'" he says, "but I think I'm too jacked up on adrenaline and unadulterated fear to be witty."

"Speaking of which," I say, stooping down next to Bok Choy. "If you can move, now'd be the time to show us some of that genetically superior Jin'Kai stamina."

Wincing, Bok Choy allows Chloe to lift him off the floor. "Can do," he says.

We use the sound of gunfire and screaming as an indication of which directions *not* to travel as we make our way through the installation and back to the main ozone plant. Scoring from blaster fire marks the walls our entire way, and whatever security may have been in place before has been completely blown to hell. It seems Marsden wasn't exaggerating about how much the Jin'Kai command would disapprove of his secret genetic tinkering. The ozone plant's backup lights are flickering and fading, and it's clear that whatever forces hit the station, they hit it hard and fast.

We clomp along the high suspended catwalks until we reach a segment that's completely collapsed in what appears to have been a very one-sided firefight.

"Now what?" Ducky asks.

"I could jump down," Cole offers. "Catch you one at a time."

"It's too high," I tell him. "Even for you." I look around, and then my eyes rest on perhaps the worst idea I have had in a long time. Which is really saying something.

"The power's down," I say. "Machinery is offline. These compressors have conduits that lead straight to the loading bay in the hangar, right?"

"You're bat shit," Chloe says. "You want to crawl *through the compressors*?"

"You have a better idea?" I ask.

"Isn't any idea better than going through machinery that houses highly explosive and completely unbreathable gas?" she counters. "Like, literally any idea?"

"The ozone in the conduits is in brick form," I say. "We should be able to climb through without too much trouble."

"Assuming that the bricks are stable," Chloe says. "The temperature is probably already rising with the power off. If the bricks break down, we blow up."

"That sounds bad," Ducky puts in helpfully.

"Look," I argue, "our way is blocked, and there's an army of two-and-a-half-meter-tall space monsters swarming everywhere, just waiting for another chance to cut us to bits. This is the fastest way out. And if the temperatures really are rising, then it's in our best interest to get the flip out of here before the whole place explodes, don't you think?"

"I'm with Elvie."

And spank my tooshie and call me a cab, it's none other than Britta who says it.

"If Elvie says it'll work," she continues while I stare at her, mouth agape, "I believe it. She totally saved all of us on the *Echidna*. Well, *most* of us, anyway."

"Uh, thanks?" I say.

Finding a panel weak enough to jimmy open without using one of the blasters takes a little while, but after we've pried it open with one of the Devastator swords, climbing inside is relatively easy. At least Marnie has the good sense to wake up in time for the trek. I was having visions of tugging her behind us by her shoelaces. To her credit, as soon as Marnie hears that we'll all be crawling through a series of narrow ducts filled with highly unstable explosives, she simply nods and says, "Somethin' fer the songs, yeah?"

The metal ducts that house the conveyors are narrow, but

I'm able to squeeze through by keeping my elbows tucked tightly under my chest.

"Hey, Elvie," Ducky calls from behind me. "Now I know what a TV dinner feels like."

"A what?" Marnie asks from behind Ducky.

"Come to outer space," I join in. "We'll get together, have a few laughs."

Ducky starts chuckling, and I crack a smile myself.

"What in the hell are you two talking about?" Chloe shouts. She's taken the lead, followed immediately by Bok Choy and then myself.

"Don't worry about it," comes Cole's echoey voice. He's holding up the rear, in an effort to herd all of the Brittas as quickly as possible. "You'll get used to those two eventually. They have their own language."

The acrid ozone smell stings my nose, and I squeeze my eyes shut to push the tears away.

"When we're out of here, Chloe," I grunt, squeezing around a difficult bend, "back on Earth, I'm going to have to educate you on the rich dramatic oeuvre of the genre-redefining thespian Bruce Willis."

"If you exercised your tub of an ass as much as you talked, you wouldn't be holding us up back here," says a familiar catty voice. But I can't tell if it belongs to one of the Brigade or to Original Britta.

As we continue—and I do my best to block out the incessant jabbering of the Brittas quizzing Cole about his hair products—I begin to notice something wet beneath me.

"What is this sticky stuff?" I ask. "It's not ozone, is it?"

"I thought if the bricks broke down, we'd go boom," Ducky says.

"Want to get the lead out in front there?" Cole calls. "I'm not super-excited about the 'going boom' part."

"Keep your pants on!" Chloe shouts back to her father. "Some of us are injured."

Ahead of me, Bok Choy says not a word. I can hear him grunting quietly as he moves.

The wetness underneath me is starting to soak through my tunic now, and I'm getting a very bad feeling in my gut. Sure enough, as we pass over a grated portion of the duct, a dim light shimmers through, and I see that the viscous liquid running down my fingers is bright red. Instantly I feel nauseous.

Bok Choy's breathing is slow and labored. With some difficulty I manage to push my arm forward to grab his calf and give it a squeeze. Bok Choy simply pauses for a second. I can see his head dip slightly as a quiet sigh escapes him. He flexes his calf under my hand. I know immediately to stay quiet. Tears are welling in my eyes suddenly, and I realize that they're not for Bok Choy, as sad as his condition makes me. They're for the girl who's in love with him, crawling just ahead of him, totally unaware that he is bleeding out. The girl, I realize with a mixture of guilt and fear, who is helping us all only so that I'll help him.

The last portion of our crawl through the chlorine-smelling pipeline is a sharp vertical drop. Without any real room to maneuver otherwise, we're forced to wiggle headfirst down the tube and slide the rest of the way. After Chloe and Bok Choy lower themselves, it's my turn. I make my way to the edge and look down. Below I watch as Bok Choy lands on a gelatinous receptacle pad no doubt designed to absorb the impact of the ozone bricks sliding through. Chloe swims through the goo to cradle him, and I can tell from the way her face darkens that he's doing even worse than I feared.

"Shit," I whisper, watching my daughter choke on her sobs.

"What's going on?" comes Ducky's voice from behind me. "Don't tell me you're stuck. This is so *not* where I'm dying."

"I'm not stuck," I tell him. I push myself forward and start working my way over the edge. The entire passage is slick with blood now, and I force back the bile that rises in my throat from the sticky-sweet smell. I'm doing my best to shimmy around the bend, my head and shoulders already over the edge and tilting downward, when my right arm slips and, thanks to a luck only I seem to possess, lodges itself at an incredibly painful angle beneath my chest.

"Okay," I tell Ducky. "*Now* I'm stuck."

Groans from the entire length of the duct.

"What's going on up there?" Chloe calls. "Hurry up! We've got to get to the ship!"

"Just . . . hold . . . *on*," I grunt, trying out various uncomfortable contortions to try to pull my arm free. But no luck. The worst part is that I can feel the pull of gravity on my body, and the sensation is giving me a Ducky-size case of vertigo. As the blood rushes more quickly to my head, I really begin to panic. Is this how I finally die, as a clog in a drain? Is this how we *all* die?

That's when I hear Ducky thumping forward in the passage behind me. I feel pressure on my feet and soon realize that he's nuzzling my boots with his head.

"Duck?" I ask as I feel him parting my feet slightly with his noggin. "What are you doing?"

"I'm sorry," Ducky says, and I can tell he means it. But what in the world is he—

"Ducky!" I scream, jolting up and hitting my head on the top of the duct. Ducky has slid my feet to the edges of the narrow tube and is currently *crawling headfirst between my legs.*

"Sorry!" he says again. "I'm so sorry! Really! Sorry!"

The repeated exclamations of apology do very little to allay the incredibly uncomfortable situation that we find ourselves in.

"What are you *doing?*" I say again. Broken records, the two of us.

"We've got to get you moving," he says. "I can't move my arms. This is the only way I can . . ."

And then, with no further warning, my best friend in the whole world has the top of his head pressed squarely into my butt.

"Sorry!"

"It's working!" I cry as I feel my body slide a few centimeters. "Keep it up, Duck!"

"Donald!" Marnie calls from behind him. "Careful, love! I'm quite fond of that head of yers."

Two more bumps, and my elbows have cleared the edge, joining my head and shoulders in the very downward dog position. Gravity finally grabs hold of me, and now I slide slowly along until I'm completely upside down and falling toward the receptacle bin.

I pop out like a gumball from a candy dispenser and

come down with a squishy *plop* into the bin. Bok Choy and Chloe have climbed out already, but Chloe's too busy comforting her friend to help me clear the edge as I slip and slide on the Jell-O-like padding.

"He's hurt," Chloe says, rather needlessly, when I land beside them on solid ground.

Bok Choy shakes his head. "There'll be time to deal with it later," he tells her. But the rag, sopping wet with blood, seems to imply otherwise.

Ducky flops down into the gelatin bin behind us. He climbs out and lands next to me, his face all different kinds of red. "Again," he mumbles. "Sorry."

The others follow, one by one, and we find ourselves in the loading bay for the factory's private hangar, where the bricks are gathered, tagged, and loaded onto the ships that will deploy them into the atmosphere. Bok Choy gathers his strength and leads us, as quietly as you can move with a bunch of confused and genetically- and intellectually-challenged clones, up a large, wide flight of stairs to the control room between the loading bay and the hangar.

The control room is long, probably twenty-plus meters across, with a transparent aluminum window panel looking out over the hangar. Cole edges up to the window and peeks down over the edge.

"Well?" Marnie asks.

"Shit," he says.

I creep up alongside him, hoping to embellish his commentary with a little more detail.

"Shit," I add helpfully.

Below us the smoking wreckage of dozens of small ships litters the deck. At first I wonder if the Devastators targeted the hangar with some sort of ship-to-ship missile, but the damage is too specific, with ships lying in useless fiery heaps while the cargo loaders and flatbed trolleys remain untouched—presumably because the Jin'Kai determined that it's difficult to escape into outer space on a forklift.

"Careful," Marnie says from beside me. "They're still wandering around down there." I spot roughly a dozen Devastators on the floor. They're all hovering around one ship, the sight of which fills me with excitement and dread both at once.

"That's our ship!" I cry.

"You came here in that thing?" Britta asks. "How did you expect to fit us all into that little tin can?"

"I didn't," I snap back. "If you want, we can leave you here."

Ducky's comment is slightly more helpful. "It looks like they didn't blow it up or anything."

"They're probably right confused about why it's there," Marnie says. "It's not Jin'Kai or human. They might be tryin' to find out if there's an Almiri presence aboard the station."

"Well, our ship's in one piece, so that's good," Cole says. "But I hate to point out that it's also crawling with those things."

"That's not all," Bok Choy says, grimacing. Chloe offers a concerned hand to steady him at the console, but he shakes her off. "They've attached something to the ship. Some sort of docking clamps. It'll take me a while to disable them."

"You start fiddlin' with those, and they'll know we're here," Marnie says.

"Not if we distract them," I say. I flick on the console next to Bok Choy and bring up the inventory screen for the loading bay.

"There's more than two thousand ozone bricks sitting in here waiting for a stack and pack," I say. I turn to Chloe. "You feel like setting off any more fireworks?"

"You can't detonate those bricks," Ducky warns. "If we can't get the ship to fly, you'll block our only way out."

"If the ship doesn't fly," I point out, "then we're all dead anyway." I hold out my hand to Chloe, who smirks and drops a long, pointy blaster into my grip. "Bok Choy, you work on those clamps. Cole, you and the others take the Brittas—" At the sound of their name, all of their perky blond heads turn to me in unison. "Wait down in the access corridor until the coast is clear. Chloe, let's go shoot this place to hell."

Chloe and I make our way back into the loading bay. A floor console stands near the front loading gate that connects the bay to the hangar. I activate it and initiate the loading sequence. Immediately, shielded panels begin sliding open on the three walls, frosty mist rolling out from the refrigerated storage compartments. Inside each compartment, rack after rack of dark purple bricks begins to automatically extend into the bay, where normally a loader would be waiting to install them on a deployment craft. The bricks themselves are actually quite pretty. They look like a cross between colored quartz and grape-flavored Popsicles.

"Okay. We're only going to get one chance at this," I say.

"Well, now's not the time for cold feet," Chloe says. She positions herself in front of the loading gate and cocks two big guns, one in each hand, like the little Rambolina I always dreamed of rearing. "Open sesame."

I tap in the commands, and the gate groans and creaks open, rusted metal screeching against rusted metal.

"That got their attention!" comes Bok Choy's voice over the comm in the control panel. "They're sending two your way."

"Well, they're going to love this, then," Chloe replies. As soon as the gate is fully open, the two Devastators come into view and see her. Before they can react, she opens fire. "Die, you sap-suckers!" she cries, unleashing unholy hell on them with their own advanced firearms. The two giant creeps stagger backward under the barrage of fire. From behind them enraged voices fill the air.

"Here they come!" Bok Choy warns.

Chloe runs back inside the bay, sending random fire toward the gate, being careful not to shoot anywhere near the bricks. I hightail it back up the stairs toward the control room and crouch by the door. Chloe races my way.

"Now!" she says.

Not yet, I tell myself. I square up my gun and balance it on my knee.

Once Chloe reaches me, she spins around, looking back down at the empty bay below us. "What are you waiting for?" she asks.

"This," I say.

As the Devastators come barreling into the bay, I take aim and fire my weapon, straight past the aliens, at the stack of bricks at the opposite end of the room. The bricks explode one after another in a chain reaction, cascading around the room from one stack to the next. The concussive force knocks both me and Chloe to the ground, but the Devastators on the floor are completely engulfed by the maelstrom, and they wail in pain. Still, blaster fire seeks us out as we scramble on our hands and knees back to the control room. The door slides shut behind us as soon as we're inside.

I'm pretty sure mani-pedis would've been a more stress-free form of mother-daughter bonding.

Bok Choy is still working intently over the docking controls.

"Are the others aboard?" I ask.

"They're at the ship," he informs me. "They're under fire from a few stray hostiles."

"What about the docking clamps?"

"I need another minute."

"We don't have a minute!" Chloe shouts.

Bok Choy doesn't look up from his work. "Just get to the ship," he says. "Stick close to the left wall there. You'll be able to flank them and create cover so the others can get aboard."

"What about you?" Chloe asks, her voice strained.

Bok Choy pauses for the first time and looks up at her. "I'll be with you soon," he tells her, then immediately returns his focus to the control panel.

"But . . . ," she starts, but she can't get any more words out. I grab her arm and tug her toward the exit.

"Chloe, we have to help the others," I say.

Chloe reluctantly exits with me, but she keeps her gaze on Bok Choy as we move. He never looks up.

I can hear the blaster fire as we move quickly along the

left wall, weaving around the rubble that was once a small fleet of crappy fliers. As we zoom around a long block of loading equipment, I make out Cole and Marnie exchanging fire with the Devastators from behind the ship's loading ramp, while the others use the ramp as cover. There are three baddies returning fire. Our vantage point creates a triangle among all three parties; we're slightly behind the Devastators but still obscured by debris.

Without a word between us, Chloe and I open fire. As soon as we do, the Devastators pivot and discover us, sending a return volley before retreating to cover. This gives Cole, Marnie, and the others a chance to scurry up the gangway into the ship. Once everyone else is aboard, Cole and Marnie emerge halfway back down the ramp and fire again at the Devastators' position. Pinched between two sets of foes, the Devastators can't line up any good shots, and Chloe and I are able to make a dash for the ship, the Devastators' fire clearing wide of us and exploding harmlessly against the hull of a ruined ozone flier.

"Get in!" Cole says, waving Chloe and me past him into the main hold.

I run inside to find Ducky trying to calm the Brittas. "We're fine," he tells them. "You're all fine. Remember how cute Cole is? His, uh, butt and everything? Just concentrate on that."

The Brittas, rattled like a group of puppies during a thunderstorm, settle slightly at the thought of Cole's posterior. Well, save one.

"I hate every last one of you," Original Britta tells her gaggle of clones.

Ducky spots me as I come up the ramp. "Elvie, thank God," he says.

"We've got to get this tub in the air," I say.

"We can't leave yet," Chloe says, shadowing me to the cockpit. "He's still back there. We're not leaving without him."

"Of course not," I tell her. I slide into the pilot's chair and begin the takeoff sequence. "Go back out there and help Cole and Marnie hold those scumbags back."

Chloe doesn't look wholly convinced, but I give her a good mom-glare, and she retreats back to the ramp.

"Ducky!" I shout back into the hold. "Get your ass up here!"

He runs in at breakneck speed. "What is it?"

"I know you don't know how to fly this thing, but I need a co-pilot."

"What about the Brittas?" he asks.

"Let Britta handle the Brittas."

Ducky slips into the seat next to me without further hesitation.

"Check that our thrusters and stabilizers are all online while I fire up the engines," I tell him. And when he gives me a *Wha-huh?* gaze, I elaborate. "Think *Tech-a-Mecha Revolutions 3*. Heroic mode."

"Now you're talking my language," Ducky says. He begins deftly flicking through the touch screen controls. But after just a few seconds he lets out a low whistle. "Um, hey, Elvie? What is this?" He flicks the display toward me, and his screen slides onto my display. At first I think that Ducky has accidentally accessed some weird redundant system, but when I give it a second look, I realize what it is.

"Jesus, Mary, George, and Ringo," I gasp. "Bricks. A full load of ozone bricks. At least a hundred."

"On this ship?"

"The Governor's men must've had the ship retrofitted after Marsden handed it over," I say, cycling through the system. "They've installed a launcher into the aft section too."

"A ship this advanced, and they use it like an ordinary junker?" Ducky asks. Then a troubling expression washes over his face. "The bricks can't blow up once they're loaded," he says. "Right?"

I don't bother answering, because I think we both realize how dead we're all about to be. The Governor's men—who, in my very brief encounter with them, didn't strike me as overly careful about their work—have done a really, really shitty job of installing the new system into our ship. Try as I might, I can't get the rear repulsors to light up on my board.

Bust out the label maker and mark us BONED.

"Bok Choy, are you there?" I say, patching into an open channel on the comm.

"I'm here, Elvie," comes his voice. It is weak and shaky. "The clamps are disabled. You should be able to start the take-off sequence."

"That's the thing," I tell him. "I can't. The back repulsors are offline. I'm not going to be able to get her off the deck."

"Can't we just start up the engine and slide out?" Ducky asks.

"With a half ton of explosive ozone in the hold?" I say. "We'll light up like a Girl Scout campfire before we've moved half a meter."

"So, that's a no, then."

"Elvie!" Cole screams from behind me, racing through the gauntlet of Brittas. "There's more of them coming. We need to get out of here!"

"What do I do?" I ask Bok Choy into the comm.

There's nothing but silence on the other end for several seconds.

"Bok Choy?" I repeat, growing more and more frantic. "What do I do?"

After what feels like a century, I hear Bok. He exhales a long, drawn-out sigh, one that sounds almost like relief.

"Bring up your ramp," he tells me.

"What?" I reply. I must've misheard. "How will you—"

"Bring it up," he interrupts. "Set your ignition cycle on standby and put all of your power into the aft dampeners."

"But why . . ." But I know why. I stop asking questions and start following instructions. Behind me I can hear the ramp rising.

"Elvie?" Ducky asks.

I ignore him. "Do you want me to tell her?" I ask Bok Choy.

There's another slight pause.

"Thank you," he answers.

Outside in the hangar the red alert lights begin strobing just as the launch siren rings.

"What are you doing?" Chloe says as she barges into the cockpit. "Lower the ramp. Now!"

"Sit down and hold on tight," I tell her, finishing the preparations Bok Choy gave me.

"Did you hear what I said?" she shrieks, her voice shrill.

"I heard you."

"What's happening?" Marnie asks as she enters, stepping up next to Ducky.

"Bok Choy is decompressing the hangar," I say. "Strap yourself down if you value your unbroken bones. Cole, go help the Brittas."

"*What?*" Chloe screams. "*No, no, no.* Lower the ramp. I said, lower the ramp. We're going to get him."

"Please sit down, Chloe," I tell her as calmly as I can.

In response Chloe raises her gun and points it at my head. "Lower that ramp," she instructs me again.

I stand up slowly and turn to face her. "Marnie," I say, and without another word Marnie slides into the pilot's chair and resumes where I left off.

"Open that ramp right now," Chloe says, tears streaking her cheeks, "or I'll kill you."

"Chloe," I say. *Calm, Elvie. Your baby's crying. Channel your calm.* "He has to do this. For you."

"I swear I'll shoot you right now," Chloe says, but her gun shakes in her hands. "You know I will."

"Chloe," I say one last time. Then I knock the gun from her trembling hands, and it crashes to the floor. Chloe takes a swing at me, which I deflect—but her second strike catches me right on the nose. I grab hold of her wrists and push her backward. Chloe falls hard into a chair behind the pilot's seat, me on top of her. She pulls me toward her, and I smack my mouth on the back of the chair, cutting the inside of my upper lip against my teeth.

But I don't let go.

"I'll kill you!" she wails.

I wrap my arms around her tightly, linking my hands together behind the seat.

"He wanted me to tell you."

"I'll *kill* you!" She is nothing but sobs now.

I close my eyes and squeeze my daughter as tightly as I can, swaddling her like in those first few weeks before I lost her.

"I love you," I tell her.

She kicks, scratches, bites, sobs. Still I hang on.

The main hangar door slides open, exposing the hangar to the vacuum of space. The ship shakes violently and rolls, shuddering each time a loose piece of wreckage slams into us as it is blown out into space.

"Hold on!" Marnie shouts.

When I feel my stomach go into my throat, I know we're upside down. We're off the deck and spinning like a top toward the door. I slide back and forth, my grip tight on the chair, pressed against Chloe. There's so much turbulence that I don't initially understand that the high-pitched sound in my ear is my daughter. I can feel her arms clutching my back, and I squeeze her even closer as we continue spinning toward the void.

"I love you," I tell her again. Soft in her ear. "I love you."

Chapter Eleven

WHEREIN IT BECOMES CLEAR THAT OUR HEROINE'S FRESHMAN GUIDANCE COUNSELOR WAS TOTALLY WRONG ABOUT PLAYING VIDEO GAMES NOT COUNTING AS A "LIFE SKILL"

"We're na' clear yet!" Marnie screams. The ship has stopped spinning, and I can feel the engines kicking into full burn. We haven't exploded or anything, so I count that as a plus.

Chloe pushes me away from her. Her face is streaked and her eyes are red and raw. But right this second I can't worry about consoling her on the loss of her would-be love.

Right now they're trying to shoot us out of the sky.

The ship shudders with a *crack!* and Marnie veers sharply to one side, trying to avoid the next volley from whoever or whatever is behind us. As we come about, I can see one ship out of the corner of the front viewport bearing down on us.

"Just one ship? I'm insulted."

Marnie coughs and points to the tactical display.

"Oh," I say. "Four ships. Well that's . . . more like it?"

"Hold on," Marnie barks. "They're lookin' to cut us off!"

The only sounds that follow are the engines straining and

the Brittas moaning. Then another *crack!*—this one harder than before.

"What are they hitting us with?" Ducky screams. His eyes are darting around the copilot console, the confidence he had only a few moments ago now lost in the panic of an actual spaceship chase.

"Ducky, move it," I command. Ducky bolts out of his seat like it's covered in spiders, and I slide in and bring up the environmental scanners.

"Looks like they're using some sort of particle cannons," I say. "Assuming I'm reading this right."

"Well, what do *we* have?" Ducky asks.

"This isn't a combat ship," I reply.

"What? I thought this was an Almiri attack ship. Where are the phasors? The photon torpedoes?"

"We stole a shuttle, Duck, not the *Millennium Falcon.*"

"I'm very scared right now, so I'm going to overlook your franchise conflation. This time."

"Elvie, can ye get our stealth field up?" Marnie asks me. "I dunnae if we'll be completely invisible to whatever sensors they've got, but we might be able to lose 'em."

"No go," I say. "The shield is still charging. Apparently our fancy new ozone system is leeching energy from the same cells, so it can't . . ."

"Elvs?" Cole asks as I trail off. "What is it?"

"Marnie," I say slowly, "I need you to straighten out."

"They'll have a clear shot lined up if we do that!" she screeches in response.

"Just do it. And get ready to break when I say."

Marnie straightens out our course, although there's a stream of what are obviously Scottish obscenities escaping from under her breath as she does so.

"I sure hope you know what you're doing, Elvs," Cole says.

"Me too. This is my first space battle."

"Two of 'em on our six," Marnie tells us. "Three thousand meters. . . . Fifteen hundred meters. . . . They're locked on!"

I slap the release button on our new shipment of ozone bricks. The clumsy gears grind and groan, but thankfully within seconds the display reads *Payload deployed*.

"Break now!" I cry.

Marnie pulls up on the controls, pushing us all back hard into our seats. A split second later the ship shudders more violently than ever before.

"They're hitting us again!" Ducky shouts.

"No," Marnie says. She glances from the tactical display over to me. The look on her face can only be described as dumbfounded respect. "Tha' wasn't us. It was them. Two ships destroyed."

"What happened?" Ducky asks. "Are they crashing into each other or something?"

"At these speeds," Marnie tells him, "the impact of a few hundred bricks a ozone was enough to blow 'em to kingdom come."

"To be fair," I say, trying not to gloat in the middle of the crisis. "I thought at best it would distract or disable them."

"There are still two more of them out there," Chloe chimes in from her seat behind us. It's the first time she's spoken since takeoff, and her voice is so low and even that I get a chill up my spine. "Unless you think they'll fall for that again, I think this bucket is out of tricks."

"And out of bricks," I say. A shot across the bow jolts us, and I wince. "At least we're less likely to explode if they hit us square in the ass."

As if on cue, another shot rocks us. I scan the navigation charts. "Marnie, take us to these coordinates," I say, tapping the screen to bring up the course I want and sliding the screen over to her display.

Marnie looks at the screen like I just sent her a mash note asking if I "like-like" her. "Elvie, there's not a chance in bloody hell we'll survive a run through that," she says.

"Through what?" Cole asks.

"There's a lane filled with derelict stations, ships, and other space junk," I explain. "A lot of clutter, but it's the shortest path out of the Rust Belt headed back to Earth."

"It's called the Gauntlet," Marnie says. "And they call it that fer a reason. It'd be suicide."

Another blast smacks into us.

"We're losing hull integrity," I say. "We don't have time to debate this, Marnie. With any luck they won't bother to follow us in there."

"We fly in there, and they won't need to," Marnie replies, on the verge of yelling now. "We'll be smashed to smithereens!"

There's a bright white flash in the viewport, coming from behind us. The ship swings around, and I see what remains of the space station, combusting like a giant goldfish at high altitude.

"Holy Moses," Ducky gasps. "Did they just blow up the entire station?"

"Take us into that run now!" I shout at Marnie.

"Elvie, I cannae fly us through all that," Marnie says. "I'm no fighter pilot. I've flown maybe two transports in me whole life."

"Give me the controls," I say. Marnie obliges, with only a "Saints preserve us" as she slides the flight protocols to my console.

As soon as I have control, I turn us toward the Gauntlet, keeping the Devastator ships on the display in the corner of my eye.

"They're closing in fast," Ducky says.

I put the engines into full burn and use the thrusters to zigzag us jarringly around. "Time to put those hundreds of hours of *Jetman* to good use," I say.

Our readout shows several energy blasts coming from the Devastators, but none of them land. The only casualty of my daredevil piloting is Ducky's stomach. Squeals of disgust shower down from the Brittas. It's all doing wonders for my concentration.

"Marnie's right," Chloe says, staring at the heads-up. "You'll never be able to clear all that." And it's true that our path is filled with more junk than a Macydale Black Friday sale. As we enter, I manage to avoid several large hunks of disintegrating hull fragments, only to collide with several smaller floaters, which scrape and scratch as they drag along the top of the ship.

"You ever fly something like this?" Cole says. And it takes me a second to realize he's asking our *daughter*.

"Cole, she's, like, a month and a half old or something," I point out.

"I think I can figure it out," Chloe replies. She takes the other pilot's seat from Marnie, who follows Ducky's barf trail to the main hold, presumably to care for her weak-stomached paramour. Or perhaps to smack all the Brittas into silence— either one would be fine by me.

"I'll focus on steering," I tell Chloe. "I need you to fire the thrusters when I say. Got it?"

"Stop telling me what to do," Chloe snaps.

"Chloe," I say, forgoing an eye roll only because I need to focus on the field in front of us. "I know you're going through a major growth spurt and everything, but now is a poor time for teenage sass."

"You're not the boss of me!"

"Actually," I say, "that's *precisely*—"

It's Cole who breaks in. "You've got this, Chloe," he says calmly. "I know you can do it."

"I can do it," she repeats.

Despite my best efforts to outmaneuver the Devastators, their ships are too fast for our little shuttle. The only weakness that I can see is that they don't bank well. However, given enough open space, they can easily correct for any overshots, making up the distance in a matter of nanoseconds. Up ahead the junk is clearing somewhat, offering us a safer path, but it also means fewer obstacles for the Devastators to work around. And soon I see the reason for the sparse debris field—an old L.O.C., similar class to the *Echidna*, maybe slightly bigger. Years of bouncing around in the debris field has punched several enormous holes through the hull, leaving it a massive floating skeleton.

"What are you doing?" Chloe asks as I turn us onto an intercept course. "There's a clear path directly to port!"

"Well, at least we know you've got your nautical terms down," I say. "I'd hate to think this was a wasted learning moment."

"You're crazy," Chloe says.

"Get used to it, sweetie. It's genetic."

I pilot us directly into the wreckage of the cruiser's hull, hoping that its interior is as worm-eaten as the outer hull suggests.

The Devastators remain in pursuit.

"Stern thrusters now!" I shout. "Port! Stern! Port!"

Chloe follows each command instantly, lurching the ship to and fro as I thread the needle.

And then, suddenly, our path is blocked. I don't have time to call out for thrusters. There's an open gap to our right, and I put my whole body into the turn. We're all sideways in our seats like we're on an old-timey sci-fi television show. The bottom of the hull scraping against metal sounds like a million forks being drawn slowly across a million china plates. We clear the ship, just barely, and fly out into the clear. The ship shudders slightly.

Chloe looks at the tactical display. "They're toast," she says. "Both hostiles are down." She turns to me, her face stoic. "Nice flying. For a maniacal, heartless nut."

"Nice copiloting," I reply. And call me mature or something, because I only *think* the *for an immature, snotty brat* part. "Couldn't have done it without you," I say instead. Something dangerously close to a smile nearly creeps across Chloe's face.

"Guys," Cole says. "I hate to interrupt this touching mother-daughter moment, but . . ."

Chloe looks at the tactical again. "*Rikslamma,*" she spits, in what I can only assume is the foulest of Jin'Kai epithets.

I don't need the tactical to summon my own swear words. Through the viewport approximately *eighty bajillion Devastator ships* come into focus, ranging from what look to be single-pilot fighters to enormous juggernauts three times bigger than the largest orbital cruiser I've ever seen, forming a blockade between us and our home planet.

"Does it count that I got us *pretty close* to not being dead?" I ask.

"It looks like they're already engaged," Chloe says, eyes on the tactical. "I've got readings on two unique power signature types coming from that fleet."

"Byron," I say. "I didn't think the Almiri built that many ships." Cole shrugs.

"They've spotted us," Chloe cuts in. "Three bogeys are breaking off and are in pursuit."

"Didn't we just play this tune?" I mutter. I come about and try to make a break for it, back into the belt, but these ships are bigger and faster than the ones that had been tasked primarily with taking out a defenseless space station.

"They're right on top of us!" Chloe shouts.

Which, actually, I'd already pretty much figured out, because now our ship is rocking under a constant barrage of fire. The tactical and heads-up displays go dead—and just like that we're flying blind.

"Port thrusters gone!" Chloe informs us. "Secondary engine offline!"

"This is it, then," I say. I turn to her. "Chloe, I just want you to know that I love you and—"

"Cut the sap and look straight ahead!" Chloe screams, pointing. Through the viewport a ship is materializing right before my eyes. It's easily twenty times as big as us.

It's also awfully familiar.

Two large turrets on either side of the hull open up a barrage of fire, visible only as brief blue muzzle flashes. The shots fly right past us, clearly intended for someone else. I turn the ship as best I can to get clear of the cross fire, and as I do, we all get a view of the Devastator vessels exploding silently in the void. The comm crackles to life on the console.

"Elvie? Is that you, dearheart?"

"Daddy?" I screech. I'm sobbing and laughing at the same time, barely able to form words.

Beside me Chloe snorts. "*Daddy*," she mutters.

I clear my throat. "Dad, don't tell me you're flying that thing?"

"Well, technically, your grandfather is," my father replies. "And you have Oates to thank for the fireworks display. I suppose you could say I'm the resident science officer aboard."

"Dad, I found Chloe. Olivia. Long story. But the Devastators are chasing us."

"I know, dearheart, I know. The Almiri and Earth military forces are already engaged with the enemy."

"The military?" I ask. Stunned murmurs pop up around me. (Well, except from the Britta Brigade—they're still busy complaining about Ducky's puke on their shoes.)

"A lot has happened while you've been away," Dad tells me. "Crazy, world-altering stuff. Someone could write a doozy of a novel about it someday, perhaps. We can cover you out of the fire zone. I'm sending you coordinates now."

"Our tactical computer is offline."

"Then I'll give you the coordinates over the comm and you can dock with us. Don't worry. We'll get a head start on these sons of guns."

"Where are we going?" I ask.

"Elvie, dearheart, we're going to Mars."

Chapter Twelve

IN WHICH OUR MERRY BAND OF MISFITS GET THEIR ASSES TO MARS

"Dearheart!" Dad shouts, waving like a madman as Chloe and I walk down the shuttle's ramp into the hangar of Byron's command ship like we just returned from a two-week vacation cruise, as opposed to a daring and intestine-twisting escape through a debris field in space. A team of three Almiri passes us and makes its way up into our (okay, technically *their*) ship, pulling a hover cart loaded down with fancy alien doozy-whatsits.

"Where are they goin'?" Marnie asks as they brush past her, Cole, and Ducky at the top of the ramp without so much as a "Pardon me."

"They're going to take a look at your hyperdrive," Dad says.

"Oh. Well, then, Harry, I think I'll join 'em an' get a better jog o' how this girl's wired, if it's all the same t' ye."

"I'll join you," Ducky says, his face still green. "Just as soon as I make use of the facilities one"—he pauses midsentence for a seriously rancid burp—"more time."

I look at Cole, who's just standing there, and the look I give him must say, *Why are you just standing there?* because he smirks and nods at my father.

"So, this is my granddaughter?" Dad asks, examining Chloe like he's inspecting a new motherboard for his computer.

"I'll babysit the Brigade for a while," Cole says. "Holler if you need me."

Chloe glares at my father, squirming her face away when he touches her cheek. "*This* is my genetic lineage?" she asks, grunting. "Human. Ugh. Let me guess—your knees give out all the time, or something equally ridiculous."

Dad looks from Chloe to me. "Quite the resemblance," he says.

"There will be time for the family reunion later," I say. "Dad, tell me what's going on. The short version, please. I don't have any patience for exposition at this point."

Dad clears his throat. "Come with me," he says ominously.

Dad leads me and Chloe out of the hangar and down a tight corridor. While the bones of the ship's interior are unmistakably alien and advanced, there's also no question that this is Byron's personal flagship, with all of his decorating flair on display. Hung between access panels and computer node stations is a series of familiar oil paintings, mostly of dogs, that clash terribly with the otherwise clean white metallic décor. Just as I'm about to make a crack about Gramps's Achilles heel for lousy art, we pass by a large mural of—literally—Achilles.

Note to self: when you're not so busy fighting for your life, remember to check if you're related to Achilles.

As we walk, Dad takes his best stab at explaining to me

what's been going on Earth-side as of late. "Shortly after you, ahem, *parted ways* with us," Dad begins, "Byron and Oates and the rest of us rendezvoused with the surviving Almiri leadership. Byron and Oates were able to convince them that current circumstances dictated a change in policy regarding the Enosi resistance and their sub rosa relationship with the rest of mankind."

"*This* is the short version?" Chloe mutters.

"Dad," I say. "Cut to the chase, will you? Earth, happenings, you guys, Mars. Just tell me how this all ties together."

Dad nods and continues. "A little more than a week ago, the Jin'Kai invasion force entered expanded satellite range—which, as you can imagine, made it a perfectly horrible time for the Almiri to reveal to the United States government that the president and several key members of the cabinet weren't technically human—"

"Wait," I interrupt him. "President *Holloway*?" Then I pause a moment and consider the leader of the free world's perfect single dimple. "Okay, yeah, that makes sense. Move on."

"Despite the unfortunate timing," Dad continues, "the Almiri's 'coming out' to most of the world's governments has thus far been largely without incident." He grins. "I like to think that I played a crucial role, given my unique position as a human with intimate understandings of the Almiri. I maintained the position—agreed upon by our elected leaders, I might point out—that our only hope in the days to come is to postpone any public revelation about aliens among us, and the inevitable fallout, in the hopes of coming together to valiantly repel those who would destroy us. It was a most inspiring bit of captaincy on my part, and a riveting story that I will tell you about in full at a more appropriate time—"

"Please tell me that being long-winded isn't genetic," Chloe cuts in.

"Good for you, Dad," I tell him. He is still grinning, clearly pleased with himself. "Now skip to the part where they're reenacting the act-three space battle from Return of the Jedi over New Jersey."

Dad nods. "Yes. I was getting to that. As you already know, the Almiri have been developing advanced offensive and defensive technologies for some time, in the hopes of slowly doling them out to the rest of us in a way that felt organic to our own technological growth. Some of these technologies had already found their way into the military, thank goodness, seeing as your grandfather's attack fleet consisted of only about one hundred small to midsize vessels. When the Jin'Kai invaders arrived on the horizon, Byron's force was deployed to repel them, along with any human-built ships that might be remotely up to the task. So the fleet you saw back there, engaged with the Jin'Kai? It consists mostly of human orbital military craft."

"Which aren't going to be able to survive in a sustained conflict," I surmise.

"Precisely," Dad agrees. "On a positive note, from what little evidence I've been able to gather so far, the Almiri ships have a decent edge in maneuverability over the enemy."

I nod at that. "We found that out for ourselves."

"Up until now the Almiri have been losing roughly one ship for every twelve enemies neutralized," Dad says. "An excellent win-loss ratio. Unfortunately, simply due to

Jin'Kai numbers, we're bound to lose in a war of attrition."

We come to the end of the corridor, and Dad flicks a security card to open the door blocking our path. The door *swooshes* open to reveal the bridge. Unlike before, now not all of the bridge crew are Almiri. There are several men and women wearing American and French military uniforms running their stations side by side with their alien counterparts.

"Cool, huh?" Dad asks.

It is, but I've got other things on my mind. "So why Mars? If things are going so badly, then what are we doing running off to the red planet?"

"Isn't it obvious?"

It's not my father who says it.

The command chair swivels, revealing the cool, confident star of *East of Eden*, wearing a tight red uniform so covered in shiny baubles that he looks like an extra from Hansel Wintergarten's Christmas video "Hey Girl, I'm a Tree, Come Decorate Me . . . as a Friend."

"Mars holds the key to rescuing the world!" Byron says dramatically.

"And this," I say to Chloe, "would be *my* grandfather. Hey, Gramps. Long time no see. Sorry about, you know, stealing your ship and stuff."

He does not look mad. Byron rises from his chair and walks over to me, reaching out his arms in a super-awkward gesture to hug me. I hesitate perhaps a moment too long, and he starts to pick up on it, so finally I just rush over and wrap my arms around him. Byron gives me two hard claps on the back, which I can feel reverberating throughout my skeleton.

"It's good to see you," he says.

"You too," I say. I pull away and clear my throat. I point toward Chloe, who is hanging out in the doorway, observing the entire scene with about as much emotion as you'd have watching a yogurt commercial. "This is Olivia," I tell Byron.

"Chloe," she corrects me. Her voice is harsh, but she's shifting her weight uncomfortably from foot to foot, splitting her gaze between us and the floor.

"Chloe, right," I say, turning back to Byron. "Long story. She's your great-granddaughter."

"Is she now?" he says. He walks over to Chloe, staring at her intently as he does, making her visibly more uncomfortable with each approaching step. Standing directly in front of her, Byron raises his hand and offers it to her.

"Hello, young lady," he greets her. "Welcome aboard."

"Whatever," Chloe replies, self-consciously hugging herself while admiring the fine welding work on the floor plating. "You were saying? About saving the world?"

Byron adjusts a shoulder bauble as he explains. "Ah, yes, that. You see, a hundred years ago I was doing research for an epic poem I was writing."

"Dammit, it *is* genetic," Chloe says, more astonished than anything else.

Byron appears not to notice. "I had in mind a poem that focused on the Almiri's early days on Earth. A heroic retelling of how we came down to live among a species bursting with potential yet held back by their rather quaint grasp of the universe."

"And you thought somebody was going to want to *read* that?" Chloe asks.

"The intention was to perform it aloud," Byron continues, undeterred. "I was trying to 'unearth,' if you'll pardon the pun, the earliest records we had of our journey through the cosmos— landing, making first contact, et cetera, et cetera. Records that should have been contained in our primary historical data bank. However, when I tried to access these records, I found none. I tried employing the assistance of our archivists, but they could not—or would not—help me. Through some sleuthing on my own over the next several decades, I was able to recover data entries whose time codes put them at or near the dawn of our arrival on Earth. The entries, however, were badly damaged. The damage appeared to be the result of energy surges and environmental corruption. Accidental in nature."

"A little *too* accidental," Dad chimes in.

"Exactly, Harry," Byron says. "Upon further investigation it became clear to me that these entries had been intentionally destroyed. But why would anyone want to erase the most momentous event in the history of our race?"

I'm finally beginning to see where all this is headed. "They had something to hide," I venture.

"Precisely," Byron agrees. "From that discovery I launched into a nearly thirty-year long endeavor to recover anything that I could from the records. I was mostly unsuccessful, until just recently, when I was able to avail myself of your father's rather impressive faculty for computer wizardry."

The fact that Lord Byron/James Dean/his father-in-law just gave Dad the ultimate compliment is giving Dad's ego a near pornographic level of stroking. His goofy grin appears to be lifting him several centimeters off the floor.

"So what mysterious secrets did you discover?" I ask. "And what does this have to do with Mars or the Jin'Kai or anything? I mean, not that I don't love superlong stories about history and poetry, but the thing is that I *really* don't."

"We weren't able to glean much. But what we did find was telling. Geographical references to the colony ship's initial landing site, fractured descriptions of the landscape, climate. None of these meshed with the commonly held beliefs of the Almiri, or the history passed down in our Code. And then we found a single instance of the name of the host planet."

Dad cuts in like a kid who can't keep from revealing the punch line to his older sibling's joke. "Barsoom!" he cries. And I swear he squeals when he says it.

"What the crimson crap," Chloe says, "is a Barsoom?"

I am clearly better versed in pre-turn-of-the-century sci-fi pulp novels than my daughter, because I recognize the forgotten nickname of the familiar planet immediately.

"Mars? You mean the Almiri didn't land on Earth originally? Why? And why bother to go to such great lengths to change their history?"

"Perhaps they were ashamed," Byron says. "From what I can gather, the Almiri were quickly repelled by the indigenous resistance. I wouldn't be surprised if my ancestors wanted to keep the defeat under wraps. We're not exactly known for being great losers."

"This is all purely speculation at this point," Dad reminds me.

But I'm stuck on another tiny detail. "Hold up. Did you just say 'indigenous'?" I've met all sorts of alien creatures over the past several months, but for some reason the existence of *martians* is what's threatening to blow my circuits.

"The point is," Byron says, gazing at me like *I'm* the one who's getting us off topic in this conversation, "it appears that someone or some*thing* convinced the Almiri to abandon their originally designated host planet, and the circumstances were such that my forefathers thought it best to erase all evidence of the fact and create a false history for my people."

"And if there was something powerful enough to chase off the Almiri," I say, slowly putting it all together, "you think this something might be useful against the Jin'Kai."

"It is a desperate shot in the dark, I will readily admit," Byron says. "But at this point it's all we have left in reserve. The alliance of Almiri, human, and Enosi fights bravely against unimaginable odds, but our time is quickly running out."

"How quickly?" I ask. "It will take us weeks to get to Mars. Not to mention the time it's going to take us to convince the martians—I repeat, *martians*—to let us use their superweapons."

"With our hyperdrive engaged, we should be there in a matter of hours," Byron tells me. "We should have an adequate head start on the Jin'Kai, even if they are in pursuit. And as to the planet's inhabitants," he says, "as far as we can discern, Mars was long ago abandoned."

"Then why the hell are we going there?" Chloe asks.

"The planet is devoid of *life*. Not artifacts."

"And how could you possibly know a thing like that?" Chloe asks.

"The Ares Project," I say, queen of the obvious realizations. "You've had your people searching for weapons for a while."

"Well, not *weapons* specifically," Byron says. "Not until recently. But remnants, yes. Pieces of the puzzle. And all the pieces we have point to one very particular spot. We will be landing at Terraforming Station 1-1-3-8. Prior to being evacuated, the team there had reported unusual power readings below the surface. They'd been in the process of tunneling toward the source."

"And you think these power readings will lead us to some sort of Jin-Kai-killing deus ex machina?" I ask.

"We can only hope."

"And here I'd always thought poetry was a complete waste of time."

"Don't go knocking old Byron's verses, now, miss," comes a sturdy voice from behind me. "A man needs something to occupy his mind during long trips to the loo."

I spin around and embrace Titus Oates, who wraps me in a massive bear hug.

"I'm so glad you're okay!" I say, squeezing him. He squeezes back.

"I should say the same," he tells me. Then he leans back to look me in the eye. "In the future, Miss Elvie, if you could refrain from absconding with any vehicle that isn't expressly yours . . ."

I hug him again. Chloe leans over to my dad and stage-whispers.

"Don't tell me that's my great-great-uncle," she says.

• • •

e our way down to the surface of the planet, it's _____ being behind the controls. But I don't think Lord _____ particularly keen on having his granddaughter behind the wheel.

"You're coming in a little hot," comes Oates's voice over the comm. He's still up on the command ship, tracking our landing. Our dinged-up little jalopy is coming in blind, since the terraforming stations' systems have all been powered down to avoid detection by the Jin'Kai. "Bring her up a titch and start firing your front thrusters."

"How exactly does one quantify 'a titch'?" I ask Dad nervously. Dad, ever the champion of precision, simply shakes his head in dismay. Our descent has been bumpy enough that Ducky has been in the bathroom since we disembarked, and the entire Britta Brigade hasn't missed an opportunity to *eeeewwwww* after each upchuck.

"Fret not, Elvie," Byron says jovially. "Oates and I speak the same language. Look! Down below! You can see the station."

Indeed, as we approach the ground, the station comes more clearly into view through the sandstorm that has kept us blind till now. The station itself is fairly small and non-descript: from this altitude it almost looks like a metallic wedding tent, although I know that in reality it's a prefab building with living quarters and an engineering bay. What stands out is the atmospheric generator that towers above the station. It's an enormous orb, with intricately crosshatched paneling running down its sides, making it look something like a baseball the size of a baseball field. Along the top runs a series of vents from which the generator—dormant now—would pump the gaseous cocktail necessary to start the process of transforming Mars from an "uninhabitable rock" to a "prime real estate opportunity."

"You look like you can handle things from here," Oates chimes over the comm again. "If you won't be needing us any further, we'll be off. I hope you find what you're looking for, old sport."

"I do too," Byron says. "Be safe, my friend."

"Good-bye, Miss Elvie," Oates says. "I'll be seeing you before long."

"You be careful," I say, my eyes welling up against my will.

With that, the comm cuts out, and Byron begins our final descent. Ducky enters the cockpit, wiping his mouth and looking very much the worse for wear.

"I still don't see why they're taking the ship with all the guns," he says drearily.

"They're needed back in the fray," Byron says. "*The Albatross* is our fittest fighting vessel. They'll buy us the time we need."

"You hope," comes Chloe's cheery answer.

"He could have at least taken Britta and the rest with him," Ducky moans. "As if puking weren't bad enough, I have to do it with an entire cheerleading squad listening in."

"Truly you've suffered above all others," Chloe says. Ducky starts to respond, but a jolt of turbulence sets him off again, and he rushes back out of the cockpit without another word, holding his hand over his mouth.

"Eeeeeewwwwwww!" comes the chorus of Brittas.

coming in for a landing," Byron says. "Elvie, rry, you're with me."

"I think I should stay behind to look after the repairs, don't you?" Dad says. "We've got the hyperdrive working again, but if the Jin'Kai show up, I'd sure like to have that stealth field operational."

"You're my resident computer wizard, Harry. How am I supposed to access any foreign systems we come across without you?"

"I can't be in two places at once, and I've got more time under the hood with these babies than anyone else here other than yourself. Besides, with a totally foreign system, you'll need someone with a more intuitive feel than I have. In which case, Elvie's your woman," Dad says. I nearly choke on my surprise. "What?" he says. "You know I've always been extraordinarily proud of your acumen."

"I know," I say. "I've just never heard you say I was *better* than you."

"I have every faith in your abilities," Dad tells me.

I think my cheeks are burning.

"You'll need help," I say.

"Donald and Marnie can stay to assist me."

There's a pang in my chest at the thought that I won't be sharing my first martian experience with Ducky. But if Dad actually approves of him as an assistant, I know that will be a good consolation prize in his eyes.

"Fine," I say. "But then you have to keep the Brittas as well. I'm not going anywhere with that lot."

• • •

After activating the station's environmental systems and giving them enough time to pump the station full of breathable air, Cole, Byron, Chloe, and I head down inside. With caution we step into the station via the long entry corridor, which, if my love of schematics and my more-than-decent memory are correct, leads directly into the living quarters—a sparsely furnished area for the initial terraforming crew to sleep and eat in while not operating the massive machinery at the heart of the base. Byron takes the lead, clearly anxious about what we'll discover.

I'm on Mars, I keep having to remind myself with every step. I always dreamed I'd be a part of the Ares Project one day. This isn't exactly the way I envisioned it, but hey, dreams change.

Up ahead Byron comes to a doorway. "Archer, give me a hand with this, would you?" he asks. Cole runs over to his superior, and the two of them attempt to pull the unpowered door open. I stand with Chloe behind the two as they grunt and strain, and Chloe mumbles something under her breath.

"What was that?" I ask.

"I said I don't even know what I'm doing here," she says.

"Well, we're trying to uncover . . . ancient martian secrets . . . that will . . . do something. We hope. Or not."

"It's pointless. Even if you find something, the Jin'Kai are the superior race. They'll win this fight precisely because of their superiority."

"Superior, my occasionally bruised behind," I say. "They might be all burly and, okay, occasionally covered in a slimy impenetrable exoskeleton, but they are *totally* evil."

"Your morality is subjective."

think it's subjective morality to say you shouldn't
girls and use them like cattle."

lmiri do it," she says.

"Well," I start. "That's different." She gives me a look, and I swear it's like looking into a mirror. A really judgy mirror. "Okay, it's not different. But that's one of the things we're going to change."

"I should be with them," Chloe says.

"Them?" I ask, dumbfounded. "'Them' who? The Jin'Kai? Marsden? The ones who stole you from me, messed with your DNA, brainwashed you?" After all this time, I cannot believe that she'd still consider those intergalactic dickheads as her preferred team.

"They didn't brainwash me. You keep treating me like I'm some stupid little kid."

"You're, like, two months old!"

"I have my own mind."

"Yeah, well, tell me when you decide to use it."

Instantly my brain locks up. Because those aren't my words streaming out of my mouth like some uncontrollable verbal diarrhea.

They're my mother's. The one person in the universe I swore I would never be like.

"Look," I say, trying to reset. "I know you don't like me all that much. But trust that I want what's best for you. You are the whole reason I'm doing any of this. Not for the Almiri. Or even the Enosi. Or even flipping mankind. It's all for you, kiddo. So that, when all this is over, nobody gets to decide your fate but you. I'd lay down my life for you, annoying brat that you are. Bok Choy *did* lay down his life for you."

I can see from the clenching of her jaw that I may have just pulled the last stable Jenga peg out from under her wavering reserve of restraint.

"*He* didn't lay down anything," she says, sharply enough to cut my heart out in one fluid swipe. "*You* left him." I feel air escape from my lungs, but I can't form any words. My vision goes blurry, and I realize that my eyes are filling with tears. "And *you're* trying to decide my fate right now!"

"Th-that's not true," I stammer. "I . . . tried . . . with Bok . . . I *tried* . . ."

"That's enough!" Cole shouts suddenly. He storms up to Chloe, getting right in her face. "I don't want to hear another shitty thing out of you, or so help me, I might just put you over my knee. That is *your mother*, do you understand? Your mother, who carried you for nine months, who gave birth to you, cared for you under unbelievably hard circumstances, and when you were stolen away from her, stopped at nothing—*nothing*—to get you back. Now, we're all sorry about what happened to Bok Choy. He was incredibly noble and brave. But don't you dare crap on what both he and Elvie have done for you."

"She could have waited," Chloe says, suddenly crying. "She could have—"

"She could have done jack shit. He was already dying, Chloe. He was bleeding out from his gut. And if the stab wound didn't get him, all that messed-up weird science Marsden played with his DNA would have. You know that. He knew what he needed to do, and that was save you and your mother, because he loved you. The way we love you."

Chloe is a ball of tears now. She takes a halfhearted swing at Cole, only to fall into his arms without resistance. As she sobs into his chest, I wipe my own tears away and take in the lovable doofus whom I've been so hard on the past year. It's as if he's suddenly blossoming into an honest-to-goodness father right in front of me.

"It's okay, sweetie," Cole tells Chloe in a hushed tone, rocking her gently. "It's okay. I mean, it's not, because we're all probably going to die soon, but you're okay."

Ah, Cole.

"We need to keep moving," Byron announces. He has jimmied the door open far enough that we can all fit through. "The strange power sources were reported down this way. The crew was excavating the area when they were recalled."

Cole guides Chloe as she slips through the doorway after Byron and starts down the stairs. I tap Cole on the shoulder, and when he turns around, I surprise him with a big hug.

"What's that for?" he asks.

"You're going to be a great dad," I tell him. "Check that. You *are* a great dad."

Cole grins. "Guess my paternity suit had to kick in sometime."

I pause, mentally accessing my Cole-to-English translator. "Cole," I say slowly. "Did you by any chance mean 'paternal instinct'?"

He nods. "Yeah. That thing."

And with that, Cole squeezes his way through the doorway. I follow closely behind.

The stairs spiral downward for several dozen meters before

they disappear and give way to a red, ashy rock path.

"We must be getting close," Byron says. He carries a sensor pad in front of him, much like the tracker we used to find Chloe back on the ozone station. "The readings are getting . . . for lack of a better term, weird. There's definitely a power signature down here, and it's not one of ours."

"So, did these guys find something underneath their station by sheer dumb luck?" I ask.

"No," Byron answers. "Each station was positioned in an area that seemed likely to have supported life at some point in the past. While the surface of Mars had been lifeless for eons when we first began the Ares Project, it seemed reasonable to assume that if there had been a native species, that species would have developed a subterranean civilization. And the most likely starting points for building such a system would have been below where the native species had lived prior to the environment's becoming uninhabitable."

"Of course," I say, vowing never to ask for explanations from an epic poet again. (Seriously, there's a reason the guy never took up haiku.)

"Here," Byron says. We are facing a large rock front.

"Are you sure?" I ask. "The path continues down this way."

"The signature is coming from behind this wall." Byron pockets the sensor pad and exchanges it for two wonky-looking pistols. He hands one to Cole.

"Concentrated pattern, Archer," Byron says. "Let's try not to cave the whole tunnel in around us."

I flinch at the sound of the weapons echoing through the corridor as Cole and Byron fire into the rock face, zigzagging their shots from the ceiling down to the floor. The rock crumbles away more and more rapidly, and after a few moments they stop firing to let the dust settle.

"Wow," Chloe says as the results of their labor come into focus. "More rock. Great job, guys."

"Wait," I say. I step forward. It's true that the surface looks nearly identical to the rock that was just cleared away. But something seems . . . off. I place my hand on the surface. It's cool to the touch, but the longer my hand stays in place, the warmer the surface gets. I place my other hand on the rock, and suddenly a low humming begins to emanate from the rock.

"Incredible," Byron says.

"Well, what do I do now?" I ask. "Say something in old Elvish?"

Where's Ducky when you need someone to laugh at your hilarious nerd jokes? Not a peep from these guys. Nothing.

But soon I've stopped caring that my humor goes unappreciated, because the rock begins to slide apart down a middle seam, and it becomes clear that it isn't a rock wall at all but a door. It parts all the way, revealing a large circular room crafted out of more red mineral, similar to the door. We step inside, our footsteps echoing in the empty space.

And then the wall/door slams shut behind us.

"Shit," I say. I place both hands on the door again, but nothing. There's no visible seam to work either.

"So here we are, in a pitch-black cave, under Mars," Chloe says. "Now what?"

As if in response to her question, the room springs to life. Lights flash along the sheer walls without any hint of a source.

It appears as if the rock itself is illuminating the space. Along the curved walls, large sections begin to flicker with strange, scrolling symbols.

"Did I do that?" Chloe asks in a whisper.

Cole is more direct. "Helllllloooooo?" he calls loudly. "Who's there, please?"

I place a hand on his arm. "It's not a who," I tell him, amazed. "It's a what." I point at the scrolling imagery around us. "It's a screen. This is a computer."

"Then what's that say?" Cole wonders, tracing a few of the gibberish symbols with his finger. "Is it Martian?"

"I don't think it's a language, per se," I reply, slowly examining it. "It looks more like code."

"Very astute, Earth child."

The voice is so otherworldly that even Byron jumps at the sound. We all look around the room frantically but see no one.

"Who's there?" I ask, not even bothering to feel silly for pulling a Cole Archer.

"There is no one there, Earth child. It is simply me. The 'computer,' as you put it. Here. Perhaps this will make for a more fluid exchange of data."

The center of the ceiling begins to glow, and a cone of red light shoots down to the floor and begins spinning around. After a few moments the light takes shape as a tall, humanoid form, almost like a regular person but thinner, hairless, and with large, oblong black eyes.

"Greetings, travelers. You have come very far. I am Merv. How may I assist you?"

Chapter Thirteen

WHEREIN, IF YOU THOUGHT THAT THERE WAS NOTHING FURTHER TO LEARN ABOUT ALIEN LIFE, YOU WOULD BE WRONG. SOOOOOOO WRONG.

"*You seem confused by my appearance,*" Merv says as he looks at each of us in turn. Well, not looks, I guess—I'm assuming this room-slash-computer has camera sensors recording our every move, embedded somewhere unseen, along with the magically appearing monitors, but the holographic projection is doing a good imitation of "looking" with its massive dark eyes as it registers our movements.

"What's to be confused about?" I say. "You're a computer. This is what martians looked like. End of story."

"*Ah, yes, 'martians.' Perhaps I should clarify—*"

"I said *end of story*. There are too many different alien species to keep track of already. We're kind of on a tight schedule here, and I honestly don't care anymore. So, you're a martian. Let's move on."

I don't know if holographic representations of AI can get offended, but apparently they can *look* offended. Merv's eyes widen in what I'm assuming is a martian expression of indignation.

"*Very well,*" he says at last. "*Tell me, then. What is your purpose here?*"

"Well, like you said, we're from Earth. But we're not all, strictly speaking, earthlings. This here"—I point at Byron—"is my grandfather. He's what's called an Almiri."

Byron is staring, mouth agape, at Merv. "I've waited a very long time for this," he tells the holograph earnestly.

"*Accessing . . . ah. 'Almiri. Long-range colony seed ship, planetary arrival 2656.8 cycles ago. You have taken the name of your vessel. When your kind arrived here, you called yourself Klahnia.*"

"That's correct," Byron replies. He seems pleased that Merv knows so much about his people.

"*Why have you returned? Doing so violates our pact.*"

"Pact?" Byron asks. "We come seeking help. Earth is under attack."

"*Activating external sensors . . . Accessing . . .*" Merv seems to stare blankly at the far wall for several moments. "*Yes, it appears that Earth is indeed under attack,*" he says as he refocuses on us. "*I am detecting three distinct engine signatures. Two are significantly more advanced than the other.*"

"Those are our ships helping the humans," Byron explains. "The aggressors call themselves Jin'Kai."

"*Analysis suggests they are Klahnia.*"

"Yes," Byron admits. "It's a long story."

"*Your female companion does not care for long stories.*"

"And yet that's all I ever seem to get," I mutter.

Merv turns back to me, his eyes rotating upward slightly. *"You are not Klahnia."*

"Good eye."

"You are not human."

"Two for two. Want to cash out now, or try for the Kia?"

"Your query does not compute. However, it appears hybridization was a success."

That jolts all of us, even Cole, who has been way more focused on the flashing lights than the conversation with the sentient computer.

"You know about the hybrids?" I ask.

"Yes. Shall I explain? Or do you prefer again to rest on assumptions?"

"Explain away."

"I could use pictures and small words if that would help."

"When did you get so snarky?"

"I am programmed to adapt my interface to communicate more readily with the user."

"Score one for the ancient computer guy," Chloe mutters.

"Right," I tell Merv. "So, speaking of adaptation?"

"The Klahnia ship Almiri arrived on Barsoom expecting to find a primitive peoples they could easily conquer and use for the purpose of procreating their species."

"Conquer?" Byron starts. "We would never—"

"There will be time for baseless indignation after I have completed my expository. To continue, the Klahnia did not find this to be the case. The society they intruded upon was a flourishing and advanced species, considerably more developed in many regards than themselves. The attempt to subjugate the

native population was drawn-out, bloody, and fruitless."

"So you guys defeated the Almiri?" I ask. Dreams of martian superweapons once again dance in my head. "Do you still have the weapons you used to beat them?"

"There are no large-scale weapon systems left operational on this planet. If this is what you came seeking, then may I suggest you . . . Accessing Earth cultural databases . . . 'Go Fish.'"

Well, that's that, then. As nifty as this history lesson has been, it's all been for nothing. No martian weapons. No answer for the Jin'Kai fleet. No hope.

"Please do not exhibit an outwardly defeatist attitude. Your problems would not be solved by finding weapons here."

"Is that a fact?" Chloe says. Merv considers her, his eyes rotating like when he was looking at me earlier.

"Our conflict with the Klahnia had no victor. Neither side had definitive technological superiority, at least where the arts of war were concerned. After a time neither side had the ability or desire to continue. A treaty was agreed upon, including several stipulations. First, that the Klahnia would depart, never to return. In exchange, we would provide them with an alternative home suitable to their needs."

"Earth," I say. "So if you got the Almiri to leave, why aren't there any martians running around? What happened?"

"The planet was determined unsuitable for the further development of the species, and so it was abandoned."

"Where did they go?" Cole asks.

Look who just started paying attention.

"My programming does not include this information."

My wheels are spinning. "But I thought there were only

six species in the galaxy that the Klahnia could use as breeding hosts," I say. "That was the whole point of the six colony ships, wasn't it, Byron?"

"That's what we've always believed," Byron says.

"There are more than six galactic species compatible with the Klahnia's breeding requirements."

"And humans just happened to be one of them, sitting right next door to you martian folks?"

"No."

I scratch my head. Cole apparently feels head-scratchy too.

"Okay, I'm lost," he says. "I know this comes as a shock."

Merv's eyes twist in his head again, and suddenly one of the monitor displays pushes away from the wall and hovers in three dimensions in front of us. A stream of data scrolls over the screen, and maps that appear to be star charts arrange themselves around the edges of the text.

"My information banks contain the histories of 4,672 sentient species throughout the known universe. We have been observing and studying other worlds considerably longer than the Klahnia— or Almiri, as they now refer to themselves. Of these known species, one in ten exhibit the genetic markers that would make them suitable hosts for the parasitic breeding cycle of the Almiri."

"You're saying there are more than four hundred species out there that they could be breeding with?" Chloe asks, sounding as incredulous as I feel. "Marsden doesn't know that. I'm sure none of the other Jin'Kai do either."

"More than four hundred viable species, yes. However, there was never any intention of offering up another defenseless species to the fate the Klahnia had intended for us."

"What do you call siccing them on the humans, then, huh?" I ask.

"*Earthlings were chosen with a different purpose in mind.*"

"And what purpose would that be?"

"*The Klahnia were a brutal, violent, unpredictable race. They were also, colloquially speaking, not great planners. If they were to succeed in their goal of finding a suitable host species, because of the nature of their procreation cycle, they most likely would have exhausted their potential hosts within a few hundred years, thereby forcing themselves to move on to another planet, and then another, and another, leaving nothing but husks in their wake.*"

"Sounds familiar," Cole says.

"*While not a perfect match for Klahnia breeding, humans appeared*"—Merv emphasizes the word "appeared," even raising his holographic eyebrows—"*on many levels to be exactly that. So much so that the Klahnia were fooled into believing humans could indeed be used to help spawn future generations of their species. However, given enough time, the dominant species' genetic traits would surely exert their will. And the strongest evolutionary trait in all the universe is the ability to adapt.*"

"Hybrids," I say. I feel like I've been struck by lightning, my body vibrating as the current runs across my skin. "You sent the Almiri to Earth because you knew that they'd start producing hybrid children. The mutation that produced the Enosi didn't come from the Almiri. It came from humans."

"Yes," Merv says. "*The will to adapt and survive is stronger on Earth than on nearly any other planet recorded. If environmental factors threaten a species, that species simply adapts to the new variables to continue to thrive. Failure to do so leads to extinction."*

"But humans aren't stronger than the Almiri, or the Jin'Kai," Chloe argues. "They're weaker, slower. They live a fraction as long."

"And yet they survive. The enormous dinosaurs of Earth's past were more powerful than any other species within half a million light years. Yet when disaster struck the planet—literally— those who could not adapt perished. And what mighty animal took their place? The chicken. Do not mistake the strength of an individual as indicative of the strength of the species."

Beside me Byron lets out a bemused chuckle. "'Veni, vidi, vici,'" he says, shaking his head.

"Who's Vinny Vidivici?" Cole asks.

"It's Latin, dear boy, from one of our forbearers. 'I came, I saw, I conquered.' It's all so terribly ironic now, isn't it? First we were gods. Then kings, emperors, conquerors. Then we discovered science, the arts, social justice. All the while, we thought we were influencing mankind. We thought ourselves their betters. But it was man who changed us." Byron strikes a pose, one arm crooked, hand resting on his hip, while the other arm shoots out dramatically in front of him. "'How happy is the blameless vestal's lot! The world forgetting, by the world forgot.' How cruel that this wondrous revelation comes to us at the twilight hour of our story."

"Is he always like this?"

"As long as I've known him," I tell Merv.

"What I don't understand," Cole says, "is why our ancestors didn't just wipe humans out completely, the way they tried on Mars, the way the Jin'Kai have done over and over again?"

"*For a time we kept watch. Envoys were sent periodically to make sure that your people upheld our agreement and followed the Code.*"

"You wrote the Code?" Byron asks. He's surprised, sure, but almost giddy at the revelation. More fodder for the poem, I suspect. "All of our laws, all of our dearly held beliefs, found their origin here?"

"*It was necessary to ensure that your kind did not over-populate too quickly. The mutation would need adequate time to spread organically through human-hybrid mating.*"

"I don't think time is going to be a luxury afforded us by the Jin'Kai," I say. "With their numbers they'll make the entire planet infertile within a single generation."

"*That is impossible. The mutation has already achieved biological dominance. The movement toward the new species is now inevitable. Human parents or Klahnia parents, the major-ity of births will be the same. Hybrid. The unification of all. It cannot be avoided.*" Merv pauses. "*It appears we have more visitors.*"

"Visitors?" Cole asks. "Who?"

"Who do you think?" I reply, looking at the display. "Jin'Kai. Devastators. Three ships landed right outside."

"The others will be sitting ducks out there!" Cole cries.

I examine the sensor readout—the martian systems turn out to be quite intuitive—but I can't seem to find our shuttle anywhere.

"Dad must have gotten the stealth shield activated," I say.

Byron looks over my shoulder. "If the Devastators are

scouring the area, it won't be long before they find the ship, stealth shield or not."

"You're right," I agree. "We've got to get them in here before the Jin'Kai discover them. Merv, open the doors so we can get our friends."

"I'm afraid I cannot do that," Merv says.

"What? Why not?"

"The new arrivals appear to be very aggressive. My preservation protocols prohibit me from willfully allowing such forces access to my data banks."

"My father's out there, you stupid holographic twit!" I yell. "And my best friend, and his girlfriend. And . . . a bunch of annoying cheerleaders. But they're people too, and if you think I'm going to let you—"

"I'm sorry. The entrance must remain sealed."

I watch the display helplessly as the motion sensors pick up several signals spreading out in military formation outside the entrance to the terraforming station. The Devastators are dangerously close to where our ship is most likely sitting, cloaked. It's only a matter of time.

"I can't sit here and just watch," I say.

"Don't worry," Cole says. "The Jin'Kai will probably follow the same power source we did. Maybe your Dad and the others can take off safely while the Devastators attack us here."

"Very comforting, Cole," I tell him. Damn. We were so close. I could practically taste the deus ex—

"Pardon me, but would you like me to activate this installation's defensive systems?"

We all turn and stare at Merv, mouths agape.

"I thought you said there were no weapons left on the planet!" Cole screeches.

"There are no weapons that you could use off-planet in a conflict. However, this installation is fortified with energy shielding, several direct-energy turrets, and—"

"Yes. Yes! Activate them!" we all shout.

"*Very good. Shall I transport your friends on the stealthed vessel inside before raising the shields?*"

"You have *molecular transporters*?" Byron asks. "I'm most impressed."

"Could have used that information *before* my heart attack, Merv," I say. "But, yes. Beam them up, Scotty."

"*I am not sure I understand the command. Accessing . . .*" Merv's eyes twist in his head for several seconds. "*Ah, yes. 'Scotty.' Charming. There is interference from the rudimentary stealth field. I cannot ascertain if they are all friendlies. There are more than a dozen life-forms aboard. Perhaps these 'Jin'Kai' have already boarded?*"

"No, that would be our in-house cheerleading squad," I say. "They're not exactly friendlies . . . but I guess you'd better beam them all in anyway."

Beside me Chloe lets out a groan. And I can't even blame her.

"*Very well. Initiating transport.*"

There is a flickering light in the center of the room, and forms begin to take shape. At first they're transparent, but as the shimmering light around them fades, they become more solid. But something's wrong. Only a handful of them are standing up. Most of them are lying flat on the ground. As they come into focus, it looks like all of the Brittas are out cold on the floor. Then I spot Marnie, also unconscious. The hairs on the back of my neck prickle.

"What the hell?" Chloe asks.

Standing next to the unconscious girls are three people—Dad and Ducky, wearing some sort of hooded suits, and behind them . . .

"You just won't stay dead, will you, Doc?"

Marsden looks discombobulated. Which I guess is to be expected when you've just been de- and re-molecularized.

"What is this?" he asks. His muscles are coiled and his eyes wide. Then, as though it's the only logical move, Marsden swiftly grabs Ducky and pulls him into a headlock, brandishing a weapon and pointing it directly at Duck's noggin.

"Easy with that thing," I say. The blood in my veins runs ice cold, but I try to explain things as calmly as I can to the madman with the ray gun. "You're on Mars. Or, well, under it." He still seems confused. "Lemme guess," I continue. "You hid on the shuttle when we blasted our way out of the Rust Belt, like a rat leaving a sinking ship."

"Such a way with words," Marsden says, quickly returning to his usual evil-scientist-in-charge shtick. "You wouldn't believe that I always forget that." He makes a quick survey of the room. "Weapons. All of them. Kick them over."

Reluctantly Byron and Cole take the blasters they used to carve the rock face and slide them across the floor toward Marsden.

"What did you do, Marsden?" I ask. "Are they all dead?"

"What, the cattle?" Marsden asks, darting his eyes down

toward Marnie and the Brittas. "No. The plan was to gas everyone and then commandeer the ship."

"Donald and I were outside doing repairs," Dad explains, pulling his shielded hood back so that he can be heard. "When we reentered the ship, we found the girls unconscious and our friend here trying to start up the engines."

You'd think I'd be insanely pissed about this new development. But the fact that I don't have to listen to a bunch of Brittas prattle about Cole's butt in this tense moment is lessening my rage.

Marsden's still got my bestie in a headlock, though, so there's that to deal with.

"Mind telling me what is going on?" Marsden asks. And given the gun and all, I'm inclined to answer him.

I point to the hologram who's been taking in our standoff with fascinated detachment. "This is Merv," I explain. "He's kind of the resident record-keeper here on Mars. We came here looking for a superweapon to blast your buddies to smithereens with, but what we found instead was a big old truth bomb. It's all pretty long and convoluted, but the short version is: You're done. It's all over. Your experiments are based on bad science, Doctor. You let your prejudice blind you to the truth. The mutation responsible for the Enosi hybrids does not originate in the Almiri but in man."

Marsden slits his eyes at me. "That's impossible," he says. "The mutation appears in the gestating Almiri fetus."

"See for yourself," I say. I flick through the screen in front of me. "Merv, put the pertinent info up for the good doctor to read, would you?"

"This has been the strangest day," Merv replies, but he follows orders. The data streams on a holographic display in front of Marsden.

Marsden's eyes scroll over the text, and you can practically see his conviction melting away with each line he reads.

"This is impossible," he repeats.

"It doesn't matter how many times you try to graft your own DNA onto any of us," I tell him. "The stronger species will always win out. And humans are the stronger species. So suck on that until it tastes like candy."

"I am not in the mood for games, Elvie."

"Neither am I. The writing is literally on the wall, Doc. So maybe you should just put down the gun and go to your Devastator buddies out there for an honorable beheading, or whatever."

"Speaking of which," Merv interjects. *"The encroaching aliens have come into contact with the first line of turrets. Shields at ninety-three percent. Analysis suggests defensive systems will hold for ten minutes."*

"They're here?" Marsden asks, his face going white.

"Dearheart, what exactly is going on?" Dad asks.

"Same old stuff, Dad. Aliens. Revelation. Drama. Put the gun down, Doc."

Marsden ignores me, staring intently at the genetic analysis scrolling in front of him. "My work . . ." I've got to give it to him, the man sounds truly gutted. "If all this is true . . . If we had known, we never would have come to your backward planet."

And there it is. The cartoon lightbulb going off above my head. "I guess you wouldn't have, would you?" I say. I turn to my new buddy the hologram. "Merv, maybe you can help us out after all."

"*As I mentioned previously, there are no weapons systems left on the planet that would be of use to you in a planetary conflict.*"

"We don't need to beat the Devastators," I say, thinking things through out loud. "We only need to make them realize how pointless beating us would be."

Byron shakes his head. "I don't follow," he says.

"What are you getting at, Elvie?" Marsden asks. His grip on Ducky has not loosened in the slightest.

"The whole point of this stupid invasion is for the Jin'Kai to find a new source of baby mommas, right? But if we could get a signal out, share the info about the mutation, let them see that hybridization is an inevitable and systemic thing at this point, and there's no reason to stay . . ."

"Then they'll just exterminate the whole planet," Marsden says.

"That sounds bad," Cole puts in.

"They wouldn't waste their time with extermination if they have somewhere better to be," I say. "Heck, this might even save *your* bacon, Doc."

"Elvie . . ." Ducky starts to ask. But Marsden squeezes more tightly, and he shuts up.

"Merv," I say, attempting to keep my cool. *A plan, Elvie. All you need is a plan.* "You said there are, what, four hundred some species out there compatible with the Klahnia? I'm assuming they're pretty far away, right? I mean, seeing as the Almiri never found them before."

"The species are a considerable distance from this system, yes."

"And you have broadcast capabilities, right? If I wanted to transmit a message on an open frequency, the Jin'Kai fleet would be able to pick it up and understand it?"

"That is correct."

"So if they're so desperate to start making babies, there'd be very little reason to stay here and fight before they left. If we could send them coordinates . . ."

"It is against my programming to allow you to expose a vulnerable species to an aggressor."

"Yeah, that makes sense," I say. "Do you have a user interface I can operate manually?"

"Yes, but—"

"Can you activate it, please?"

"It is against my programming to—"

"I got that part. Just open the goddamn interface."

"Very well." Merv's eyes widen and spin, and a three-dimensional holographic keyboard panel appears in front of me, complete with a monitor. But when Marsden retrains his gun on me, I take a step back from the keyboard, arms raised.

"What are you playing at?" Marsden asks.

"I'm not playing, Doc. What you're seeing here is a last ditch effort to keep us *all* alive."

Marsden appears very unsure—an unusual look for him. His gun arm relaxes ever so slightly, which I take to mean that I momentarily have his attention. I move back to the keyboard. The cryptic martian code scrawls in front of me.

"I slept through Beginners' Martian freshman year, Merv," I say, already furiously scrolling through the data in front of me. "Mind throwing a universal translator my way?" Cole and Chloe crowd around me as English appears on the screen. "Show me star charts for the nearest compatible species." Merv complies.

Embedded in the charts are data about each inhabited planet, detailing varieties of plant and animal life, sentient species (some planets, remarkably, have more than one), and levels of technological advancement. It's pretty much the most astounding discovery in history, but I'll have time to contemplate it later. Hopefully. In the present I need coordinates. The *right* coordinates.

"Elvie, don't," Byron says. "This is wrong."

"He's right, Elvs," Cole says. "You can't just shove the Jin'Kai off onto some other unsuspecting race because it's convenient."

For his part Ducky makes a gagging noise that I take as agreement.

"Look, I don't know about you all," I say, "but I just met my daughter, like, a week ago, and for most of that time she's been a real bitch. No offense, sweetie."

"None taken."

"I'd like a little more time to get to know her better, and worldwide annihilation would seriously get in the way of that. I mean to survive this. I mean for us all to survive."

"If we were to sacrifice another planet's freedom to save our own skins," Byron warns—and I swear I will knee him in the groin if he starts in on the poetry right now—"that would make us no better than the Jin'Kai."

"He's right, dearheart," Dad says gently. "While I cannot

contemplate oblivion, I find it a sweeter fate than that of being an accomplice to mass genocide."

"All right. That's just about enough, I think." It's Marsden who says it. When I look up, his gun is trained steadily on me, his forearm still firmly pressed into Ducky's windpipe.

"Doc, this will work, I swear. You just have to—"

"Trust you? I think not." He takes a step back toward the sealed door. "You are all quite convincing, but I'm not about to be hoodwinked by a half-assed ruse concocted by the Almiri and their pets."

"This is the only way, Marsden," I plead, doing my best to stay calm. "What do you think you're going to do, just walk out there and fly away happily with the monsters who want to kill you?"

"That's exactly what I intend to do. But they won't lay a finger on me," he says, throwing his glance to Chloe. "Not once I have her."

My heart does a nosedive straight to the pit of my stomach. "Forget it, Doc. She's with us now. You burned that bridge when you revealed yourself as the cold, calculating prick that you are."

Marsden trains the gun on Chloe.

"I don't care if I have to carry her out in pieces. She's coming with me."

"This may not be the best time," Merv interjects, *"but the intruders have crossed the first threshold and have engaged the secondary turret position. Shields are at sixty-seven percent."*

"I don't think you've thought this through, Doc," I say. "Taking my daughter with you won't change any of the facts that we've learned here today."

"This is not your daughter," Marsden says. His tone is so matter-of-fact that it sounds like a smirk.

"What do you mean?" I feel breathless. "Of course she is."

"Your troublesome mother took your mewling infant when she abandoned my facility weeks ago," Marsden tells me. "This one is of my making."

Chloe and I lock eyes with each other, and I'm not sure which of us is more terrified.

"A clone?" Cole asks. His voice is weak, nearly defeated. It's a tone I don't think I've ever heard from him.

"But the tracker . . . ," I say. "It led me right to her. It . . . it *beeped*."

"The tracer is genetic," Byron offers. His voice is gentle, as though he knows that what he's about to explain will gut me. "If Chloe is really a clone, it's possible the tracer could have been transferred into her DNA as well."

I spent all that time rescuing my baby girl, and now I've lost her all over again. And my mom has her? Where? Are they safe?

No. No time for this. You're in a cave underneath the surface of Mars, Elvie Nara. You have an evil alien doctor holding you at gunpoint. The lives of your father, your friends, and yes, even the clone of your daughter, are at stake. Push it down. Push it deep down and save that worry for later. Right now you have to save the world.

"Marsden," I say. "You're a putz."

"Not your best insult, Miss Nara, but given the circumstances I'll let it slide."

"Taking Chloe won't help you one bit."

"It is my fifth attempt at splicing your offspring's hybrid

DNA with the superior Jin'Kai code, and the only one to survive this long," Marsden says. "My best shot at creating a sustainable breeding population lies in her cells."

"Marsden, haven't you listened to a single thing that I've been saying?" I snap. "Your DNA *cannot overwrite the hybrid gene*. This was all by design. You lie with Enosi, and Enosi is all you're going to get."

"*Lies!*" Marsden booms. "I will unlock the secret! Make it viable. We will never need to depend on an inferior race again. We will be eternal!"

"*I should point out,*" Merv butts in, "*that the intruders have engaged the final line of turrets. Shields at twenty-nine percent. If this room is breached, I will be forced to terminate life support.*"

"Do you plan on being a complete racist idiot the rest of your soon-to-be-very-short life?" I rage at the doc. "There's still a way for everyone to walk away from this!"

"You know, Elvie, now that I think about it, I don't find you all that charming anymore. Perhaps your particular brand of snark has grown old." He tightens his grip on his gun. "Maybe it's time that we shut you up once and for all."

"Stop!" Chloe shouts. She looks at me for a brief second, then turns to Marsden, her mind made up. "I'll go with you."

The surprise is written all over Marsden's face, as I'm sure it is on mine.

"I'll come without a fight, all right?" Chloe tells him. "Just don't hurt anyone."

"I'm not in the mood for tricks," Marsden warns.

"No tricks. You leave them be, and I come with you. You

don't, and you'll have to extract the DNA you need from your ass, 'cause that's where my foot will be."

"Chloe," I say, suddenly choked up. "You don't have to do this. There must be some other—"

"If there's one thing you taught me, it's that I have the right to choose my own path," she says. "So. This is my choice. Besides, I'm not even really your daughter."

"I might not have given birth to you," I say. "But either way, you're my daughter. That foot-up-the-ass remark seems to prove it."

I get a slight smile out of her with that. "I hope you find your real daughter," she tells me. Then she turns back to Marsden. "We have a deal?"

"We have a deal," he says.

Chloe walks slowly over to him, her hands raised. As soon as she gets close to him, Marsden shoves Ducky away and grabs hold of her, pulling her against him into the same headlock.

"Of course, you realize I can't just leave them here to continue what they're doing," Marsden says, raising the gun toward me again, his finger on the trigger.

"And of course you realize that you should have checked me for a weapon," Chloe says. Her hand flies into her tunic and she squeezes. The blaster shot sizzles through the loose fabric on her back and catches Marsden in the ribs. "How's that free will taste, scumbag?"

Marsden cries out, stumbling back a few steps. Chloe tries to pull the gun free to get off another shot, but Marsden kicks her squarely in the face, knocking her out cold.

"Chloe!" I scream, rushing to her on the ground.

That's when Cole and Byron make their move on Marsden. The doctor gets off a shot that hits Byron in the shoulder, sending him sprawling. Cole collides with Marsden, whose gun falls to the ground, and Ducky makes a beeline for it, nearly overrunning the weapon, fumbling it, and kicking it ahead of him as he stumbles, bent over. Even Dad tries to get in on the fisticuffs, grappling with Cole and Marsden, but one well-placed kick into his bad knee, and he crumples to the floor in agony. Marsden turns over and rolls Cole into a choke hold. Cole's face turns purple, the veins throbbing in his throat and forehead.

"I expected a little better after our first sparring match," Marsden tells him.

"Stop it!" I cry. I'm cradling Chloe's head in my lap on the ground, tears streaming down my face. "You're killing him!"

"That is the general idea," Marsden says.

"Let him go. Now."

Marsden turns to see Ducky training his own gun on him. Ducky's sweating and trembling. I want to tell Duck to step back, that he's too close to Marsden, but before I can open my mouth, the doctor reaches out and snatches the gun right from Ducky's hands. He flings Cole to the floor, where he gasps desperately for air, unable to move.

Marsden grins at me as he trains the gun on Ducky. "Perhaps I'll let you watch me kill everyone you love before I get to you," he says. "How would you like that, Elvie?"

"Please," I whimper. "No."

Dad has crawled over to me and is wrapping me and Chloe in a protective embrace. Ducky looks at me wistfully and smiles.

"Elvie . . . ," Dad whispers. "Listen."

That's when I hear the humming sound. Marsden hears it too—a split second too late. Ducky drops and covers his face just as the blaster explodes in the doctor's hand, flinging him across the room, where he crashes into a bloody heap on the floor. The blast knocks Ducky in the opposite direction and throws me and Dad back on the floor as well. The ceiling is spinning above me, until I focus in on the red hologram staring down at me.

"*Are you badly injured?*" Merv asks, blinking.

"I don't think so," I say.

"*Good. I just wanted to inform you that shielding will fail in approximately ninety seconds. It's been nice getting to know you.*"

"Don't write me off just yet, Merv," I say, rising unsteadily from the ground. "Show me that manual interface again."

"Did you see that?" Ducky asks a little too loudly. His ears are probably ringing even more than mine are. "Elvie, did you see what I did? I did it! I totally did it." He tries to stand up too quickly, and winces, holding his shoulder.

"I saw, Ducky," I say without looking away from the display. "Great job."

"I overloaded the pistol, just like Chloe did before." He's still beaming with excitement. "I tricked him into grabbing the gun, and then it blew up right in his hand!"

"Like I said, I saw. Cole, make sure Chloe is okay."

"I hope that guy stays dead this time," Cole mutters. His voice is hoarse, and he rubs his throat as he makes his way over to Chloe. As if in answer, a moan emanates from Marsden's slumped mass, and the doctor shifts slightly on the ground.

"Oh, come *on!*" Cole says. "Are you kidding me?"

Merv considers Marsden. *"This one is badly damaged. Disintegrated limb. Ruptured internal organs. Heavy blood loss. He will be deceased in moments."*

"Good," Ducky says, but then he stops himself. "I mean, not 'good,' but . . . I never killed anyone before." He looks at me. "I don't think I like it, Elvie."

"How . . . do you think . . . I feel?" Marsden manages to flip himself over, and the sight of him is enough to make me sick. The left side of his face looks *melted*, and his left arm has been blown off past the elbow. His stomach is a mass of leaking organs, and his shirt is so slick with blood that I can't even remember what color it was originally. Upon looking at the doctor, Ducky immediately barfs on the ground.

"Done in . . . by a human," Marsden croaks.

"Just die already," I say. "I'm so done with you."

"He really does seem like quite the anal orifice," Merv remarks.

So I guess there's a little tweaking needed in the AI's colorful metaphor subroutine.

"Elvie." Dad puts his hands on mine, halting my typing. "Stop, dearheart. It's over."

"I really wish I had time to debate this with you guys, but I don't. You're just going to have to trust that I know what I'm doing." I put the last touches on the info packet. "Merv, prepare to upload the packet."

"While I am impressed that you have managed to override the considerable safeguards in my programming in such a short amount of time, I still must protest this course of action."

"Listen to the ancient artificial intelligence, dearheart." •

"I just need a few more seconds," I say through gritted teeth.

There is a sudden blast from outside. The lights momentarily flutter, and red dust falls from the ceiling. The unmistakable sound of blaster fire can be heard, each shot sending another shudder through the room.

"Shielding has failed," Merv states. *"The door will hold a few seconds only. You have my sympathies, truly."*

"Elvie, enough!" Byron grabs me and pulls me away from the keyboard. "Look at what we've learned here today. My species believed that they were a benevolent, enlightened people who bestowed their goodness on mankind. Our forefathers buried the truth about how we really came to live as we do, and that arrogance has lead to our undoing. Let the cycle of madness end here. Do not sentence another people to our fate."

"You're forgetting that the martians pushed the Almiri off onto Earth in the first place. They didn't have a problem making their problems our problems. So it's not just you who's getting boned here." I struggle against his grip, but he's too strong.

"They did so in an effort to change us for the better. They were motivated by something greater than mere self-preservation. They had a plan. You can't do something as reckless as this without thinking it through! You don't have a plan."

I stop struggling and look Byron dead in the eye.

"I'm Elvie Nara. I *always* have a plan." I turn to Merv, who is watching our struggle with detached curiosity. "Merv, send the info packet."

"Don't do it!" Byron shouts.

"*I am sorry,*" Merv says, "*but she has overwritten my programming.*"

Merv's eyes spin in his head.

"*The packet has been delivered.*"

Suddenly an enormous blast shakes the entire room, and the door crumbles away in shards of red ore. An entire squadron of decked-out Devastators bursts through, weapons at the ready. They train their weapons on us and bark indecipherable commands at us in their own language. They seem slightly confused by the pile of Brittas lying, unconscious, on the ground, not to mention the pile of Marsden.

"We surrender!" Ducky cries, hands in the air.

I simply grasp my father's hand and squeeze. "We were so close," I say.

"I love you, dearheart," Dad replies.

I feel someone take my other hand. I look down. It's Chloe. She smiles at me and shrugs, and I can't help but laugh. It seems to confuse the lead Devastator. He charges toward me and picks me straight up off the ground with one monster claw, despite the protests from my friends. The Devastator barks something at me, its long dagger right in my face.

"*Excuse me?*" Merv says. The Devastator turns and glares at him. "*I have an incoming message from the alien fleet.*"

Suddenly Merv's image disappears, and in its place stands a tall, imposing Devastator wearing some sort of cape. The death squad immediately stands at attention. The image barks at them for a few seconds, and the lead Devastator responds, his tone confused-sounding (well, as confused-sounding as mangled spoons in the garbage disposal can get). The answer he receives sounds incredibly angry, even by Devastator standards. Then the image blurs once more and Merv reappears.

"The transmission has ended."

The Devastator with the kung fu grip on my throat looks at me and narrows his yellow eyes. His jointed teeth ripple in a cascade from one side of his mouth to the other, a sort of disdainful Jin'Kai sneer, I suppose. I feel his putrid breath on my face and prepare myself for the worst. Then, without warning, the gnarly creep drops me roughly to the ground. He barks a command to the others, and to my great shock, they all turn and head out of the room.

"What are they doing?" Dad asks. "Is that it?"

"The package was received and acknowledged. The intruders have received orders to fall back immediately."

"Then it's done," Byron says glumly.

"That's it? The invasion is over?" Ducky asks. "We won?"

"No . . . you . . . can't . . . *leave* me," Marsden gurgles from the floor. "It's a trick. . . . Don't . . . a trick . . ."

Most of the Devastators head out of the room without acknowledging Marsden in any way, but as their leader pulls up the rear, he turns and spits a nasty alien loogie right on the expiring villain. With that, the last of the baddies disappear through the hole in the door. All that's left of our would-be executioners is the sound of their footsteps plodding toward the surface.

Merv's eyes spin in his head. *"It appears that the encroaching fleet has broken off their attack on Earth and is falling back. The 'Devastators,' as you call them, are preparing for immediate departure to the coordinates contained within the data packet."*

"I don't even know what to say," Ducky says, shaking his head. "But didn't that feel . . . *extremely* too easy?"

"The hard part will be living with what we did here," Byron says, staring grimly at the star maps. "You realize we have blood on our hands now," he tells me. "You've doomed an entire planet to a fate of enslavement."

"Have I?" I say. "Or did I just send the Jin'Kai coordinates to a dead moon that could take them hundreds of years to get within sensor range of?"

"What?" Cole asks.

"*Accessing . . . Hmm, yes. Very clever. Very clever indeed. You have a deft hand for programming. The alteration to my data is seamless. I have only been able to detect it by comparing it to the file redundancy.*"

"The code couldn't have fingerprints on it," I say. "It had to look like the original data entered years ago."

Dad is the first to catch on, the lightbulb slowly illuminating over his head. "So they think they're headed to an inhabited planet," he says. And if he doesn't sound proud of his only daughter, then I'll be a clone's mother. "When in fact they're off on a wild goose chase."

"The best way to lie to someone is to give them ninety-nine percent of the truth," I reply.

From the corner Marsden laughs weakly. We all turn to look at him.

"Oh right," I say. "I forgot that you aren't all the way dead yet."

"You're too clever by half, Elvie Nara," Marsden says. "You may have fooled them for a time. But what do you think will happen when they realize you tricked them? They might easily discover another viable planet on their own, or simply realize they were duped. In either case, what's to stop them then from coming back and finishing what they started?"

"When that day comes, we'll be ready for them," I say. "A few hundred years is a good head start on anybody."

"*I would be happy to provide your peoples with any information in the depository that may be of use to them.*"

"See that?" I say. "We even have Merv on board."

"You will fail," Marsden spits. Blood speckles his lips. "You cannot deter my brethren with smoke and mirrors. We will come for you. We are strong."

I kneel down next to Marsden and look him in the eye.

"You are a dinosaur," I say. "I'm the chicken." And I get right in his evil bastard face then, before I let out a triumphant, "*Ba-cawk!*"

The hate rises in Marsden's eyes as he looks at me. He can't move, but his body trembles with rage. He starts to cough, and blood sprays from his mouth, flecking my face. The hate in his eyes clouds over, and his gaze goes blank as his death rattle escapes from his lungs. And then . . . that's it. I stand up and move to Chloe, slip an arm around her waist, and rest my head on her shoulder. To my surprise Chloe offers me a small hug in return.

It's over. Dr. Marsden is finally over.

Murmurs from across the room inform us that the gas Marsden used to dope Marnie and the Britta Brigade is wearing off. Slowly the girls rise from the ground, rubbing their eyes and whining about bed hair. After a few seconds the first of them spots Marsden, which sets off a chain reaction of shrill shrieking and gagging.

"Wha's all this, then?" Marnie says, rising off the floor.

"You missed it!" Ducky says, rushing to her.

"Missed what?"

"Elvie totally saving the entire world. Of course, she couldn't have done it without me. You should've *seen* me with Marsden." Marnie gives Ducky a enormous squeeze of a hug, and he flinches away in pain. "Careful with the ribs," he says. "Most likely they're broken."

"Well, then I guess I best be kissin' ye instead," she replies, and that said, she plants a fat, wet kiss on Ducky, smack on the mouth.

And Ducky, bless him, he doesn't flinch or turn red or anything. He kisses that girl right back.

I look at everyone standing around me. My adoring, adorable father. My pretentious, centuries-old grandfather. My best friend in the whole world. His way too worldly and awesome girlfriend. A young woman who is as much a part of me as if I'd given birth to her myself. And my Cole.

Well, not *my* Cole. But Cole. He offers me that trademark lopsided grin, and it releases any pressure that might still have been lingering in my shoulders. Now that I'm relaxed, I can allow myself to admit that I'm tired. And I need to rest. But not just yet.

There's one more thing I need to do.

Chapter Fourteen

IN WHICH OUR HEROINE CONFRONTS HER PAST AND RECOVERS HER FUTURE

"So, this is the place, huh?" Cole asks, looking around. "I expected something a little more, I dunno, secret-y."

"This is the place," I tell him. The smell of the sea is a refreshingly salty alternative to the stale, canned O_2 I've been breathing lately, first on New Moon and then on Mars. The sun is just starting to poke up over the horizon, sending a cascade of shimmering orange and purple lights across the ocean's surface. The early spring breeze is still bitingly cold, but it feels revitalizing more than anything else. We walk along the sandy beach — me, Cole, and Chloe — our spaceship parked in stealth mode farther down the beach next to the boardwalk, which is completely deserted so early in the season.

"You're sure they're here?" Chloe asks.

"Trust me," I say, glancing at the tracker in my hand. "They're here."

Ahead of us lies a large groyne, rocks held together by

concrete, forming a jetty that juts away from the beach and into the water. I can just make out the silhouette of someone at the edge of the groyne, but I don't really need to get up close to know who it is.

Leave it to my mother to escape from outer space and hightail it directly to *New Jersey*.

We climb up onto the rocks and start the long walk to the edge. Zee sits cross-legged with her back to us, looking out at the waves, rocking back and forth. Sitting next to her is a small radio, and I catch snatches of a low, garbled news report as we approach. I can't quite make it out, but I can guess what they're talking about. Since the Jin'Kai ran off and the Almiri came out publicly to the world, that's pretty much been dominating the news cycle. World news. Local politics. Postulations about how this will impact the tenuous real estate market in "high alien" population areas. The only reason the news anchors ever take a break to talk about March Madness is because Villanova's starting backcourt can trace their ancestry to the other side of the galaxy.

As we get closer, I catch the tail end of the report.

"*. . . the only known survivor of the doomed space station, single-handedly slowing the alien invaders as they made their way toward Earth. So stay tuned for our exclusive interview with Huxtable, the hero of New Moon.*"

Seriously, who *is* that guy?

"Elvan," Zee says without turning around. "I knew it would be only a matter of time before you caught up with us."

It's hard to know exactly how to greet the woman who gave birth to you, faked her own death, let you grow up motherless, then snuck back into your life only to steal your daughter from you. "Hi, Mom!" just sounds like you're repressing things that will boil over at Thanksgiving ten years later. "Hey, you deceitful, double-crossing bitch"—while perhaps appropriate—seems a little too vulgar. So I decide to go with a classic.

"Put your hands up where I can see them."

"May I stand?" Zee asks, rising without waiting for an answer.

"I said hands *up*. These Almiri ray guns don't have a hammer to cock or anything, so just imagine a dramatically slow 'click' and use it as motivation to do exactly as I say."

She raises only one hand. "I'm not trying to be difficult," she says, turning slowly. "It's just that my hands are presently occupied."

"*Olivia!*" I screech. I immediately forget that I'm supposed to be pulling a calm, cool, collected badass-cowboy impersonation and run, elbows flailing, toward my baby girl, who is curled up in the crook of Zee's arm.

"Is she okay, Elvs?" Cole asks. His gun is still firmly trained at my mother's head. "Please tell me she's okay."

"I'd hate to have come all this way just to shoot my pseudo-grandmother in the face," Chloe adds. "I mean, it'd be a nice topper, but . . ."

Zee doesn't even fight me as I scoop Olivia from her.

Oh God, she's so warm. So beautiful. She's grown since I've seen her. Not grown enough to be an ex-Jin'Kai youth cadet or anything, but the appropriate amount of development for the time we've been apart. I begin laughing and crying, both at once, snot shooting out of my nose in disgusting bubbles. I don't care. Who cares? She's back. She's here. After all this time, missing her, thinking I'd found her, then realizing I hadn't and missing her triple, I've finally, finally got my baby girl back.

"She looks good," I tell Cole. "Come see. Doesn't she look good?" I check her all over. Ten fingers, ten toes, two ears. Nose fine.

And then I get to the stomach.

"What?" Cole asks in a near panic when he sees the fire hydrant's worth of tears that come pouring out of me. "What is it?"

"Oh, I wasn't—" I begin, trying to explain the tears. But I am becoming quickly hysterical. I hold up our daughter so he can see for himself.

I ♥ Momy!

It's still there, the smeared remnants of the message Cole scrawled on our baby's stomach in indelible marker, all the way back in Antarctica, a few dozen lifetimes ago.

"I told you that marker was permanent," I say, laughing. More snot shoots out of my nose. Olivia lets out a tiny giggle and reaches a fat arm out for me, clenching my hand in hers.

"Aren't there three *m*s in 'mommy'?" Chloe asks.

"Oh God, I'm just so glad you're okay." I squeeze Olivia as tight as I can without damaging her precious internal organs. I may just keep squeezing until she leaves for college.

"I wanted to show her this spot," Zee tells me softly. "While I still had her. It's very special. Your father proposed to me right here. Did you know that? Right here on the rocks."

"You *kidnapped* her," I snap.

"Stop being dramatic," Zee says, waving a dismissive hand. "You should be thanking me for rescuing her from Marsden and his thugs."

"Are you really that delusional?" I ask in disbelief. "You're the one who turned her over to Dr. Marsden in the first place!"

"You want me to shoot her now?" Chloe says. "Or is there something we're waiting for?"

"No one's shooting anyone, Chloe," I reply.

Suddenly a look of horrified realization spreads across Zee's face. "What is *she* doing here?" she demands, eyeing Chloe up and down like she's some sort of infectious disease. "What's going on?"

"Chill out. Chloe's not with Marsden anymore," I tell her. "No one's with Marsden anymore. He's perma-dead."

"She's not even real, Elvan. She's a, a . . . a *thing*." Zee can hardly get the words out. She's gone from calm and collected to unjustifiably morally outraged in the span of ten seconds.

"She's been there for me a lot more than you ever were," I say.

"They grew her in a test tube. They pulled the DNA from your daughter, corrupted it with their own filthy genes, and created an abomination. You can't trust something like that. She's not a real person."

"Hey, watch it," Cole says. "That's my daughter's clone you're talking about."

Chloe takes Zee in, a wicked smile spreading across her face. "You're starting to sound a lot like my old boss," she says. "And by the end he and I *really* didn't see eye to eye."

"I'm just trying not to laugh at the idea of you thinking

someone *else* is untrustworthy," I tell my mother, rocking Olivia gently in my arms as she coos.

"I did what I thought was best for our people. My mistake was believing that the Jin'Kai would be any different from their Almiri cousins. I won't make that same mistake again." She takes a few steps toward me, and instinctively I back away. Cole is immediately beside me, a hand on my shoulder, and Chloe flanks me on the other side, her gun trained directly on Zee.

"Elvan, there's still time. Come with me."

"Come with you?" I ask. "Come with you where?"

"There's an Enosi enclave not far from here. People will be gathering, making preparations. It will be safe there."

"Safe? Haven't you been listening to that radio of yours? The war's over. It's the dawn of a brand-new day."

"You're being foolish. The real war has just begun."

"Do you, like, *ever* have a cheery thought?" I ask. "You should be overjoyed. The mere existence of hybrids has saved the entire planet from annihilation. Dad and Byron are even cowriting a poem about it. They're calling it 'The Defeat of Devastation.'"

In my arms Olivia wiggles around. She wants a better view of her daddy. When she sees him, she breaks into a broad grin. *She smiles now,* I realize. *I missed her first smile.*

But at least I get to see the rest of them.

"Oh, everyone's happy now," Zee says. "The humans are more than willing to accept the presence of a people that have been exploiting them for millennia, and the Almiri are more than happy to receive that acceptance. But how long do you think it will last? How long before they both start seeing the existence of the hybrids as a threat to their respective species?"

"Wow," I say. "I feel really sorry for you. I know you've been out of the loop for a little bit, what with hiding under a rock—I'm guessing somewhere in the Rust Belt?—so let me fill you in. We discovered life on Mars. Well, a computer on Mars, at least, with records of life there. And those records told us a lot of things. Like how we—you, me, and now Olivia— aren't some accidental mutation but a planned evolution of not one but two species. We're the future now."

"And just how do you think they'll react to that, huh? Any of them. You think mankind has a real capacity to accept something so new and different? You think the Almiri will stand for sullying their perfect race?" She gestures back toward the radio. "The news already has stories of protests in the cities, of Almiri ships taking off to find another home separate from the 'lower' species. How long before unrest and disdain lead back to the path they always take—fear and loathing? How long before the Almiri's solution—extermination—is back on the table?"

Zee takes another step toward me. This time I don't shrink away. She puts a hand on my arm and looks me in the eye.

"There's still time. You can come with us. We won't be on the sidelines anymore. We'll be prepared for whatever comes."

"What makes you so sure we *can't* all live harmoniously?" Cole asks her. "How can you possibly know that we can't live together in peace?"

"Because I *know*!" Zee is shouting now, enraged. "I've *seen* it. Don't you understand? Elvan, your daughter's place should be with her own people. That's who she can trust to protect her. Come with us, and I can help you raise her, the way I should have raised you."

"You had no idea we'd find you," I say, the realization suddenly hitting me. Olivia gurgles and grips my thumb, squeezing it tightly. "You weren't waiting for us here, in this place. You were going to take Olivia, go underground. Teach her to be a distrusting, paranoid crazy person, just like you."

"Elvan—"

"She's not your daughter. *I* am your daughter. At least I was." I turn and walk back toward the beach. Chloe falls into place beside me, giving Zee a sarcastic good-bye wave as we go. Zee starts after me, but Cole blocks her path.

"You're being stupid, Elvan!" Zee screeches at me. "This is the only way! You're making a mistake, and it's your daughter who'll pay for it."

I spin around and glare daggers through my mother. I want to shout a lot of things at her, especially about how she shouldn't exactly apply for a guest lecturer position in the field of How Not to Suck at Motherhood. And I'd like to illustrate my point with some of the choicest curse words I've ever had the good fortune to come across. But I steel myself, try to reach some inner calm, or at least lower my blood pressure to normal levels. This is not about me anymore, I tell myself. It's about Olivia.

"You know," I say calmly. "You're right about one thing. There *are* Almiri leaving. There are definitely some who don't want to see the big picture, still think they're the big cheese. And so they're leaving. And you know what? They'll die. There are humans who are scared of change, scared of something different. But you know what? They'll adapt. And guess what else, Zee? There are Jin'Kai already turning themselves in, surrendering to authorities, willing to pay the price for their crimes. Because they want in on the 'grand experiment.' They understand the stakes of the game, a lot better than you. I've met some Almiri who are real douche bags, and I've met some who are extraordinary heroes. I've met Jin'Kai who wouldn't think twice about killing just to prove a point, and I've met one who died to protect the girl he loved. I've met Enosi I would trust with my *life* . . . and I've met you. Your problem, Zee, is that you can't get past where people come from, when all that really matters is where they're headed."

"Don't come running to me when your brave new world disappoints you," she spits at me.

"Well," I say. "I've met you. And I've met the world. And I think I'll put my faith in the world."

And with that, I turn again, and walk off with Chloe by my side. Zee is shouting something while Cole holds her back, but the crashing of the waves against the rocks drowns out whatever hollow protests she might be making.

"So, is that it?" Chloe asks. "You're done with her?"

"It would appear so," I say, trying to keep the tears welling in my eyes from spilling down over my cheeks. Olivia makes a high cooing sound and stares with wonder at Chloe. Chloe makes a sort of fish face, and Olivia giggles, and I can't help but laugh.

"But you never know," I continue. "Sometimes people can surprise you."

EPILOGUE

"We're here," Dad says as he pulls the car into the private lot. "Donald, I trust you'll feel better with a little fresh air."

"I'm okay, Mr. Nara," Ducky says, not entirely convincingly, as he opens his door and exits the car. I begin to fiddle with the straps on Olivia's car seat, a ridiculous contraption that Dad researched and purchased and insists on using whenever we drive the baby around in the old car. It takes me five minutes, minimum, to figure out how to dismantle the many redundant belts and harnesses every single time we go anywhere.

"Need a hand?" Cole asks. He sits on the other side of Olivia, playing the "spinning finger" game that seems to amuse him more than it does her.

"No," I say. "I've got it. Why don't you help them with the bags?"

Cole gives me an awkward half smile and obliges. I feel a

little bad for blowing him off when he's just trying to be helpful, but right now every reminder of what he *could* be doing is making me more and more miserable.

It's not that I still love Cole. At least in a romantic sense. I don't. It took me a while, but I've come to a definite conclusion on that front. But that doesn't mean I won't miss him when he's gone. After all, not being in a relationship with your child's father is one thing. Having him blast off into space on a dangerous mission with no end point is something else entirely.

When I finally get Olivia free from the Dad-approved safety seat, I lift her out of the car and make my way with Dad, Ducky, and Cole across the lot and toward the flightport that will shuttle us to the takeoff site for the *Nautilus*, the spanking new deep-space craft they'll be trekking on. Waiting for us at the shuttle stop are Marnie and Chloe, engaged in an animated conversation.

"Hey, you two," I say. "Everything cool?"

"It's fine," Chloe says. "Just a disagreement on the best way to incapacitate an attacker. I still say it's the groin."

"Not if ye dinnae wanta be seen comin' from a light-year off," Marnie replies. She grabs Chloe's shoulder and makes to jam her heel down on the top of Chloe's foot, in a weird slow-motion demonstration. "Ye go fer the instep, always," she insists.

"Right," I reply. "Obviously." Chloe and Marnie have gotten to be fairly close as they've prepared for their journey into the cosmos. I guess being the only two women aboard, they've decided that they should form some sort of alliance.

"Well, will ye look at tha'?" Marnie coos, calling off her

assault demonstration and bringing her face down to meet Olivia's. "She's learnt to wave already! By the time we get back, she'll be flying her own ship, and tha'."

"Olivia won't be flying any ships until she's at *least* two," I reply. And I don't tell Marnie, but I don't think Olivia's waving so much as flapping her hand in front of her face in an attempt to land it in her mouth. I've been watching her carefully for signs of supergrowth, but as far as I can tell, all Marsden did was extract her DNA. Thank goodness. I plan to be along for every milestone, big or small, from here on out.

I can see Chloe focusing on the baby with that poorly veiled intense stare that she's developed whenever we're together.

"Would you like to hold her?" I ask, already knowing exactly the response I'm going to get.

"Well, um, sure, if your arms are tired," Chloe answers, straining to sound completely uninterested.

"Oh, *exhausted*," I say, smiling. Chloe eagerly accepts the wriggling baby and rocks her gently in her arms. As always when being held by her doppel, Olivia focuses in on Chloe like her gaze is laser-guided, her brow crinkled in wonderment, her mouth pursed into a perfect little *o*.

"So, I haven't decided what she should call you when we communicate," I say. "I mean, if we're able. Do you want to be Aunt Chloe, Cousin Chloe? I guess 'sister' would be the closest thing to true, but that might raise too many questions too soon."

"Whatever. Like I care," Chloe says. Her eyes dart up at me quickly before falling back down onto Olivia. "Aunt Chloe's fine."

"Great, then it's settled."

Chloe's mouth goes thin. "You're not going to be one of those moms who sends vidcaps, like, every twenty seconds, are you?" she asks. But even with the rehearsed disdain in her voice, the way she bounces Olivia like an old pro undercuts her apathetic posturing. "Like, 'Here's the baby farting!' 'Here's the face she makes when she smells mustard.' 'Here she is at—' Wow, did you see that? She went right for my nose! *Such a strong grip, Wivvie. You're such a strong girl!*" She stops herself when she realizes we're all staring at her, smirking, and she blushes sheepishly.

The shuttle pulls into the stop, the doors slide open, and we all step inside to be whisked toward the takeoff pad.

"You don't even need the vidcaps," Cole tells Chloe, smiling and cooing at the baby just as big as everyone else. Olivia really is a happiness magnet. "You already know she's going to turn out exactly like you."

"Well, probably not *exactly* like me," Chloe replies. She bounces the source of her genetic material on her hip. "Nature versus nurture, and all that."

"Just *when*, precisely, in your two-week growing-up period did you have time to learn about nature versus nurture?" Ducky cuts in.

Chloe rolls her eyes. "It was an exhaustive course," she explains.

"Olivia may not be *exactly* the same as you," I tell Chloe. And I offer her a genuine smile. "But she sure could do a lot worse."

Chloe blinks and turns her face to the floor.

"This is, like, the weirdest, sweetest thing ever," Ducky says.

The shuttle comes to a halt, and the doors swing open onto the launch pad. The rest of the crew of this crazy mission is standing at attention, waiting for us. Oates tips his cap to us politely as we disembark and start toward the *Nautilus*.

"Ladies, gentlemen. Shall we?" he says in that wonderful British lilt.

"Just promise me to come back not-blown-up," I say, looking at each of them in turn. And goddamn that lump in my throat. "That goes for all of you."

"I shall do my utmost, miss," Oates tells me.

"Are ye sure ye cannae join us?" Marnie asks. "I woulda thought ye'd be jumping at the chance, an adventurer such as yerself."

At that, I snort. "Flying off into the great unknown? Keeping tabs on the entire Jin'Kai fleet while avoiding capture? Trying to find clues as to where the ancient martian civilization scampered off to? All in a ship too small to transport a varsity soccer team? No thanks." I let Olivia grab my finger. "I just saved the planet," I tell Marnie. "The universe can manage without me for a little while. Besides"—Olivia giggles that perfect, heartwarming laugh of hers, as if on cue—"there's another tiny matter that requires my attention at the moment. I mean, *someone's* got to make sure she grows up in the spirit of interspecies cooperation. We'd hate for her to take after her grandmother. *Wouldn't we, Wivvie?*" I tickle her chin, and she blows a spit bubble out of the side of her mouth in reply.

"You shall be with us in spirit, miss," Oates puts in.

"Oh, you'll have so many badasses on board, you won't even miss me," I say. I grin at Oates. "I mean, any killer whales out there, I *dare* them to get by you guys. And Cole here"—I punch his arm playfully (when was the last time I did *that*?)—"I think he's proven he's more than just a cute butt."

Cole wrinkles his nose at me.

"Okay, sorry," I say. "I take it back. You *are* just a cute butt."

"No." He shakes his head. "It isn't that. I . . ." He blinks at me. "I'm not going. On the ship. I'm staying here. I . . . I thought you knew that."

Perhaps I shouldn't be, but I am flabbergasted. "You're staying here?" I ask. The action hero star? "But . . . why?"

"Why?" he repeats. Now it's his turn to look confounded. "I thought that would've been obvious." He glances down at Olivia, who returns his warm smile.

Oh yeah. The baby. *Cole's* baby.

Dur.

"We're a family," Cole tells me. "I plan on having it stay that way."

For one of the very few times in my life, I'm utterly speechless. To think, I once worried I'd have to raise this little girl all on my own, and now here the little squirt has a whole *family*.

"But . . ." A new worry has popped into my head. "I mean, I just want to clarify . . . I, like, don't plan on getting back together with you. I mean, we can be Olivia's family without . . . It's not that I don't *like* . . . I just don't have *romantic* feelings . . ." I stop babbling when I realize that literally everyone is staring at me.

"Wow," Ducky puts in. "Maybe your dad and Byron

should write an epic poem about you sticking your foot in your mouth."

Cole just smirks. "No worries, Elvs. I know I can be slow on the uptake, but I think even I've figured out that I like you better when we're not a couple."

Call the fire department, 'cause my face is burning. "Uh. Good," I say lamely. "Just, uh, don't get back together with Britta or anything. Any of the Brittas."

"You're not the boss of me," he says.

"Seriously, Cole, last I heard from them, they were legitimately considering forming a band called Britta and the Brittas."

"I promise nothing," he says with that perfect smile of his. I smile back, suddenly overjoyed to know that I'm not losing my ex-boyfriend to the dark reaches of the outer cosmos.

But then I remember something.

"Wait, then what was with all the suitcases in the car?" I ask.

"They're mine," Ducky says.

The words hit me so quickly and so sharply that I feel like someone just fired a carving knife into my heart using some sort of high-powered knife-propelling device.

"*You're* going?" I ask, incredulous.

"Well, don't sound too surprised," he says. "After all, who took out Dr. Marsden with his quick thinking?"

"But you're not a space commando!" I protest.

"Not yet, maybe," Ducky says. "But I'll get there. I want to be the hero of my own story, Elvie. No more sidekicking. I'll be the first man to barf in multiple solar systems!" We laugh at that. "Besides, I won't be alone. I'll have Marnie looking out for me. And Merv, of course."

Right. Before departing from Mars, the AI construct requested that he be brought back to Earth with us, now that his duties in the alien data depository were no longer needed. Dad and I figured out a way to transfer him from the martian computer system onto the world's biggest memory drive (thank goodness for Almiri high tech), and he's been integrated into the *Nautilus*'s computers to serve as the only "crew" member with any firsthand knowledge of the mysterious race they'll be seeking out.

"Trust me," I say. "A few days with Merv up there, and you'll be trying to swim home."

"I dunno," Ducky says. "We've already discussed programming our own *Jetman* game to pass the time."

There's no point even pretending that I'm not going to be all weepy about this, so I just let the waterworks burst forth as I wrap Ducky in an enormous hug.

"I love you *so much*," I say, crying into the crook of his neck. "Like, bonkers sauce."

"I know," he says. I can feel his own tears on my cheek.

"I'm sorry if I ever made you feel like a sidekick," I say. He pulls me back, and we look at each other through weepy girly eyes, the both of us.

"Hey, you never did that. I'm doing this for me. It's the opportunity of a lifetime. I just hope that you'll understand, and be proud of me."

"I'm already proud of you, you dumb idiot," I say, and we fall back into another big, soppy, wet hug.

. . .

Standing at the base of the ship's ramp, Chloe is the last to say good-bye before boarding. She shuffles her feet awkwardly, not looking at me or Cole but instead focusing all her attention on Olivia, who rests comfortably in her arms.

"It's so weird," she says. "She's, like, older than me, but not."

"Of all the weird crap over the past year, you holding your infant self is definitely in the top five," I agree.

"I'm glad we were able to get her back," Chloe says. "I'm glad at least one of us will get to have a childhood. Make it a good one, all right?"

"Cross my heart and blah, blah, blah," I say. "We'll do our very best. And when you come back—"

"*If* I come back," she interrupts.

"*When.* We'll be here. And you can make sure we did everything right for your 'niece.'"

"I know you will. You're a great mom."

She leans in close to my ear, so only I can hear. "Not every twenty seconds," she tells me. "But a vidcap every now and then probably wouldn't be the worst thing."

"I promise," I say.

She carefully hands Olivia off to Cole, and to my surprise she pulls us all into a Cole-Elvie-Olivia-Chloe sandwich.

"You guys aren't the worst," she says.

"Thanks?" Cole replies.

She disengages from the family group hug, turns, and, just like that, walks up the platform and disappears inside the ship. I wonder if it's the last I'll ever see of her.

. . .

The start-up sequence is mostly a blur to me. A haze of tears. I'm mildly aware of Cole settling Olivia back into my arms, and of her clinging to my arm, blowing cute little raspberries at my cheek. At some point Dad and Byron wander over to me. Dad sets a hand on my back, and Cole moves in closer too. Together we watch as our friends and family shoot off into the great unknown.

"You going to be okay, dearheart?" Dad asks me softly.

I sniffle, watching the ship dart higher, higher, *highest* into the atmo. It is quickly less than a speck, leaving a trail of vaporized exhaust in its wake. Then it's gone. I look down at Olivia. Her beautiful face. "I think so," I reply.

We are silent for a while, all of us watching the empty sky, until a horrifying thought occurs to me.

"Do I have to go back to high school?" I ask. "'Cause I'm not sure Lower Merion is going to transfer my credits from the evil alien academy."

"Your grandfather and I were discussing that," Dad says.

"Really?"

"Well," Byron says with that rakish grin of his, "I know it's always been your dream to join the Ares Project someday."

"You're going forward with the terraforming?" I ask. "You think people will still want to colonize the surface even after the discovery of an underground martian civilization?"

"I'm optimistic that the terraforming and archeological interests will dovetail together nicely," Byron says. "Now, you're not really in a position to join the team right now, of course, but seeing as the provost of the Armstrong School is a personal friend of mine . . ."

"The Armstrong School?" I gasp. "Really?"

"What's the Armstrong School?" Cole asks

"Only the single best and hardest-to-get-into aeronautic engineering program in the world!" I gush. I turn back to Byron. "You know the provost?"

"I should say so. I did save his life during the Franco-Prussian War. If you want to go, there's a spot for you in the fall class."

If my jaw dropped any lower, I'd need Olivia to scoop it up and push it back into place.

"You cannot be serious."

"And yet I am."

My dad is grinning too. "Great news, right?" he says, rubbing my shoulder.

"What about Olivia? Cole?"

"We can place Mr. Archer in a position nearby, if he likes," Byron replies. "And my great-granddaughter will not want for care."

"Wow, I just . . . Wow," I say. It's like getting exactly the Christmas present you asked for, immediately after learning that Santa is an old man in a fat suit. But I have to slow down, think everything through.

"Can I have some time to think about it?" I ask.

"Dearheart?" Dad says.

"I'm not saying no," I tell them. I shift Olivia on my hip. "God, I'm not saying no. It's just . . . I've been thinking . . . well, I guess I've come to realize lately that, despite everything, I've lived a very fortunate life, and that there are a lot of people who haven't. That ozone factory that blew up—there are hundreds more places like it, and maybe millions of people living lives that until recently I couldn't even conceive of. The kind of poverty I saw there, that was more alien to me than any pretty boy Almiri or monster-looking Devastator. I think . . . I think maybe I'd like to help people the way I've had people help me. Maybe that still means Ares. Maybe more. But I need a little time to think. Like what you were talking about on Mars. 'The world forgot' and all that."

"Yes, about that," Byron says. "Maybe don't mention to Alex that I was quoting him. It'll go straight to his head."

When I look back up, my father is beaming. "You're a wise woman, Elvie," he says. "That's for sure."

I lean my head on his shoulder and snuggle my daughter closer into my side. Cole wraps an arm around the two of us, and together with Byron we go back to watching the sky. In the upper atmosphere I think I catch the glint of something shining briefly, and then disappearing the next moment. Perhaps it's the flash from the *Nautilus*'s hyperdrive, pushing my loved ones into the final frontier. Perhaps it's a satellite for HBO. Regardless, my friends are beginning their greatest journey, just like I'm about to embark on mine. Who knows what lies around the bend, what calamity we'll have to deal with next? How will we handle all the unknown perils our new life has in store for us?

In my arms Olivia giggles—the kind of sweet, charming, delightful baby giggle that travels all the way through you. I kiss her head.

"You're right," I whisper to my daughter. "Whatever comes, we'll adapt."

SAGA PRESS

MYTHS MADE DAILY.

THE GRACE OF KINGS
KEN LIU

The debut epic fantasy novel from Ken Liu, one of the most lauded fantasy and science fiction writers of his generation; winner of the Hugo, Nebula, and World Fantasy Awards.

PERSONA
GENEVIEVE VALENTINE

Nebula Award finalist Genevieve Valentine's acerbic thriller, set in a near-future world of celebrity ambassadors and assassins who manipulate the media and where the only truth seekers left are the paparazzi.

CITY OF SAVAGES
LEE KELLY

Lee Kelly's startling debut novel, a taut drama set in a post–WWIII POW camp in Manhattan.

THE DARKSIDE WAR
ZACHARY BROWN

How will a band of criminals and co-opted rebels become Earth's legendary first line of defense?

Born in Canada in 1966, Susanna Kearsley has been writing since the age of seven. She read politics and international development at university, has worked as a museum curator, and has had two short novels published in the US. She lives in Ontario.

Susanna Kearsley's previous novel, *Mariana*, is also published by Corgi and was the second winner of the Catherine Cookson Fiction Prize which was set up in 1992 to celebrate the achievement of Dame Catherine Cookson.

The Splendour Falls

Susanna Kearsley

SEAL BOOKS
McClelland-Bantam, Inc.
Toronto

THE SPLENDOUR FALLS
A Seal Book/published by arrangement
with Mary Lynne Williamson

Seal edition May 1996

ISBN: 0-770-42718-9

Reproduced, printed and bound in the United Kingdom by
Cox & Wyman Ltd, Reading, Berks.

0 9 8 7 6 5 4 3 2 1

The splendour falls on castle walls
    And snowy summits old in story:
The long light shakes across the lakes,
    And the wild cataract leaps in glory.
Blow, bugle, blow, set the wild echoes flying,
Blow, bugle; answer, echoes, dying, dying, dying.

This and all other quotes contained herein are taken from
Tennyson's *THE PRINCESS*

Author's Note

If you walk the streets of Chinon, you will find each setting and each building mentioned in this story. Because of this, I wish to remind the reader that while the places may be real, the people who inhabit them are entirely fictional.

To the Chinonais, I offer my apologies, for moving their *gendarmerie*. To Paul Rhoads, who became my guide, and to Dorothée Kleinmann, who shared her Chapelle with me, I give my heartfelt thanks.

And to all my friends at the Hotel de France, both past and present, I dedicate this book.

Prologue

. . . when all was lost or seem'd as lost . . .

The first night had been the worst. They had come on so violently, and without warning. One moment she'd been peacefully at prayer within the chapel, and the next the captain of her guard was pounding at the door, with orders she should seek in haste the safety of her chamber. And then someone had whispered 'siege' . . .

It had been dreadful, that first night – the darkness and the shrieking of the wind and the fires burning everywhere, it seemed, upon the plain below. But daylight came, and still the castle held. Of course it held, thought Isabelle. This was Chinon. Like the Plantagenet kings it sheltered, Chinon Castle had a will of iron. It bowed before no man.

At first, she had not wanted to believe that Guillaume des Roches could be so bold, so callous, as to try to hold her hostage. He'd been an ally of the king her husband, and in return he had been used most fairly. Had John not made des Roches warden of Chinon? And yet she'd seen the evidence with her own eyes, she'd seen des Roches himself among the men, striding freely through their ranks as though such treason were a thing to make him proud.

If John were here, she thought, he'd teach the traitor otherwise. If John were here . . .

She drew the velvet robe more tightly round her shivering body, and looked again towards the west. The sun had slipped much lower, now. Already it had flattened on the purple haze of hills, spilling its brilliance into the darkly flowing river. Soon, she knew, there would be only darkness left. Four nights now she had stood here in this high and lonely tower, watching while the dying sun sank weakly in the western sky. This time she found herself looking for the fires, her own eyes seeking out the places where the rebels kept their camps.

'They are quite close, tonight,' she said aloud, and one of her women stirred beside the hearth.

'My lady?'

Isabelle glanced round, her long hair tangling on the crimson velvet. 'I said the fires are close, tonight.'

'Yes, my lady.'

'It must be very cold . . .' She looked away again, thinking on the madness that might drive a man to leave the comfort of his own warm hearth in this, the depth of winter.

Her women were watching her, she could feel their eyes. Her calmness, she knew, surprised them. They thought her still a child, as she had come to them three years ago, when John had brought her here, to Chinon, for the wedding. He'd scandalized the court, that summer – she had heard the whispers. A man past thirty marrying a girl of twelve . . .

But even then, she had not been a child. She had already been betrothed to Hugh of Lusignan when John had met her first at Angoulême. No matter. As in the game of chess, a king outranked a knight, and Isabelle had known from their first meeting how the game would end. Some said that she yet wanted Hugh, but they were fools who thought so. In all her fifteen years, she had loved one man only – a quiet man, a caring man, with midnight eyes that smiled for her alone. And had it been her choice to make, three years ago, she would have chosen John.

He was not like his brothers, not like Richard. She'd met the fabled Lionheart – an armoured giant with a beard of gold. The image of his father, people said, the image of the Lion himself, King Henry, that raging intellect who, with indomitable Eleanor of Aquitaine, had bred a line of princes unparalleled in time.

It was, thought Isabelle, the strangest family. They loved and hated one another, wept and warred and plotted, moving always in a weird diagonal between deceit and truth. It had left scars on all of them, especially John. He did not speak of it, but many times she'd seen him standing silent in the chapel here at Chinon, brooding on the very spot where old King Henry, sick at heart, had finally died.

'Twas rumoured it was John's fault that the Lion ceased to roar – John's fault because he had been Henry's favourite, and because the king had seen John's name upon a list of those who stood against him. But Henry's heart was not so weak, thought Isabelle. He'd fought his sons before, unflinching. He'd dungeoned up his wife. He'd played John and betrayed him until no-one could with any certainty say how his feelings lay. And yet John loved him. When he stood so sad and solemn in the chapel, Isabelle had but to look upon her husband's face to know whose heart had broken there those many years ago.

Still, people would persist in rumours. They

whispered now about young Arthur of Brittany, held captive in Rouen for laying siege to the old queen at Mirabeau. John had once been fond of Arthur, his brother Geoffrey's only son, and Geoffrey, who died young, had been of all the brothers closest in both looks and age to John. But Arthur was not Geoffrey. Where his father had been cunning, Arthur failed to think at all, and his rash behaviour left John with no option but to take him prisoner.

And so the rumours shifted, day to day. Arthur of Brittany was free . . . he was in fetters . . . he was planning his escape . . . he was too weak to raise his head . . . he had been moved in secrecy from Rouen . . . Some said – she'd heard it only yesterday – that Arthur was already dead, that John had had him killed. What foolishness, thought Isabelle. John could not kill the boy.

She might have told that to the men camped now around the walls of Chinon Castle, if they had been like to listen, since it was for Arthur's sake that they had come. They thought to hold her hostage for the freedom of the reckless young pretender. Fools, she thought. They knew John not at all.

The wind struck chill through the high narrow window. It had a voice, that wind – half human and half demon, that numbed the soul and turned the heart to stone. Isabelle turned slowly from the dimming view and crossed the great round room to where a smaller window gazed upon the north. The northern sky was deepest blue and full of cloud, without a star to pierce the gloom. Did they have stars, she wondered, at Le Mans? Her message would, by now, have surely reached him. Le Mans was not so very far away. She had but to hold out a few more days, and help would be at hand. Isabelle smiled faintly in the firelight. Even if John had loved her not at all, she knew he would not lose his precious Treasury. Indeed, she might have thought he loved his Treasury above all else, had it not been for the day she'd teased him about it and he'd caught her to him, there in front of everyone, and told her: '*You* are my treasure.' She could still taste his kiss upon her lips . . .

Her hand moved, unthinkingly, to the gold and pearl pendant at her throat, and she frowned. 'Alice,' she said quietly, over her shoulder, 'I would have my jewel casket.'

'Yes, my lady.' The woman by the fire rose obediently.

'And Alice . . .'

'Yes, my lady?'

'Which of the servants knows the tunnels best?'

They did not need to ask which tunnels she was speaking of. Chinon Castle was riddled with them. John often said it was a mystery that the walls did not collapse.

'Old Thomas, my lady,' came the answer, finally. 'He works in the kitchens.'

'Then I would have him brought to me,' said Isabelle, 'without delay. I have need of him.'

The women stared at her, and murmured, but they knew better than to question her wishes. For all her youth, this waif-like figure by the window was yet Isabelle of Angoulême; she was their queen, and she would be obeyed. Old Thomas would be fetched with haste.

Content, Isabelle turned back to the small window and the fires burning brightly on the blackened plain below. She did not hear the door behind her close, nor hear the footsteps of the women ringing down the cold stone passage. She only heard the wind. She was still standing motionless, her eyes upon the northern hills, when Alice came to set the small jewel casket down beside the bed.

Alice was the oldest of her women, and her gaze fell very gentle on the sad-eyed little queen. 'He will come, my lady,' she said softly, and they both knew it was not Old Thomas that she meant.

Isabelle nodded, without words, and blamed the stinging winter wind for the sudden trail of dampness on her face . . .

Chapter One

. . . and thus a
noble scheme
Grew up from seed . . .

'And did he come?' I curled my feet beneath me on the sofa, and poured another cup of tea.

My cousin was idly contemplating my sitting-room window, where the raindrops chased one another down the panes in ragged paths. He pulled his gaze back to mine, with an effort. 'What?'

'John,' I prompted, patiently. 'Did he finally come to rescue Isabelle?'

'Oh.' He smiled. 'Naturally. He sent his best knight, Jean de Préaux, with a group of mercenaries, to bring poor Isabelle back safely to Le Mans.'

I pulled a face. 'How very noble of him.'

'You would have seen the romance in that, once,' Harry said, passing me his own teacup to be refilled. It was a gentle reprimand. He was quite right, I knew, but I pushed the thought aside.

'So tell me,' I said, 'about this new theory of yours.'

'My dear girl, it isn't theory – it's been published in three quite prestigious journals.'

'Sorry.'

He forgave me, leaning back. 'Well, you remember

when they turned up that new chronicle last year, at Angoulême?'

'By William de What's-his-name? Yes, I remember.'

'Right. It tells us Isabelle hid something when she was besieged at Chinon, something so valuable that she didn't want the rebel barons to find it. At least we can infer that much. She asked for her jewel case, and then she asked for someone who knew the tunnels, and then she disappeared for nearly an hour with this Old Thomas, to where, nobody knew.'

I frowned. 'But surely when the threat was over, she'd have got back what it was she hid.'

'Not necessarily. Chinon was hardly secure, remember, and John lost it completely not long afterwards, so Isabelle might never have had the chance. The chronicle,' he told me, 'clearly states that in her later years our Isabelle spoke often of the "treasure without price" she'd left in France. Put two and two together—'

'—and you've got your lectures packed with students for the term,' I teased him, smiling.

He grinned. 'Not this term. I'm on half-time now, remember? One term off, one on. And this one's off.'

'Nice work if you can get it.'

'Well, I need the time for writing. I've been working on this book . . .'

'Let me guess. Plantagenets.' That was no great effort to deduce. My cousin Harry had been potty for Plantagenets since we were both in the nursery. I'd paid the price for his obsession many times in childhood games, condemned to die a Saracen at Richard the Lionheart's crusading hand, or playing Thomas à Becket, a role I thought was rather fun until I learned the fate of the Archbishop. The only truly juicy part I'd been allowed to play was that of Eleanor of Aquitaine, which I'd played often, until Harry one day locked me up in 'Salisbury Tower' – an old bomb shelter at the back of his neighbour's garden – and left me there till dinner time. To this day, it was all I could do to force myself to take the tube in London, or to spend more than ten minutes in my own basement.

My cousin smiled. 'Not all of the Plantagenets – just John. A sort of revisionist approach to his biography. The misunderstood king. Which reminds me, did I show you what your father sent me?' Without waiting for my answer, he dug into his pocket and produced a circle of hard plastic, within which nestled a small and perfect silver coin. 'That's John himself, in profile. Must be worth a bloody fortune, but your father just put it in the post.'

I took the encased coin from him, turning it round. 'Wherever did Daddy pick this up?'

'God knows.' My cousin shrugged. 'Uncle Andrew has so many friends in odd places, doesn't he? I sometimes think it's better not to ask too many questions.'

I agreed. 'He doesn't answer questions well, at any rate. He'd likely say he bought it at a car boot sale.' He'd say it with a straight face, too, I thought. My father was a charming liar when he chose – a trait that he'd acquired through his lifetime in the diplomatic corps. I'd learned the trick of it myself, these past few years.

'He says,' my cousin informed me, 'you ought to ring him more often.'

I looked up, eyebrows raised. 'I ring him every month. He *is* in Uruguay, you know – if we talked any more frequently I'd drain my savings, such as they are.'

'I know. I just think he worries about you, that's all.'

'Well, there's no need.' I flipped the coin over to study the reverse. 'You'll be off to France then, I expect, to do more research?'

'Yes, at the end of the month.'

'Just in time for the wine harvest.'

'Precisely.'

I took a sip of tea and sighed. 'I'm envious, I really am.'

'So come with me.' He dropped the comment casually, then slid his eyes sideways to watch my reaction.

'Don't be daft. You know I can't.'

'Why not?'

'Some of us,' I explained mildly, 'do work for a living, you know, and I can't just pick up any time I like and leave.'

'Give over,' was my cousin's blunt response. 'You work for my dad, for heaven's sake. I'll not believe that Braden Glass would fall to pieces if you took a fortnight's holiday. Surely Dad or Jack could answer their own telephones . . .'

'And then there's the house to think of,' I went on stubbornly. 'I'm supposed to be looking after it for Daddy, not leaving it unattended so some burglar can break in and strip the place.' I saw his unconvinced expression, and I frowned. 'Look, I'm sorry if you think I'm boring . . .'

'It's not that you're boring, exactly,' Harry corrected me, 'it's just that you're not very exciting. Not any more. Not since . . .'

'This has nothing to do with my parents' divorce. I'm just getting older, that's all. Taking some responsibility.'

'There's responsible,' said my cousin drily, 'and then

there is responsible. Mother tells me it's been six months since you so much as stopped in at the pub for a drink.'

I rolled my eyes. 'The curse of living in a small community. What else does your mother tell you?'

'That she hardly ever sees you smile, and that last month in London you walked straight past the fountains in Trafalgar Square without tossing in so much as tuppence.'

I looked down. 'Yes, well. Only tourists throw coins in fountains.'

'That never used to stop you.' He set his empty teacup on the table at his knees. 'Which reminds me, may I have my King John coin back? Thanks. You might have stopped believing in good luck pieces, Emily Braden, but I haven't. I'd rather lose my right arm than this little chap. So,' he said brightly, tucking the silver coin safely back into his pocket, 'that's settled, then. You're coming with me to Chinon.'

I shook my head. 'Harry . . .'

'Cheap flights right now, out of Heathrow, but you'll have to book this week I think. Dad says the end of September would be fine with him, just so he knows . . .'

'Harry . . .'

'And I've found the most wonderful hotel, sixteenth-century and right on the main square, with a view of the castle.'

'Harry,' I tried again, but he'd already pulled out the brochures. The photographs made Chinon look like something from a childhood dream – pale, turreted houses and winding cobbled streets, with the castle rising like a guardian from the cliffs against a lavender sky, and the river Vienne gleaming like a ribbon of light at its feet.

'There's the tower where Isabelle would have waited out the siege,' Harry said, pointing out a narrow crumbling column at the castle's furthest edge. 'The Moulin Tower.'

I looked, and shook my head with an effort. 'I can't come with you.'

'Of course you can.'

I sighed. My cousin had the rare ability to solve the whole world's problems single-handed. My father did that too, sometimes, and my Uncle Alan. At the moment, I sensed I was the victim of a triumvirate of conspiracy. I hadn't changed that much, I reasoned . . . had I? It was just that when one's parents, after thirty years of marriage, chose to go their separate ways, it made one view life rather more realistically. So what, I asked myself, was wrong with that? So my parents' happy marriage hadn't been so happy after all. So love was never meant to last for ever. It was better that I'd learned that lesson young, instead of making their mistakes all over again.

And I didn't carry any bitterness towards my parents. A little disappointment maybe, but no bitterness. My mother was . . . well, she was just my mother – vibrant, headstrong, independent. Every now and then she sent me postcards from Greek ports or Turkish hotels or wherever she and her latest boyfriend were at large. And Daddy . . . Daddy went on working as he always had before, only now instead of his London office he had his office at the British Legation in Montevideo. He'd hardly seemed to notice the divorce.

But then, he'd never really grown up, my father. Like all the Braden men, my father had a child's innocence and simple faith and depthless well of energy. My Uncle Alan was the same, and Harry too. It made them all three rather charming, and I loved them for it, but it put them on a plane of life one couldn't always reach, or share.

Harry was the worst of them, come to that. Though I was terribly fond of my only cousin, he'd driven me to the brink of murder more times than I cared to remember. Unreliable, my mother called him. I might instead have termed him 'easily distracted', but it amounted to much the same thing when one was left stranded at the airport because Harry had gone off exploring, somewhere. The memory made me smile suddenly, and I looked across at him with affection.

'I'd be a proper idiot to go on holiday with you,' I said. 'God alone knows what trouble you might lead me into.'

He grinned at that. 'Maybe that's what you need, a good adventure. Bring you back to life.'

'I'm perfectly alive, thanks very much.'

'No you're not.' His eyes were serious behind the smile. 'Not really. I miss the old Emily.'

I looked down at the spreading tangle of coloured brochures. It was a trick of light, I knew, that made me see the shadow of a woman waiting still within that tower at the ruined castle's edge, yet for a moment she was plainly there. A young woman, staring blankly out across the years, waiting, wanting, hoping . . . For what, I wondered? Brave Prince Charming on his pure white charger, riding to the rescue? More fool her, I thought – he wouldn't come. *You're on your own, my girl*, I told the shadowed figure silently, *you'd best accept the fact. Those happy-ever-afters never stand the test of time.* The shadow faded and I looked away, to where the raindrops were still dancing down my window panes.

Harry poured the final cup of cooled tea from the pot, and settled back in his chair, his blue eyes oddly gentle as he tapped my thoughts with maddening precision. 'If you don't believe in fairy tales in Chinon,' said my cousin, 'then there's no hope left for any of us.'

Chapter Two

Arriving all confused . . .

I should have known better. Experience, as everyone kept pointing out, had taught me nothing. Even my Aunt Jane had raised her eyebrows when I'd told her I was going on holiday with Harry.

'My Harry? Whatever for?'

'He thinks I need a holiday,' had been my answer. 'He's promised me adventure.'

'How much adventure,' she had asked me, drily, 'were you planning on?'

I'd shrugged aside the warning. 'I'm sure we'll do just fine. Besides, I do like Harry.'

'My dear Emily, that's hardly the point. We all like Harry. But he has a habit of being, well, rather . . .'

'Unpredictable?' I'd offered, and she'd smiled.

'That's being kind.'

I'd reassured her it was only France that we were going to, not darkest Africa. What could possibly happen in France? And if something were to happen I was well equipped to handle it – French was at least a language I could speak, thanks to my father's years of service at the Paris Embassy. Besides, the thought of spending two whole weeks in Chinon was terribly seductive.

Aunt Jane had listened to it all, her blue eyes twinkling, and quirked an innocent eyebrow. 'You've taken out insurance, have you?' And then she'd laughed and turned away to make the tea.

My Uncle Alan had been less cynical. 'Just what you need,' he'd pronounced with satisfaction. 'Change of scenery, eh? Bit of romance.' He'd winked at that and nudged my arm, and I had smiled as I was meant to, thinking all the while that romance was the last thing that I needed. A holiday fling perhaps, quick and painless, but real romance . . . well, that proved as reliable as Harry himself, and, like my cousin, it could only lead one into trouble.

Harry, for his part, had done his level best to confound our suspicions these past weeks. He'd gone ahead of me to do some of the 'boring bits' of research on his own – I never had liked reading rooms. But he'd been almost conscientious with our travel plans, had sent me maps and confirmation of our reservations at Chinon's Hotel de France. He'd even telephoned on Sunday last from Bordeaux, with my final instructions.

'Not the Gare Austerlitz, love,' he'd corrected me cheerfully. 'Montparnasse. You still know your way around Paris pretty well, don't you? Just take the bus in from the airport, and then the TGV from Montparnasse to St-Pierre-des-Corps, that's the quickest way to do it. You'll be there before lunchtime.'

I'd stopped scrawling down directions and tapped the pen against my notepad, frowning. 'And you *will* come to meet me?'

'Certainly. I'll be driving right across the top of Tours – that's where St-Pierre-des-Corps is – so I'll pick you up right at the railway station. I've got the red car; you shouldn't have any trouble spotting me. Shall we say noon?'

'That's noon on Friday?' I confirmed. 'Friday the twenty-fourth?'

'Don't worry,' he'd said, sounding amused. 'I won't forget. I'm not a total idiot, you know. Besides, I've had this letter, did I tell you?' He hadn't, as it turned out, so he went on to elaborate. The writer of the letter was some fellow history buff who'd read one of my cousin's academic journal pieces on the lost treasure of Isabelle. 'So presumably he reads English,' said my cousin, 'though his letter was in French. He's rather cryptic, but it seems he has some information that might interest me, about the tunnels underneath the castle. Asks me can I get in touch with him. It's wonderfully intriguing – just like that Watergate informant chap, you know the one . . .'

'Does your man have a code name, as well?'

'No.' Harry had sounded a shade disappointed. 'No, just his real name . . . Didier . . . Didier something. I'd have to look it up, I don't remember. Well anyway, he lives in Chinon, so that's why you needn't worry I'll forget to pick you up. I'm rather keen myself to get up there and find out what this fellow knows.'

'Fine, then I'll see you on Friday.'

'St-Pierre-des-Corps at noon. I promise.' It had been that final word, oddly enough, that struck a warning note, but the phone line was already crackling, breaking up. I'd heard my cousin's voice saying, 'Must dash, sorry,' and something that sounded vaguely like 'Till Friday', and that was that.

I should have known.

'Bloody Harry,' I said aloud. The young woman

25

seated at the table next to mine looked up, surprised, then glanced away again discreetly as she raised her dainty cup of coffee. My own cup was long since empty, and cold against my fingers. I pushed it away with idle irritation and, resting my chin on my hands, stared out through the wall of windows in front of me. The view from the café of the rail station was less than inspiring – a wide sweep of concrete slabs set in a square geometric pattern, curving rows of futuristic lamp standards perched on thick concrete pillars, and a long, low concrete fountain filled with foaming white jets of water that only emphasized the coldness of the architecture. Across the street three large blocks of flats rose like blemishes from the landscape, pale and impersonal, with rows of windows staring blankly back at me through the prison railings of their balconies.

I sighed.

This section of the city of Tours was depressingly modern. Chinon itself lay somewhere to the southwest – not far, though at that moment it seemed a thousand miles away. I could almost hear it beckoning, that lovely castle in the river's curve, beneath a violet sky. 'The flower of the Garden of France', the brochures had promised me. I sighed again, with feeling. Because I wasn't in Chinon – I was here, and St-Pierre-des-Corps looked nothing like a flower.

He wasn't coming, I thought glumly. Harry never came an hour late. He either showed on time or not at all.

'Well, bother it,' I said, and once again the woman at the next table turned her eyes upon me warily. She seemed relieved to see me counting out the change to pay my bill, and even more relieved a moment later as I took a firm grip on my suitcase, pushing back my chair. I felt like telling her I didn't normally talk to myself; that it was all the fault of my rotten bounder of a cousin . . . but then it didn't really matter what she thought, as I was leaving anyway. Harry or no Harry, I would find some way to get to Chinon.

Outside, the air was cool against my heated skin. The skies had threatened rain all morning and the breeze was brisk, but still one wistful, optimistic patch of watery blue had broken through the unrelenting grey. With lifting spirits I headed for the taxi rank.

There were three taxis parked along the curved arcade of concrete columns in front of the station, but only one of them – the one at the rear of the rank – appeared to have a driver. He was standing not ten feet away from me, leaning against the bonnet of a smoke-grey Renault Safrane, eyes fixed upon the fountain in mild contemplation. One hand was thrust deep into the pocket of his tailored wool trousers, while the other held a half-finished cigarette. He wasn't tall, but the dark and handsome labels certainly applied. He wasn't young, either – perhaps a decade older than my own twenty-eight years. Distinguished, my mother would have branded him, and rather elegant in that unaffected way that the French alone seem to have mastered.

As I drew closer, his gaze slid sideways from the fountain to my face, and something flickered behind the dark eyes before they drifted on, taking in my clothes and, most tellingly, the British Airways tags still dangling from my suitcase. Before I'd had a chance to use my French he spoke to me in flawless, fluid English. 'May I help you, Madame?'

He knew I wasn't married. His glance had rested on the fingers of my left hand – more from habit than anything else, I imagined, as I never looked my best when travelling. But it was a matter of politeness, to address me as 'Madame'.

'Well, yes. I need a taxi, please.'

He frowned. An odd response, considering he was leaning against one. It wasn't until he cast a quick glance along the taxi rank that I understood.

'I know you're last in line,' I told him, 'but the other taxis don't have drivers.'

He looked back at me and smiled. 'Where do you wish to go, Madame?'

'To Chinon.'

'Chinon?' He lifted the cigarette, narrowing his eyes against the smoke. They were very thoughtful eyes. 'But it is almost an hour away, Chinon. An expensive trip by taxi.'

'Oh.' I tried to look as if it didn't matter, but of course it did. I couldn't throw my budget out of whack.

Again he glanced along the idle taxi rank, then back at me, as though he were trying to decide something. I saved him the bother.

'Is there a train to Chinon, then?' I asked him.

'Not from this station, no.' His face cleared. 'But there is the *autocar* . . . the bus. I think that it departs at thirteen hours and a half, from over there.' The dark head nodded once, towards the fountain. 'You can buy a ticket from inside the station, there is time.'

I checked my wristwatch, making the conversion to the French twenty-four hour system. I had fully fifteen minutes to buy my ticket and catch the *autocar* – plenty of time. 'Thank you, Monsieur,' I said, lifting my single suitcase from the pavement. 'Thank you very much.'

'You are welcome.' He inclined his head gallantly, then leaned back against the sleek grey Safrane and looked away, lifting the cigarette. When I came out of the station the second time, he was deep in conversation with an older, red-faced man sweating beneath the burden of a rich-looking set of luggage.

I passed by swiftly, without looking up, and scurried on towards the waiting *autocar*, where I settled myself in the vacant front seat behind the driver. I had every intention of enjoying my clear view of the passing scenery, but the rolling motion of the bus defeated me, and before we'd even driven the few miles to the centre of the city of Tours I was asleep. It was wholly understandable – I'd been up before the birds that morning, caught the plane to Paris and endured a bumpy bus ride, high-speed trains, and two full cups of railway station coffee the consistency of river mud.

I might have kept on sleeping straight to Chinon, but for the sudden blare of a car horn directly beneath my window. The second blast of sound brought my head round with a jolt that rattled my teeth, and my eyes flew open in time to see the Safrane cut smoothly in front of us, travelling at twice the necessary speed. So, I thought smiling, my dashing taxi driver had found himself a fare after all. Good for him. He had long disappeared down the road ahead by the time the bus reached the next town.

'Azay-le-Rideau,' the driver announced over his microphone. Fully awake now, I held my breath as the bus folded itself around the narrow, sharply twisting streets, pressing pedestrians back against stone walls or into the shelter of doorways. Down we went at a dizzying angle, disgorged a handful of passengers in front of a row of shops, and swept on over a bridge that offered an intriguing glimpse of a jewel-like château that seemed to have been built on water, a perfect island perfectly reflected in a pale, quiescent lake.

Here at last, I thought happily, was the Loire Valley of the brochures and guide books – and the France that I remembered from my childhood. The town gave way to forest, and the forest fell in turn to field and vineyard. I sat forward in my seat, reading the passing signposts with interest, and then with eager recognition. *La Devinière* . . . surely that great block of a building was the birthplace of the writer Rabelais. I remembered reading about it in one of my brochures, somewhere. Which meant that Chinon itself must be just around that . . .

'Oh,' I said suddenly, and with rather more force than I'd intended.

The bus driver smiled at my reaction, understanding. He slowed his speed a little. 'It is your first visit to Chinon?' he guessed, in French.

I somehow managed a nod in reply, and the bus slowed still further.

'It should be savoured, then, this first approach,' he told me.

Savoured indeed. The yellow-white ruins of Chinon Castle rose majestically above us like the crumbling scene of some great Shakespearean tragedy, an unbroken sweep of blind wall and decaying towers bleached with age, jaggedly spearing the grey and ever-shifting sky.

Despite the bus driver's best efforts, I barely had time to register the image before the road tipped sharply downwards, hugging ancient walls hung thick with ivy as we dropped towards the level of the town. The castle hung high on the cliffs above us now, all but forgotten in my first view of the river Vienne and the wide avenue of towering plane trees that ran along the riverbank, marking the approach to the town centre. Nothing

– neither Harry's descriptions nor my own faded memories of the French countryside – had prepared me for such a sudden, breathtaking explosion of sheer beauty.

'Oh,' I said again.

It was, I realized, an inadequate sort of comment to make, but the bus driver seemed quite pleased by it.

'It grabs, does it not? It grabs you here,' he said, making a fist with one hand over his heart, to illustrate.

I found my voice at last. 'Yes, it does.'

And it did. It grabbed me so completely, in fact, that when the driver announced: 'Place Jeanne d'Arc' and another handful of passengers filed off the bus, I scrambled off after them without thinking, bumping my suitcase down the steps. It was only after everyone had scattered purposefully that I realized I hadn't the faintest idea how to get to the Hotel de France.

I stood for a moment with the river to my back and the plane trees stretching off to either side, and looked for someone to direct me. The square across the street was, I presumed, the Place Jeanne d'Arc, a great broad crossroads filled with a confusing swirl of bodies and faces and the half-familiar sounds of speech and laughter. I'd just prepared myself to grab the nearest person when, quite by accident, I saw a face I recognized.

He had parked the Safrane in a no-parking zone beside the curb, and was leaning up against the bonnet as before, frowning slightly as he watched the milling crowd. I don't know what impulse it was that made me cross the street towards him – simple weariness, perhaps, or maybe just his handsome face. I caught him this time unawares.

'Is it also an expensive taxi ride,' I asked him, in English, 'to the Hotel de France?'

His head came round, startled, and the frown dissolved into a genuine smile. 'No,' he conceded. '*That* is not expensive. I will take you.' He pitched the stub of his cigarette into the street and levered himself away from the car, coming round to open the passenger side door for me. 'You have only the one suitcase?' he asked, taking it from my hand.

'Yes.'

There were already suitcases in the back seat of the taxi, the same expensive cases that I'd seen the round and red-faced man struggling with at St-Pierre-des-Corps.

'But you already have a fare, Monsieur,' I said, looking at the suitcases. 'I'm sorry, I didn't realize . . .'

'It is no problem,' he assured me. He shoved the costly luggage aside, unconcerned, to make room for my less impressive bag. 'The gentleman has business to attend to. I will return for him. He will not miss me; your hotel is not so far.'

It was, in truth, the shortest ride I'd ever taken in a taxi. A few moments along the river, back the way I'd just come, then up a narrow square wedged tight with plane trees to a still smaller square shaded by leaning acacias.

'The Hotel de France,' my driver announced, with a smile that was wholly understandable. I could probably have walked the same distance myself in less than five minutes, and for free. I looked at the meter on the dashboard, and his smile deepened. The meter was blank.

'There is no charge, Madame,' he told me.

'Of course there is.' I reached for my wallet. I didn't like to be in debt.

'But I insist. The taxi, it has hardly moved at all.'

'How much do I owe you?'

He looked at me a long moment, silently weighing my will against his, and then he tipped his head, considering. 'Ten francs.'

'A cup of coffee costs ten francs,' I reminded him.

'Fifteen francs, then.'

I handed him twenty-five, and he took it with a thoughtful glance at my face. 'I hope that you enjoy your stay in Chinon, Madame.'

I'd have no problem doing that, I thought a moment later, as I looked around the quiet hotel lobby. For all my cousin's failings, he did have his brilliant moments, and he'd chosen the Hotel de France in one of them.

It was an older hotel, lovingly restored and decorated in rich classic tones of rose and cream, with an elegant hardwood staircase spiralling upwards from the entrance hall. To my left a few steps led up to the sunlit breakfast room, while on my right a door stood open to the bar. Both rooms were empty.

The young woman at the front desk was amiable and pretty, if a little dim. No, Monsieur Braden had not yet arrived, but our rooms were all prepared . . . two rooms . . . I was sure that we wanted two rooms? *Very* sure, I told her, and with a small, perplexed shrug she handed me the key. 'Your room is on the second floor, Madame. Room 215.'

And so my holiday begins, I thought drily, with Harry, as I'd half expected, nowhere to be seen. I could almost hear Aunt Jane's mild voice saying, *Didn't I tell you, dear?* as I climbed the two flights of curving stairs to the second floor.

My room, at least, was all that I'd been promised – bright and fresh-smelling, with a soaring, white-painted ceiling and walls papered in a soft, restful gold. And best of all I had a window, a huge casement window that looked out over the square and the clustered rooftops of the old medieval village.

Swinging one half of the window inward on its hinges, I leaned out as far as I dared and inspected my view. There was a fountain nestled among the acacia trees in the square below me. I hadn't noticed it on my arrival, but there it was, a large bronze fountain ringed by sculpted figures. Even above the confused noise of the street and square I could hear the steady dancing splash of water cascading from the two-tiered basin into the gathering pool below. The sound set off a rush of memory, and for a fleeting moment I was five years old again, my fingers trailing in another fountain while my father urged me, 'Make a wish . . .'

I pressed the memory firmly back, and focused. A man was sitting on the rim of the fountain's pool with a spotted dog sleeping at his feet, and beside them a flower-seller was starting to dismantle his display of drooping marigolds and roses. I was drooping a little myself. Another wave of weariness swept over me, and I pulled myself away from the open window, turning my wrist to see the time. Three o'clock, nearly. Fifteen hours, I corrected myself with a faint smile. Time all travellers were at rest.

It was sheer heaven to crawl between the sheets of the sprawling bed and draw the blanket to my chin. I was so completely and utterly exhausted that I would not have expected to dream. But I did dream, all the same. I dreamed that an angel was playing the violin outside my open window. It should have been a lovely dream, but it wasn't.

The angel wore my cousin's smiling face.

Chapter Three

We were seven . . .

I awoke refreshed, completing my revival with a half-hour in my private bath. The small tiled room was thick with steam when I finally switched off the shower spray and emerged, my skin the colour of a boiled lobster above the plush white hotel towel. The steam followed me in a swirling great cloud as I dripped my way across the carpet and round the corner of the rumpled bed to push the window open wider.

I had only slept an hour or so, but it might have been a different day. The grey sky had broken to reveal a clear, unblemished field of blue, through which the sun blazed its determined way towards the west. Bright sunlight touched the feathered tops of the acacia trees in the square below and glittered in the pools of the fountain. In the place where earlier I'd seen the flower-seller, a weary trio of tourists now sipped pints of beer at a little white table with red plastic chairs, one of a dozen or more such tables that seemed to have sprouted from nowhere in the square.

I drew back again from the window, combing my fingers through my drying hair. The air was biting still, despite the sun – too cool, perhaps, for an outdoor table, but the idea of a drink appealed to me.

Downstairs, I found the hotel bar no longer empty. A handful of people were taking advantage of the invitingly intimate modern decor – sectioned seats and ottomans arranged round tables of pale laminate, the rich terracotta tones of the upholstery glowing against grey linen walls and charcoal carpet. Enormous plants and artwork softened the modular angles, and the late afternoon light poured slanting through the floor to ceiling windows facing out upon the fountain square.

The conversation dipped, paused, and began again when I walked in, and I found myself facing the not unfriendly stares of two young men who sat together by the nearest window. One of them, a black-haired lad with gentle eyes, smiled cautiously and greeted me in French.

'Would you care to join us?' he ventured. 'There's plenty of room.' At my hesitation his smile grew charming. 'We're quite well-behaved, I promise. It's only that we've been travelling together for four months, now, and we're tired of hearing each other talk. Please,' he urged me, indicating the vacant seat across from him. 'Let us buy you a drink.'

His companion sent me a vague but pleasant smile as I took the offered seat, reminding me a little of a chap I'd known at school – he, too, had worn tie-dyed shirts and let his hair grow straggling to his shoulders, and he'd carried with him something of the same distracted aura of a young man who has chosen to remain young, like the hippies of the sixties. The dark-haired lad, by contrast, was cleaner-cut, conservative, and better-schooled in manners. He raised his hand to get the bartender's attention. 'You're new at the hotel, aren't you?' he asked me. 'I haven't seen you before.'

I nodded, trying without success to place his accent. Not Provençal, I thought – it was lighter than that. Not Breton, either, but something decidedly rustic, rather loose about the vowel sounds . . .

'I've only just arrived,' I said, 'this afternoon. From England.'

He lowered his hand and grinned. 'You're English?' he said, in my own language. 'I should have known. Every time I try to start up a conversation with someone . . .'

'Good heavens,' I cut him off, astonished. 'You're American.'

The long-haired youth winced visibly. 'Canadian, actually,' he corrected me. It was the sort of stubborn, pained response that Hercule Poirot made in the detective books, when someone called him French instead of Belgian.

His friend forgave me my mistake. 'The accent sounds the same, I know.'

'The hell it does.' The hippie grinned. 'We don't sound like the Whitakers.'

'Well, true. But then, they're from the deep South, so that's hardly surprising.' The dark young man glanced over at the gleaming oak-topped bar, where a middle-aged couple sat in conversation with the young bartender.

Middle-aged, I decided upon closer examination, was perhaps the wrong label for them. The woman would certainly have resisted it. She was quite pretty, in a brittle sort of way, with artfully arranged auburn curls and fluttering hands that glittered with rings. At first her husband looked much older, until one noticed that

37

his silver hair was not matched by his tanned and vital face.

'I'm sure you'll meet them,' the long-haired youth assured me. 'Garland likes to keep up to date on new arrivals. She's kind of . . . well, kind of unique.'

'Her husband's really nice,' the dark one added. 'His name's Jim.' Which reminded him he hadn't yet introduced himself. 'I'm Paul, by the way. Paul Lazarus. And this is my brother Simon.'

'Emily Braden.' I shook hands with each of them in turn, relaxing back into the thick cushioned seat. Dark-haired Paul, I decided, was the younger of the two, despite appearances. I'd found that between siblings there was always a clear pattern of interaction, of deference and command, that set the first-born apart. Simon Lazarus might look the less mature but he was restless, more aggressive, and now that our conversation had switched to English he assumed the role of spokesman for both of them – assumed it with a natural ease born of long familiarity and habit.

He sent me a friendly grin. 'We're doing the Europe thing. Paul finished university last spring and neither one of us could find a job, so we decided to squander our savings instead. We're planning to go all the way around the world, if the money holds out. And if I can ever get Paul away from this place.' Simon grinned wider. 'I had a hard enough time dragging him out of Holland, and now here we are,' he told me, 'stuck again.'

Paul smiled and would have said something, but he wasn't given the chance. The bartender, having excused himself from the American couple, descended upon us in a whirl of youthful vigour.

Seen at close range, the bartender appeared even

younger than I'd first suspected. He couldn't have been above twenty, but it was easy to see how I'd been deceived. Only in France, I thought, could a teenager look suave, even worldly. He would break a lot of hearts, this one. He probably had already.

I watched in open admiration as he exhaled the expressive 'pouf' of breath that was so undeniably French, muttered some brief comment about *les américains*, and winked conspiratorially at Paul Lazarus. 'What can I bring you?' he asked, in flowing English.

'Thierry will tell you,' Simon said positively, his accent anglicizing the bartender's name so that it came out sounding like 'Terry'. 'Thierry, tell Miss . . .'

'Braden,' Paul supplied.

'Emily,' I said, over both of them.

'. . . tell Emily what the difference is between Canadians and Americans.'

The bartender looked down at me with a serious expression. 'The Canadians, Madame, are much more difficult,' he confided. 'They are impossible. This one,' he pointed at Simon, 'makes always the curtain in his room to fall down, and always I must get the ladder to replace it.'

'Twice,' Simon defended himself. 'I've only done it twice. And it's your own fault for putting a curtain in front of that window to begin with. Windows like that are meant to be opened, to be enjoyed. I can't help it if your stupid curtain rod gets in the way.'

'You see?' Thierry winked again. 'Most difficult, these Canadians. But you, Madame, you are not Canadian?'

'Worse.' I smiled up at him. 'I'm English.'

'*Non!*' He clapped a hand to his heart in mock agony, but his eyes twinkled at me. 'You would like a *café au lait*, Madame? All the English, they enjoy the *café au lait.*'

Only, I thought, because that's what we learned to say at school. Until I'd lived in France I hadn't known there were so many different kinds of coffee, from thickly fragrant *café* on its own, to the decadent richness of *café crème*. I considered my options. 'Could I have a *crème* instead, please?'

'*Bien sûr*,' he said. 'With pleasure.'

'Thierry,' Simon informed me, as the bartender left to fire up the gleaming monster of a coffee machine sitting behind the bar, 'is the nephew of the proprietors, Madame and Monsieur Chamond. Have you met them yet? No? Well, don't worry, you will. They're terrific people, very easy to talk to. I'm surprised they're not in here now, they usually are. Anyhow, Thierry's their nephew. He's a bit of a drain on them, I think, but he's lots of fun. Just don't let him know you speak French,' was Simon's advice, 'or he'll talk your ear off. He kept Paul going for three hours our first afternoon here.'

'You don't speak French?' I guessed, and Simon shrugged.

'Just the basics. Hello . . . where's the bathroom . . . I have a blue hat – that sort of thing. Paul's the expert. He spent a year in Switzerland, on a Rotary exchange.'

I assured Paul that he'd done his sponsors proud. 'You sounded terribly French, just now.'

He smiled. 'So did you.'

Thierry had returned with my *café crème*. He set it with a flourish on the table in front of me, sent me a thoroughly disarming smile, and swept off again to take the order from a clustered group of older tourists – Germans, from the snatches of their conversation I could overhear. It wasn't easy to hear things at a distance. The radio crooned steadily above our heads, not loudly but persistently, and Edith Piaf had just begun to sing 'La Vie En Rose' when my wandering gaze came to rest upon the solitary figure in the far corner.

Had I been drinking anything but coffee I'd have blamed it on the drink – that blinding moment of illumination that made time, for one long heartbeat, cease to be. It was as if my mind said, see now, *this* must be remembered . . . this single moment, with Piaf's voice rasping out the haunting lyrics and the clink of glasses fading to a far-off sound no louder than the trickle of a fountain.

Time blinked. The moment held. There was no reason for it, really – none at all. None, at least, that I was willing to admit. The world, I thought, was full of handsome men.

This one sat close against the tall French windows that opened to the street and fountain square. He looked German too, I thought, or maybe Swedish. His hair was so amazingly fair, the same whitish-gold colour that one sees sometimes on very young children, and where it brushed against the collar of his crisp white cotton shirt it seemed to blend into the fabric. His eyes looked oddly dark in contrast, though of course I couldn't tell their colour. He looked too handsome to be human, really, sitting there – like some youthful middle-aged pop star, narrow-hipped and long-limbed, his classic face unlined.

Simon Lazarus caught me staring. 'That's Neil,' he told me helpfully. 'He's English too, like you. He's a musician.'

I'm sure my face must have shown my reaction because Paul laughed, a short, soft laugh of understanding. 'No, not *that* kind of musician,' he said. 'He's a violinist. Plays with a symphony orchestra, I think. You'll hear him practising if you're around the hotel in the afternoon.'

So this, I thought, was my mysterious angel with the violin. He certainly looked the part, with that face and his loose white shirt and the sun turning his hair to a halo of light.

'I think I heard him playing earlier,' I said, to Paul. 'I was half asleep at the time. I thought I'd dreamed the music.'

'He sounds like a recording when he practises,' Simon put in. 'He's that good. His room's right underneath ours, on the first floor, so we can hear him pretty clearly. Hang on, I'll introduce you.'

There wasn't time to voice a protest, he was already taking charge, turning his head to call across the bar, and a moment later I was being introduced. 'Neil Grantham,' Simon said, 'meet Emily . . .'

'Braden,' Paul supplied, for a second time.

'Braden,' Simon echoed. 'Emily, this is Neil.'

I had to look a long way up. He was older than I was, though I couldn't have placed his age with any certainty. Thirty-five, perhaps? Forty? I watched his smile cut a cleft in one clean-shaven cheek, and crinkle the corners of his eyes. Black eyes. How odd, I thought. Like his hair, they seemed to glow with some strange inner radiance. I mumbled something banal and shook his outstretched hand.

'She heard you practising this afternoon,' Simon went on, conversationally.

'Did you really? I hope I didn't disturb you.'

I shook my head. 'It was lovely, actually. I like Beethoven.'

The crinkles round his eyes deepened, and he took the seat beside me. 'I'm flattered you could recognize it,' he said. 'You've just arrived?'

'This afternoon.'

'From England, I gather?'

'Yes.'

It was difficult to carry on small talk with a man who looked at you like that, I thought. This was not the sort of man that one could flirt with. Those eyes were far too level, far too serious, and because of that they made me feel uneasy. I smiled at him even as my own defences slammed down stoutly into place, and to my relief Neil Grantham didn't try to bridge the distance. He rubbed an absent hand along his outstretched thigh and shifted his gaze to a thick paperback novel sitting on the table next to Simon. I'd noticed it earlier myself, and smiled at the title: *Ulysses*. The sort of book, I thought, that young men like Simon Lazarus went in for – the sort of book that thumbed its nose at polite convention. Which is why I was surprised when Neil addressed his question, not to Simon, but to Paul. 'Haven't you finished that, yet?'

Paul smiled lazily, but it was once again big brother Simon who answered for him. 'Give him a chance.' Simon's grin was broad. 'He's only been reading it for two years.'

'Experiencing it,' said Paul. 'I'm experiencing it. You don't just read James Joyce, you know.'

Simon seemed ready to make some argumentative reply, but something he saw over my shoulder distracted him. 'Damn.' He glowered into his wine glass. 'Don't look now,' he muttered, 'but we're about to be invaded.'

It must be the couple from the bar, I thought – the

43

couple from America. Either that, or Scarlett O'Hara herself had just snuck up behind my back. 'Hel-*lo*,' drawled the feminine voice at my shoulder. 'Is it all right if we join your little party? I was just saying to Jim how *tiring* it is to have to speak in French all the time. Boys, you don't mind, do you? Hello, Neil. I heard you playing this afternoon and I said to Jim it's just like being in Carnegie Hall – no, really, it *is*. Hello, I don't believe we've met. I'm Garland Whitaker.'

'Emily Braden.' I briefly clasped the ring-encrusted hand, feeling somewhat dizzy after that introductory speech. Jim Whitaker shook my hand firmly and sat down beside his wife, facing the window to the street. His solid, almost stoic figure made an intriguing contrast to his wife's gushing mannerisms. They were both in their mid-forties, I decided, although Garland fancied herself younger.

'The boys have picked you up, I see,' she said to me. 'You have to be careful with these two, you know. They look harmless, but they're really *not*. Oh, Paul,' she shifted in her seat, '*do* you think you could be a dear and make that Thierry understand that the heater in our room is just too hot for us? I tried to explain it to him, but I don't think he knew what I was saying and his English is really *so* awful . . .'

It hadn't sounded awful to me, but then the French did have a mischievous tendency not to speak well when it suited them. I'd watched many a Parisian waiter play the game with unsuspecting tourists, particularly tourists who were difficult to deal with. Garland Whitaker, I thought, might just qualify for that distinction.

Her husband, on the other hand, appeared to be a different sort of person entirely. He had kind eyes.

44

'Thierry speaks English perfectly well,' Jim Whitaker informed his wife in a calm voice. 'If you'd stop talking to him like he was a two-year-old with a hearing problem, you'd find that out.'

Garland Whitaker ignored the rebuke and smiled brightly at all of us. 'Jim's mother was French, you know. Or so he says.' She cast a teasing eye upon her husband. 'I never met your parents, darling, so I have to take your word. But really,' she told Paul, 'Jim can only speak a little French, and you get along so well with Thierry, I'm *sure* you'd have no problem . . .'

'I'll see what I can do,' Paul promised.

'Oh, wonderful. Now, listen,' she continued, leaning forward in her seat, 'while everyone's here . . . I'm thinking we should all take Christian out to dinner tonight. You know, a sort of going away party.'

Paul looked surprised. 'Christian's going away?'

Neil Grantham smiled, and answered, 'Not exactly. He's moving out of the hotel, though, into a house.'

'The house *her* husband used to live in.' Garland flashed a gossip's eyes. 'Can you believe it? Apparently she owns it, though she hasn't lived in it herself for ages. She let *him* use it, instead.'

I didn't know who 'him' was – 'her' husband, obviously, but that hardly helped. Still, I didn't think it polite to ask.

'I suppose it will be nice for Christian, having a whole house to himself,' Garland went on. 'Mind you, *I* wouldn't want to live where somebody had *died* . . . can you imagine how awful? And in a sense it's kind of tasteless, don't you think, for Martine to even offer? Out with the old, in with the new. I mean, her husband isn't even buried . . .'

'Ex-husband,' Simon cut her off abruptly. 'He was Martine's ex-husband.'

Paul finally looked across and noticed I was all at sea. 'A woman that we know,' he told me, quietly. 'Her ex-husband killed himself night before last, by accident. He tripped and fell down the stairs.'

'Not down the stairs,' Simon made the correction in authoritative tones. 'Over the bannister. Broke his neck.'

'Ah,' I said.

Garland Whitaker smiled slyly. 'Maybe it wasn't an accident. Maybe Christian did it, just to make sure . . .' She broke off suddenly and twisted round in her seat as the hotel's front door slammed. 'Why Christian, darling, we'd almost given up on you! Come on in and join the gang.'

I had the distinct impression that the man hovering in the open doorway would have preferred to face a firing squad.

He appeared to be around my own age – a lanky, soft-eyed man with rough blond hair that looked as if he'd cut it himself with a pair of garden shears and a beard that seemed more the result of simply forgetting to shave than of any concerted effort to grow one. His clothes, too, were rather rumpled and oddly matched, his denim jeans stained with small splotches of bright colour.

'I must go and change my clothes,' he excused himself self-consciously. His voice was quiet, edged with a German accent that kept it from being soft. 'I have missed the bus connection back from Saumur, and it has made me late.'

'You will join us for dinner, though?' Garland Whitaker pressed him, then turned her smile on all of us. 'We are going for dinner, aren't we? To give Christian a proper send-off?'

It wasn't so much an invitation as a stage direction, I thought. The man named Christian wavered a moment longer in the doorway, then gave in like the rest of us.

'Of course,' he said politely, and faded into the hallway. The heavy clump of his shoes on the stairs had a faintly defeatist sound.

Simon slouched back in his seat, scowling blackly, and opened his mouth to say something. I didn't actually see Paul's elbow move, but I did see Simon jump a little in his seat, and whatever he had meant to say he kept it to himself. Garland Whitaker, triumphant, turned her attention back to the rest of us, and started talking about some day trip she and her husband had taken, or were planning to take . . . I'll admit I didn't really listen.

She just went on talking anyway, red curls bobbing with the motions of her head, that honeyed Southern voice giving way to grating trills of laughter. Like Simon, I was not impressed. I felt the frown forming on my own face, and could have used Paul's elbow in my own ribs to remind me of my manners. Instead, some instinct made me glance upwards, at the face of the man sitting beside me.

The look Neil Grantham slanted back at me was privately amused.

But he wasn't smiling, and he didn't say anything to me. So there really was no reason why I should have looked away as quickly as I did, face flaming, like some prudish Victorian spinster. Or why I should have felt, all of a sudden, a ridiculous urge to run.

Chapter Four

. . . let the past be past; let
be . . .

The restaurant was packed to the rafters with the Friday night supper crowd, but I didn't mind waiting for a table. It was a cosy sort of restaurant – small and warm, filled with glorious smells and furnished with a tasteful eye for detail. Besides, I thought, one had to like the name: *Le Cœur de Lion*. In honour of Richard the Lionheart, I presumed. Plantagenets again. Harry, when he stayed in Chinon, probably ate here every night.

While the seven of us waited, packed like sardines by the door, I introduced myself to the shy young German. His name was Christian Rand, he told me, above a firm but fleeting handshake.

'Christian's an artist,' said Simon, who had dressed up a bit for dinner, topping his T-shirt with a thick black jumper and smoothing back his hair into a sailor's pigtail. 'He's not a tourist, not like us. He's lived in Chinon for . . . how long, Christian? Five years?'

'Six.'

'Really?' I looked at Christian Rand with interest. 'At the Hotel de France?' I'd read of all those great

48

composers, poets, writers, who had lived in hotel rooms, of course, but I'd never actually met someone who . . .

'No.' He shook his tousled head and smiled. 'For these past two months only. I had until July a small house, not too far from Chinon, but my neighbours they were not so good. And so my friends the Chamonds said that I could stay at their hotel while I am looking for another house.'

It was the longest speech I'd heard him make, and the effort appeared to leave him exhausted.

'And now you've found one,' Garland piped up, her tone bright.

'Yes.' Christian looked down silently. He wasn't as slow as he looked, I thought. He knew quite well that Garland Whitaker was dying to draw him into conversation, to learn as much as she could about his dealings with this Martine woman, whoever she was. But Christian Rand was not prepared to play.

The waiter finally managed to find us a table tucked well away from the other patrons, where we wouldn't disturb the quieter, more reticent French at their evening meal.

Garland Whitaker perused the menu with an expression of vague distrust. 'Maybe a pizza,' she decided. 'Though they're not *real* pizzas here, you know. Not like we get back home. Jim ordered a pizza here a couple of nights ago and when it came to the table it had an *egg* in the middle of it. Can you imagine? A runny egg. I tell you, I nearly *died* . . .'

'Sounds kind of good, actually,' Simon mused, leaning forward. 'Which one was that, Jim?'

Garland was mortified. 'Oh, Simon, *don't*. If there's anything I can't stand, it's the sight of a runny egg.' She

49

looked away, missing Simon's smirk, and turned enquiring eyes on Christian Rand. 'You'll be moving into your new house tomorrow, I take it?'

'Yes.'

Garland turned to Neil and smiled sweetly. 'Then I guess you'll be our only artist left in residence, darling.'

I'd been trying, since we left the hotel, not to notice Neil at all. For reasons I chose not to explore, I found it easier to talk to Simon or to Paul – or even to the taciturn Christian – than to meet those quietly intense dark eyes. But I couldn't keep it up for ever, especially not since he'd taken the chair directly opposite mine. I glanced up, in time to see him shrug off Garland's comment with a small, indulgent smile. 'I'm hardly in Christian's league.'

'Nonsense,' Simon said. 'You had Paul reciting poetry today, in the stairwell.'

Neil's eyebrows lifted. 'Poetry?'

'Yeah. In French, of course, so I didn't understand it. What was it you said, Paul?'

Paul lifted his head, looking faintly embarrassed, and shrugged. 'Just a quotation I remembered. Not poetry. Just something George Sand wrote in her diary about Liszt.'

'What was it?' I asked him, curious myself now. He sent me such a look as Caesar must have given Brutus, and repeated the quotation out loud. It was a lovely phrase, almost lyrical in its sentiment, and it told me rather more about the boy Paul Lazarus than it did about Neil's violin playing.

'Are you going to share it with the rest of us?' Garland Whitaker prompted, a trifle impatiently.

It was only when I looked up, into Neil Grantham's blank expectant face, that I suddenly realized Paul and

I must be the only ones who understood the French language on that level.

'Sorry,' I apologized. 'It means: "My griefs are etherealized, and my instincts are . . ."' I faltered, and looked to Paul. 'How would you translate that last word?'

'Exalted?'

'That's it.' I nodded. ' "My instincts are exalted." '

'How pretty.' Garland eased back in her chair, satisfied.

'Indeed.' Neil looked sideways at Paul. 'Thank you.'

Paul shrugged again. 'It's what I felt, that's all.'

'Well, it's no small praise, that, for a musician. I can't say as I've ever etherealized anybody's grief before.'

'Do you practise every day?' I asked Neil.

'Every day. Not as much as I ought to, of course, but as much as I'm able.'

'Neil's not really on vacation,' put in Garland. 'He's recuperating. He broke his hand.'

'Tell her how,' Simon dared him.

Neil grinned. 'Stupidity. I let myself get dragged into a fist fight, in some bar in Munich.' He held his left hand up to show me. It was a nice hand, square and long-fingered, neatly kept. 'It's getting better, but I can't do all my fingering properly yet. So my employers kindly gave me some time off. On the condition,' he added, 'that I don't enjoy myself too much.'

'And is this your first trip to Chinon?' I asked him.

He shook his head. 'No. This would be my eighth visit, I think – maybe even my ninth. It's an addiction, really, Chinon is. You'll understand, if you stay long enough.'

Beside me, Simon nodded. 'Monsieur Chamond says

once you've been to Chinon, you're hooked for life. He says you'll keep on coming back.'

'He sounds like a wise man,' I said. 'I haven't met him yet.'

'I'm sure you'll meet them eventually,' Jim Whitaker assured me. 'They're nice people, both of them.'

'*They* speak English,' Garland said. 'Not like that nephew of theirs. Honestly, you'd think with all the tourists they get around here, more people would take the time to learn English. It's so *frustrating*, trying to communicate.'

At the far end of the table, Paul smiled gently. 'I'm sure the French feel the same way,' he said, 'when they visit America.'

Our waiter seemed to understand us well enough. He took Paul's order first, then Neil's, then waited while Garland tried to choose a wine and Simon tried to learn which pizza had the egg on it. I settled on a galette for myself – a buckwheat crêpe filled with cheese and mushrooms – washed down with a half bottle of sweet cider.

The food, when it arrived, was excellent, and yet the meal itself was slightly off. I tried, and failed, to put my finger on the cause. The atmosphere around our table was, at its surface, entirely normal for a group of people who'd just met on holiday – a little forced, perhaps, but normal. And yet, I thought, there was a tension here . . . a tension spun from more than my awareness of the man across the table. One couldn't shake away the sense that something deeper flowed beneath the smiles and salt-passing, some darker conflict hinted at but never quite revealed. It made me feel excluded.

I ate my meal in silence, for the most part, and let

the others talk. In time the conversation dwindled to a kind of battle between Simon and Garland Whitaker, both of whom seemed fully capable of carrying the standard single-handed. Garland proved the more experienced combatant, and more often than not her voice came out on top.

She had remarkable stamina, I had to admit. The table conversation had exhausted several topics, and still she showed no sign of wearing down. Her husband, though, I noticed, had stopped listening. He went on eating quietly, his gaze occasionally focusing with mild interest on someone or something at another table – a laughing child, an old man eating alone, a frilly woman slipping titbits to a poodle underneath her chair . . . But he'd tuned his wife's voice out completely. It was, I assumed, a defence mechanism he'd acquired over the years.

Garland chattered on about the château that they'd visited that morning. 'We stay in one place,' she said to me, 'and take our day trips out from there. So much easier than jumping from place to place, don't you think? And I can actually unpack my clothes, which is a blessing. This time we're doing all the Loire châteaux. We always like to have a theme for our vacations, don't we, Jim? Always. We did the D-day beaches on our honeymoon.'

'How romantic,' muttered Simon. He tore a piece of bread in half to mop up what remained of his runny egg, and looked towards Jim Whitaker. 'Were you in the Army, during the war?'

It was the first real smile I'd seen from the American. He looked rather nice, when he smiled. 'I'm not that old, son,' he said. 'I wasn't even born until after the war ended.'

'Oh,' said Simon. 'Sorry.'

Garland laughed her tinkling laugh. 'Your father fought in France, though, didn't he?' she asked her husband. 'That's how he met your mother.'

'Yes.'

'And Jim was in the Army, Simon, when I married him. We lived in Germany for two whole years.' She shuddered. 'God, that awful little apartment, darling, do you remember it? But then I guess it was just fine, for Germans.'

Christian flicked a brief look down the table, but made no comment. It was Neil who asked the Whitakers just where in Germany they'd lived, and nodded when they told him. 'I do know it,' he said, smiling. 'There's a wonderful music festival not far from there, every June. Lovely place.'

'I hated it,' said Garland with a shrug. 'The people were so unfriendly. Nazis, probably, most of them.'

Her husband pushed his empty plate away and smiled at her with patience. 'Now come on, honey, you know they weren't.'

'Darling, it's *true*. Don't you remember all those little holes someone kept digging, all over town? Mrs Jurgen's dog fell into one, and the police got suspicious? Well, *that* was Nazis, the police proved it.' To the rest of us she explained: 'There'd been money hidden there, or something, at the end of the war, and these people were coming back to find it thirty years later. Incredible. And then there was the time . . .'

She was still going, like a wind-up doll on overload, when we finally paid the bill and rose and wound our way through the labyrinth of tables to the front door.

It was heavenly to breathe the outside air. The restaurant fronted on the long and narrow Place du

Général de Gaulle, and against the dark green trees the streetlamps glowed a softly spreading yellow. Further up the square the fountain gurgled merrily, and I saw the sign of the Hotel de France illuminated through the shifting leaves.

Christian apparently saw it too. He mumbled some faint words of thanks for dinner, and wandered off towards the beckoning lights. A moment later Neil Grantham followed suit. He had a long, unhurried stride, and watching him I felt again that strange unbidden twinge of interest. I pushed it back, and tried to hold my thoughts to what was going on around me.

Simon and Garland had switched from Nazis now to neo-Nazis, and the rising tide of tension in Europe. 'It's all the immigration,' Garland was saying. She tossed her auburn head. 'It's the same everywhere, I think, all these foreigners moving in and taking over. It's like the Jews all over again, isn't it? I mean, you can't *condone* what the Nazis did, don't get me wrong, but you can almost understand it. These immigrants can get so uppity . . .'

It was an ugly thing to say. I stared at her, and Jim burst out: 'God, Garland, *honestly* . . . !' and then to my delight Simon recovered from his own stunned silence with a vengeance and began to give her proper hell. In the midst of all this Paul turned placidly to me and smiled. 'Feel like taking a walk?' he asked.

'Sure.'

I don't think anybody even noticed us leaving. Paul turned towards the river, away from the hotel, and I ambled along beside him, content to let him set the pace.

We walked past a statue that I recognized from my travel brochures – a seated figure of the great humanist Rabelais, once a traveller and a lover of life, now confined to one small patch of garden at the end of the Place du Général de Gaulle. Bathed by floodlights, the seated scholar seemed immense, brooding in gloomy silence as the river murmured on behind him.

Paul sauntered across the road and round the far side of the statue, where a narrow breach in the river wall revealed a long fall of sloping stone stairs that vanished into the dark water below. On the seventh stair down, he sat and waited for me.

'I lied,' he confessed, with a sheepish smile. 'I didn't really feel like a walk. I felt like a cigarette.' He shook one loose and offered the pack to me, but I declined, watching his face in the brief flare of the match.

'I didn't know you smoked,' I said.

'Only when Simon's not around. He's got opinions on all kinds of things, and smoking's one of them. I try to avoid arguments when I can. In case you hadn't noticed.' He grinned suddenly, and I knew that he was thinking not of his brother but of Garland Whitaker, and the little scene we'd just escaped from.

I envied him his self-control, and told him so. 'I'm afraid she makes me lose my temper.'

'Bad luck to lose your temper on the Sabbath – that's what my mother always tells me.'

'I'm safe, then. It's only Friday.'

'After sundown on Friday.' He smiled. 'My Sabbath.'

It took me a moment to digest that. 'You're Jewish?'

He shrugged, still smiling. 'With a name like Lazarus I'd better be.'

To be truthful, I hadn't noticed his surname at all. But then, I fancied myself a different sort of person than Garland Whitaker. I thought again of what she'd said, of how she'd said it . . . 'She really is a hateful woman.'

56

'No she isn't. Not really. She just gets a little bit much sometimes, that's all.' His eyes touched mine briefly, warmly, then drifted away again, out across the wide expanse of river to the shadowed line of trees that rimmed the opposite shore. 'She doesn't mean anything by it. It's simple ignorance with her, not spite.'

I wasn't convinced. 'Sure about that, are you?'

'Pretty sure. Besides, you get used to it, after a while.' He paused, drawing deeply on the cigarette, still gazing out over the swiftly flowing water. 'You see those trees over there? That's not the other side of the river, it's an island. You can't tell, really, unless you see it from the cliffs, or walk across the bridge, there.' His voice was soft and even, storytelling. 'They burned the Jews of Chinon on that island in the fourteenth century. Accused them of poisoning the town's wells. It didn't just happen here, of course, it happened everywhere. Women, children, no-one cared. They just burned them.' He glanced at me and half smiled in the darkness. 'The Nazis weren't the first, you know. It's been around for ever, prejudice.'

'That's hardly an excuse for it.'

'No,' he agreed, exhaling a stream of smoke that caught the shifting light from the street behind us. 'But sometimes taking the historical perspective helps you understand a little better why people do the things they do. That's what life's all about, I think – understanding each other. Now Simon,' he told me, his mouth curving, 'sees things differently. If someone spits at Simon, he spits right back. An eye for an eye. But that doesn't accomplish anything.' He turned his head to look at me. 'People hate too much, you know?'

His face, in that instant, seemed suddenly older than

my own. Centuries older. And then he laughed and looked away, and the moment passed.

'God,' he said, 'I sound like my father.' He pitched the stub of his cigarette away, and it died with a hiss in the dark water. 'Come on, I'll take you for a real walk, across the bridge. You get a great view of the château from over there.'

He rose, the boy again, and led the way. The bridge was an impressive one, a gentle arc of pavement raised on heavy piles sunk deep into the river Vienne, and the river seemed to be doing its level best to wear away the unwanted obstacle. From the arched openings beneath us the roar of the rushing water rose fiercely to our ears.

I saw what Paul had meant about the island. It was a small island, to be sure, little more than a wedge of trees and scattered houses stuck oddly in the middle of the broad river, like the lone oaks one sometimes sees stranded in the ploughed stretches of a farmer's field. It looked quite peaceful, really, pastoral, as if its murderous past had never been. And yet, and yet . . .

'There,' Paul announced proudly, 'now turn around and look at *that*.'

It was spectacular, as he had promised. The soaring walls of Chinon Castle rose in floodlights from the cliffs, its long, majestic outline standing sentry over the huddle of ancient houses below. In the river at our feet, the blinding image was reflected clearly, with scarcely a tremor to disturb its still perfection.

'Beautiful, isn't it?' Paul asked me.

I nodded dumbly, gazing up at the pale outline of the tower that marked the furthest jutting corner of the castle walls. The Moulin Tower. Isabelle's tower.

Again I saw the shadow moving softly past the window, but before the shadow formed a shape, a wind arose and rippled down the river, and the bits of bright reflection broke and scattered on a rolling surge of darkness.

Chapter Five

'Come out,' he said . . .

The telephone was ringing as I stepped from the shower early next morning. Still dripping, I grabbed a towel and made a lunge for the receiver.

'Hello?'

The line crackled unhelpfully for a few seconds, and then a deep familiar voice came booming down the line. 'Emily? Is that you?'

'Daddy?'

It would have been difficult, at that moment, to judge which one of us was more surprised to hear the other.

'What the devil are you doing in France?' demanded my father. 'You ought to be in Essex.'

'I'm on holiday,' I told him.

'What?'

'Holiday,' I said, raising my voice above the static of the transatlantic line. 'In Chinon.' I frowned. 'How did you get my number?'

'Didn't know it was your number, did I? They must not have heard me clearly at the front desk, I suppose . . . put me through to the wrong room.'

My frown deepened. 'What are you talking about?'

'I was trying to reach Harry.'

'Harry?' My voice was swallowed by a sudden burst of static that didn't quite disguise my father's sharp oath.

'Blast these telephone lines,' he said. 'We can put a man on the moon, but we can't *talk* to him, there's the tragedy. Can you hear me now? I was saying,' he went on, speaking more distinctly, 'that I was trying to reach Harry. Trying to return his call, rather.'

'Harry telephoned you?' I repeated, stupidly.

'Apparently. He left a message on the machine.'

'When was this?'

'I've no idea, love. Yesterday, I suppose, or perhaps the day before. I've been in Buenos Aires for a few days, on business.'

'What, golfing with Carlos again, you mean?'

'Carlos *is* business, my girl, so don't you go sounding all superior,' my father set me straight. 'Anyhow, I've not rung to talk to you, now have I? So fetch me Harry, will you? Put him on the phone.'

'He isn't here.'

'He's not out in the ruins at this hour, surely? It can't be breakfast time there, yet.'

'Half six,' I told him. 'And he really isn't here. He was supposed to meet me yesterday, but he hasn't turned up yet.'

'Hasn't turned up?' My father feigned surprise. 'Our Harry? Now, there's an item for the evening news.' His voice was dry. 'We are talking about my nephew, aren't we? The same boy who kept you waiting seven hours at the airport because he wanted to see where a footpath went?'

I smiled. 'Yes.'

'The same boy,' my father went on, 'who was

supposed to meet you at the festival in Edinburgh, that one year?'

'The very same.' I'd gone to Edinburgh, as it happened. Harry had made it as far as Epping, where he'd met up with an old girlfriend . . . but that was, in itself, another story.

'Well,' said my father, 'when he does turn up, tell him I'm waiting with bated breath to find out why he rang.'

'I will.'

'Mind you, he didn't sound too urgent in his message. He's probably forgotten all about it, now. Gone off on the trail of King John's coat buttons, or some such other nonsense.'

I smiled. 'That reminds me . . . wherever did you find that coin for him? That King John coin?'

My father coughed, pretending not to hear me, and asked a question of his own: 'What *are* you doing there on holiday? You haven't gone on holiday in years.'

'It was Harry's idea. He thought it would do me good to get away.'

'Well,' said my father, faintly pleased, 'he might be right at that. The village life's no good for you, you know – not healthy, stuck down there away from everything.'

I could have reminded him that he had turned out healthy enough, having grown up in that same village, and that I'd only gone there in the first place because he'd asked me to mind the house for him, but I wasn't given time to answer back.

'Must go now, my dear. Enjoy your trip.'

'Daddy . . .' I said, but the line had already crackled and gone dead. With a sigh, I set the receiver back in place. Honestly, I thought, they were all the same, the men of my family. Cut from the same cloth.

I shrugged my arms into my dressing gown and yanked my window open to let out the steam from my shower. Leaning out across the sill, I drew a deep breath of the morning air, drinking in the peaceful scenery.

I couldn't see the castle from my room – that view was blocked by another building squared against the hotel wall, its windows tightly shuttered still against the morning sun. But if I leaned a little further out and looked off to my left, across the tops of the trees that filled the square, I could just see the river, shining silver, beyond the head of the Rabelais statue.

Somewhere close by a bell was counting out the hours. Seven times the bell rang out, then silence. I was straining further across the sill, trying to get a better view, when the silence was abruptly shattered by a reverberating crash from the room next door. The window just beside mine on the left had opened inwards, and after a long moment's pause I heard a burst of helpless laughter followed by a cheerful curse that floated out into the clear morning air.

I must have made some sound myself, because Paul's dark head came round the painted window frame, his expression apologetic.

'Sorry,' he said, in a hushed voice. 'Simon's knocked the curtain off again. Did we wake you up?'

I shook my head. 'I was awake already.'

Simon's head joined Paul's at the window. 'Some crash, eh? I swear Thierry hangs the thing low on purpose, just to make life difficult for me. Don't you have any problem opening yours?'

'No.' I glanced upwards at my own curtain rod, which hung a good inch clear of the top of the frame.

'I told you,' said Simon to Paul, his chin defiant. 'It's only us. He does it on purpose.'

Paul shrugged and grinned. 'Yeah, well, you're on your own this time. You can tell him yourself.'

'I don't know the word for curtain,' Simon hedged, a little hopefully, but Paul stood firm.

'So go look it up in the dictionary. It's the only way you'll learn the language.'

After a final glance at his brother's face, Simon withdrew from the window, and Paul turned back to face me, still grinning.

'Beautiful day,' he commented. 'You must have brought the sunshine with you; we've had nothing but rain for three days.'

It was beautiful, I conceded. The shadows hung sharp and clear on the turreted houses and tightly clustered rooftops of the medieval town centre, and the pale stone walls gleamed brightly above the tufted green tops of the acacia trees. Two cars swung round the square below us, but the noise of traffic was muffled in the distance and the cheerful gurgle of the fountain carried over everything.

A second bell began to chime, quite near and rich and ringing, and I looked at Paul in some surprise.

'I thought the bell just went,' I said.

'There are two bells. I've been trying to figure out exactly where the second one is – it's either at the Church of St Maurice, just up the rue Voltaire, or it's at the City Hall, which is that big building over there.' He pointed out the large square building to our left, at the spot where the fountain square narrowed into the Place du Général de Gaulle. 'I can't quite make it out. But the first bell, the one you heard a few minutes ago, that's up at the château.' He used the proper French word for the castle. 'Which reminds me,' he went on. 'Do you have any plans for this morning? Because

Simon and I are going up to the château to putter around for an hour or so, and we thought if you didn't have anything else to do . . .'

Well, I certainly wasn't going to waste my first full day in Chinon hanging about the hotel in the hope that Harry would show up. He'd be here soon enough, I thought drily, and in the meantime there was no law that prevented me from touring on my own. 'I'd love to come,' I told Paul. 'Thanks.'

'Terrific. It's really something to see, and you shouldn't waste this sunshine. The weather here can be kind of unpredictable.'

We both heard the stern knock from the corridor.

'That'll be Thierry,' Paul said, with a wink. 'He'll be irritated.'

'Wouldn't it be simpler to just leave the curtain off, instead of always hanging it back up again?'

'Oh, sure.' He shrugged. 'But it's sort of a game for them, I think, and Simon considers it a personal challenge. Simon,' Paul told me in a positive tone, 'loves a challenge.'

Which was, I learned as we set out after breakfast, quite a thorough summing up of Simon's character.

He took charge of our impromptu tour party the moment we passed through the front doors of the hotel and stepped onto the pavement. 'OK,' he began firmly, 'since this is Emily's first real day in Chinon, I think we should take her down the rue Voltaire first, and then up to the château from there. It's a lot easier than going straight up those steps, anyway.'

He meant the broad, inviting flight of cobbled steps that cut between the buildings to our right, in a direct line with the fountain. The steps themselves didn't appear to be particularly steep, but it looked a long way up. I could just see the small cluster of yellow-white houses peering over the edge of the cliff that rimmed the town.

'What is this stone, do you know?' I asked my self-appointed guides. 'All the buildings here seem to be made of it.'

Simon proudly supplied the answer. 'It's tufa-stone. *Tuffeau* in French. It's the same stone they used to build Westminster Abbey, as a matter of fact.'

'He's been reading the guide books,' Paul explained. 'It's just a porous limestone, really. That's what the cliffs round here are made of.'

Tufa-stone. I filed the name away in my memory. On some of the buildings it almost looked like marble, hard and smooth and faintly reflective, cut in enormous blocks that had been fitted so expertly one could hardly spot the seams. Coupled with the pale grey pointed roofs, it gave the town a certain unity of colour and style that lovingly embraced the eye. Most of the shutters were open, now – painted metal shutters stained with rust, and older wooden ones, unpainted, that hung unevenly on their hinges, fastened back against the walls of their respective houses by ancient iron latches. I could understand why Simon found his curtain rod such a nuisance. French windows begged to be flung wide – it seemed a crime somehow to keep them closed.

The rue Voltaire led off the square as well, a narrow cobbled street that cut a line between the cliffs and the river. It was a lovely street, tastefully restored and rich in atmosphere, but I only caught the briefest glimpses of its tight-packed houses as Simon drove us past them at a breathless pace.

'And here,' he said, coming to a full and sudden stop

where a narrow street angled across the rue Voltaire, 'is the Great Crossroads. Well, it was a lot greater in the old days, I guess. This,' he told me, pointing up the smaller, sloping street, 'was how people used to get to the château back then. And that well over there, against the wall, is where Joan of Arc got off her horse when she came to Chinon to see the Dauphin.'

'Ah.' I smiled. It wasn't that I didn't like Joan of Arc – I had in fact been fascinated by her in my younger days, but having lived in France I'd gorged myself on Joan of Arc relics and Joan of Arc books and Joan of Arc historic sites until, in the end, it had produced the same effect as had the one too many Rusty Nails I'd drunk the night of my twenty-first birthday. All these years later, I couldn't face a Rusty Nail without a shudder.

Still, so as not to ruin Simon's tour I dutifully inspected the well and made the proper noises. Satisfied, he turned to lead the way up the tilting little street. 'We go up here. Just watch your step, it's pretty rough.'

And pretty steep, in spite of the fact that the road bent back upon itself several times in an attempt to soften the grade of the ascent. Halfway up I stumbled on the jutting cobblestones and paused to catch my breath.

'Small wonder Joan of Arc got off her horse,' I said, between gulps of air. 'No self-respecting horse would want to make this climb.'

Paul laughed and moved steadily past me. 'You get used to it.'

I wasn't so sure. 'Is this really easier than going up the steps?'

'Yes,' both boys averred, in unison.

Simon grinned, and pushed the hair back from his

face. 'Neil goes up and down those steps a few times a day,' he informed me, 'for exercise. He says musicians need to keep in shape.'

'Bully for Neil,' I muttered, and forced my wobbling legs to push onwards. Just when I thought they couldn't possibly carry me any further, we cleared the final corner and found ourselves gazing out across the rooftops to the gently snaking river. It was a breathless view. The gardens of the closer houses had been terraced upwards to the level of the cliffs, a chequerboard of trees and flowers hemmed by ivied walls turned crimson in the autumn air.

A final slope, five paces more, and out we stepped onto a modern road that ran along the level of the cliff. Facing us, a cracked and crumbling wall rose starkly up one level more, its sheer bulk draped with clinging clumps of ivy broken here and there by leaning doors that marked the entrance to some long-abandoned dwelling.

'There's the château,' said Simon, pointing.

'Give us a chance,' I pleaded, slumping back against the wall. 'Wait till my vision clears.'

Simon wasn't listening – he was already several steps ahead, walking with a brisk and purposeful step, but Paul hung back to wait for me. 'Not far now,' he promised. 'We're almost there.'

I glanced after Simon, noticing not the soaring, narrow tower that served as gateway to the château, but the alarming slope of the black asphalt road ahead. 'More climbing?' I asked, weakly.

Paul laughed again. 'I thought you Brits were used to hills.'

'Yes, well,' I excused myself, 'I'm from the flat part.'

Simon finally noticed we weren't keeping up.

Frowning, he turned and called, 'Come on, you two.'

Paul shot me a rather paternal glance. 'You ready?'

'Have I a choice?'

The final approach wasn't all that bad, as it turned out, mainly because my attention was focused on the strange tower ahead of us. The *Tour de l'Horloge*, Paul told me when I asked him – the Clock Tower. It was tall and curiously flat, like a cardboard cut-out of a tower, with a grey slate roof and wooden belfry. The bell that chimed the hours, I thought, must hang within this tower.

A stone bridge spanned the grassy moat that once had barred invaders from the tower's high arched entrance gate. Today, the wooden doors stood open wide, inviting us to leave the road and cross the narrow footbridge to where Simon waited by the postcards, impatient.

'They do have guided tours,' Paul said, as we paused at the entrance to pay, 'but Simon and I usually just wander around on our own. It's up to you, though, if you'd rather take a tour . . .'

'I hate guided tours,' I assured them, 'thanks all the same. Much more fun to wander.'

And wander we did. I'd always liked castles. I'd expected this one to be little more than a ruin, but many of the rooms and towers had been preserved intact within the shattered walls. One could almost hear the footsteps of brave knights and ladies, kings and courtiers, echoing round the empty rooms. The white stone, bathed in light from mullioned windows, lent a bright and airy feel to the sprawling royal apartments and made them look much larger than they were. From every corner twisting stairs led up to unexpected rooms with hearths and windows of their own, small private

69

sanctuaries where a queen could comfortably retire to do her needlework or dally with her lover . . . at least, I thought, until the king found out, and had the lover killed.

In the next tower on, Simon pointed to a large framed painting of the château, just like the view Paul had shown me from the bridge. 'That's one of Christian's paintings. Pretty good, eh?'

'It's marvellous.' I leaned closer, amazed. 'Christian did this, really?' It was a bold and sweeping painting in the true romantic style, and he had caught exactly the unusual pale colour of the tufa-stone gleaming bright against a stormy violet sky.

'He's incredibly talented,' Paul said, beside my shoulder.

'So I see.' With a vague prickling feeling of being watched, I slid my gaze from the painting to the figure looming in a shadowed recess of the tower wall. Not a real person, thank heavens – just a statue, and a massive one at that. 'Good heavens,' I said. 'It's Philippe.'

Paul looked up as well, at the young heroic face. 'Who?'

'Philippe Auguste. One of the early kings of France. He was the first real French king to own this château, actually,' I went on, recalling Harry's countless lectures.

Simon frowned. 'Who owned it before?'

'The counts of Blois and Anjou, I believe. And then the Plantagenets.'

'What, like the Black Prince, you mean?'

I smiled. 'A little earlier than that. Richard the Lionheart and that bunch. Richard's brother John was the last to own Chinon.'

'As in Robin Hood?' Simon checked, his eyebrows lifting. 'Bad Prince John? That guy?'

'The very same.'

'Neat.'

Paul looked at me with quiet interest. 'You know a lot about the history of this place, then?'

My smile grew wider. 'Rather. I'm lectured on it constantly. My cousin,' I explained, to both of them, 'is something of an expert on Plantagenets. It's his fault, really, that I'm here at all – he talked me into coming on holiday with him.'

The brothers exchanged glances. 'But he isn't here,' said Simon, pointing out the obvious.

'Not yet, no. But then, that's not unusual for Harry. He does race off on tangents when he's working on a theory. Which reminds me,' I said, turning, 'how does one get to the Moulin Tower?'

Someone was coming. Isabelle raised her head, all thought of sleep forgotten, as the heavy stamp of boots on stone drew nearer. Oh, please, she prayed, dear Mother of God, please let it be John.

Beside her, the old woman Alice roused herself, alarmed. 'My lady—'

'Hush.' The whispered word held urgency. The boots were at the door now. She held her breath.

A rough knock, and a rougher voice . . . a voice she knew. 'Your Majesty, are you awake?'

He hadn't come. She swallowed back the bitter taste of tears and felt in darkness for her gown. He'd promised he would always come, whenever she sent word . . . with solemn eyes he'd sworn it, always. But the man who stood outside her chamber now was not her husband. She stood, shivering in the velvet gown, and crossed to unbolt the door, raising a hand to shield her eyes from the sudden glare of torchlight. The tall man in the passage looked more fierce than she remembered. He frightened her, he'd always frightened her, and yet she'd rather die than have him see it. By force of will she kept her voice composed. 'My lord de Préaux.'

'Majesty.' He knelt, and took her hand. The torchlight traced an old scar on his cheekbone as he raised his head. She saw no mercy in his eyes, no warmth – they were the hard eyes of a ruthless man who made his living by the sword. 'You are to rise, and come with me,' he told her. 'I am to bring you safely to Le Mans.'

'John sent you?'

'Yes.'

She only had his word, she thought, and the word of such a man was hardly comfort in these troubled times. If he'd turned traitor, like the others . . .

Still, she was alone, with John not here – she had no choice but trust. Besides, she thought, de Préaux was a soldier – soldiers had no cause to lie. To take her hostage, he had but to seize her where she stood. And if he desired her dead he'd simply kill her and be done with it. The fact that he'd done neither proved de Préaux spoke the truth.

She raised her chin. 'My lord,' she said, 'the rebels do surround us.'

'Yes, I know.'

'May I ask, how did you . . . how . . .'

'With difficulty.' He stood, impatient. De Préaux never stayed long on his knees. 'Do you come or no? I've twelve men freezing round the fire in your courtyard. They've ridden long and hoped for sleep, but I'd think it less than wise to wait till morning.'

She shivered in a draught of air that swept along the passage. 'What would you have me do?'

'Dress you warmly, and make haste.'

'My women . . .'

'Only you.' He shook his head. 'We have but one horse spare. Your maids must wait.'

She glanced at Alice. 'But my lord—'

'Queen Isabelle.' He was not moved; his ugly face was resolute. 'Upon your life my own life hangs. I am not sent to save the household – only you. It is yourself the rebels seek,' he reminded her, 'and once they learn their prize is flown, the castle will be safe. The siege will end.'

'There is the Treasury, still.'

'These men have no desire for treasure.'

No, she thought. They had one cause, and one cause only – to force John to release his nephew Arthur. And so he would, in time. Frowning, she drew back, gathering the folds of her robe about her. 'What news of Arthur of Brittany?' she asked, slowly. 'Is he well?'

The eyes that touched hers held a fleeting trace of pity. And then he looked beyond her to where Alice stood in silence by the bed, and for a moment understanding passed between the dark knight and the old woman. 'See that your mistress dresses warm,' he said. He bowed and turned away.

Watching the last faint flickering of torchlight vanish down the twisting stairs, it seemed to Isabelle that every stone around her breathed a sigh of cold despair, as if by sorcery her own bedchamber had become a prison . . . or a tomb.

Chapter Six

From all a closer interest flourish'd up . . .

'You've done it now,' said Paul, as we watched Simon bounding off away from us.

'Whatever do you mean?'

'That story you just told us, about Queen Isabelle. You mentioned treasure. *Big* mistake.' With Simon safely out of sight, he rummaged in his pocket for his cigarettes, shifting clear of the shadow cast by the tower at his shoulder. It was in ruins now, the Moulin Tower – an empty hull of stone with dark weeds sprouting in the roofless chambers. And no-one walked those chambers, any more. A sign beside the bolted door said sternly: *Danger!* so we leaned instead against the low, lichen-crusted wall that formed the western boundary of the château grounds. Behind our backs the slumbering Vienne flowed seaward, unconcerned.

Paul cupped the match against the breeze. 'Telling a story like that to Simon,' he advised me, 'is kind of like waving a red flag in front of a bull. He's all fired up, now.'

'He's only gone to find the toilet, Paul.'

'Don't you believe it. Not my brother.' He grinned. 'He has the bladder of a camel. No, you wait and see

– he's sneaked off down to the entrance booth to see what he can learn about the tunnels.'

I looked along the empty path, intrigued. 'But he doesn't speak French.'

'That wouldn't stop him.' Stretching his legs out in front of him, Paul dug his feet into the gravel and braced his hands beside him on the sun-warmed stone. 'So,' he said, 'what happened?'

'When?'

'To John and Isabelle. You never finished the story.'

'Oh, that.' The breeze blew my hair in my eyes and I pushed it back absently. 'It's not the happiest of endings, I'm afraid. John did kill Arthur, or at least he had him killed, depending on which chronicler one reads. The King of France – Philippe – you remember the statue? Well, Philippe went rather wild. He'd raised the boy, you see. He'd been great friends with John's big brother Geoffrey, Arthur's father, and when Geoffrey died Philippe took Arthur back to Paris, brought him up. John might as well have killed Philippe's own son.'

'So he started a war.'

I nodded. 'A terrible war. It cost John nearly everything. Chinon was one of the first castles to be captured, actually – it fell to Philippe not long after Arthur died.'

'And Isabelle?'

I looked up at the Moulin Tower, lonely and abandoned, the green weeds grasping at the crumbled window ledge. 'He lost her too, in the end. John had foul moods and jealous rages, like his father. He even followed in his father's footsteps in another way – kept Isabelle locked up and under guard, just as his mother had been kept.'

Paul frowned. 'How sad.'

'Yes, well,' I shrugged, 'it's not a fairy tale, I'll grant you. But then real life never is.'

He turned his head to look at me, squinting a little against the sun. 'You don't believe, then, in a love that lasts a lifetime?'

'I don't believe,' I told him drily, 'in a love that lasts till teatime.'

'Cynic,' he accused me, but he smiled.

We sat on several moments in companionable silence while Paul smoked his cigarette, his eyes half narrowed, deep in thought. I couldn't help but think again how different he was from his brother Simon. One had room to breathe, with Paul.

'Tragic,' he said, quite out of the blue.

'I'm sorry?'

He shrugged. 'It's just a kind of game I play, finding the right adjective to suit a place. I try to distil all the feeling, the atmosphere, down to a single word. Château Chinon's been a tough one, but I've got it now – it's tragic.'

He'd hit the nail precisely on the head, I had to admit. In spite of all the sunshine and the blue sky, and the brilliant golden walls, the place did seem to be pervaded by an aura of tragedy, of splintered hopes and unfulfilled desires.

The swift breeze stole the sunlight's warmth and, shivering, I glanced up.

'Simon's coming.'

'Damn.' Paul stubbed his cigarette against the wall, setting off a shower of red sparks that died before they reached the ground. By the time Simon reached us, the telltale evidence lay crushed deep in the gravel underneath Paul's shoe.

'I got a map,' said Simon cheerfully.

Paul's eyes were knowing, but he held the innocent expression. 'Map of what?'

'The tunnels, stupid. Now, according to the woman at the gate, there should be something we can *see*, just over here . . .' And off he went again, with purpose, heading for a spreading box tree several yards away. 'Come on, you two,' he called back.

With a sigh, Paul straightened from the wall and stretched. 'I told you so.'

I smiled. 'Well, not to worry. When my cousin turns up he'll be glad of the help.'

It took us some few minutes to find Simon, round the far side of the box tree. At first it seemed he'd vanished into thin air, until we stumbled on the narrow shaft sunk deep into the well kept lawn. A flight of stairs, worn smooth with age, and damp with fallen leaves, descended here to end abruptly at a blank stone wall. And at the bottom of those steps stood Simon.

'Hey, come down here,' he invited. 'This is really neat.'

I frowned. 'But it doesn't go anywhere.'

'Of course it does.' He pointed off to one side, into darkness. 'Come and see.'

I wasn't really going underground, I reassured myself. The sky was still above me, calmly blue. But when I reached the bottom step the air was dank, and the only thing that kept me from bolting right back up the steps was the fact that I'd have flattened Paul in the process. He leaned in now, behind me, looking where Simon had pointed. One had to focus past the iron bars to see the dimly stretching corridors beyond. 'You're right,' he told his brother. 'This *is* neat. Where does it lead?'

Simon consulted the hand-sketched map he held. 'I'm not sure. The woman at the gate said there are tunnels all over the place, not just under the château but all around Chinon. I think she said Resistance fighters used them in the war.'

It was easy to imagine that. Easier still to imagine the echo of earlier times. I could almost see the torchlight casting shadows on the arched stone walls, and hear far off the furtive rustle of a velvet gown against the eerie silence. I wondered if this was the tunnel Isabelle had passed through, on her way to hide her treasure . . .

I was so deep in my imaginings that the sound, when it came, caught me unawares. A sound quite real and not imagined: the quiet closing of a door, somewhere in the dark and stretching shadows.

I cleared my throat. 'Did you hear that?'

'Hear what?' Both brothers looked at me blankly.

'It sounded like a door.'

Paul tipped his head and listened, but the dusty walls stayed silent. 'Maybe the château workers use the tunnels,' he suggested, 'to get around the place. Or for storage.'

It seemed logical enough, I thought. But I felt a good deal better when we'd clambered up to ground level again, up in the sunshine where the breeze could blow the shivers from my skin.

'Oh, hey,' said Simon, looking at his map, 'I think that might have been the tunnel that goes to the vineyard.' Brow furrowed, he followed the tracing on the map and tried to match it with his own steps, so deep in concentration that he didn't seem to notice when he left the grass and walked onto a broad paved circle that jutted out from the château walls. It might have been a tower once, or some such other fortification, but time had worn it level with the lawn. And Simon might have kept on walking, clear off its edge, had Paul not whistled sharply.

'What?' Simon raised his head, enquiring. He stopped two inches from the railing and leaned over, with a nod. 'Yeah, that's where it leads, all right. If Isabelle hid her treasure there,' he told me, as we joined him at the railing, 'your cousin can kiss it goodbye.'

Below us ran the road that had brought me into Chinon yesterday, now busy with a blur of passing traffic. And on the other side of the road was the most incredible estate I'd ever seen. It was a vineyard, a huge and wealthy vineyard – so huge, in fact, that the rows of dark green vines rose up the rolling slope to the horizon and beyond, protected by a tall unbroken boundary wall that ran along the road. Well, almost unbroken, I corrected myself. There was a gate, a great iron thing that would have suited Buckingham Palace, and from the gate a broad drive swept imperiously up the hill to meet a Grecian mansion, gleaming white.

Above our heads a cloud raced underneath the sun and sent a shadow swiftly up the deeply furrowed hill, as the shadow of a hawk might chase its prey across a trembling field.

Paul understood my awe. 'The *Clos des Cloches*. It's really something, isn't it? I'm told they make the best wine in Chinon.'

The *Clos des Cloches* – the vineyard of the bells, I translated in my own mind. 'It's beautiful.'

Simon shifted closer. 'Martine says they give tours in the summer, and wine-tastings, but it's out of season now. Everyone's too busy with the harvest.' Elbows on the railing, he hung forward, heedless of the dizzying drop. 'Hey, look,' he said, 'there's Neil.'

I looked. The bright gleam of Neil Grantham's hair

made him easy to spot on the narrow path beneath us, by the road. Two other men were with him, and a woman with short dark hair. I couldn't see their faces from that angle, but Simon gave a low whistle.

'Damn Neil,' he said, good-naturedly. 'He always beats my time.'

Paul smiled. '*That*,' he told me, with a downwards nod at the dark-haired woman, 'is Martine Muret.'

Martine Muret. I frowned. Oh, right . . . the woman Garland had been gossiping about in the hotel bar yesterday afternoon. The one whose former husband had just died . . . what, three days ago? I watched her now lean close to Neil, her hand possessive on his arm. She had a quick recovery time, I decided drily.

Simon shouted down and waved, and I pulled myself up quickly, taking a step back from the railing. 'Listen, it must be nearly lunchtime. I'd better go back down, in case my cousin's come.'

'Are you sure?' Simon turned around, distracted. 'Because there's a Joan of Arc museum in the Clock Tower, if you'd like to . . .'

I hastily assured him I'd seen plenty for one day, and it was always best to leave something for the next time . . .

'Well, it is your first day,' Simon conceded with a shrug. 'We probably shouldn't wear you out.' He checked his watch. 'And you're right, it is lunchtime. Hey, Paul, let's go ask Neil and Martine if they want to try that Chinese place across the river.'

Paul smiled. 'She's too old for you.'

'Age,' his brother said, indignantly, 'is completely relative. You're the physicist, you ought to know that.'

He bounced off, energy renewed, and Paul sighed. 'You're sure you don't want to join us?'

'Well . . .'

'Joke,' he said. 'I wouldn't do that to you. Two hours with us is long enough for anybody. Just don't forget to warn your cousin.'

'Warn him?'

'That Simon's after Queen Isabelle's treasure.'

'Oh, that.' I promised him I'd not forget. 'I'll see you later, then.'

I left him on the road outside the château. Instead of going back the way we'd come, along the path that wound down through the ancient part of town, I walked a few steps further on and found, as Paul had promised, the entrance to the *escalier de la brèche*, a steep flight of stairs that led back into the fountain square.

It was far easier going down, I decided, although the steps were too broad to take at a normal pace. I had to take them like a child would, one foot down and then the other, following their steeply twisting course between stone walls hung thick with ivy. Here and there a wooden door gave a glimpse of someone's terraced garden, or a fruit tree leaned across the wall to drop its leaves.

One final twist, a straight descent, and there I was, safely back at the fountain square with the hotel angling off beside me, its fanciful wrought-iron balconies webbed like pure black lace against the yellow-white stone of the façade.

The fountain sang and beckoned from the centre of the square. I stopped and paused, and took a step towards it. But the man sitting on the edge of the fountain's basin changed my mind.

He had been sitting in that same spot yesterday, when I arrived – I'd seen him from my window. There couldn't be two men in Chinon with a dog like that, a little spotted mongrel curled around its owner's feet. And he wore the same clothes, leather jacket over tattered shirt, his blue jeans soiled and frayed. He looked, I thought, a shade less than respectable. Not threatening, exactly, but . . . something in his roughened face, some quality I couldn't place, put me on my guard.

The man himself appeared to take no notice of me. He went on smoking, gazing placidly at nothing in particular. At his feet the small dog shifted, raised its head, and pricked its ears up, suddenly alert. It stared, I thought, directly at my face. And as I crossed to the hotel I felt those silent eyes upon me, watching steadily, as a hunter sights its prey.

Chapter Seven

Nor knew what eye was on me . . .

Monsieur Chamond rose from behind the reception desk to greet me with a smile smooth as silk. In middle age he was a handsome man, neat and compact with an efficiency of movement that I much admired. In his youth, he would have rivalled his nephew Thierry as a breaker of women's hearts. Most certainly he would have broken mine.

We exchanged our formal greetings, and because I answered him in French he kept on in that language, a little cautiously, poised to switch to English at my first sign of difficulty. 'I'm sorry that I was not here to meet you yesterday, myself. You are enjoying your stay in our hotel, I hope?'

'Very much.'

'And your room, it is satisfactory?'

'It's lovely, Monsieur,' I said, and was rewarded with a warm smile of pleasure.

'I'm glad. Room 215, is it not?' He handed me the key. 'And you have another message, Mademoiselle. Just this morning.'

I took the narrow envelope he handed me and turned it over, frowning slightly. It was addressed, quite simply, 'Braden', in a bold black hand I didn't recognize. 'Another message . . . ?'

Monsieur Chamond proved most perceptive. At the tone of my voice his eyes moved with sudden apprehension to one corner of the desk, below the counter, and whatever he saw there made him shake his head. 'I am so very sorry, Mademoiselle, I had assumed . . .' With the shrug of one resigned to suffering, he retrieved a small square notepad with a message scrawled upon it. 'Our regular receptionist Yvette, she is on holiday for two weeks, and so her sister Gabrielle is filling in. She tries, poor Gabrielle, but she is not Yvette. She is . . . easily confused, and sometimes when I tell her things, she forgets.' His smile held an apology. 'Your cousin telephoned last night, while you were out at dinner.'

Wait for it, I thought drily. 'Oh, yes?'

'He speaks good French, your cousin – like yourself. He said he would be late, perhaps a few days. If you did not mind . . .'

'I see.' My host, I knew, had made that last bit up. Harry would hardly have cared whether I minded. 'And did he say where he was ringing from?'

'No, I'm afraid not.' He looked at me more closely, perhaps surprised that I'd received the news so well. 'This will not spoil your plans, I hope? Your holiday?'

'Good heavens, no.' I'd rather expected it. In fact, when Harry hadn't met me yesterday, as promised, I'd braced myself for the inevitable. My cousin rarely kept to schedules. Hours turned into days with him, and days to weeks, and by the time he did show up in Chinon I might well be safely back in England, sorting through my holiday snaps. I smiled at Monsieur Chamond. 'I'm sure I'll manage, on my own.'

'But I am sorry that you were not told last night. We might have saved you worrying.'

Worry? About Harry? Hardly likely, I thought. 'No harm done,' I said, looking down at the envelope he'd given me. 'And is this from my cousin, too?'

'No, Mademoiselle – that came this morning, as I said. By hand.'

'How curious. I wonder who . . . ?' I tore the flap, and drew a printed card from the envelope. It was an invitation, of all things. I was invited to a guided tour and wine-tasting, the card informed me, at a time of my own choosing, although a written note along the bottom edge asked would I please be kind enough to telephone for an appointment. How *very* curious.

Monsieur Chamond was watching me. 'It is from the *Clos des Cloches*, I think?'

'Yes.' I showed it to him. 'That's the vineyard on the hill, isn't it? The one behind the château? I saw it just this morning.'

'Yes. The white house.'

'Odd. I wonder where they got my name.'

'Ah, no,' he said, 'that is my writing, Mademoiselle, on the envelope. The boy who brought it told me it was for the English lady staying here. And you,' he explained, with a small shrug, 'you are the only English lady that we have.'

'But surely . . .' I let the protest hang, unfinished. I could hardly accuse my host of making a mistake – that would be rude. And anyway, it hardly mattered. It was just an invitation; probably some sort of marketing ploy delivered round the hotels. Come and taste our wines, and bring your wallet with you – that sort of thing. Strange, though, that they should still be holding tours at harvest-time. I dropped the square card into my handbag and forgot about it.

Well, *nearly* forgot about it. One couldn't quite forget about the *Clos des Cloches* in Chinon, I discovered. The name leapt out at me again half an hour later, from the menu of the restaurant where I'd chosen to eat lunch. 'May we suggest,' the menu read, 'a red wine from the *Clos des Cloches*?' Why not, indeed? A half bottle of the youngest vintage could be squeezed within my budget, I decided. The waiter took my order down approvingly, then vanished, leaving me to watch the ebb and flow of passersby along the narrow cobbled street outside the window.

The restaurant was tiny, just six tables and a narrow bar, but Monsieur Chamond had recommended it so strongly I had gamely searched the streets until I'd tracked it down. The French, I reasoned, knew their restaurants. And lunches were a serious affair. Most businesses closed down in France from noon till two, so everyone but cooks and waiters could observe the ritual. I had forgotten how enjoyable it was to sit and eat at leisure, not to hurry, with the warm smells swirling lazily around me and the hum of conversation drifting past from nearby tables. I'd forgotten how wonderful the food in France could be – how even a salad could be stunning, filled with unexpected textures and a subtle trace of spice. And I'd completely forgotten about the wine.

At home I rarely drank wine with my meals, but here in France it seemed so natural, and the half bottle seemed so harmlessly small, that I'd already drunk three glasses by the time I thought to count. And by then I couldn't do much, anyway – I was feeling quite pleasantly foggy.

So foggy, in fact, that when I'd finally paid the bill and stepped outside, I found I couldn't quite remember just which way I ought to go. Looking round, I tried to get my bearings. There was the château, off to my right, which meant I should head that way, surely . . . except it seemed to me I'd come along a wider road than that one . . . and I had changed direction twice . . . or was it three times? *Blast*, I thought, *you're lost*.

The tourist map I'd tucked into my handbag proved no help at all. It only showed the central part of town, and the unnamed streets and alleys formed a mysterious web on the glossy paper. It was no use, I decided – I'd have to ask someone.

It was no small thing, here in France, to ask someone directions. The rules of etiquette were very clear – the person you asked was obligated to help, even if they didn't have a clue, themselves, exactly where to send you. Wrong directions, to the French, were better than no directions at all. When all else failed, they'd pull another stranger into the discussion to assist. I'd caused a pile-up on a Paris pavement, once, by asking someone where to find the nearest bookshop.

So it was with a certain caution that I scanned the passing faces now, waiting for the proper sort of person. The morning's sun had disappeared behind a swell of slate-grey cloud, and people walked by briskly with their collars pulled tight against the damp. I chose a woman slightly older than myself, smartly dressed and carrying a briefcase. She glanced with mild horror at my map, and I remembered how the French disliked maps – they preferred to ask a person. Calmly, I refolded it and stuffed it in my handbag, listening in patience while she told me how to get back to the Hotel de France.

It sounded rather more complicated than I remembered, but I thanked her, careful not to slur my words, and toddled off in the appropriate direction. The problem with medieval towns, I thought some twenty minutes later, was that the streets all ran whichever way they wanted. Which meant, I thought as the asphalt gave way once more to cobblestone, that following directions proved nearly impossible.

The pavement shrank until there was barely room for one person to walk, and I crowded close against the leaning buildings. These houses had not been scrubbed clean like the houses on the rue Voltaire, and the passing centuries had weathered their walls to a sort of uniform dun colour. Here and there, where the houses didn't quite meet one another, a darkened crevice lay concealed by broken boards, or a snatch of garden glimmered through the narrow opening.

An old woman with suspicious eyes, her thick, shapeless body lurching from side to side, passed by me in indifferent silence, and I felt bolder stares from a cluster of young men who moved more swiftly and with purpose.

Around the corner, the street was quieter. The human noise of shouts and speech and motors grew steadily more faint behind me, until my own footsteps sounded intrusively loud. On every house the shutters were pulled back and fastened; lace curtains fluttered at the open windows. Painted doors sagged on their ancient hinges, over steps that had been swept spotlessly clean. The evidence of human life was everywhere, but I saw no-one. The twisting street was empty, lonely, silent.

I might have been the only soul alive.

And so the cat, racing past me in a sudden blur of

black and white, nearly scared me to death. I jumped aside as a great lolloping mongrel of a dog came tearing up the street in hot pursuit, but the cat was even quicker. In the blink of an eye it hurled itself over a high stone wall, leaving the dog standing in frustration on the other side. After barking its displeasure, the dog slunk sourly off in search of a more co-operative quarry.

The wall over which the cat had vanished formed part of a narrow alleyway whose name, *Ruelle des Rêves*, was plainly marked for all to see. The Lane of Dreams. It seemed too grandiose a name for such a tiny thoroughfare.

Curious, I crossed the street. Standing in the lane, one could easily see how the cat had managed its escape. The wall was thickly hung with ivy – not the dark English ivy to which I was accustomed, but the other kind so common here in Chinon, a tangled mass of paler green that brightened at its outer edge to crimson, where the smaller leaves spilled down in curling tendrils.

No windows peered into the little lane, and there appeared to be just one door, painted green and set so deep in ivy that one almost didn't notice. It would open, I thought, into the garden of the house that rose behind the high stone wall.

The house itself looked less than friendly. Even as I took a step backwards to view it from a proper angle a window slammed above my head, and looking up I saw a face against the glass. Only for an instant, the briefest glimpse, and yet I recognized the face and knew the man who owned it: the young German artist, Christian Rand.

This must be his house, then. The house that had

been loaned to him by Martine . . . what was her name? Martine Muret. The house in which, three days ago, a man had died. I remembered Garland Whitaker saying cattily, *Maybe it wasn't an accident. Maybe Christian did it* . . . One wouldn't need much fancy to imagine murder here.

It was enough to give one the creeps, really – the silent street and the dingy, claustrophobic Lane of Dreams, and the touch of death still hanging heavy round the house. Like ivy, I thought, dropping my gaze to the wall.

The cat's unblinking eyes locked with mine. I hadn't heard a sound, yet there it was, settled comfortably among the red-tinged vines that rustled along the top of the high wall. After a moment's hard stare the cat, like Christian, chose to ignore me. The pale eyes closed.

Twice snubbed, I turned away. Since I was, by this time, quite hopelessly lost, it hardly seemed to matter which direction I chose, and so I walked on through the narrow lane and came into another street as quiet as the one I'd just been on. Unlike the first street, though, this one was packed with cars and people, and the silence made me curious until I saw the cause of it.

At the street's end stood an old church, pale and plain and solid. And in front of the church, almost blocking the road, a long hearse stretched dead black against the yellowed walls of the houses. The mourners, sombre in their dark overcoats, milled about the pavement, exchanging subdued kisses and handshakes.

One face among the many drew my gaze. It was the smoothly handsome face of my taxi driver, his classic profile turning a fraction away from me as he bent his head to say something to the young woman standing by the church door – a young woman with short black hair and fragile features that were almost tragic in their beauty. I frowned. I'd seen her somewhere, too, just recently . . . but where? And then she placed her hand upon his sleeve and I remembered.

I looked with deeper interest at Martine Muret. This morning, from the château walls, I'd seen her laughing, leaning close against Neil Grantham, full of life. She looked sedate now, solemn, though I couldn't find much sadness in her lovely face. But then, I thought, perhaps she wasn't sad. Paul called the dead man her ex-husband, so they must have been divorced. She might have hated him, for all I knew. She might have wished him dead.

Respectfully, she looked down as they carried out the flowers – great elaborate racks of flowers, red and gold, that were laid with care inside the waiting hearse. A woman, not the widow, started weeping audibly, and not wanting to intrude further I pulled my gaze away.

And then I froze.

Across the narrow street, not ten feet from me, the dark, unshaven man from the fountain square leaned one shoulder against the stuccoed wall of the house behind him, and calmly lit a cigarette. Expressionless, he met my eyes. For a long unnerving moment we just stood there, staring at one another, and then the church bells set up a great clanging peal of sound that made the dog at his feet throw back its head and howl, joining the general lament.

The burst of noise broke the spell. I turned and walked on rapidly, away from the church and the press of mourners. Foolish, I thought, to be nervous of a stranger in broad daylight, in a public street. Foolish to find myself listening for a sinister fall of footsteps on the pavement behind me. Still, foolish or not, I kept on walking faster and faster, and I was very nearly running by the time I reached the river.

Chapter Eight

*. . . on the spur she fled; and
more
We know not,—*

I would have walked straight on past Paul, had he not
called to me. He was sitting where we'd sat last night,
near the top of the steps leading down to the river, his
body folded in unconscious imitation of the brooding
statue behind him. Resting his book face down upon
his outstretched leg, he called again and waved.

Even with the zebra-striped pedestrian crossing, it
took some minutes for me to cross the busy street and
join him.

'You've been drinking,' he said, in a brotherly
tone.

'Only a little wine with lunch.' I raised one hand to
touch my flushed cheek. 'Is it really that obvious?'

' 'Fraid so. Your eyes are kind of glazed.'

'Oh, well.' I took the news in stride, not overly
concerned. Stepping with care over his leg, I settled
myself on the next step down and linked my hands
around my knees. It was a lovely place to sit and watch
the world go by, to watch the river coursing past and
hear the ducks call out to one another as they paddled
round the reeds that edged the sloping river wall. One
could sit here all the afternoon and never be disturbed.

I sighed, my worries sliding from me as I smiled up at Paul. 'And how was your lunch?' I asked.

'Don't ask.' He grinned. 'The Whitakers decided to go for Chinese food today as well.'

I laughed. 'Oh, Paul, what rotten luck.'

'You're telling me. Martine and Garland spent the whole meal taking shots at one another – all terribly polite, you know, and smiling – and when Martine started scoring points Garland suddenly developed one of her headaches and made a big dramatic exit. You should have been there.'

'Just as well I wasn't,' I replied. 'Theatricals don't impress me.'

Paul tucked one hand inside his jacket, searching for his cigarettes. 'I don't think they impress Jim much, either. He didn't seem too upset when Garland left. He just ordered another drink.'

They were a most unlikely couple, Jim and Garland Whitaker. When I said as much to Paul, he smiled in agreement.

'I like Jim, though,' he said, placing a cigarette between his lips. 'He's a lot smarter than he lets on. And he really takes an interest in things.'

'What sort of things?'

'Oh . . . history, architecture, local food. He's the one who wanted to tour the Loire Valley, you know – not Garland. Garland couldn't care less. And this trip is definitely not her style.'

'Oh?' I looked up, interested. 'In what way?'

'Every way. Garland stays at the Ritz when she's in Paris. Christmas in the Swiss Alps. Easter on the Italian Riviera. Chinon,' he told me, 'would not have been her first choice for a holiday.'

'Are the Whitakers rich, then?'

'Disgustingly rich.' He nodded, blowing smoke. 'Of course, they'll never say as much directly, but Jim's clothes aren't off the rack, they're tailor made. And he's got one suit that's worth at least a thousand dollars.'

My expression must have been questioning, because he laughed and, mimicking a New York Yiddish accent, said: 'My family's in the garment business, *Mäusele*. I know from menswear.'

'What's a *Mäusele*?' I wanted to know.

'Little Mouse.'

'Oh.' Is that what I reminded him of, I wondered? A little mouse, afraid to come out of her hole? But I didn't ask him that. Instead, I asked: 'What does Jim Whitaker do, anyway? Do you know?'

'He says he works for a private engineering company, but Simon thinks that's just a smokescreen, a cover story to hide Jim's real occupation.'

'Which is?'

'CIA, of course.' He winked. 'Simon gets a little paranoid sometimes – he's studied politics too long. He sees conspiracy in everything and everybody, and the worst part is that it's contagious. I've spent so much time listening to Simon that even *I* look at Jim sometimes and think, yeah, he does look kind of secretive, you know? It catches.'

'Maybe that's my problem, then,' I said, hugging my knees more tightly. 'My own imagination's been working overtime this afternoon. It must be Simon's paranoia rubbing off.'

'Why? What have you been imagining?'

'I rather fancied I was being followed.' Said like that, I thought, it sounded ridiculous. I smiled.

'Who was following you?'

As I described the man, Paul's eyebrows drew

together in a frown of recognition. 'What, the gypsy, you mean? The one with the little dog about that big?' He held his hands a foot and a half apart, to simulate the size of the dog.

'That's the one. He's a gypsy, really?' I'd never seen an actual gypsy before – only fake ones in films.

Paul nodded. 'There are a lot of gypsies around here. Some of them live in campers – caravans, I guess you'd call them – down by the beach. They're not the cream of society, to be sure, but that guy you saw is pretty harmless. At least, he's always been nice to Simon and me,' he said, shifting his legs. 'Simon always stops to pet the dog. So I wouldn't worry about . . . oh, damn, there goes my book!'

I caught it for him as it came bouncing down the steps beside me. 'There,' I said, handing it back to him. 'No damage done. But you've lost your place.'

'That's OK, I can find it again.' He grinned. 'I have a very intimate relationship with this book.'

'Well, I should think so, if you've been reading it for two years.'

He turned the paperback over, balancing it carefully in his hand. 'That was always my favourite poem, you know, when I was a kid. Tennyson's *Ulysses*. I used to know it by heart.'

From what I'd seen so far of his memory, I was willing to bet he knew the poem still. I'd memorized it once myself, years ago, at school. I remembered how romantic it had seemed – the aged Ulysses throwing off the chains of boredom, leaving his dull hearth in search of new adventure. *To sail beyond the sunset . . .* I'd thought that beautiful, once. But now I knew it was a wasted effort, chasing sunsets. There was nothing on the other side.

96

Paul was watching me with those wise eyes that saw too much. I glanced away, quite casually, and asked him: 'But however did you make the leap from Tennyson's *Ulysses* to James Joyce? They're not a bit alike.'

'That,' he told me, 'was my sister's fault. She saw this book in a used bookstore a couple of Christmases back, read the title, and bought it for me. She thought one Ulysses was the same as the next. I didn't want to disappoint her, so I started reading it.' He smiled again, and set the book aside. 'It's become sort of an obsession. I won't be able to rest until I've finished the damn thing.'

I was vaguely surprised to learn that Simon and Paul had a sister. Not that it mattered, but for some reason I'd thought there were only the two of them. The curious thing about meeting people on holiday, I told myself, was that one formed opinions based on first impressions, or past experience. And one was so often wrong. I looked up at Paul. 'How many brothers and sisters do you have?'

'There are six of us, altogether.'

'Six!'

'Yeah. Simon's the oldest, then Rachel, Lisa, Helen, me and Sarah. Sarah,' he added, having counted everyone off in order on his fingers, 'is the one who bought me the book.'

'Six,' I repeated, incredulous.

My reaction amused him. 'Let me guess. You're an only child.'

I admitted that I was. 'But then my cousin was usually around at holidays and half-terms to keep me company. People used to mistake us for brother and sister, we looked so much alike.' We still did, come to that.

Especially around the eyes. The thought of Harry triggered a more recent memory. 'I've had a message from him, by the way. He'll be a few days late.'

'Don't worry,' Paul said. 'Simon will have the next few days planned out for us, just watch. He's a man with a mission now.'

'Queen Isabelle's treasure, you mean?' I smiled. 'Well, he can hunt if he likes, but I doubt he'll find it. Harry says the research alone could take years.'

'God, don't tell Simon that. The more impossible something is, the more he wants to do it.' He stubbed out his cigarette, fraying the end of it, and lit another. 'And don't tell Simon you saw me doing this, either. He'd have my hide. He thinks I just come down here to feed the ducks.'

There were an awful lot of ducks, now that I noticed it. They seemed to be clustered mostly upriver, where a cobblestone ramp for launching boats slanted gently down to meet the water, although a handful of adventurous ones had ridden the current down to where we sat and were paddling now around a flat-bottomed punt moored by chains to the river wall. The ducks were noisy little creatures, scolding and complaining as their feet beat time against the dragging river.

I'd often fed ducks myself, as a child, but now I simply put my chin on my hands and watched them, while Paul smoked his cigarette in mellow, undemanding silence. At length he stood and stretched, picking up his book. 'Come on,' he said. 'Let's go and see if Thierry's got the bar open yet. I could use a coffee or something.'

I walked back with him, but when he would have bought me a drink I shook my head, yawning. 'Have a heart,' I begged him. 'I only got here yesterday, remember, and I've been on the go ever since. I'll never make it through to suppertime if I don't have a nap.' The thought of supper made me frown. 'Do you all eat together, every night?'

He laughed, and shook his head. 'No, we usually end up doing our own thing. Why, did we scare you last night?'

'Well, I wouldn't want to . . . heavens, is that Neil?' I broke off suddenly to stare in wonder at the floor above us.

'Yeah. He's good, isn't he?' Paul listened for a moment, then flashed a sympathetic smile. 'And he's just getting started, from the sounds of it. I hope you can sleep through Beethoven.'

I couldn't, as it happened, but it was my own fault more than Beethoven's. My restless mind would not keep still enough for sleep to settle on it. It conjured images of gypsies and of castles and of dark-eyed men with blindingly fair hair. In the room below, Neil finished playing the symphony's opening *allegro*, and moved smoothly on into the funeral march. A new set of images rose to join the ones already swirling behind my closed eyelids – a black-and-white cat and a mournful church and a spray of flowers, red as blood. And through it all, the gypsy's face turned, watching me with a strange and secret smile.

I opened my eyes, and sat up.

It was no use, I thought. I wasn't going to sleep. I might as well go down and have that drink with Paul. What happened next, I later decided, was *entirely* Beethoven's fault. If he hadn't written such a beautiful piece of music, I wouldn't have paused on my way downstairs to listen to it. And if I hadn't paused, there on the first floor landing, I wouldn't have been anywhere in sight when the Whitakers' door opened further down the hall, and Garland came out into the passage. She hadn't seen me yet – she was looking down, one hand shielding her forehead – but I felt a moment's panic. I didn't like the woman, didn't want to be drawn into conversation, didn't want Neil Grantham to hear her piercing voice and know that I was standing there, outside his room . . .

I looked round, seeking some escape. Not down the stairs, I dismissed the obvious. There wasn't time, and she was bound to see me. But beside the stairs a glass door stood propped open to the outside air, and, feeling a proper coward, I ducked my head and darted through it. Behind me, the rustle of footsteps swept by without stopping, and a heartbeat later I heard a sharp knock. The violin fell silent. Cautiously, I edged along the wall, away from the open doorway, away from the murmur of voices.

I hadn't picked the best of hiding places, really. I was standing on a sheltered terrace, built upon the flat roof of the hotel's garage – a broad, square stretch of pavement bordered by a wooden portico and hugged on three sides by the bleached stone walls of the hotel. One couldn't truly hide, out here. All someone had to do was poke their head around the door, and there you were, in plain view. But for the moment, at least, the terrace was deserted, except for me.

The voices stopped. A door clicked shut. The rustling steps retreated down the corridor. But instead of going back inside, I crossed on tiptoe to the centre of the terrace, where a neat grouping of table and chairs basked in the fickle sunlight of the afternoon. Wiping the dampness from a chair. I sat down. From here I had a panoramic view along the cliffs, from the wedge-shaped Clock Tower guarding Château Chinon to the wilder fringes of the hills beyond the town.

High above me on the cliff path a small cluster of sightseers had paused against the waist-high wall, and their red and purple jackets made a splash of welcome colour on the drab white rise of rock behind them. One of the couples was holding hands and laughing, and I hated them without reason.

The violin began again. I closed my eyes against the beauty of it, settling back with a sigh. He wasn't playing the Beethoven any more. No, this was stranger music, sweeter, more seductive . . . yet familiar. I searched my memory for it. Elgar, I decided. That was it. Edward Elgar. The *Salute d'Amour*.

Neil played it beautifully, with such emotion that the air around me trembled from the sound. I remember wishing he would stop, because I didn't want to think of love just now. I remember squeezing my eyes shut tighter still, and feeling the sudden damp of tears upon my lashes. And after that, I don't remember anything.

I hadn't meant to sleep. But when I next opened my eyes the terrace was in darkness, and a scattering of stars gleamed faintly where the clouds had been before. The chill had penetrated to my bones. I rose and flexed my stiffened shoulders, picking my way cautiously across to the glass door into the hotel. Someone, while I'd slept, had closed that door. I tried the handle. 'Damn,' I said, aloud. They'd locked me out.

Hugging my arms to ward off the cold, I pressed my face against the glass and peered along the corridor. I knocked twice, loudly. No-one came. 'Damn,' I said again, cursing my own stupidity. And then, quite by chance, I saw the stairs. It was a narrow flight of stone stairs, nearly invisible in the dark, curving downwards from the level of the terrace. Remembering that the hotel's garage was underneath me, I plucked up my courage and started down, my hand clutching at the railing, expecting at any moment to miss my footing on the uneven stone. It was a relief to feel the ground again, safe and solid beneath my feet and, after a moment's search, to find the door that I had hoped would be there.

It didn't open into the garage, as I'd expected, but straight onto the street itself. The fountain gurgled placidly in front of me, bathed in the golden glow of street lamps, and the hotel's front doors, brightly lit beneath the awning, beckoned me from several yards away. I shivered again and headed for those doors.

But before I reached them, I saw the child.

I stopped, and hovered, hesitating. *It's not your business*, I warned myself. *Don't get involved.* But I couldn't help myself.

She was so young, I thought, no more than six or seven years of age, and so pitifully alone. A miserable figure all in black, sitting still as a statue on the bench at the far side of the fountain square, her large eyes fixed upon the doors of the hotel. She looked up as I approached, and my heart turned over tightly. She'd been crying.

Hunching down on my knees, I spoke to her as gently as I could, in French, and asked what was the matter.

'I can't go home,' she said.

'Why can't you? Don't you know the way?'

She shook her head, setting her short cap of dark brown curls bouncing around her pale face. 'Papa will be so angry.'

Tears swelled again in the big eyes and I rushed to reassure her. 'I'm sure he won't be angry, really he won't. You can't help being lost.'

'I'm not lost, Madame,' she said, with another toss of her head. 'I know how to get to my house. But my papa, he will be angry.'

'Tell me why.'

'Because I left them. They looked the other way, and so I left them. Papa, he said I was to stay with her until suppertime, but they did not want me there, you see . . .'

'I see,' I said, although of course I didn't. 'And who are "they"?'

'My aunt and her friend. Her man friend.'

'Ah,' I said, comprehension dawning.

'I was sorry, afterwards, for leaving them, but when I went back they had already gone, and so I came here to wait for them. My aunt's friend stays at this hotel, and so I thought . . . I thought . . .' Her lower lip quivered. 'But they have not come. And I cannot go home.'

'Nonsense.' I rose to my feet, stretching out one hand. 'Of course you can. I'll take you home.'

The big eyes were imploring. 'But my papa . . .'

'Just you leave your papa to me.'

She sniffed and thought a moment, and then the small cold fingers curled around my own, trustingly.

'Now, where is your house?'

'It is up there,' she said, and showed me. 'Behind the château.'

She was pointing at the steep stairway leading upwards from the square. Wonderful, I thought with an inward groan. Why couldn't I have been called to play the Good Samaritan to a child who made her home on street level? With sinking heart I started up the steps, the little girl in tow.

Simon and Paul had been quite right, I decided – the

stairs were definitely more difficult to manage than the more gradual ascent from the rue Voltaire. By the time we neared the top my lungs were burning, and my heart was pounding wildly against my ribcage. I felt an old woman beside the child, who climbed with irritating ease. At the summit of the steps I paused, trying desperately to buy a moment's rest. 'Where now?' I gasped.

'This way,' she said, and pointed. I let her lead me up the long slope to the château, then round the sheer and silent floodlit walls and down again. I would have gone on further but she held me back.

'No, Madame,' she told me, 'it is here. This is my house.'

'*This* is your house?' My jaw slackened. I felt rather like someone who'd become lost and was wandering now in circles, forever coming round again to the same familiar spot. It was, after all, beyond the bounds of mere coincidence . . . wasn't it? 'This is your house,' I echoed, as if the repetition might convince me, and I lifted disbelieving eyes to stare at the great imposing gates that rose before us – the gates of the *Clos des Cloches*, the vineyard of the bells.

Chapter Nine

A feudal knight in silken masquerade . . .

The gates were locked. I would have pressed the buzzer, but the child stopped my hand.

'No, no, Madame – this way,' she said, and led me through a smaller door set in the high stone wall. We came out in a dark and peaceful garden, heavy with the scent of roses. Still slightly dazed, I let my young friend pull me up the wide, well-groomed approach to the white mansion, shining whiter in its floodlights, looking nearly as impressive as the château ruins that it faced.

With every step the house grew larger, and I felt smaller by comparison, scarcely taller than the child who held me by the hand. Even the front door, when we finally reached it, looked disproportionately huge.

'The door, it will be locked,' the girl informed me, matter-of-factly. 'You must push the bell, just there.'

She pointed, and I pushed.

After what seemed an eternity of silence, the door swung open on its hinges, trapping us in a slanting slab of blinding yellow light. The face of the man who stood in that doorway was faintly grey and sternly lined, his mouth a deep horizontal slash beneath a hawk-like nose. It was easy to see why the child had feared his reaction, I thought. I rather feared it myself.

Which was why, when I finally found my voice, I heard myself stammering out the little girl's predicament, or at least the essence of it, in a rapid rush of speech, ignoring the persistent tugging at my sleeve.

'. . . and so naturally I assured her, Monsieur, that you would not be angry,' I concluded, rather lamely.

Beside me the child gave another tug. 'But Madame,' she hissed, in a stage whisper, 'this is not my father. This is only François.'

I looked in surprise from the tall grey man to the child, and back again. 'Oh,' I said.

The man had been staring at me steadily, his eyes in shadow, but now, as if awaking from a trance, he bent his head, the corners of his hard mouth lifting in a smile that surprised me with its kindness. 'It is true, Madame,' he told me gravely. 'I am not the father of Mademoiselle Lucie. But please, do come in.'

Numbly, I stepped into the brilliantly lit foyer, and felt the child's fingers loosen from my grasp. The man named François shut the door firmly behind us, and I noticed for the first time that he was an older man, in his sixties, perhaps, or even early seventies. Old enough to be the child's grandfather. He drew himself up gravely and looked down at the small figure beside me.

'So, Mademoiselle, you have had an adventure tonight, have you not? A bath, I think, and then to bed.'

'I have not had my supper . . .'

'Just water and dry bread, tonight,' he threatened her, but he didn't look as if he meant it, and she wasn't a bit fooled. 'Say thank you to the kind lady, Lucie, for bringing you home.'

She turned to me, her dark eyes noticeably clearer and less miserable. 'Thank you, Madame.'

'You are most welcome.'

I solemnly shook the hand she offered me, before François sent her off with a playfully imperious sweep of his hand. Giggling, she galloped up the elegant staircase that curved upwards from the foyer, her small feet making no noise on the thick red carpet as she trailed her hand along the painted wrought-iron railings of the bannister.

I felt the man's eyes on my face again, with a curious intensity, but as I met his gaze the impression vanished. He cleared his throat and spoke. 'This is a very kind thing you have done, Madame. The streets can be quite dangerous for a small child, and her adventure might not have ended so pleasantly. I am grateful to you for bringing her home.'

'It was no trouble, honestly.'

'You will wait here, please, Madame,' he commanded me, as I turned to leave. 'Monsieur Valcourt, I am sure, will also wish to thank you.'

My hesitation must have shown, because he said to me again: 'Wait here, please,' before he finally left me. The tone of his voice left no room for argument. I linked my hands behind my back like a chastened schoolgirl and did as I was told, feeling a childish twinge of apprehension, as though it had been myself and not the girl Lucie who'd gone wandering off against the rules. This was, I thought, what happened when one got involved in other people's problems.

Still, I had to admit that my situation was not entirely without interest.

The inhabitants of the *Clos des Cloches*, like Jim Whitaker, evidently bought their clothing tailor made.

The tangible evidence of wealth met me here at every turning. Not only wealth, but old and polished wealth, generations of it, handed down with pride from time immemorial. The plush red carpet, the marble floor on which I stood, the golden sconces on the white-painted walls, the rich, dark tones of the gilt-framed portraits – all this spoke to me of money and of privilege.

A portrait by the staircase drew my eye, and I moved closer to examine it. It showed a boy just entering his teens, a boy with thick black hair and great dark eyes that watched me, lifelike. Those eyes, I thought, were faintly familiar . . .

'Good evening, Madame.' The deep voice spoke suddenly out of the air behind me.

I had not heard him come into the foyer, but my startled reaction was not due solely to the unexpected nature of his entrance. Pulling my eyes away from the portrait, I turned slowly round to face Monsieur Valcourt, and had the satisfaction of seeing his own features change abruptly.

'You . . .' he said, the flash of surprise in his dark eyes quickly swallowed by a spreading warmth.

I lifted my chin a fraction and summoned up the brightest smile I could muster. 'You owe me twenty-five francs, Monsieur,' I told him.

I ought to have been furious, I told myself. No doubt he had thought it a marvellous joke to be mistaken for a taxi driver, and he had certainly enjoyed that joke at my expense. It was a rotten thing to do, and I should have despised him for it. But the best I could manage was a kind of limpid irritation, and even that would not hold up beneath the smooth persuasion of his smile.

'I owe my daughter a debt, I think,' he said, coming forward. 'I am Armand Valcourt.'

'Emily Braden.' I shook his hand stiffly, keeping the contact as brief as possible.

'You're angry with me.' I did not answer, and his breath escaped him on a sound that wasn't quite a sigh. 'I never said, you know, that the taxi was mine. If you had asked, I would have told you no, I was just waiting for the driver to collect my luggage from the train, that's all. But,' he spread his hands, in self-defence, 'you didn't ask.'

'You might have told me, later. When we met the second time.'

'I might have, yes. But by that time you were convinced I drove the taxi. I thought it would embarrass you to find out who I was. And it was no great sacrifice for me to drive you to your hotel.'

'You took my money,' I reminded him.

'You were most insistent, as I recall.' His eyes were gently mocking above his smile. 'I did not keep your money, Mademoiselle. I gave it to my friend, Jean-Luc, who owns the taxi. And if it matters, he also was not pleased with me, when he found I'd taken his taxi. So I have been twice reprimanded.' Not that he looked particularly remorseful. He thrust his hands in his pockets and tilted his head to one side. 'Am I forgiven?'

'Possibly.' I softened, noting he had switched to calling me 'Mademoiselle' in place of the more formal 'Madame'. The change implied a subtle move in our relationship as well – no longer strangers, but acquaintances.

'But you are right,' he said, 'I must repay you. Have you eaten yet?'

'No, but—'

'Then please, you must dine with me, tonight. François always cooks far more than I can eat alone. Do you like veal?'

'Yes, but—'

'Good. You can leave your coat there, if you like, beside the door. Here, let me help you.'

I hesitated, and he smiled again. It was a damnably persuasive smile. 'Please,' he said again. 'I've upset you, and my daughter has dragged you across half of Chinon. The least that I can do is give you dinner.'

It would be harmless enough, I thought, to accept the offer. I *was* rather hungry, and the fact that he was flirting with me openly convinced me just how harmless it would be. Flirtatious men I could handle. It was the serious ones, like Neil, who made me nervous – the ones who looked straight at you and spoke simply and had no use for games. Men like Neil, I thought, might talk of love and mean it, while flirtatious men demanded nothing, promised less, and never disappointed. There could be no danger, I decided, in a dinner with Armand Valcourt.

'Of course,' he said, 'if there is someone waiting for you back at your hotel . . .'

I shook my head. 'No, I'm all on my own.'

'Good,' he murmured, cryptically, as I followed him from the foyer into a long, expansive room half shadow and half light, its understated elegance both soothing and surreal. It had been decorated with an eye to detail – the artistic arrangement of chairs and sofa, the graceful antique writing-desk, the swan-like pair of table lamps . . . but it looked more like a stage set than a sitting-room. A place where no-one really *lived*. The image was compounded by the fact that one whole wall seemed made of windows, black as pitch at this late hour. As we moved, the glass threw back our images, distorted.

'I eat in here,' he told me. 'It's my habit, when I'm alone. Unless you would prefer the dining-room?'

I shook my head. 'Here is fine.'

He must have already been sitting down to dinner when François had interrupted him. A table at the far end of the room was set for one, its polished surface scattered with an odd assortment of china bowls and chafing dishes.

I'd seen so many films about the rich that I was half expecting serving maids in starched white caps, but it was Armand Valcourt himself who fetched me an extra plate and cutlery, and filled my wine glass from the open bottle on the table.

'It's last year's vintage,' he explained, as he poured. 'Not a great wine, I'm afraid, but sufficient for François's cooking. The real cook is off this evening.'

He took the chair across from me and raised his own glass in a toast. 'To small deceptions,' he said, with a slow deliberate smile.

The wine, to my untrained palate at least, proved excellent, as did the meal itself. I thought François a smashing cook, and said so.

'François has many talents,' my host told me. 'He's a good man and a loyal one. But you will learn this for yourself, I think.'

'What do you mean?'

'You've made a friend of him tonight, make no mistake. He does not forget a kindness, and he's very fond of my daughter.'

'Oh, I see.' I nodded. 'Well, that's understandable, Monsieur. She is a charming child.'

He smiled a little, lowering his eyes to the food on his plate. 'Her mother's doing, and not mine. Brigitte was much more sociable than I am.'

I thought it impolite to ask the question, so I didn't, but he answered it for me anyway. 'My wife had a weak heart, Mademoiselle. She died three years ago.'

'I'm sorry.'

He was still looking down, and I couldn't see his eyes. 'Life moves us onwards, does it not? More wine?'

I held my glass out while he poured. 'How many children do you have?'

'Just Lucie. I think it must be lonely for her, sometimes.'

'I rather enjoyed being an only child, myself,' I confessed. 'I was spoiled rotten.'

Briefly, his enigmatic gaze touched mine. 'François tells me I'm not to be angry with my daughter. Your words, I think.'

'Yes, well . . . I did rather promise her that you wouldn't be.' I suddenly developed an intense interest in my own plate, pushing my vegetables round with the fork. 'I shouldn't have interfered, perhaps, but if you'd seen her you'd have understood. She looked so small, and so unhappy, I thought surely no parent would want to . . .' My voice trailed off and I speared a carrot with my fork. 'Besides, she wouldn't have come with me, otherwise. She was afraid.'

He raised an eyebrow. 'Afraid of what?'

'Of your reaction, naturally.'

That surprised him, and he frowned as he dismissed the notion with a classic Gallic 'pouf'. 'I don't beat my daughter, Mademoiselle.'

'Of course you don't. But your daughter was very tired,' I reasoned, 'and upset. And things always do seem quite a bit more frightening when one is lost. Not that she was ever lost herself, really, but she'd lost the people she was with, which rather amounts to the same thing.'

His mouth curved, and I had the distinct impression he found me amusing, but the tone of his voice betrayed nothing. 'She would not have lost anyone if she had done as she was told. I gave her clear instructions to remain with her aunt.'

'Yes, but she told me . . .' I broke off suddenly, realizing my error. It was really none of my business, I thought. This was a family matter, and I ought not to get involved.

Armand Valcourt raised his eyebrow a second time, expectantly. 'Yes?'

'Nothing. It's not important.' I scooped up a forkful of seasoned meat and tried to ignore his suddenly curious eyes, watching me across the table.

'Where exactly was my daughter, Mademoiselle, when you found her?'

I glanced up, saw he wasn't going to let the matter drop, and sighed. 'She was sitting by the fountain just in front of my hotel.'

He frowned. 'And did she tell you why she went there?'

'She told me her aunt's . . . friend was staying there. I think she hoped they'd come back to the hotel, so she was waiting for them. Forgive me for asking, Monsieur, but the child's aunt . . . your sister . . .'

'My wife's sister,' he corrected me.

'Shouldn't someone notify her that your daughter is safe? She must be frantic with worry by now.'

My statement was punctuated by a loud bang from the front hallway, and Armand Valcourt reached, smiling, for his wine glass. 'I don't think that will be necessary,' he said. 'This will be Martine now.'

Martine . . .

At first I thought, *it couldn't be*, and then an image flashed into my mind of Armand Valcourt standing close beside the widow at today's funeral, and I thought, *of course it must be*, and I turned expectantly as Martine Muret burst in upon us.

I believe I'd been preparing myself to dislike her, for her beauty if nothing else, but the moment the door from the hallway flew open all my preconceived notions went out of the window. In place of the coldly glamorous woman I'd expected, I saw someone who seemed scarcely older than her wayward niece, with cropped black hair and large eyes liquid in her bloodless face. And 'frantic with worry', I now saw, was an understatement. Martine Muret was terrified.

'Armand, I cannot find her,' she broke in, ignoring me completely in her distress. 'Lucie, she is gone. I have looked everywhere, but—'

'Calm yourself, Martine,' her brother-in-law said, raising one hand to stop the woman's flood of speech. 'Lucie is fine, she's safe in bed.'

'Oh, thank God.' Her knees caved weakly in relief and she dropped suddenly onto a tapestry-covered chair by the long windows. Touching a hand to her brow, she seemed to notice me for the first time, and the look she sent her brother-in-law was faintly quizzical.

In a few brief, unembellished sentences, he explained who I was, and how I'd come to be there.

'I am so grateful to you, Mademoiselle.' Her smile was a fleeting shadow on that lovely, fragile face. 'You cannot know how I have suffered these past hours, searching for my niece. One reads such horrible things in the newspapers, you know, and I was so afraid . . .' She couldn't even finish the thought out loud. Her pale hand brushed her temple once again, and she said quietly: 'I would never have forgiven myself.'

I mumbled once again that it was nothing, that I'd been only too glad to help Lucie, that they'd already been too kind . . . And pushing aside my empty plate, I glanced down at my wristwatch. 'But I'm afraid I really must be getting back to my hotel.'

'I will drive you,' Martine said, as if determined to repay the debt. 'Where are you staying?'

'The Hotel de France.'

I caught the flicker of surprise, the too-bright smile. 'Oh, yes?'

'Martine has friends there,' said Armand Valcourt. Leaning back in his chair, he lit a cigarette, and the lighter's click was as violently loud as the cock of a loaded gun. 'But I think, perhaps, that I should drive you down myself. To see you get back safely.' He stressed that last word, 'safely', and Martine's eyes flashed a quick response.

I glanced from one face to the other, sensed the coming storm, and diplomatically excused myself to use the bathroom. In spite of the fact that arguing was to the French what complaining about the weather was to the English, I'd never learned the knack of it. I hated arguments. I particularly hated being in the middle of them, and so I loitered as long as I could in the little washroom under the front stairs. Which rather backfired when Martine and Armand came into the hall. Trapped, I could only stand and wait, pretending not to hear the angry voices.

'I've already told you I was sorry,' snapped Martine Muret. 'What more do you want?'

'I want you to behave responsibly, to show some consideration for my feelings, Lucie's feelings, instead of thinking only of yourself.' He wasn't really shouting, but his voice was cold and hard and carried clearly. 'Do you realize what can happen to a child, alone at night? Do you?'

'Of course I do,' she shot back. 'What do you think, Armand, that I wasn't worried myself? That I wasn't sick with fear when I realized she was missing? Is that what you think?'

'I think you were too occupied with other things to notice she was gone. Which one was it, this time?' he asked her. 'The German or the Englishman? Or have you grown bored with them already, and found someone else?'

'I don't see that my private life is any of your business.'

'When it affects my daughter, it's my business. My God, Martine, what were you thinking of? We buried him today, or have you forgotten this?'

A silence followed, stung by the echo of those words. 'I forget nothing,' said Martine, at last, in a calm and quiet voice. 'And how dare you judge my feelings, Armand. What do you know of love?'

I heard her cross the foyer and start up the staircase, her footsteps treading lightly over my head. Still, I waited until those footsteps were completely out of earshot, until I'd heard the click of Armand Valcourt's cigarette lighter, before I decided it was safe to emerge.

He was standing at the foot of the stairs, his expression quite relaxed and natural. Only the jerking movement of the hand that held the cigarette betrayed his anger. By the time I reached him, even that small action had been brought under control. His eyes, on mine, were normal. 'Ready?' he asked me. 'Yes? Then let us go.' And handing me my jacket, he ushered me out into the waiting night.

Chapter Ten

. . . the Graces, group'd in
threes,
Enring'd a billowing fountain . . .

He drove a Porsche. That didn't surprise me overmuch
– the flashy red sports car rather suited him – but it did
set me wondering. If Armand Valcourt owned a car,
why had he taken a taxi from the station yesterday
morning? Come to think of it, why had he taken the
train? I only wondered for a moment, then I asked him.

He shrugged. 'I always take the train when I go to
Paris. Martine might need the car, you see, if there were
some emergency with Lucie. And anyway, I'd be a fool
to drive the Porsche in Paris.' He shot a sideways glance
at me. 'Why the smile?'

'Was I smiling? Sorry. It's only that I used to live in
Paris, so I understand completely. My father once
backed into a Mercedes. The owner wasn't very . . .
understanding.'

Armand laughed. 'No, I don't suppose he would have
been.' I felt again the flashing glance. 'How long were
you in Paris?'

'Five years. But it was ages ago. I was only twelve
when we left.'

He smiled and swung the Porsche round the hairpin
bend that plunged towards the river. 'I had wondered,'

he confided, 'where you learned to speak your French.'

It took a minute for his words to hit their mark. I'd spoken French to little Lucie, when I'd first approached her in the fountain square, and then . . . well, I suppose I'd simply gone on speaking it. In all the confusion, I hadn't really noticed. I shrugged now, suddenly self-conscious. 'My father's in the foreign service,' I explained. 'He wanted me to have a second language.'

'You have one. Your French is very beautiful.'

'Thank you.'

He didn't ask me what I did for a living, but then the French didn't ask such things, as a rule. It was considered impolite, a means of pigeonholing people before one really got to know them. Since the Revolution, everyone was meant to be equal anyway. *Almost* equal, I amended, leaning back against the glove-soft leather of the Porsche.

Armand Valcourt had missed the Revolution. There was a certain feudal gallantry about the way he dropped me at my hotel door, coming round to help me out of the car as if I were royalty. His handshake lingered, by design, and his smile was deliberately charming. 'You have your key?' he asked me.

'Yes.' I rummaged for it in my handbag, pushing aside a stiff white card with printing on it. 'Oh,' I said. I'd quite forgotten, in all the confusion, about my mysterious invitation to taste wine at the *Clos des Cloches*. 'This was from you, then, I presume?' I held it up to show him. 'It was left for me this morning.'

'Was it?' The charming smile broadened, refusing to take responsibility.

'Yes.'

'Ah. That is very curious, you know, because we don't give tours this time of year.' Taking the card from my hand, he assumed a mock-serious expression. 'Still, it appears quite genuine. I am sure,' he said, as he gave it back, 'that we would honour it.'

'So you did send it, then.'

His dark eyes held a deep amusement. 'Well, if I did, I could have saved myself the trouble.'

'Why?'

'Because you came to see me anyway.'

Definitely a flirt, I thought, as he walked back round to the driver's side of the car. Smiling faintly, I watched the Porsche's back lights twinkle out of sight along the Place du Général de Gaulle.

It was a lovely night for late September, crisp and clear, filled with the drifting scents of autumn – pungent leaves and petrol fumes and slowly burning coal. My watch read ten past eleven, but there were still people passing me by on the pavement – young people, mostly, in boisterous clusters, making their way to the lively bar on the nearest corner. The mingled sounds of dance music and laughter spilled out across the square. Saturday night, I thought. I thrust my hands in my pockets, feeling suddenly at a loss. I could almost hear my cousin's voice reminding me, in disapproving tones: *It's been six months since you so much as stopped in at the pub for a drink*.

Frowning, I hovered there a moment, trying to decide whether to go out for a drink or go up to my room. In the end I did neither. I crossed to the fountain and sat on the bench where I'd found Lucie Valcourt.

Here, beneath the whispering tangle of acacia branches, it was easy to go unnoticed. I sat back, facing the brilliant glow of the Hotel de France and the bustling bar on the corner, and focused on the pleasantly murmuring fountain in front of me.

The bottom pool was perhaps two feet deep, a stone hexagon raised on a sloping step. Water cascaded into it from a bronze basin set high overhead like an upside-down umbrella, and that basin in turn was fed by the overflow from a smaller bronze bowl above *it*. From the centre of the fountain rose three women, cast in bronze, supporting the entire structure. Back-to-back the women stood, arms lowered to their sides, their fingers linked in an eternal show of sisterhood. There was no mistaking their classical origins – even without their flowing draperies and tightly coiled hair, there was a depth of beauty to their faces that told me they belonged in ancient Greece.

A hopeful nudge against my legs disturbed my contemplation. It was a cat, a rather familiar-looking black-and-white cat, and when the green gaze locked expectantly with mine I fancied that I recognized it. It was the same cat, surely, that I'd seen that afternoon perched on the high wall of Christian Rand's house. It rubbed itself against my legs a second time, more demanding now than hopeful, and I tapped my fingers on my lap. 'All right, then,' I coaxed it, 'it's OK.' Pleased, the cat leapt up and padded round in circles on my knees, pausing once to sniff my face in a delicate sort of greeting.

It was clearly a stray – one stroke of my fingers along the dirt-encrusted back told me that – but it was nonetheless affectionate. And trusting. It stopped circling and curled itself inside my jacket, claws working against the stiff fabric, and within seconds the green eyes closed. Head nestled heavily against my breast, the cat breathed deeply with a steady, rumbling purr that vibrated up through the thick fur to my caressing hand. Surprised, and oddly moved, I crooked my neck to stare down at the sleeping animal.

I ceased to be aware of time. I don't know for certain how many minutes had passed before I heard the footsteps coming down the steps from the château, between the shuttered buildings.

Neil Grantham's hair was almost white beneath the street lamps, white as his shirt beneath the soft brown leather jacket he was wearing over faded jeans. *Oh, damn*, I thought, feeling again the unwanted stirring of emotion, like a persistent hand tugging at my sleeve. I shrank back further into shadow, hoping he'd go straight into the hotel without seeing me. His head came round as if I'd called to him, and with easy strides he crossed the square to join me on my bench beside the fountain.

'You'll get fleas,' he said, looking at the cat.

'I don't care,' I tightened my hold protectively, lifting my chin. 'He just wants some attention, poor devil. I've a soft spot for strays.'

He smiled and stretched his long legs out in front of him, elbows propped against the top rail of the bench's back. His presence, like the cat's, was very peaceful, but for some reason that only made me more nervous. If only he would flirt, I thought, like Armand Valcourt had, then I'd be fine. But Neil was not Armand. He just went on sitting there, perfectly still, as though he were waiting for something.

I stroked the cat's head, and cleared my throat. 'Were you just up at the château?'

He nodded. 'My nightly walk. It's the only exercise I enjoy, really – walking. You ought to come with me some time.' I glanced at him then, but he still wasn't flirting. His face was dead serious.

I made a non-committal noise and swung my eyes

back to the trickling fountain with its trio of lovely bronze women.

Neil followed my gaze. 'Enjoying the fountain, are you?'

'Yes,' I said, and then because the silence stretched so long I cleared my throat again and told him, childishly: 'There used to be a fountain in our garden when I was very small. My father worked in Rome, then, and we had this marvellous house, with a court-yard and everything, and the fountain in the middle of it. A wishing fountain, my father called it – he used to give me a coin at breakfast, every day, for me to make a wish with. Anything I wanted.'

Now why, I thought, had I told him that? It was a foolish thing to tell a total stranger.

Neil went on looking at the dancing fall of water. 'And did it work?'

Did it work? I remembered the day I wished for a kitten, and found one wandering in our back lane. And the day the horrid girl next door fell off her bike. I tucked my jacket round the sleeping cat and shrugged. 'I don't remember.'

He brought his quiet gaze back to my face, and I hastily changed the subject. 'Are these women in the fountain sculpture Greek?'

'That's right. Splendour, Joy and Beauty. The three Graces.'

'Oh, I see.' I peered more closely at the downturned faces. 'Which one is which, do you know?'

'Lord, no.' His smile was disarming. 'I only know their names because I looked them up last Tuesday. Simon asked me, and I didn't want to appear ignorant, not when I've been coming to Chinon for so long.' His eyes slid from me, looking at the figures with new interest. 'Still, I imagine there's some way to tell them apart, if we approach it logically. Splendour means brilliance, doesn't it? So the lady facing into the sunset would be my choice for Splendour – she'd get the best light, vivid colours. And the prettiest one is round the other side, facing the hotel, so I'd say she's Beauty. Which leaves Joy, and that fits,' he decided, 'because she's got the widest smile.'

I frowned. 'She's not smiling.'

'Of course she is. They all are. That's what Graces do, you know. They smile upon you and make life beautiful.'

'Oh.' The man was seeing things, I thought, as I stared back at the nearest statue, the one Neil had pegged as Splendour. She certainly wasn't smiling. Not at me.

High above, in the ruined château, the midnight bell began to toll, disturbing the sleeping cat. The green eyes opened and stared at me with a deeply disappointed air, then in one fluid motion the cat rose and stepped, stretching, from my lap onto the pavement. Stiff-legged, it wandered off into the shadows.

Neil watched it go, then looked across the square at the noisy corner bar. 'Listen, since we're both still up, can I buy you a drink?'

Five years ago, I would have told him yes. Five years ago, I would have done a lot of things.

Tonight I stammered some excuse about being tired, and faked an unconvincing yawn.

'Another time, perhaps,' he said.

'Perhaps.' I rose from the bench, and said goodnight, and his dark eyes gently called me coward.

'Goodnight, Emily.'

It seemed a long walk across the little square to the

hotel door, mainly because I felt those eyes upon me every step of the way, but when I turned at the door to glance back, Neil wasn't watching me at all. He wasn't even looking in my general direction. His face was turned the other way, towards the château steps.

The black-and-white cat had returned, weaving itself nimbly around Neil's outstretched ankles. As I watched, he leaned forward and scratched the animal's ears absently, but he didn't look down. He just went on looking with narrowed eyes at something . . . or someone . . . I couldn't see.

Chapter Eleven

'O long ago,' she said, 'betwixt these two
Division smoulders hidden;'

Next morning the young bartender, Thierry, looked a
little the worse for wear. He set the basket of croissants
and bread between the boys and me, and leaned against
the spare fourth chair at our breakfast table.

'. . . but no,' he went on, 'they do not come down
for breakfast today. Madame Whitaker, she has the
headache since yesterday afternoon – the migraine. She
stays in bed today. And Monsieur Whitaker, he went
out very early.'

It was still only nine o'clock, and Simon looked with
interest at the empty corner table where the Whitakers
liked to sit. 'By himself?'

Thierry admitted that he didn't know. 'But then, I do
not always pay attention. I think that he is gone to hear
the Mass somewhere.'

'I'm surprised you haven't gone to Mass yourself,'
Paul said. 'You could use a confession, my friend.'

Thierry merely grinned and raised his shoulders in
a carefree shrug. 'But I must work on Sundays,' he
excused himself. 'Who else would serve your break-
fasts?'

Which was probably just as well. Judging by the

shadows beneath his dark eyes and the rather wickedly rumpled look he was sporting after what had obviously been a wild Saturday night, I decided Thierry's soul was very likely past redemption.

'He's superhuman,' Simon said, with grudging admiration, as Thierry left us to attend an older couple seated by the window. 'He wore us out completely last night, at the disco. You should have been there, Emily.'

I pulled a face. 'I'm much too old for discos.'

Paul stopped pouring his second cup of coffee long enough to roll his eyes. 'Oh, right. What are you, thirty?'

'Twenty-eight.'

'Positively ancient,' he said drily. 'They'll be fitting you for false teeth next, I guess.'

'Besides,' Simon added, 'age is no excuse. Neil's come out with us a couple of times, and he's forty-something. He dances pretty good for an old guy.'

'Pretty well,' Paul corrected him, automatically.

'Whatever.' Simon grimaced. 'Remind me to get some aspirin later.'

'I've got some,' I offered, reaching for my handbag. 'Somewhere, that is. I don't know why I carry all this, I can never *find* anything.' Rifling through the over-stuffed bag, I started to remove things, one by one, piling them beside my empty plate. My bulging wallet, sunglasses, two pens, a packet of tissues, a crinkled tourist map of Chinon, a square of thick paper with printing on it . . .

'Hey,' said Simon, pouncing on the latter. 'What's this? You've been holding out on us.'

I glanced up. 'What? Oh, it's just an invitation.'

'Yeah, right.' Simon flipped the card around to show his brother. 'To the *Clos des Cloches*.'

Paul whistled, impressed. 'Who'd you have to kill to get that?'

'No-one.' I smiled. 'They just gave it to me. Aha!' I found the aspirin at last, and handed the bottle to Simon.

He took it absently, tapping the edge of the card with one finger. 'The *Clos des Cloches* is where that tunnel leads, from the château.'

Paul caught my eye. 'Oh, here we go.'

'No, no,' said Simon, 'I was only thinking that it might be kind of neat to get inside, you know. To find out what the tunnel looks like at that end.'

'I would think it looks a lot like a wine cellar,' was Paul's dry comment. 'And they probably would have noticed by now if Queen Isabelle's jewel box was lying around.'

'Not if she buried it.'

'You are not,' Paul said firmly, 'going to dig up the poor guy's wine cellar.'

Simon ignored him and rocked back in his chair, deep in thought. 'I wonder if there's any place in town that rents out metal detectors.'

Paul looked at me. 'I told you this would happen.'

I laughed. 'I don't mind, honestly. And Simon, if you want to use the invitation—'

'Oh, no, it's yours, I wouldn't steal it from you. But,' he added, with a grin, 'there's nothing here that says you can't bring guests.'

He was quite right. The card wasn't even addressed to a specific person. A small, mischievous thought began to glimmer at the back of my mind. Armand Valcourt had flung a challenge down last night – he expected me to come. I didn't doubt that he was used to having women swoon in all directions when he smiled. He was probably sitting up there now, waiting for me to ring him, and feeling smug about the whole affair. And I knew just the way to wipe that smug look off his face. 'All right. I'll ring the *Clos des Cloches* and arrange a tour for the three of us. For today, if you like.'

'But no metal detectors,' Paul instructed, turning knowing eyes on his brother. 'And no shovels.'

Simon promised nothing. 'This morning would be good,' he said. 'We don't have anything planned for this morning.'

Indulgently, I checked my watch. 'I'll see what I can do.'

Paul had been right about Simon, I thought – once he set his mind to something, he was rather like a great shaggy dog with a bone. When I would have dawdled an extra minute over my coffee cup, he pushed and prodded me up the stairs instead. He would probably have followed me right to my room, to see that I dialled the telephone properly, if he hadn't been distracted by the sudden, shocking oath that greeted us on the first floor landing.

'Careful, Neil,' Paul called out. 'It's Sunday.'

'I don't bloody care,' Neil's voice came back, and then his head came round the open door to his room. 'Do any of you know anything about hi-fis?'

Forty-something? I thought, looking at his longish hair and unlined face. I'd not believe it. He looked half that age this morning. Something had clearly irritated him – his mouth was set in a thin, tight line, his dark eyes narrow with impatience.

'Stereos, you mean?' Simon asked. 'What kind of stereos?'

'The kind that don't bloody work.'

Paul couldn't keep the smile from showing. 'Yeah, I have a little experience with those. Want me to take a look?'

'Please.' Neil relaxed a little in response, pushing the door wider to let the boys in. Catching my eye, he flashed a brilliant smile. 'I don't bite, honestly.'

I hung back, and was relieved when Simon boldly came to the rescue. 'She has to make a phone call.' One couldn't argue with that tone of voice, I thought, and with a tiny shrug that absolved me from blame, I turned my back on Neil and continued up the stairs.

The man at the *Clos des Cloches* picked up the phone on the second ring. It wasn't Armand Valcourt. The older man, perhaps – François. At any rate, his voice was kind. Yes, he assured me, it was possible to take a tour that morning. Would ten-thirty be agreeable? That gave them nearly an hour to prepare. And for one? For *three*. That threw him for a moment, and he asked again, just to be sure.

'Three,' I repeated, and thanked him. Replacing the receiver, I sat back and waited for Simon and Paul to come upstairs.

The minutes stretched.

Finally I crossed to my door and opened it a crack, listening. They were still one floor down, in Neil's room – I could just hear the murmur of voices. I was about to close my door again when I remembered what Paul had called me, yesterday: *Mäusele*. Little Mouse. *I'm not afraid of anything*, I told myself stoutly. Convinced of that, I stepped into the corridor and headed downstairs.

The door to Neil's room was wide open, as he'd left it, and I could see the three of them inside, clustered round what looked like a bedroom dresser.

'Well, that's not it,' Paul was saying, his own voice losing patience. He shifted and I saw that he was frowning at a great gleaming metal hi-fi system sprawled atop the dresser. It was truly a monster – all dials and wires and separate components. Neil rummaged among the wires, pulled out a red connecting line and plugged it in somewhere else.

'What about that?' he checked.

Simon slotted a cassette tape into the machine and pushed a button. Nothing happened. 'Nope. I hate to say it, Neil, but I think you're out of luck.'

I hadn't made a sound, but Neil looked up and over his shoulder, his eyes seeking mine unerringly. 'Hullo,' he said. 'I don't suppose that you . . .'

'Sorry.' I shook my head. 'I'm hopeless with electronics.'

Simon grinned. 'Well, you can't do any worse than the three of us.'

Neil's mouth curved wryly, and he dropped the wires, admitting defeat. 'Come in,' he invited me. 'Don't be shy.'

I came a few steps into the room, keeping the door to my back. It was a larger room than my own, with a soaring ceiling and cool shadows dancing on the papered walls. It was quiet, like him, and it smelled of him – of soap and freshly-ironed cotton and the faintly woodsy scent of aftershave. I concentrated fiercely on the window facing on the fountain square. His window, too, was more beautiful than mine. It was a door, really: arched glass panels that touched the floor, swinging inward on their hinges so that one could walk straight out into the narrow balcony beyond. The rustling branches of the acacia trees seemed near enough to touch.

Neil followed my gaze, understanding. 'Nice, isn't it?'

'And you'll notice,' Simon pointed out, 'that Neil doesn't have any stupid curtains blocking his view.'

Neil smiled at that. 'Yes, well, I'm afraid I had Thierry take them down. It improves the acoustics when I practise.'

'You hear that?' Simon asked his brother. '*Thierry* took them down. Favouritism,' he pronounced. 'That's what it is. Though I don't imagine Thierry'll be too happy when he finds out you busted his stereo.'

'Probably not, but I'm sure he'll find me another. I'd just as soon have a smaller one, anyway,' he confessed. 'This one's rather too powerful for my needs. Can't set the volume higher than three, or it makes your ears bleed.'

'That's your age showing, old man,' Simon teased.

I looked from the jumble of cassette tapes on top of the hi-fi to the sleek violin case propped on a corner chair. 'Do you tape your practice sessions, then?' I asked Neil.

'Lord, no, I spend enough time listening to myself. No, my orchestra in Austria is learning a new piece,' he explained, 'by a young composer – very strange stuff, very difficult. And with a newly written piece I find a tape more helpful than just looking at the score. Actually,' he said, rubbing the back of his neck, 'this is the second system I've ruined. I brought my own portable one with me, but it barely lasted two days.'

'Maybe someone's trying to tell you something,' Paul suggested, tongue in cheek.

'Maybe. But if it keeps up, it'll drive me to drink.'

'Hey!' Simon suddenly remembered his treasure hunt. He turned to face me, hopeful. 'Did you get through to the *Clos des Cloches*?'

'Yes.'

Something chased across Neil's face, some flicker of emotion that was gone before I could identify it. 'The *Clos des Cloches*?' he echoed, lightly. 'Why were you ringing there?'

Simon answered for me. 'They gave Emily an invitation for a tour and wine-tasting. So we're all going.' Cheerfully, he looked in my direction. 'Was this morning OK for them?'

'Yes. Ten-thirty.'

Paul glanced at his watch. 'God, that's only half an hour from now. We'd better get a move on.'

Neil folded his arms across his chest and looked down at me, his eyes faintly searching. 'They gave you an invitation?'

I nodded. 'I met the owner, you see, quite by accident, and—'

Simon cut me off. 'You met the owner? Really? Great! Then you can ask him for me.'

Neil pulled his eyes from mine, eyebrows lifting. 'Ask him what?'

'If I can see his cellar.' I was watching Simon's face when the next thought struck him, and my heart sank, because there wasn't a thing I could do to prevent it. 'Hey,' he said brightly, turning to Neil, 'why don't you come with us? You know the guy, too, don't you?'

Startled, I glanced up at Neil, and he met my eyes with a curious smile. 'Yes, I know him,' he said, sliding his gaze to Simon. 'And thanks. I'd be delighted to join your tour.'

Armand Valcourt didn't look especially delighted when he met us at the gate. He hid it well, but I caught the hard line of his smile as he returned Neil's handshake.

'It's been a long time,' Armand said.

'Yes.'

'Martine told me you were back. I was surprised you did not come earlier, to the house. You are avoiding us, perhaps?'

'Not at all.' A curious tension grew and stretched between the two men, like a tightly strung wire, until the air around us fairly hummed with silent friction. It felt, I thought, almost like hate . . .

Paul must have felt it, too. Ever the peacemaker, he took a step forward and introduced himself, and the moment of unspoken combat passed.

Armand shook Simon's hand next, then mine, his dark eyes knowing. 'So,' he said, in French, 'you decided to use your invitation, after all. And you have brought your friends. How . . . nice.'

I smiled up at him, innocent. 'Did I mention, Monsieur, that my friend Paul can speak the most beautiful French?'

'Can he?' The dark eyes laughed, left mine and looked at Paul. 'Can he, indeed?' He let go of my hand, and took a step backwards. He looked different again by daylight. The working man's outfit of chinos and sweater suited him rather well, I thought.

Simon nudged me. 'Ask him.'

Armand arched an eyebrow, intrigued. 'Yes? You have a question, Mademoiselle?'

Again I smiled. 'More of a request, actually. Simon here was hoping to see your wine cellar.'

'Ah.' He looked from me to Simon, and back again. 'Naturally, the cellars are included in the tour, but at the end, yes? For the tasting. We must follow the process in its proper order, beginning, I think, with the vines.'

He turned to lead us along a narrow, straight-edged

path, cool in the shadow of the high stone wall that bounded the vineyard. Simon, impatient as always, kept close behind Armand, and Paul ambled along behind. Neil fell into step beside me, matching his pace to mine.

We walked in silence to begin with, but then my own awareness of him made the silence uncomfortable, and I tried to think of something neutral to talk about. 'You've been here before, then?' I asked.

'Yes. I knew his wife.'

I bent my head hurriedly. 'Oh, I see.' So much for neutral, I told myself.

'Brigitte, her name was,' he went on, in a mild tone. 'We had mutual friends in Vienna. I knew both the sisters, Brigitte and Martine.'

Curiosity pricked me then, and against my better judgement I asked: 'And were they very much alike?'

I felt the glancing touch of his eyes on my downturned face. 'That's right, you've met Martine, haven't you? Yes, Brigitte was very like her to look at, but as far as personality . . .' He smiled a little, thinking back. 'Brigitte was wild. Unpredictable. She met Armand and married him, all in one weekend. Destiny, she called it. She believed in destiny.' He spoke the word almost as if he believed it, too. He cast a quick glance up the ridge towards the white house, remembering. 'She used to hold these huge dinner parties,' he told me, 'all artists and writers and poor musicians like myself, and she'd fill us full of food and wine and set us talking. Bright minds and brilliant conversation, that's what Brigitte wanted. Like Madame Pompadour.'

Still looking down at the path, I stole a sideways look at the denim-clad legs striding evenly beside mine, and the beautiful, long-fingered hands, and I thought I knew exactly what Brigitte Valcourt had wanted from Neil

Grantham. The sudden stab of feeling rather shocked me. I hadn't felt jealous in years. Aloud I said: 'It must have been fun.'

'It was. Brigitte brought us all together, Christian and myself and . . . oh, there was a gang of us, in those days. I don't know what happened to most of them. When Brigitte died the group just fell apart, stopped meeting.'

I kicked a pebble on the dirt path. 'How did she die?'

'Heart failure.'

'Oh. I'm sorry.'

'It happens. She'd been in and out of hospital since giving birth to Lucie – she used to make a new will nearly every week, I think,' he said, with a brief smile. 'I don't think any of us was particularly surprised.'

Armand was still walking briskly alongside the wall, several paces ahead of us. He turned his head to say something to Simon, and glanced idly back at Neil and me, his expression unreadable.

The corners of Neil's mouth tugged upwards. 'We never did get on, Armand and I. It's not your fault.'

I flashed a quick look up at him. 'I don't see that I have anything to do with it.'

'Don't you?' He slanted a kind smile down at me. I struggled for a response, but before I could collect my thoughts, the others ahead of us stopped walking, and I had to step smartly to avoid running over Paul. The vineyard tour was about to begin.

Chapter Twelve

. . . past a hundred
doors
To one deep chamber shut from sound,

Armand had led us to a spot halfway along the imposing wall, where the rows of stunted vines began their orderly climb to the crest of the hill. The noise of the passing traffic was muted here, a muffled humming on the far side of the wall, and nothing more. There was only the deep green hill, and the great sun-drenched sky with its speckling of cottonwool clouds, and at our backs, the ever-watchful presence of Château Chinon. The modern world seemed but a distant dream.

'Of course,' Armand was saying to Simon, 'you know that it was an American, like yourself, who nearly ruined the wine-making in France?'

'We're Canadians.'

'But that is the same thing, surely?'

Paul stepped in once again to keep the peace, his calm voice riding smoothly over Simon's ruffled feathers. 'What did the American do?'

'He ate our vines,' Armand replied, then to our puzzled faces he explained how the tiny phylloxera beetle, nearly a century and a half ago, had crossed the wide Atlantic aboard the newly-invented steamship, and landed like a conqueror upon the shores of France.

In the 1860s, Armand told us, that one microscopic pest, undetected, had ravaged vineyard after vineyard, bringing the noblest of estates near to ruin. The French wine industry had very nearly collapsed, until it was discovered that by grafting French vine stalks onto American roots – immune by nature to phylloxera – the devastator could be held at bay.

'It is a truce only,' Armand admitted, fingering a broad leaf. 'We must still graft, and spray, and be on guard. The danger, it has not entirely disappeared.'

Paul peered closely at the base of one of the gnarled vines. 'These have American roots, then?' he asked. 'All of them?'

Armand nodded. 'Yes. In my father's time, such grafting was done by hand, but now we have a machine to do the work.'

'Wouldn't it be simpler,' I put in, 'just to grow American vines?'

Armand grinned at that. 'The native vines of North America, Mademoiselle, produce the wine like vinegar. Even the roots, they change somewhat the character of our grafted vines, but,' he added, philosophically, 'we must make sacrifices sometimes, to preserve a way of life. And what lies beneath the surface, no-one sees.'

Still conscious of Neil standing close behind me, I took the opportunity to move away a few steps, venturing into the row of vines. 'What kind of grapes are these?'

'They are the Cabernet Franc,' Armand said. 'That is the grape of Chinon's wines, the red wines.'

'But there aren't any grapes,' Simon complained, as though he'd been somehow cheated.

'No, we have already harvested, last week. I had a . . . how do you say it . . . a hunch that there would be rain, and at this time the rain can be most harmful to the grapes. The water rises through the roots, you understand, and swells the grapes, and so the wine it has no colour, no substance – it is spoiled.'

Simon, who had only come to see the cellar anyway, lost interest quickly after that. When Armand led us in between the vines, Simon wandered after us, hands in his pockets, his mind on other things.

The vines stood chest-high on the men and reached very nearly to my shoulders, their spreading branches trained around strong wires strung between short posts. Trained, I thought, was the operative word, for despite the twisting tangle there was pristine order here. The rows climbed the sloping hill like soldiers, each vine pruned with such precision that when I looked out across the field of fluttering green I might have been looking out across a level, square-clipped hedge.

Neil walked behind me, silently, and seemed content to listen while Armand explained the workings of the vineyard. Paul was the only one of us who truly paid attention. His intelligent questions pleased Armand, who took his time in answering them, his technical language punctuated by beautifully expressive gestures.

I had thought Armand Valcourt in his element when I'd seen him in his home last night, but here in the fragrant hush of the vineyard another aspect of his being came quietly to the surface, surprising me with its intensity. He spoke proudly of the superior qualities of the *Clos des Cloches* – the south-facing slopes that captured each ray of the summer sun, the limestone soil that kept those slopes well-drained, the age of the vines themselves . . . 'The *appellation contrôlée* requires that a vine be four years old before wine can be made from it, but we wait until our vines have eight years.'

'What is the *appellation contrôlée*?' Paul wanted to know, and Neil's voice drifted lazily over my head.

'A kind of committee that sets the standards for the making of French wine.'

Armand accepted the definition, adding only that the rules were very strict. 'We must not harvest before a certain date, nor after a certain date. We must grow a certain variety of grape, and then we may call our wines Chinon. If not, if we choose to break these rules, the penalties are hard. There are heavy fines, and they will come and uproot our vines.' He shrugged. 'It is truly the end of the world, I think.'

That was the farmer talking, not the aristocrat, just as it was the farmer who knelt now among the vines to demonstrate to Paul how each gnarled branch was pruned by hand to catch the sunlight.

'I am sorry,' he was saying, to Paul, 'that I cannot spare the time today to show you how our wine is made, but I can at least show you the result. It is the most important thing, I think. The process of wine-making, the machines we use, these are things you can learn from a book, but the wine . . .' He gave a pointed shrug. 'The wine, it is like life itself. It must be tasted at the source.'

Simon perked up behind us. 'So we're going to see the cellar now?'

'Yes. I have set out a few good vintages for you to taste.'

'Terrific.' The bounce was back in Simon's step. Moving past us, he assumed the lead, his eyes fixed with a hunter's single-mindedness upon the huge white house.

I wished I could share his enthusiasm. Wine cellars might be interesting places, and impressive, but underground was underground no matter how one viewed it, and the French didn't call their cellars '*caves*' for nothing. The only thing that cheered me was that Harry wasn't here to announce to everyone that I was phobic. 'She has a thing,' he would have told them, 'about going underground.' He always said it just like that, as if it were some random illness, inexplicable, and though I sometimes did remind him of the day he'd locked me in the neighbour's bomb shelter, Harry never would admit he was to blame. 'I shot an arrow at you, too,' he'd once retorted, 'and you didn't develop a phobia about *that*.'

He had a point, I thought. Given the choice between facing a field of archers or spending an hour in someone's basement, I'd pick the archers every time. But now, without a single bowman in sight, I found myself with no real option but to take a deep breath and follow along with the tour.

The cellars of the *Clos des Cloches* lay deep within the cliffs beneath the house. They were enormous, high-arched and spacious like the soaring nave of some fantastic cathedral. The ghostly limestone caught the light and cast it back upon us, and when I let my breath go I inhaled the sweeter scent of oak and wine above the dank aroma of the stone. Along one curving wall the bottles ran in ranks, neatly stacked, awaiting labels, their glass dark green beneath the thickly sifted dust. But the barrels dwarfed them easily.

They were everywhere, those barrels – great monstrous ones that might have served Gargantua himself, and row on row of smaller ones that seemed to stretch for ever, an aisle of darkened oak illumined softly on all sides by countless burning candles whiter than the walls. The candles, set with care upon the rim of every barrel, seemed to be the main source of light in this medieval hall of wonder. Beyond their reach the shadows crept, to claim the farther corners and the dimly rising stacks of bottled wine.

In the middle of it all stood François, tall and grey and elegant, arranging polished glasses on a small table that already groaned beneath the weight of several vintages. He looked round as we came in, his inscrutable face relaxing as he noticed me beside Armand. Only a statue could have failed to be flattered by his smile. 'Mademoiselle,' he greeted me, in French, 'it is indeed a pleasure to see you again.'

To my surprise he welcomed Neil with similar warmth, framing his words in halting English. There was no hint of the bitterness, the tension, that had marked Neil's conversation with Armand. In fact, I thought, they spoke like friends.

Paul, at my shoulder, waited patiently to be introduced, gazing at the arching dome of the *cave's* ceiling with eyes half-closed in rapt appreciation. I'd only known him two days, but I fancied that I recognized that look already.

'Go on, then,' I teased him, with a nudge. 'Shatter me. What's the word for this place?'

He smiled. 'That obvious, eh?'

Armand looked sideways at the two of us. 'The word . . . ?'

'Oh,' said Simon, 'it's just this kind of game Paul plays, trying to find the perfect word to describe a place. He's pretty good, most of the time, except he hasn't got the word for Château Chinon, yet.'

'Yes he does,' I said. 'It's "tragic".'

Armand studied Paul's face closely, as though he hadn't seen him properly, before. 'That is indeed the perfect word. Tragic . . .' He tasted the feel of it, on his tongue. 'And my *caves*?' he asked. 'How would you call them?'

Paul looked a shade embarrassed, but he met the challenge squarely. 'Clandestine,' he said, in his quiet voice.

'So,' Armand said, softly. 'So . . . a place for intrigue, yes? Or secret lovers.' His eyes slid past me, smiling, and came to rest on François. 'Well, who can say you are not right? There is much history here, and in my family there are many secrets.' François glanced up, and Armand looked away again. 'The making of wine,' he said to Paul, 'it is an art wrapped well in secrets. As in your game of words, one tries to find the essence of each vintage, removing that which complicates. Come, I will show you.'

It was more work than I'd imagined, tasting wine. With François guiding me, I sampled the estate's great vintages, trying to follow each instruction – how to hold the glass, how to inhale the wine's 'nose' – there were so many things a true wine-lover ought to notice.

And I did try, really I did. I swirled and sniffed and scrutinized, and in truth I very nearly saw the purple edge that Armand said was such a telling characteristic of his clear red wine. But when he spoke of complex structure and of 'legs', and breathed the scents of strawberries and vanillan oak, I had to admit my own deficiencies. It was a lovely wine, I thought, a great one even, but to my untutored palate it tasted . . . well, like *wine*. And the more I drank the more like wine it tasted.

Neil knew. His eyes touched mine and held, smiling, and the faintest shiver crawled between my shoulders.

'Cold?' Paul checked, missing nothing. He was well into the fourth vintage. Paul, I felt sure, could see with ease the violet edge, and catch the scent of strawberries. I shook my head, and shrugged to clear the shiver.

'No, not really.'

Simon looked at Armand, his expression casual. 'How old,' he asked him, 'would your cellars be?'

Armand shrugged. 'Older than the house. Our *cave*, our cellar, it was once used by the kings who stayed at the château.'

Paul eyed his brother warningly over the rim of his wine glass, but Simon had already seized the opening. 'Really? So this was connected to the château, somehow?'

I might have imagined the flickering glance François sent his employer, and the careful pause before Armand replied. 'Yes. The kings built many *souterrains*, or tunnels, as you call them. Ours is among the oldest, I believe.'

'It still exists?' Simon feigned surprise. 'You mean you have a tunnel that goes straight to the château?'

Before Armand could answer that, Neil set his own glass on the table. 'I haven't seen the *souterrain* in years,' he said. 'Perhaps, Simon, if you ask him very nicely, Monsieur Valcourt will show it to us.' There was a sort of challenge in his voice, and in the way his level eyes met those of our host.

'It is kept locked,' Armand said, finally.

Neil smiled his quiet smile, and the challenge became a dare. 'Surely, just this once.'

There was a moment's silence, then Armand's mouth hardened and he picked the gauntlet up. 'Why not?' He turned to François. 'Do you have the keys?'

I would have preferred not to go with them. The *cave*, at least, was brightly lit and full of air, and I could half convince myself I wasn't underground. But once again,

I didn't have much choice. The others swept me with them, through the *cave* and past a small group of incurious workmen, to a darker, narrow passageway behind.

Above our heads the pallid rock, its surface scarred and pitted by the chisels of ancient craftsmen, closed round us like a tomb. The smell of damp was stronger here, and Neil was forced to duck his head. There were at least a dozen doorways bolted shut on either side of the passage.

Simon stopped, excited, at the first one. 'Is this the entrance to a tunnel?'

'No.' Armand laughed, and shook his head. 'It is a . . . how do you call it? A broom cupboard. This,' he told us, walking a few steps on and fitting his key into a lock, '*this* is the door you want.'

The tunnel was just that – a tunnel, hung with cobwebs, strewn with dirt, and smelling of decay. I took one look and stepped back hastily, bumping into Neil. He kindly took no notice.

'But it's stone,' said Simon. He sounded disappointed, and I realized he'd expected to see walls of earth or clay. One didn't, as a rule, dig holes in solid rock to bury treasure. 'Is it stone all the way through?'

Armand assured him that it was.

'Can I go in?'

'I am afraid,' Armand replied, 'that I cannot allow it. This *souterrain* is old, and there is now a road overhead that weakens it. To use it now would not be wise.' He swung the door shut and the key in the lock clicked firmly. 'It is not safe.'

Nothing underground was safe, I thought. It was a relief to surface once more into sunlight, and to feel the whisper of the wind upon my face. I stood a moment enjoying the sensation, while the boys walked on ahead with Neil. Armand hung back as well, his face expectant. 'So, how do you like my vineyard?'

I told him it was fascinating, and he looked pleased. 'It is my pride, you understand. This estate has come to me from many generations of Valcourts, and one day it will belong to Lucie.' He looked out, as I had done earlier, across the flat-topped vines. 'The greatest part of me lies in this place,' he told me. 'I'm glad it fascinates you.'

Simon turned ahead of us. He appeared to have recovered quickly from his setback in the cellar, and having ruled out Armand's tunnel as a hiding place for Isabelle's lost treasure, he was eager to get on to other things. He beckoned me impatiently. 'Emily, come on. We're going to the Echo next.'

Armand's eyes narrowed, sliding sideways. 'He has much energy, that young man.'

'Yes.' I couldn't help the smile. Armand walked with me to the gates, and after a confusing criss-cross of handshakes and thank-yous, he turned to take my hand.

'You must come back another time.' *Alone*, his dancing eyes said, and his smile was a sinful thing. 'And you must tell me how you enjoy seeing our Echo. It is quite unique.'

I wasn't entirely sure how one could see an Echo in the first place, but everyone promised me that it was indeed possible, and that there was a lovely view from the Echo, and that I would be suitably impressed.

And so I kept an open mind as I followed my companions through the gates. Neil left us there. 'Sorry, but I promised to meet someone,' was his excuse, and looking like a man well pleased with the day's work, he strolled away, head bent and humming to himself.

Simon, happy to be back in charge, turned sharply in the opposite direction and, keeping his shoulder to the high wall of the *Clos des Cloches*, led Paul and me around a curve of deserted road to a desolate place where the wind wept softly through the long grass. 'Here it is,' he announced, proudly.

There was no mistaking it – a sign posted to one side of a raised viewing platform clearly read: *Ici l'Echo*, and the platform itself, though small, looked rather official.

'It really does work,' said Paul. 'Just stand up there and yell something.'

I climbed the few steps obediently and turned around. The view, as I'd been promised, was a postcard panorama stretching from the château on the one side, out across the silver river and the patchwork roofs and gardens, to the distant hills beyond. Closer than that, across the road, treetops and a tiled roof peeked above an unkempt, rambling hedge. 'But I'll be yelling into someone's yard,' I protested, and Simon hopped up beside me with a laugh.

'It's OK, really. People do it all the time. Here, I'll show you.' And he bellowed out an enthusiastic yodel that would have done credit to a native of the Swiss Alps. The sound soared out and came back, crashing loud against the green hills and the ruined walls of the château, like waves striking rocks on a wild shore.

'Neat, eh?' Simon grinned. 'You can even ask it questions, like this . . .' Again he filled his lungs, and yelled: 'Will I ever get Paul to leave Chinon?'

The answer flowed back, faintly questioning in itself: '*Non . . .*'

'Very funny,' said Paul. 'Why don't you let Emily give it a try?'

I smiled. 'I wouldn't know what to say.'

But they weren't about to let me off that easily. Put on the spot, I closed my eyes tightly and tried to think of something clever. Perhaps I ought to call out Armand's name, I thought wryly, in case he was standing on the other side of the vineyard wall, listening. It might be good for his ego. But the dark eyes that smiled at me in my thoughts were not Armand Valcourt's. I tried to push the image from my mind. Oh, damn and blast, I thought. Oh, *help*. So that was what I yelled, in French. '*Au secours!*'

It was a foolish thing to do. If I'd been in a public place, I might have caused a panic – people hurrying to help me; cries for the police.

But here, I only startled Paul, who turned to stare at me while Echo stirred in far-off fields and called back her advice.

'*Cours*,' was what she told me.

Run.

Chapter Thirteen

From out a common vein of memory . . .

'The day gets better and better,' Simon said, as we filed out between the houses at the foot of the cobbled stair. I saw straight away what had pleased him.

It was already afternoon, and the sun had grown uncertain, but Thierry, in a burst of optimism, had set the hotel's tables out around the fountain square. It made a cheery showing, the bright white tables and red chairs. And directly ahead of us, at a table beside the fountain, sat Martine Muret. She was so lovely, so strikingly lovely, with her fashion-model features and cropped black hair. Neil had said that Armand's wife had looked like that, and pushing back another pang of jealousy I looked more closely at Martine, with eyes that sought to see beyond her to a woman three years dead. Had Brigitte Valcourt's hair been short as well? The cut certainly suited Martine, and her simple dark clothes set off her beauty as a plain frame enhances an exquisite painting. Head up, she sat watching the idle activity of the square through expensive sunglasses that hid the expression of her eyes. She looked entirely unapproachable.

Undaunted, Simon raised one hand in cheerful

greeting and blazed a path across the square towards her.

Paul looked at me. 'He never gives up.'

'Well, one can't really blame him.' I stopped, and bent to tie my shoe, tipping my face up towards him. 'Paul, what does Martine Muret do?'

'What do you mean?'

'For a living. Does she work, or . . .'

'Oh. She owns the local gallery.'

'Art gallery?'

He nodded. 'Yeah. It's just around the corner there, in one of the smaller squares.' He pointed off to one side of the hotel. 'You can't miss it. There's a Christian Rand self-portrait in the window.'

'They're a couple, then, I take it?' I tried to ask the question quite as if I didn't care, as if it hardly mattered which of the hotel guests Martine had been out with, when Lucie had wandered off.

Paul shrugged. 'I wouldn't say so, no. In fact I'm sure they're not. Good friends, I think – that's all.'

'Oh.' I yanked on my shoelace, tying it too tightly. *Which one was it?* I'd heard Armand ask Martine, last night. *The German or the Englishman?* And I'd been hoping, for some foolish reason, that it was the German. I sighed and stood, and looked again at that lovely face. The face that reminded Neil of Brigitte Valcourt. 'I wonder if she chose that chair on purpose?' I asked.

'Why?'

'Well, she's sitting next to Beauty.'

'What? Oh, the Graces, you mean.' He scrutinized the fountain sculpture. 'How can you tell which one's which?'

'Neil named them, last night. He thought Splendour

faced the sunset, and that one there was Beauty, and Joy had the biggest smile.'

'That makes sense.'

I folded my arms and frowned. 'Only they're not smiling, are they?'

'Of course they are. That's what—'

'—Graces do. I know.' Still, try as I might, the only smile I saw belonged to Martine Muret herself. And even that smile looked faintly strained.

'So,' she said, as we descended on her table. 'Simon tells me you have toured the *Clos des Cloches*. And how did you enjoy it?'

Simon grinned. 'It was great, thanks. Mind if we join you?' His arm was promptly nudged from behind, and he turned round, frowning. 'What?' he demanded of Paul.

'I think she has company already, that's all.'

There was no-one with her at that moment, but it was obvious from the glasses on the table that she hadn't been drinking alone. Her glass held red wine, but whoever had been with her had been drinking *Pernod*. Martine hesitated for a moment, only a moment, then shook her head. 'No, it is all right. Please,' she moved her hand, inviting us to sit down.

I took the chair facing the fountain, where I could watch the spring-fed water tumble gently past the bowing Graces like a jewelled, transparent veil. Across the table from me Martine Muret smiled pleasantly, expectantly.

'So, what did Armand show you?'

Simon summarized our tour. He didn't mention anything about the tunnel, though, which surprised me, until I remembered that Paul had termed his brother 'paranoid'. Perhaps, I reasoned, Simon was afraid to talk about the treasure in case someone else started looking for it. When he came to the end of his animated account, he leaned back in his chair and raked the hair back from his forehead. 'But I could really use a coffee,' he concluded. 'He gave us these huge glasses to taste with. I always thought wine-tasting meant an inch of wine in the bottom of the glass. Who knew?'

Martine's laugh was a tinkling echo of the fountain spilling down behind her. 'So Armand has made you drunk, today?'

'Well, he certainly tried to,' said Paul. 'But I've still got room for a beer. Emily?'

I shook my head. 'You don't have to buy me a drink, it's quite all right.' But Paul insisted, and he would have kept right on insisting if I hadn't finally given in and opted for my favourite drink of white wine and black-currant cordial. 'I'll have a *kir*, then, please.'

My own wine-tasting flush seemed to have worn off, but Thierry, when he came over to take our order, wasn't altogether convinced. He sent me a piercing, faintly paternal look. 'You have eaten lunch, Mademoiselle?' he asked me.

'Well, not exactly . . .'

He shook his head, disapproving. 'No food at all?'

'Well, no, but—'

'It is not good,' he chastised me, 'to drink the wine without food first.' But he brought me my *kir* in the end, along with a small dish of peanuts that he'd smuggled from behind the bar. 'These are for you,' he said, setting the dish down in front of me. 'Do not let Simon steal them.'

Simon sent him a wounded look. 'You never bring me peanuts,' he complained.

'This is true,' agreed Thierry, without apology. 'Is there anything else your table is missing? No? Then I leave you to enjoy. I have promised to Monsieur Grantham that I will find for him my little stereo so he can listen to his tapes.'

Martine frowned. 'Did he not have a stereo already?'

'My big one, yes,' said Thierry with a wistful nod. 'But this morning, it has broken, and so . . .' His shrug was resigned. 'He is lucky it is only the machine that breaks, and not his violin. I warned him of this yesterday.'

When I asked him what he meant by that, he shrugged again and grinned. 'Only that he plays every day his . . . how do you say it in English . . . *les gammes*?'

'Scales,' said Paul and I, in unison.

'Yes, his scales, and then the symphony by Beethoven. But yesterday,' he shook his head, 'yesterday, he also plays the song of love, and Isabelle, she does not like to hear such songs.'

I heard the sharp clattering of a glass against the tabletop. Across from me, Martine Muret quickly righted her wine glass and reached for a paper napkin to mop up the small spill. 'How stupid of me! No, it is all right, it is nothing . . .'

His offer of help refused, Simon took advantage of the moment of confusion to sneak a handful of peanuts from the dish in front of me. 'Queen Isabelle, you mean?' he asked Thierry, showing off his knowledge, but the bartender shook his head emphatically.

'She is no queen, this Isabelle. She is our *fantôme*.' He cast his eyes upwards, searching for the English word. 'Our ghost.'

'No kidding?'

'I do not kid,' he said to Simon, stiffly. 'She lived here, in the last war.'

Definitely not Isabelle of Angoulême, I thought. Not King John's young and tragic queen, but someone else, some later Isabelle, who couldn't bear to hear Neil play a love song. I felt a sharper twinge of curiosity. 'Have you ever seen her, this ghost?'

'Of course he hasn't,' said Simon, mumbling through his mouthful of peanuts. 'There are no ghosts.'

'Ah,' said Thierry, 'are there not?' He slanted a superior eye down on this upstart sceptic from the New World. 'Then it will not upset you to know that you sleep each night in the room where Isabelle died.'

'Isabelle.' Madame Chamond curled herself gracefully onto the seat opposite me and tilted her head to one side, smiling faintly. She was a lovely woman, tall and dark and elegant, with all her husband's grace and charm and then some. 'But this is such a sad story to tell, Simon, and I do not wish to spoil the evening for everyone.'

Which was a rather hollow argument, I thought, considering what a sorry-looking bunch we were, the lot of us. The boys and I had just come back from dinner at the *Cœur de Lion*, and the food had made me drowsy. Paul, too, was leaning back with half-closed eyes, while beside him Neil lounged in his corner seat, unmoving. Even Christian Rand, who'd dropped in for a nightcap at the bar, looked rather like he might fall off his stool from sheer exhaustion. Simon appeared normal enough, but then nothing seemed to tire Simon. And Garland Whitaker, recovered from her headache, was back in full voice, snuggled like a kitten on the chair beside her husband.

She smiled a faintly pouting smile of encouragement at Madame Chamond. 'You won't spoil our evening one bit. Anyway, you've got us all curious now, about this Isabelle person.'

'Think of how I feel,' Simon chimed in. 'She died in our room, for Pete's sake.'

Behind me, at the bar, I heard Monsieur Chamond's low and pleasant laugh. 'Isabelle did not die in your room,' he said. 'Who told you this?'

'Thierry.'

'Ah.' Our host nodded. 'Well, he does not know the story very well. Even I do not remember all of it. It was so long ago, before I myself was born, you understand . . .'

'She was a Chinon girl,' Madame Chamond began, relenting. 'She worked here as a chamber maid, during the war, the occupation.'

Garland raised her eyebrows. 'Occupation? I thought France collaborated.'

'Not all of France. Not Chinon,' Madame Chamond answered firmly. 'We were occupied. This hotel was used to garrison . . . that is the right word? . . . garrison the German officers. And that is how Isabelle met her Hans.'

'A romance!' Garland's eyes gleamed victoriously. 'Oh, how wonderful! I always *love* a wartime romance, don't you? That's how Jim's parents met, when his father was stationed in . . . where was it, darling?'

Jim Whitaker balanced his second double Scotch with care on his outstretched knee. 'Normandy.'

Madame Chamond smiled rather gently. 'This was happy for your parents, that they could find each other. But war is not so kind to many people. Not to Hans and Isabelle.'

Cradling her wine glass, she settled back against the cushions, warming to the tale. 'They met in 1944, in the spring. They say that Isabelle was very beautiful, a beauty one does not forget, though she had only sixteen years. The German officers noticed this, of course, but Isabelle guarded well her reputation. She had no love of Nazis. Her older brother had joined already the *Maquis*, the Resistance. In time Isabelle might herself have joined them. But instead, she met Hans.

'He came from a good family, Hans. He spoke French and English also, not just German. He was educated. The other officers would bother Isabelle when she was working, say things to her, but not Hans. Always to Isabelle he was a gentleman, a quiet, handsome gentleman. She did not wish to think of him, but . . .' Her shrug was philosophical. 'Life does not always let us choose. And so they fell in love, the French girl and the German officer. For both of them the risks were very great. Always they would meet in secret, for an hour of stolen happiness that could not last.'

Madame Chamond paused to sip her drink, quite calmly, though she must have known she had drawn every one of us into the web of her story. Like an audience waiting for the curtain to rise on the second act, we sat in silence until the wine glass was lowered and once more that lovely, lulling voice took up the narrative. I leaned back, listening, my eyes fixed on the dancing flame of the candle on the low table in front of me, and as Madame Chamond went on speaking, my own mind conjured up the images like something seen through darkened glass. I saw young Isabelle, alone and waiting, listening for the familiar footsteps of her lover. And I saw the German officer slip through the sleeping town, heart pounding . . . saw him reach

the cliffs and find again the hidden door behind the fall
of rock . . .

He turned the corner of the tunnel, blindly. Six steps
on, and then another right . . . He counted off the paces
in his mind. It wasn't safe to use the torch, not yet –
the faintest glimmering of light, the smallest shadow,
would bring the sentries running. The tunnels had made
them all nervous at first. They'd made him nervous,
too, the thought of them, the thought that underneath
his feet the earth was riddled with the things, with
hollow caves and passages that twisted off, unseen, into
the darkness. But now he knew the tunnels well, and
welcomed them, and on this night he was more worried
about meeting one of his own men than he was afraid
of the *Maquis*.

Two paces more, then left . . . he switched the torch
on, blinking in the sudden brightness of the ghostly
limestone walls that curved round him like the walls of
a tomb.

'Hans?' Her voice, uncertain. 'Oh, God, I was so
worried . . .'

How could he have known life before, without her
in his arms? He pulled back, smiling . . . touched
her face. 'You must be brave for me.'

'I don't want to be brave.' Her eyes seemed very large,
there in the darkness.

'Please. For me.' They would both have need of
bravery, he knew, before the month was over. It had
been weeks now since the enemy had come ashore upon
the Norman beaches to the north. Weeks, and still the
Reich was fool enough to stand its ground. They knew,
they all knew, it was over. Just last night, Jurgen –
strong, solid Jurgen who had been there longer than

anyone – had turned world-weary eyes on Hans above his glass of whisky. 'We're finished, you know,' Jurgen had told him. 'Finished. Only the Führer won't admit it. He thinks we'll win it back for him, the fool.' It was treason to talk like that, but Hans hadn't said anything. Jurgen had looked at him again, and smiled wryly. 'Ah well, I've lived enough, I think, and there is no-one left at home to miss me when I'm gone. Tell me, do you still see that girl?'

'What girl?'

'I do have eyes, you know. Do you still see her?'

'Yes.'

Above the whisky glass the weary eyes had grown curious, and almost kind. 'Do you love her?'

'Yes.'

A moment longer Jurgen had watched him, and then he'd thrown something on the table, a small black bag of velvet cloth, tied with a cord. It rattled when it landed, like a sack of shifting pebbles. 'Then give her these. I have no use for them.'

'What are they?' he had asked.

He'd been stunned, then, and even tonight his hand shook slightly as he felt inside his jacket for that same small velvet bag. 'I have brought something for you,' he said to Isabelle. He held out the bag and she looked at him.

'I don't need anything.'

'This is not anything. It's diamonds.'

She echoed the word back at him, her dark eyes flashing disbelief. 'But where would you get diamonds?'

'From a friend. He was given orders to bury them below the hotel, for safety. So they will be there when our Army comes back.' Again he touched her face, he couldn't help himself. 'Only, we won't be coming back . . .'

'Don't.'

'I said you must be brave. I do not plan to die, my love.' His smile was a promise. 'I will come back when this is over. I will come back for you.'

He felt the longing in her kiss, and the dampness of her tears against his own skin, but when he opened his eyes she was smiling. He murmured something soft, in German, that she couldn't understand, and closed his fingers over hers, around the velvet bag. 'You keep these safe, for us,' he told her. 'They are our future.'

Our future, he thought sadly, and he reached for her again . . .

The night was nearly over when he wound his way back through the tunnels. Six steps on, then left . . . this must be how the blind felt, he thought, with the darkness thick against his face and the sound of his own breathing harsh in that still space. It was a despairing sort of feeling. Fourteen steps . . . he put out his hand, trailing it along the dry and dusty stone, feeling for the iron ring of the door. His hand touched cloth instead.

Warm cloth, that breathed.

He felt the fingers groping at his throat, cutting off his choking gasp of surprise, but five years of army life had made his own reactions swift and automatic. This was no fellow soldier, standing sentry – the shirt he felt was soft, not stiff. Not a uniform. And the words of hate were hissed in French, not German. Deprived of breath, Hans moved from instinct. Up came his own hands, feeling, finding, then one sharp twisting motion and a sickening crack. The fingers at his throat relaxed, fell away, and he breathed a painful breath.

This time he found the iron ring and wrenched the thick door open, letting in a singing rush of air. Beyond the door the road and roofs were silent. Nothing stirred. The sky was something less than black, a creeping greyness edging out the stars, but still he had to risk the torch to see the body at his feet. The yellow light touched a torn shirt, and brown long-fingered hands, and travelled upwards to the staring face.

Her face. Oh, God. Her brother's face. She'd shown him once, a photograph. 'You wouldn't get along,' she'd said.

'Isabelle . . .' His hand jerked and the torch fell from it, shattering upon the ancient stone.

Chapter Fourteen

Before me shower'd the rose in flakes;
behind
I heard the puff'd pursuer;

．

Beside me, Jim Whitaker bent his head to light a cigar, and the scrape of the match sounded loud in the quiet room.

Garland shifted in her seat, her eyes gleaming like the eyes of a satisfied cat. 'Oooh, it's just like something out of a movie. He really killed her brother? How exciting.'

It was not, I thought, the word I would have chosen. Not exciting. It was, as Madame Chamond had warned us, a story of great sadness. Of all the fighters of the French Resistance, why did it have to be Isabelle's own brother who met Hans in that dark tunnel? Fate had a heartless sense of humour, sometimes. One death, I thought, and three lives ruined. So it had been with John and Isabelle, more than seven hundred years earlier, when young Arthur of Brittany's murder had brought John's great empire crashing to the ground. How many times had they relived those moments, John and Hans, and wished the deed undone? Two men in separate centuries, both loving Isabelles, bound by a single destiny that sent its unrelenting echo down the years.

A tiny chill swept fleeting through the room, and Simon fidgeted, unable to stand the suspense. 'So what happened?' he asked Madame Chamond. 'What happened to Hans and Isabelle?'

'Ah, well, it was most difficult. A few days later came the liberation and everything was changed. Hans I think was killed, or captured, in the fighting, and Isabelle . . .'

Simon reacted sharply. 'She killed herself? In our room?'

'No, not in your room,' said Monsieur Chamond, unable to mask his quick smile. 'No, Isabelle drowned herself, did she not, in the river?' He looked to his wife for confirmation. 'At least, that is what I have heard. No-one has ever died in this hotel, not like that.'

Neil turned in his chair. 'And what became of the diamonds?'

'No-one knows,' said Christian quietly. It startled me a little, to hear the cadence of the German voice, so soon after surfacing from my imaginings. It was as if Hans himself had spoken to us.

'Diamonds . . .' Garland Whitaker breathed the word like a prayer. 'Wherever did the Germans get diamonds from?'

'From . . . displaced persons.' Christian's eyes touched Simon and Paul for the briefest of moments before he lowered his gaze and went on. 'The Nazis hid many such things during the war. But you know this, you were talking of it at the restaurant on Friday, of the place you lived in Germany.'

Garland nodded. 'And no-one's ever tried to find these diamonds? Well for heaven's sake, where was this tunnel that Hans and Isabelle used to meet in?'

'I do not know,' Madame Chamond replied, her smile indulgent. 'Chinon is not so large, Madame, but the tunnels, they are everywhere. And it is just a story, after all. It happened many years ago. The diamonds might just be invention, added later to the story. Who can say?'

Jim Whitaker gave his Scotch a swirl. 'So Isabelle left her ghost behind, did she?'

Monsieur Chamond looked over at him from behind the bar. 'If she did, she is a quiet ghost. She does not bother us.'

'She's murder on my electronic equipment,' Neil said drily, and Monsieur Chamond laughed.

'Apart from that.'

Simon sent our host a suspicious look. 'And you're sure she didn't die in our room?'

'Quite sure.'

Paul smiled finally, in his quiet way. 'I thought you said,' he reminded Simon, 'that there were no such things as ghosts.'

'Well, yeah, but—'

'Then it really doesn't matter where she died, does it?'

Neil Grantham's dark eyes moved thoughtfully from Paul to me. 'I think our Miss Braden believes in ghosts, though. Don't you?'

It was quite unsettling, the feel of those eyes on my face, and I answered without looking up. 'On occasion,' I admitted, 'yes, I do. I'd think Isabelle would have every right to haunt this place, after what happened. I mean, war is so futile, isn't it? So inexcusable, the things it does to people's lives.'

Garland widened her eyes. 'Oh, but it's necessary sometimes, Emily. The Germans – excuse me, Christian – but the Germans just had to be put in their place, don't you agree?'

Simon spoke up in my defence. 'But I think I know what Emily is saying. My grandfather never talks about the war. It hurts too much for him to think about it. And that was over fifty years ago.' He looked across at Jim Whitaker, with a vaguely curious expression. 'You said your father fought in Normandy. Does he ever talk about it?'

'No.'

'My father talks,' said Christian, unexpectedly. 'He was a child in the war. He talks in his sleep. He has dreams.'

We were all silent a moment, reflecting on the wreckage of a war that none of us had lived through. For me, the war meant only grandad's faded ration book and the neighbour's horrid bomb shelter and musty gas masks gathering dust in the cupboard under the stairs. It all seemed so distant from me, really – an hour or so of film in black and white, and stories told by old men at the local, when the winds of November came cold off the Channel.

So distant, and yet . . . for a moment, there in the bar of the Hotel de France, the echoes of the past came calling, calling, and trailed a haunting trace of laughter through the air.

It was Christian who spoke up first, shifting his position at the bar, his soft eyes thoughtful. 'But this war,' he said, 'it is over now, and now we all sit here and talk, French and German and American . . .'

'And Canadian,' said Simon.

'. . . and Canadian. It is strange, is it not?'

Paul smiled at him. 'It's reassuring. Nice to know we can all move forward, once the scars heal over.'

Half swallowed by the shadow in the corner, Neil calmly pointed out that all old scars felt twinges now and then. 'You can't erase the memory altogether, unfortunately.'

After another full minute of thoughtful silence Simon leaned forward, reaching for his beer glass. 'It's kind of sad, really, when you think about it,' he said, 'but I guess for some people the war is never really over, is it?'

It was Jim Whitaker who answered him, but he wasn't looking at Simon. He wasn't looking at any of us. Eyes fixed unseeing on the darkened windows, his voice came absently, almost as if it didn't quite belong to him. 'No,' he said, slowly. 'I don't believe it is.'

I didn't sleep well, tossed by dreams. I heard the tramp of soldiers' feet across the fountain square, the sound of German voices in the rooms below, the lighter running rhythm of a woman's feet along the corridor. I sighed and shifted restlessly upon the bed, the covers tangling round my legs. Isabelle may not have died in the Hotel de France, but she had left her shadow here. I felt it passing over me, as though she stood beside my bed, and then the curtains at my open window fluttered while the fountain's song grew louder, lulling me to dark oblivion.

I woke early, feeling vaguely melancholic and decidedly unsociable. And so I rose and dressed, and went alone to walk beside the river.

Monday mornings in France had a peaceful silence all their own. Most shops stayed closed out of tradition, and people clung a little longer to their pillows. In all my hour's walk, I only met two people in the shuttered winding streets. From the river's edge, I turned along the road and sauntered up around the château walls to where the white house of the *Clos des Cloches* slumbered in its field of green; then round and up again, past the château's entrance tower with its silent bell, to the narrow breach in the cliff wall, where the steps from the fountain square wound their breathless way upwards.

Here I rested, tucking my hands into the pockets of my jeans and lifting my face to the warmth of the morning sun. Below me, in the patchwork jumble of turrets and church steeples, tightly walled gardens and blind shuttered windows, I heard a swallow singing. *O Swallow, Swallow, if I could follow* . . . What was the rest of that poem? I couldn't remember. Tennyson, again, at any rate – I'd read it at school. Something about a prince wanting the swallow to carry a message to his true love, to tell her he was coming.

A bird, perhaps the same one, broke, rustling, from a fruit tree in the garden just beneath me, and went winging out across the town, its dancing flight and joyful song dissolving my clinging mist of melancholy. 'So my prince is coming, is he?' I asked the swallow, just a speck now in the brilliant sky. Well, I wouldn't hold my breath.

But when, a moment later, I heard footsteps coming up the steps below me, that's exactly what I did – I held my breath for no good reason and leaned forward to peer over the wall. My chest relaxed. I exhaled, and it sounded like a sigh.

Not a prince, certainly. Only Garland Whitaker, labouring upwards, her fingernails flashing blood-red on the iron handrail. The auburn hair, I thought, looked artificial in the sunlight – too bright, too tightly curled. She puffed a little, and her face was flushed.

More footsteps echoed to my right, punctuated by a trill of childish laughter. I straightened away from the wall and turned in time to see a tall man coming round the corner further up by the château, with a lively child swinging on his hand. The man's dark head was bent low, to catch the chatter of the little girl. He hadn't seen me yet.

Thinking fast, I ducked my head and scurried off, away from the château, away from the steps, away from all of them. I was *not*, I thought firmly, going to hang about while Garland and Armand bumped into each other, with me in the middle. She was a hopeless gossip, he was a hopeless flirt, and I'd never hear the end of it.

My getaway would have done credit to a bank robber, I moved that quickly, though no doubt a bank robber would have had a better sense of direction. It should have been easy to find my way down into town, but the first sloping crossroad I came to was blocked, completely blocked, by an idling lorry, and instead of waiting for the driver to move on, I decided to walk along the cliff a little further. Surely there'd be other roads, or even stairs . . .

The narrow road curved upwards and became a lane. Still hopeful, I moved briskly between the silent houses and garden walls, past thick falls of fading ivy and red clay-tiled roofs, painted gates and painted shutters. The houses crowded closely on both sides, parting now and then to give a glimpse of the dizzying drop to the terraced gardens on the cliffside, and the quiet river snaking past the rooftops far below.

I appeared to be the only person about, which was just as well, since there wasn't room for two on the narrow strip of pavement. For a short while I enjoyed the solitude, the scent of roses drifting from the gardens, the spectacular view. But when I reached the first cluster of troglodyte caves, I began to feel uneasy.

I blamed it, to begin with, on the caves themselves. They were not the neatly chiselled cliff dwellings pictured in my Loire Valley guide books, cosily supplied with curtains and carved fireplaces. These caves, cut from a thrusting rise of rock, were eerie and abandoned, black windows crumbling over hollow doors, broad chimneys giving way to the grasping growth of weeds and vines that spilled down from the burning, cloudless sky. It was an easy thing, in this apocalyptic settlement, to fancy eyes that watched from every yawning door.

All right, I admitted, so maybe it wasn't too clever of me to be walking up here, on my own. When I crossed the next path cutting down from the cliff, I'd descend to the safety of town.

The path that I was on grew more wild and lonely the further I walked. There were few houses now. On my right, a low rubblestone wall, spattered with lichen and moss, was the only barrier between me and a sheer vertical drop through cedar-scented scrub and tangled weeds. Even the roofs of Chinon, far below, seemed somehow less hospitable.

The paved path turned to yellow soil beneath my feet, and a second crumbling cliff of troglodyte dwellings rose from the weed-tangled hill beside me. A warning prickle chased between my shoulder blades. *Oh, bloody hell*, I thought. I turned. The breeze caught a withered leaf and sent it tumbling end over end across the dirt path, until it was trapped by the long waving grass. Nothing else moved. 'Hello?' I called, just to be sure. 'Is anyone there?'

Silence. Slowly I turned around again, pushing on more cautiously. The solitary house that rose blackly from the path ahead did nothing to reassure me. It was an ugly house, unwelcoming, its sagging door wrapped round with barbed wire coils. As I passed by, the wind swept past, rattling the tightly-shuttered windows like a viper's warning to the unwary. Again the shiver struck me and again I turned my head to look behind. The path was empty.

But this time, when I started to walk on, I heard a sound. The faintest shuffling footfall, and a breathing that was nothing like the wind. Behind me in the house some creature flung itself against the door with a savage growl, and I broke into a half run. I stumbled twice on the uneven ground, and my shoulder brushed a trailing vine and loosed a shower of small white petals that clung to my skin, but I didn't slow my pace until I reached a less neglected place.

There were troglodyte houses here, as well – a neat, low line of them, fronted by a level sweep of gravel. But these houses looked inhabited, not ragged and abandoned. At their farthest end one lovely tree spread green against the white stone walls, and beside the tree a carved and ancient archway sheltered a wooden door with heavy iron hinges.

Here, in this oasis of ordered beauty, I stopped running. There was no logic to it, really, but my racing mind said: *Sanctuary*. Here, I knew beyond all reason, I was safe. With trembling legs I leaned against the wall and drew a ragged breath. I didn't move, even when the sound of footsteps rose above the pounding of my heart. This was not the sound that had pursued me down the path. These steps were different, sharper, climbing from the bottom of the cliff, and there was nothing furtive in their measured tread. Stairs, I thought. There must be stairs nearby. My eyes searched out and found the spot. The steps grew louder, mingling with a voice I recognized, and I felt myself relaxing.

I believe I looked quite normal when Martine and Christian finally appeared above the tangled grasses of the cliff edge.

Martine recovered first from the surprise. 'Hello!' Her widow's veil had been emphatically cast aside this morning, in favour of a yellow windcheater so bright it almost hurt one's eyes to look at it, worn over smartly-pressed black denim jeans and a yellow roll-neck jersey. Even in casual clothes, I decided, she outshone me fairly, but the only thing of which I was truly jealous was her smile. She had perfect teeth. I hadn't ever met a person with really perfect teeth before.

I returned the greeting, straightening away from my supporting wall. 'Out for a walk, are you?'

'Yes. Christian is bored with moving,' Martine told me, 'and so he makes today the sketches for his painting.' Which would explain, I thought, the decidedly battered leather satchel he was lugging about with him this morning, its broad strap digging into his hunched shoulder. He looked half-asleep still. Martine, on the other hand, was wide awake and talking brightly. 'You are admiring the chapelle, Mademoiselle?'

'Please,' I said, 'call me Emily.' And then I frowned. 'What chapelle?'

'The Chapelle of Sainte Radegonde, behind you.'

I looked round at the silent wall, the bolted door. 'Is that what this place is? I didn't know.'

'But yes, this is most famous, here in Chinon. Christian often sketches here. You must come in with us, and see it. The chapelle,' she informed me, 'is not to be missed. Is it, Christian?'

'What?' His head came round a quarter turn, the blue eyes vague as he pulled them away from a contemplation of a floating tuft of clouds. 'Oh, yes, of course. You must come.' He didn't sound particularly enthusiastic, but I didn't take it personally. He seemed to move in a solitary world of his own creation, did Christian Rand.

'The chapelle is kept locked, now,' Martine said. 'Most people, they must ask at the Tourist Office if they wish to see inside. But Christian has a key.'

He was fiddling with it now, in the lock – a long, old-fashioned key like something from a Gothic film. At last it turned, but before he opened the door he did a most peculiar thing. He looked at me with a serious expression, and said: 'You will close your eyes, please.'

'I beg your pardon?'

'I am sorry,' he looked half embarrassed, 'but it is . . . you will only have one chance to be seeing this for the first time, and it is better to be surprised. Please.'

I shrugged and stepped up to the door, screwing my eyes tightly shut like a child waiting to receive a present. I heard the creaking of old iron hinges as Christian pushed the great door open, and I caught a gentle breeze upon my upturned face, a breeze that faintly smelled of flowers and warm stone.

'There,' said Christian. 'You may look.'

At first I couldn't seem to move at all, I could only stand there with my face uplifted to the naked sky and stare and stare until my eyes grew moist. Before me, framed by the open doorway, rose two colossal pillars, smooth and richly white. They seemed to soar towards the heavens, supporting on their curving capitals the

171

arched remains of a ruined wall, capped softly by a golden fringe of grass. Tall iron gates set in between the pillars shielded the inner sanctum, within whose cool and sloping shadows slender columns stretched along a sacred aisle, and the eyes of sculpted saints gazed blindly back at me.

Between the saints and me a garden grew, a wild garden, mindless of man's will or rules of order. Here and there the sunken forms of graves spoke of the time when this wild place had been a proper church, with nave and transept, altar and aisles. But the graves were empty now, the bodies moved and buried elsewhere. Above where they had lain the roof had long since fallen and been cleared away, and the once-high walls had crumbled to uneven contours, their jagged stones yet softened by a trailing growth of ivy.

'My God,' I whispered.

Christian seemed to understand. 'It is most beautiful, this place.'

I scarcely heard him. I finally managed to free my frozen limbs and take a cautious step inside the door.

Here a bay tree arched above a broken baptismal font, and delicate wild flowers quivered at my feet. Everything was green and living, even the soil sprouted moss, and the silent air around me seemed to hum with vital energy.

I nearly didn't see him, to begin with.

He might have been a statue himself, propped against the sunlit wall. The pale hair, the white shirt, both seemed to blend into the ivory stone behind him, and his outstretched legs were buried in a waving sea of green. Only his eyes, when he opened them, commanded attention. They stared, blinked slowly, tried to focus. And then one hand came up to pull the wired headphones from his ears, and I heard the jarring click of a portable tape player being switched off.

'Good morning, everyone,' Neil Grantham said.

Chapter Fifteen

. . . silent
light
Slept on the painted walls . . .

The three of us reacted rather differently, although in my own case it wasn't so much a reaction as a lack of one. I don't think my expression even changed. Martine, beside me, simply laughed, a short, delighted laugh, and said, 'Neil, you idiot! How ever did you get in?'

Christian's response was by far the most dramatic. 'You will *not* move!' he ordered, in a forceful tone that sounded not a bit like him.

Neil, who had been leaning forward as if to rise, sank back against the wall and watched benignly while Christian dropped to his knees in the damp earth and swung the bulging satchel from his shoulder, searching through its contents. I'd never seen an artist in action. It was fascinating to watch him clasp an ink pot to the edge of his sketchbook and boldly dash a straight-nibbed pen across the virgin page.

Fascinating to me, at least. No-one else took any notice. Martine Muret had doubtless seen it all before, and Neil was looking, not at Christian, but at me. 'You gave me quite a turn just now,' he said, mildly accusing. 'I didn't hear you come in.'

'I'm surprised you didn't hear us opening the door. That lock goes off like a shotgun.'

'I was listening to my music.' The small movement of his head provoked a stern look of reproach from Christian.

'Neil . . .'

'Sorry.' Neil's head stayed very still against the glowing stone, but his eyes swung back to me. 'Thierry loaned me this little machine to replace the one I broke yesterday. It's working rather nicely.'

'At this moment.' Martine came forward, smiling, to stand between the two of us. 'And how did you get in?' she asked again. 'The door, it is kept always locked.'

'I have my methods.' His dark eyes crinkled at the corners.

Christian sighed. 'Martine, please, you block the light. Thank you,' he said shortly, when she'd backed away a step. The pen went scratching across the drawing paper and Christian huddled over it, frowning with the force of his concentration. Neil seemed quite unaffected by all the attention. He didn't stir against the wall, and when his gaze came back to mine it held a quiet resignation.

'It isn't me that interests him,' he said. 'It's something that I'm doing, without knowing it. Isn't that right, Christian?'

The painter looked up, briefly. 'You make this good shadow on the column, just there. This shadow I can use.'

'You see?' Neil smiled at me, vindicated.

Christian lowered his head. 'And also,' he went on, 'you have a quality quite unique that I try to capture. This most amazing stillness.'

'Well, naturally,' said Neil. 'You won't let me move.'

But I knew what Christian meant, and it was something deeper than the seated man's motionless hands or his calm, deliberate voice. It was a thing intangible, yet clearly felt – the sense that time was moving round him, past him, leaving him untouched. Even when the drawing was completed and Neil was finally able to stand, rising stiffly from the hard ground and stretching, the aura of stillness clung to him.

Martine smiled. 'You are too old, I think, for climbing walls,' she told him.

'Have a heart, love,' was Neil's reply. 'I've only just turned forty-three – I'm not quite ready for the eventide home.'

Not by a long shot, I agreed, turning my gaze from his boyish face and snugly fitting denim jeans to the crumbling wall above his head, which at its lowest point must still have been some ten or twelve feet tall.

'You climbed that wall?' I asked, incredulous. 'Is that how you got in?'

'Could be.' He smiled again, refusing to appease our curiosity. Turning to Christian, he asked: 'Have you got the keys for this gate with you? Emily might like to see the murals.' He said my name so easily, as though we were old friends, or something more. I thought I saw a flash of curiosity in Martine's sideways glance, but Christian found his keys again and came forward to unlock the towering black grille that sealed the sculpted saints within their inner chamber. They had an odd effect on me, those saints. Though they were trapped in shadows, while I had open sky above me, I felt somehow that it was me, not them, shut in behind the iron bars; that their eyes saw a wider world than mine.

The blind stone faces stared at me as Christian swung

the great gate open and we passed into the chapel proper, where our voices echoed as we walked between stone columns soaring high to meet the ceiling many feet above our heads.

'This has been carved from the cliff,' Martine told me. 'You can see here the marks of the chisel. It is very old, this chapelle. Christian,' she said, turning, 'you must tell the story of Sainte Radegonde. I never can remember it properly.'

Christian shrugged uncomfortably and hurried through an abbreviated version. 'She was a German, like myself – a princess. In the sixth of centuries her people were destroyed by the Frankish king, Clotaire, who took Radegonde for his bride. She was then eleven years old. But she was not happy with Clotaire, and so she left him and became a nun. She founded, here at Chinon, a small convent.'

I looked around. 'What, in this spot?'

'No, not here. The hermit Jean was living here, a holy man. I will explain.' He frowned a little, trying to collect his thoughts. He was clearly unaccustomed to the role of tour guide. 'When Radegonde was living at Chinon, there came an order from Clotaire, her former husband, that she should be going south to Poitiers to make a convent, for which he would provide the money. But Radegonde, she was not certain this was good, so she came here to visit Jean the hermit, to ask him what to do.'

'And what did he tell her?'

A second shrug. 'He said that this was a good idea, to go to Poitiers. And so Sainte Radegonde went there, as Clotaire wanted, and built in Poitiers a great church. It is there that she is buried.'

There was an altar of sorts at the end wall, a heavy

stone table laid with a white lace covering, set in a hollowed niche that glowed with ancient paintings.

'This mural,' Martine said, pointing to the flaking pigments, rich blue above a deep wine colour, 'this is not the oldest here. This one is only seventeenth century.'

There were fresh flowers on the altar, and a wooden standing crucifix flanked by bronze candlesticks. Beneath the drape of lace, a broken sculpture bore the likeness of a medieval woman lost in meditative rapture, a royal crown upon her head.

'Is this her?' I asked, bending for a better look. 'Is this Sainte Radegonde?'

Christian nodded. 'Yes. And also this,' he said, showing me a daintier statue that graced a second table in the adjoining painted niche. At the feet of this Radegonde were more cut flowers, and a shallow plate with several coins laid in it. Offerings to the saint, I thought, until Christian set me straight.

'Those are donations to the Friends of Old Chinon,' he said. 'To help with the upkeep of the chapelle.'

Always the practical intruded into the romantic, I reminded myself with a wry smile.

Martine was at my shoulder, pointing. 'The chapelle, it goes even further into the rock, through there.' She showed me a smaller iron gate that spread to fill an opening in the rear wall. There were no saints behind this gate, no kind benevolent eyes, only a few feet of visible stone floor and then an inky darkness. 'There are more caves, and many fine museum items, and an ancient well, from Sainte Radegonde's time. She must see the well, Christian. Do you have the key?'

But the young German shook his head, expressionless. 'No, I have not brought it with me. We can show the well to her another time.'

'But Christian, surely . . .'

'I have not brought the key, Martine.' His tone was firm. 'I am sorry.'

I wasn't overly disappointed, myself. The dank smell of stone that rose from behind the iron gate was acrid and unwelcoming. Besides, my roving gaze had just that moment fallen on a painted frieze at the opposite end of the covered aisle.

'I don't believe it,' I said abruptly. 'There's John.'

Martine, interrupted in her train of thought, looked at the end wall and frowned. 'Yes, that is Jean the hermit,' she said. 'It is a reproduction of his tomb, you understand. The sleeping statue, it is not as old as—'

'No, I didn't mean that,' I broke in. 'I meant the fresco higher up, at the back. That's John Lackland, King of England.'

'Oh, I see. Yes, you are quite right, that is a painting of the Plantagenets.' Her face cleared, and she led us across the neatly swept floor to the corner where the painting was. It was only a fragment of a fresco, really, with a fair chunk missing along the bottom edge, but the colours were brilliant and stunningly true.

'I've seen this before,' I said slowly, admiring the artist's skill. I remembered it from one of Harry's books.

Martine, the art expert, assured me it had been much photographed. 'Many people came to see it thirty years ago, when it was found. It is believed to have been painted when this John came here to marry his queen. That is her there,' she pointed out, 'on the horse behind her husband's. Not the older woman at the back, but the young girl riding in the front.'

Neil came up behind me, closer to the wall, his breath

stirring the hair on the top of my head. 'She looks young to be a queen,' he commented. 'And she isn't wearing a crown, is she? The crown is on the older woman.'

'That's Eleanor,' I told him, absently, my eyes fixed on the vibrant painted figures. 'Eleanor of Aquitaine. She was John's mother.' But I wasn't looking at the famous queen. I was looking at the lovely, tragic girl in front of her, the great dark eyes that gazed towards the future with such hope . . .

'It was by luck alone that this survived,' Martine was saying. 'Just after it was painted Chinon came to the French king. This John of England, he killed someone, I think, and it was not so nice to have his picture in the church. And so this fresco, it was covered up with plaster. It was not seen again until 1966, when some of the plaster fell down.'

I heard her only dimly. I went on studying the painting, and as my eyes passed over Isabelle it seemed she was now staring straight at *me*, as though she yearned to tell me something. The quiet shadows wrapped cold hands around me, and I quickly looked away. It was, at any rate, the end of the impromptu tour. We wandered back into the sunlight of the walled and roofless yard.

Christian took up a position by the baptismal font, beneath the waving branches of the bay tree, and began to sketch again in ink, his upward glances swift and keen as he traced the broken architecture onto paper. Not wanting to disturb his concentration, I settled myself between Neil and Martine, against the great pillars opposite. I don't believe I did it purposely, sitting between the two of them . . . I don't *believe* I did . . . but then, my actions and reactions where Neil

Grantham was concerned were becoming increasingly unpredictable.

He levered his head away from the curved white stone to toss the thick fall of fair hair back out of his eyes, and the noonday sunlight struck him full across the face. 'This is as close to Eden as it gets,' he said. 'I daren't come up here too often, or I'd never get anything accomplished. In fact I'd probably never leave Chinon, come to that.' He started to smile, but my expression stopped him. 'What? What's the matter?'

'Nothing.' I looked away rather quickly. It would sound foolish to tell the truth, to tell him that I'd only just now noticed that his eyes weren't black at all. They were blue, a pure dark blue, deep as the still sea at midnight. Not that it much mattered what colour his eyes were. What mattered was that I'd noticed it at all.

Harry had always laughed at me for noticing men's eyes. 'I can always tell when you're smitten, my love,' he'd teased me, more than once. 'I only have to ask you what colour his eyes are.' And he was right, as always. If I wasn't interested I answered 'brown', not knowing, but if a man had struck my fancy I could describe his eyes in embarrassing detail.

I felt my face growing warm, but Neil didn't notice. He'd looked away again, towards the far wall, where he'd been sitting earlier. 'There's that bloody bird again,' he said, his voice mildly amused.

Martine, at my other shoulder, turned her head to look. 'What bird?'

'Just over there. The swallow. He was hopping round like mad this morning – made me tired just watching him. He must have his nest around here somewhere.'

I stared at the little fork-tailed bird, and for a moment – just a moment, mind – I almost wanted to believe . . .

Don't be an idiot, I told myself firmly. It wasn't the same swallow I'd seen, it couldn't possibly be, and it certainly hadn't brought me a message from any prince. There were no such things, I reminded myself, as princes. Neil rolled his head sideways again, as if to tell me something, but I pushed myself upright and rose to my feet. 'I think I'll leave my own donation at the altar,' I said, my voice sounding unnaturally bright. 'This is a lovely place, I'd hate to see it go to ruin for lack of funds.'

I wasn't the only one who felt that way, obviously. Beside the statue of Sainte Radegonde, the small chipped saucer held a generous scattering of coins. Among the thin French francs I saw a few larger pieces that proved to be American, and half hidden below those was a smallish coin of beaten silver . . .

I stared at it a moment, disbelieving. It couldn't be, I thought, it simply couldn't be . . . but there it was, all the same – a small, round coin of tarnished silver, with the image of a dead king raised on one side. The image of King John of England, third of the Plantagenet line.

The breeze blew suddenly chill within the sheltering walls, and I heard again my cousin's laughing voice, and saw him close his fist protectively around that coin, drawing it back and up, out of my reach. 'You might have stopped believing in good luck pieces, Emily Braden,' he'd told me then with an indulgent smile, 'but I haven't. I'd rather lose my right arm than this little chap.'

Numbly, without thinking, I fished the coin from the saucer and closed my fingers round it, pressing it into the soft flesh of my palm until I could feel each contour of its worn surface. It was no longer in its round protective casing, but it was obviously Harry's coin. I wouldn't think too many tourists carried King John coins about. He had been here, then, just recently. I frowned. Harry had been here . . .

My own five-franc piece tumbled with a noisy clatter into the saucer and Martine looked round, blinking in the sunlight. She couldn't have seen me clearly, there in my shadowed corner, but still she asked: 'Something is wrong?'

Beneath the saint's accusing eyes I slipped the coin into my pocket, and shook my head. 'No, nothing's wrong.' Satisfied, Martine turned away again to talk to Neil, and I clenched my trembling hand into a fist. *Nothing's wrong*, I repeated, silently. I only wished I could believe it.

Chapter Sixteen

Henceforth thou hast a helper, me . . .

It was nearly dark when I left my room and went to look for Paul. I found him sitting alone in the bar, his shoulder to the wall of windows fronting on the square. *Ulysses* lay open on the low table at his knees, the spread pages pinned beneath a heavy glass ashtray.

He looked so peaceful, sitting there, that I hated to disturb him, but there was no help for it. My aunt's telephone had been engaged all afternoon, and when I'd rung my father I'd been greeted by his answering machine. Which left only Paul. I wouldn't have felt comfortable discussing my problems with anyone else, but Paul already seemed an old friend. As I entered the bar he surfaced from his book and sent me a welcoming smile. 'You've got good timing,' he said. 'I was just about to put this down and have a drink.'

'What page are you on now?'

'Five hundred and forty-six.'

'And how many pages are there?'

'Nearly eight hundred,' he admitted, repositioning the ashtray to hold his place while he stretched his cramped shoulders. 'I'm doomed.'

'You could always skip some bits, you know. You'd

hardly miss a passage or two, surely, in a book that size.'

'But that would be cheating,' said Paul, as I sat down on the sofa opposite him. 'Besides, I don't do anything half way. Once I start something, I have to see it through – it's just the way I am. I hate leaving anything unfinished.'

'Is it really such a difficult book?'

'Not difficult, no.' He frowned, thinking. 'No, complex would be a better word, I think. There are lots of layers in Joyce's prose, and you can't go too fast or you miss things. For instance,' he said, turning the book towards me with his finger on the open page, 'what would you say that means, exactly?'

I read the passage twice and shook my head. 'I haven't the faintest idea.'

'Neither do I. But I know I'll work it out eventually. That's how you have to read this book, you see. You wade through a few sentences, then stop and think about them, then wade through a few more.'

'Well, you're a better man than I am, Gunga Din.'

'Pardon?'

'You've far more patience than I'll ever have,' I explained.

'Simon wouldn't call it patience,' he said, with a shrug. 'He'd just call it another one of my annoyingly obsessive personality traits. He says I'm a typical physicist, that I always have to force everything to make sense.'

'And do you?'

'Sure.' He grinned at my question, unashamed. 'Because everything does make sense, when you look at it from the right angle. All you have to do is find out what that angle is, for whatever it is you want to understand,

and bang, the universe becomes a rational place.'

'Does it really?' I remained unconvinced, sagging back against the seat cushions as I brushed the hair back from my forehead. There was a pink geranium growing in a planter outside the window, behind Paul's shoulder, and I frowned at it without really seeing it. 'Well, I've tried every angle I can think of, and I still don't know what to think.'

'About what?'

Dragging my gaze from the window, I dug into my pocket and held out my hand, palm upwards. 'This.'

Paul frowned. Leaning forward, he took the little coin and raised it to catch the slanting light from the overhead fixture. 'What is it?'

'It's a King John coin.'

'Really? Where on earth did you get this?'

I was ashamed to say I'd stolen it from a donation plate, so instead I told a half truth. 'I found it, up at the Chapelle Sainte Radegonde.'

'Wow.' He turned it slowly, studying the ancient image. 'I can't imagine many people would have one of these.'

'My cousin has one.'

He caught on quickly did young Paul. His upward glance held total comprehension. 'But your cousin isn't supposed to be here yet.'

'I know.'

'So.' He handed the coin back to me, watching my face with careful eyes that were older than his age. 'So you think that this is his, then? That he's been and gone already?'

'I don't know what to think. I rang up the other hotels and they've never heard of him. I checked round the hospitals, but he hasn't been admitted. From all accounts, he hasn't been within ten miles of Chinon. Not recently, at any rate.'

'Did you try the tourist office? They keep the keys, you know, for the Chapelle of Sainte Radegonde.'

I nodded. 'They said no-one had asked to see the chapelle for at least a month.' Christian had a key, of course, but if Christian had met Harry he'd have mentioned it to me, surely. My cousin and I were alike enough to be brother and sister, one could hardly miss the resemblance. And while Neil had apparently managed to scale the walls somehow, I doubted whether Harry could have done the same. Harry, for all his energy, was no athlete. 'It's this coin, you see,' I said to Paul, 'this bloody coin, that bothers me.' I rolled it pensively between my fingers. 'His good luck piece, he called it – to help him with the book he was writing. He'd never have left it behind.'

'Maybe he dropped it without knowing.'

I shook my head. 'No, not where I found it. Someone would have had to place it there deliberately. Besides, he couldn't have dropped it loose like this. He carried it round in a plastic case, the kind collectors use.'

'He'd have dropped the whole thing, you mean.'

'Yes. Of course, the obvious answer is that this isn't Harry's coin at all, that it belongs to someone else. But still, it's solid silver, and terribly old, and you'd have to be mad to put it in . . . well, to put it where I found it.'

Paul was silent for a minute. Shaking a cigarette loose from his nearly empty packet he lit it with a thoughtful frown. 'If you're really worried, you could call the police.'

'And tell them what? That I've found a coin that may or may not be my cousin's?' I smiled, knowingly.

'They'd send me packing for wasting their valuable time.'

'So you don't want to bother the police,' Paul summarized. 'OK. There must be some other way of finding out whether he's been here.'

'Well, I can't think of any.'

'You said he was coming here to do some research.'

'Yes.'

'And where would he go to do that?'

I shrugged, a little helplessly. 'I don't know, really. The library, perhaps, or the château . . . no, wait,' I broke off suddenly, remembering. 'He did say he was meeting someone. Some man who'd read one of Harry's articles and was offering some useful information about tunnels.'

'You're sure it was a man?'

I thought back, closing my eyes as I replayed the week-old conversation in my head. 'Yes, positive.'

'Remember his name?'

'No.' I opened my eyes again, faintly frustrated. 'No, I don't. I think he only said the first name.'

'Is he French or English?'

'French,' I said with certainty. 'He wrote his letter in French, I do remember that, only Harry said the fellow must know English because the article – the article about Queen Isabelle's treasure – had been published in an English journal.'

'Right,' said Paul. 'So we're looking for a local history nut who knows the tunnels pretty well and reads British history journals.' He smiled at me above the burning cigarette. 'Sounds like a case for Sherlock Holmes.'

'Impossible, you mean.'

He grinned. 'I mean it's something I could probably

look into for you. I don't think there'd be too many guys in Chinon fitting that description, and the few who do must hang around the library. It's just down the street, here,' he nodded out the window. 'I can drop in tomorrow, if you like, and ask around. And if you want to take another look around the chapelle to see if your cousin left anything else there, I'm sure I could sweet-talk Christian into lending me the keys.'

'Would you?'

'Sure. Sweet-talking is one of my specialities.' He smiled, blowing smoke. 'I have to do a lot of it with my brother.'

I smiled back. 'Where is Simon, by the way?'

'Don't know. He took off after lunch, treasure-hunting, and I haven't seen him since. After last night's ghost story, he's been unstoppable, you know – two Isabelles, two hidden treasures, twice the chance of finding something.'

'Look on the bright side,' I told him. 'At least he won't be quite so eager to leave Chinon, now. You'll get to stay a few more days.'

'Longer than that,' he reminded me, sagely. 'Don't you remember? The Echo told Simon he'd never get me to leave.' Leaning back, he stretched his arms above his head. 'Listen, do you want a drink or something? Coffee?'

I looked round the deserted room. 'Is the bar open, then?'

'Oh, sure. Thierry's in the back room, doing paper-work.'

'Paperwork?' It seemed an odd thing for the bartender to be doing, and Paul smiled at my reaction.

'Yeah. I think the receptionist, Gabrielle, is helping him.'

'Oh, I see.' I smiled back, as comprehension dawned. 'I'm supposed to whistle if I want anything.'

He had to whistle twice, in fact, before we heard a stirring from the room behind the bar, and a slightly muffled voice said: 'Ho-kay, just a moment.'

Across from me, Paul struck a match to light another cigarette, his eyes faintly apologetic. 'Chain-smoking, I know. My mother would have a fit. But I have to enjoy it while I can, before Simon gets back.'

I bit my lip, thinking. 'Paul . . .'

'Yes?'

'You won't tell anybody, will you, about my cousin's coin?' If he'd asked 'why not?' I would have had a devil of a time explaining. One couldn't very well explain a feeling. And that was all it was – a feeling, an irrational suspicion that things were not quite what they seemed to be among my fellow guests. I'd felt it that first night at dinner, and again last night, here in the bar – that sense of something darker running underneath the surface, some troubled current that I couldn't understand. It reminded me of the time, years ago now, when my father had taken us to London to see a play, only he'd read the tickets wrong and we arrived just as the second interval was ending. I'd sat through the final act in absolute confusion, with the motivating plot-lines of the characters long since laid out and set in motion, so that while I felt their conflict and the atmosphere of tension, I had no idea what was going on.

But whatever the cause of the atmosphere of tension here at the Hotel de France, it didn't seem to have touched Paul Lazarus. 'Of course I won't tell anyone,' he said. 'Not if you don't want me to.'

'Not even Simon?'

'Not even Simon.'

'Thanks,' I told him. 'You're an angel.'

Smiling, he balanced his cigarette on the edge of the ashtray and leaned back in his seat, arms folded complacently across his chest. 'I do my best.'

'Aha!' Simon, coming round the bar door, skewered Paul with a smugly triumphant look. 'I knew I'd catch you at it sooner or later, I just knew it!'

I couldn't resist. I reached innocently across for the lit cigarette and raised it to my own lips, inhaling with perfect nonchalance. 'Catch him at what?' I asked Simon.

His face fell, and even Paul looked faintly shocked, but I managed to hold the innocent expression long enough to convince Simon.

'Nothing,' he said. He glanced uncertainly at Paul. 'I only thought . . .'

He wasn't allowed to finish telling us what he thought. Behind him in the entrance hall the front door blew open and shut and I braced myself as the Whitakers came into the bar, shattering what little remained of the companionable peace that had settled between Paul and myself.

'Why, Emily!' Garland raised her eyebrows in a calculated arc and widened her eyes. 'I didn't know you smoked.'

I didn't, actually. I had given it up three years ago, as part of my more responsible approach to life, and I was somewhat relieved to find it tasted awful, but I sent Garland an almost cheerful shrug. 'Well, we all have to have one vice, don't we? That's what my father says.'

'Only one vice? Darling, how *boring*!' She sank gracefully onto the soft chair nearest the door and gave a tiny, self-satisfied sigh. 'I won't be able to get up again, now,' she pronounced. 'We must have walked a hundred miles.'

'Just over the river and back, actually,' Jim Whitaker put in, as he joined us by the window, 'but my wife's not used to walking. And those shoes don't help.'

Garland lifted one delicately arched foot, the better to examine her tight Italian pumps. 'I know. I really *must* invest in a pair of sensible shoes like yours, Emily,' she said, sending me a smile designed to soften the cutting compliment. 'You English always wear such practical clothes.'

Paul's eyes laughed at me as he positioned the ashtray nearer me, closing his unfinished book and pushing it aside. He looked at Simon, curious. 'And where did you take off to, this afternoon?'

'Oh, nowhere in particular,' Simon answered, swinging his lanky frame into the chair beside me. He whistled a snatch of something through his teeth and looked around. 'Where's Thierry, by the way? Isn't he working?'

'He's in the back, doing paperwork.' The lie came easily in Paul's unhurried voice. 'He knows we're here, though. He'll be out in a minute or two.'

'Thank God,' said Garland. 'I could certainly use a drink after all that marching around. I prefer places we can drive the car to, you know. What about you, Emily?'

'Oh, I don't mind walking.' I smiled politely, folding what was left of the cigarette into the ashtray with exquisite care. 'I rather enjoy it, actually.'

Garland smiled. 'Like Neil. Honestly, he makes me tired just watching him. Up and down those stairs all day, and he never even breathes hard. It's disgusting. Jim used to be fit like that, didn't you darling? When I first met you. The Army,' she sighed, 'does wonderful things to a man's body. Oh, *there* you are, Thierry, we were beginning to think you'd disappeared.'

Thierry looked rather flushed, and more than a little pleased with himself. Garland mistook his cheerful distraction for an inability to understand.

'We . . . thought . . . you'd . . . disappeared,' she repeated, in a louder voice.

'Ah.' He grinned, and broadening his accent so that he sounded exactly like a music hall actor pretending to be French, he asked her very slowly: 'Would . . . you . . . like . . . a . . . drink?'

Even Jim smiled at that, but Garland missed the joke completely. 'Oh, that's very much better, Thierry,' she congratulated him. 'You see? I told you if you kept on practising, your English would improve in no time.'

Thierry shrugged, a modest little shrug. I didn't trust myself to look up again until after he'd brought the drinks.

For the next half hour I sipped my *kir* and smiled politely. When it became apparent that the Whitakers were rooted to their seats for the remainder of the evening, and that Paul and I would have to wait until breakfast to talk any further about Harry, I excused myself with a rather convincing yawn and started up the winding stairs.

Alone in my room, I closed my fingers thoughtfully round the little silver coin, still nestled deep within my pocket, and wandered over to the window. The night air was thick and full of dampness. In the square below, the street lamps spread warm yellow pools of light upon the smooth black pavement, and water spilled from the fountain like an iridescent rain.

Beside the fountain, the little spotted dog yawned and

stretched as the breeze went shivering through the acacias.

The gypsy glanced swiftly upwards, expressionless, at my window, then looked away again and lit a cigarette with unhurried fingers. It was only the darkness, I told myself, that was giving things this air of melodrama. The gypsy had every right to be sitting in a public square, and he might have been looking at anything, really, not just at my window. But still I latched the window firmly, securely, and twitched the heavy curtains closed before I crawled beneath the covers of the wide bed, shutting my eyes tightly into the pillow like a child seeking comfort in the long uncertain night.

Chapter Seventeen

'. . . we give you, being
strange
A license: speak, and let the topic die.'

Paul answered my knock at the door next morning with the telephone slung from one hand and the receiver cradled close against his cheek. Smiling, he motioned me in, not missing a beat in his conversation. He was speaking in French. 'Ah. I see. Yes, I'll wait, it's no problem.' Fingers cupped round the mouthpiece, he smiled again. 'Come on in,' he told me. 'Have a seat.'

Which was easier said than done. The boys' room was the mirror image of my own, except that where I had one huge bed they had two narrow ones, one neatly made and strewn with maps, the other rumpled and half buried beneath a set of curtains, still anchored firmly to the curtain-rod. Three spreading piles of clothing, sorted by colour, rose like miniature alps from the carpet at my feet. There was very little room to stand, let alone sit.

Paul had solved the problem by sitting on the cluttered desk, feet braced against a chair that had been buried thick in newspapers. He resumed his seat now, while I made my cautious way around the mounded clothing to perch upon a corner of the neater bed by the window.

Simon, I thought, had a point – the window did look better without curtains. It stood fully open to the morning air, and the jumbled sounds of traffic, talk and fountain drifted upwards from the square beneath, like some discordant modern symphony.

Paul was still on hold, and humming to himself.

'Any joy?' I asked him.

'Sort of. The library isn't open yet, but the staff is there. This guy's just gone to ask the librarian if he knows anyone who—' He broke off suddenly, and bent his head. 'Yes, I'm still here.' A shorter pause, and then: 'Yes. I'm a student, you see, and I'm writing a paper on . . . that's right. And I was told there might be someone here who might be good to talk to. Pardon?' He leaned forward to scribble a few lines on the pad of paper at his side. 'Yes, I've got that. Belliveau, that's B-e-l-l . . . ? You don't have the telephone number, do you? Yes, of course, I understand. Well, I'm sure it won't be a problem. Thanks so much.' He replaced the receiver with a smug expression, and struck a match to light a cigarette. 'Well, that was fun.'

'You want to watch out, Sherlock,' I said drily. 'Big brother might walk in and catch you smoking.'

'Simon,' Paul informed me, savouring the words, 'isn't here. He left half an hour ago, with the Whitakers.'

'Simon's gone off with Jim and Garland?' I couldn't quite believe my ears. 'Why on earth would he do that?'

'Because they were going to Fontevraud, where your Queen Isabelle is buried. Simon thought there might be clues there, as to where she hid her treasure.' Paul shrugged. 'But mostly he went because I reminded him today is Tuesday, our weekly laundry day, and Simon really hates the laundromat.'

I smiled slowly. 'You're a whopping sneak.'

'I know.'

'And how are we supposed to play detective, might I ask, if we have to do your laundry?'

'Thierry and I have it all under control.'

'You didn't tell Thierry?' I asked, startled.

His eyes held soft reproach. 'Of course not. I promised, didn't I? I only told him you and I were taking off to do some sightseeing on our own, and could he help us keep it secret from Simon?'

I smiled. 'Well, that's torn it. He'll be thinking we've gone sneaking off to do something romantic.'

'Nah.' Paul grinned. 'We could do that right here at the hotel. Besides, Thierry knows me better than that.'

'What, I'm too old for you?' I teased him.

He shook his head. 'Hardly. But I'd never hit on someone else's woman.'

'Someone else's . . . ?'

'Anyhow,' he changed the subject, picking up his notepad. 'Do you want to know what I've just found out?'

I stopped frowning and leaned forward. 'Please.'

'Well, the librarian only knows of one man who reads foreign history journals and takes an interest in the tunnels – a local poet by the name of Victor Belliveau.'

'Victor . . .' I tried the name, experimentally.

'Was that the name your cousin mentioned, on the phone, do you think?'

I shook my head. 'I can't remember.'

'Because it sounds like this might be our guy, it really does. Apparently he's been poking around the tunnels for years, making maps and things. Kind of a personal obsession. So if this Belliveau did write your cousin, then your cousin might have met with him when he was here in Chinon. Assuming, of course, that he *was* here.

It can't hurt to ask.' Paul checked his notes again. 'He lives just outside Chinon, sort of. I've got the address, but there isn't any phone number. The librarian doesn't think he has a phone. Our Monsieur Belliveau is a true artiste – a little bit eccentric.'

'But you said he doesn't live far from here?'

Paul shook his head. 'Just up the river, past the beach. A fifteen-minute walk, maybe. Do you want to go there first, then? Or would you rather start by taking another look around the Chapelle Sainte Radegonde? I've got the key.'

'How did you manage that?'

Another shrug, more modest than the first. 'I just went round to Christian's house this morning, before breakfast, and asked him for it. Christian's like Neil, he wakes up with the birds, and I figured he wouldn't mind.'

'Well, I'm most impressed, I really am. You've had a busy morning, Sherlock.'

'Morning isn't over, yet,' he reminded me. 'So where do we start? The poet or the chapelle?'

I took a moment to consider the options. The Chapelle Sainte Radegonde, I thought, was the more appealing prospect, and I was quite certain Harry had been there, but then again . . . I rubbed my thigh unconsciously, recalling the hellish climb along the cliffs, and the endless winding steps that led back down again.

I smiled at Paul. 'The poet, please.'

The house of Victor Belliveau stood on the fringe of the community – a sprawling yellow farmhouse with an aged tile roof, set off by itself with a scattering of crooked trees to guard the boundary fence.

Thierry had confirmed the man's artistic status. 'He was a famous man, this Belliveau,' Thierry had said in response to Paul's casual question. 'Not just in Chinon, but in all of France. I read his poetry at school, in Paris. But now he drinks, you know, and he is not so well respected.'

His property reflected that, I thought. The yard was pitted and unkempt, and the stone barn, built long and low to match the house, was tightly shuttered up. And the rubbish! Peelings rotted everywhere among the weeds, and paper wrappers cartwheeled in the wind to fall exhausted in the rutted muddy lane before us.

'Oh, boy,' said Paul.

'My thoughts exactly.'

'I guess poets don't make much money, do they?' Paul strolled across the road and tried the fastening of Victor Belliveau's gate. It was a long gate, stretched across what might have been a drive, and it was unlocked. One push sent it creaking back on its hinges. The sound spoke of loneliness and isolation, and I'd not have been surprised to see a snarling dog come slinking round a corner, but the only animal that came to greet us was a small black chicken. Keeping its distance, it turned a round and curious eye to watch us cross the lawn towards the house.

It was a farmer's house, square and sturdy. Great blocks of smooth pale stone framed both front windows and the door that stood between them, but the rest of the walls were made of rubble. Much more economical, I supposed. It might have been made quite a pretty house, if someone had cared enough to take the trouble. It only wanted some new roof tiles and a lick of paint on the sagging shutters, perhaps some curtains and a flowerpot or two to brighten things.

But I could clearly hear the rattling of the cracked and greying tiles, and on the wall see places where the years had worn away the mortar so the dampness could creep in between the dirty yellow stones. The windows, staring out across the littered yard at the still and shuttered barn, had a blank and empty look.

No-one, I decided, had cared about this house for a very long time.

I had already conjured up a vivid mental picture of Monsieur Victor Belliveau, and so I was completely unprepared for the sight of the man who actually opened the door to Paul's polite knock. This was no unkempt, wild-eyed poet, half mad with drink and raving in his solitude. Instead a tidy, dapper little man with crisp grey hair and a shaven face that smelled of soap, looked back at us in pleasant expectation.

Paul did the talking for us both, in flawless French. He didn't tell the whole truth, mind. He was careful not to contradict the tale he'd spun for the librarian, about being a student working on a paper, only this time he did mention he was trying to find my cousin. 'Braden,' he said. 'Harry Braden. He's from my university. I believe he was here in Chinon last week, doing research, and I thought he might have come to talk to you . . . ?'

Victor Belliveau raked us with a measuring look. 'No, I'm sorry, he did not come here.'

'Oh. You didn't write him a letter, then?'

'No.' Another long and penetrating look. 'You say it is something to do with the tunnels, this paper you are writing?'

'Well,' Paul scuffed his shoe against the step, 'sort of . . .'

'Then perhaps I can help you myself,' said Victor Belliveau, with a rusty smile. He pushed the door a fraction wider. 'Please,' he told us, 'do come in.'

The French did not ask strangers into their homes as a matter of habit, and it would have been unspeakably rude to have refused his invitation. Feeling slightly guilty for intruding on the man's privacy in the first place, I followed Paul across the threshold.

There were only two rooms on the ground floor, a large square kitchen and a second room in which a bed, a coal stove and a sofa were the only furnishings. The far wall of the kitchen groaned beneath the weight of rustic bookshelves, stacked two deep in places, an intriguing mix of paperbacks and expensive-looking volumes leaning wearily on one another. The other walls were bare, with jagged cracks that ran from the ceiling like thunderbolts. In one corner some plant – an ivy branch, it looked like – had actually worked its way through the heavy plaster and been unceremoniously hacked off for its trouble. Still the rooms, while spartan, were surprisingly clean, and the tile floor had recently been swept.

Victor Belliveau seated us in the kitchen, round a large scrubbed table spread with newspapers. 'Would you like a drink?' he offered. 'Wine? Coffee? No?' He shrugged and poured himself a glass of thick red wine. 'I had some brandy here the other day, but I'm afraid it's gone. They took it,' he said, jerking his head towards the window and the tangled yard outside. 'Damned good taste, if you ask me.'

At Paul's blank look the poet smiled again. 'I'm sorry, of course you wouldn't know. I meant the gypsies,' he explained. 'I have a family of them, usually, living on my land. That's why the yard is such a disaster. Good people, gypsies, but they don't believe in guarding the environment.'

'*Gypsies?*' The word came out rather more sharply than I'd intended, and the bland and guileless eyes shifted from Paul to me.

'Oh, yes. We've plenty of gypsies round here, my dear. Mine stay here several times a year. One's never sure exactly when – they just turn up when the mood strikes, with their caravans. Not everybody likes them, but they don't much trouble me.'

'I see.' The scarred table felt suddenly damp beneath my splayed fingers.

'But what was it you needed to know, about the tunnels?' he asked, his glass trailing moisture on the table as he leaned forward in his own chair, helpfully.

Paul played his part extremely well, I thought. Having only just left school himself he made a most convincing student – even borrowed pen and paper to make notes, his face attentive, serious. I tried to listen to what Victor Belliveau was telling Paul about the history of the tunnels, but my mind kept wandering off to other things.

Like gypsies, for example. Of course it was coincidence, and nothing more, that Victor Belliveau let gypsies on his land. There must be half a dozen other people living in these parts who had a gypsy caravan parked down their back lane. And besides, I reminded myself, the gypsy with the little dog who haunted the fountain square had nothing at all to do with me. Nothing at all.

'. . . up to the Chapelle Sainte Radegonde,' Belliveau was saying, 'but that has long since fallen in. One has to use imagination . . .'

His mention of the chapelle set my mind wandering

again, this time to Harry. Bloody Harry. I ought to have that printed on a T-shirt, I thought. He'd probably be quite amused by all the trouble I was going to, just because I'd found that King John coin. There was bound to be a simple reason why the coin was here and Harry wasn't.

'He died last Wednesday,' Victor Belliveau said, shrugging, and I came back to the conversation with a jolt.

'I beg your pardon?'

'A friend of Monsieur Belliveau's,' explained Paul, for my benefit.

'Well, I knew him, let us say,' the poet qualified drily. 'We were not friends. But this is why the gypsies left, you see. We'd had the police round a few times, asking questions, and gypsies don't much care for that. Not that I was a suspect, or anything,' he said, smiling at his own joke, 'but as I said, I knew the man quite well. It was a sad case. He drank too much.' He shrugged and raised his own glass, which I noticed had been filled again.

Paul raised his eyebrows. 'You don't mean Martine Muret's husband, do you?'

'Yes, Didier Muret. You know them, then?'

'Only Martine,' said Paul. 'I never met her husband. Ex-husband, I should say.'

'Ah, she is a lovely woman, Martine, don't you think? I believe I wrote a sonnet to her, once. But she chose Muret. God knows why,' he said, smiling above his wine glass. 'He was an idiot.'

I frowned. 'Didier Muret – that was his name?'

'Yes, why?'

Didier . . . I turned it round again, concentrating. It rang a bell, that name. I was sure it was the name Harry had mentioned – either that, or something very like it. It was a common enough name. There were probably dozens of Didiers living in Chinon. Still, I thought, it never hurt to try . . .

'He wasn't a historian, by any chance?' I asked.

The poet laughed at that. 'God, no. Didier? He took no interest in such things. He was a clever man, don't get me wrong – he worked once for a lawyer, so he must have had a brain. But I don't think I ever saw him read a book. Now me,' he confessed, 'I have too many books.'

Paul turned to admire the shelves. 'There's no such thing.'

'I have some books, old books, about the history of Chinon, that make some mention of the tunnels. I'm afraid I can't lend them, but if you'd like to look . . .'

It was a good excuse to stand, to bring our rather pointless visit to a close, and I loitered patiently to one side as Paul leafed through the offered books with polite interest.

It was too bad, I thought, that Harry hadn't known about Victor Belliveau. My cousin would have coveted this collection of books – old memoirs, bound in leather rubbed bald at the edges; some odd assorted plays and books of poems; an old edition of *Cyrano de Bergerac*; a copy of a British history journal . . .

I blinked, and peered more closely at the shelf. The journal was a recent one, with a revisionist slant. And there upon the cover, bold as brass, I read my cousin's proper name: *Henry Yates Braden, PhD*.

'What's that?' asked Paul, behind my shoulder. I tilted the cover to show him.

Victor Belliveau leaned in to look as well. 'Ah, yes,' he said, 'that talks about the tunnels, too. I had forgotten . . .' He looked a little closer, and his eyebrows lifted. 'Braden . . . isn't that the man you asked me about? The man from your university?'

Paul nodded. 'Harry Braden, yes.'

'Then I'm sorry he didn't come to visit me,' the poet said, his tone sincere. 'I enjoyed his article very much. He has an interesting mind, I think.'

I put the journal down again, frowning faintly. 'I don't suppose that Didier Muret would have read this article as well?'

The poet shrugged. 'I wouldn't think it likely.'

'Because he didn't read much, you mean?'

'Because he knew no English.' The poet's smile was gentle. He walked us to the door and shook our hands. 'You must come back again, if I can be of any help,' he said. But he didn't linger for a goodbye wave. He closed the door behind us as we stepped onto the grass, and I heard the bolt slide home. The sound seemed to echo back from the abandoned barn opposite, where a padlocked door creaked in the slight wind as Paul and I trudged thoughtfully across the pitted, overgrown yard.

'He certainly didn't seem a drunkard,' I remarked.

'Yeah, well,' Paul smiled faintly, 'that doesn't mean anything. My Uncle Aaron soaks up liquor like a sponge, but you'd never know it. He only slurs on days he's stone cold sober.' We'd reached the leaning gate. Paul pulled it open and stood aside to let me pass through first.

I looked at him, curious. 'Do you think he was telling us the truth? About not writing Harry the letter, I mean?'

'Why would he lie?'

Why indeed? I looked back one final time at the

dismal yellow farmhouse, at the crumbling walls and sagging roof. The curtains of the kitchen window twitched, and then lay still, and the only movement left was that of the lone black chicken, stalking haughtily across the yard through the long and waving grass. I felt a faint cold shiver that I recognized as fear, although I didn't know its cause.

'The chapelle, next,' said Paul, and slammed the gate behind us with a clang that sent the chicken scuttling for cover.

Chapter Eighteen

Two plummets dropt for one to sound
the abyss . . .

Paul pulled the jangling ring of keys from the iron lock and swung the great door reverently, as though he hated to disturb the peaceful atmosphere laced with the songs of unseen birds and the whispering of wind in shadowed alcoves. Above the old baptismal font the bay tree rustled gently, while the wild flowers nodded drowsily along the edges of the empty, grass-filled graves. Soft weathered faces watched us from each corner of the architecture, from every ledge and pediment and every vaulted niche, and in the shadowed aisle behind the tall black iron gates the pensive saints gazed through the bars as one stares at a lion in its cage.

It should have been unnerving, having all those eyes upon me, but it wasn't. Oddly enough, it was reassuring. I felt again that rush of pure contentment, of childlike wonder, and the sense of beauty stabbed so deeply that I had to blink back tears.

'Wow,' said Paul. 'It doesn't lose its impact, does it, second time around?'

I shook my head. 'You've been here before?'

'Yeah. It was one of the first places we discovered after the château. Simon read about it in a book, I think, and when he found out Christian had a key . . .' He shrugged, and left it at that, moving past me to the soaring grille of iron.

'And what's the word for this place, then? Secluded?' I guessed. 'Sacred?'

He grinned. 'Sanctuary.'

I recalled my own first reaction to the place, and felt an even closer kinship with this quiet young man I'd only met three days ago.

The iron gates swung open, and we stepped into the cloistered aisle with its peeling frescoes and fragile-looking pillars. 'Sacred,' Paul informed me, as he shuffled the ring of keys, 'is just through here.'

'Just through here' lay beyond the altar, beyond the second iron gate – the gate that Christian hadn't had the key to, yesterday. The tunnelled passage in behind looked every bit as uninviting as I remembered, and even when Paul had successfully sprung the lock I hung back, hesitating, peering with a coward's eyes into the darkness. 'I haven't brought a torch.'

'A flashlight, you mean? That's OK, I've got one.' It was a pocket torch, a small one, hardly any help at all, but he snapped it on and stepped into the passage- way ahead of me. 'I think the main switch is around here somewhere. Yeah, here we go.' A flood of brilliant yellow light dissolved the lurking shadows.

I blinked, surprised. 'Electric light?'

'Sure. This place is kind of a museum, you know. They do take tourists through, during the summer, and I guess they don't want people stumbling around. Here, watch your step.' He guided me over the uneven threshold. The passageway was filled on either side with artifacts and curious equipment, neatly laid out on display. Ancient tools for farming and for wine-making shared equal space with emblems of religion and broken statuary, the whole effect being one of wondrous variety. 'This is where the hermit lived, originally,' said Paul. A few steps on, the passage turned and widened briefly in an arched and empty room of sorts, where more pale statues stared benignly down on us.

My claustrophobia eased a little and I paused to draw a deep and steady breath. 'Is this the sacred part?'

'No. Behind you.'

I turned, and saw what looked like another tunnel running down into the rock, its entrance barred by an ornate black metal barrier, waist-high, anchored in the scarred and worn limestone. Curious, I went as close as the barrier allowed, and peered over it at the flight of crudely chiselled stairs that steeply dropped towards a glowing light. It made me dizzy, looking down. 'Like Jacob's ladder in reverse,' I said to Paul, as he joined me at the railing.

'It's a well,' he said. 'A holy well.'

'But where's the water?'

He smiled. 'Come on. I'll show you.'

I had no great desire to go still deeper underground, but neither did I want to seem a coward. And at least I trusted Paul to bring me safely out again.

Climbing the barrier proved simple enough, no different than climbing a stile back home, but the stairs were a different matter. They were irregular in shape, some only several inches high while others fell two feet or more, and my fingers scrabbled in the dust and chips of rock to find a firmer handhold as I made my slow descent. Paul, who had clearly done this before, went down like a mountain goat, his steps sure and even. I was more ungainly, and brought the dust with me, a great whoofing cloud of it that swirled on even after I had stopped to join Paul on the narrow ledge at the bottom of the stairs.

'This,' he said, 'is the sacred part.' His hushed voice sounded hollow, like the echo round an indoor swimming pool. Intrigued, I braced one hand against the paper-cool stone and leaned forward for a proper look.

The water was there, as he had promised. Clear, holy water, pale turquoise in the glare of an electric light that hung from the stone arch overhead. It was, Paul told me, a Merovingian well, meaning it dated back to the time of the Franks – older, he thought, than Sainte Radegonde herself. The shaft sank deep and straight and true; several metres deep, I would have said, and yet the water was so amazingly clear that I could see the scattering of pebbles at the bottom.

'You can even see the footholds,' Paul said, pointing, 'that the well-diggers used to climb out again, after they'd struck water.' The footholds ran like a makeshift ladder, straight to the bottom of the well – small, even squares the width of one man's boot, gouged in the yielding yellow stone.

I sighed, and the surface of the water shivered. 'Well,' I said, 'at least we know that Harry isn't anywhere down here.'

'A cheerful thought,' Paul smiled. 'But you're right, it'd be pretty hard to hide something in that water. Even a King John coin.' He flipped a tiny half-franc piece into the well to demonstrate, and we watched until it came to rest upon the bottom, clearly visible. 'Here, make a wish,' Paul told me, handing me another coin.

He sounded just like my father, when he said that. For a moment I was five years old again and standing at the rim of the fountain in the courtyard of our house in Italy. But then I caught my own reflection in the water of the well, and the child vanished. I shook my head. 'I don't have anything to wish for.'

'Everyone has something to wish for. Besides, how often do you get a chance to make a wish in holy water?'

'No, honestly, you needn't waste your money . . .'

'Has anyone ever told you you're a terrible cynic?' He grinned and closed his eyes. 'OK, never mind. I'll make a wish for you. There,' he said, and tossed the second coin into the waiting well. It hit the water with a satisfying plunk. End over end my unknown wish tumbled, glittering, and landed close to Paul's one on the smooth and level bottom.

'So what did I wish for?' I asked, curious.

'Bad luck to tell,' he reminded me. Turning, he offered me his hand to help me up the stairs again. 'Right,' he said, 'let's give this place a proper search, and see what we can find.'

We found a treasure trove of slightly dusty artifacts displayed in every crevice of the caves. We found a smaller chamber at the tunnel's end, where someone evidently lived from time to time. 'There's a caretaker in the summer,' Paul informed me, 'on and off. I think she stays up here.' But no-one had been staying here recently. The bed was stripped, the cupboards empty, and dust lay thickly settled on the floor, marked by no sign of footprints save our own. We found a working wine press tucked in one high corner of the largest cave.

What we didn't find, of course, was anything that Harry might have left. There wasn't so much as a chewing-gum wrapper or a shred of tissue dropped in that bright, winding underground maze. I was, by turns, relieved and disappointed. Relieved because I hadn't turned up any evidence that Harry was in trouble, disappointed because I hadn't turned up any evidence that Harry was here at all. There was only that blasted coin.

Paul poked at the donation saucer as we paused before the simple altar on our way back out. 'Is this where you found the King John coin?'

My face flamed with embarrassment, but I didn't bother to deny it. The problem with Paul, I thought, was that he was too damn clever. He had a quiet but persistent way of finding out the truth. 'Yes. I . . . I put in a donation of my own,' I added, as if that made my theft acceptable, but Paul didn't seem to be listening.

'There's got to be an explanation.' That was the physicist talking. He furrowed his brow and stared hard at the plate of jumbled coins. 'There's got to be. We just aren't looking at this from the right angle.'

He was still standing there, thinking, when the faint sound of the noonday bells came drifting up from the town below and broke the peaceful silence of the chapelle. There was nothing more for us to do here, I decided. I tugged at Paul's sleeve. 'Come on, Sherlock, time for lunch.'

'Yeah, OK.' He glanced at his watch. 'I guess I ought to check the laundry, anyway, before Simon gets back. Thierry's probably shrunk everything beyond recognition by now.'

His gloomy fears turned out to be unfounded. From the pristine pile of folded shirts and jeans that met us in the hotel's entrance lobby, it appeared that Thierry had done quite an expert job.

He flashed his quick disarming smile and ran his thumb along a trouser crease. 'I cannot take the credit,' he confessed. 'I gave the clothes to Gabrielle for washing.'

Paul raised his eyebrows. 'Gabrielle?'

'The girl who does reception this week. Me, I am not good at washing things.'

He'd never have to worry about it, I thought, as long as he could aim a smile like that at a member of the opposite sex. It was a difficult smile to resist. I couldn't help but feel a pang of sympathy for Gabrielle – small wonder she was so confused, sometimes. 'You don't play fair,' I said to Thierry.

'*Comment?*'

'She means you take advantage,' Paul explained. 'Is Simon back yet?'

'No, he is still with the Whitakers, I think.' Again the grin. 'It has been quiet here, today.'

Paul turned from the front desk and looked a question at me. 'You sick of my company, yet?'

'Of course not. Why?'

'Feel like having a drink or something? I know I could use one.' Paul glanced back at Thierry. 'The bar is open, isn't it?'

'Of course. You have had a nice time, sightseeing?'

'Very nice.' Paul smiled. 'But don't forget, now, it's a—'

'—secret,' Thierry finished. 'Do not worry, I am good at keeping secrets. If I had a franc for every secret in this hotel,' he said, grinning, 'I would not be needing to work.'

But he condescended to serve us anyway, before vanishing once more into the back rooms. Paul sipped his beer and leaned an elbow on the stack of freshly laundered clothes, which he'd set carefully beside him on his customary window seat. Behind his shoulder I could see the concrete planter outside, with its single pink geranium. It made a pitiful splash of colour against the shadowed backdrop of the busy fountain square.

Paul reached for his cigarettes and offered me the packet. 'Want one?'

'What? Oh, no thanks.' Smiling, I shook my head. 'No, I gave up smoking, years ago. Last night was just a momentary lapse.'

'A momentary lapse that saved my butt,' he pointed out. He lit one for himself and settled back. 'So, what's our next move?'

I gave a faint, defeatist shrug. 'I don't know. I'm rather tired of thinking about Harry, actually.'

'So take a break,' was his advice, 'and drink your drink.'

It was, I decided, sound advice from one so young. I leaned back in my chair and sighed. But I couldn't let it drop entirely. 'What did Martine Muret's ex-husband do for a living, do you know?'

Paul smiled at my obstinacy. 'He was unemployed, I think. Simon actually met the guy once, he might know. Simon didn't like Muret – thought he was a real jerk. He was drunk, you know, when he fell over that railing. That's how he died. And I guess he gave Martine a hell of a rough time when they were married. He didn't hit her or anything, I don't think, but he was . . . well, he was pretty rude. Embarrassing. The kind of guy who likes to play the big shot, you know?'

Like Jim and Garland in reverse, I thought. No wonder Martine hadn't been upset by her ex-husband's death. To her, it must have been almost a deliverance.

Close by, a car door slammed and Paul craned his neck to peer out of the window, beyond my line of vision, towards the hotel's front entrance. 'So much for our quiet drink,' he said, stubbing out his half-smoked cigarette.

'Why? Are they back already?'

'Do you know,' he mused, his dark eyes twinkling, 'I think I'll just slip round to Christian's and give him back that key.'

'Coward,' I teased him. But he just laughed, and winked, and ducked like lightning through the back door as the returning tour party from Fontevraud descended upon the Hotel de France in a blur of sound and motion.

The transatlantic line hummed thick with static, and it seemed an age before my father picked the phone up at his end. It was suppertime in Uruguay, and I'd obviously caught him in mid-meal. His voice at first was hard to understand.

'Mmwamph,' he said, when I apologized for calling at this hour, and 'Barrrumph-ba' was his comment after that. He cleared his throat, and coughed. 'You're still in France, then, are you?'

'Yes.'

'Still on your own?'

'Yes. Actually, that's why I called . . .' I twined the phone cord round my fingers, then in a rush of explanation told him what I'd found.

'The King John coin? You're sure of that?'

I nodded, not caring that he couldn't see the gesture. 'I've got it right here, in my room. And I don't think he'd have left it anywhere unless he meant to leave it, only that doesn't make much sense, does it?' I sighed, plucking at the coverlet of my bed. 'Honestly, Daddy, I don't know what else I can do.'

'Well, it sounds as though you've handled things quite sensibly.'

'I thought I might just ring Aunt Jane—'

'Good Heavens, no!' My father's voice came booming down the line, emphatic. 'No point getting her upset for nothing – and it may well be for nothing, knowing Harry. No, I think you'd better leave it all with me. I've still got friends you know, in Paris. I'll ask some questions, stir around, see whether they can track him down. All right?'

Which meant, I thought, he'd likely make some notes, then forget all about it before tomorrow morning. I smiled. 'All right.'

'Just leave it all with me,' he said again, in charge now, reassuring. 'And Emily?'

'Yes, Daddy?'

'Don't let it worry you too much, either, will you? Comes sailing clean through any crisis, does Harry. No point in losing sleep over him.'

That, at least, seemed sound advice. I repeated it to myself that night as I lay restless underneath the covers of my bed, my dry eyes fixed upon the mottled shadows dancing on my ceiling. *No point in losing sleep*, I thought firmly, but it didn't help.

Close by, the bell tolled one o'clock, a solemn sound above the chuckling fountain. Through the open window swept a sudden breath of cold night air, and the shadows on my ceiling stilled their motion as the street lamps were extinguished. All the shadows, that is, except one.

It might have been the moon, passing high among the clouds outside, that made the dim reflection on my wall, and what I heard I blamed on my imagination, or the wind. 'Follow,' said the shadow, as it slipped across my bed. 'Follow . . .'

A sudden breath of chill air blew my window open wider, and the curtains flapped and fluttered like a wild, tormented ghost. My heart leapt, frightened, to my throat, but I forced it back again. *Fool*, I called myself, as I rose and hugged my blanket round me. *There's nothing there.*

But just to make absolutely certain of that, I leaned across the window sill and looked down at the sleeping square.

The black-and-white cat moved stealthily between the rustling acacias, from shadow into light and back again, carefully avoiding the spray of the glittering fountain. On soundless feet, the cat traversed the empty square and crossed to sniff the planter set beside the hotel door. My gaze followed, and fell and with a startled jolt I saw that I was not the only one awake and watching the cat.

Neil Grantham's hair looked white in moonlight. Ruffled by the night breeze, it was the only thing that moved. His hands lay still upon the railing of the narrow balcony, and beneath the leather jacket his shoulders were immobile, carved of stone. He didn't seem to breathe.

And then his head began to turn and I drew quickly back, away from the window, and the curtains drifted past me on a sigh that was not mine.

Chapter Nineteen

I rose and . . .
Found a still place.

The cat came to me early next morning. How it found me I'll never know; I'd walked some distance from the hotel to the hushed and peaceful Promenade, where the plane trees grew tall and regal by the river's edge. But the black-and-white cat came to me nonetheless, and curled itself wearily into my lap with a wide, indulgent yawn.

He'd had a hard night, from the looks of it.

He looked, in fact, much like I felt: tired and rumpled and out of sorts. I always felt like that when I hadn't slept well. It was an inherited curse, insomnia. My grandad had it, and my father, and they'd kindly passed it on to me, so that from time to time I found myself counting sheep into quadruple digits while I tried to will my aching brain to stop its restless thinking. It didn't happen often any more, but when it did it always brought me to a place like this, a quiet place where I could watch the sunrise. Things seemed less important, somehow, once the sun was up.

Behind me, on the cliffs, the château bell sang seven times – they'd just be starting breakfast service back at the hotel. I ought to be getting back. But not just yet,

I thought. Not yet. I smiled as I gently stroked the sleeping cat, and lifted vague unfocused eyes to gaze along the Promenade.

Row facing row the plane trees stood, ghostly pale and thick with green, mute sentries from an age long past. Beneath the arching canopy of leaves a raked red gravel path invited idle footsteps, like my own, and garden benches beckoned one to pause and watch the world drift by.

From my own bench I could see clear across the Vienne, past the jutting point of the little island to the darkly wooded shore that lay beyond. And in between, cold and still like a sheet of ice, the river breathed a veil of mist that caught and spread the dawning spears of sunlight.

Earlier I'd watched a yellow kayak cleave that mist, dancing the current down towards the bridge. Earlier still, a woman with a dog had passed me by, her step brisk and purposeful. But now there was only me, and the cat, and the ducks chattering noisily along the riverbank.

My mind had begun to drift idly along with the river when the cat suddenly shifted position, claws pricking through my woollen jumper. I winced, and looked to see the cause of its alarm.

I didn't have to look far. Four trees away a little spotted dog, nose fixed to the ground, came trotting round a metal litter bin. It was obvious that the dog hadn't yet taken note of us, and even more obvious that it posed no immediate danger to my bristling cat – this because the dog was attached by a bright red lead to a man standing, slouched, with his back to the river, his face cast half in shadow by the flat morning light.

The gypsy wasn't alone. Another man had stopped beside him on the blood-red path, a tall, long-limbed man with hair so fair it shone in that soft morning light like silver. The gypsy spoke, and gestured, and I saw Neil shake his head, and tossing back some smiling comment he came on towards me.

'Good morning,' he greeted me. 'Mind if I join you?'

There seemed no escaping the man, I thought, despite my best efforts. I shifted to make room for him on the bench and he sat down with a decided thump, angling himself against the armrest so he could look at me. 'You have a thing for cats, I take it? Or are you out to comfort every stray in Chinon?'

'Not every stray. Just this one.'

'Is this your chap from Saturday night, then?' He reached a careful hand to scratch the dirty black-and-white head. The cat, less nervous, subsided into my lap and stared at him through half-closed eyes. 'Well, what do you know.' Neil's own eyes crinkled at the corners. 'He gets about, this one. I think I saw him prowling about last night, as well.' Withdrawing his hand, he stretched his long legs out before him, ankles crossed. 'He seems rather affectionate, for a stray.'

'Yes.' I looked up and past him, to where the gypsy and his dog still loitered. 'What did that man ask you?' I wanted to know.

'He wanted a match, that's all. I didn't have one.'

I set a calming hand upon the deeply purring cat. 'Spoke to you in English, did he?'

'No, French.'

'I thought you didn't speak French.'

He slanted a curious look in my direction. 'I don't, beyond the limits of my Oxford phrasebook,' he said, 'but when a chap comes up to me with an unlit cigarette in his mouth and pantomimes the striking of a match, I've a fair idea what he's wanting.'

'Oh.' My gaze dropped defensively. When I raised my eyes again the path was empty. The gypsy and his dog were nowhere to be seen. I gathered the cat closer and summoned up a cheerful smile to show to Neil. 'I didn't expect to see you up and about this early,' I told him. 'I thought you did your walking in the evenings.'

'Dustmen woke me,' was his excuse. 'Four o'clock in the bloody morning, they come barrelling round the square like it's a parade ground.'

I sympathized. I'd heard them myself, that morning. I'd heard a great many things, actually, from the tiniest rustle of a dead leaf scuttling across the asphalt to the quiet talk and measured footsteps of two gendarmes patrolling on the graveyard shift. Sleeplessness always heightened my senses.

'They wake me every time, those dustmen,' Neil went on. 'Most mornings I just drop off again, but this morning . . .' He shrugged, and fitted his shoulders to the worn back of the bench. 'This is a lovely place, isn't it?'

'Yes, quite lovely.'

'The whole town is, really. I always hate to leave it.'

'Your holiday's almost over, then?' *Blast*, I thought. I could hear the trail of disappointment in my own voice.

'Next week, I think. I'm very nearly back to normal.' He flexed his hand to demonstrate. 'Besides, I'm pushing my luck as it is. I'm not paid a salary to sit around and do nothing.'

'But you've been practising,' I argued in his defence. 'Every day.'

His eyes slid sideways, unconvinced. 'Only for an hour or so.'

'Isn't that long enough?'

'Back home my normal work day lasts six hours, sometimes more. I'm only playing at it, here.'

'Oh. Well, it sounds nice, anyway. I like the sound of a violin.'

He thanked me for the compliment. 'But you'll probably think differently in a few days' time. Even Beethoven loses some of his appeal after the first hundred playings. I'm getting rather bored with him myself, but then I'm only using him for exercise. I know that piece like the back of my hand.'

'You ought to choose something else, then. You're learning something by a new composer, aren't you?'

'I'd never subject the hotel guests to that.' The midnight blue eyes crinkled a second time. 'It's not the nicest piece to listen to, in my opinion – the composer doesn't much like harmony. No, I only listen to the tape of that one, to learn it better, and even then I have to watch my step. The first time I put that tape in Thierry's monster hi-fi I nearly cleared the hotel,' he admitted with a grin. 'Sounded like the whole bloody orchestra was playing in my room, it was that loud. I kept it turned low, after that.'

My mouth curved. 'I'm beginning to think you played the *Salute d'Amour* on purpose on Saturday, so the ghost would break poor Thierry's hi-fi.'

He looked at me with interest. 'I did play it on purpose, actually. But not to upset the ghost.'

I didn't respond to that, but he didn't look away. 'You've just surprised me, Emily Braden. Some people might recognize Bach, or Mozart, but to spot old Elgar takes a certain depth of knowledge.'

'Yes, well,' I glanced down, flushing, 'my mother quite likes classical music. She was always dragging me to concerts. I didn't pay as much attention as I should have, but I do remember what I liked.'

'You've put that in the past tense, I notice. Don't you go to concerts any more?'

I shook my head. 'Terrible, I know, but I never seem to have the time, these days. My mother goes often enough for both of us. Her boyfriend,' I explained, with a dry smile, 'is a conductor.'

'Oh, really? What's his name?'

I told him. 'Do you know him?'

'I know of him, yes. We've never met.' His eyes were mildly curious. 'So then your father—'

'—lives in Uruguay.'

'I see.' He looked away again, but I had the distinct feeling that he *did* see; that he saw rather more than I wanted him to. I tried to steer the conversation back to neutral ground, by asking him which orchestra he played with in Austria – which didn't help much, as I didn't recognize the name.

'That's what everyone says,' he assured me. 'We're not exactly the Vienna Philharmonic, but we've eighty-six members and we hold our own. And speaking of conductors, ours is just this side of brilliant.'

'You like living in Austria, then?'

'Very much.'

'No desire to move back to England?'

He raised his shoulders in an almost Gallic shrug. 'If you had the choice of living in Austria or Birmingham, which would you choose?'

'If I were a violinist?' I smiled. 'I'm not sure. Birmingham has a cracking good orchestra.'

'And if you weren't a violinist?' He asked the question

223

quietly, and slid his serious eyes to mine, and all of a sudden I felt I'd been tossed into deep water, over my head. I found I couldn't answer him, even in jest, and after a long moment he calmly looked away again, towards the river. 'Damned noisy this morning, those ducks,' was his only comment.

The silence stretched. I was just beginning to think I couldn't bear it any longer, that I'd have to invent an excuse and leave before I did something foolish, when the cat, apparently deciding that I'd suffered long enough, woke from its nap and stirred. Arching its back in a reluctant stretch it dropped gracefully from my lap to the gravel path and stalked off without so much as a backward look, melting like a shadow into the grassy riverbank.

I watched it go. 'Time for breakfast, I suppose,' I said. Standing up, I brushed my hands against my legs to clear off the clinging strands of cat hair, suddenly aware of the rattling hum of traffic from the boulevard behind us. It seemed a harsh intrusion, in the scented stillness of the Promenade.

'I'll walk back with you.' Neil rose and stretched as the cat had done, and fell into step beside me.

The red gravel path led us into the modern world, where cars and lorries lumbered noisily up and down the boulevard. All along the far side of the street the shopkeepers were running through their daily ritual of opening up, polishing windows and scrubbing down awnings and sweeping the pavement in front of their stores.

We kept to the river walk. There were plane trees here, too – not as ancient or peaceful as those of the Promenade, but nearly as tall, and the breeze blowing through them was idle and cool. It had blown the mist from the murmuring river that danced past in sharp, sparkling ribbons of light, and the pavement was dappled with shadow and sunlight, both shifting in time with the whispering leaves.

Despite the bustle of the boulevard, no-one seemed to hurry on the river walk. Several people had stopped to lean against the low stone wall and watch the yellow kayak I'd seen earlier come smoothly stroking by on its return trip. Further on a young man struggled up a flight of steps in the sloping river wall, fishing rod in one hand and creel in the other, looking well satisfied. And further on still, not far from the steps where Paul usually sat, a little girl skipped down the cobbled boat launch towards the chattering ducks. They let her come quite near, indeed – so near that the older man lounging some distance behind her stirred in mild alarm. Raising his voice, he called her back a few steps from the swift-flowing water.

Beside me, Neil smiled. 'Just like her mother. She has no proper sense of danger.'

My head jerked round before I remembered that he would know Lucie Valcourt. Lucie could hardly have remembered him from his visits to the house – she wouldn't have been more than four years old herself when her mother died, and three more years had passed since then. But she obviously knew Neil now, and knew him well. When she came dancing back happily up the ramp to say hello, she greeted me in singing French but spoke to Neil in clear, if halting, English. 'Good morning, Monsieur Neil,' she said. 'I feed the dukes.'

'Ducks, love. And yes, I see that. No school today?'

The dark curls swung from side to side, emphatically. 'No. It is Wednesday.'

'Wednesday already?' He raised his eyebrows. 'You

know in England, children go to school on Wednesday.'

Lucie wrinkled her nose at the thought. It was an expression, I decided, that must have crossed many a French face down through the ages – the civilized person pondering the ways of the barbarian. Even her comment, that she would not like to live in England, was hardly without precedent.

François turned his dry, indulgent gaze on Neil. 'But in England, a man like me would have some rest,' he said, also in English. 'Instead this little one, she takes me every Wednesday for a walk, like a dog.'

'I feed the d . . . ducks,' she chimed in, careful with the new pronunciation. She thought of something, looked at me. 'Mademoiselle, you would like also to feed the ducks? I have much bread.'

If anybody else had asked me that, I'd have said no, but then I'd never learned the knack of saying no to children. Neil stayed behind with François, and Lucie lapsed into French again as she led me down the broad boat launch, her small feet bouncing on the cobblestones. 'Monsieur Neil is a friend of yours, Mademoiselle?' she asked, and then without giving me a chance to answer, 'He was a friend of my mother's, too. He lives in Austria. Last summer I went there with Aunt Martine, and he came to visit us. He speaks German,' she informed me, 'but he can't speak French. I heard him try to, once, with Aunt Martine, and he got all his words mixed up. It was funny. Do you like him?'

'Yes, I do. He's a very nice man.'

'Is he your boyfriend?'

'No.'

'Oh.' She bounced a little higher. 'He is very pretty, I think. Prettier than my papa.' With the candid eyes of childhood she looked back at Neil who stood, arms folded, talking now to François. 'But he is not perfect.'

I smiled. 'No?' If Neil Grantham had a flaw, I certainly hadn't been able to find it.

'No.' Lucie shook her head. 'He has a space, a little space, between his teeth, right here.' She bared her own front teeth and pointed to the spot. 'He says it is to whistle with.'

'Ah.' Fortunately, I was spared the need for further comment. We had come nearly to the bottom of the ramp now, and Lucie tugged at my sleeve, her voice dropping to a solemn whisper. 'François says it is not good to scare the ducks.'

I took the hunk of bread she gave me and began to throw out crumbs in my best non-threatening manner. It was rather like dropping a chip in Trafalgar Square. From everywhere, it seemed, the ducks came flapping. A small Armada of them massed in the shallows of the river while others tumbled over one another on the cobblestones, adding their full-throated pleas to the general mayhem. They fluttered, they splashed, they begged and demanded and, like the pigeons of Trafalgar Square, they didn't show the slightest fear of people. How had Neil put it, exactly? No proper sense of danger . . .

'. . . and this one, this is Jacques,' said Lucie, pointing out her favourite birds among the bunch, 'and that one with the funny legs I call Ar-ree.'

The bird in question did have funny legs, quite long and skinny, together with a rumpled and dishevelled look that reminded me instantly of my cousin. Something unseen broke the surface of the water beside us and sent a spreading wash of ripples out, unstoppable and oddly sinister.

The gawky duck stared at me and I tossed a crumb towards it. 'Why Ar-ree?' I asked, casually.

'It's an English name,' she told me, with a proud upward glance. 'My Uncle Didier, he has an English friend . . . well, he's dead now, of course, but his friend is called Ar-ree. Last week he came to feed the ducks with me, and he said this duck looked just like him.'

I tore the bread between my fingers, with a jerking motion. 'Harry?' I checked. 'Was his name Harry, Lucie?'

'Yes, Ar-ree. It's such a funny name. Are many people in England called this?'

'Quite a few.' I frowned, thinking hard. Her Uncle Didier, she'd said. I put the names together in my mind – Didier Muret and Harry. Didier and Harry, *here*. 'Was it last Wednesday that he came to feed the ducks with you?'

She nodded. 'François had a headache last week, so he couldn't walk with me. But after lunch my Uncle Didier said he could take me out, instead. He's dead now,' she said again, quite matter-of-fact. 'He's not as nice as François. François always lets me stay here a long time, and then we have an ice cream. But Uncle Didier had his friend to talk to last week, and he didn't let me give the ducks all my bread. He was in a hurry, he said.'

A duck flapped against my foot and I took an absent step sideways, flinging down another scattering of crumbs. My bread was very nearly finished. 'Your uncle's friend, did he look anything like me?'

'Yes, very English,' she said, squinting up at me to check. 'But his nose was not so straight.'

'I see. What else do you remember about him?'

'He was very funny, and he likes to feed the ducks, like me. *And* he can make his ears wiggle.' Which obviously raised him above the level of the common man, in her opinion. I looked down at the scruffy little duck with the long ungainly legs, and tossed him my last breadcrumb.

He really did remind me of my cousin, that duck. And if Lucie had her story right, then Harry had been here, in Chinon . . . Harry had been *here*.

I wasn't given time to ponder this new piece of information. Lucie grabbed me by the hand and pulled me back up the ramp to where François and Neil waited, chatting like old friends. Neil laughed at something François said, and turned to look at me. 'Still standing, are you, after that attack? We couldn't see the two of you for feathers, from up here.'

Lucie looked up at him, her brown eyes curious. 'Monsieur Neil,' she asked, in careful English, 'do your ears move?'

'I beg your pardon?'

The tone of his voice penetrated my troubled fog of thought, and I smiled in spite of myself. 'I think she's asking if you can wiggle your ears.'

'Oh. Of course I can.' He crouched to Lucie's level, and demonstrated. I leaned against the low wall, next to François. I wanted to ask him about Didier Muret, but I couldn't summon up the courage, so I tried to slide into the questions sideways.

'She is,' I said in French, 'a lovely child.'

'Yes. I'm very fond of Lucie.'

'She talked to me a bit about her uncle. She seems to be taking his death well, for one so young.'

I felt the brush of his eyes and he lifted his shoulders. 'Didier Muret,' he told me, cryptically, 'was not the sort

229

of man one mourns. And anyway, she didn't know him well.'

'Was he a historian?' I kept the question lightly curious. For after all, I thought, we only had Victor Belliveau's word . . .

'A historian?' He turned that time, to look at me directly. 'No, Mademoiselle, he was a clerk – a lawyer's clerk – when he worked at all.'

'Oh. I must have got it wrong, then.' The doubting flooded back, and what had seemed so certain moments earlier now hovered in the realm of the improbable. Why would an unemployed lawyer's clerk, who reportedly read no English, be interested in a British article on Isabelle of Angoulême, I wondered? It simply made no sense.

François looked back at Neil and Lucie, his weary eyes softening. 'She is just like her father sometimes, very charming. And she doesn't take no for an answer.'

The child was giggling at the moment, a delighted and infectious sound. 'Again,' she commanded, and Neil sighed in mock despair.

'They'll fall off, you know, and then you'll be sorry.'

But he wiggled his ears again, anyway, and was rewarded with another fit of giggles from his appreciative audience. It was a difficult sound to resist. So it was odd that François's smile faded, the lines on his face deepening as though something had pained him.

Concerned, I touched his arm. 'Are you all right?'

I saw the shiver, hastily suppressed, and fancied for a moment that his gaze seemed faintly questing on my face, but when he spoke he looked himself again.

'Yes, I am fine, Mademoiselle. I am an old man, that is all. Sometimes I see the ghosts.'

Chapter Twenty

Thro' her this matter might be sifted
clean.

I didn't go straight back to the hotel. Instead I turned along a narrow street and went in search of the smaller square where Martine Muret kept her gallery.

It wasn't difficult to find. A few acacias grew here as well, draped over cobbled stone, well pitted and grown dark with age. The sun shone warmly, cheerfully, upon the clustering of leaning shops and houses, reflected in the gleaming glass front of the little gallery.

Even without Christian's paintings hanging in the window, I believe I would have known the place belonged to Martine. It looked like her, somehow – so smart and neat and elegant, with everything in perfect order. But Christian's oils clinched the matter. They stood out from the other paintings easily, the bolder brush strokes and exquisite play of light and shadow lending them a warm, romantic feel. Stepping closer, I peered with interest at the softly swirled self-portrait Paul had mentioned. Christian, I thought, had a master's touch. He'd shown himself no quarter, tracing every jutting outline of his sharply contoured face, the pale eyes gently sombre and the golden hair uncombed.

He'd breathed similar life into his landscapes. I saw

the walls of Château Chinon shiver under storm clouds, and the idle spreading peace of fields flecked liberally with grazing cows, but my favourite of his paintings was the one that showed the river.

He had painted it at sunset, not far from the steps where Paul often sat. The steps themselves were plainly there, beneath the looming silhouette of Rabelais, and on the placid water three ducks drifted round a weathered punt, moored close against the sloping wall, while further off the gleaming arches of the bridge stretched like a golden thread from shore to shore. The only thing missing from that picture, I thought, was Paul himself, sitting halfway down the steps with his back to the traffic above, reading *Ulysses* and smoking an illicit cigarette.

It wasn't often that a painting so transported me, and when Martine herself came out onto the doorstep to greet me, she had to speak twice before I heard her.

'It is a lovely painting, that one, is it not?' She smiled, understanding.

'Very lovely.' I bit my lip. 'Is it very expensive?'

'Not so expensive as his others. It is a smaller canvas, and there are no cows in it. Tourists,' she informed me, 'like the cows, and so the cows have higher prices than the river. But if you like, I have a price list.'

I came inside and waited while she went to fetch the list. The gallery's interior was bright and white and spotless, meant to show off every sculpture, sketch and painting to advantage. Martine had a clever eye for art, I thought. I didn't see a single work that I would not have wanted to own myself. Still, I fancied most of it was well outside my price range, and when Martine finally found the list and ran her finger down it, I braced myself for the inevitable. Not that it mattered, I consoled myself. I hadn't come to buy a painting, anyway. I'd only come to ask Martine some subtle questions about her ex-husband, Didier Muret.

'Painting number 88,' she said at last. 'Yes, here it is.' The sum she quoted was almost twice what I earned in a month.

I heard a quiet footstep on the polished floor behind me. 'Perhaps Christian will reduce his prices, for a friend.' A man's voice, but the accent was distinctly French, not German. I hadn't seen Armand Valcourt come in. Martine had, though; she didn't bat an eyelid as she shook her head, a smile softening her sigh.

'Christian,' she said, 'would give them all away, I think, these paintings. He has too generous a nature. Always I must watch him and remind him painters, too, must eat.'

I glanced round at Armand, and said good morning. 'I saw your daughter earlier, by the river.'

'Yes.' He smiled. 'This is her morning with François. The ducks, I think, and then the ice cream . . . such a simple way to happiness. She likes her Wednesdays, my Lucie.'

His eyes were quite unhurried as they roamed the quiet gallery, and he didn't seem in any rush to move. So much, I thought, for my chance of a private chat with Martine. I tried to hide my disappointment by asking him how old his daughter was, exactly.

'Lucie? She has nearly seven years.'

'And already she has genius,' said her slightly biased aunt. 'She can tell you every step of how the wine is made, that little one.'

'She is a Valcourt,' Armand said, as if that explained everything. 'It will be hers one day, the *Clos des*

233

Cloches, and so I pass traditions down, as I learned from my father.'

Martine smiled. 'But she is half her mother's child, remember. She likes the vine but also likes the art. Perhaps one day she will begin the home for artists that Brigitte so often talked about.'

'God help us.' Armand shuddered. 'The artist by himself, he can be interesting. A few of them at dinner, when they are not fighting, that also can be interesting. But a house of artists,' his eyes rolled heavenward at the thought. 'They would drive me mad.'

'You will forgive my brother-in-law,' Martine said, her dark eyes teasing. 'He likes only the art on his wine labels.'

Armand looked offended. 'That is not true. I like this painting very much.' He nodded at a watercolour hung behind the cash register, a sweeping vista of a vineyard with a mellow-walled château nestled in the distance. 'This shows great talent.'

'This shows grapes.' Martine's voice was dry. 'But no matter. I'm sorry, Armand, was there something that you needed?'

'No, not really.'

'Oh.' Surprise flashed momentarily across her lovely, fragile face, from which I gathered that Armand Valcourt didn't often visit the gallery without a reason.

'No, I was just passing, and I thought I would come and see what you have done. Lucie says there are sculptures, somewhere, that are new.'

Martine considered; shook her head. 'Not new ones, no. I do not think . . .'

'Ah, well. You know Lucie, she sometimes gets her story wrong.' He didn't seem concerned. Hands in his pockets, he leaned closer to me, his breath feathering my neck as he studied a smaller pen-and-ink drawing on the counter. 'And this is also nice, Martine. It is by Christian, yes?'

She looked, and nodded. 'Yes.'

'It looks like Victor's place.' He reached to pick the drawing up, his arm brushing casually against my shoulder. 'Yes, so it is. I wonder sometimes what Victor does with himself, these days. Do you ever hear from him?'

Martine shook her head. 'Christian sees him, now and then. They have a drink and talk.' She smiled at me, in vague apology. 'This is a friend of ours we speak of, an old friend.'

Victor Belliveau, I nearly said. Of course, they all would know each other from the days when Brigitte Valcourt had held her magnificent parties up at the *Clos des Cloches*. A poet would have been included on the guest list, I decided, alongside musical Neil and clever Christian. I longed to ask Martine about those parties, just as I longed to ask her if her former husband ever talked of history, or of Englishmen named Harry. But even as I tried to summon up the nerve, a telephone rang shrilly in the gallery's back room, and Martine excused herself to answer it, her heels clicking on the hard tile floor as she walked away.

Armand shifted at my shoulder, looking down at me. After a moment's silence, he cleared his throat and spoke. 'I have a confession.'

'Oh, yes?' I glanced up.

'I have not much interest in art. And sculpture bores me.' He moved around to lean against the counter, facing me, and raised one hand in an automatic gesture before remembering he shouldn't smoke here. The hand went back inside his pocket. 'When I said that I was

235

passing, that was true. But I only stopped because I saw you here.' He grinned. 'It is no easy matter, in a town this size, to find someone.'

Harry always said I had a talent for deducing the obvious, and I displayed it now. 'You were looking for me?'

He shrugged. 'I thought, if you had not made plans already, you might let me buy you lunch.'

'Lunch.' I repeated the word rather stupidly, and he brought his smiling eyes back to mine.

'Yes. Most days my lunch hours are reserved for Lucie. My work, it keeps me very busy, so I try to keep this hour for her, our private time. You understand?' Convinced I did, he carried on. 'But on Wednesdays, François takes Lucie for half the day, and they eat lunch together, so I am left with no-one.'

No-one? On the contrary, I thought, the women must be queueing up.

'You don't believe me?' His eyes were warm behind the coal-black lashes. 'It is true. I am a rich man, Mademoiselle, but the price one pays for influence is isolation.'

It was a blatant attempt to play upon my sympathies, and while it didn't work, I must confess I couldn't see the harm in having lunch. Besides, I thought, Armand Valcourt had also known Didier Muret. Perhaps I could ask him the questions I had meant to ask Martine.

'All right, then,' I said, on impulse, 'I'd be happy to have lunch with you.'

'Good.' He flashed a smile briefly, raised his eyes, then dropped them to his watch. 'Good, then I shall pick you up at your hotel at noon, if you like?'

My own watch read nine forty-five. 'All right.'

'Good,' he said again, pushing away from the

counter. 'In that case I will leave you for the moment, to enjoy the paintings. I have business still to do before we eat. You will excuse me?' His smile was very charming, but it wasn't serious. It didn't mean anything.

He showed the same smile to the rumpled young man who bumped shoulders with him in the doorway. 'Morning,' Simon said cheerfully, as Armand slipped past him into the shaded street. Whistling an aimless, happy tune, Simon stepped into the gallery and stopped short at the sight of me. '*There* you are!' From his tone, one would have thought I was some errant schoolgirl, late for lessons. 'Paul's been looking everywhere for you, you know. You missed breakfast.'

'Yes, well—'

'He's back at the hotel now, waiting for you to turn up.'

Martine emerged from the back room, having dealt with her telephone caller. Her dark eyes, dancing, travelled from Simon's face to mine. 'You are much in demand, I think, this morning. All these men come looking for you.'

Simon, bless his heart, said: 'I'm looking for Christian, actually. Thought you might know where he is.'

She arched a curious eyebrow. 'Christian?'

'Yeah. I wanted to borrow . . . something.'

'If he is not at home . . .'

'He isn't.'

'Then you might try in the next street,' she advised him, 'around this corner. He talked last night about making a drawing there.'

Simon, to my surprise, showed no desire to hang about chatting to Martine. Thanking her, he turned to me. 'You should probably come with me,' he decided, 'so we don't lose you again.'

There was little point in staying, I thought glumly, as heavy footsteps sounded on the front step and an elderly couple entered the gallery, calling out a greeting to Martine. She saw us graciously to the door, her eyes faintly puzzled as they met mine over our handshake. 'Was there something else, Mademoiselle, that you were wanting to ask?'

'No.' The lie fell heavy as a lump of lead.

'It's only that . . .' She stopped, and shook her head, and the bemused expression cleared. 'No matter, it is nothing. Enjoy your day, the both of you.'

The day, I found, had swiftly changed its character. The sun now hung, suppressed, behind a screen of dull grey cloud, and the air smelled faintly of motor oil and coming rain.

Simon took the lead and I followed him, head down and deep in thought. So deep in thought, in fact, that at the next corner I nearly ploughed straight into Christian Rand without seeing him. Not that it would have mattered to Christian – he probably wouldn't have noticed. The young artist was lost in contemplation of a different kind, staring with half-seeing eyes at the bakery across the road.

Neil Grantham was something of a recurring theme this morning. He was standing next to Christian now, head back and hands on hips, his calm gaze focused on the same building. I looked, saw nothing too remarkable, and offered my apologies to Christian for so nearly tripping over him.

At first I thought he hadn't heard, but then the roughly cropped blond head dipped forward slightly, in a silent nod of acknowledgement.

'Working, eh?' asked Simon, and again the artist nodded, not moving his eyes.

'I must tear down this building,' he said, slowly. 'It spoils my composition. But how . . . how . . . ?'

I shot Neil a quizzical glance.

'He doesn't mean it,' he assured me. 'He does it all in his head, you see – pulls things down, or lumps them closer together, to make a better picture. Artists can do that sort of thing.'

'Oh.' I hadn't really taken Christian literally, if only because knocking down a building required a physical energy that seemed quite beyond him, somehow – but it always helped to have a proper explanation.

Neil smiled, understanding. 'I only know because my brother paints, and he tears things down all the time. He's very much like Christian, actually, my brother is, though his paintings aren't nearly as good.'

'You've a talented family, then.'

He shrugged. 'It comes from my mother, I suppose. She used to sketch, and teach piano.'

'So what did your father do?' Simon asked drily. 'What was he, a writer? Actor? Opera singer?'

'He worked for British Rail.' The boyish grin was like a flash of light.

I looked away and checked my watch again. 'I'd best find Paul,' I said. 'Excuse me.'

I left the three men standing like a mismatched group of statuary in the middle of the street, with Simon chattering on to Christian about borrowing a shovel and bucket. Rather like a child going to play at the seashore, I thought with a smile. Well, perhaps he'd find his treasure, after all. No harm in trying.

The hotel bar was closed until the lunch hour, but I found Paul sitting in there anyway, reading in the semi-darkness. He put *Ulysses* down when I came in, and stretched, his expression relieved. 'Well, it's about time. I was starting to get worried.'

'Sorry.' I sat down, stretching out my own weary legs. 'I went out rather early, for a walk along the river.' I didn't mention meeting the cat, or Neil – for some reason, that part of my morning seemed private and not for sharing. But I did tell Paul about Lucie Valcourt, and how we'd fed the ducks together earlier, and what she'd said about her uncle's English friend.

'Wow,' he said. Leaning back, he absently rumpled his hair with one hand. 'So you think Muret might have been the guy who was supposed to meet your cousin here in Chinon?'

'It certainly sounds like it, don't you think? I mean, he could have read the journal article at Victor Belliveau's house. They knew each other.'

'Only everybody so far says he didn't know English.'

'I know.' I frowned. 'And I haven't figured out yet why he would be interested at all in what my cousin wrote about. There are so many questions. I was going to ask Martine about it, actually. I went round to the gallery this morning.' I smiled. 'But it was rather too crowded to talk properly, and I'm not sure I would have had the nerve to ask anything, anyway. I mean, it isn't done, is it? Not when you hardly know a person, and it's her ex-husband you're asking about, and he's only been dead a week. Still,' I told him, brightening, 'I'm having lunch with Armand Valcourt, and he might be able to—'

'I beg your pardon?' Paul cut in, with an incredulous smile. 'You're what?'

'Having lunch with Armand Valcourt,' I repeated.

'And you can wipe that smug look off your face, Paul Lazarus, because I really don't—'

'OK, OK.' Paul lifted both hands in self-defence. 'And it's not a smug look, I'm just jealous, that's all.'

Jealous? Heavens, I thought, he surely didn't think of me that way, did he? 'Paul—'

'Hardly seems fair, you eating lunch with a rich guy while I'm stuck with cheese-on-a-bun and Simon.' He grinned at me. 'Where's he taking you?'

'I haven't the faintest idea.'

'Somewhere disgustingly expensive, I'll bet. There are a couple of gourmet restaurants down the rue Voltaire, the kind of restaurants where they have six forks, you know the type. What time are you meeting him?'

'At noon.' I turned my wrist to read my watch. 'Oh, Lord, it's just gone eleven now, and I haven't even showered.'

'Go on then, I'll cover for you.' He leaned back in his seat and reached for the tattered paperback. 'Just remember your mission, Dr Watson.'

'And that is?'

'Get the man drunk and ask him about Didier Muret.'

'Right.' I smiled, and turned to leave. 'Let's hope he tells me something useful, then.'

'Let's hope he doesn't. I, for one, would feel a whole lot happier knowing there was no connection between Martine's husband and your cousin.'

He didn't need to tell me why. My own mind had already gone this route a few hours earlier, and reached the same unsettling impasse: if my suspicions were correct, then Harry had been here in Chinon last Wednesday, feeding ducks with Lucie and chumming with her uncle Didier. And by Thursday morning, Didier Muret was dead.

Chapter Twenty-One

*. . . call'd mine
host
To council, plied him with his richest
wines,*

He didn't choose a gourmet restaurant, after all, and I only had to muddle through three forks, a simple feat recalled with ease from my days of eating at Embassy dinners. Except for the forks, my lunch with Armand Valcourt bore no resemblance to those plodding Embassy events.

For one thing, the surroundings were more comfortable. The restaurant's dining-room was rustic, whitewashed country French, its deep-silled windows stuffed with flowers blooming pink and red in the slanting midday sunlight. Pine tables, artfully distressed in keeping with the country theme, were set at discreet intervals around the room, and the russet tile floor gleamed warmly mellow, spotless, at our feet.

They'd seated us beside the fireplace. Not yet in use, it too was filled with flowers, shell-pink roses mixed with ferns and feathered pale chrysanthemums. The smell of roses, delicate, seductive, clung to every breath I took. It swirled around the scent of wine, the whiff of garlic, and the tender, tempting fragrance of the shellfish jumbled on my plate.

Exquisite food, a charming ambience, and the close,

attentive company of a handsome man who, if not exactly an aristocrat, was clearly near the top rung of the social ladder, as evidenced by the quietly respectful service we'd received. It was a shade surreal, the whole affair, which was perhaps why I felt so terribly relaxed. That, or the fact that Armand had twice refilled my wine glass.

He was holding out the bottle now, dividing the remaining wine between our empty glasses as he finished off an anecdote about his daughter and her bicycle.

'She looks like you, you know,' I told him. 'Not feature for feature, but the smile is the same.' We were speaking English, mainly I think because it gave us the illusion of privacy, encircled as we were by three tables of French-speaking patrons.

'Thank you,' he said, and looked at me. 'You have no children?'

'No.'

He didn't push it, didn't pry. 'They are like nothing else, children. Nothing can prepare you for the feelings they create. You would do anything.' He pried a mussel from its shell and chewed it thoughtfully. 'I was not sure, myself, that I wanted a child, but when Lucie was born . . .' He set his fork down with a shrug. 'Everything was changed.'

'It must be difficult, though, raising her alone.'

'Not quite alone.' He smiled, a smile that forgave my ignorance of the privileged world he lived in. 'There was a nurse, in the beginning, to take care of her. Then, when Brigitte died, Martine came back to live with us. And of course, there is always François.'

'He's been with you a long time, has he, François?'

'A long time, yes. His parents worked for my

grandparents, and François himself was born the same year as my father – 1930.' He caught himself and winked at me. 'Don't tell him I told you this. He likes to be most secretive about his age. My wife said always François was like those men in films, you understand, the valet faithful to the family who counts their needs ahead of his.'

I told him I could understand her point. 'He looks the perfect butler, and he does seem rather loyal.'

'Perhaps. But he is more like family, François, and he stays because the vineyard is his home as much as mine. He does not serve without the questions, like the valet of the films, and if he serves at all it is because he likes the person he is serving.'

'He must like you, then.'

Armand smiled above his wine glass. 'I try his patience, sometimes, but this is natural for people who have passed a life together. Lucie he adores.'

I remembered the way François had watched his young charge by the ducks that morning, how his weary eyes had softened on her face. But even as I thought of that another image rose to take its place – of François staring, startled, at the laughing little girl. Seeing ghosts, he'd told me. For a moment I debated asking Armand if Lucie looked very like her mother, but then decided it might be easier to ask him about Didier. If I could only find some plausible excuse, some way of leading him round to the subject . . .

Toying with my glass, I tried the indirect approach. 'You said Martine came back to live with you when . . . when you were widowed. Where did she live before that? Here in Chinon?'

'With her husband, yes. You know that he is dead?' The dark gaze flicked me, moved away. He shrugged.

'One should not be speaking ill of the dead, I know, but he was not a pleasant man, her husband. Already when she came to help with Lucie there were problems with the marriage.'

I nodded, pleased that my tactic had worked. 'Yes, I'd heard they were divorced.'

'Annulled. There is a difference, to the Church.' The wine swirled like liquid gold in his glass as he lifted it and smiled faintly. 'If you believe in that sort of thing.'

'And you don't, I take it?'

'Me? No, I believe in the things that I can touch – my land, my family, old traditions and good wine. And you?'

I had to admit I hadn't the faintest idea. 'I'm a sceptic, I'm afraid.'

'You have no religion?'

'No.'

'People, then. You must believe in people.'

'People aren't permanent,' I answered drily, and he raised his eyebrows in surprise, a slow smile forming at the corners of his mouth.

'You are indeed a sceptic, as you say. Tell me, did you always think this? As a child?'

'Good heavens, no.' I grinned. 'I was the most believing child that ever lived. I wished on stars and everything.'

'So what has happened?'

'Life.' I gave the answer with a shrug. My last mussel had grown cold in its shell, and I pushed it away with my fork. How had we got on to this subject from Didier, I wondered? The conversation wanted steering back to more productive ground. 'And Martine's husband? What did he believe in?'

'Money,' came the answer, then he tempered his

quick judgement with an even-minded shrug. 'That is not fair, perhaps, because I do not know what it is like to be coming from nothing, as Didier did. He had, I think, an ugly childhood. Martine had money, so he married her.'

I found it rather difficult to imagine any man marrying Martine Muret simply for her money, but Armand assured me this was so. 'It is the thinking of most people, of Martine herself. But then,' he admitted, 'most people, they think this is also why I married my wife.'

'You?' I stared, surprised. 'But you're . . .'

'Rich? Yes, now, but when I married things were not so well for the *Clos des Cloches*. I managed badly in the early years, the harvests were not good, and everybody knew this. I'm not surprised that people think I chose Brigitte for money.'

'And did you?' It was too late to withdraw the question, however much I kicked myself for asking it. Already Armand was leaning back, head tilted, considering his answer.

'In part.' He smiled without apology. 'This was no burning passion, between Brigitte and myself. It was more business, an exchange. She wanted a nice house, where she could play the hostess, hold her parties. And me, I wanted a beautiful wife of good family. That she had money was one more attraction. At that moment, we suited one another, but later . . . I was sorry for her death, but I did not suffer with it.' His smile softened. 'Do I shock you? I should keep to the politics in conversation, or you will not come to lunch with me again.'

But he didn't keep to politics. Instead he asked about my family and my childhood, so I favoured him with a few of the better anecdotes I'd gathered growing up a Braden. I finished with the one about the day Harry tried to burn me at the stake. We'd been playing in the garden – Joan of Arc, as I recall – with me strapped to the rose trellis for an added touch of authenticity. The blaze had been spectacular, and for a few long moments, while Harry was off looking for my father's garden hosepipe, I had felt uncomfortably close to poor St Joan.

Most people laughed when I told them that story, but Armand looked rather shocked. 'He is alive still, this cousin of yours? Your father did not kill him?'

'No, he survived. He lectures in history, on and off, in London.'

'I see.' He smiled then, and leaning back he felt for his cigarettes. 'Then I am glad you did not bring him with you. The history of my family, that is one thing, but the wars, the kings and queens . . .' His shrug dismissed such trivialities. 'I find them always boring.'

Here was my opportunity, I thought, to swing the conversation round again. 'Your brother-in-law was quite the historian, though, from what I hear.'

'Didier?' The cigarette lighter clicked shut. Leaning back, Armand narrowed his eyes as the smoke curled upwards. 'A historian? Who has told you this?'

'I don't remember,' I hedged, keeping my voice light. 'Someone at the hotel, I imagine. I thought they said he had a love of history.'

He lifted the cigarette and inhaled smoothly, but I saw the line of his jaw tighten. 'You have been misinformed, I think. My brother-in-law loved nothing but himself. And money. Always money.' His voice sounded hard. Didier Muret, I was learning, had that effect on people. 'He couldn't keep a job, because he stole. Brigitte, my wife, she once found him work with her own lawyer, for Martine's sake, but it was no good.

247

The money went missing there, too. Martine left him after that. She let him stay in the house, but he got no more money from her.'

Well done, Martine, I thought. 'Actually,' I went on, trying to make the white lie sound convincing, 'I think it was young Simon who told me your brother-in-law liked history. They'd met each other once, I think.'

'Simon?' Armand looked sceptical. 'The boy with the long hair, who came to tour my vineyard? But he does not speak French, not like his brother. And Didier, he spoke no English. They might have met, but they could not have talked to one another.'

'I must have got it wrong, then,' I said brightly. Three people had now told me the same story, and three people, I thought, couldn't be mistaken. Which meant that Didier Muret could not have read my cousin's article, would not have had a reason to contact him, had probably never met him. What had Armand said that morning, about his daughter? *Lucie, she sometimes gets her story wrong*. And a duck named 'Ar-ree' was hardly the best evidence, I reminded myself with a wry smile. 'It must have been some other Didier he was talking about. Simon's less than clear in conversation, sometimes.'

Not that I was very much better. I really *must* go easy on the wine while trying to investigate, I thought. It took all my effort, as we left the restaurant, just to walk a straight line without tripping over cobblestones.

I don't think Armand noticed. He strolled easily beside me, along the half-deserted rue Voltaire. I smiled when I saw he walked with one hand in his pocket, his cigarette held loosely in the other. Most French men walked like that. It was a sort of national identity badge, a wholly unconscious habit they acquired at some early age and carried till they died. In my younger days in Paris I'd often passed a lazy hour at the Luxembourg gardens, spotting the *français* among the tourists by the way they walked.

'I have enjoyed this,' Armand said, when we came out into the fountain square. 'I enjoy your company. We should have dinner one night before you leave.'

It was a non-committal sort of invitation, and I responded in kind. 'I'd like that.'

The light goodbye kiss caught me slightly off guard, I must admit. Things naturally progressed this way, of course, among the French: from smiles and nods to handshakes to *la bise*, the friendly double kiss, but they didn't usually progress this quickly. Armand Valcourt, I thought, worked fast.

He was only a flirt, and a harmless one, and I was decidedly single, but still I felt a twist of guilty conscience. I cast a quick glance upwards at the hotel, along the row of empty balconies, to where the tall and graceful windows of Neil's room reflected back the calmly drifting clouds. I thought I saw a flash of something pale behind the glass, but I might have imagined the movement.

I must have imagined it. The château bell was chiming three o'clock when I entered the hotel lobby – it was Neil's normal practice time, but there was no violin this afternoon. There was only Thierry, looking very bored behind the desk. No, he told me, nobody was back yet. There was only him, and the telephone, and . . . He broke off, brightening. 'You would like a drink, Mademoiselle? In the bar?'

I shook my head. 'The last thing I need, Thierry, is a drink. I'm floating as it is. No, I think I'll go upstairs and have a nap.'

He rolled his eyes. 'The naps,' he said, 'are for old women, and for children.'

He was quite wrong, I thought later, buried deep beneath my freshly-ironed sheets and soft wool blanket. An afternoon nap was a glorious indulgence, tucked into the middle of a long and active day, with rich food and fine wine fuzzing round the edges of one's drifting mind. I sighed and snuggled deeper.

Few sounds rose to drown the murmur of the fountain underneath my open window. Now and then a car passed by, or someone shouted to a friend across the square. Nearby a dog barked sharply and was silenced by a quick command. But nothing else disturbed the peace, the perfect peace that filled my shadowed room. The fountain's voice grew louder still, subtly altering pitch, becoming low and deep and lulling like the darkly flowing river to the south.

It was so close, that sound . . . so close . . .

It was beside me. I hardly ever dreamed, not any more, so I was rather surprised to find myself moving in that strange, disjointed way that dreamers do, not in my room but down along the river, where the plane trees wept like mourners in the wind beneath a grey, uncertain sky. I moved with no real purpose, no true course. One moment I was standing on the bridge, and then there was no bridge, and I was sitting on the riverbank, my arms hugged tightly round my upraised knees. Across the calm water I could see my cousin Harry, pacing back and forth along the tree-lined shore of the little island. He wanted to cross, but without the bridge it was impossible.

'No point in worrying about Harry,' my father said beside me. Smiling, he reached into his pocket and handed me a King John coin. 'Here, make a wish.'

I took the coin from Daddy's hand, without thinking, and tossed it in the water. It changed, too, as it fell, no longer silver but a diamond, and where it sank the river ran pure red, like blood.

Alarmed, I looked up at the place where I'd seen Harry, but he wasn't there. The only person standing on the far shore was a lean, tall man with pale blond hair, his eyes fixed sadly on my face. He was trying to tell me something – I could see his lips moving, but the wind stole his voice, and all that reached me was a single word: 'Trust . . .'

A cold shadow fell across the grass beside me, and I looked up to meet the gentle gaze of the old man François. 'Seeing ghosts?' he asked me. Then, incredibly, he raised a violin to his shoulder and began to play Beethoven.

I opened my eyes.

One floor below, Neil stopped his practising a moment, tuned a string, began again. I listened, staring at the ceiling. Ordinarily, I found Beethoven soothing, just the thing to clear my mind of stray and troubling dreams, but this afternoon it proved no help at all.

At length, I simply shut it out. Closing my eyes to the light, I turned my face against the pillow and felt the unexpected trail of tears.

Chapter Twenty-Two

*There moved the multitude, a thousand
heads:*

'You've got a snail on your sleeve,' Neil pointed out, quite calmly, as if it were an everyday occurrence. I looked down in surprise.

'So I have. Poor little thing. Making a break for it, that's what he's doing.' Gently I detached the clinging creature from the slick material of my windcheater. I ought to have put him back in the bucket with the others, I suppose, but I just couldn't bring myself to do it. Instead I closed my fingers softly round the snail and wandered on, away from the fishmonger's stall. The noisy Thursday market crowd pressed in on all sides, but Neil managed to stay close by my shoulder.

'Thief,' he said, grinning.

'I'm not stealing him, I'm liberating him,' was my stubborn reply. 'Bravery should be rewarded.'

'Well, I'd hardly think that chap back there with the tattoo and the cleaver would agree with you. He's charging a good penny for his escargots.'

I shrugged. 'Plenty more in the bucket. Do you see a planter anywhere about?'

'Whatever for?'

'I can't put him down here, now can I?' I explained, patiently. 'He'd be trodden on.'

Neil sent me a lopsided smile and lifted his eyes to look over my head. 'Would a flower pot do?' he asked. 'There's a flower seller over there, by the fountain.'

The fountain square was not so crowded, and one of the benches was actually free. Neil sat down with a grateful sigh while I set free my pilfered snail among the potted geraniums.

I was rather glad myself to be out of the crush for a moment. For all its festive fun and colour, the market was a confusing sort of place, with everybody jostling and disagreeing over the price of a bolt of calico or a hunk of cheese, and children coming loose from their parents and being chased down with a stern warning *not* to wander off again, and the vendors themselves doing everything short of a strip-tease to make one stop beneath the bright striped awnings and take notice.

Some of the vendors had gone high tech. With microphones shoved down their shirt-fronts they kept their running patter up and drowned the ragged voices of their neighbours, while from every corner of the Place du Général de Gaulle came blaring music, blending like a weird discordant symphony by some off-beat composer.

I didn't mind the noise – it was the crowd that was a nuisance. We'd started off in company with Simon and Paul, only to lose them several minutes later. I'd tried myself to lose Neil, once or twice, but it hadn't worked. He was tall enough to see above the milling heads, and my bright blue jumper made me easy to spot. And, to be honest, I hadn't really tried *that* hard.

'I must be getting old,' said Neil. 'I haven't the stamina for market day that I once had.'

'I know what you mean.' I turned, leaning against the bench, and found him watching me. The strong midday sun caught him full in the eyes, making them glow a strange iridescent blue before he narrowed them in reflex.

'How many pets do you have, back in England?'

I stared at him. 'Not a one. Why?'

'I just wondered. Animals do seem to follow you about, don't they? First the cat, and now a snail.' Again the brief and tilting smile. 'I'd have thought your house would be stuffed to the rafters with strays.'

I shook my head. 'No, there's only me.'

'I saw your cat last night, by the way, when I went for my walk. Quite an adventurous chap, isn't he? He'd gone clear across the bridge to the other side of the river, the Quai Danton.'

I heard the hint of admiration in his tone, and glanced up sideways, struck by a sudden thought. 'I don't suppose you ever adopt strays, yourself . . . ?'

Neil intercepted my look with knowing eyes. 'Much as I'm sure your little friend would enjoy the train ride back to Austria, I'm afraid I couldn't take him. My landlady doesn't allow pets.'

I'd been tempted to take the cat home with me to England, only it wouldn't be fair to put him through the quarantine. I thought of winter coming on, and sighed. 'He ought to live in Rome,' I said. 'They have whole colonies of cats there, running wild, with women to feed them.'

'That reminds me,' Neil said, shifting on the bench to dig one hand into the pocket of his jeans. 'I've got a present for you.'

I blinked at him. 'A what?'

'A present. I meant to give it to you at breakfast, but

Garland trapped me at my table . . .' He dug deeper, frowning slightly. 'Don't tell me I've bloody lost it, after all that . . . no, there it is.' His face cleared, and he drew the whatever-it-was from his pocket.

It didn't look like anything, at first – I only saw his hand stretched out towards me. And then his fingers moved, and a disc of bright metal glinted between them, and he dropped the coin into my upraised palm.

It was the size of a tuppence but twice as thick, with a gold-coloured centre surrounded by an outer ring of silver. Absently I rubbed my thumb across the bit of braille close to the coin's edge. 'It's Italian,' I said, faintly puzzled.

'Yes, I know. Five hundred lire. Last night at dinner I sat next to a kindly old Italian gent,' he explained, 'who found that for me in the pocket of his overcoat. He charged me rather more than the going rate of exchange, I think, but I simply couldn't let the opportunity pass.'

'You mean you actually bought this from someone?' I stared down at the coin, feeling the weight of it, the warmth. 'For me?'

'You said your father gave you coins to wish with every morning, when you lived in Italy.' He turned his mild gaze upon the dancing spray that veiled the three bronze Graces. 'Different fountain, of course, but I thought if the coin were the proper currency, you might still get your wish.'

I was stunned that he'd remembered such a small thing, that he'd gone to so much trouble. My vision misting, I tucked my head down, mumbling thanks. The spectre of my five-year-old self danced happily beside me. *What should I wish for, Daddy?* And again I heard his answer: *Anything you want.* Anything . . .

I hadn't heard Neil move, and so the touch of his fingers on my face startled me. It was a light touch, warm and sure and faintly comforting, as if he had every right to tip my chin up, to fix me with those understanding eyes and brush his thumb across the curve of my cheekbone, wiping away the single tear that had spilled from my wet lashes. 'It's really not that difficult,' he said. 'Believing.'

'Neil . . .'

'Whenever you're ready.' His smile was strangely gentle. 'It'll keep.' His thumb trailed down my face to touch the corner of my mouth, and then he dropped his hand completely and the midnight eyes slid past me to the crowded market square. 'There they are,' Neil said.

The boys had spotted us as well, but it took them a few minutes to push their way through. I was grateful for the delay. By the time they reached us, I was looking very nearly normal.

Paul's hands were empty, tucked into the pockets of his bright red jacket, but Simon had evidently fallen victim to the vendors. '. . . and you can't tear it or wear it out,' was his final proud pronouncement, as he held up a perfectly ordinary-looking chamois cloth to show us. 'You should have seen it, Emily – the sales guy even set *fire* to it, and nothing happened.'

I agreed that was most impressive. 'But what is it for?'

'Oh, lots of things,' Simon hedged, shoving the miracle cloth back into its bag.

Paul grinned. 'He's pathetic,' he told us. 'He nearly bought a radiator brush, of all things. Every salesman's dream, that's Simon.'

'Mom and Dad have a radiator,' his brother defended himself.

'And I'm sure that's what they've dreamed we'd bring them home from France – a radiator brush.' Paul's voice was dry. 'Have you still got my bread, by the way? I'll need it to feed the ducks.'

'What? Oh, yeah.' Simon rummaged in a carrier bag, tugging out a long piece of baguette. 'I'm surprised those stupid ducks haven't sunk to the bottom of the river, the way you feed them.'

'Ducks need to eat, too.' Paul took the bread and turned to me, his dark eyes slightly quizzical. 'You're welcome to come with me, if you want, unless you'd rather—'

'I'd love to come,' I cut him off, relieved to find my legs would still support me when I stood. Neil settled back against the bench, the soft breeze stirring his golden hair. He met my eyes and smiled. I was running away, and we both knew it, but he didn't try to stop me. He seemed quite content to stay behind with Simon and peruse the bulging carrier bags, while I scuttled like a rabbit after Paul.

The crowd surged in around me, swept me on, and shot me like a cork from a bottle onto the Quai Jeanne d'Arc, where Paul stood waiting at the foot of the Rabelais statue.

We sat on the steps, as we had before, with the sloping stone wall to our backs and the river spread like a glistening blanket before us, stretched wide at either end to the horizon. The ducks were clustered out of sight at the end of the boat launch, but the cacophony of paddle and squawk still rose loudly to our ears, nearly drowning out the constant drone of traffic on the quai. The same flat-bottomed punt bobbed gently to the rhythm of the current at our feet, its chain moorings trailing clots of sodden, dead-brown leaves.

Paul reached for his cigarettes, nodding at my hand. 'What have you got there?'

Vaguely surprised, I looked down at my tightly clenched fist. 'Nothing,' I said, a little too quickly. 'Just a coin.' I dropped it loose into my handbag, and heard it fall to the bottom with a reproachful clink. Frowning, I ran a hand through my hair. 'Listen, could I have a cigarette?'

'Sure.' He held the packet out, unquestioning, and struck the match for me. 'That must have been some conversation, back there. He looked like he could have done with a cigarette, too.'

I inhaled gratefully. 'Who did?'

'Who, she says.' Paul shook his head and looked away, smiling through a drifting haze of smoke. 'OK, since you don't want to talk about it . . .'

'There isn't anything to talk about,' I told him, stubbornly. 'We've fifteen years between us, Neil and I, and he lives in a different country. And he's a musician, for heaven's sake.'

'What's wrong with musicians?'

'They're unreliable.' I reached to tap the ash from my cigarette, my expression firm. 'Besides which, he's blond.'

Paul didn't even waste his breath trying to figure out what *that* fact had to do with anything. He simply looked at me with quiet sympathy, the way a doctor might look at a patient with a terminal disease. 'You're not making sense,' he pointed out.

'Yes, well.' I rubbed my forehead with a weary hand. 'I've not been sleeping, that's the problem. I'm not thinking clearly.'

'That's OK. It's the job of the Great Detective to think clearly,' he said with a wink. 'Trusty Sidekicks are always a little muddle-headed, don't you know.'

'Right then.' I leaned back, my eyes half closed. 'What's on the Great Detective's mind this morning?'

'Afternoon,' he corrected me, with a glance at his watch. 'It's twelve-thirty, already. And if you must know, I've been thinking about numbers.'

'Numbers?'

'Twenty-two, in particular.' He smiled. 'There are twenty-two people with the first name Didier listed in the Chinon telephone directory.'

'How do you know that?'

'I stayed up last night, counting them. It's a pretty thin directory. So if the man who wrote to your cousin does live in Chinon, he's probably one of those twenty-two.'

'Twenty-one,' I corrected him. 'Didier Muret is out of it.'

'Is he?' Paul sent a smoke ring wafting through the pregnant air. 'I've been thinking about that, too. I asked Thierry what he knew about Martine's ex-husband, and it's kind of interesting, really.'

I leaned back, hands clasped around my bent knees. 'Oh yes?'

'Yeah. It seems apart from being a colossal drunk, Didier Muret was one of those guys who likes to flash his money around. You know – expensive clothes, expensive car, buying drinks for everybody.'

'So?'

'So where did he get the money from?' Paul asked. 'The lawyer that he used to work for fired him for stealing from the petty cash, and Martine cut him off completely, except for the house. So how could Didier Muret afford his lifestyle?'

I had to admit no easy answer came to mind. 'But I don't see how that connects to my cousin, at all.'

'It doesn't, really. It's just one of those things that I tend to wonder about.'

I smiled, remembering his belief that everything ought to make sense. 'Looking for the angle, are you?'

'Always.'

'What else did Thierry tell you?'

'Oh, lots of things. It's hard to shut Thierry up, once he gets going. He said the death was ruled an accident, but the police originally thought someone else was with Muret that evening, because of the number of wine glasses they found. Which probably explains,' he said, 'why they questioned poor old Victor Belliveau, and people like that.' He rubbed the back of his neck, thoughtfully. 'Your cousin's not a violent person, is he?'

I raised my eyebrows. 'Harry?'

'Suppose he'd been drinking, or someone made him really angry . . .'

I finally caught his meaning, and rose bristling to my cousin's defence. 'Paul, you don't think for one minute that *Harry* killed Martine's ex-husband?'

He shrugged. 'Not really. I just think it's a hell of a coincidence . . .'

'It's ridiculous,' I argued. Harry would never hurt anyone, he hated fighting, and besides, what possible motive would there have been? Even if Didier Muret *had* somehow read that article, and written to Harry, and met with him . . . how could that lead to anything like murder? And even if it was an accident . . . I shook my head. 'Ridiculous,' I told Paul, resolutely. 'Harry's got a great respect for justice. He would never run away from something that he did.'

Paul looked at me, amusement in his eyes, and handed me another cigarette. 'OK, OK. I'm sorry I brought it up.' His smile punctured the balloon of my righteous indignation.

'Well, anyway,' I said, softening, 'the point is moot, isn't it? You said the death was ruled an accident.'

'Accident,' Paul replied, 'is just another word for chance.' But when I asked him what he meant by that he only shrugged, turning his gaze thoughtfully across the river. 'I don't know, exactly. Just a hunch I have. Tell me again about this theory of your cousin's. About the lost treasure of Isabelle of Angoulême.'

I told him, and he listened, quietly, attentively. My father looked like that, I thought, when he was doing crosswords. One could almost hear the wheels at work. 'So what,' I asked him, 'are you thinking?'

'Nothing important.' He lifted his cigarette. 'Like I said, it's just a hunch. Simon's paranoia rubbing off again, most likely. Gypsies, Nazis, treasures in the tunnels . . .' He smiled. 'This really is a case for Sherlock Holmes.'

'Well, don't get too carried away with your investigations,' I implored him. 'I'd hate for you to spoil your whole holiday on my account.'

'Don't worry so much,' was his advice. 'I'm hardly spoiling my holiday. Here.' He handed me a hunk of bread. 'Feed the ducks.'

When all the bread was gone, he stretched and checked his watch. 'I'd better go find my brother. He said something about having lunch with Christian – I don't know. Simon thinks that every German is an expert on the Nazi empire.' Paul smiled. 'He never gives up, my brother. He's bound and determined to find one of those treasures, before we leave.'

'You might never leave, then.'

'Suits me. Hey, are you going back to the hotel?

Could you take this with you?' He shrugged his jacket off and held it up to me. 'It's getting kind of warm, with all this sun.'

'Sure. Paul . . .' I frowned. 'I know you like playing detective and all that, but you will be careful, won't you?'

'What could happen?' Paul stood up, pitching his spent cigarette away. The breeze caught it and sent it tumbling down the steps into the brackish water, where it landed with a soft and final hiss. For a brief instant, with the sun at his back, he looked like some young hero from the Old Testament, a David yearning for the battlefield. But then I blinked and there was only Paul, with his black hair flopped untidily across his forehead and his dark eyes deep and quiet as the river at our feet. 'I'll be careful,' he promised. 'Want to meet for drinks in the hotel bar? Say, three o'clock?'

'OK.' I climbed with him to the top of the sloping steps and leaned, half sitting, on the low stone wall, watching him walk back towards the market place. At the other side of the zebra crossing he turned back, grinning, and called out something that I didn't catch. He seemed to be pointing at the Rabelais statue beside me, but I couldn't see anything out of the ordinary. I nodded anyway, and waved. Satisfied, he turned away again and vanished in the crowd.

My cigarette had burned down nearly to the filter. It left an acrid, bitter taste upon my tongue, and I bent to crush it out against the wall, holding the torn stub lightly in my fingers while I looked round for a litter bin. There was one not far from me, at the edge of the busy road. Gathering Paul's jacket in my free hand, I pulled myself away from the river wall with a small sigh, and wandered the few steps forward.

The jacket felt a good deal heavier than it ought to have been. It hung awkwardly to one side, and for a moment I thought he'd left his wallet in it, until one pocket gaped to reveal the dog-eared pages of a thickish paperback, with a cracked, disfigured cover. I was smiling as I tossed my dead bit of cigarette into the bin.

The prickling at the back of my neck was my only warning. I barely turned in time to see the gypsy step from the shadow of the brooding statue and cross the boulevard, walking back towards the market square. He didn't look at me. I might have been a ghost, invisible. Paranoia, I thought, was a sign of creeping age; and yet I did feel more at ease when man and dog had disappeared, and the shifting sea of faces swirled and flowed to fill the wake behind them.

Chapter Twenty-Three

. . . the heralds to and fro,
With message and defiance, went and
came;

Thierry set my second *kir* on the low table at my knees, propped one foot against the carpeted step up to my section, and picked up his story where he'd left off. '. . . and they cannot eat or bathe, or do anything for pleasure – not until the sun has set, tomorrow night. It is a most important holiday. Paul calls it Yom . . . Yom . . .'

'Yom Kippur?'

'Yes, that is it.' Thierry nodded. 'The Day of Atonement. Paul says it is a day for remembering the dead, and for confessing sins.'

'I see.' I took a sip of my drink. 'And this begins tonight, then, does it?'

'When the sun goes down, yes. Paul and Simon, they will have to eat like giants before then, if they are to fast all day tomorrow.' Thierry placed a sympathetic hand on his own flat stomach. 'I would not like to be a Jew, I think.'

'Didn't you ever fast for Lent?'

His dark eyes danced with mischief. 'My sins, they are so many, Mademoiselle – the fasting, it would do no good. Besides,' he added, 'the Jewish holiday is more than just not eating. Paul says it is forbidden to be angry, or to hold an argument, or to think bad thoughts about someone. It is not possible.' He dismissed the notion with a 'pouf'. 'Not if I must serve Madame Whitaker.'

One level up, the violin ran through a series of scales and then began its mournful song. Thierry frowned. 'He has not listened to me, what I said. He plays today the love song.'

Sure enough, the strains of the *Salute d'Amour* came drifting down the empty stairwell and into the bar. I tried to shut it out, leaning back in my chair. 'Where is Madame Whitaker today, anyway?' I asked Thierry. 'I haven't seen her at all. Does she have another headache?'

He shook his head. 'She has gone with my aunt and uncle, to see the church at Candes-St-Martin. It is a nice church, very old.'

'Did her husband go, as well?'

'I do not think so. But he is also out, somewhere.'

Hiding from his wife, most likely. Happy marriages, I thought, seemed something of a rarity these days. Especially in Chinon.

'Ah.' Thierry glanced upwards, approvingly, as the violin shifted tunes. 'This is the symphony by Beethoven, is it not?'

I listened, and nodded. 'Yes, the Eroïca.'

'*Comment?*'

I repeated the name more clearly. 'Beethoven's Third Symphony. He wrote it for Napoleon.'

Thierry raised his eyebrows. 'So it is French, this symphony?'

'Well, in a way. But Napoleon went and had himself crowned Emperor before this piece was finished, and

Beethoven wasn't at all pleased about that.' In fact he'd been so disillusioned that he'd changed the dedication – no longer for Napoleon, but simply 'to the memory of a great man'. Every age, I thought, had mourned the loss of heroes.

Thierry smiled. 'You know much about this music, Mademoiselle.'

'Not really. I just remember certain pieces, and the stories that go with them.'

'Me, I do not listen to the type of music Monsieur Grantham plays. I take him into Tours, to the disco-theque, so he can hear real music, but . . .' The young bartender shrugged again, amiably. 'He says he likes better the violin.'

Silently, I sided with Neil. 'What time is it now, Thierry, do you know?'

He turned his wrist to look. 'It is just after fifteen hours.' He sighed. 'Two hours more before my work is finished for today.'

Work or no, I thought, the hotel bar wasn't the worst place one could spend an afternoon. The long polished windows stood open to the scented breeze and the glowing sunlight of an autumn afternoon fell warm upon my neck and shoulders. Outside, the market crowds had thinned and I could clearly see the fountain scattering its rain of diamond drops through which the Graces gazed, serene.

Thierry was looking out the window, too, and thinking. 'Yesterday, that was Monsieur Valcourt you lunched with, was it not? I did not know you knew him.' The trace of envy in his tone puzzled me, until he went on, 'He has the best car, the very best.'

I smiled, remembering that bright red Porsche that purred like a great cat and gleamed like any young man's dream. 'It is a nice car,' I agreed.

'Madame Muret, she has promised she will take me for a fast drive in this car one day. When Monsieur Valcourt is gone to Paris.'

'Has she really?'

'Yes. He lets her drive the car, when he is gone. She brought it here last week when she came once to see Christian, and she would have given me the ride then,' he confided, 'only I could not leave until my work was finished and by that time the police had telephoned.'

I frowned. 'The police?'

'Yes. To say they had found the body of her husband.' He sighed, shaking his head. 'It was most sad.'

Presumably he meant his thwarted efforts with the Porsche, and not the death of Didier Muret. I sympathized. 'I could ask Monsieur Valcourt, if you like. He might have time to take you for a—'

'No, please,' he broke in hastily. 'It is not so important. And besides, it would be more pleasant, I think, to drive with Madame Muret.'

Et tu, Brute, I thought drily. Were there any men around who *weren't* smitten by Martine? Smiling, I swung my gaze beyond the tumbling fountain. There was that blasted spotted dog again, I thought. Without its owner, this time. It snuffled round the edges of the phone box at the far side of the square. Now who, I wondered, would a gypsy be telephoning?

When the phone behind the bar burst shrilly into life, I think I jumped as high as Thierry did, then caught myself and smiled. Paul was right, I thought. Simon's paranoia was definitely spreading.

'A moment,' Thierry begged the caller, as a trio of customers came through the door from the street. He cupped his hand over the receiver and sent me an imploring look. 'Mademoiselle, I wonder . . . ?'

'Yes?'

'It is a call for Monsieur Grantham, but he is practising, and when he practises he always takes his telephone off the hook. I wonder, would you be so good . . . ?'

'You want me to fetch him for you?'

'Please.' He flashed the charming smile at me, the one the poor receptionist, Gabrielle, had such trouble resisting. I was a little more immune than Gabrielle to Thierry's charms, but his dilemma was very real. The new customers settled themselves at the bar, expecting service. I sighed, and rose half-heartedly to go and break up Neil's practice session.

A shiver struck me on the twisting staircase, but I shook it off again, blaming it on the cool breeze that drifted through the open door to the terrace. On the first floor landing the air felt distinctly chilly. Here the violin was sweeter, stronger, and even though I knocked two times it kept on playing. He couldn't hear me.

My third knock was so forceful that it moved the door itself – the handle hadn't latched properly – and I felt like an intruder as I watched the door swing inward on its hinges. It didn't open all the way, just far enough to show me one angled corner of the room. And Neil.

It was easy to see, then, why he hadn't heard me. I doubt if anyone could have reached him at that moment – he was locked in a world that no-one else could touch or even visualize. He looked a different person when he played. His eyes were closed as if it somehow pained him, the fleeting and elusive beauty of the music that would not be held, but slipped past the listener almost before one's ear could register the notes. Neil's hands moved lightly over the familiar strings, sure as a lover's touch and twice as delicate. And the strings responded in a way no human lover could, singing pure and sweet and achingly true. It was disquieting to watch.

The violin faltered, and stopped, and my ears rang in the sudden silence. Neil opened his eyes. They were brilliant and beautiful, unfocused, the eyes of a dreamer surfacing. And then he looked towards the open door and saw me and he smiled, a broad exhausted smile that included me in its happiness. 'Bloody Beethoven,' he said. 'He does make one work for it.'

It was my own fault, I thought later. He'd as much as told me, by the fountain, that whatever happened between us would be up to me, that I would have to come to him. 'Whenever you're ready,' he had said. And now here I was, standing in the doorway of his room, not saying anything, trying desperately to remember what message I'd been sent to deliver, while Neil set down the violin and came towards me. Even when he took my face in his hands, I couldn't say a word. I only stared at him, and thought *He's going to kiss me . . .* and then, in a rush of panic, I remembered. 'You have a telephone call,' I blurted out.

My eyes followed Neil's mouth as it halted its descent. 'I beg your pardon?'

I cleared my throat, and repeated my message. 'Thierry sent me to tell you.'

'I see,' he said. But he didn't take his hands from my face, and he didn't move away. We might have gone on standing there indefinitely, staring at one another, if it hadn't been for Garland Whitaker.

It was difficult to say which sound came first – they

269

seemed to happen all at once, like tracks laid down upon the one recording. I heard the front door slam, and Garland's voice half screaming and half sobbing words without apparent meaning; and then somewhere someone smashed a glass and through Neil's window came the first faint wail of sirens in the fountain square.

Chapter Twenty-Four

*And some were push'd with lances from
the rock,*

Neil moved with calm, deliberate speed. He was downstairs in the entrance lobby before I'd even reached the stairs, and by the time I followed, he and Thierry had between them coaxed some sense from Garland Whitaker. Her eyes were still half wild in her pale, bewildered face, and her voice held traces of a shrill hysteria, but her words came easily enough, between small sobbing breaths. I heard the words, of course, but I didn't for a moment believe them. It simply wasn't possible.

'No.' My voice, half strangled, made Neil pause and turn his head, but for all his swiftness he was not in time to stop me.

I didn't seem to touch the ground. I felt the heavy door swing to my desperate push, and heard the screech of tyres as I dashed across the narrow road. At the edge of the fountain square, where the château steps wound down between the lovely ancient buildings, the bright red ambulance stood waiting, blue light flashing, doors flung wide. The square was crowded, full of people, questioning and murmuring and elbowing each other for a better view. I pushed my way with purpose to the fountain, searching for one face among the many . . .

'What is it?' asked a man, ahead of me, and his companion answered, 'Someone's hurt.' Just hurt, I thought. I knew it. Somehow Garland Whitaker had got the story wrong.

But then my eyes found Simon.

They had moved him to one corner of the square, to one of the benches, where he sat huddled like a child with a blanket round his shoulders. Someone had given him a cup of coffee, and a kind-faced man in uniform knelt by him, talking, but Simon didn't respond. He looked so young, so unutterably young, his frozen face beyond emotion. I shivered in the chill spray of the fountain as the gathered crowd increased the tempo of its murmuring, excited.

The medics were bringing the body down.

'No, don't look.' Firm hands took hold of me and turned me round, away from the spectacle. Above my head Neil's voice spoke low and steady. *'Don't* look.'

Dry-eyed, I focused on the weave of his crisp white cotton shirt, and the tiny frayed bit at the point of his collar, and the way it moved with his breathing. He didn't speak again, didn't try to comfort me or stroke my hair, and yet the comfort flowed out from him anyway and kept me standing still.

Around us the voices swelled, loud and confused. The doors of the ambulance slammed shut, an engine roared and rumbled off, and then it was all over.

Neil let go of my arms, breaking the spell. My gaze shifted upwards from his collar, and our eyes locked. For a long moment we just stood like that, staring.

'He isn't dead,' I said, at last.

His voice was gentle. 'Emily, don't.'

'He isn't dead!' I felt the bitter sting of tears at that,

and pushed him off, stumbling blindly up the square towards the château steps. It was a foolish thing to do, I knew, a foolish thing to say. I'd caught a glimpse of the stretcher as they brought it down the steps, and I'd seen as well as anyone the swaddled figure strapped to it. The sheet had been drawn up over the face, which plainly meant . . .

But I couldn't bring myself to even think the words.

The crowd of people on the steps had thinned, and those remaining moved obligingly aside to let me pass. It must have been my face that made them move aside with quiet words and pitying glances. My face, I thought, must look a bit like Simon's: cold and bloodless, empty-eyed. I pushed on, lungs burning, to the uppermost angle of the steps, where the high cliff wall rose stark and merciless in front of me, sharply outlined in the harsh sunlight. A bit of street lamp and a sign peered over the wall's top edge, and at its base the cobblestones spread rough and jagged in the shadows.

There was very little blood on those stones. I consoled myself with that, and with the knowledge that it would have happened quickly. For all it was a wicked drop, he would have fallen faster than his mind could register the fact. It helped a little, thinking that.

There were people talking round me and from both below and overhead the noise of traffic rose and fell, but oddly enough the only sound that truly penetrated was the closer whining of bees – not the portly, languid insects so familiar to my garden, but a smaller, nastier-looking variety, as pale as the stone of the high wall behind them. They were everywhere, those bees, drifting amongst the white, mist-like flowers of a grasping vine hanging from the weathered stone. The flowers were nasty as well, and the smell of them clawed at the back of my throat. It was an evil, putrid scent, like roses left to rot on the rubbish heap.

I turned away from it. Neil was standing two steps down, his shoulders propped against the wall. He straightened as I came back down towards him, but he didn't say a word – he just fell into step beside me, understanding. With one last ragged backward glance, I turned and let him lead me down to the fountain square, away from the place where young Paul Lazarus had died.

The brandy burned. My second sip was much too large, but I coughed a little, forced it down, and raised the glass again. It was odd, I thought, how the mind behaved so differently in times of stress. Mine grasped at detail, any detail, anything that might distract it from the thoughts that brought it pain.

I counted three pink petals clinging to the lone geranium that drooped against the window of the hotel bar. Four cigarette ends jumbled in the ashtray in front of me: two left there by Madame Chamond, edged with rich red lipstick; two taken from the pack I'd found in Paul's coat pocket, stuffed beside *Ulysses*. I had smoked them to the filter, till the paper curled and burned. Another sip of brandy washed the acrid taste away.

The Chamonds had moved off a discreet distance to the cushioned bar stools, respectfully out of earshot, yet near enough to lend support. Madame Chamond had cried. I saw the smudge of shadow at the corner of one eye, and the specks of black mascara that bore witness to her tears. Monsieur Chamond, grim-faced, reached out to shield her hand with his. I looked away.

Across from me the young policeman with the tired eyes made one more scribble in his notebook. He was sitting in the place where Paul usually sat, and I hated him for it. But then, I thought with a sigh, I was tired myself and still in shock and anything but rational. And we'd gone over all these questions once, already.

The policeman glanced up, reading my mood. 'I know, Madame, this must be trying for you, but it's necessary that I ask these questions, you understand. The boy's brother can't tell us much. He was in the château when it happened. And you have spent much time with the . . . with Monsieur Lazarus.'

'Enough time to know he didn't kill himself.' The police, I knew, thought differently. It didn't take an expert to interpret all those questions. Was Paul a happy person? Had he been depressed of late? Did he have a stable family? On and on the questions probed and prodded, dozens of them, variations on a theme. 'He wouldn't kill himself,' I said, to make it absolutely clear. 'He was very happy with his life.'

'I see.'

'He loved his family very much.' I looked away again, and focused on the pink geranium. The sun was nearly gone now, and the light was weak. It would be early afternoon in Canada. Paul's mother would no doubt be busily at work somewhere, preparing for the holy day of Yom Kippur, not knowing that her son . . . I struck a match and the flame trembled as I touched it to my third cigarette. 'I can't believe,' I said, 'that no-one saw what happened.'

'It is unfortunate.' He nodded in agreement. 'But this is market day, of course, and most people are down here, in the Centre Ville. They aren't up visiting the château.'

'But there must be residents, surely. People who have houses on that road.'

'They saw only your friend sitting alone on the wall.

It's a low wall, where the road is – waist-height, but on the other side . . .' He shrugged, and let the image form itself. Not that I needed reminding. I'd seen the deadly drop, myself – I knew the likelihood of somebody surviving.

'If he did not jump, this friend of yours,' said the policeman, 'then he must have fallen. Perhaps he lost his balance, sitting there.'

'Or perhaps someone pushed him.'

'Perhaps. It is my job to look at all the possibilities.' His face looked almost kind at that moment, and I gathered my courage, drawing a deep breath so that my next words came out on a kind of endless rushing current.

'Then you might want to ask questions of another man, Monsieur. A gypsy, with a dog, who often hangs about the fountain square.'

'Oh, yes?' The pencil halted on the page, and he raised his eyebrows expectantly. 'And why would I wish to question him?'

I told him everything, beginning with the man who'd written to Harry – the man Paul had believed was Didier Muret – and ending with our final conversation by the river, just that morning, when the gypsy had followed Paul into the market-day crowd. The young policeman took notes politely. He even asked me, once or twice, to clarify a point. But it was plain from his expression, so carefully-schooled, so bland about the eyes, that he thought I was off my trolley.

'I see.' He flipped back a page in his notebook. 'You say your cousin left a message, Madame? And that you did not worry about him, at first, because it was his habit to change his mind, is that correct?'

'Yes.'

'Ah.' The single syllable spoke volumes. 'I can make enquiries, if you like, about your cousin. And I know this gypsy well, I'll talk to him, although I don't think he will tell me much. I know he looks rough, but he doesn't make much trouble.' He glanced at me. 'Perhaps, Madame, your cousin's absence . . .'

'Disappearance.'

'. . . has made you, how shall I say, sensitive to things that are not there?'

I swallowed that small rebuke, along with a mouthful of brandy, and felt the muscles of my jaw tighten. No point in wasting my breath, I told myself. It was obvious that my suspicions hadn't been taken very seriously. I watched in silence while he made a final entry in his notebook and flipped it closed.

'I must thank you, Madame, for your time and for your patience. You've been most helpful.' It was a lie, I knew, but he told it well. I hadn't helped at all, unless he counted holes poked in his suicide theory as evidence of my helpfulness. I smiled faintly at him and he nodded, rising to take his leave of the Chamonds with both respect and muted sympathy.

He hadn't been gone from the bar thirty seconds when Garland Whitaker swept in, looking rather like Lady Macbeth, with just the proper touch of déshabillé and an air of drama hanging over her. Behind her Jim moved silently, tall and stoic.

Garland took the chair the young policeman had been sitting in. Paul's chair. She leaned in closer, placing one hand on my sleeve in a gesture that was meant to be comforting. 'Oh, Emily, how *awful* for you,' she sympathized. 'I simply couldn't have done it, not this soon after . . . Well, you know. Did he ask very many questions?'

I looked sideways, at the wide blue eyes so greedy for a breath of scandal, and felt my patience slipping from me. 'No,' I said, 'he didn't.' Something of my contempt must have shown in my face, because she dropped her hand, and shifted a little further away from me on the plump cushions.

Madame Chamond crossed over from the bar and took a seat, her warm, low voice like balm upon my blistered nerves. 'You must be tired,' she said. 'And you have finished your brandy. Edouard . . .' Turning, she called her husband's attention to my empty glass, and in an instant he was at my side as well, bottle in hand. He had brought glasses for his wife and the Whitakers as well, but when Garland urged him to take a seat he straightened up with a courteous shake of his head, and tightened his grip on the brandy bottle.

'No, I cannot stay. I must go back and see how Simon is, if you will please excuse me.'

He went out through the door behind the bar, into the passageway that led back past the office to the Chamonds' private quarters. 'Simon spends this night with us,' Madame Chamond explained. 'We could not leave him in that room alone. Tonight he sleeps in Thierry's room, and Thierry keeps him company.'

'Poor kid.' Jim Whitaker frowned. 'Shame it had to be him that found the body.'

'Another five minutes,' his wife said, 'and it would have been *me*, darling. Oh, what a horrible thought.' She shuddered with feeling, and I looked at her again.

'What were you doing on the steps?' I asked her. 'I thought you were in Candes-St-Martin.'

'I was. Monsieur Chamond wanted to stop in at the hardware store, you see, to do some shopping, so I said they should let me off at the château, and I'd walk back.

It's not far, I said, not when you use the steps. And I thought Jim might be lonely.' She sent her husband a vaguely questing look. 'But of course, you weren't even here, were you darling?'

'No.'

I thought she hesitated, waiting for some explanation, but it was clear Jim Whitaker was not in a communicative mood. 'Well, anyway,' she went on, 'I started down the steps and ran smack into Simon and . . . well, you know. It was a horrible shock, let me tell you.'

For a brief moment I thought I caught the faintest glimmer of distaste in Madame Chamond's normally immaculate expression. 'It is a shock for all of us.'

'It just doesn't seem real, does it?' Garland went on, unable to leave the wound unprobed. 'I mean, one minute you're talking to someone, and the next . . . ' Her eyes moved to the low round table at her side, and her train of thought was interrupted. 'Isn't that Paul's book?' She reached to grasp *Ulysses*. I'd had to pull it from the pocket of Paul's jacket to get at the cigarettes.

Garland didn't ask how the book had come to be there. She simply turned it over, with a sigh. 'I guess he'll never finish this, now. Not that it really matters. Poor Paul, I can't believe—'

'For God's sake, Garland.' Jim Whitaker leaned back against the window wall, and rubbed his forehead with a weary hand. 'Just shut up.' He spoke the words quietly, as though he had exhausted all his energy. To my surprise, it worked. Garland actually stopped talking, but her jaw compressed with irritation and I knew she'd give him hell come morning.

I held out my hand. 'I'll take that, please.'

She handed the book over in silence with a small,

uncaring sniff and, rising, said good night to us and left.

Jim sighed, a heavy sigh. 'I'm sorry,' he said simply. 'Truly sorry.' And pushing himself to his feet, he followed his wife out into the hall.

With downcast eyes I trailed my fingers across the lettering of the book's cover, blinking hard. *Not that it really matters*, Garland had said. But it did matter. It had mattered to Paul. I saw again his flashing smile, and heard his cheerful voice telling me: 'It's kind of become an obsession. I won't be able to rest until I've finished the damn thing.'

Madame Chamond leaned forward, concerned. 'You haven't touched your brandy. Would you prefer another drink?'

'No, that's all right.' I looked out the window again, at the darkening sky. The sun was gone. Yom Kippur had begun. A time for fasting, Paul had told Thierry – for remembering the dead. 'I really don't want anything. I think I'll just sit up for a while on my own.'

My hostess looked in silence from my face to the book, and back again, pressed my shoulder with a gentle hand and rose with the grace of a dancer, leaving me alone in the quiet bar. I heard her talking to someone in the entrance hall, and then I heard the lower timbre of Neil's voice, and then they both moved on and there was only silence.

My fingers found the turned-down corner on the page where Paul had stopped. The book wanted concentration, so I curled myself against the seat and did my best.

I sat there all night, reading.

At four o'clock the dustmen rumbled in the darkness round the square, but I paid them no heed. The first pale streaks of dawn had just begun to split the steel-grey sky when I finally closed the worn covers of the book and lowered it to my lap. It was done, now. Finished. I spoke the word again, out loud, though there was no-one there to hear me: 'Finished.' No more labours for Ulysses, no more voyages to make. Paul, wherever he had gone to, could find rest.

I felt the warmth of tears upon my face, and my body ached with a hollow weariness that was almost more than I could bear, but I felt better, all the same.

Wiping the wetness from my cheeks, I turned my head. Outside the window, the three pink petals clung and trembled on the bowing geranium, the only spot of colour in that grey and dreary morning. The wind was rising from the distant river, chasing the wall of cloud before it. It caught a handful of dry, twisted leaves and sent them scuttling across the deserted fountain square. It caught the lone geranium as well, and set the pale pink petals dancing.

And as I sat there watching, one by one they, too, were torn away, swirling past my window out of sight, until only the stripped and naked stem remained.

Chapter Twenty-Five

*That morning in the presence room I
stood . . .*

I had met death before, in different forms – I knew quite well the pattern of my grieving. First came shock, and then the tears, and then a bitter anger, followed by a softer grief that time would wear away. As I stood alone now on the steps to the château, looking down on the spot where Paul had died, I felt the anger come creeping up inside me. The Jews might call it a sin, being angry on their Day of Atonement, but I welcomed the emotion. It was something real, at least – something warm and hard and tangible, where before there had been nothing, only numbness.

Someone had washed the step, since yesterday. A crumpled mass of yellow leaves lay rotting in the crease between the stone steps and the wall, and except for a few spots of darker colour in their midst everything was as it had been before. It might have been imagined, what I'd seen here yesterday afternoon, and Paul himself might never have existed.

'It isn't fair,' I said. There was no-one there to hear me. It was too early yet for anyone to be wandering about. Back at the hotel, the kitchen staff would be only just beginning now to set the breakfast tables and brew the first pot of morning coffee. I was thankful not to be there. It would have only made me angrier still, to watch the daily routine unfold with all its petty rituals, as if nothing had happened. It had to be that way, of course, I knew that – but understanding something didn't make it easier.

It was strange, I thought. On a different level, I'd faced the same grim tangle of emotions when my parents had divorced, five years ago. I'd grieved then, too. But where that loss had deadened me, killed dreams and hope together, losing Paul had sparked some part of me to burning life.

Don't get involved. It had become my motto, almost, that small phrase. Safer not to care too much, and better not to love at all than risk a disappointment. But with Paul, I thought, how could one help but care?

'Damn,' I whispered.

I don't know how long I stood there, looking down at the unspeaking stone. I had no way of telling time. The sky, I thought, grew faintly brighter, but the sun stayed tucked behind its veil of clouds and the wind on my face promised rain. After what seemed a minor lifetime I raised my eyes and, turning, climbed the final flight of steps up to the road.

The château bell began to strike the hour and I turned to watch it ringing, a small black swaying silhouette high in the narrow, wedge-shaped tower that loomed at the bend of the road. Seven times the bell rang out; the last note hung and quivered on the morning air.

It wasn't difficult to find the place where Paul had been sitting. The wall here was indeed the perfect height for sitting on, its broad top capped with rougher stone. There was a sign here, slightly dented, warning people that the road ahead was not for common use. Paul must have sat beneath that sign for some time. Three spent cigarettes lay clustered at the base of the wall, their frayed ends showing that he'd stubbed them out against the stone, as was his habit. He had sat here, and smoked, and then . . .

I forced myself to take the short step forward, to the wall, and gazed down at the sheer, relentless drop to the hard steps below. It was more difficult to look at than I'd thought. I took a hasty step back from the low wall, shoving my hands in my pockets in a gesture that was unconsciously defensive. I was wearing Paul's red jacket over yesterday's rumpled clothes, and although I'd left *Ulysses* in the bar, the left-hand pocket still held something firm and full of angles. My fingers brushed it, recognized it. Cigarettes. There couldn't be too many left, after my self-destructive binge last night. I drew them from my pocket now, not because I craved one but because a tiny thought was troubling me.

If Paul had left his cigarettes behind, forgotten for the moment in the pocket of his coat, then how had he smoked three here yesterday afternoon? He might, I thought, have simply bought another packet, but then he would have bought the same brand, surely? It was a popular French brand, sold at every corner store – a longish cigarette with a plain white paper filter and the brand name stamped in simple black. I'd never seen Paul smoke a different type.

And yet here before me was the evidence – the three spent ends on the pavement had dark spotted yellow filters. I picked one up to look, but there was no clear name or logo visible. Not only were the cigarettes a stranger's brand, but there were no match stubs anywhere. Paul had always used matches, and I thought it unlikely he'd have bought himself a lighter all of a

sudden. Not impossible, of course, but decidedly unlikely.

Which meant, to me, that someone else had given
Paul those cigarettes; that someone else had held the
lighter for him. That no matter what the witnesses had
said to the police, Paul hadn't been alone here yesterday,
not all the time. He hadn't been alone.

Knowing this myself was one thing; telling it to the
police was quite another. In my mind I could already
hear the quiet tolerance, the kind but oh, so firm
dismissal by the weary young inspector. If only someone else could speak for me, instead – someone with a
bit more clout, and knowledge of the system. The
Chamonds, perhaps, or maybe even . . .

I bit my lip. What was it that Armand Valcourt had
said to me in Martine's gallery? 'The price one pays for
influence is isolation.' Influence . . .

The bell below me in the town began to chime the
hour, a tardy echo of the older peal from the château.
With thoughtful eyes I raised my head again to look
along the steeply rising road.

If François thought the hour an early one for visitors,
he gave no indication of it. 'You may wait here,' he
said, politely. 'He will not be long.'

I thanked him and he withdrew, leaving me alone in
the quiet room. This was not the glittering sitting-room
into which I'd been shown on my first visit to the *Clos
des Cloches*. The windows here were thickly curtained,
and the room itself was small. It appeared to be a study
of sorts, or an office, with richly panelled walls and
shelves for books. A writing desk stood angled in one
corner, and on its surface, neatly dusted, a row of
framed photographs stood waiting for inspection.

The photographs were all of Lucie, at different ages, solemn and smiling. There was no-one else. I moved closer to examine them, brushing the glass of one with wondering fingertips. My mind drifted back, I don't know why, to the argument I'd overheard last Saturday, between Armand and Martine. 'What do you know of love?' she'd taunted him. Lord, I thought, how could she ask that, having seen these photographs?

Behind me the door to the study opened and closed again, quietly. I spun round, hands laced nervously behind my back, to face him.

He'd obviously been dragged from the course of his morning routine. His hair was damp from the shower, and he hadn't finished buttoning his shirt, but I fancied he looked more presentable than I did. He, at least, had slept. The memory of that sleep still lingered round his heavy-lidded eyes, and the way he looked at me was unconsciously intimate.

'I'm sorry,' I began, speaking French from instinct. 'I shouldn't have bothered you, this early.'

'It is no problem.' He fastened the last few shirt buttons. 'What did you want to talk to me about?'

'My friend is dead.' To my dismay, I felt the tears come burning up behind my eyes. I blinked them back, determined not to cry, but Armand saw them anyway. He stepped quickly away from the door, muttering a soft recrimination that was, I gathered, directed at himself.

'I didn't think,' he said. 'I'm sorry. That was the young boy yesterday, who fell, yes? I didn't realize . . .' He broke off, stiffly. 'It must be very difficult.'

I nodded dumbly, and took the chair he offered me. He didn't sit behind the desk, but pulled a second chair across the carpet, facing mine, and sat so that his knees were only inches from my own. His dark eyes gently searched my face. 'You have not slept.'

He had dropped the formal manner of address, and used the more familiar 'tu' instead of 'vous'. It was not a change that the French made lightly, signifying as it did a deepening of one's relationship. At any other time I might have noticed, and been flattered, but today it scarcely registered.

'No,' I said, 'I couldn't sleep. Too many thoughts.'

'I understand. Myself, I've worried many times about Lucie playing near that wall. I was afraid that such an accident might happen.'

'But it wasn't an accident, that's just it.' I took a breath and squared my shoulders. 'Someone pushed him.'

He stared, incredulous. 'What?'

'I . . . I'm not sure who did it, but I think I do know why, only the police wouldn't listen. They were very polite, and all that, but they wouldn't listen.' My voice was bitter, laced with more emotion than I'd heard in it for years. 'Somebody pushed Paul.'

He studied me. 'You saw this happen?'

'No.'

'Then how can you be sure?'

I sighed, and looked away. 'It's a long story.'

'I have time.' He smiled, faintly. 'Have you eaten, yet?'

'Yes,' I lied.

'Well, I have not. So I will find François, and while I eat my breakfast you will tell me this long story of yours. All right?'

It didn't take as long as I'd imagined, after all. I'd finished talking by the time he pushed his plate away. We had moved into the sitting-room, to the same dining table where we'd shared our first meal on Saturday. Across the table from me, Armand lit a cigarette in contemplative silence. He smoked a yellow-filtered brand, I noticed. But then, so did half the population of France.

'Your cousin is in danger, you think?'

'I don't know what to think,' I answered honestly. 'I only know that Paul was trying to help me find him. And now Paul's dead.'

'Like Didier.' He lowered his gaze to the tablecloth in brow-knit concentration. 'So this is why you asked so many questions about Didier, last time we met.'

'Yes.'

'You might have told me then, that you were worried for your cousin.'

'It's not the sort of thing one drops on strangers, is it?' I replied. 'And anyway, you seemed so sure that Didier could not have known Harry.'

'I'm not perfect,' he said quietly. 'And I'd hardly call us strangers, you and I.' He lifted his eyes, then, and I met them squarely, aware that in the hard pale light of day I must look something less than human. 'You have told this to the police, you said?'

'Every word.'

'And they did not think it serious.'

'Yes, well,' I shrugged, 'that's why I've come to you. I thought, perhaps, if you could talk to them, a man of your standing . . .'

His mouth twisted. 'You overestimate my influence, I think.'

'Then you won't help?'

'I didn't say that.' He turned his head and spoke over his shoulder. 'François.'

The older man appeared around the doorway with

such alacrity that I didn't wonder Armand's wife had thought François the classic, flawless butler come to life. 'Yes, Monsieur?'

'Would you telephone to the police station, and tell them that I wish to speak to . . .' He paused to look at me. 'This policeman that you met, was he young? A tall young man, dark-haired? Inspector Fortier, then, François. I'll wait until he's on the line.'

'Thank you,' I said, as François quietly left the room. 'You're very kind.'

'You're very young,' he told me, smiling. Leaning forward, he reached across the table and smoothed a wayward strand of hair behind my ear. 'It's nothing to do with kindness.'

A small cough sounded in the doorway behind us, and Armand lowered his hand from my face, turning.

'Inspector Fortier is not there,' said François, 'but there is a Chief Inspector Prieur who would be pleased to speak with you.'

'Prieur.' Armand searched his memory for the name. 'He is not local, surely?'

'No, Monsieur. He says he comes from Paris.'

'Oh, yes?' Armand pushed back his chair. 'Thank you, François, I will use the telephone in my study.'

He wasn't gone long. When he came back he didn't sit; he lit another cigarette and sent me a self-deprecating shrug. 'You did not need me, after all. Inspector Fortier seems to share your doubts. He has begun a full investigation and he's out now looking for your gypsy friend, to ask him questions.'

'You're joking.'

He assured me that he never joked. 'And I will look myself for this gypsy, so you may stop worrying so much and try to get some rest.' He glanced at his watch.

'I will drive you back to your hotel. But first, I must make one more phone call, a business call – it may take some minutes. Will you be all right if I leave you here with François?'

'I'll be quite all right.'

'Good.' He smiled, a slow and charming smile that warmed his shadowed eyes. 'I won't be long.'

In the silence that followed his departure, while the pressing weight I'd felt earlier slowly eased with the relief of burdens shared, François moved forward to clear away the remains of Armand's breakfast, his eyes concerned and watchful on my tired face. 'I'm very sorry, Mademoiselle.'

I knew what he meant. 'Thank you.'

'Death is always difficult, but the death of the young . . .' He sighed, and set the dishes on the sideboard. 'There is no justice in it.'

'No.'

He slanted a look down at my empty plate. 'You do not wish a cup of coffee, Mademoiselle?'

'No, thank you.'

'A piece of toast?'

I shook my head. There was no easy way to explain that I couldn't eat, that I was fasting for Paul, so I simply said: 'I'm just not very hungry.'

'I know, it's very difficult, but the dead, they are beyond our care. It is to life that we must turn our energy.' He fixed me with a philosophical eye. 'You must still sleep, and guard your health. And you must eat.'

It was his tone, and not his words, that made my mouth curve, and though I quickly dipped my head his eyes were keen enough to spot the smile, just the same.

'It's only that you sound so much like my mother,' I

explained, with a shake of my head. 'She used to talk to me like that.'

'Ah. Well.' He looked faintly embarrassed. 'With you I'm always too familiar, I know. Please forgive me. Sometimes I look at you and see instead my sister – you are very like her. She also had this sadness that does not belong in one so young.' His eyes grew soft, remembering. 'Life was not always very kind to Isabelle.'

My smile died. A faint, prescient shiver chased along my spine. 'Isabelle?'

François nodded. 'My sister. There were three of us, born in this house: myself, and Isabelle, and Jean-Pierre, my brother. I was the youngest, and the only one to carry on in service to the family Valcourt. My brother died in the final days of the last war, and my sister . . .' He shrugged, and looked away. 'She left Chinon not long after the liberation.'

It seemed too wild a thought, but having lived enough to know the world could be quite small at times, I asked the question anyway. 'Did your sister ever work at the Hotel de France, Monsieur?'

'Why, yes, but how did you . . . ?' His eyebrows lifted and then fell again with a sudden nod of comprehension. 'Of course, you're staying there. You will have heard the story about Isabelle and Hans. It is romantic, don't you think? I thought so myself, when I was a boy.'

I agreed that it was most romantic. Except for the ending, I added silently. 'Where did she go, your sister,' I asked him, 'when she left Chinon?'

'She went away.' A door closed, firmly, and I didn't venture further. Instead I asked him whether the diamonds had really existed. 'Oh yes,' he told me, 'they were real diamonds. My sister showed them to me.'

'And they've never been found?'

'Isabelle hid them well.' His mouth quirked slightly, with a hint of pride. 'Monsieur Muret, he always said that he would find the diamonds. It was for him an obsession, the thought of money. He dug everywhere little holes, down in the cellars and up on the hills, looking for that fistful of jewels, but of course he never found them.'

I sent François a curious look. 'Why, "of course"?' I asked him.

He smiled cryptically, and shrugged. 'Isabelle hid them well,' he said again. 'She was very clever, my sister.'

'And very beautiful, I'm told.'

'Yes.' He cleared the coffee pot away and set it with the dishes on the sideboard. 'I could find you a photograph, if you would like to see one. Perhaps you will see then why I am reminded of Isabelle, when I look at you.'

'I'd like that,' I said. 'I've a fondness for old photographs.'

'Then I shall find one for you,' he promised me. 'Perhaps tomorrow, when I have time to sort through my albums.'

'I believe,' I told him, slowly, 'that I've already seen your sister, in a way.'

He arched an eyebrow. 'Yes?'

'Yes. She haunts the hotel corridors.'

His eyes forgave my superstition. 'That is a legend, Mademoiselle, nothing more. And it is quite impossible. There are no ghosts.'

I wasn't so sure. I saw again that gentle shadow

drifting past my bed, its soft voice urging me to 'Follow
. . .' Follow what?

'Unless,' said François, reconsidering, 'you count the
living. Then I would have to say that you were right.'
His lined face softened as he looked at me. 'The Hotel
de France this week is filled with ghosts.'

Chapter Twenty-Six

. . . notice of a change in the dark world
Was lispt about the acacias,

The hotel's entrance lobby seemed dim and deserted for the time of day. Most mornings, cleaners bustled round the bar and breakfast room, the Hoover doing battle with both typewriter and telephone to see which of the three could outperform the others. But this morning there was silence. Thierry, slouched behind the reception desk, was the only sign of life.

His eyes were strained and rimmed with red, and when he greeted me his voice sounded rough, as though his throat were hurting him. I wanted to say some word of comfort, but my own nerves were still raw and vulnerable and I was much too tired for tears. Besides, I thought, we each of us knew how the other felt. There was no need to say the words. 'You're on your own again, are you?' I asked him. 'Where have your aunt and uncle gone?'

'They take Simon up to Paris, to meet his parents at the airport. They will be back tonight, I think.' He paused a moment. 'The police came here at breakfast. They have taken everything of Paul's, everything but this.' He reached beneath the counter and lifted the forgotten item up, to show me. It was Paul's copy of

Ulysses. 'I found this in the bar. My aunt said that you finished reading it. You finished it for Paul.'

My own throat felt rather painful, just then. I coughed to clear it. 'Yes.'

'I wondered, maybe . . . do you want to keep it? Because, if you do not, then I would like . . . ' he broke off, frowning, and tried again. 'I thought that I might like to read this book. To learn the English better.'

I didn't bother telling him that Joyce's tangled prose was not the best source for a student of the language. It wouldn't have mattered anyway, not to Thierry. I knew what he was struggling to say. 'You keep it, Thierry,' I said gently. 'I think Paul would have liked that.'

'Thank you.' He tucked the book away again, out of sight behind the overhanging counter. He didn't meet my eyes.

'Where are the others?' I asked him.

'I don't know.' He shrugged, uncaring. 'Out.'

Thank heaven for that, I thought. Aloud I said: 'I'll just go on upstairs, then. If anyone asks, tell them I'm sleeping, will you?'

'Yes, of course.' He pulled himself back with an effort, and showed me a smile that held a hint of his old cockiness. 'Don't worry,' he assured me, 'I will see that you are not disturbed.'

I did sleep, as it happened – a restless sleep of troubled dreams that ended as the sun was striking full upon my window. My first thought was that the château bell had woken me, because even as I turned my face from the light I heard the deeper echo of the sister chime from City Hall.

It didn't penetrate too fully. The memory of sleep

lingered like a drug, tangling my thoughts and weighting me to the wide bed. I was still lying there, listening to the fourth and final chime fade ringing through the rooftops, when I heard somebody moving in the room next door. A faint thump, followed by the unmistakeable crash of a curtain rod falling from its hooks. I smiled faintly into the pillow, and thought: *The boys are back.* And then, in a painful rush that burned like blood returning to a frozen limb, I remembered.

I opened my eyes.

The noises in the next room had grown louder, now. I heard a scuffling footfall and a burst of boyish laughter, and the creaking of the window swinging inward on its ageing hinges. Stumbling to my feet, I tugged on jeans and a loose sweater and went out into the hall to investigate. I'd probably not have done it if I'd been awake; but I wasn't awake, not really, and this tiny part of me still hoped . . . still hoped that . . .

'Yes?' The door to the boys' room opened to my knock and a tall young woman, blonde and florid and full of life, peered politely out at me. 'Can I help you?' She spoke in English, but it wasn't her first language. Swedish, I decided, or perhaps Danish. Something Scandinavian.

I shook my head, my smile an unconvincing cover for the stab of disappointment. 'No, I . . . I was looking for someone else. I'm sorry.'

That only made it worse. She looked at me with feminine suspicion. 'There is only my husband.'

I rushed to fix the blunder. 'Oh, no, I meant that I must have the wrong room. Sorry to have bothered you.'

I don't think I completely reassured her. The round

blue eyes were rather glacial when she finally shut the door, and I felt a twinge of guilt. Her husband, poor chap, was no doubt going to be called upon to answer a question or two. Stupid, I chided myself. What had I been expecting? Some sort of miracle, that's what – Paul Lazarus . . . Lazarus, risen from death . . . only I was old enough to know that miracles didn't happen.

I suddenly felt very much alone.

Downstairs, the cool and shadowed bar was empty. On the radio, a folk-rock balladeer was strumming out a sad poetic tune, and the candles burned for no-one on the low round tables. The tall glass doors stood open to the afternoon breeze. I walked on through and crossed into the fountain square, into the sunlight, where the bright white tables and red chairs were clustered, waiting, underneath the acacias.

I wanted to sit alone, but Garland wouldn't hear of it. She all but dragged me to the table she was sharing with her husband, and I was much too tired to argue with her. Apart from which, I rather liked Jim Whitaker. He smiled kindly at me as I took the chair beside him. 'Can we buy you a drink?' he asked.

'No, thank you. I'm quite fine.'

'Well, I could use another,' he confessed, raising his hand to catch the server's eye. To my surprise it wasn't Thierry who came over, but the flustered, pretty Gabrielle.

'Such a bother,' Garland said, as Gabrielle went off to fetch Jim's *Pernod*, 'when Thierry isn't working. I mean, he's a pain sometimes, but at least he gets your order straight. I ask you, does this look like a Manhattan?'

I confessed I'd never seen one. 'Where is Thierry?' I asked.

She took a look around, leaned forward and stage-whispered the answer: '*Police*. They came to get him after lunch, to ask him questions. About Paul. Do you know,' she leaned in closer, 'they've started an investigation. That's what Martine said. They don't think that it *was* an accident, Paul falling off that wall.'

'Garland . . .' Jim warned.

'What? It's common knowledge, dear, she's bound to hear about it. Nazis,' she said, turning back to me.

'I beg your pardon?'

'That's who did it, just you watch. They've come back for the diamonds, the way they did in Germany, where Jim and I used to live. Don't you remember? I told you all about—' She paused, distracted by a scene just past my shoulder at the entrance to the rue Voltaire. 'Well, well, *well*, isn't this interesting? Look who's here.'

Jim and I turned to look, as we were meant to. In front of the phone box, two police cars had drawn up to park against the curb. The drivers got out first, young officers in uniform who both deferred respectfully to an older, plain-clothed colleague whose calm, unhurried movements marked him as a man of high authority.

'His name's Prieur,' said Garland, when I asked. 'I think he's a Chief Superintendent, or something – someone important, anyway. From Paris. He came to the hotel this morning, during breakfast, to ask us all some questions about Paul. *Very* nice man,' was her considered opinion. 'Real class, if you know what I mean. And he *smiles* at you when he's talking, not like those other policemen. I gather,' she added, leaning towards me, 'that the local boys aren't too happy to have him sticking his nose into their investigation.'

I glanced again at the two young officers. They didn't look disgruntled, but appearances meant nothing. One of them was walking back towards the second patrol car. 'But surely,' I said, frowning, 'if they called the poor man down from Paris, they'd be pleased to have him here.'

'Well, that's just it, darling. They didn't call him down. He was already here, at his country house . . . where did he say it was, Jim, do you remember? Oh well, anyway, it's near Chinon. And he heard about Paul's accident, and thought he'd see if he could be of any help. It's because of him,' she told me, 'that they started the investigation. Or at least, that's what I hear.'

I didn't think to question where she'd heard it. Women like Garland Whitaker always seemed able to tap into the local grapevine with shocking efficiency, unhindered by barriers of language and culture. She'd been kept well occupied, this morning. 'This Prieur man,' she went on, having fortified herself with a sip of her unsatisfactory Manhattan, 'was the fellow who came to drag away poor Thierry, for questioning.'

Her husband smiled. 'Come on now, honey, I'd hardly call that dragging. The man was pretty polite about it, from what I could see.'

'Well,' Garland sniffed, 'Thierry didn't want to go, you could tell. And anyhow, my *point* was that since Mr Prieur was the one who came for Thierry, I'd have thought that he'd be busy right now asking Thierry questions, but it looks as though he's found some other person now . . . look, just who is *that*, I wonder?'

She meant the middle-aged man climbing from the rear of the second patrol car, straightening his back with a motion that spoke of weariness and apprehension. I could have told her, from that distance, who the man was. I could have said: 'That's Victor Belliveau. He's a poet, quite a famous poet, and he lives just up the river.' It might have been my own distaste for gossip that kept me silent, or the fact that it satisfied me knowing and not telling her, denying her that bit of information. Whatever the reason, I said nothing.

'He must be *somebody*.' Garland lifted her chin like a hound sniffing the quarry's elusive scent. 'A suspect, maybe, do you think? Really, it's just so exciting, to be in the middle of a murder case.'

'If it was murder.' Her husband took the rational point of view. 'In which case, we're probably all under suspicion. Even you.'

She looked vaguely surprised at the thought. 'Me? Oh, I don't think so, darling.' The four men had moved off now, out of sight, along the rue Voltaire. Deprived of her entertainment, Garland sighed and turned round again in her chair, facing me across the table. She was drawing breath to speak when voices raised in argument came filtering down through the feathery branches of the acacias, from an open hotel window. The voices spoke neither English nor French, and so I didn't understand a word of what they said, but the passionate delivery promised some fresh scandal, and Garland tipped her head appreciatively. 'That sounds like the young couple that just arrived. The ones that Gabrielle put into the boys' room – and Thierry isn't going to like *that*, I can tell you, there'll be feathers flying when he finds out what she's done. But like I said to Jim, it's just a room, and you can't keep shrines when you're supposed to be making a profit.' She paused, and listened to a few more lines of unintelligible arguing, and clucked her tongue. 'Such a shame, they were a cute couple. Swedes, I think she said. On honeymoon. I wonder what she's mad about.'

I rather suspected she was giving the poor chap the devil on my account, demanding to know why some other woman had come knocking at the door, but I kept my suspicions to myself. Fortunately, Garland Whitaker wasn't seeking my opinion.

'Maybe it's the room that's unlucky,' she mused. 'Maybe Thierry was right after all, about that French girl killing herself in that room at the end of the war. You know, we only have Monsieur Chamond's word for it that there isn't a ghost. I think . . .' A glimpse of movement through the windows of the hotel bar interrupted her train of thought. I twisted round and saw, as Garland did, the tall proud figure of the Swedish woman, seating herself at the deserted bar with an indignant flip of her long pale hair. Garland's eyes grew predatory. 'Will you excuse me, for a minute? I think I need to freshen up my drink.'

She bustled off, clutching her empty glass with purpose. Across the table, Jim Whitaker's gaze held kind apology. 'She can't help it,' he said. 'It fascinates her, other people's lives.'

I summoned up a smile for him. They were very different, Jim and Garland. I'd rarely met a couple so ill-matched. The stray thought made me look again towards the open window of the room beside my own, where the honeymooning husband was presumably now sitting by himself.

'She's wrong about the room, you know,' I said, remembering what François had told me earlier about his luckless sister. 'Isabelle didn't kill herself there. In fact, I don't believe she killed herself at all.'

'I know.' He lifted his drink, slowly. 'She died of cancer in Savannah, Georgia, twenty years ago.' Above the glass, his eyes swung calmly round to lock with mine. 'She was my mother.'

Chapter Twenty-Seven

See that there be no traitors in your camp:

'It made a nice enough story,' said Jim Whitaker, 'in the bar, the other night. And it was accurate, for the most part – all except the ending. Hans may have died at the end of the war, but Isabelle . . .' He shook his head. 'She wanted to, she thought about it, but she couldn't bring herself to offend God any more than she had already. So she did the next best thing. She married my father.'

Above our heads the sunlight filtered through a cool and trembling canopy of green and set the shadows swaying, and the fountain sprayed the pavement beside us. The chattering confusion of the patrons at the other tables blended into one soft muted background, like an artist's wash upon a coloured canvas. And Jim Whitaker, who'd always seemed to me so bland, so indistinct, now stood out clearly in relief.

'He met her just after the liberation,' he went on, still in that calm and quiet voice. 'Here in Chinon. He felt sorry for her, I think. The French didn't have much sympathy for collaborators of any kind, and everyone knew that my mother had been fooling around with a German officer. She didn't have an easy time of it. My father offered her an out. He married her in private, took her home to the States, and that was that.'

The dappled sunlight danced across my face, and I shaded my eyes as I looked at him. 'So the story has a happy ending, then.'

'In some ways, yes. She lived a good life – three children, a nice home, a husband who took care of her. But I'm not sure that I'd ever have called my mother happy.' He slung one leg over the other and leaned back in his chair, considering. 'I don't know – is happiness a thing we choose, I wonder? Or is it something handed out to some, and not to others?'

'A bit of both, I should think.'

'My mother would have said that it was God's will she and Hans were separated. But I'm not so sure.' His gaze swung gently to the open door of the hotel bar, through which he could plainly see his wife's sharp silhouette bent close in conversation with the Swedish bride. 'I think we all make choices in our lives that set us down the road to happiness or disappointment. It's just that we can't always see where the road is leading us until we're halfway there.' There was a hint of regret in his calm voice; regret, too, in the way he dragged his eyes around to look at me. 'My mother chose her road.'

Somebody laughed beside us and the breeze blew past a fleeting whiff of roses. I breathed it in and sighed a little sigh. 'She must have missed it terribly, this place.'

'I guess.' His shrug was very French. 'She never talked about it, not to me. I didn't know a thing about my mother's past until she died. The day of the funeral my Dad got drunk, and the whole damn story came pouring out of him.' He narrowed his eyes in remembrance. 'Since then, I've always wanted to come here, to see the place where it all happened. I should have done it years ago. I was stationed at a base in Germany back then – it would have been so easy just to hop on a train, but . . .' His smile also held regret. 'I just never got around to it, somehow. I kept on saying next year, next year . . . and then last spring Garland said that she was bored with going to the Mediterranean, she wanted to vacation someplace else, so I said what about Chinon.' Again his gaze searched out the animated figure of his wife. 'She doesn't know,' he added. 'Garland, I mean. I've never told her about my mother.'

I stared at him. 'But . . . I mean, you've just told *me*.'

'Yes. It doesn't make much sense, I know, but it's different somehow, telling you. There were times, and I hope you won't take this wrong, but there have been times this past week when you've made me think of her. Of my mother. I don't know what it is, exactly, but there's a resemblance.'

I smiled. 'You're the second person who's told me that today.'

'Oh, really? Who was the first?'

'This man I know, up at the vineyard . . . Heavens,' I broke off suddenly, as the realization struck me, 'he'd be your uncle, I suppose. Your mother's younger brother, a rather nice old man named—'

'François. Uncle François, yes.' He nodded. 'Yes, he used to write us letters, when I was a kid. And then Mom died and the letters stopped coming. I thought he must be dead himself.' He shrugged, self-consciously. 'I'm still working up my courage to go and see him. There are questions I want to ask, about my mother but . . .' He looked down. 'Fifty years is a long time.'

'Well, you needn't worry about François. He's sharp as a tack and he speaks very fondly of your mother. I'm sure he'd love to meet you. In fact,' I said, 'I think he knows already that you're here.' And I told him what François had told me earlier that day, about the Hotel de France being full of ghosts.

The silver eyebrows rose a fraction. 'And you think that he meant me?'

'You're the only person here with ties to Hans and Isabelle.'

'Am I?' He frowned and squinted briefly upwards at the canopy of green. 'I wonder,' he mused, so quietly I almost didn't catch it. 'Yes, I wonder . . .'

A flash of motion from the hotel bar distracted him. Garland had moved to the open doorway, and was beckoning her husband to come inside and join her at the bar. He caught her eye and nodded slightly, exhaling on a tight-lipped sigh. 'Excuse me please,' he told me, 'I'm being summoned. Listen, I'd hate for her to know . . .'

'I won't say anything, I promise.'

'It isn't just the privacy, you know. It's self-preservation. Especially after that storytelling session Sunday night.' A smile faintly creased the corners of his mouth. 'If Garland ever knew that the Isabelle we talked about was my mother, I'd never have a moment's peace.'

'Why not?'

'The diamonds, honey.' His tone was dry. 'Garland has a thing for diamonds. She'd be like a dog with a bone – she'd never let it go. She'd have me out there digging little holes in the hills, hoping to find the damn things.'

Like Simon, I thought. 'Your mother never told anyone . . . I mean, she never mentioned—'

'Where they were?' He smiled sadly and pushed himself to his feet. 'She told my father they were stained with blood, they'd only bring unhappiness to anyone who touched them. She didn't want them to be found.'

I watched him walk across to the hotel, his shoulders very straight as though he'd braced himself to carry something heavy. It must be difficult, I decided, for a man like that to spend his life with Garland. He seemed to have no peace at all – she hadn't even left him alone long enough to finish his drink. His glass was still half full of *Pernod*. I looked at it, my forehead creasing in a slight frown. I'd seen a glass like that just recently, I thought. Now where . . . ?

And then I remembered. I remembered coming down from the *Clos des Cloches* on Sunday afternoon with Paul and Simon, and finding Martine Muret sitting all alone beside the fountain. There had been a glass of *Pernod* on her table, then – half finished, just like this one. And Garland . . . my eyes moved thoughtfully to the shadowed figures in the hotel bar . . . Garland had been in bed with one of her headaches, as she had been on Saturday night. The night Lucie Valcourt slipped away from Martine and her 'man friend'. 'He stays at this hotel,' Lucie had told me. And I'd assumed that it was Neil, or Christian . . . but I'd never thought of Jim.

The puzzle pieces slid and fitted, locked in place, and I felt the oddest sense of satisfaction, to think that Jim might find some happiness in spite of Garland. He was right, I thought, not to tell her the truth about his mother. Garland was the sort of woman who'd be dazzled by the thought of diamonds, the promise of riches. Like Didier Muret, who'd married for money.

I frowned again. There was something else that Jim had said, that also made me think of Didier Muret. Now what on earth . . . ? *Digging little holes in the hills*, that was it. François had said that, too, this morning – he'd said Didier had dug holes everywhere, looking for the diamonds. An obsession, François had called it. Only Didier hadn't found them.

Or had he?

A sudden, creeping thought took hold and turned within my troubled mind. Everything makes sense if you look at it from the right angle, that's what Paul had promised me. And Paul, last time I'd seen him, had been searching for the right angle from which to view Didier Muret. Unpleasant, out-of-work Didier Muret, who still had money left to throw around. That's what had bothered Paul. But then if Didier *had* found the diamonds, that might explain a great deal. Where he got his money from, for one thing, and maybe . . . maybe even why he'd died, last Wednesday.

I heard again Garland Whitaker's decided voice, saying 'Nazis'. I'd thought her foolish at the time, but now it seemed less fanciful. Not Nazis, necessarily, but someone who had known the tale of Hans and Isabelle, someone who had come to find the diamonds, and found that Didier Muret had been there already. People did murders for less, I knew, and greed was a powerful force.

Paul, I recalled, had thought that Harry might have been with Didier last Wednesday night – the night Didier died. And if it had not been an accident, if someone had pushed the unpleasant Monsieur Muret down the stairs . . . what then? Had Harry seen the culprit? Was he now himself in danger, and had he dropped his King John coin on purpose, as a warning to me? And Paul . . . had Paul perhaps guessed all this yesterday, and pressed too close upon the murderer? I pressed my fingers to my forehead, trying to make sense of things.

A crowd of young men came jostling around the corner and funnelled into the hotel bar, their voices raised in energetic conversation. They were mostly blond, and their words weren't French. Germans, I identified them. It all kept coming back to Germans, and the Hotel de France.

The Hotel de France was full of ghosts, this week, so François said. Living ghosts. Like Isabelle's son, who might have had his own good reasons for wanting Didier Muret out of the way; who might have come back for the diamonds; who had been out somewhere, alone, when Paul was killed. But I couldn't cast Jim Whitaker as a murderer, somehow, and I doubted he'd have told me who his mother was if he'd wanted to avoid suspicion.

My thoughts turned over, slowly. If Isabelle was here in spirit, through her son, then what of Hans? Was he here, too? In Christian, maybe – of an age to be his grandson, to have heard about the diamonds. It couldn't be Neil, I thought, with a feeling of relief I preferred not to analyze. Neil's father worked for British Rail, he'd said. And anyway, he'd been in his room when Paul was killed. I'd seen him there, I'd heard him playing the Beethoven. It couldn't have been Neil.

The thought was still resonating in my head like the final quavering note of a sonata, when Neil himself came out of the hotel – not through the main door, but the small, half-hidden door beside the garage. The same door I had used last Saturday, when I'd fallen asleep on the terrace and found myself locked out. It made a rather handy escape route, actually – if I hadn't been looking straight at that corner, I might not have noticed Neil at all.

As it was, he didn't notice me. Head down, his

movements purposeful, he passed by swiftly on the far side of the fountain and vanished up the rue Voltaire, beyond my line of vision. I was unprepared for the sudden stab of longing that twisted in my chest at the sight of his long tall figure, pale hair ruffled by the wind, his hands tucked deep within the pockets of the weathered leather jacket. Oh, *hell*, I thought. I hadn't asked for that, it simply wasn't fair, it wasn't . . . I broke off suddenly, in mid-thought, as the significance of what I had just seen finally penetrated.

Turning, I stared hard at the hotel, at the wall by the garage, at the little door. I nearly hadn't seen him, I reminded myself. He had left the hotel, and I nearly hadn't seen him. Which meant that someone from the hotel could have done the same thing yesterday . . . could have climbed the steps, to where Paul sat . . .

I rose and crossed the square. The door creaked inwards at my touch, then gently closed behind me as I started up the winding stone stairs. I had just set foot upon the broad deserted terrace when the violin rose suddenly in plaintive song, from inside the hotel. And then, as unexpectedly as it had started, the tune was silenced. A prickling shiver struck between my shoulders. There were no such things as ghosts, I reminded myself . . . and yet, that couldn't be Neil playing, because I'd just seen Neil leaving the hotel.

I heard a snapping sound, a whir, and then the eerie performance was repeated – two bars of music, and a queer unfinished ending.

Gathering my courage, I moved to look around the corner of the open terrace door. Neil's door was also open, but he wasn't in his room. Instead it was Thierry who looked up as I came to stand in the doorway.

'Hi,' he greeted me, looking none the worse for wear

from his afternoon of being questioned by the police. 'You are looking for Monsieur Neil?'

'I thought I heard the violin.'

'That was just me.' He held up a cassette tape, to show me. 'I am looking for the tape I gave for Monsieur Neil to listen to. My friend Alain, he wants to make the copy.' There was a small stack of home-recorded tapes piled neatly on the dressing table beside the sprawling hi-fi, and Thierry shuffled through them with a frown. 'I thought that I had found it, but no . . . maybe this one . . .' Choosing another from the stack, he slotted it into the machine and pushed the play button. A full orchestra sounded the opening strains of a Strauss waltz at an alarming volume, and Thierry quickly punched 'stop', his frown deepening.

I took a small step forward, staring at the hi-fi. 'I thought this was broken.'

'What?' He glanced up. 'No, I fix it for him two days ago. Ah!' His hand closed round the errant tape with satisfaction. '*This* one, this is mine.' A brief sound check confirmed the fact, and he returned the first recording to its rightful place in the tape player. '*Bien*, I put everything back as it was, and Monsieur Neil will not be missing my tape, I think.'

'Thierry,' I asked him, slowly, 'could you play that one again, just for a moment?'

'Sure.' He touched the button, and the stirring strains of Beethoven's *Eroïca* swept past me into the hallway. Not the full, orchestral version, but a solo violin – the part Neil practised nearly every afternoon. The part he'd told me he knew like the back of his hand.

'He likes to play it loud, yes?' Thierry raised his voice above the piercing sound, and I nodded. Only that was somehow wrong, I thought. Neil didn't like to play it loud. *Can't set the volume higher than three, or it makes your ears bleed*, he'd complained. Thierry went on talking, proudly. 'It gives a good sound, this stereo. It sounds exactly like Monsieur Neil playing, does it not?'

It did, at that – exactly like Neil. I hugged myself, trying to ward off the cold cloud of suspicion, refusing to admit the possibility. 'All right,' I said to Thierry. 'That's enough.'

Flashing me the irrepressible grin, he switched the recording off. He looked round suddenly, remembering something. 'Oh, there is a message for you, downstairs.'

'A message?'

'Yes, an envelope. The man who brought it, he came while you were sleeping, and he said I should not wake you up. He said it was not urgent.'

'Who was it, do you know?' I asked, cautiously.

Thierry shrugged. 'The valet from the *Clos des Cloches*. I do not know his name.'

François? Hugging myself tighter, I followed Thierry downstairs. I could hear Garland, still sitting in the bar, her high-pitched laughter grating like a nail drawn down a blackboard. But her laughter was the only sound that rose above the din of German voices – all those young men, I thought, that I'd seen from outside. Thierry rolled his eyes at the noise. 'There is a . . . how do you say it? A congress this week, here in Chinon. These men do not like the bar at their hotel, so they come here instead. Poor Gabrielle, she should have Neil here, yes? To take the orders for her. Neil speaks good German,' Thierry told me. 'Christian says so. But me, I do not like to learn that language. It is not pretty.'

Not pretty, no, but powerful. I started feeling cold again and closed my eyes a moment, letting the jangle of voices mixed with laughter swell around and over

312

me. These walls, I thought, had heard those sounds before: the voices of the German officers who'd lived here in the war. Like living ghosts, the German tourists went on talking, laughing . . .

'Ah,' said Thierry, jolting me back to the present. 'Here is your message.'

It was in truth from François. Not so much a message as a bit of handwriting wrapped round a faded photograph. *I thought that this might interest you*, the writing read, in French. *You see how you resemble her.*

There were two people in the photograph, a man and a young woman. The woman was laughing, looking off to one side as though the photographer hadn't been able to hold her attention long. The picture was black and white, a little scuffed and taken on an angle, but the image was very clear. I had to admit that I did look a bit like Isabelle. We weren't by any stretch of the imagination twins, but there was something similar about our eyes, the way we held our heads, the line of our noses.

But it wasn't Isabelle's face that made me stare. It was the face of the man beside her.

'My God,' I said.

It might have been a portrait taken yesterday. He was gazing straight into the camera lens, his dark eyes calm and composed, and although in the faded photograph his close-cropped hair looked white, I knew it wasn't. It was blond. Just as I knew those dark, dark eyes were blue.

With shaking hands, I turned the picture over and read the pencilled line of writing on the back: *Hans and Isabelle, June, 1944.*

I had forgotten Thierry. He looked across the desk at me, vaguely puzzled. 'Mademoiselle?'

'Thierry,' I said slowly, 'where is Monsieur Grantham, do you know?'

'I do not know. He went, I think, to the police station to talk to Monsieur Belliveau. The poet – you remember? When I was leaving from the police, they had just brought Monsieur Belliveau for questioning. Not about Paul, you understand. It was about some Englishman who had gone missing. And Monsieur Neil, he tries to help because they were friends, once.'

Of course they were friends. Neil and Victor Belliveau and Christian Rand: they'd all been part of Brigitte Valcourt's grand artistic parties at the *Clos des Cloches*. And Belliveau now shared his land with gypsies, so no doubt Neil had met the gypsy with the dog – the one who followed me. 'My God,' I said, again. Blinking back the foolish, senseless tears of shock, I stared down at the damning photograph. Neil's own eyes smiled up at me, from the face of another man, his image nearly creased beneath the pressure of my fingers.

There must have been a reason why he hadn't mentioned his relationship to Hans. Just as there was a reason why he'd put that tape in Thierry's hi-fi, and set it at a volume that he couldn't stand. Because it *had* been Neil playing the Beethoven, it *had* . . . I'd seen him. At the end of his practice session, perhaps, but nonetheless . . . And it was a difficult piece to play – that's why he'd looked so exhausted when I'd interrupted him; why his hair had been so damp around his face; why he'd been breathing with such effort, as if he'd just been running . . . running . . .

'Ah,' said Thierry, glancing beyond my shoulder. 'You see? You speak of the wolf, and you see his tail. Here comes Monsieur Neil.'

I looked round wildly, and then, to Thierry's sheer

astonishment, I dropped the photograph and ran. I ran like a rabbit pursued by a hawk, up the curving stairway to the first floor landing, and out onto the empty terrace through the door that still stood open, as it had been open on the afternoon that Paul had died. I ran across the terrace and down the narrow stairs and out of the little door into the crowded square. No-one paid me any attention. They kept on sipping wine and drinking coffee at their tables round the fountain while I turned and bolted up the breakneck steps to the château.

I didn't stop running until I'd reached the top, and I only stopped then because I thought my lungs would burst if I went one step further. With my back to the low wall I slumped forward, hands on my knees, drawing in deep, sobbing, painful breaths of air.

The sudden scraping of a match in front of me brought my head up with a jerk, in time to see the gypsy's black eyes smiling at me as, against the cliff face opposite, he touched the brief flame to his yellow-filtered cigarette.

Chapter Twenty-Eight

'Would rather we had never come! I dread
His wildness, and the chances of the dark.'

The match flared in the breeze and died abruptly.

'It is not safe, Mademoiselle,' he told me, in coarsened English, 'to stand so near the edge.'

I was gathering breath to cry blue murder when he moved. But he didn't move towards me. Instead he turned and started slowly up the road, towards the château, with the little mongrel dog trotting on ahead of him.

I hadn't expected that.

Stunned, I let my breath escape without a sound and felt my fear flip over into fascination. By the time he'd gone ten paces from me I had found my voice again. 'Wait!' I called after him. 'Please wait!'

He stopped walking, looked back. The dog stopped too, impatiently, close by his master's feet. I cleared my throat and asked the question.

'You know what happened to him, don't you? You were here.'

It was a rather ambiguous question, but he didn't pretend to misunderstand me. He met my eyes and nodded slowly. 'But I,' he said, 'was not the one who pushed him, Mademoiselle.'

At that he turned away again and walked on a few steps to where a wooden door hung scarred and derelict in the face of the yellow cliff. Through that door both dog and gypsy went without a backward glance. 'Wait!' I cried again, but it was too late. They were gone. A swiftly moving cloud passed over the sinking sun and in its shadow the breeze struck chill upon my face. 'Follow,' the wind whispered, swirling against the ancient stone. 'Follow . . .'

My brain resisted. *Don't be an idiot*, it told me. *Go right back down those stairs, my girl, and straight to the police* . . . But the unseen forces calling me, compelling me, did not respond to rationality. They pulled me numbly to that door and sent me through it like Alice on the trail of the White Rabbit. The door swung wide, and in a slanting triangle of light showed me a shallow flight of steps descending into darkness, a darkness that grew palpable as the door creaked gently to behind me.

Oh, hell, I thought. Why did it have to be a cellar? I held my breath, and swallowed down the cowardly swell of panic. Think of Paul, I told myself. The gypsy knows what happened . . .

There were only six steps in all. I counted them as I went down, with a hand braced on the cool stone wall to guide me – six steps and then a level stretch. The wall at my hand fell away, and I moved onward cautiously, only to be brought up short by another wall directly to the front.

Confused, I took a small step backwards, reaching out my hands to feel the inky blackness that surrounded me. Deprived of sight, my other senses rose to fill the void. The lingering smell of the gypsy's cigarette bit sharply at my nostrils, as did the dank sweet smell of stone that never sees the sun. Above the rasp of my own breathing my straining ears picked out the faintest clicking of the little dog's toenails on the stone floor, a sound that echoed and receded steadily along the passage to my right.

My groping hands touched chiselled stone above my head, as dry as parchment, brushed with dirt, a ceiling arched and rounded like the one I'd seen in Armand's cellars. And then I knew, with a strange instinctive certainty, where I was. Not a cellar, I corrected myself. This was no ordinary cliff house. I was in the tunnels.

My first thought was to turn back while the door was still just steps behind me. A labyrinth, that's what everyone I'd met had called the tunnels of Chinon. A labyrinth of twisting passageways that burrowed through the hills, unsafe, uncharted, half of them forgotten and collapsed through lack of use. *You'll get lost*, warned the nagging little voice inside my head. *You'll get lost down here and no-one will ever find you.* The wave of panic swelled again and I hesitated, heart pounding.

Some distance off, the clicking footsteps of the dog paused in their progress, as if the beast had sensed my indecision. The gypsy whistled softly and that echoed, too, along the stone walls back to me. '*Allez!*' he ordered. Come along! He was speaking to the dog, I knew, but nonetheless the single command shifted me. I set my face in that direction, squared my shoulders, and plunged on into the darkness.

I didn't stumble, which surprised me, since the floor was anything but even. I slid one hand along the wall, to keep my bearings as best I could, and strained my ears to hear the gypsy's steps in front of me. He knew I was following. I fancied that he kept his pace deliberately slow to aid me, and just before I reached a turning in the tunnel where I might have lost my way, the gypsy started whistling in the darkness up ahead, drawing me onward as a beacon draws a ship.

For the most part, though, the tunnel ran straight on with neither bend nor break, and only the straining muscles of my legs to tell me when we sank deeper into the rock or rose again towards the surface.

We were rising now. Ahead of me the little dog's staccato rhythm altered to a sort of surging scrabble and the gypsy's boots fell heavily with measured sureness on the stone. My brain, attuned to darkness, told me: *Stairs, they're climbing stairs.* I slowed my pace expectantly. My searching hand trailed off the wall and into emptiness, and a sudden spear of light came hurtling down to trap me where I stood.

My ears had not deceived me. I had reached the bottom of a long and narrow flight of stairs, like cellar stairs, that stretched invitingly towards the world above. Someone was standing on the upper landing, poised against the open door – the gypsy, I presumed, although he was at best a silhouette. I couldn't see his face. He pushed the door wide and left it open, passing through into whatever lay beyond.

It had seemed a good idea at the time, I reminded myself as I climbed the stairs – now, I wasn't so sure. God knows where I would find myself when I emerged, and what would happen to me there. My feet dragged just a little up the final few steps. And then I thought again of Paul, and why I'd followed in the first place, and squaring my shoulders I stepped across the threshold.

I was completely unprepared, coming from the cold

and ancient darkness of the tunnels, to find myself standing in a one-roomed house with fridge and cook-stove and a cheery fire burning in the fireplace. I'd expected a cave, I think, some sort of wild dungeon of a place, with sullen eyes that peered at me from the corners. But this was no cave, and the only eyes I saw belonged to the gypsy, the dog, and the young man lying on a bed in the far corner. A pale and rumpled young man who smiled and sent the gypsy a look of congratulation.

'Oh, well done, Jean,' my cousin said. 'You found her.'

'Feel better now?'

I pressed my fingers to my forehead and nodded, refusing the gypsy's offer of a stout brandy and water. Harry settled back against his pillows with the air of a penitent. 'I didn't think . . .'

'You never do.'

'Well, how was I to know you'd go all weak-kneed on me? You're not the swooning type, my love.'

'Yes, well,' I pushed my hand through my hair with a tired sigh. No point in telling Harry I'd been fasting, either, I decided. He'd only try to feed me something. Instead I opted for a general explanation. 'It's been a devil of a week.'

'My fault, I expect.'

'Mostly.' I looked at him. 'Harry, what on earth—'

'I can explain,' he promised, cutting me off with an upraised hand. 'I suppose it's easiest to start at the beginning, when I arrived in Chinon.'

'Last Wednesday morning, was it?'

He gave me a curious look. 'Yes. I drove up overnight from Bordeaux, and got here shortly after breakfast.

Rather proud of myself, I was, arriving two whole days before you.'

'But you didn't go to the hotel.'

'Well, no.' His tone implied it was an odd suggestion. 'It's not as if I was expected, after all. Our reservations didn't start till Friday. And one doesn't usually check into hotels at breakfast time, Emily love. Not when the tourist season's over with, and rooms are easy to come by. I figured there was no real hurry, so I parked the car and went to find this chap who'd written to me.'

'Didier Muret.'

'That's right. How did you . . . ?'

'Just go on. I presume you found him?'

'Yes. He wasn't at home, but his neighbour said I should look down by the river. Said he'd gone out with his niece to—'

'Feed the ducks,' I finished calmly.

'Yes.' He sent me a faintly irritated, sideways glance before continuing. 'Anyhow, I found him, but it didn't take me long to figure out he'd got it all wrong, somehow. He didn't read English, you see, he'd only seen the journal article in someone else's house, and read the title: *Isabelle's Lost Treasure* – I guess one could translate that easily enough – and so he'd written to me. Only it wasn't Isabelle of Angoulême he was interested in, it was—'

'—another Isabelle. I know.'

Harry's eyes narrowed on my face. 'Perhaps you'd like to tell the story.'

The gypsy laughed, a soft laugh, at my shoulder, and hitched a second chair up to the bedside next to mine. 'I told you,' he said, 'she has been well occupied, this past week. She might have found you on her own, without my help.'

'No doubt.' My cousin's voice was dry.

'I only know,' I said in self-defence, 'that Didier Muret was after diamonds. A stash of diamonds, hidden at the end of the last war by a girl named Isabelle. I'd assumed he found what he was looking for, only . . .' I paused, frowning. 'Only if he had, he wouldn't have needed you.'

'Well, I can't have been much use to him, as it was,' Harry confessed. 'He kept asking me about the tunnels under the *Clos des Cloches*, and I hadn't a clue. He'd said, in his letter, that he had information to give to *me*, but it certainly felt the other way around. Still, I felt bad about it – not being able to help him, I mean. I even rang your father, from a public call box.'

'But he wasn't home.'

'How the devil do you know that?'

'He rang back, wanting to know why you called. I confess, I was rather curious myself.'

'Well, no great mystery. Your father's got a network strung through Europe that would put our Secret Service men to shame, you know. I thought he might know someone who knew someone who could be of some assistance to this Didier fellow.'

'But you left the hotel's number on Daddy's answering machine.'

'I thought I'd *be* in the hotel by lunchtime, didn't I?' he told me, patiently. 'Only Didier Muret insisted that I lunch with him, and he seemed so damned disappointed by the treasure mix-up that I couldn't very well refuse. So I went back to his house, had a drink.' He flashed his old familiar smile. 'A few drinks, actually. I tried to cheer him up. And then, before I knew it, there it was suppertime, and I offered to go and get a take-away for the two of us. And on the way back, with my pizza,' he told me, 'I got this.'

He tilted his head to one side, showing me a patch of bruising that spread darkly underneath the fair hair just behind his ear.

I stared. 'He hit you?'

'No.' My cousin smiled. 'It's rather complicated, actually, I'd better let Jean tell it.'

The gypsy leaned back in his chair and lit a cigarette. It was odd, I thought, to be sitting here so calmly with a man that I'd been trying to avoid these past few days. A man I'd suspected of murder. His voice, when he spoke, was coarse but musical, his English remarkably good. 'That night,' he said, 'the night Monsieur Muret was killed, I am walking with Bruno,' his dark eyes glanced downwards, at the little dog, 'and I see that the door to Muret's garden, it is open. This is luck, I think. Muret, he keeps much whisky in the house, and the street is very dark there.' His shrug was casual, as though thieving were a wholly respectable pastime. 'So Bruno and I, we go into the yard, but before we are in the house we hear voices. Loud voices. I look in the window, and I see the two of them arguing. So I wait. I watch. Muret and the other, they go upstairs. Muret is very angry. Then . . .' He made a violent gesture with a hand across his throat. It was quite ugly. 'Muret he falls, and I see that he is dead. The other man, he sees this too. He comes out of the house, out the back door, into the garden where it is very dark. He does not see Bruno and me – we hide up by the wall – but your cousin,' he paused, and smiled at Harry. 'Your cousin, he comes at that moment through the garden door, with his pizza.'

'Bad timing,' Harry admitted.

'There is a little light from the house. And so the

killer, he looks at your cousin. Your cousin, he looks at the killer. And—' Again a telling movement of the hand. 'He is badly hurt, your cousin. He says to me: 'Hotel de France', and so I try to help him there, but when we turn the corner I see the car, the killer's car, and so I bring your cousin to my family, where he will be safe.'

I looked at Harry. 'So you saw him, then. The man who murdered Didier Muret.'

'That's just it, I didn't. It was too bloody dark, and the lights of the house were behind him. I couldn't see a thing. He knocked me on the head for nothing.' Harry rubbed his bruises ruefully.

My gaze swung back to the gypsy. 'But you saw him.'

'Yes.'

'And the man who murdered Paul.'

'Yes.'

I had to ask the question, even though I knew the answer. 'The same man?'

'Yes.'

'And you didn't go to the police?'

He looked at me as though I had two heads. 'The police? This is not England, Mademoiselle. The police, they will not listen to a man like me. They think I tell the lies. And your cousin, he did not see the man who hit him. So . . .' He shrugged, and blew a puff of smoke. 'We talk, we think, we wait.'

'You might have come to me,' I said, a shade reproachfully. I would have known then not to get involved with Neil. I wouldn't feel this aching emptiness inside me, as though my heart had shrivelled to a useless lump of ice. And Paul . . . Paul might yet be alive.

'I tried this,' was the gypsy's calm response. 'Your cousin, he is not so good the first few days – he cannot

324

keep awake. But he keeps saying "the Hotel de France", and "Emily", and in his wallet I find this picture.' He showed me a less-than-flattering snapshot of myself, a few years out of date. 'And so I go to the Hotel de France. I look for you. On Friday, finally, you arrive, but it is not possible to speak to you. And so I wait until you go to dinner, I telephone to the hotel, I pretend to be your cousin.'

'Why?'

My cousin answered that. 'Jean had to think rather fast that day, I'm afraid. He had to come up with a story that would keep you from worrying, without tipping off the murderer. So he left a message that I'd been delayed – brilliant, really, considering he hardly knew me – and then he kept an eye on you, to see that you weren't harmed.'

The gypsy smiled. 'We frighten you, Bruno and I, I see this. But it is difficult, you understand. Always the killer he is very close to you.'

'Yes, I know.' I looked away more sharply than I meant to. A log fell into the fire with a hiss, and it was an ugly, mocking sound, like an old woman's wheezing laugh in that stale room. My eyes stung and I blinked the wetness back.

'I see the way you smile at him,' the gypsy said, 'and I think no, she will not believe me.'

'Well, you're wrong.' I felt the stubborn lifting of my jaw. 'And you could have warned me when I first arrived, you know. I hadn't met him, then.'

The gypsy frowned. 'But . . .'

Behind us, on the bed, my cousin shifted. 'My dear girl,' he said, quite clearly, 'of course you'd met him. The bastard dropped you off at your hotel.'

Chapter Twenty-Nine

. . . the gates
were closed
At sunset,

'It didn't half give me a shock, I can tell you,' my cousin went on, shaking his head. 'I mean, of all the bloody people for you to meet, your first day out!'

I slowly turned to stare at him, feeling rather stunned, like a racing driver who'd gone almost round the course at top speed only to slam into a brick wall at the final bend. 'But it can't be Armand.'

The two men shared a knowing look. 'Look, love,' said Harry, 'I know you like the man, but—'

'No, it isn't that.' I shook my head, impatient to make him understand. 'It's just that I know who killed Paul, you see, and it wasn't Armand Valcourt. It was Neil.' There, I thought, I'd said it; I'd finally put a voice to the painful thought. I stilled the treacherous quivering of my mouth, aware both men were staring at me. Couldn't they see, I thought, how much I wanted to believe . . . ?

My cousin frowned. 'Who the devil is Neil?'

'Neil Grantham. He's a violinist, staying at my hotel.'

'Ah.'

'Only he wasn't playing the violin yesterday, it was a tape, and the opening allegro to Beethoven's Third is at least fifteen minutes long, so he had heaps of time to run up the steps and push Paul off . . . I doubt if it takes me more than a couple of minutes myself to climb those steps, and I'm not nearly as fit as Neil.'

'Ah,' Harry said again, as if my explanation were perfectly clear. 'And why would this violinist want to push a Canadian kid off the château steps, pray tell?'

'Because . . . because . . .' My chin trembled, and I realized the motive was no longer clear, not after what the gypsy Jean had told me.

'You're way off beam, love,' Harry told me, gently. 'It was Valcourt who did the killing.'

I didn't take that in, at first – I only felt relief, that nearly shook my body in a deep and swelling surge. *It wasn't Neil*, my inner voice rejoiced, but I was half afraid to listen to it. I turned to the gypsy. 'You're absolutely sure?'

He nodded, his black eyes calm and certain. 'Yesterday afternoon,' he explained, 'I am coming down from here to the town, through the *souterrains*, the tunnels. I stop at the door in the cliff. There is a space between the boards in the door, and so I look, like always, to make sure the way is safe.' He drew one finger along the line of his eyebrow, frowning. 'But it is not safe. *He* is there.'

'Monsieur Valcourt?'

His nod this time held sadness. 'He is sitting on the wall, beside your friend, the young *canadien*. They smoke, they talk – they talk like friends. But the boy, he is not on his guard. He is not watching Valcourt's face, as I am, so he does not see the danger. When Valcourt gives to him another cigarette, the boy lifts up both hands to light it, and . . .' No brutal gesture, this time, just a small regretful shrug. 'It is so quick, there is no time for noise. The boy falls and Valcourt walks very fast towards the château. When I cannot see him any more I open my door, I come out. It is terrible, what I have just seen, you understand?' A brief pause while he lit another cigarette himself, still frowning. 'I go down at once to see if the boy . . . but he is dead. He is dead.' The gypsy glumly shook his head, and sighed a spreading pall of smoke.

There was something unfinished about that story, I thought, but I couldn't quite put my finger on it. The little dog Bruno yawned with gusto and jumped onto my cousin's bed, stretching himself into the blankets. And then I remembered. I remembered very clearly how I'd seen that dog the afternoon before, outside the phone box at the corner of the fountain square. Spurred by that memory, I took a stab in the dark. 'So you went down and telephoned Monsieur Grantham, didn't you?'

'To Monsieur . . . ? Ah, the one who plays the violin. No, I do not telephone to him, Mademoiselle. I telephone to the police, to say there has been an accident.' He shrugged. 'And then I leave as quickly as I can. I come back here, to tell your cousin.'

'I was asleep, I'm afraid,' Harry said, with a regretful smile, 'and by the time I'd heard the tale from Jean all hell had broken loose at your hotel, which made it rather difficult to contact you.' His eyes were very gentle as he met my gaze. 'I am a selfish bastard, aren't I, love? I was so busy feeling sorry for myself I didn't stop to think you might yourself be in some danger. I thought you'd be quite safe with Jean to keep an eye on you, and from what I heard I gathered Valcourt rather fancied you. I thought,' he said, a little sadly, 'that it would be all right, you see. But when Jean told me

Valcourt had just pushed your friend right down the château steps, I realized I was wrong. Of course, by then,' he went on, pushing himself upright on the pillows, 'the word was out that the police were looking everywhere for Jean. His sister came to tell us that. So I could hardly send him down . . .'

'I told you,' said the gypsy, 'that your cousin, she would come to us.' He shrugged with the complacency of one who trusts the mystic course of fate.

Harry smiled. 'So you did.'

It hardly mattered, I thought, whether I'd found them or they'd found me. What mattered was what all of us intended doing now. For, in spite of Harry's evidently weakened state . . .

I looked more closely at him. 'God, I never thought. Were you very badly hurt? Do you need a doctor?'

'No,' he told me, rather quickly, hitching higher up in bed. Although he looked more tired than normal, he really didn't appear too ill. 'No, I don't need a doctor.'

The gypsy also clearly thought the question daft. 'My sister, she has seen him,' he explained. 'She is better than a doctor. She finds us this empty house, to keep him hidden, and she comes each day to make for him the medicine. It is not good, she says, for him to move around too much.'

Even so, it seemed to me unthinkable to simply sit here and do nothing. Two men were dead already, and my cousin's life was hardly safe from harm. I frowned and cleared my throat and was about to speak when I was interrupted by a gentle, furtive tapping sound, like the faint patter of a branch blown by the wind against a window pane.

Jean scraped his chair back on the floorboards and rose to answer the door. A different door than the one

I'd entered the house by, but then the tapping sound had not come from the tunnels. It had come from the outside.

The door swung open and I saw for the first time just where I was – the slanting view of narrow path and waving grasses and the smudge of rooftops far below was unmistakeable. I must have walked straight past this house, I thought, when I'd come up that first day alone and by accident to the Chapelle of Sainte Radegonde, and again when I'd returned to search with Paul. I would have to see the house from the outside, of course, to know just where along the path it stood, but all the same I knew that I was on the cliffs and just a stone's throw from the lovely ruined chapelle. The tunnels had brought me this far.

I'd scarcely registered the fact before my attention shifted to the woman standing in the doorway. She was quite young, with an arresting face and a figure that begged the word 'voluptuous'. Had I met her on the street, I would have thought her looks exotic – Italian, perhaps, or even Turkish, dark hair and eyes and olive skin – but I'd not have taken her for a gypsy. She looked so . . . well, so modern, really, in her stylish jeans and jumper; so unlike my own conception of a gypsy, and yet seeing her beside her brother Jean one couldn't possibly mistake the family likeness.

This was, I thought, without a doubt Jean's helpful sister with the healing hands, who came every day to nurse my cousin's wounded head. Which probably explained why Harry had been so content to stay hidden, I thought drily. Already he had slumped again, wanting sympathy, assuming his most appealing little-boy-lost expression as he turned to face this newest visitor.

From the exchange of greetings that followed I learned the woman's name was Danielle. We were introduced, but she was clearly too preoccupied with other things to spare me more than a few words and a distracted nod. 'They have taken Victor to be questioned,' she announced, her lovely face clouded with worry.

Her brother nodded. 'Yes, I know.'

'You know? And yet you are still here? What kind of man are you, to let your friend face trouble in your place?'

'They will let him go.'

'Oh, will they?' She tossed her head, eyes very bright. 'That isn't what I hear. I hear they think he murdered this one here,' a jerk of the jaw towards Harry, 'and that he tries to hide the evidence.'

My cousin sat bolt upright. 'What?'

'Victor Belliveau?' I checked, and the woman Danielle turned her wild eyes on me.

'Yes. They think he is a murderer because I hide the car in his old barn,' she said.

My cousin's car, I thought. Of course, it would have had to be hidden somewhere. I remembered the decrepit stone barn that faced Belliveau's house, and how the locked door had moaned and rattled in the wind.

Danielle went on, with feeling. 'He doesn't even know about the car, poor Victor. That barn, he never uses it – I thought it would be safe. It is my fault,' she cursed herself. 'And he has always been so good to us. And you refuse to help him.'

'It is too great a risk . . .' began the gypsy, but my cousin cut him off.

'All right,' said Harry, in a tone I recognized from countless lost arguments, 'that's it. I'm going down.'

And he began to lever himself out of the bed, wincing with the effort, though I couldn't be sure how much of that was for Danielle's benefit. I knew better than to try to stop him, but Jean wasn't privy to my years of experience with Harry's moods.

'The police, they will not listen—'

'Then we'll just have to make them listen.' Harry swung his feet to the floor and reached for his shoes. He had been resting fully clothed in bed, no doubt to guard against the creeping autumn chill that soaked through even these stone walls. His dusty jeans and crumpled shirt, together with his week-long growth of beard, made him look the sort of person one normally found skulking under bridges with a bottle of cheap wine – not at all respectable; yet through the rough exterior, my cousin's odd heroic quality still shone, brilliant and compelling.

Danielle moved to his side, drawn less perhaps by his heroic brilliance than by a practical and simple fear that he might fall and hit his head again. Certainly he seemed a little less than steady on his feet, although the obstinate determination in his face showed plainly that he had the will to override his weakness. If he *was* truly weak, I amended the thought, not missing his brief smile when Danielle took firm hold of his arm to help him balance.

Jean sighed. 'I will come too.'

'No.' Harry shook his head. 'No, you should stay up here I think, and out of sight, until I have a chance to clear this whole thing up with the police. Danielle can help me,' he said, brightening. 'We can take the tunnel, like you do. Danielle knows the tunnels, doesn't she?'

'As well as Jean.' The woman raised her chin with pride. 'I can guide you.'

Oh, wonderful, I thought. Aloud, I said: 'Shall I stay here, then?'

Harry frowned. 'Well, if you like. Although I would have thought . . . oh, right,' he realized, suddenly. 'Tunnels. I quite forgot. My cousin,' he informed the others, predictably, 'has a thing about tunnels. Why don't you take the outside path, instead? It's not the nicest of neighbourhoods, I'm afraid, but it is still light outside and I'm sure you'd find the way back with no trouble. You could meet up with us outside the château, where the tunnel door comes out. All right?'

'All right.' I nodded. A trace of apprehension must have seeped into my voice because Danielle looked up to meet my eyes across the room, her hands protective on my cousin's arm.

'Do not worry,' she told me. 'I will take good care of him.'

I thought that Harry looked distinctly pleased with the situation as his self-appointed nurse steered him to the cellar door. A moment later I could hear their footsteps slowly moving down the narrow stairway that led down into the darkness of the tunnels. I shuddered at the memory of that darkness, and turned my back on it. The gypsy Jean misread my action.

'They will be fine,' he told me. 'It is an easy walk down there, easier than along the cliff, and no-one will see them until they have reached the safety of the town.' He walked with me to the front door, keeping to the shadows as he held the door open for me to pass through. 'Take care, Mademoiselle,' was the only advice he gave me. And then the door was bolted once more behind me and I found myself alone on the cliff path, between the château and the Chapelle of Sainte Radegonde, with the hollow eyes of half-decayed troglodyte dwellings staring at me blackly through a tangled web of weeds and sunbleached grasses.

The house looked larger, seen from the outside. It was unremarkable in design, like a child's drawing of a house – four walls, peaked roof, two windows and a red brick chimney, with no frivolous decoration to relieve the solid, severe lines. Two storeys tall it rose, which meant two rooms; two narrow rooms, at that, and yet it still looked somehow larger, perhaps because there were no other buildings nearby to lend it proper scale. There was only the hill rising up behind it, and the gaping crumbled cliff dwellings snaking off on either side, and behind me the treacherous drop to the grey roofs of Chinon.

I remembered this house, from my first foray up the path last Monday – the day I'd felt I was being followed. I'd felt afraid, outside this house. I remembered the barbed wire, and the leaning door, and the barking dog and the sound of the wind. How differently might things have turned out, I wondered, if I had knocked at the door of the house that day, instead of running? Had I found Harry then, we might be safely home in England, he and I, while the Chinon police dealt with Armand Valcourt and left Victor Belliveau alone. And Paul would be fasting with his brother, observing the holy day of Yom Kippur.

Hindsight, I thought, was like a punishment, remorseless in its clarity and painfully unable to change what had gone before.

Turning from the house, I pressed on down the path towards the château, which I knew lay some ten minutes' walk away, although I couldn't see it from here.

Since I'd first gone into the tunnel after the gypsy

earlier that evening, the wind had shifted subtly and the clouds were drifting in to catch the brilliance of the sinking sun. The air was cold and singing past my ears. A strand of hair whipped stinging in my eyes, blinding me for a moment until I could push it back and blink the tears away. I tucked my chin into my collar, dug my hands deeper in the pockets of Paul's red jacket, and hurried on.

The path wound round and down and up again, past caves and staring houses that hunched shoulder to shoulder to watch me scurry by. And then the houses blended to a single wall that guided me along the rising slope towards the narrow, soaring clock tower at the château's gate. I bustled upwards, feeling the now-familiar burning of my laboured lungs, and glanced at my wristwatch to check the time.

Surprisingly, the walk had taken less than ten minutes – it was just past seven, which meant that, even though Harry and Danielle had started first, I was likely to arrive at the meeting place ahead of them, considering my cousin wasn't moving at top speed and was moving in the dark, on top of that. I slowed my pace a little, to ease the pressure on my pounding heart.

And then my heart, quite suddenly, seemed not to beat at all.

Ahead of me, almost at the very spot where Paul had fallen yesterday, a man was sitting on the low stone wall. He sat with body angled forward, elbows braced on knees, head bent to contemplate his loose-linked fingers. He was frowning.

Behind the pensive figure of Armand Valcourt, the château cast a stark and stretching shadow on the smooth deserted pavement. Deserted now, but not for long. At any moment now my cousin and his gypsy nurse would shuffle up the steps from the dank tunnel, and walk through that door just there . . . just *there* . . .

My gaze swung past Armand's bent shoulders to the cliff face further up the road. Fighting back the rising tide of panic, I struggled to reassure myself. There was a gap between the boards, so Jean had said, a gap that one could look through, to make sure the way was safe. *Oh, dear God, let them have the sense to look*, I prayed, in the fervent way that non-believers pray, when they hope to be proved wrong.

I wasn't the least bit worried, at that moment, for my own safety. Armand might be a killer, but he hadn't struck me as a psychopath. He must have suspected, from the very first, that I was somehow linked to Harry, to the man who'd seen him leaving the scene of Didier Muret's murder. He'd seen Harry's face, after all; any fool would have noticed the resemblance between my cousin and myself. And Armand Valcourt was no fool.

And yet, he'd always been a perfect gentleman. He didn't know I knew, I thought – that was the key. And as long as I kept up a normal front I doubted he would try to harm me now. After all, I reasoned, there was no way Armand could know that I'd just come from seeing Harry, not unless I told him myself, and I was hardly about to do that. I could just tell him I'd been walking on the cliff path – hardly a suspicious activity – and he'd have no cause to think anything had changed between us. No, he wouldn't harm me, I decided, steadying my lurching pulse with a concerted effort.

But if he came face to face with Harry, now, and Harry barely able to stand up straight, let alone defend himself . . .

A crowd of tourists would have made the roadway

safe, but it was suppertime and no-one was about, not even a straggling student or a local resident – not one soul, just as it had been the afternoon before. I flicked another watchful glance towards the door set in the cliff face, and squared my shoulders. History, Harry always said, went round and round, repeating – but the tragedy of yesterday would not be replayed tonight, not while I had the power left to stop it. Forming a smile that felt natural upon my face, I took a bold step forward, and another.

He was so deep in contemplation that he didn't hear my footsteps drawing closer, and when I finally spoke to him his head came up with a startled jerk.

'A penny for your thoughts,' was what I said. What thoughts did killers think, in private?

He turned towards me, no longer frowning, his preoccupied expression fading to a warmer look of welcome. 'My thoughts aren't worth a penny,' he said evenly, in French. 'You've been walking? By yourself?'

'Just as far as the chapelle.'

'The Chapelle Sainte Radegonde?' His eyebrows lifted a degree. 'It's not the safest walk, that, for a woman on her own.'

'Quite safe in daylight, I should think.' So many things, I thought, were safe by daylight. Even talking to murderers. Or at least, that's what I hoped. Mind you, there wasn't that much daylight left, and I was running out of time to think of some way to make Armand Valcourt move from where he sat, leaving the way clear for Harry to get down to the police.

Think, damn you, think, I ordered my racing mind, but no ideas came. My hands shook ever so slightly, and I tucked them back in my pockets to keep them still.

Armand noticed. 'You are cold?'

'No. No, it's just—' And then it finally struck me, what excuse to use. 'It's just this place,' I said, quite honestly. 'It's difficult to stand here, so soon after . . .'

'*Dieu*, I didn't think. I'm sorry.' He sent a brief look up the road and raked his hair with one lean hand, then met my eyes again and smiled. 'Have you ever seen the sunset from the walls of the château?'

The château, I thought. Public place, with lots of people. Perfect. Trying to keep the relief from showing in my voice, I replied that I had not. 'Is it very lovely?'

'It is something to be remembered.'

The walk up the hill was a short one, but to me it seemed to take an age. I held my breath as we passed the door that hid the tunnel's entrance, and fancied that I heard somebody stir behind the wooden panels, but it might have been imagination, or the wind. The wind had risen sharply with the sinking of the sun, and it caught now in my throat as I quickened my step to keep pace with Armand's longer strides.

The young guide at the château admission booth looked faintly surprised when we appeared. Her wide eyes swung from me to Armand, and she cleared her throat. 'Monsieur . . .'

Armand reached for his wallet. 'Two adults.'

'But Monsieur . . .'

'We wish to see the sunset,' he explained. He passed a bill across the narrow counter, with its tumbled stacks of coloured brochures and souvenirs. I didn't see the exact denomination of the note, but it was rather more than the price of our admission. The girl took it slowly from his hand and looked at it, hesitating, then took two pink tickets from below the counter and handed them to Armand.

I frowned as we walked up along the gravel path, past the Royal Apartments on our way to the far western wall. 'Why the bribe?' I asked him, casually. The only other visitors I could see were heading in the opposite direction, so I'd already half guessed what Armand's answer would be. And I was right.

'The château closes to the public at this hour,' he said, with an uncaring shrug. 'But it's no problem. The workers stay on for a while yet, to finish up the closing, and they know me well. We're neighbours.' He stepped aside to let me go ahead across the short bridge spanning the dry moat that split the grounds. Directly in front of me, the ruined Moulin Tower rose like a sentinel at the château's westernmost edge, its jagged, roofless silhouette a foil for the brilliant wash of colour on the billowed clouds behind.

It looked as though the very sky was burning.

'It will be still more splendid in a moment.' I heard the click of Armand's cigarette lighter and smelled the drifting smoke as he moved up to join me. 'I hope you found your cousin well?'

My mouth went dry as dust. 'What?'

'You have,' he said, 'a most revealing face.'

Some distance off a set of ancient hinges creaked a protest that was silenced by a final-sounding thud. They were closing the gates to the château.

'It was bound to happen, I suppose,' Armand went on, lifting one hand to gently touch my hair, 'but I'm still sorry he had to tell you.'

Chapter Thirty

It needs must be for honour if at all:

I felt the change in my own eyes. He dropped his hand.

'You are afraid of me,' he said. 'I didn't want that. I didn't want . . .' The dark eyes angled downwards, shutting me out, and he pulled sharply at his cigarette.

My heartbeat lurched arhythmically and for a second time I steadied it. Don't panic, I thought, just stay calm. Surely Harry would by now have reached the meeting place, the place where the steps started down to the fountain square, and he would not wait long before deciding something must have happened to me. Unlike Harry, I was never late.

No, I reassured myself, he'd realize something had gone wrong, and he'd go straight to the police, as he'd intended. And then the police would telephone the château where, somewhere, a handful of straggling staff members were still working through their closing duties, and the police would ask if anyone had noticed me upon the road, and then someone was bound to tell them . . . Yes, I thought, trying desperately to convince myself, that's how it would happen. If I only kept my head and kept Armand in conversation, then everything would be all right. It was only a matter of time before someone came for me.

He will come . . . The promise, in a voice not quite my own, flowed through my mind and over me and filled me with an oddly quiet calmness. I cleared my throat. 'May I please have a cigarette?'

I was breaking faith with Paul, I knew. *Nothing for pleasure*, that's what Thierry had said was the rule of Yom Kippur. No food, no drink, and certainly no cigarettes. And yet my request was not for pleasure, it was purposeful. It bought me time. If Armand found it odd that someone shut into a deserted ruin with a murderer would think of smoking, he didn't let on. His face remained impassive as he handed me the packet and the lighter.

The wind rose wilder up the tower walls. It took me several tries to light the cigarette, the flame kept blowing out.

Armand stood watching me. 'I wouldn't have hurt you,' he said.

Past tense, I noticed. Lovely. My own voice, to my surprise, was nearly normal. 'So what happens now?'

'I don't know.' He looked suddenly an old man, very tired. 'It's . . . difficult, this business. And so much, I think, depends on you.'

'On me?'

'What you decide.'

'I see.' I felt a fleeting stab of warmth upon my cheek from the dying sun. 'Well, I don't see how I can decide anything. I haven't heard your side of things.'

'And do you want to hear?'

'Of course.'

He looked at me a long moment. 'I don't believe you.'

'Believe what you like.'

'No, you're only saying this because you're frightened . . .'

'Well, of course I'm bloody frightened!' I shot back, against my best intentions. 'You've killed two people that I know of – maybe you killed your wife too, I don't know. My God, Armand, I'd be a fool not to be frightened!' I broke off suddenly, horrified by my outburst. Never antagonize your attacker, that's what all the advice columns said, and never let him see your fear. My heart sank miserably as I waited for Armand's reaction.

He was watching his own cigarette glow crimson in the angry wind. He flicked the end and loosed a swirl of sparks that quickly died. 'I didn't, as it happens, kill my wife.' His smile was very tight, and brief. 'I thought about it, off and on. She was most . . . irritating, sometimes, and there were days she pushed me almost to my limit, but in the end she died quite naturally – her heart . . .' He raised his eyes then, looked away. The hand that held the cigarette was very steady. 'Then Didier, my loving brother-in-law, he came to me and asked me if I knew about the will. Brigitte's will. Not the one she'd made when we were married, but the one she'd written out herself the week before her death. Didier, he was a clerk for Brigitte's lawyer, then – he'd seen the envelope addressed by her one morning in the office post, and being curious he opened it. It was a legal will, he told me, signed and witnessed, everything. Brigitte,' he said, 'had left me every cent she owned, on the condition that I turn my house, my land, into an institute for her damned artists. God!' The word came out with all the bitterness that lingered still within him. 'Without her money, I was lost – I had so little of my own. And yet, to get the money she would make me

342

give up all I *did* own. She would have robbed her daughter of the legacy we Valcourts have been born to since before the Revolution. No,' he said, his voice low and determined, 'the money, it was Brigitte's, but the land . . . the land is *mine*. It will be Lucie's land when I am gone, and no-one has a right to steal that from her. No-one,' he repeated. I glimpsed a violence in the deep black eyes, a quiet violence, carefully contained, but even as his gaze swung round to lock with mine it vanished like a thing imagined. 'Didier, he knew how I would feel. He'd counted on it. He had kept the will locked in his desk; the lawyer hadn't seen it. A little bit of money to destroy it, that's what he'd been after, and when Brigitte died, well . . . he knew he could ask for any price, and I would pay it.'

'But surely, the people who witnessed the will . . .'

'Ah yes. Your Monsieur Grantham, he was a witness, did you know? And he asked me, when Brigitte died, what happened to the will. I told him she had changed her mind, and Didier, he told this story also.'

'But he didn't keep his promise. To destroy the will.'

'No.' He shook his head, looked down again. 'No, at every turning there it was, that damned will, waved in my face. A most convenient blackmail scheme, I must admit.'

'You might have gone to the police. Explained what happened. Maybe they could—'

'No. No, you can't understand. You don't have children, Emily,' he told me softly, accusingly. It was the first time he had called me by my name. 'Children, they are everything. We owe to them a name they can be proud of, and a future with no shadows in it. Lucie deserves that much from me. I couldn't risk a scandal.'

I challenged him. 'Is that why you killed Didier?'

'It's cold,' he said. His cigarette was dead and he reached in his pocket for another. 'The wind, it's cold. You must be frozen.'

'I'm fine.'

'You're shaking. Come, let's sit down.'

The only place I saw to sit was on the broad low wall that jutted from the west face of the Moulin Tower. Beyond that wall the sun had flattened on a purple haze of hills, spilling its brilliance into the darkly flowing river, and the wind had turned electric with the threat of a coming storm. I slowly shook my head, staring at the crumbled wall and thinking of the sheer and plunging drop it masked on the other side. I was thinking, oddly enough, not of Paul being pushed from the cliff but of my mother, years ago on a family trip to Cornwall, chasing me constantly down the sea spray-slicked footpaths and warning me: 'Don't go near the edge!' She would be proud of me, I thought, for finally heeding her advice.

'No,' I said. 'I don't want to sit down.' *Stay in the open*, I told myself, *don't drop your guard.*

Armand smiled, tightly. 'Not on the wall. Just there, beside the tower. By the door.' There was a sort of trench-like entryway that led up to the Moulin Tower's wooden door. The leaves lay thick upon the pavement there, unmoving, proof that the ivy-choked walls on either side blocked out the wind with ease, and against one wall, nestled in the ivy, was a narrow concrete bench. It offered shelter, but not safety. Safety lay in staying out upon the lawn, where anyone might see us.

Again I shook my head. 'I'm fine.' I hugged my arms around my waist to stop the trembling. 'You were going to tell me about Didier.'

'Ah, well,' he shrugged, as the flame of the lighter

344

danced behind his cupped hand, 'that was an accident. Not that I regret it, but it was not meant to happen. I was that week in Paris, meeting buyers, but each lunch hour I telephoned Lucie, to talk. She likes for me to ring her when I'm out of town. Most days we talked of school, of François, but on that Wednesday Lucie asked me could she have a shovel.' His jaw tightened a little, remembering. 'I asked her why, and she said Uncle Didier was going to go digging for treasure with a man, an English man. She said she'd heard them talking just that morning, by the river, and she thought it sounded fun. Fun.' His smile held no humour. 'I felt like I'd been punched. I'd warned Didier once, you understand – I'd paid him well not to dig on my land, to ruin my vines, looking for those foolish diamonds. I told him if he ever tried again to touch my land, my daughter's land, I'd kill him. I didn't mean it,' he qualified. 'I don't believe I meant it. But I had to make quite sure he understood. So when I heard from Lucie, what was going on, it made me angry.'

Only Lucie, I thought, had got the story wrong, as usual. She'd heard Didier and Harry talking about tunnels, about digging for treasure, God knows what. And Didier, who had hoped to learn from Harry some new clue to help him find the diamonds, had no doubt been rather stunned himself to learn he'd wasted his effort. Small problems of communication, I thought, that had led to murder.

Armand shrugged. 'I had to talk to Didier, to stop him, so I hired a car and drove to Chinon. He was alone and drunk, when I caught up with him. He laughed at me . . . he *laughed* . . . and so I told him that I'd had enough, that I wasn't going to give in any longer. That I didn't think he even had the will any more. I hadn't seen it for months. That made him angry.' I saw his faint smile glimmer in the gathering dusk. 'Didier, he didn't like to be called a liar. Said he'd show me I was wrong. He went upstairs, and so at last I knew where he kept Brigitte's will. I only meant to take it back, to burn it – but Didier, he tried to stop me . . .'

'So you killed him.'

'He was very drunk. It was easy to take the will from him, but he came after me, attacked me on the first floor landing. I pushed him off – not hard, but he went back over the railing.' Armand shrugged, a short and callous shrug without remorse. 'There was nothing I could have done.'

'You could have reported it. It was an accident, for heaven's sake.'

'But why? Why let that bastard draw me into an enquiry, headlines in the newspapers, gossip in the cafés? He was dead, I owed him nothing, so I left him where he was. I don't regret what I did. If I had to do it again, I would still have left the house, only,' he admitted, 'I'd have left it by the front door, not the back. I thought the back door would be safer, not so many windows facing me, and the lane beside is always dark. I hadn't counted on your cousin coming up the path.'

'He didn't see you,' I informed him.

'Did he not? I was so certain that he did. I thought I'd killed him, too, but I did not have time to check. I could not risk a neighbour looking out and seeing me.' He lifted the cigarette, his mouth twisting. 'The next day, when Martine called me in Paris to tell me Didier was dead, I learned no other body had been found. The man who'd seen me, he was still alive, and though he had not talked to the police, he was a danger. I could not risk another blackmailer, you understand. So I came back to Chinon. And then,' he said, quite simply, 'I saw you.'

So I'd been right, I thought. He'd seen the resemblance from the very beginning. 'Is that why you sent me the invitation?' I asked. 'Because you wanted me to lead you to my cousin?'

'I wanted to find out who you were,' was his reply. 'And when I learned you had no brother, that you were in Chinon by yourself, I thought it must be just coincidence, that you looked so much like him. I was surprised, at lunch, when you mentioned a cousin – I hadn't thought of cousins – but then you said this cousin lived in England, so . . .' He shrugged, a little sadly. 'I did not know, for sure, until this morning. When you told me.'

'I see.'

He watched my face a moment, mulling something over. 'You said your cousin did not see me. And yet you knew,' he mused. 'Who told you?'

'You were seen.'

'The gypsy,' he decided, his mind sifting through what I'd told him that morning. He was very sharp, I thought. 'It was the gypsy with the dog, was it not? The one who follows you around. So, it is just this gypsy's word against my own, then.' The knowledge seemed to please him, and I kicked myself for having told him anything.

'My word as well,' I said, lifting my chin with a courage I didn't quite feel. 'You shouldn't be telling me this.'

'You won't repeat it.'

My belly crawled with sudden cold. 'Oh? And why not?'

'Because of this.' I guessed his intent even as he reached for me, but I didn't have the time to move away. The kiss was hard, and yet it scarcely registered – I was past feeling anything. I simply stood and let him kiss me, unresponsive. At length he drew back, touched my cheek. 'We have this still between us, you and I,' he said. 'From the moment I first saw you . . .'

When he bent to me again, my mind stayed stoically detached and analytical. Past Armand's shoulder I could see the little ivy-shrouded bench, with dead leaves drifted underneath it. I saw the wooden doorway to the Moulin Tower, bound firm with iron hinges, and I watched it shifting inwards as the wind went rushing past it. Impossible, I told myself. The tower was off limits, closed to tourists, it was always locked. The door could not have moved.

Armand drew back a second time and, frowning, lit a cigarette. He smoked too much, I thought absently. Like Paul . . . And suddenly my thoughts weren't absent any more. The feeling came back in a searing flood that scalded every nerve to painful rawness.

I didn't move, but mentally I took five paces back, away from Armand. I could perhaps forgive him for the death of Didier – a tragic accident, unplanned, partly orchestrated by the victim – I could forgive him that, and as for Brigitte's will I understood a father's drive to shield the future of his daughter, however much I disapproved of his methods. But Paul . . . No, I decided firmly – never. Day of Atonement notwithstanding, I could never forgive him for Paul.

'You are thinking of the boy,' said Armand. He hadn't lied about my expressive face. 'Two people, you said – I have killed two people. Did the gypsy see that as well?'

I didn't tell him, this time, but he read the answer anyway, in my stoic silence.

'Ah.' He accepted this new information calmly. 'I am sorry. Not about being seen, you understand, but about . . . I didn't know he was so close a friend.'

'Would that have made a difference?'

'No.' The black eyes touched mine briefly, honestly, and slid away. 'No, it wouldn't. I could not have let him live.'

My throat had begun to hurt. 'Why not?'

'He was too smart, your friend. Too clever. But I didn't know how clever until yesterday, when we met quite by chance upon the road, just outside there.' A nod in the direction of the sturdy château gates. 'He asked me questions, then, about Didier. About when Didier was working for the lawyer. Now, if the other boy had asked me, I might just have thought he asked from curiosity – he likes Martine, that one. I'd not have thought it strange. But this boy Paul, his questions made me curious myself. And so I sat with him, offered him a cigarette and asked him why he wanted to know about my brother-in-law. Do you know,' Armand said, unable to keep a trace of disbelieving admiration from seeping into his voice, 'he'd worked the whole thing out: the blackmail, the struggle by the stairs, the whole thing. Blackmail, he said, was the only thing that could explain how Didier got all his money, and more than likely the blackmail was connected to Didier's days as a lawyer's clerk. Your friend, he told me he thought Didier had not been by himself that night, that someone else was with him, maybe someone who had pushed him down the stairs . . .' Armand broke off and shook his head, incredulous. 'Too clever, that's what this boy was. Oh, he didn't know that it was me, of course. And

349

he didn't bring the Englishman . . . your cousin . . . into it.'

'Yes, well, he wouldn't have,' I told him. 'Paul had promised, on his honour, that he wouldn't tell anyone else we were looking for Harry.'

'On his honour,' Armand echoed, with a faint and distant smile. 'Then I should have had him promise me he wouldn't talk of Didier at the hotel. I couldn't let him do that, couldn't let him talk of blackmailers and lawyers . . . it was too dangerous.'

I didn't understand, and told him so.

'Because of Neil. Because he would remember, maybe, Brigitte's will. He would ask questions. It was too dangerous,' he said again. The last word seemed to echo from the ruined walls around us, and I turned my head away in time to see a shadow moving past the gaping window of the Moulin Tower. The shadow vanished as I looked, and yet I caught the motion at the corner of my eye. And underneath the window, as the wind swirled fiercely by, the heavy wooden door creaked further inward on its ancient hinges, beckoning.

I judged the distance silently, between the tower and myself, and knew that with a running start I might just make it. I could bolt the door behind me. I'd be safe then, till they came to find me, if they came at all . . .

Behind us, in the high and narrow confines of the clock tower that guarded the château's entrance, the great medieval bell began to toll the time. Half past seven. Hunching deeper in my jacket, I swung my troubled gaze around to watch the outline of the ringing bell. 'Who's that coming now?' I asked Armand.

And when he raised his head to look, I ran.

I heard him swear; I heard him pounding close behind me, but I ran as one possessed and when I reached the door I still had time to turn and slam it shut behind me. The only problem was, there was no bolt. Not on the inside. 'Damn,' I breathed. I couldn't hope to hold it, by myself. Already I could hear the scrape of steps upon the stone outside, I saw the heavy handle start to turn . . .

My eyes were not adjusted to the darkness, and I stumbled as I dragged myself across the barren room to where the ghostly suggestion of a staircase curled its way upwards against the wall. The door crashed open behind me.

'Emily! For God's sake, don't be stupid. I won't hurt you . . .'

I had reached the stairs. With one hand trailing on the curved stone wall to guide my steps, I started up. The stone felt damp and full of dirt – the smell of it burned sharply in my nostrils, but I was climbing far too rapidly to register the full range of sensation. I burst with trembling legs into the upper chamber, open to the sky, and groped my way around the wall in search of some place, any place, to hide. The gathered clouds, tinged still with crimson, gazed down at me with pity.

The light was nearly gone now, and the wind seemed everywhere around me. It had a voice, that wind, half human and half demon, that numbed the mind and turned the soul to stone. I'd reached the end, with nowhere left to go. A slash of brightness showed in the wall a few feet on and with desperate hands I clawed my way around to it. I found a window . . . well, a murder-hole – a crumbling, gaping murder-hole my height and width, with jagged edges framing an impressive view across the roofs of Chinon's old and peaceful heart.

In ages past an archer would have stood here, poised

with watchful eyes to hold the castle keep against all challengers from the darkening hill below. And nearly eight centuries ago a frightened girl of fifteen years might well have stood in this same spot, watching the spreading fires of the rebel barons camped around the château walls. I could almost see the fires myself, tonight – the rue Voltaire below me was a blaze of light, and I fancied that I saw a line of torches winding up the cliff. *Oh, God*, I prayed, *please let him come*.

'I'm coming up,' Armand announced, below me. He was on the stairs. 'Do you hear me, Emily? I'm coming up. Don't move.'

I slid away, along the wall, and pressed myself into the dripping stone. Armand moved very slowly, with deliberate purpose. His steps fell loud upon the worn stone. 'Please, Emily, I promise I won't hurt you. I could never . . .' His voice trailed off, and clearing his throat he tried again. 'Just don't move. The walls are weak in places, they're not safe. Please . . .'

I could see his outline now, at the top of the stairs. A few more steps, and he would be beside me. Panic froze my limbs, keeping me anchored to the stone while Armand edged his way towards me, past the murder-hole.

Then, in one flashing second, my whole world seemed to explode. The sudden stab of brilliant light came slashing through the murder-hole like lightning, and caught Armand full square upon the face. He tried to move and turned against the wall, and, frozen still, I heard the horrifying sound of grinding mortar giving way, and watched while Armand lurched to one side, out of sight. The light that had so blinded him kept shining, unconcerned, upon the settling dust and pebbles. It reflected even on the thick clouds moving low above the sharp and ragged edges of the roofless chamber I stood in.

And then I realized what had happened. The sunset, now, was nearly over. They had turned the floodlights on.

Armand hadn't fallen, not completely. With one hand he kept a death grip on the stone ledge where the murder-hole had been. Half stunned, I sidled round and watched him while he scrabbled for a foothold. He couldn't find one, but he managed to bring his other hand up to strengthen his grasp. And there he hung, suspended, muscles straining as he gathered all his energy to pull himself back up and in.

His fingers clung mere inches from my feet – I could have stepped on them, kicked at them, sent him to his death. It would, I thought, be no less than the man deserved. He'd killed Paul, hadn't he? But even as I thought of Paul I knew I couldn't do it, for in my mind I saw again Paul's gentle face, his dark eyes gazing out across the darkly flowing river, and I heard again his voice telling me sadly: 'People hate too much, you know?'

I knew.

And anyway, I thought, it was a sin to hate someone on Yom Kippur. I slowly crouched and braced myself with one hand against what remained of the wall, and stretched the other hand to take firm hold of Armand's wrist. He raised his head to look at me. With all the floodlights angled up behind him I could only see a darkened outline of his face, I couldn't see his eyes, and yet for some strange reason I believed I saw him smile at me. He turned his own hand slightly in my grasp until his fingers closed with mine. And then he just let go.

353

They told me later that when Armand fell, my group of would-be rescuers had only just arrived within the château grounds – that Harry was, in fact, still causing some kind of disturbance at the entrance booth. But somehow, when I spun away from the gaping, light-filled hole, Neil was there to catch me, his solid body shielding me from danger while his arms came round me strongly, firmly, warm as life itself.

I clung to him while, overhead, the clouds burst forth a final, brilliant streak of golden red, as if the gates of heaven themselves had briefly opened, and closed again. My trembling stilled; the wind seemed to fall silent, and some weight I didn't fully understand, a melancholy ages old, was lifted from my sobbing chest and drifted like an answered prayer into the darkness.

'It's all right, don't be frightened, now,' Neil said, his mouth moving down against my hair. 'I'm here.'

Chapter Thirty-One

> . . . *the long fantastic*
> *night*
> *With all its doings had and had not been,*
> *And all things were and were not.*

Inspector Prieur proved to be a decent man. I'd thought as much the moment I'd first met him, when he'd come walking across the château yard, calm in the midst of the confusion, and gently coaxed me out of Neil's protective hold. He'd looked like someone's grandfather come down for sports day, with a vacuum flask in one hand and a dark wool blanket in the other. 'You must be cold,' he'd said to me. 'I've brought you coffee.' And then, when I was ready, he'd begun to ask me questions, but even that had been relaxed – less an interrogation than an undemanding chat. When it was finished, he had looked at me with understanding. 'There is a child, they tell me. A little girl.'

'Yes.'

The old inspector, weary-eyed, had fixed his gaze upon the Moulin Tower. 'It can be difficult, a case like this. It can be difficult to prove. The suspect dead, and just one witness – no real evidence. And if the witness should rescind his statement, or refuse to testify . . .' The sentence hung unfinished, and he had raised his shoulders in a philosophical shrug. 'Sometimes, the scales of justice find a level of their own, without our help,' he'd said. 'And sometimes, in seeking justice, we don't always serve it. Do you understand?' Not trusting my voice, I'd nodded carefully. 'Good. Then I will see what I can do. There will be rumours, you understand; talk around the town. I can't stop that. And if, when she is grown up, she chooses to come looking for the truth, then she will find it. But perhaps,' he'd said, his grey eyes very kind, 'she will not look. It is better, I think, for a child to keep her heroes.'

A decent man, I thought again. I had blinked the tears back, smiled at him. 'Thank you.' And suddenly I'd felt a crawling sense of déjà-vu. A memory of a younger man in uniform, much larger, who had smiled at me in just that way . . . 'I'm sorry,' I had said. 'This may sound foolish, but I wonder . . .'

He'd looked pleased. 'Your father said you would remember. I told him no, that you were such a little girl in those days, but he was very sure.'

I'd blinked. 'My father?'

So he'd kept his promise, after all. He'd promised me he'd ask his friends in Paris to enquire after Harry, stir around, but I hadn't expected him to do anything. I certainly hadn't expected him to send a chief inspector straight to Chinon. Harry'd put it rather well, I thought: *Your father's got a network strung through Europe that would put our Secret Service men to shame.* I was just a bit surprised he'd actually remembered.

I'd felt an old and automatic need to apologize to the inspector for the trouble he had gone to on my family's account; for the interruption of his holiday; for everything. He'd merely smiled, and shrugged it all aside.

'Your father is an old friend,' he had told me. 'He was worried. And when Andrew Braden worries, it is rarely without reason.' Then against a blurring back-drop of black sky and brilliant lights he had tucked the blanket tighter round my shoulders, and left me with the vacuum flask of strong reviving coffee.

I could have done with that coffee now, I thought, as I nestled deeper into the cushions of my seat in the hotel bar and stiffened my jaws to smother a yawn.

For the second time that week, the bar of the Hotel de France was blazing light long after its official closing time. One would have thought it was the cocktail hour and not past midnight. How far past midnight I could not be sure – I seemed to have lost my wristwatch – but when last I'd asked Jim Whitaker the time he'd told me it was going on for one, and that had been before Monsieur Chamond brought out the second bottle of Calvados.

We were well down in that bottle now. Monsieur Chamond had abandoned his bartending duties to settle on the stool beside his wife, leaving Thierry with the job of keeping all our glasses full. Thierry, for his part, was deep in some debate with Christian Rand, and had filled his own glass rather more often than ours. It was a smashing Calvados, well aged and mellow, resplendent with the golden warmth of apples from the finest fields of Normandy. After going twenty-four hours without food, that warmth had spread through all my aching limbs, and I'd long since given up my efforts to make sense of what was going on around me.

François was there . . . now, that was strange. I wanted several times to ask him how and why he came to be there, but my tired brain kept stumbling on the question, and no-one else seemed interested, so I just let it pass. I was having enough trouble getting used

357

to seeing Harry lounging opposite among the potted palms, his lean face animated while he chatted on to Neil as though the night had been a normal one, like any other. My cousin's health had greatly improved, I'd noticed, since the gypsy woman Danielle had left us to go round to the police station, where her brother and the Chief Inspector were still sorting out the matter of official statements.

I didn't doubt they'd get it sorted. Certainly everyone here had entered the conspiracy of sympathetic silence. Oh, we could talk about it now, between ourselves, but come the morning I knew even Thierry, facing questions from his friends, would simply shrug and shake his head and say: 'A tragic accident' like the rest of us. He felt cheated by Armand's death, I could sense that – it had robbed him of the chance to take his personal revenge upon Paul's killer. But even Thierry couldn't transfer all that hatred to Lucie Valcourt. A child shouldn't suffer for her father's sins.

Martine, I thought, would see she didn't suffer. Martine had looked like a different person, up at the château, her face composed and elegant, expressionless, while she'd listened very quietly to Inspector Prieur's explanations. And then with equal calm she'd asked him: 'And my niece?'

'One of our officers is with her now. We haven't told her anything.'

'I see. Thank you.' She had nodded. 'Thank you very much. I will take care of her.' Lucie was in good hands.

Beside me, François stirred and said something to Jim. I pulled my thoughts back just in time to catch the final sentence. '. . . am looking forward,' he was saying, in his musical English, 'to showing you, while you are here. Perhaps your wife—'

'My wife will not be staying,' Jim said quietly. 'She's going on to Paris, and then home.'

I'd thought it odd that Garland hadn't joined us, but at some point between my third and fourth glasses of Calvados it had ceased to be important. Now I looked at Jim and thought: *He told her, that's what happened. He told her about Martine.*

Jim shrugged. 'But I'll be here for quite some time, I think. As long as I'm needed.'

Christian made some comment, low, in German, and I saw a warm, approving smile flash across Neil's face, his dark eyes crinkling at the corners. I quickly looked away again before he caught me staring. Not that it would have made a difference if he had, I told myself. Unless of course he'd turned that smile on me, and then . . . and then . . .

I sighed. Well, that was the whole problem, wasn't it? I didn't know just what would happen then. I only knew I'd been avoiding him since we'd come down from the château, feeling uncertain without knowing what I wasn't certain *of*. It all came, I supposed, of having someone charge to your rescue like a bloody-minded prince out of a fairy tale; of having someone take you in his arms the way a lover might, as though you really *mattered*.

I felt my cousin watching me, his blue eyes frankly curious, and with a silent curse upon all men I sipped my drink, ignoring him.

It didn't work. Instead, he turned his curiosity on Neil. 'My cousin was convinced you were the culprit,' he said cheerfully.

Neil raised an eyebrow. 'Really?'

'Mm. Something about Nazis, I think, and diamonds. I'm afraid I didn't follow it all, but then she never does make sense when she's upset.'

'Ah,' said Neil.

François looked on, benevolent. 'My fault, I think. The photograph . . .'

'God, yes.' Neil grinned. 'Wherever did you dig that up? It's quite a damning likeness, that.'

Christian swivelled round upon his stool, addressing Neil in a mild voice. 'I am very angry with you. All these years you are a German, like myself, and I am never knowing this.'

'Half German. My mum's pure English, through and through. Dad moved to England when the war was over, and she met him there.'

Madame Chamond frowned prettily. 'Except your name,' she said. 'Grantham. It does not sound a German name.'

'Dad wasn't very proud of being German in those days. He took the name of the place he moved to first, in Lincolnshire.'

'Oh, right,' said Harry, smiling. 'I've gone through Grantham dozens of times on the train. It's on the main line north to York, isn't it?'

Neil nodded. 'Mum and Dad still live there, actually, and my brother Ron.'

I tried to recall what he'd told me of his family. 'The painter?'

'No, the chemist.' Again the grin. I had to look away. 'Michael, he's the painter, lives in London. Then there's Isabelle. My sister,' he explained, as Jim and François both reacted. 'So you see, he didn't quite forget.'

Jim Whitaker frowned thoughtfully. 'But he didn't come back for her, did he, like he promised?'

'He was afraid, I think, that she would hate him. I

used to think it terribly romantic, as a boy – like something out of Shakespeare.'

François smiled softly. 'That is why you came to Chinon in the first place, was it not? To do what your father could not?'

'I put it down to destiny,' said Neil.

'Ah, yes,' said François, 'destiny has played a part. It was destiny, I think, that your old friend Brigitte married Armand, that she came to live in my house, and that she invited you to visit her.'

'Destiny, too,' Madame Chamond put in, looking from Neil to Jim to François, 'that the three of you should be together, here at our hotel.'

Jim smiled. 'That's true.'

'Although,' Neil qualified, 'if you want to be technical, that was Emily's doing.'

'Me?' I did look at him that time, eyes widening. 'What on earth did I have to do with it?'

'Well, you took off like a rabbit when you saw me coming, and no-one knew where you had gone. Poor Thierry was beside himself.'

Thierry looked up suspiciously from his post behind the bar. '*Comment?*'

'You were concerned.'

'Ah. Yes, I showed to Monsieur Neil the photograph, a photograph of him, I was thinking, and he asks me where it came from, and I told him—'

'So I rang up François,' Neil went on, recapturing his narrative. 'I thought you might have gone up there, to have a word with him, but of course he hadn't seen you.'

'And then I am worried,' François said in turn. 'Because I'm told that you were most upset, and so I called someone to come and stay with Lucie, and I came down here.'

'Where he met me,' said Jim. 'So you see, Emily, it really was your doing.'

And the rest, I knew, had happened pretty much as I had thought it would. Danielle and Harry, on arriving at the meeting place to find I wasn't there, had marched post-haste to the police station where, from all accounts, my cousin had stirred up a minor riot. The police in turn had telephoned the hotel to check my whereabouts. Naturally, that only raised the level of confusion as, with torches waving, everyone had formed a siege force the like of which had not been seen in Chinon since medieval times. In all, I'd heard, some fifteen people had swarmed up the château steps to rescue me. Odd, I thought – I'd noticed only one.

Monsieur Chamond poured out the last of the Calvados and clucked his tongue regretfully. 'Another bottle gone,' he said. 'Thierry, would you mind . . . ?'

'Not at all.' Thierry could hold his liquor rather better than the rest of us, I thought. He walked with little effort to the door behind the bar, then swore with feeling as he bumped against some unseen object in his path.

'Be careful,' Christian warned him, craning forward, 'that is fragile.'

'So is my foot. You should give it to her . . .'

'Now is not a good time, I am thinking.'

I caught the furtive sideways glance and sensed they were discussing me again. 'What should Christian give me, Thierry?'

For an answer Thierry hoisted up a flat brown paper parcel, two feet square. 'This.'

A painting, I thought. It could only be a painting. And I knew which one it was before the paper fell away beneath my clumsy hands. Christian watched my face, uncertain. Everyone, it seemed, was watching me. My fingers hardly shook as I pushed back the torn paper so that nothing obscured my full view of the lovely painting. Painting number 88, the river steps, with Rabelais a sleeping shadow in the background.

Christian cleared his throat. 'Martine, she told me that you liked that one, so I thought . . .' He knew why I liked it, too – his smile showed me that. It was a tight smile, almost forced. And then he put it into words. 'I should have painted Paul there, yes? On the steps.'

I shook my head, and touched the fifth step lovingly. 'No need,' I told him, honestly. 'He's there already.'

Harry was the only one who didn't fully understand. He frowned and looked across at me. *I'll tell you later*, my eyes promised him, *only please don't ask me now.* Still frowning, he reached out a hand. 'Can I see it?'

'God, it's brilliant, Chris,' Neil breathed, looking over Harry's shoulder. 'That river really moves.'

Jim Whitaker leaned forward, too, to look. 'It's too bad,' he said finally, 'that Didier Muret was never told what really happened to the diamonds. Think of all the trouble that it might have saved.'

François looked shocked. 'You cannot mean that.'

'Sure. If he had known she threw them in the river, he'd have never tried to find them, would he?'

'The river?' François raised his eyebrows. 'Who told you Isabelle did this?'

Jim faltered, thinking back. 'Well, she did. At least, she told my father . . . '

'What did she tell him, exactly?'

'I'm not sure, it was so long ago. I always thought . . .'

'*Not* the river,' François said, with certainty. 'She might have said "the water", but not "the river".'

His tone, his words, had finally penetrated past my fog of Calvados. I turned in my seat to stare at him. 'Do you mean . . . you don't mean that you *know* where the diamonds are?'

'Of course.' He smiled. 'I helped her, I was there. She told me they were stained with blood, those diamonds, and she knew only one way to make them pure.' He shrugged, and looked an apology at Jim. 'She didn't throw them in the river Vienne,' he said. 'She gave them back to God.'

Chapter Thirty-Two

. . . all the past
Melts mist-like into this bright hour,

The ancient door swung open with a heavy groan as
Christian's key turned creaking in the lock. A shaft of
torchlight caught a pillar's gleaming edge, then travelled
up to where the grasses waved upon the ruined wall.
Beneath the clouds that raced across the moon, the
Chapelle of Sainte Radegonde slept still and peaceful,
sacrosanct. Nothing moved.

And then the silence blinked.

Christian's keys dropped jangling to the ground and
at the muttered German curse my cousin swung the
torch around to help. 'Just there,' Harry pointed out
the keys, 'beside the . . . no, beside that clump of
flowers. Right.'

'This would be easier,' said Christian, 'in the daylight.'

Harry grinned. 'Well, we're here now, so there's no
point having second thoughts. Besides, it's all well and
good for Jim and François to put off exploring until
morning – they're old men. They've lost their sense of
adventure. Not like us.'

'Jim Whitaker's not old,' I contradicted.

'Of course he is. He must be over forty, surely.'

'Thanks,' said Neil, behind my shoulder. 'I'll just stop here and have a nap then, shall I?'

'I didn't mean . . .'

'I know you didn't.' Neil's smile forgave my cousin's blunder. 'Emily, my dear, could you just shine your torch in that direction, so Christian doesn't trip on anything? Thanks, that's lovely.'

Christian walked ahead, pinned by the torchlight like a cabaret performer in a follow spot. His shadow loomed macabre on the frescoed wall behind the sturdy iron grille. Again he clanked the ring of keys, selecting one to fit the lock. 'Let us hope that Sainte Radegonde does not mind to be awakened.'

'She won't mind.' Harry's tone was confident. 'And anyway, it's not as if we're doing anything we oughtn't. We're just having a bit of a peek, that's all. Giving in to normal curiosity.'

Still, I half expected the saint's statue to be frowning at me, disapproving, as I passed between the iron gates and entered the hushed chapel proper, where the cave-like walls arched up to rest upon the ghostly row of pillars. But when I glanced at Radegonde's stone face she looked back benignly. Evidently, I thought, even saints could understand the pull of curiosity.

Thierry would be terribly put out when he learned we'd come up without him, but he'd gone to bed before us – it was really his own fault. The Chamonds, too, had given in to weariness, and Jim as well, and François had gone back up to the *Clos*, to help with Lucie. Which had only left the four of us – Harry, Christian, Neil and me – quite pleasantly awash in Calvados and irretrievably beyond the point of being tired.

I had, for my own part, reached that magical plane

of inebriation in which time begins to float and anything seems possible, which went a long way towards explaining why, when Harry had leaned forward and said: 'Listen, *I've* got an idea . . .', instead of running in the opposite direction as experience would warrant, I had donned my jacket and trailed after him. Completely sober, I'd have had more sense. And I would never have come up that cliff path in the dark, alone or no.

'I've got it open,' Christian announced, twisting the key to the third and final gate. Harry'd wandered down the aisle to stand below the Plantagenet fresco, his torchlight angled up to catch the vibrant figures of young Isabelle and John. 'Well done,' he said, in absent tones. He stood a moment longer, looking up. 'I was afraid it might have changed, since I last saw it.'

I raised my eyebrows. 'Changed? In one week? Hardly likely.'

'Not one week, love. It's been at least two years since I've been up here, to the chapelle. Had I known my hiding place was quite so close I might have tried to sneak in another visit. One forgets how very beautiful—'

'Hold on,' I stopped him, frowning. 'You were here last week. You must have been. That's how I knew that you were missing in the first place – you left your coin, your King John coin, there on the altar, as an offering.'

'No chance.'

'You did.' My chin rose stubbornly. 'Or at least, if you didn't leave it there yourself, perhaps the gypsies . . .'

'Darling Emily.' My cousin strolled towards me, hand in pocket. 'I'm not all that daft, you know. I mean, they're lovely people, gypsies, but they will take things unless you're careful. My watch is gone, and my wallet . . . but they haven't taken this.' He held his hand out, with the coin upon it, to show me. 'With this, I was very careful.'

I stared. It was the King John coin, without mistake, safe in its plastic case. I opened my own wallet, just to be sure, and drew out the matching coin. Harry stabbed it with a beam of light.

'How curious,' he said. 'I wonder how on earth it got there.'

'I don't know.'

Christian leaned in closer for a better look. 'It is very old, yes? Somebody must have found it on the ground here, near the tombs perhaps, and put it with the other coins as tribute to Sainte Radegonde.'

'Y-yes, I suppose that's how it could have happened.'

'You don't sound terribly convinced,' said Harry, grinning. 'What other explanation is there – Sainte Radegonde herself, perhaps? A helping hand from beyond? Don't tell me that you've found religion, Em.'

'Of course not.' And I meant it, only . . . only . . .

Behind the altar, lovely pale Sainte Radegonde just went on gazing at nothing in particular, her blind, carved eyes serene and peaceful. I put the coin back in her dish of offerings, and pushed it well down, frowning. Neil moved up behind my shoulder, and his breath brushed warm on my neck. 'The world would be dead boring, don't you think, if everything were easy to explain?'

My cousin grinned. 'The true Romantic viewpoint,' he pronounced. 'Come on then, are we ready? Tunnels again, Emily. You'll have to cope. She has a tunnel thing,' he told Neil, confidently.

'Oh, yes?' Neil glanced my way. 'I'll have to remember that.'

Beyond the second gate the glare of harsh electric light seemed almost an intrusion. The chapel caves cried out for candles, I thought, or the flicker of a burning torch. The hanging bulbs and switches took away much of the mystery, and it wasn't until we'd reached the steep and crooked steps that dropped down to the holy well that I felt again the ancient and eternal sense of wonder shared by all explorers.

Harry must have drunk more than I'd thought. By the time the rest of us had slid with caution down the steps my cousin had stripped neatly to his underpants.

'What *are* you doing?' I demanded.

'Well, you can't see anything from here. Just pebbles, really. If I've come all this way to see diamonds, then I want to bloody see them, don't I?'

I looked down at the narrow shaft of clear blue water, plunging several metres deep into the rock. 'You can't be serious.'

He just grinned, stepped cleanly off the ledge and dropped feet-first into the well. The spray that came up after him was cold as ice. Neil knelt beside me, one arm braced against the pale stone wall to see I didn't accidentally topple in myself. 'We'll fish him out again,' he promised. 'Never fear.' The three of us peered over the edge, to watch as Harry forced himself towards the bottom, his hands splayed out in search of the elusive diamonds. 'Runs in your family, does it?' Neil asked idly. 'This sort of behaviour?'

'Well, yes, it seems to.'

'Ah.'

I might have asked him why he wanted to know, but our situation was already intimate beyond the comfort level, and at any rate there wasn't time. My cousin broke the surface of the water in a burst of triumph, gasping air.

'He was right,' he called up to us. 'Old François was right. Just look!' And spreading out his fingers he stretched up his hand, palm upwards, to the light. I saw the glittering before I saw the stones themselves.

'*Mein Gott*,' breathed Christian.

'Precisely.'

And then for some few minutes we were silent, all of us. I thought of Isabelle – Jim's mother, François's sister – standing here that summer evening while her world fell in around her, holding diamonds stained with blood no human hand could wash away. I thought of Hans . . . where had he been that night, I wondered? Miles away, by then. He'd sought redemption too, in different ways. He had surrendered, left his country, changed his name. Well, it was over now, I thought. Time everyone forgot, forgave, let be. Yom Kippur might have ended with the sunset, but the message of the Jewish holiday remained. *People hate too much*.

'There are some coins down there,' said Harry. 'Not old ones, but . . .'

Paul's wishing coins. 'Just let them lie,' I told him.

'Yes, Mum.' He grinned. 'And these as well, I think.' He tipped his hand to let the diamonds tumble back into the turquoise water. 'Bad luck to steal things from a holy well. Sainte Radegonde would have my head.'

I watched the flashing glitter of the gems descending. They vanished at the bottom, amid a scattering of what looked like pebbles. How many diamonds had there been? I didn't want to know. After all, they were nothing more than stones, small bits of stone that someone thought were pretty, and in that illusion lay their value. In the greater scheme of life, I thought, they didn't matter a damn. Maybe all that mattered was the tangible, however fleeting – friends and family, feelings . . .

'Oh, sod it,' Harry bit out. 'Damn, I think I broke my finger.' He'd made his way to the sheer wall of the well and had begun to climb up, using the row of footholds gouged by the well-diggers centuries earlier. He pulled his hand free, flexing it.

He was still several feet below us, and I had to lean to look. 'It doesn't look broken.'

'Well, maybe not, but it might have been. There's something jammed in here – a block of wood, it feels like.' Far more gingerly now, he placed his injured fingers back within the recessed foothold just above the surface of the water. 'Hang on,' he said, 'it isn't wood at all. In fact it feels like . . . I'll be damned.'

'What is it?' Christian leant down, curious, as Harry finally tugged the object free. I only saw a small dark square the size of Harry's hand. He passed it up to Christian. 'You tell me.'

It was filthy dirty, for one thing. My cousin's hand left black marks on the stone as he swung himself up the few remaining feet to join us on the narrow ledge above the well. Christian had turned the packet over, sniffing. 'Oil,' he pronounced. 'It has been oiled.'

'Waxed as well.' Harry pointed to the great untidy splotch of black that held the packet closed. 'Somebody didn't want this getting wet.' He was dripping water himself, but that didn't seem to bother him. He slicked his hair back, glanced at me. 'Emily, love, would you toss me my trousers? Thanks.' He rummaged for his pocket knife and prised the battered blade open. It was

371

rather tricky, since the packet seemed to crumble when he touched it, but at length he'd sliced the wax seal through and gently, oh so gently, coaxed the stiffened edges apart.

The squares of parchment had been folded up so tightly for so long that they were nearly solid lumps, and Harry didn't try to force them open. He knew better. There were specialists who did that sort of thing. But he did forget his training long enough to turn the parchment in his still-damp fingers, searching for a scrap of writing, anything. 'Oh, my God,' he said.

I looked at him, and caught some measure of his own excitement. 'What?'

'You ought to know that signature,' he told me, stretching out his hand towards me. I looked. I blinked, a long blink, looked again. And then I raised my head to stare at him.

I couldn't even speak.

Neil slid his gaze from me to Harry. 'What are they?'

'Letters.' My cousin's voice had roughened slightly, as it always did when he became emotional. It echoed back from the still water of the well. 'Love letters, I expect. Written by a king eight hundred years ago.'

Christian stroked a corner of the crumbling oiled packet. 'Eight hundred years? Incredible.'

My cousin looked at me. ' "A treasure beyond price," ' he quoted, and his eyes grew moist. 'That's what the chronicle said Queen Isabelle hid, here at Chinon. Only it wasn't jewels, or money. Damn, who would have known . . . ?' He shook his head, his dreamy gaze returning to the crudely-chiselled footholds in the soft, unspeaking stone. And then, as if he'd suddenly remembered Neil and Christian wouldn't have the foggiest idea what he was talking about, which meant that they were fair game for a classic lecture, Henry Yates Braden, PhD, promptly cleared his throat. 'You see,' he began, 'there was another Isabelle . . .'

Chapter Thirty-Three

*. . . lift thine eyes; my doubts
are dead,*

'What, no lectures?' Harry asked me, as we paused before the altar. Christian swung the iron gate shut and the sound disturbed my thoughts. I turned unfocused eyes towards my cousin.

'I'm sorry?'

'About how I shouldn't steal things from historic sites,' he clarified. 'You're rather puritan about the subject, as I recall. You read me the Riot Act that day I nicked a pebble from Tintagel.'

'That wasn't a pebble, it was a building stone, and if everybody did that there wouldn't be a castle left to . . .' I saw his smile forming and broke off with a heavy sigh. 'Anyhow, I suppose I can't talk, can I? I stole a coin from an offering plate, for heaven's sake.'

'You brought it back.'

'And you said yourself you're going to give the letters to the University of Paris.'

'Right. Just as soon as I have a chance to look at them.'

My gaze narrowed. 'Harry . . .'

'Well, have a heart! You can't expect me to just turn the damn things over without looking at them first.

Christ, I'm not a saint, you know.' His eyes flicked sideways to where Radegonde's calm statue stood behind the altar, as if he half expected to be flattened by a lightning bolt. 'Besides,' he went on, in a lower voice, 'since no-one else even knows that the letters exist, it stands to reason that no-one will miss them for a few days, will they?'

'A few days?'

'Well, a month maybe.'

'And then you'll send them on to Paris?'

'On my honour.' He swore the oath with hand upraised.

Past redemption, I thought – that's what Harry was. On his honour indeed. I smiled and looked away, out past the iron grille to where the gentle fingers of the breaking dawn touched softly on the bay tree standing sentinel beside the chapelle's door.

'Cold?' Harry asked me.

'No.'

'Then why the shiver?' And then he followed the direction of my gaze, and said quite simply: 'Ah.'

I turned around. 'What do you mean, "Ah"?'

'Just "Ah".'

He saw things rather more clearly than I liked, I thought. More clearly, sometimes, than I myself could see. I felt the colour stain my cheeks and turned my head away again, looking back towards the bay tree and the man who sat beneath it.

He was sitting comfortably stretched out against the outer wall, one leg drawn up on which to rest his injured hand. The hand hung stiffly, as though it hurt him, and I remembered Harry telling me how Neil had climbed the château walls to get inside. Actually climbed the walls. They must have been a good twenty feet high, even at their lowest point around the gates. Less than that on the inside, naturally, where the ground level was higher, but even so. He simply hadn't wanted to wait, so Harry said, for the main gates to be unlocked. It must have been a different Neil Grantham, I decided, who'd shown such a lack of patience.

It could not have been this quiet man, lost in a serenity so deep he scarcely seemed to breathe, with the faint light trickling through the bay leaves turning his hair a pale and softly radiant gold. He might have been Christ contemplating the sunrise over Gethsemene. All else was darkness compared to him, and though he neither moved nor spoke his very stillness drew the eye more effectively than motion – drew it and held it until I felt myself being pulled into the glowing centre of its reverent, breathless peace.

Harry watched me, eyebrows raised. 'I like him, if it matters.'

I faced him with a flat expression. 'I don't know what you're talking about.'

'Right.' My cousin turned to Christian, with a smile. 'Sorry to have kept you from your bed, but I really am grateful for this. And for these.' He patted the lumpy parcel wrapped with care inside his jacket.

Christian shrugged. 'It is no trouble. And now,' he announced, brushing his forehead with one hand, 'I will make for everyone some coffee, yes? So much excitement in one night, it makes the head ache.'

'Coffee,' Neil agreed, 'sounds wonderful.' He rolled his head against the stone wall to smile at us, and moved to stand up, wincing a little. 'It isn't so much the excitement,' he explained, 'as the drink. Bloody Calvados. I feel like there's a herd of horses dancing on my skull.'

My cousin laughed. 'That's age for you. You ready, Em?'

No, I thought, I wasn't ready. That was the whole problem, wasn't it? I trailed along the cliff path after them, too busy with my own confusing thoughts to join the conversation. I had some vague memory of passing by the house where Harry had kept hidden, and of brushing through the fragrant clutch of pine, and then of starting our descent into the town, but I was still surprised to find myself upon the pavement outside Christian's house, with all the houses round still shuttered tight against the pale and spreading light of day.

I looked at Harry, and at Neil, and suddenly I felt a little stifled. 'Actually,' I said, 'I don't feel much like coffee. I'd rather get some sleep.'

Harry's eyes were gently sceptical. 'Oh, yes?'

'Yes. I think I'll just go back to the hotel.'

Neil smiled at me, faintly, seeing too much, as he always did. I tried my best to make a graceful exit, but in truth it took all my effort not to break into a run as I wound my way through the narrow, sleeping streets. Each window seemed to stare at me, accusing me of cowardice, and even when I reached the fountain square the elegantly entwined Graces looked less than approving. I wrapped my arms around myself defensively, moving across to stand at the fountain's edge.

Splendour, Joy and bloody Beauty – they looked as stern as ever, those three faces. Unless . . . was that a quirk I saw, just there? I squinted through the tumbling rain of water droplets, glistening like diamonds in the slant of morning sun. No, I decided, it was nothing. And yet, I had the feeling that the statues were trying to tell me something.

'It would never work,' I answered them aloud. I wanted to tell them that the fairy tales were lies, all lies, but it was difficult to say the words when above me Château Chinon rose resplendent in the sunshine, looking every inch the castle of a fairy tale. Difficult, too, to deny the existence of Prince Charmings when one had just last night come charging to my rescue. Damn, I thought. And happy endings? A sweet wind whispered through the leaves of the acacias, and I thought I heard Jim Whitaker's voice asking me a second time, 'Is happiness a thing we choose, I wonder?'

I wondered, too, and found no answer.

My hands were cold. I rummaged in my handbag for a pair of gloves and saw a flashing glimmer at the bottom, in amongst the jumbled clutter. Gloves forgotten, I reached in deeper, and closed my fingers round the two-toned coin. Not a French coin, but an Italian one – five hundred lire, to be exact. I seemed to see Neil's eyes before me, watching me, quietly urging me to make a wish. *Whenever you're ready*, he'd told me. *Whenever you're ready*.

It had been years since I'd performed the tiny ritual, yet in the end it came so naturally. I took a deep breath, kissed the coin, and sent it tumbling with a wish into the icy water of the fountain.

I was so intent on watching it fall that I didn't notice the cat, at first. The little creature had rubbed past my legs twice before I surfaced from my thoughts and looked down. The cat blinked up at me. It came into my arms without hesitation when I bent to pick it up, and nestled underneath my chin, purring like a motorboat.

Behind me, Neil's voice warned: 'You'll get fleas.'

I stiffened, then relaxed, not looking back. 'I don't

care.' How long he had been standing there, I didn't know – I hadn't heard his footsteps. But I heard them now, crisp and even on the pavement as he came across the square to join me at the fountain's edge. I went on looking at the water, and my hands upon the cat were almost steady. Almost.

Neil glanced into the water, too, then turned his quiet gaze on me. 'I see you've used your coin,' he commented.

'Yes.'

'You didn't wish for the cat to find a home, did you?'

I looked at him then, and saw that his eyes weren't quiet at all. They were alive, intense with some unnamed emotion, and a question lurked within their midnight depths. Slowly, I shook my head.

The question vanished and he smiled. 'Thank God for that,' he said. 'I thought you might have wasted it.' And then he raised a hand to touch my face, a touch of promise, warm and sure, and as I struggled to smile back at him he kissed me. It felt so very right, so beautiful; tears pricked behind my lashes as life flowed through all my hollow limbs, and I lost all sense of place and time. It might have been a minute or an hour later when he moved, slanting a thoughtful look down at the black-and-white bundle of fur in my arms. The cat stared back at him, a trifle smugly.

'I suppose,' said Neil, 'that this beast will have to come with us?'

Just like that. I stared up at him. 'I thought you said your landlady hated cats?'

'Yes, well, she doesn't much like other women, either, but I fancy she'll get used to both of you. Even Austrian landladies,' he informed me, 'recognize the hand of destiny at work.' His own hand felt very warm as he smoothed my hair back. 'Still, we'd better see to it the little fleabag gets his injections. Have you named him yet?'

I hadn't really thought about it, but quite suddenly I knew there was just one name that would fit. 'Ulysses,' I told Neil. 'His name's Ulysses.'

A flash of understanding passed between us, and his dark eyes smiled down at me. 'Right. Put Ulysses down, then, will you?'

'Why?'

'Just put him down.'

The cat yawned grumpily as I lowered him to the pavement. A stiff breeze scattered the fountain's spray around the three bronze Graces, and the cat leapt safely out of range, moving to resume his nap beneath the nearest bench. The fountain's spray struck me as well, as cold as ice, but I didn't really mind it. Neil's eyes, his smile, his touch, were warmth enough. Maybe he was right, I thought – it might not be so difficult, believing. I lifted my own hand to touch his face, his hair, to bring his head lower. And in the moment just before he kissed me, I could have sworn that, past his shoulder, Splendour smiled.

THE END